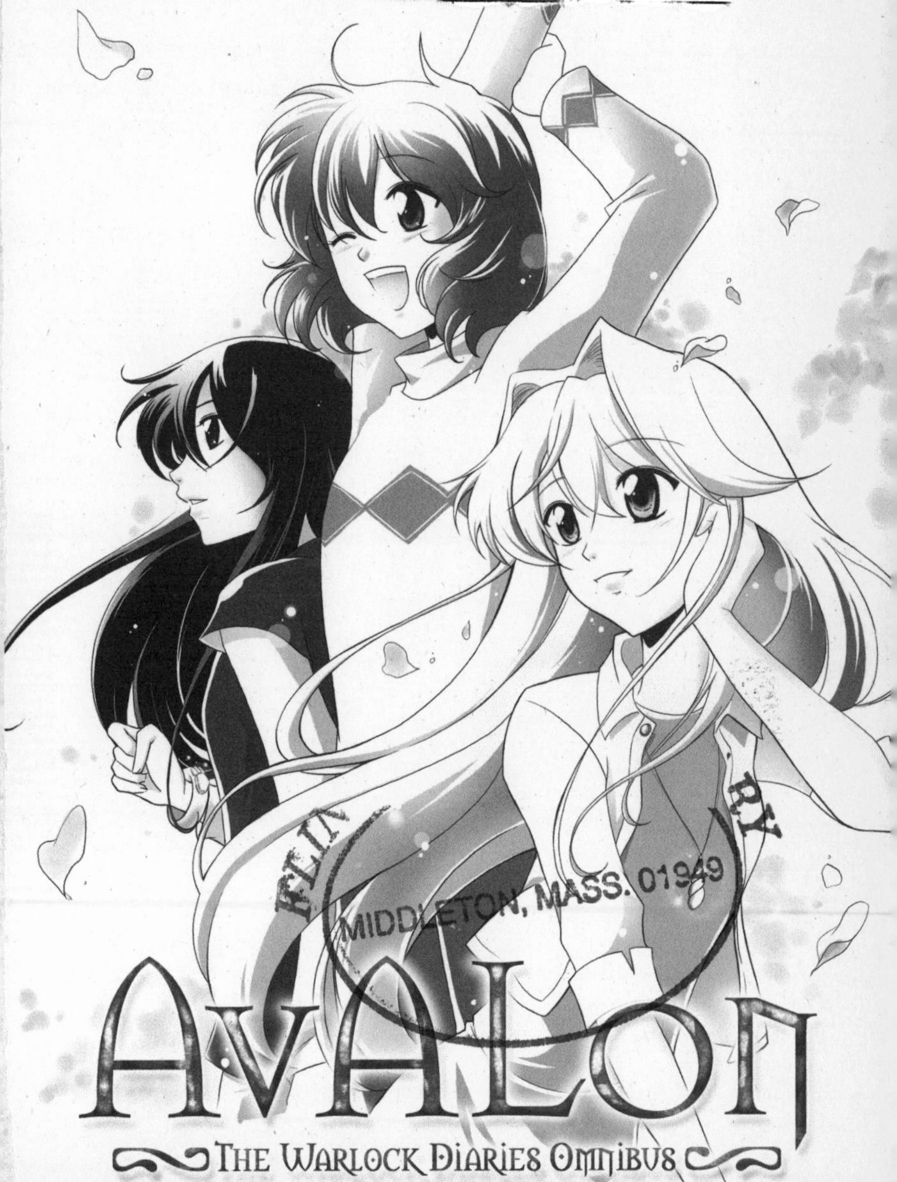

AVALON

THE WARLOCK DIARIES OMNIBUS

AVALON
THE WARLOCK DIARIES OMNIBUS

story by **Rachel Roberts**
art by **Carmela "Shiei" Doneza & Edward Gan**

GN
Roberts

STAFF CREDITS

toning	**Rhea Silvan**
lettering	**Nicky Lim**
character design	**Edward Gan**
layout	**Adam Arnold**
book design	**Nicky Lim**
editor	**Adam Arnold**
Publisher	**Jason DeAngelis**
	Seven Seas Entertainment

Explore a world of magic & fun at www.AvalonMagic.com.

ISBN: 978-1-934876-88-6

Printed in Canada

First Printing: December 2010

10 9 8 7 6 5 4 3 2 1

3 2126 00108 464 4

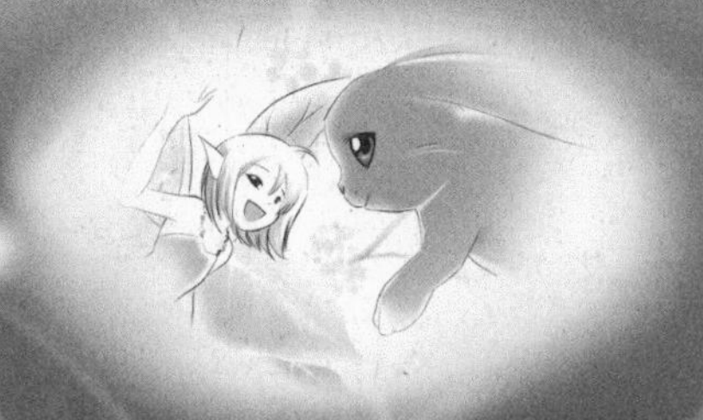

Once magic flowed freely along a vast web, the Magic Web, connecting many worlds.

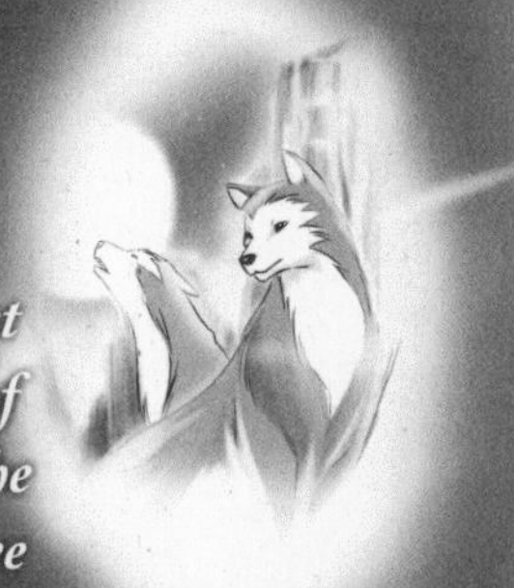

Now the magic has almost vanished. The only hope of renewing it and saving the magic web falls upon three mages—a healer, a warrior, and a blazing star.

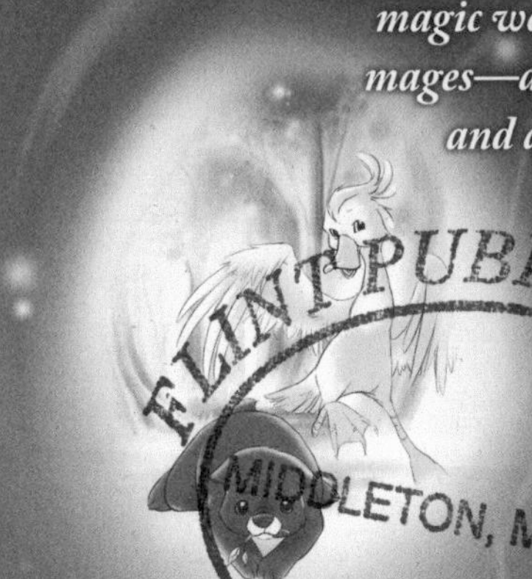

Together with their animal friends, they are on a quest to find the lost, legendary home of all magic: **Avalon.**

EMILY
The Healer

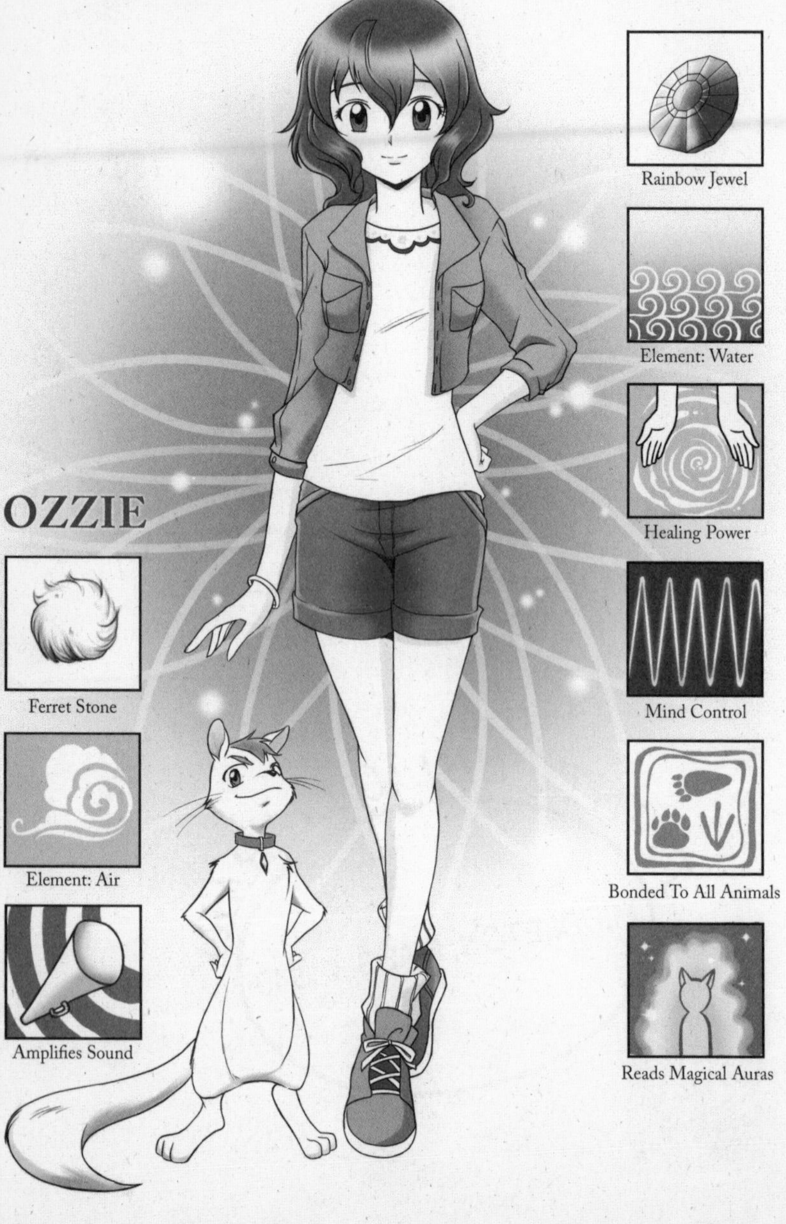
Rainbow Jewel
Element: Water
Healing Power
Mind Control
Bonded To All Animals
Reads Magical Auras
OZZIE
Ferret Stone
Element: Air
Amplifies Sound

ADRIANE

The Warrior

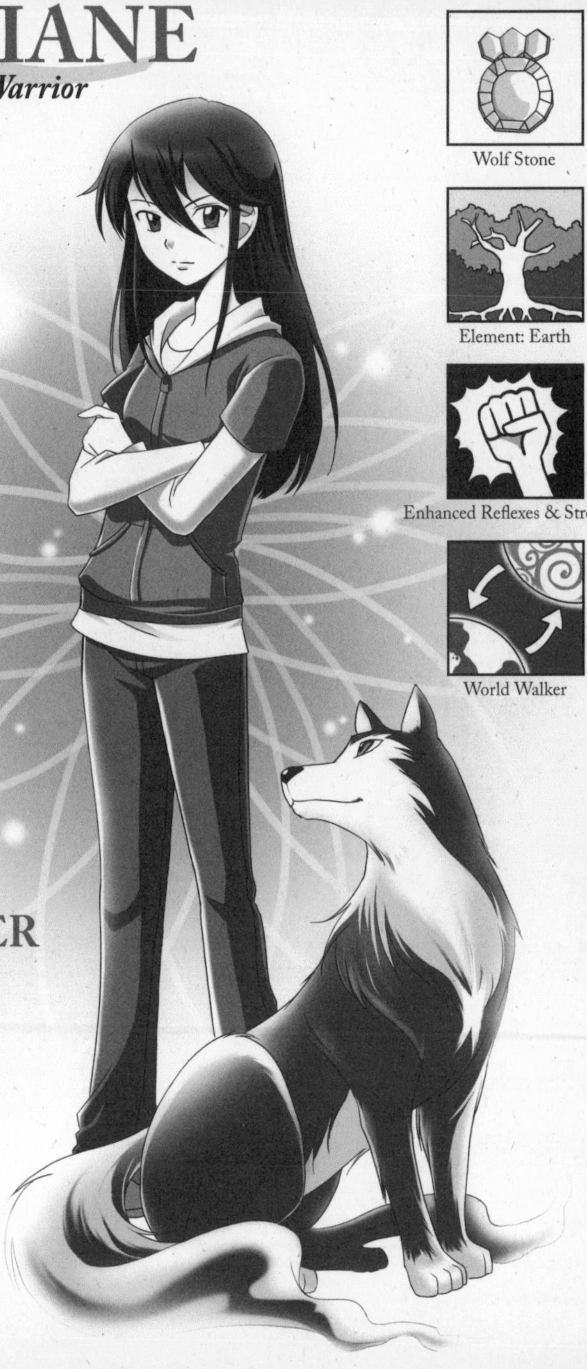

Wolf Stone

Element: Earth

Enhanced Reflexes & Strength

World Walker

DREAMER

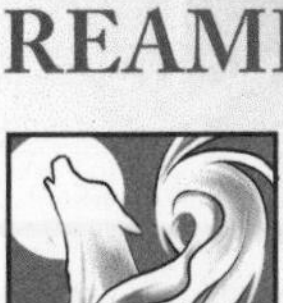

Shapeshift to Mist

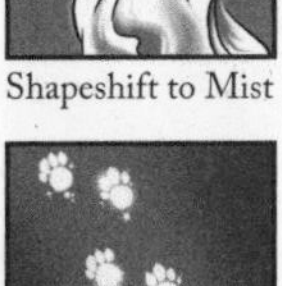

Magic Tracker

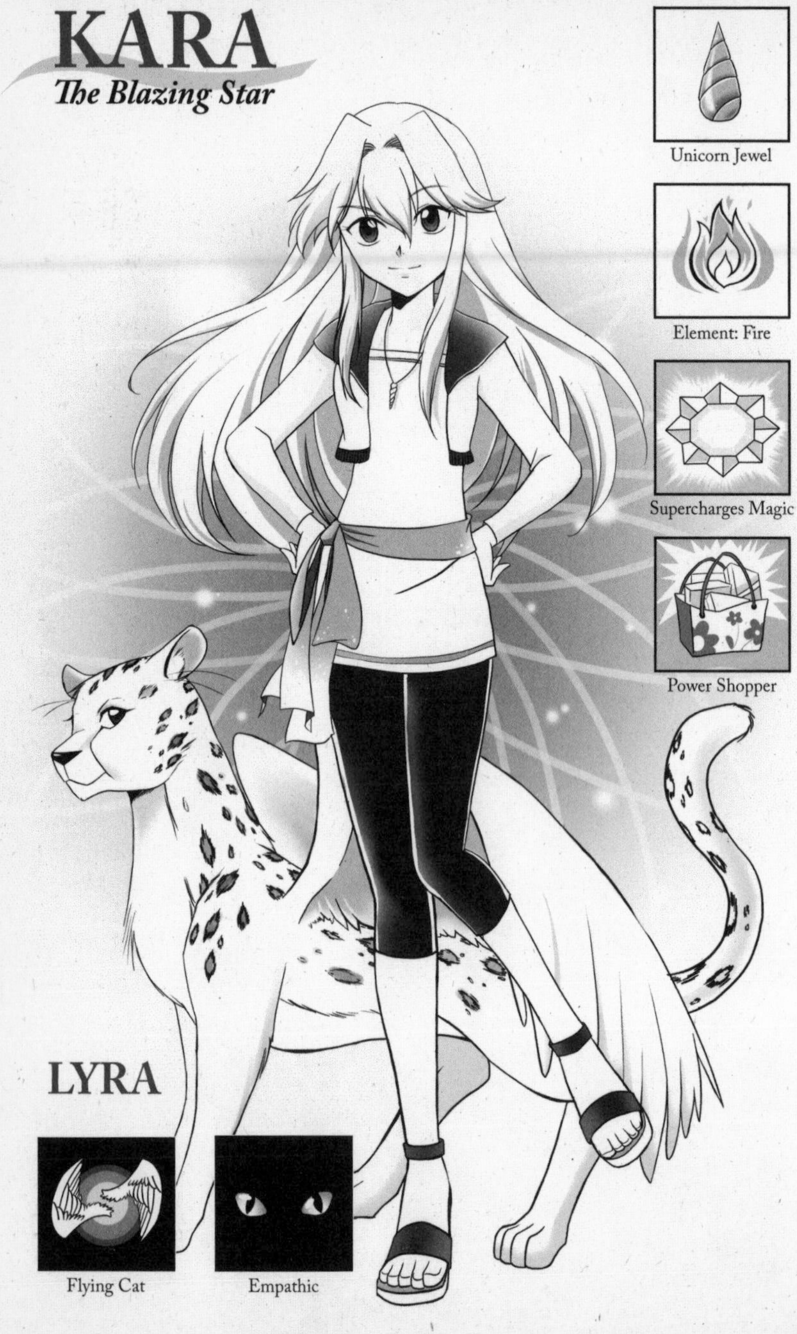
KARA
The Blazing Star
Unicorn Jewel
Element: Fire
Supercharges Magic
Power Shopper
LYRA
Flying Cat
Empathic

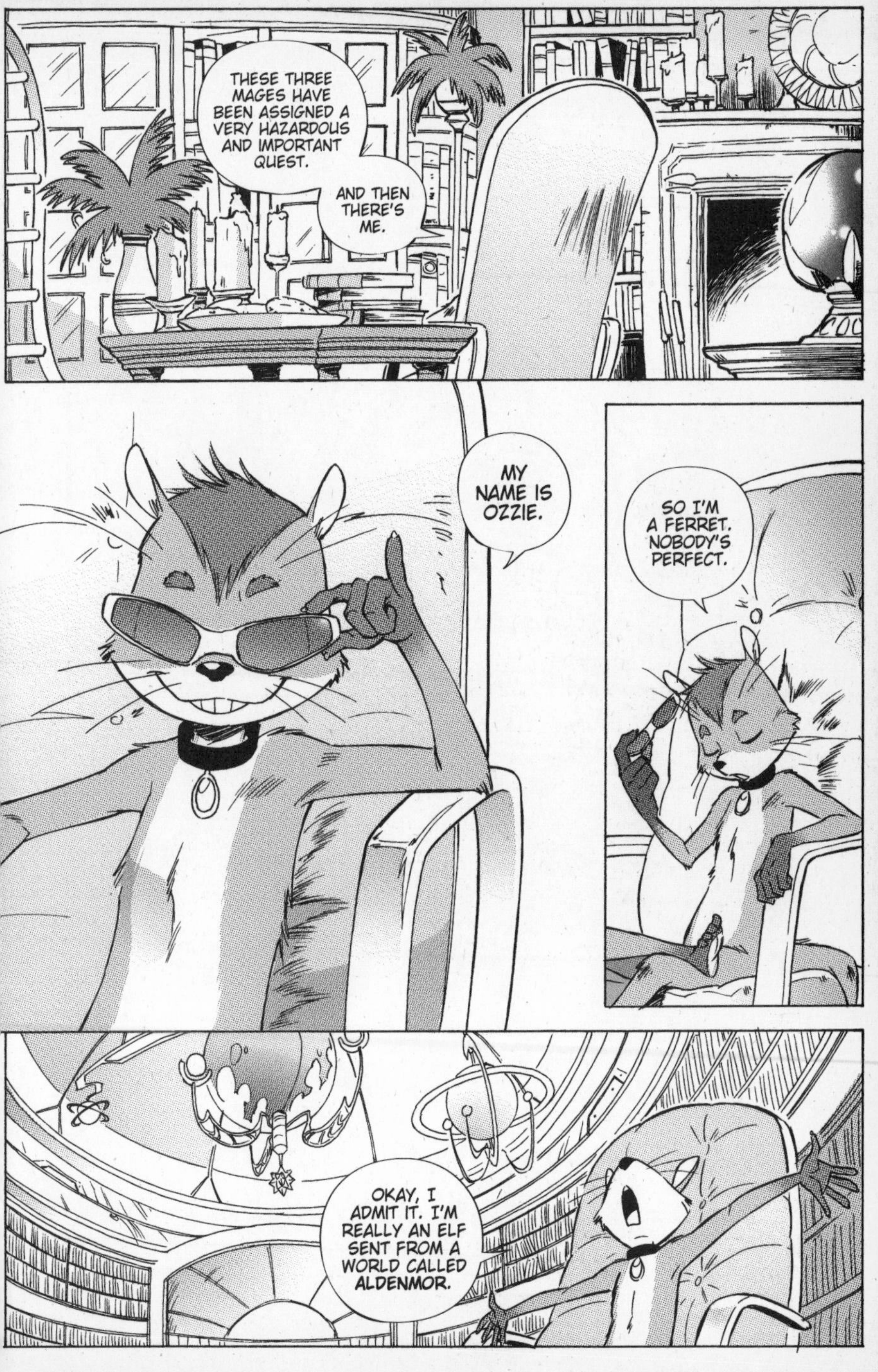
THESE THREE MAGES HAVE BEEN ASSIGNED A VERY HAZARDOUS AND IMPORTANT QUEST.
AND THEN THERE'S ME.
MY NAME IS OZZIE.
SO I'M A FERRET. NOBODY'S PERFECT.
OKAY, I ADMIT IT. I'M REALLY AN ELF SENT FROM A WORLD CALLED ALDENMOR.

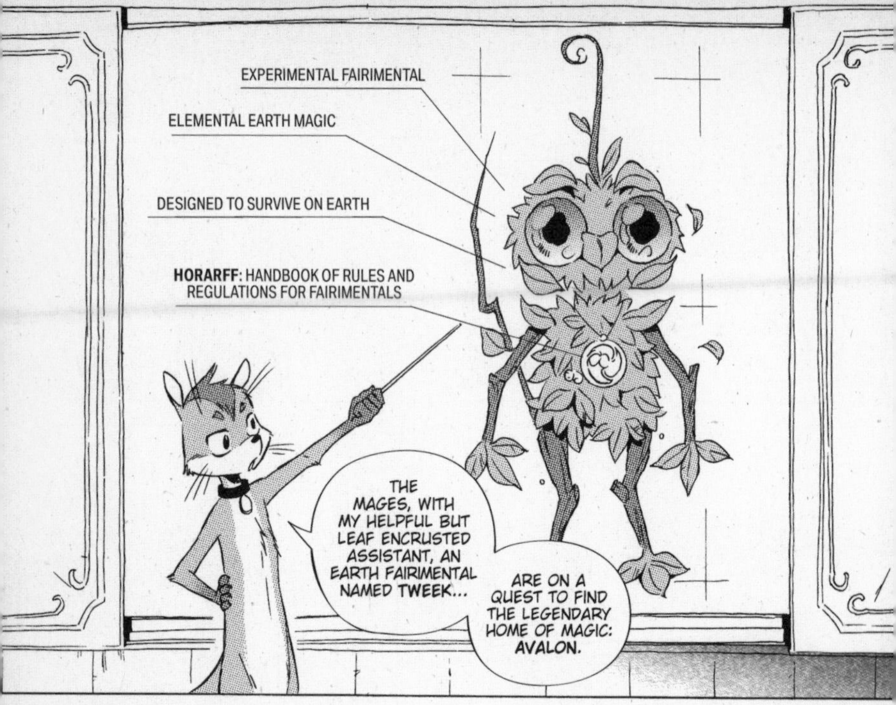
EXPERIMENTAL FAIRIMENTAL
ELEMENTAL EARTH MAGIC
DESIGNED TO SURVIVE ON EARTH
HORARFF: HANDBOOK OF RULES AND REGULATIONS FOR FAIRIMENTALS
THE MAGES, WITH MY HELPFUL BUT LEAF ENCRUSTED ASSISTANT, AN EARTH FAIRIMENTAL NAMED TWEEK...
ARE ON A QUEST TO FIND THE LEGENDARY HOME OF MAGIC: AVALON.

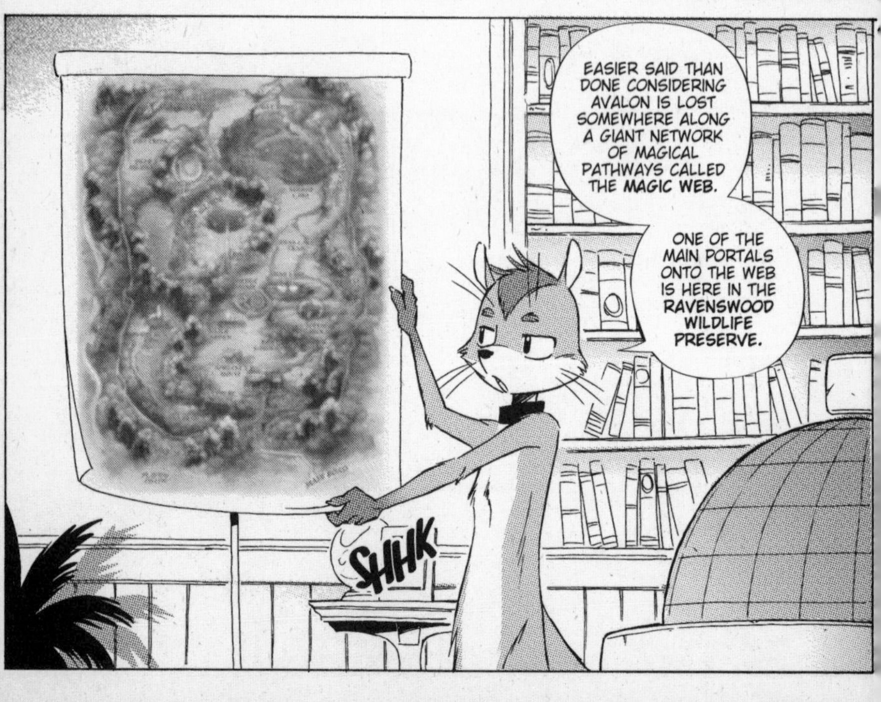
EASIER SAID THAN DONE CONSIDERING AVALON IS LOST SOMEWHERE ALONG A GIANT NETWORK OF MAGICAL PATHWAYS CALLED THE MAGIC WEB.
ONE OF THE MAIN PORTALS ONTO THE WEB IS HERE IN THE RAVENSWOOD WILDLIFE PRESERVE.
SHHK

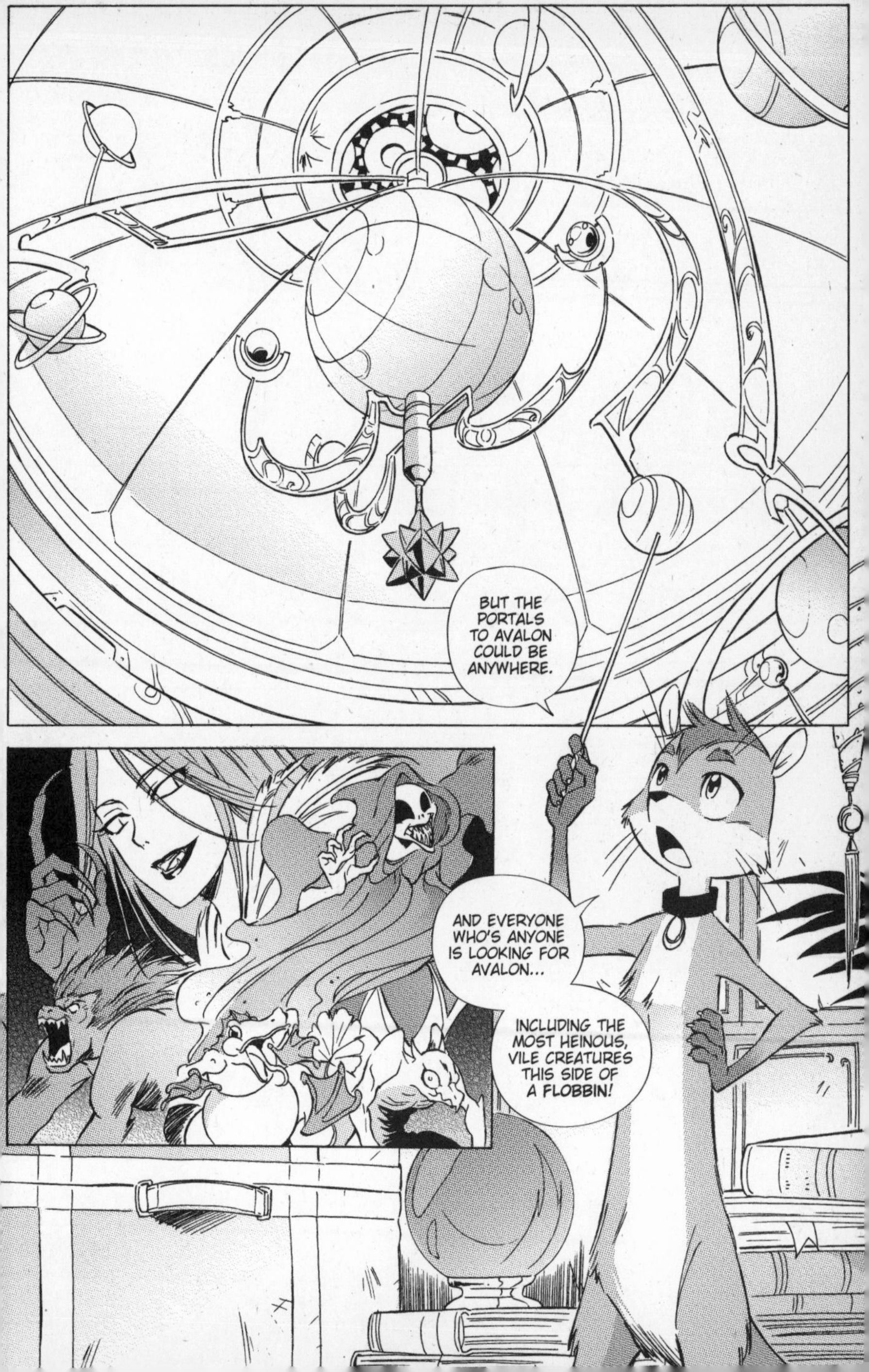
BUT THE PORTALS TO AVALON COULD BE ANYWHERE.
AND EVERYONE WHO'S ANYONE IS LOOKING FOR AVALON...
INCLUDING THE MOST HEINOUS, VILE CREATURES THIS SIDE OF A FLOBBIN!

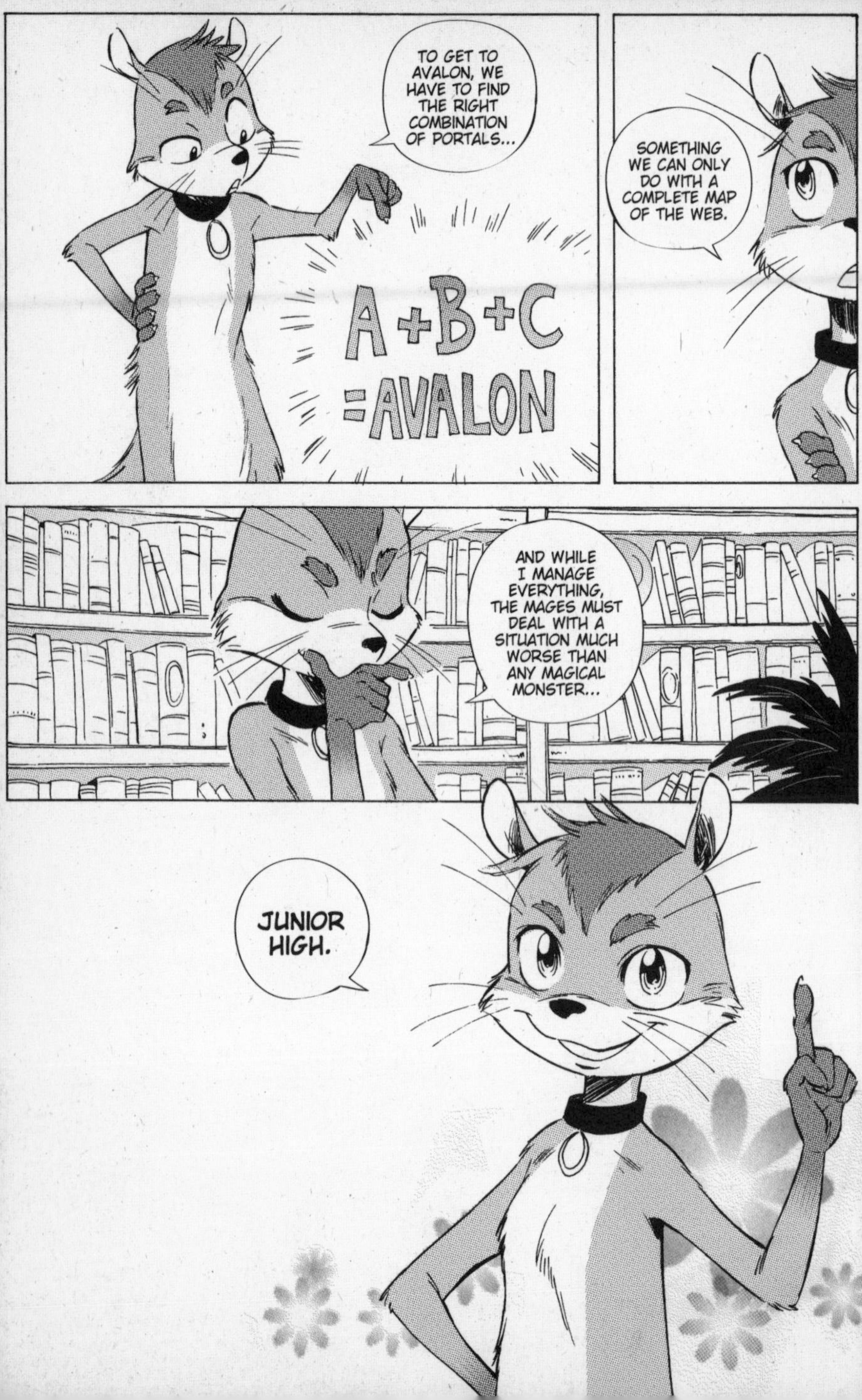
TO GET TO AVALON, WE HAVE TO FIND THE RIGHT COMBINATION OF PORTALS...
A+B+C =AVALON
SOMETHING WE CAN ONLY DO WITH A COMPLETE MAP OF THE WEB.
AND WHILE I MANAGE EVERYTHING, THE MAGES MUST DEAL WITH A SITUATION MUCH WORSE THAN ANY MAGICAL MONSTER...
JUNIOR HIGH.

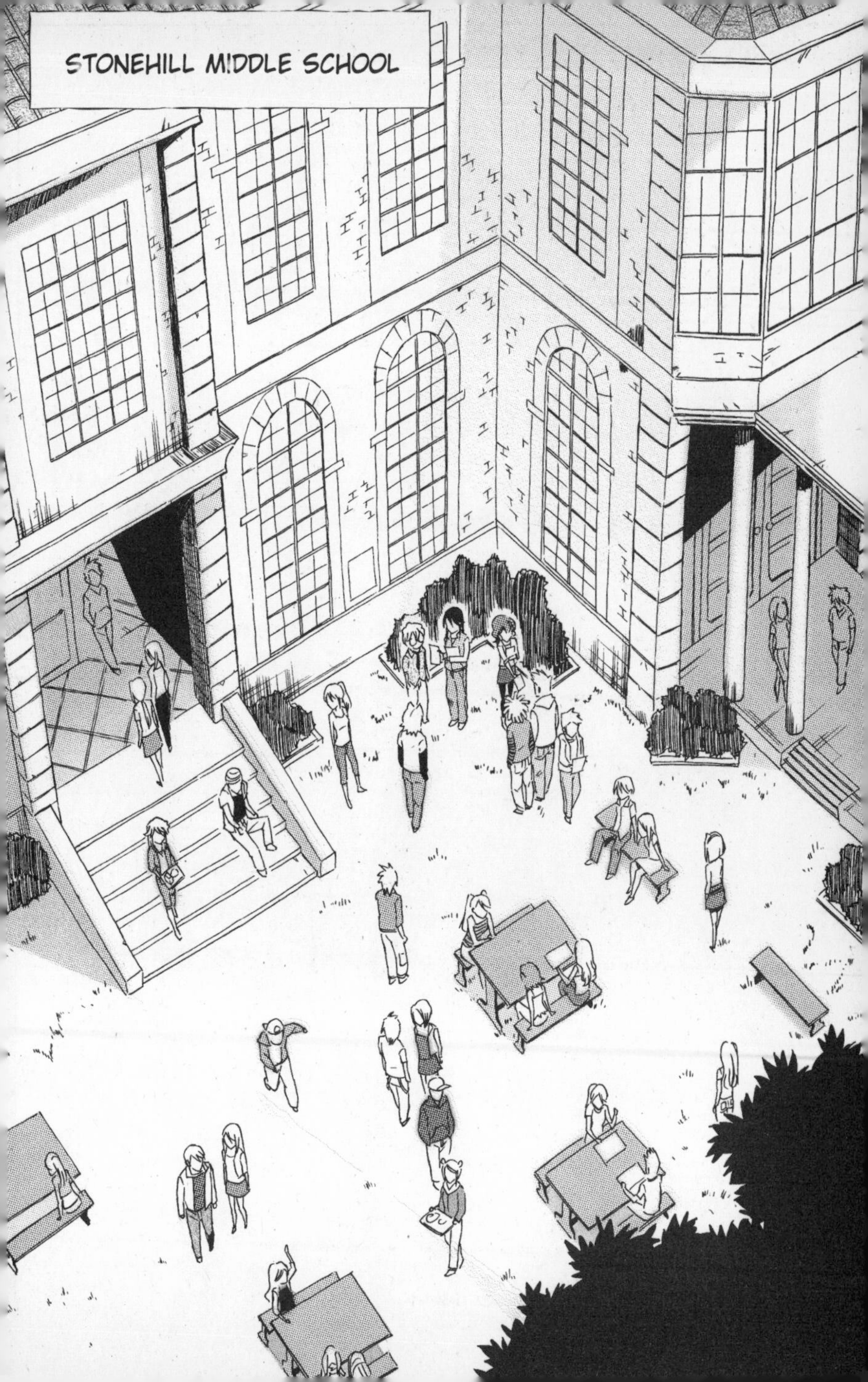
STONEHILL MIDDLE SCHOOL

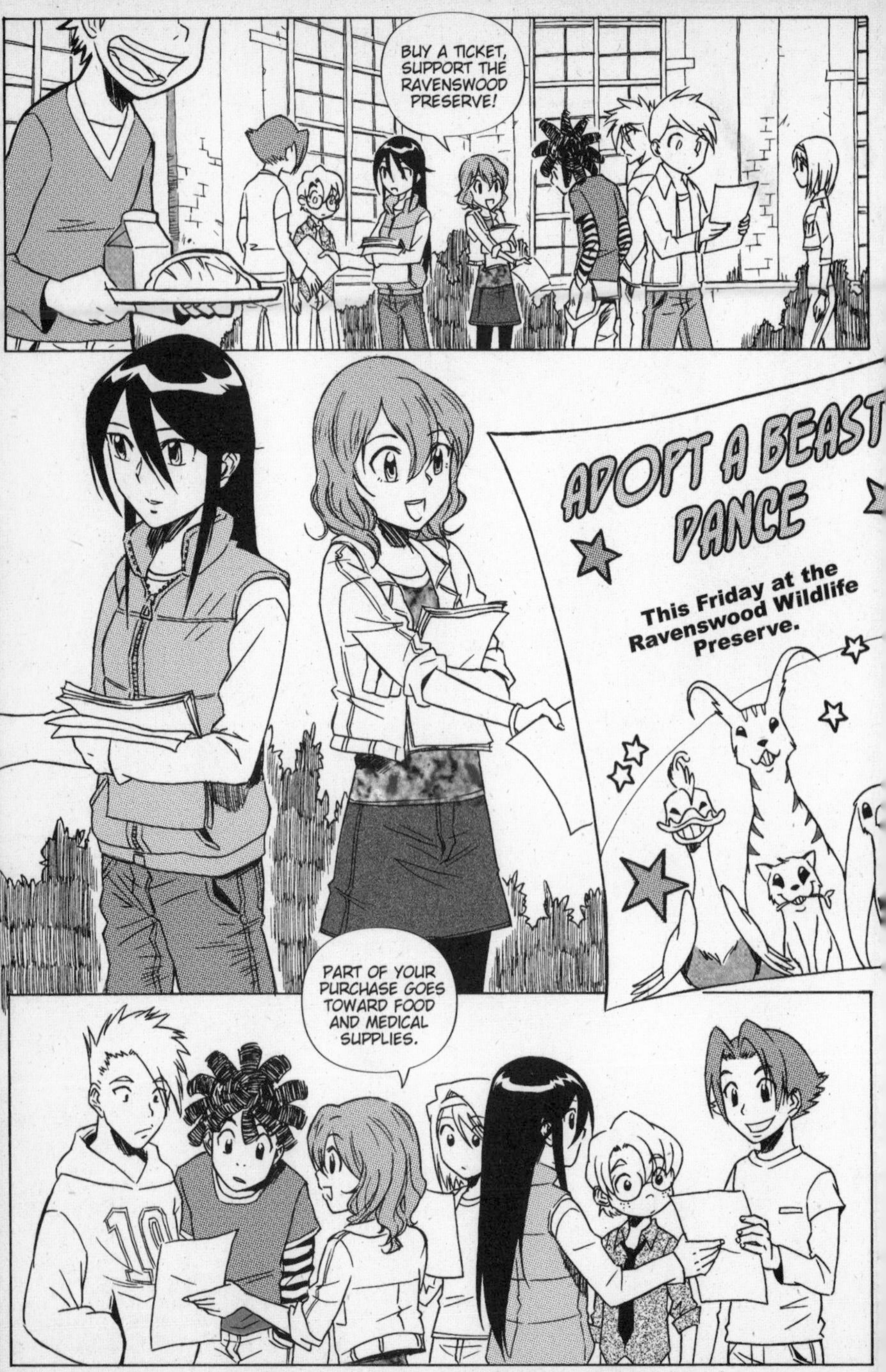
BUY A TICKET, SUPPORT THE RAVENSWOOD PRESERVE!
ADOPT A BEAST DANCE
This Friday at the Ravenswood Wildlife Preserve.
PART OF YOUR PURCHASE GOES TOWARD FOOD AND MEDICAL SUPPLIES.

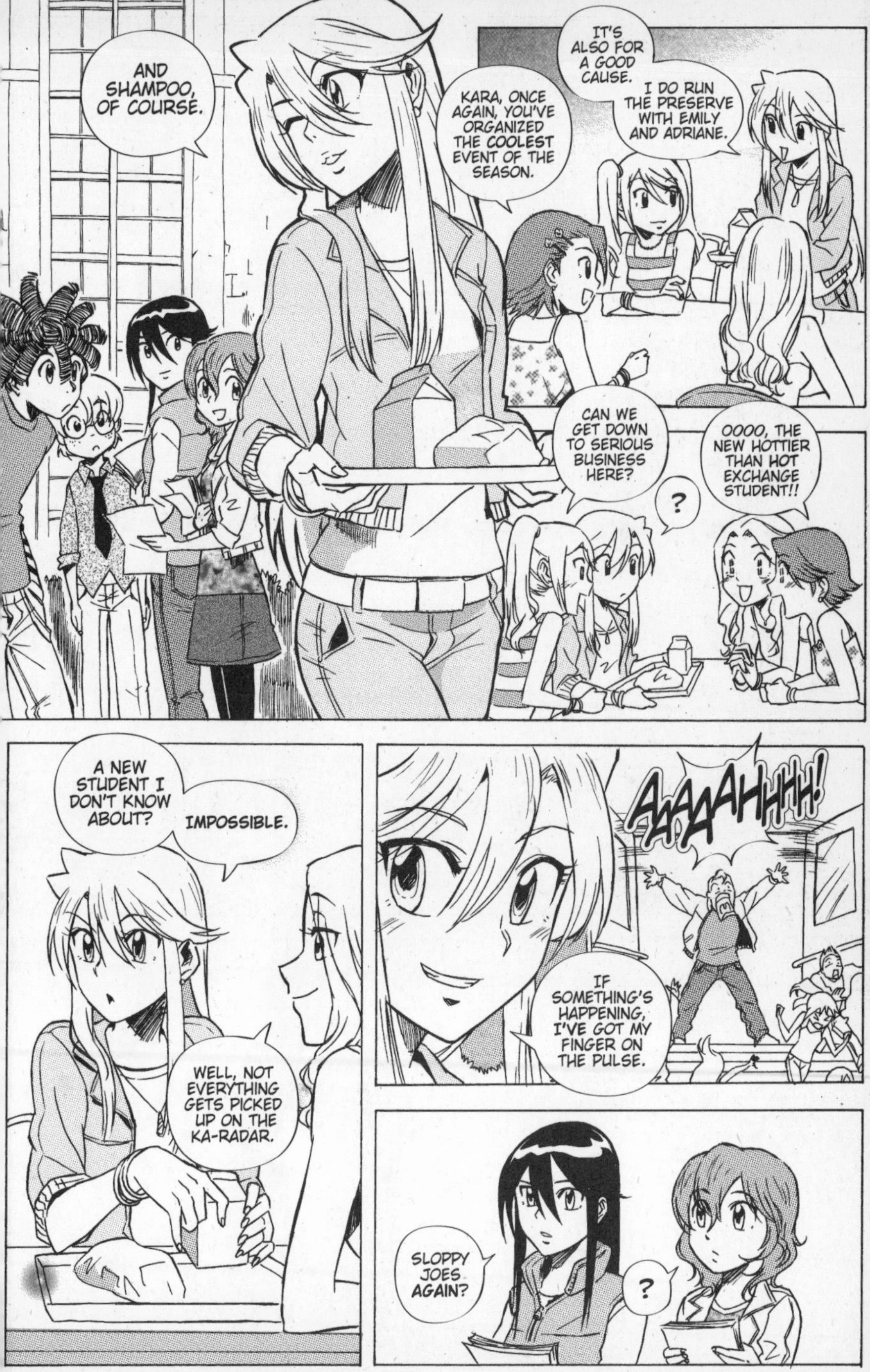
AND SHAMPOO, OF COURSE.
KARA, ONCE AGAIN, YOU'VE ORGANIZED THE COOLEST EVENT OF THE SEASON.
IT'S ALSO FOR A GOOD CAUSE.
I DO RUN THE PRESERVE WITH EMILY AND ADRIANE.
CAN WE GET DOWN TO SERIOUS BUSINESS HERE?
?
OOOO, THE NEW HOTTIER THAN HOT EXCHANGE STUDENT!!
A NEW STUDENT I DON'T KNOW ABOUT?
IMPOSSIBLE.
WELL, NOT EVERYTHING GETS PICKED UP ON THE KA-RADAR.
AAAAHHHH!
IF SOMETHING'S HAPPENING, I'VE GOT MY FINGER ON THE PULSE.
SLOPPY JOES AGAIN?
?

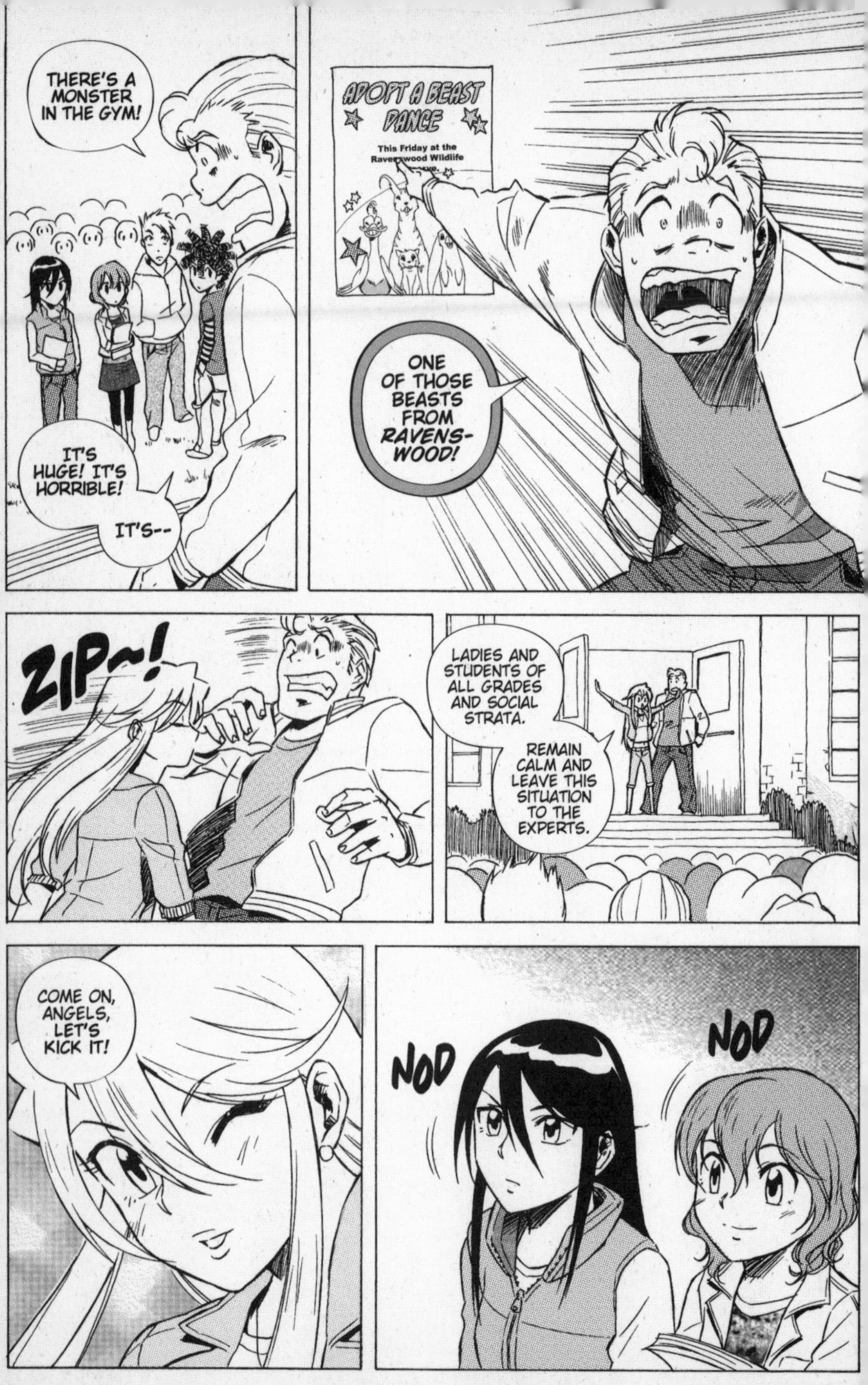
THERE'S A MONSTER IN THE GYM!
IT'S HUGE! IT'S HORRIBLE!
IT'S--
ADOPT A BEAST DANCE
This Friday at the Ravenswood Wildlife
ONE OF THOSE BEASTS FROM RAVENSWOOD!
ZIP~!
LADIES AND STUDENTS OF ALL GRADES AND SOCIAL STRATA.
REMAIN CALM AND LEAVE THIS SITUATION TO THE EXPERTS.
COME ON, ANGELS, LET'S KICK IT!
NOD
NOD

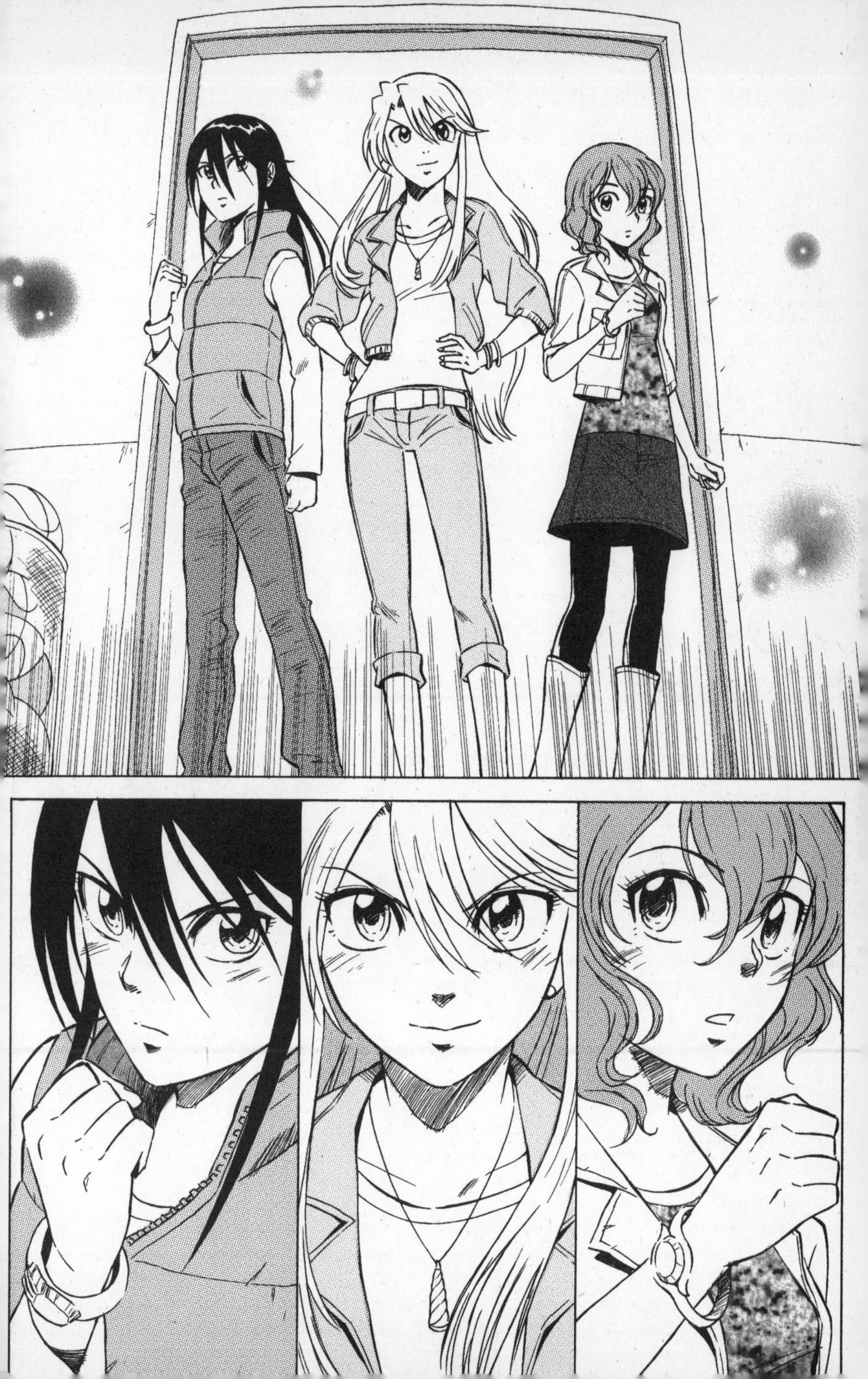

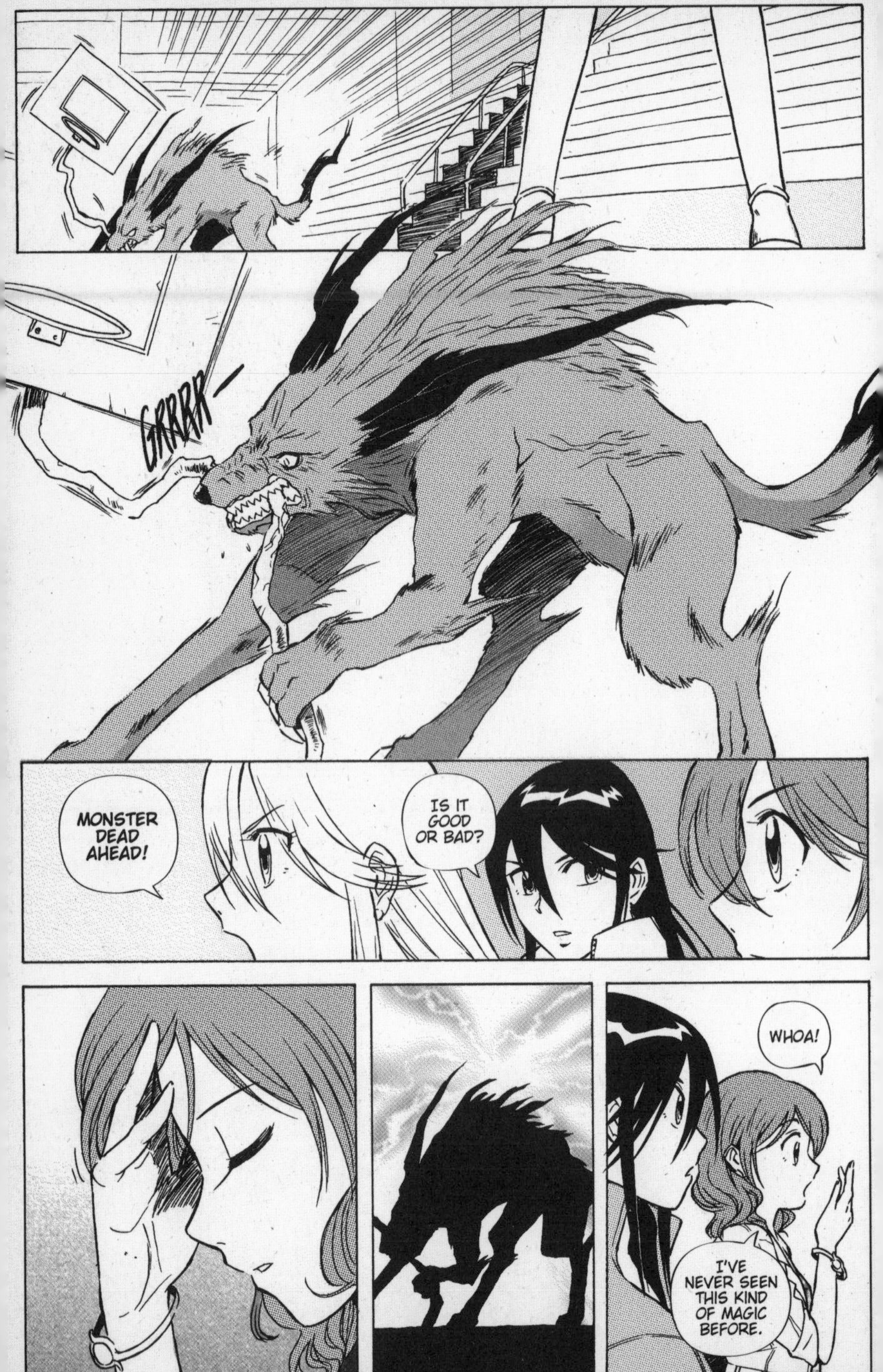
GRRRR
MONSTER DEAD AHEAD!
IS IT GOOD OR BAD?
WHOA!
I'VE NEVER SEEN THIS KIND OF MAGIC BEFORE.

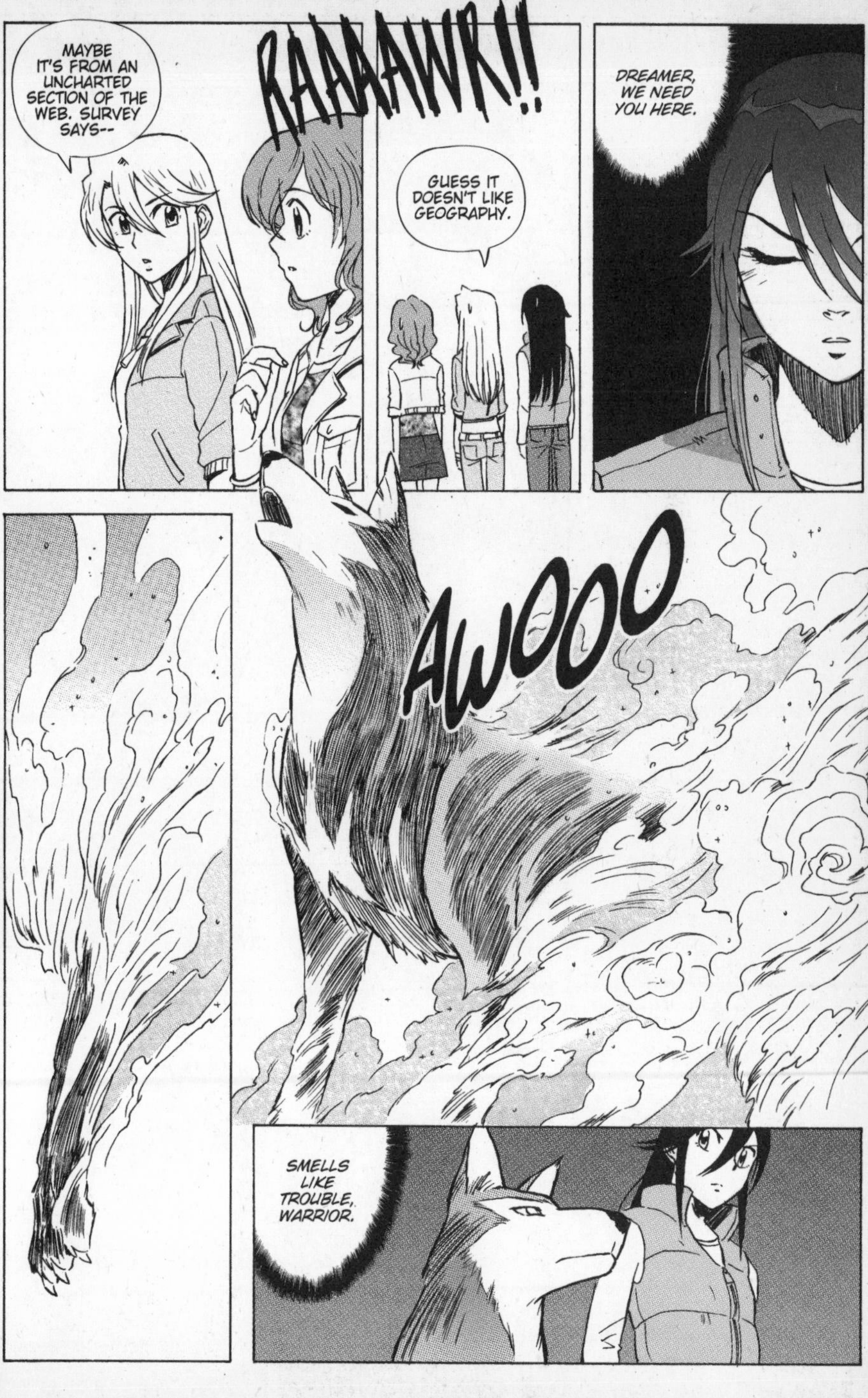
MAYBE IT'S FROM AN UNCHARTED SECTION OF THE WEB. SURVEY SAYS--
RAAAAWR!!
GUESS IT DOESN'T LIKE GEOGRAPHY.
DREAMER, WE NEED YOU HERE.
AWOOO
SMELLS LIKE TROUBLE, WARRIOR.

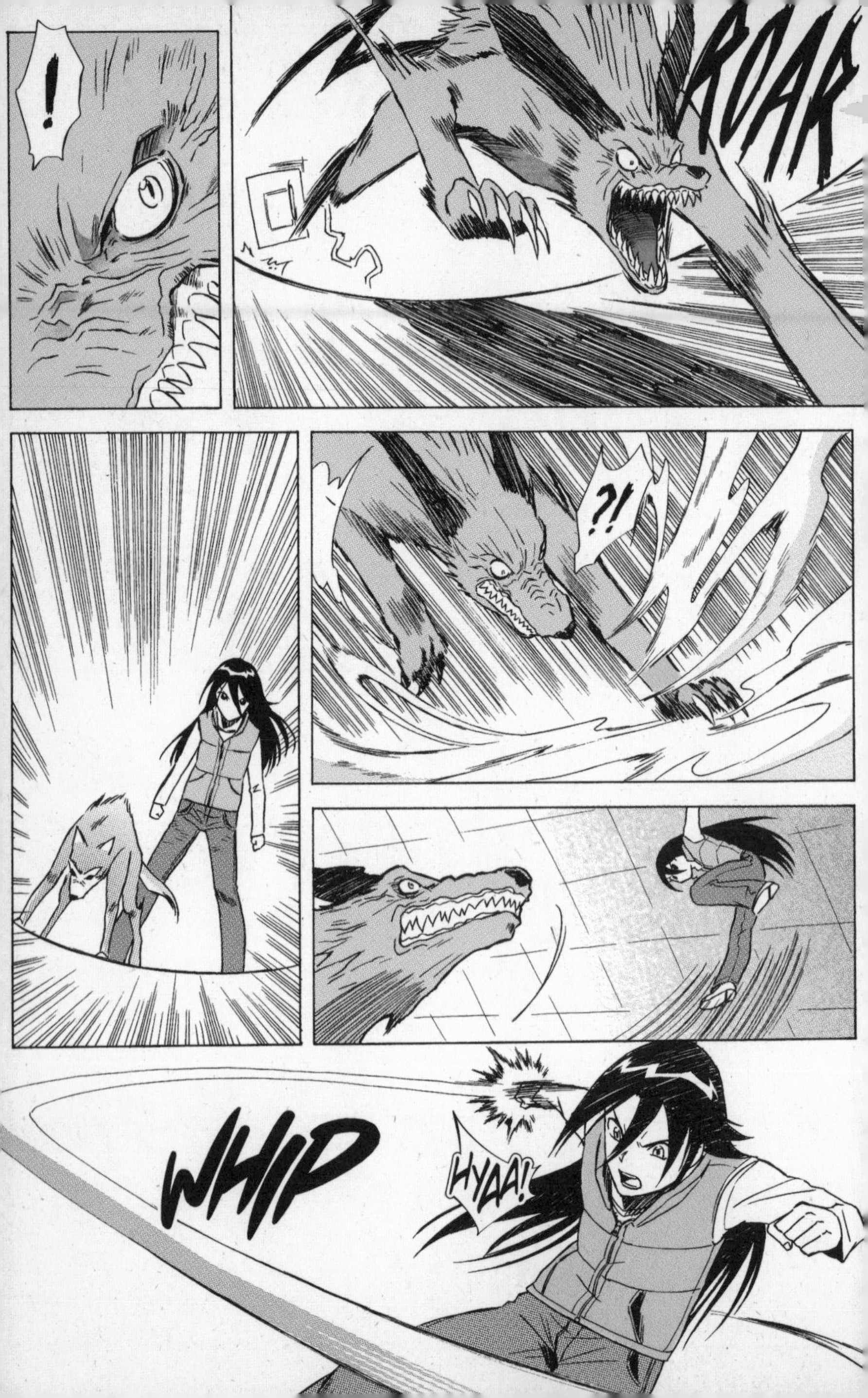
!
ROAR
?!
WHIP
HYAA!

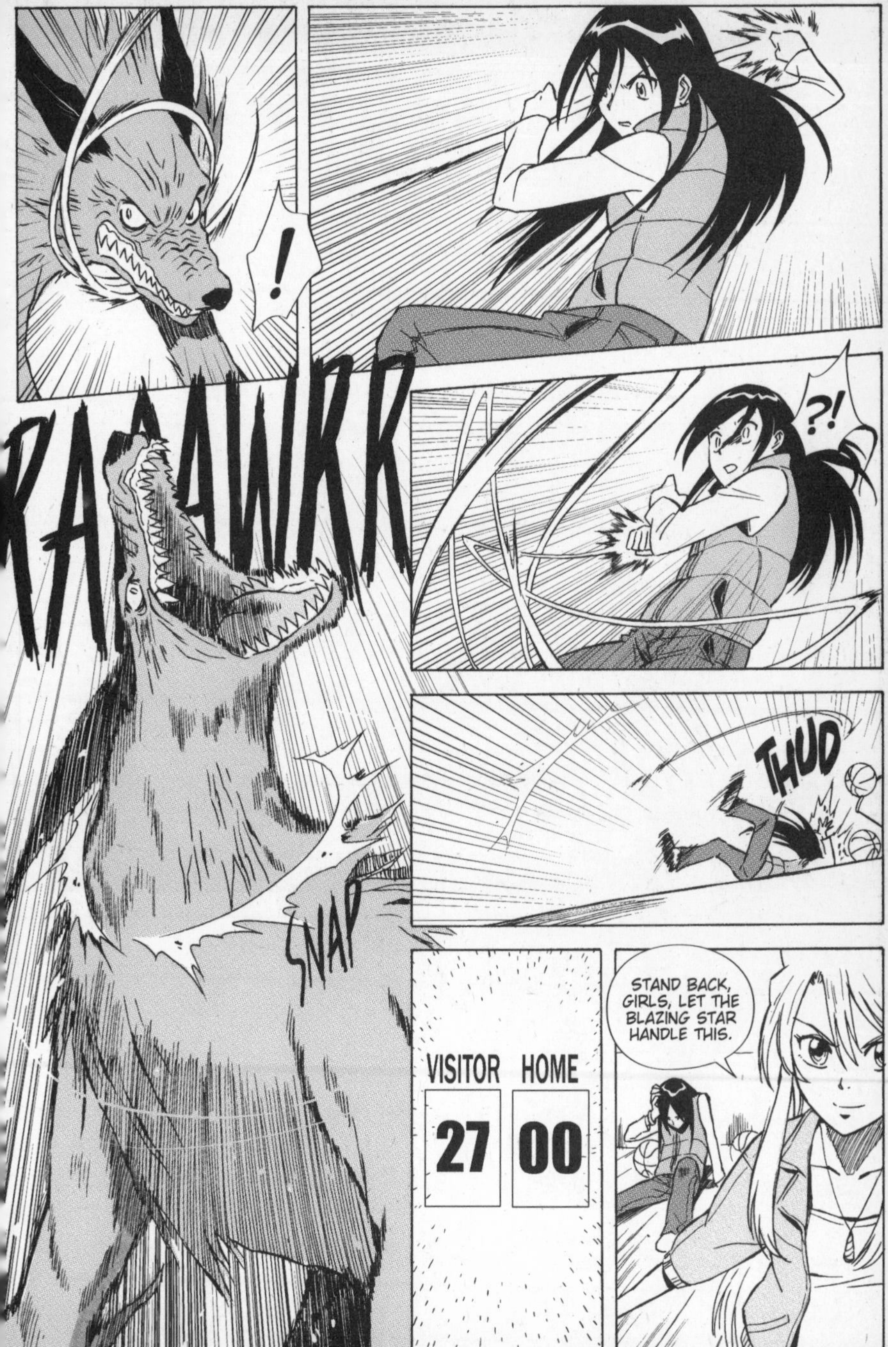

!
RAAAWRR
?!
THUD
SNAP
VISITOR HOME
27 00
STAND BACK, GIRLS, LET THE BLAZING STAR HANDLE THIS.

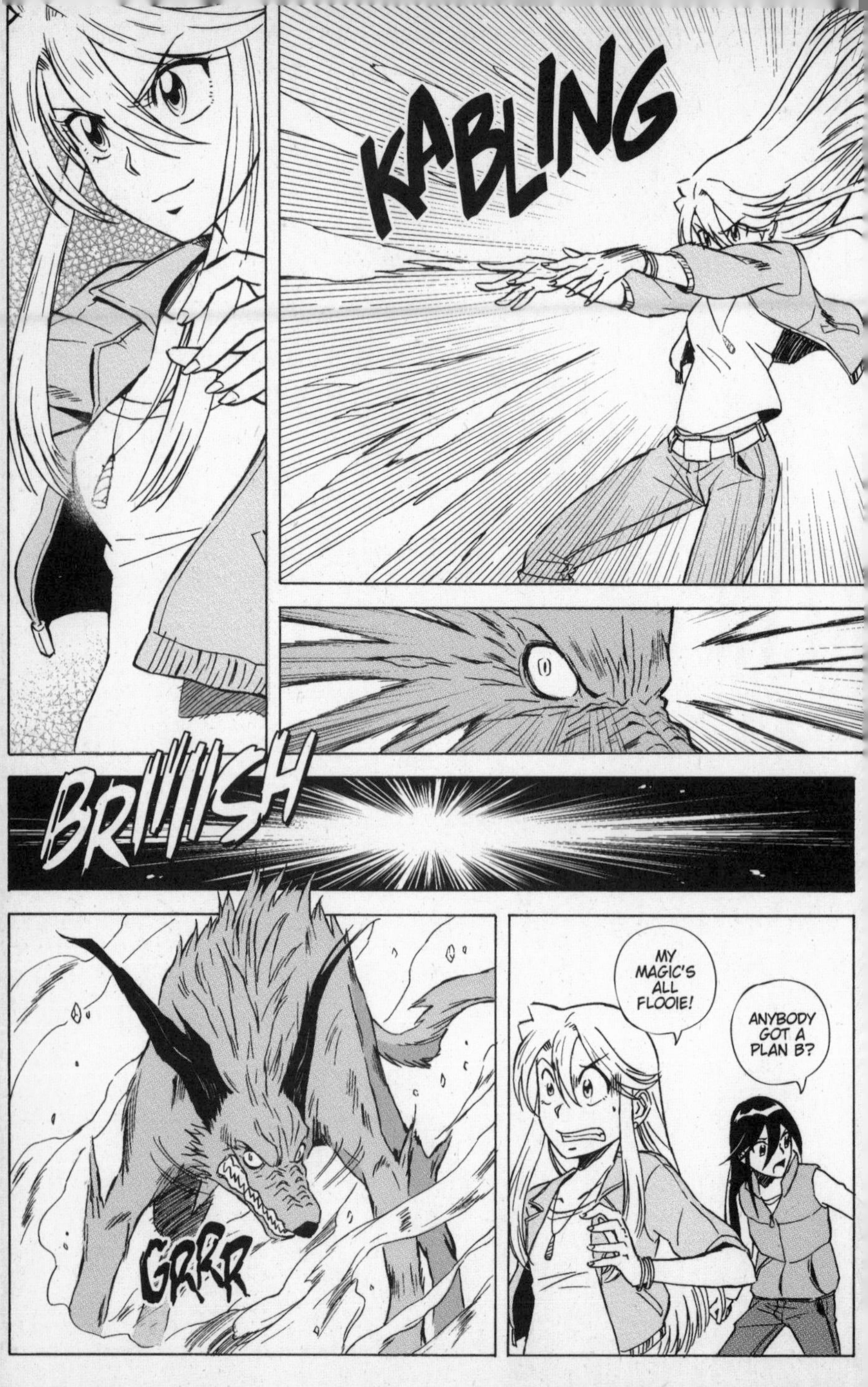
KABLING
BRIIIISH
GRRR
MY MAGIC'S ALL FLOOIE!
ANYBODY GOT A PLAN B?

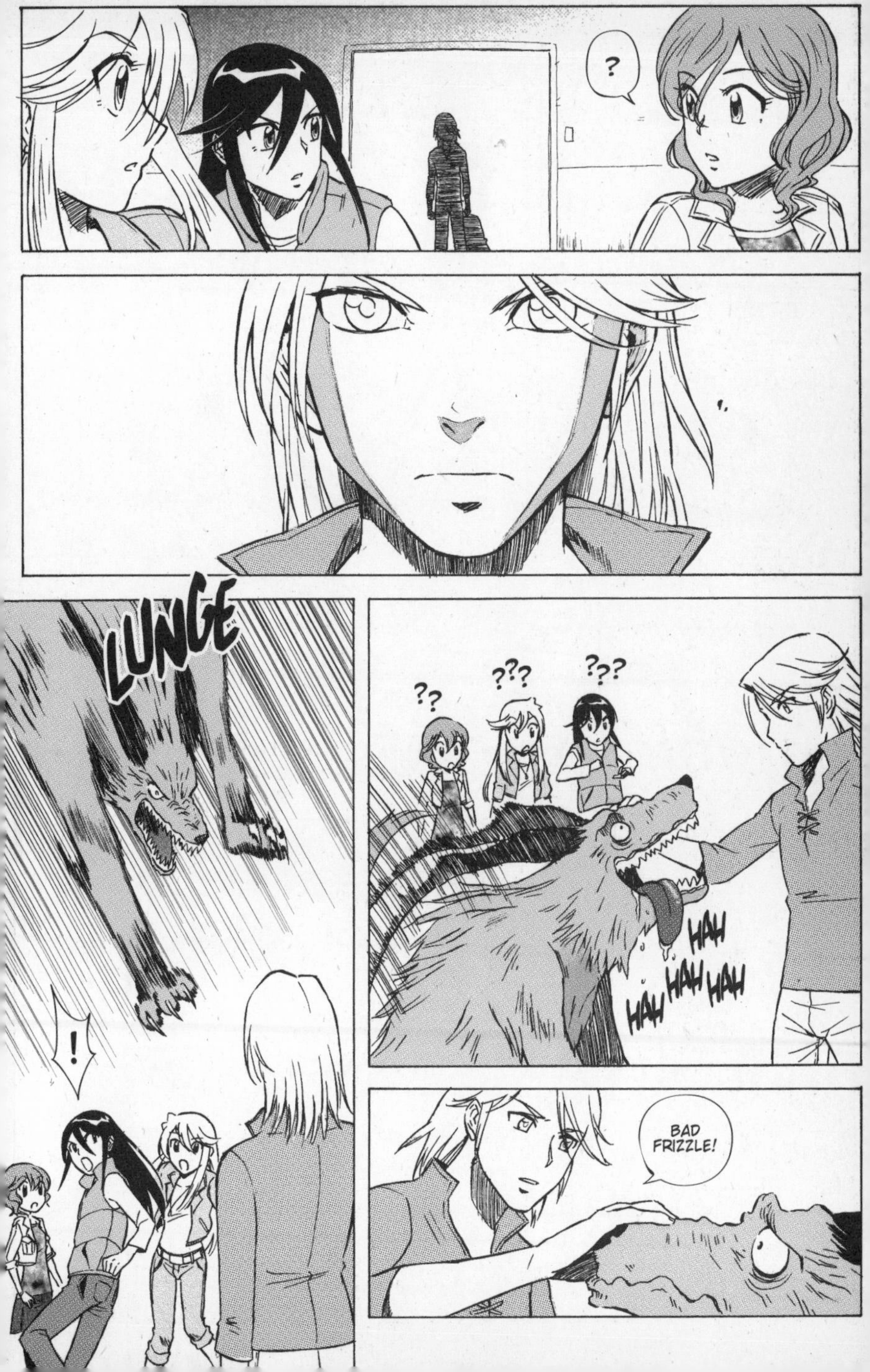
?
LUNGE
!
??
???
???
HAH
HAH
HAH
HAH
BAD FRIZZLE!

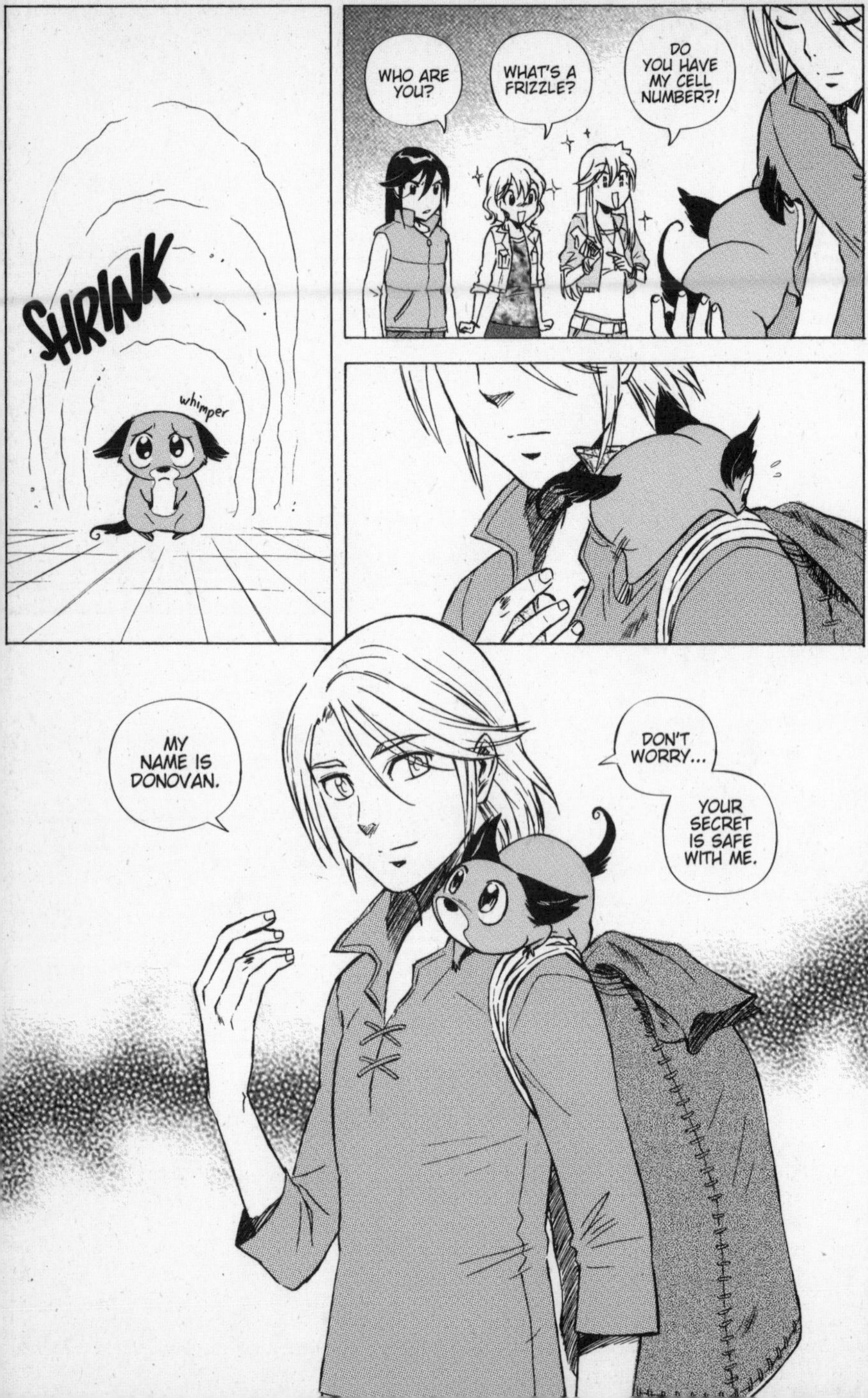
SHRINK
whimper
WHO ARE YOU?
WHAT'S A FRIZZLE?
DO YOU HAVE MY CELL NUMBER?!
MY NAME IS DONOVAN.
DON'T WORRY...
YOUR SECRET IS SAFE WITH ME.

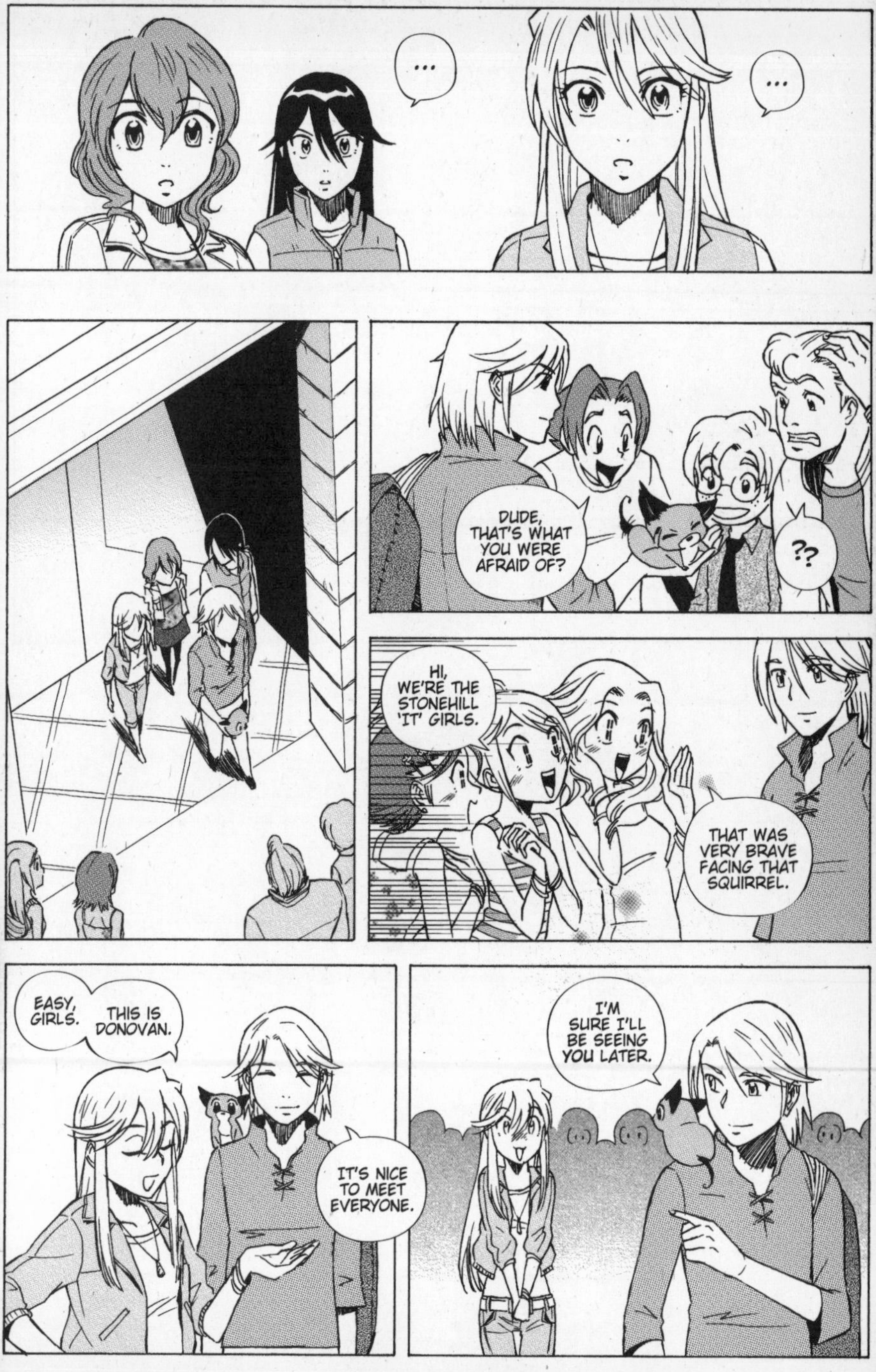
...
...
DUDE, THAT'S WHAT YOU WERE AFRAID OF?
??
HI, WE'RE THE STONEHILL 'IT' GIRLS.
THAT WAS VERY BRAVE FACING THAT SQUIRREL.
EASY, GIRLS.
THIS IS DONOVAN.
IT'S NICE TO MEET EVERYONE.
I'M SURE I'LL BE SEEING YOU LATER.

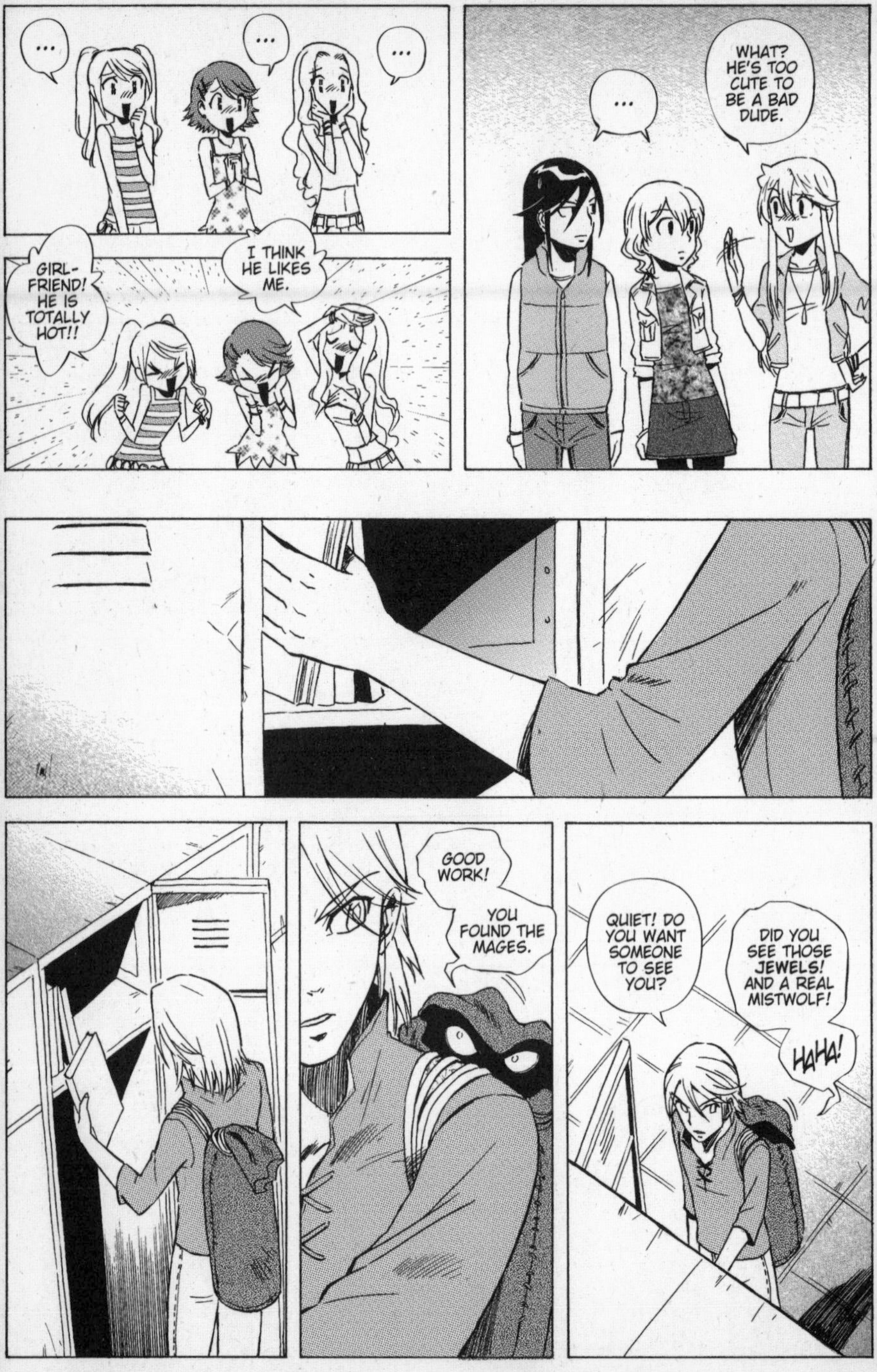
...
...
...
GIRL-FRIEND! HE IS TOTALLY HOT!!
I THINK HE LIKES ME.
...
WHAT? HE'S TOO CUTE TO BE A BAD DUDE.
GOOD WORK!
YOU FOUND THE MAGES.
QUIET! DO YOU WANT SOMEONE TO SEE YOU?
DID YOU SEE THOSE JEWELS! AND A REAL MISTWOLF!
HAHA!

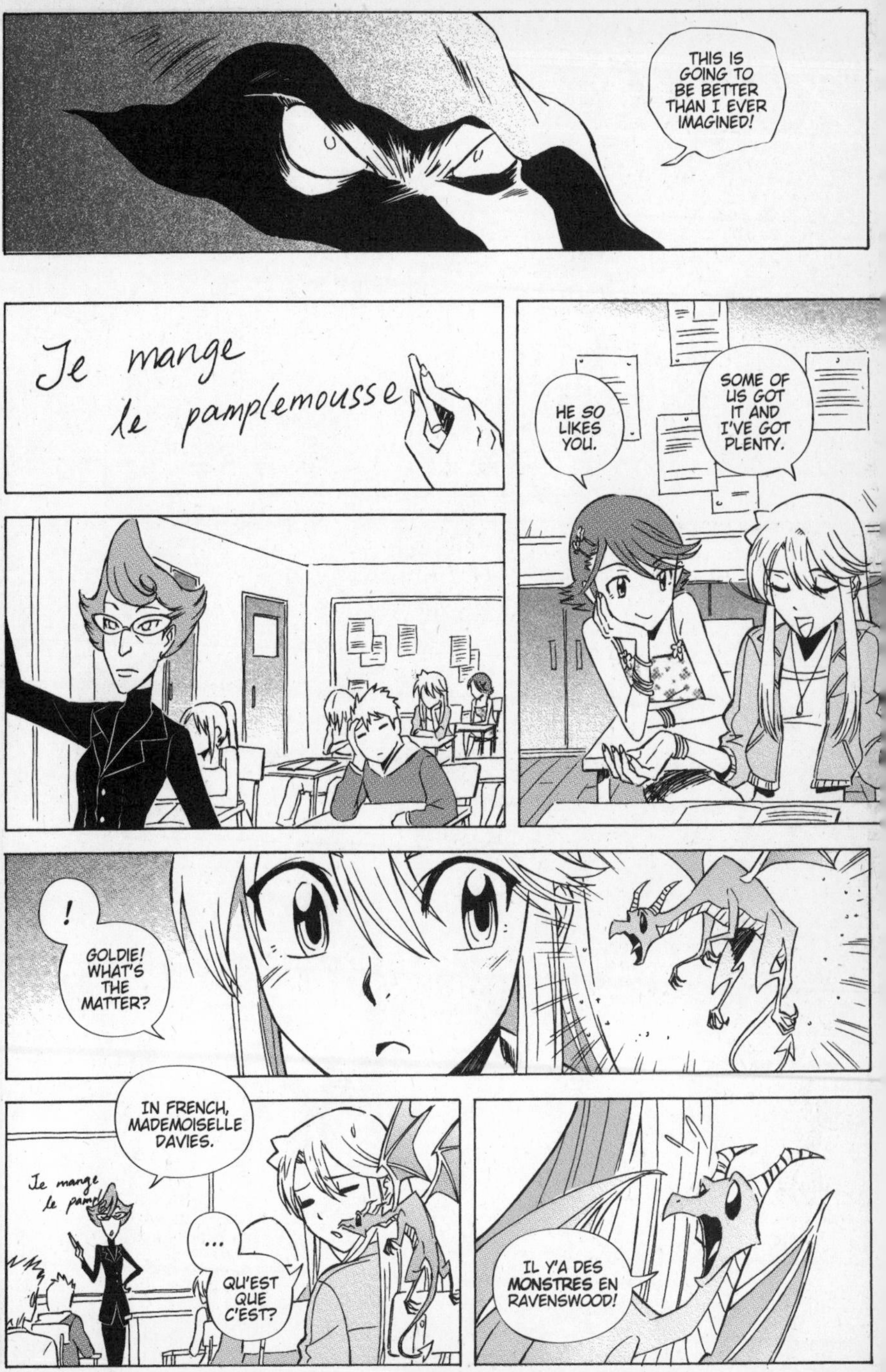
THIS IS GOING TO BE BETTER THAN I EVER IMAGINED!
Je mange le pamplemousse
HE SO LIKES YOU.
SOME OF US GOT IT AND I'VE GOT PLENTY.
!
GOLDIE! WHAT'S THE MATTER?
IN FRENCH, MADEMOISELLE DAVIES.
Je mange le pam
...
QU'EST QUE C'EST?
IL Y'A DES MONSTRES EN RAVENSWOOD!

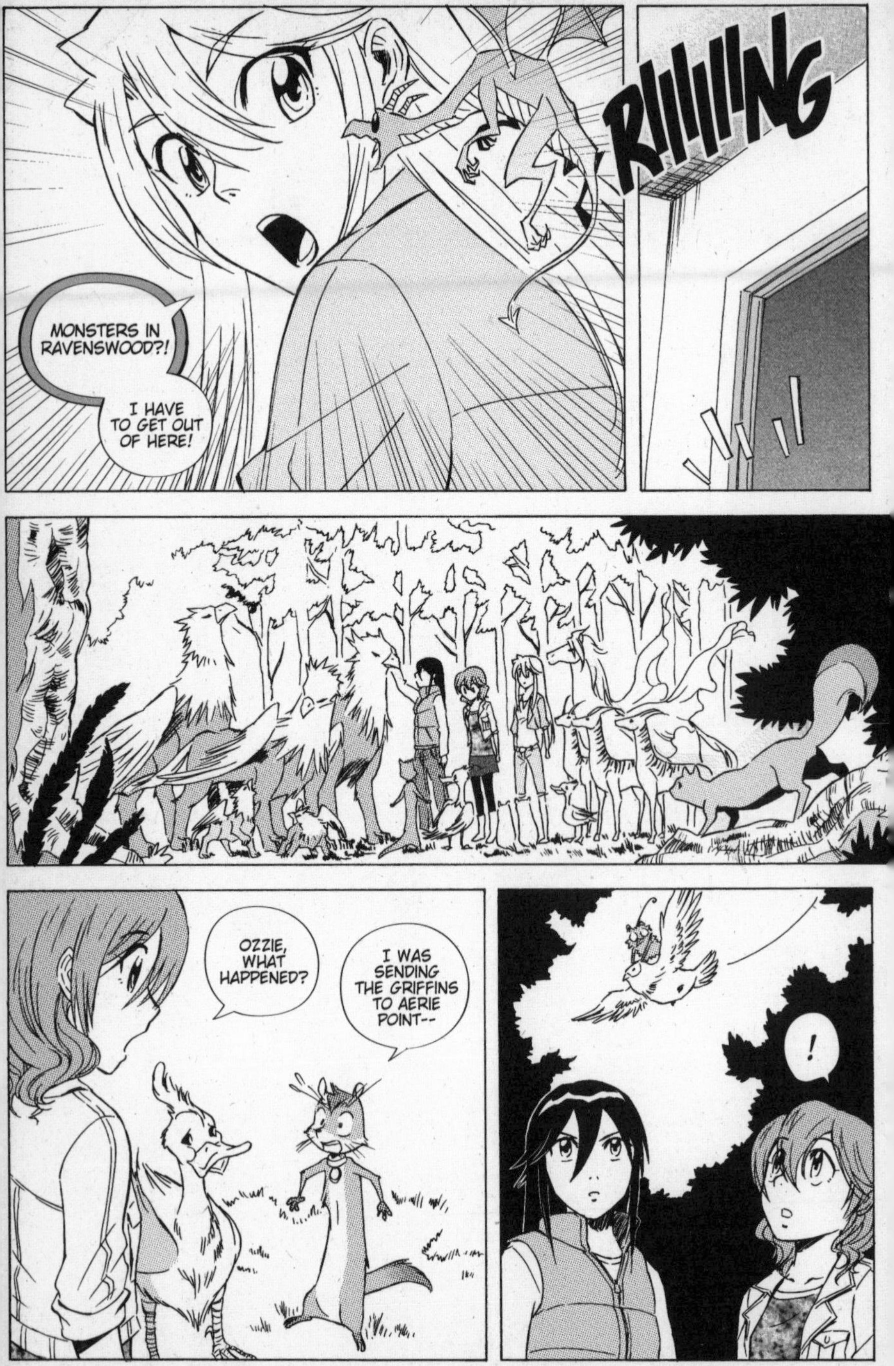
MONSTERS IN RAVENSWOOD?!
I HAVE TO GET OUT OF HERE!
RIIIIING
OZZIE, WHAT HAPPENED?
I WAS SENDING THE GRIFFINS TO AERIE POINT--
!

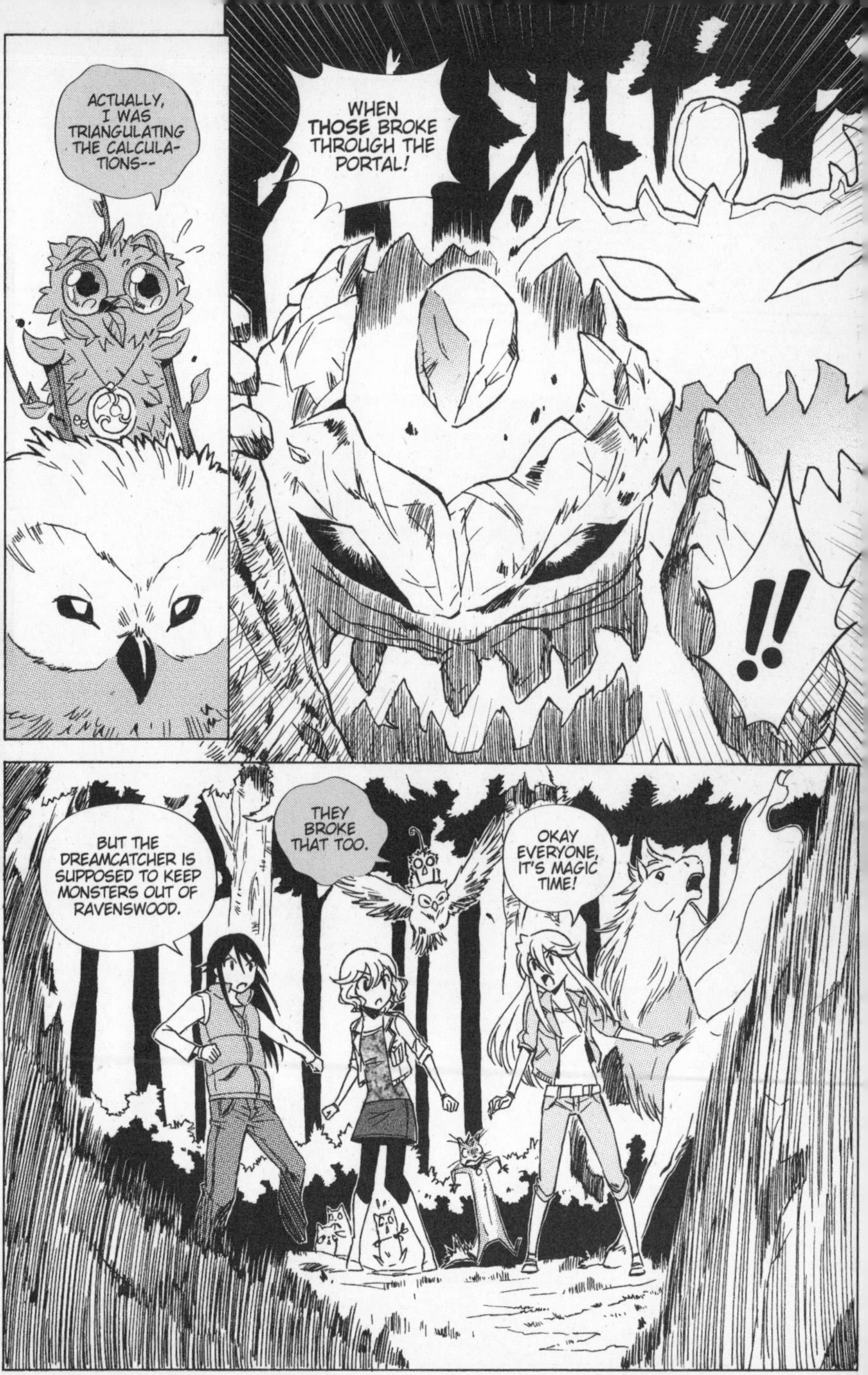
ACTUALLY, I WAS TRIANGULATING THE CALCULA-TIONS--
WHEN THOSE BROKE THROUGH THE PORTAL!
!!
BUT THE DREAMCATCHER IS SUPPOSED TO KEEP MONSTERS OUT OF RAVENSWOOD.
THEY BROKE THAT TOO.
OKAY EVERYONE, IT'S MAGIC TIME!

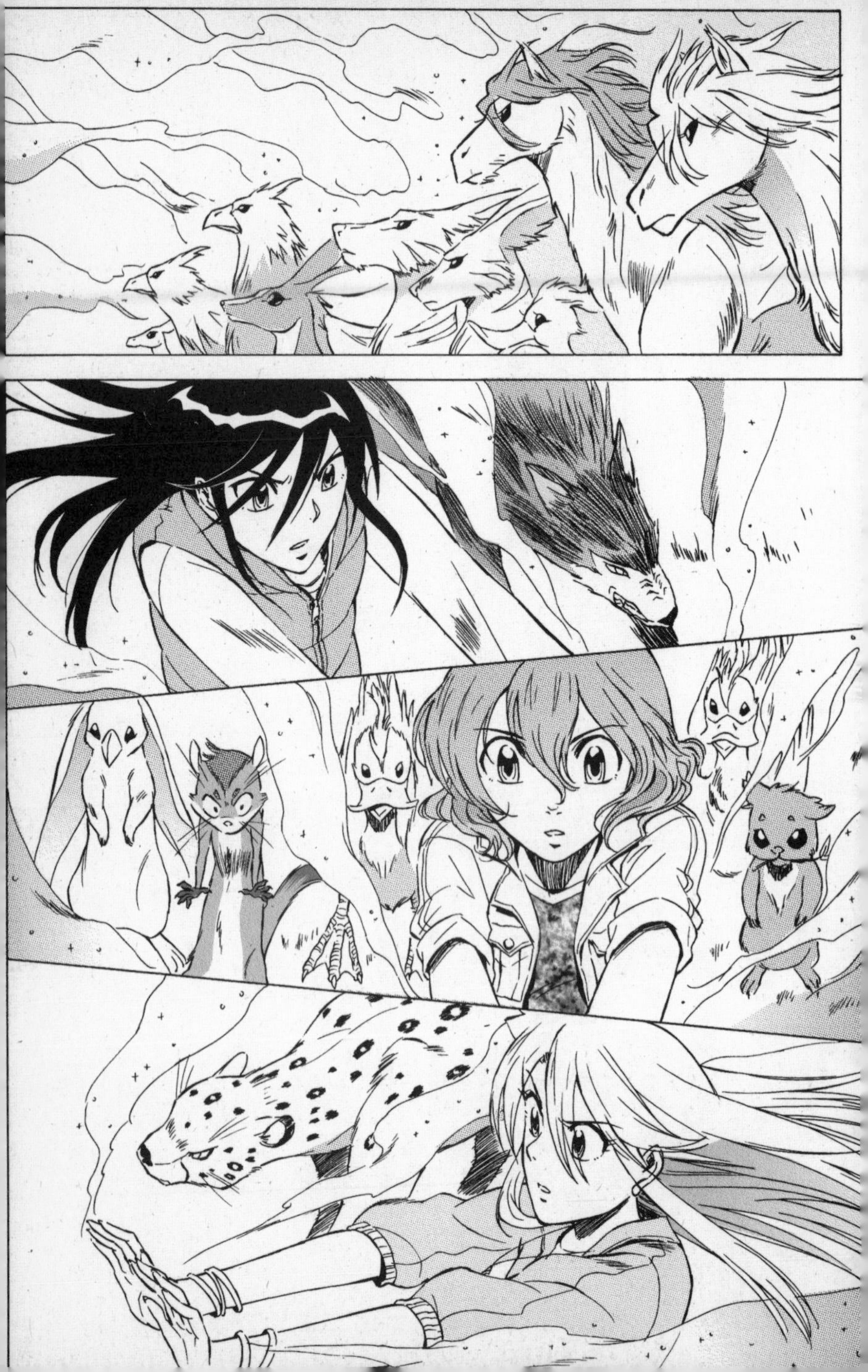

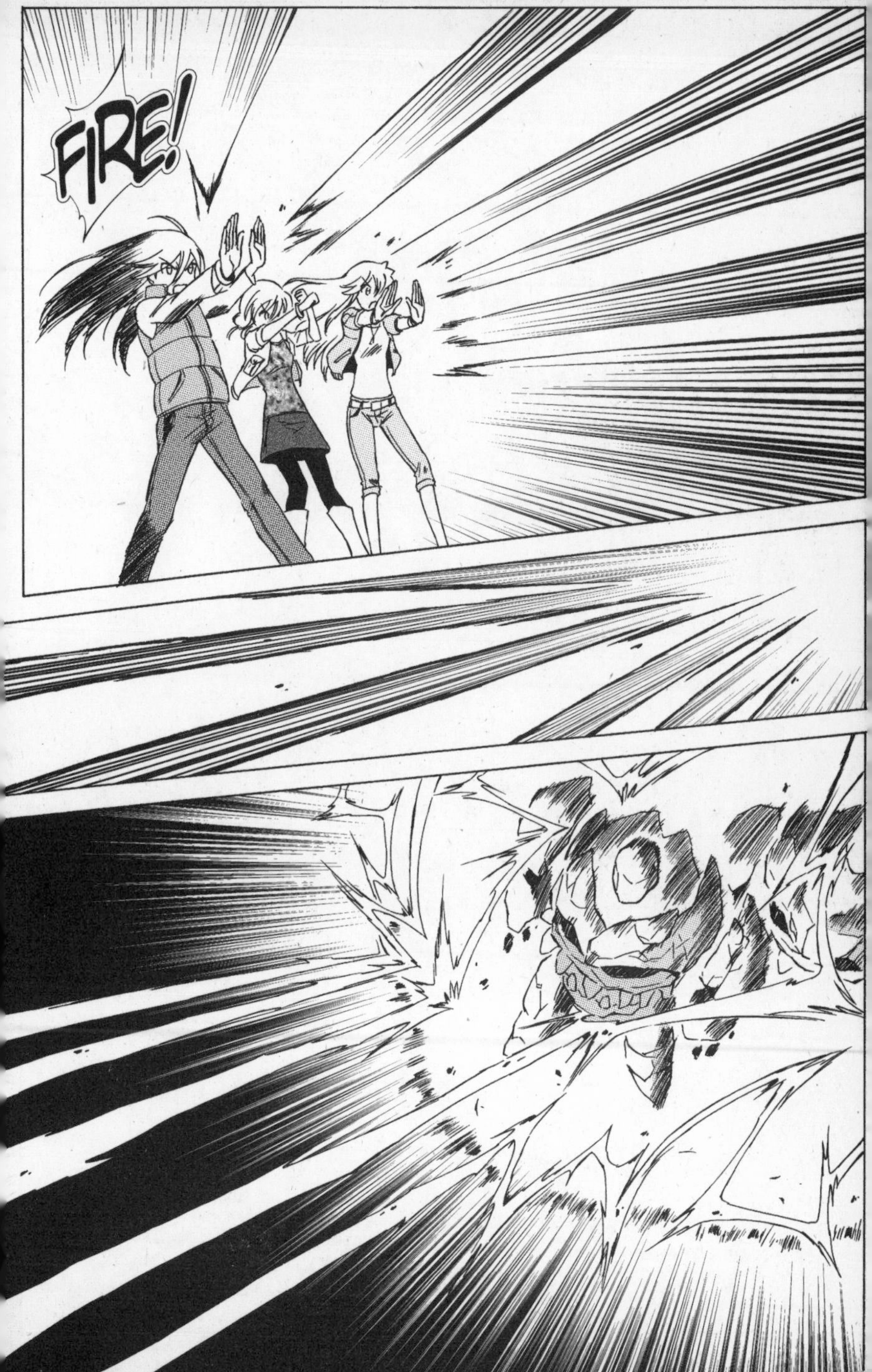
FIRE!

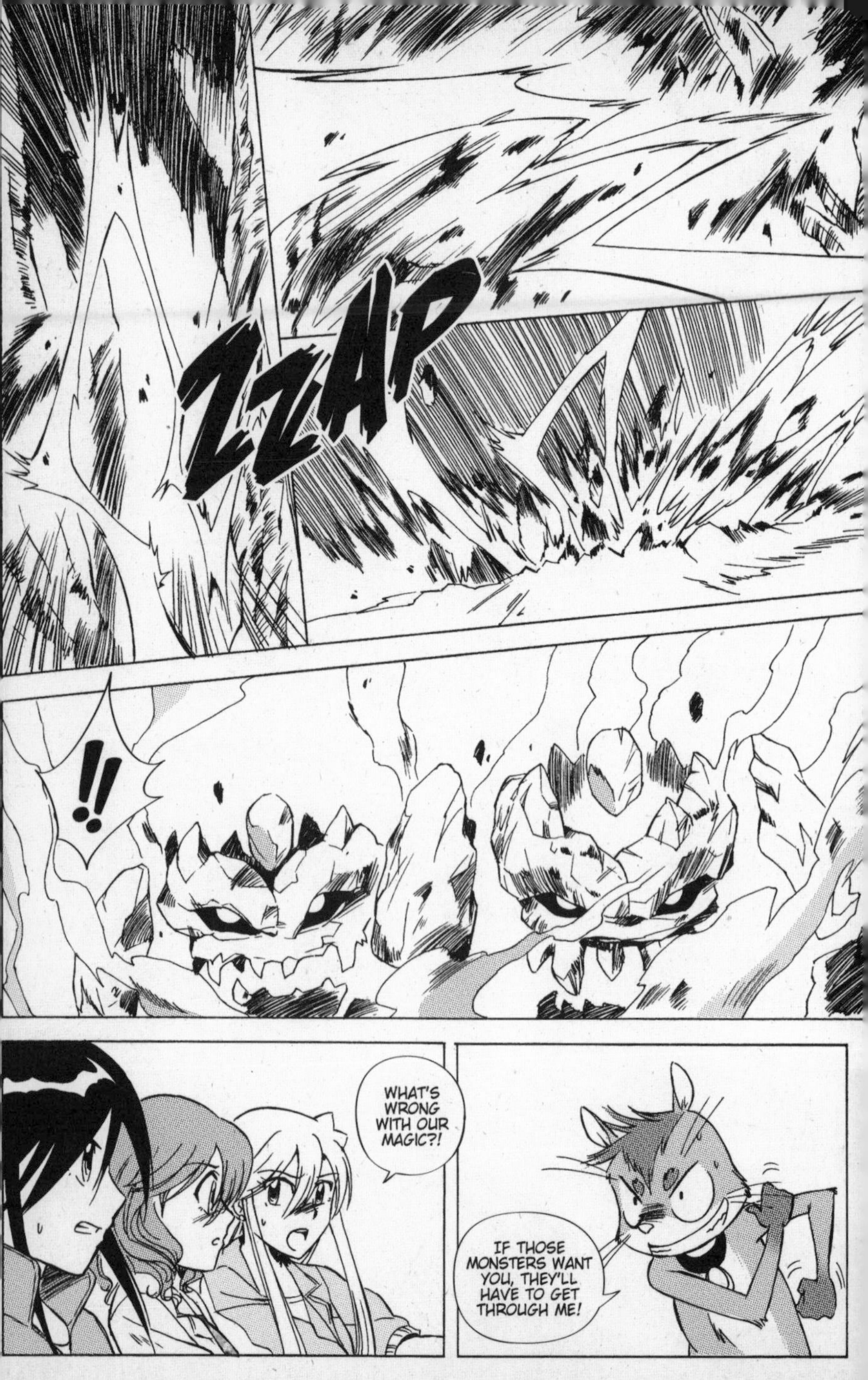
ZZAP
!!
WHAT'S WRONG WITH OUR MAGIC?!
IF THOSE MONSTERS WANT YOU, THEY'LL HAVE TO GET THROUGH ME!

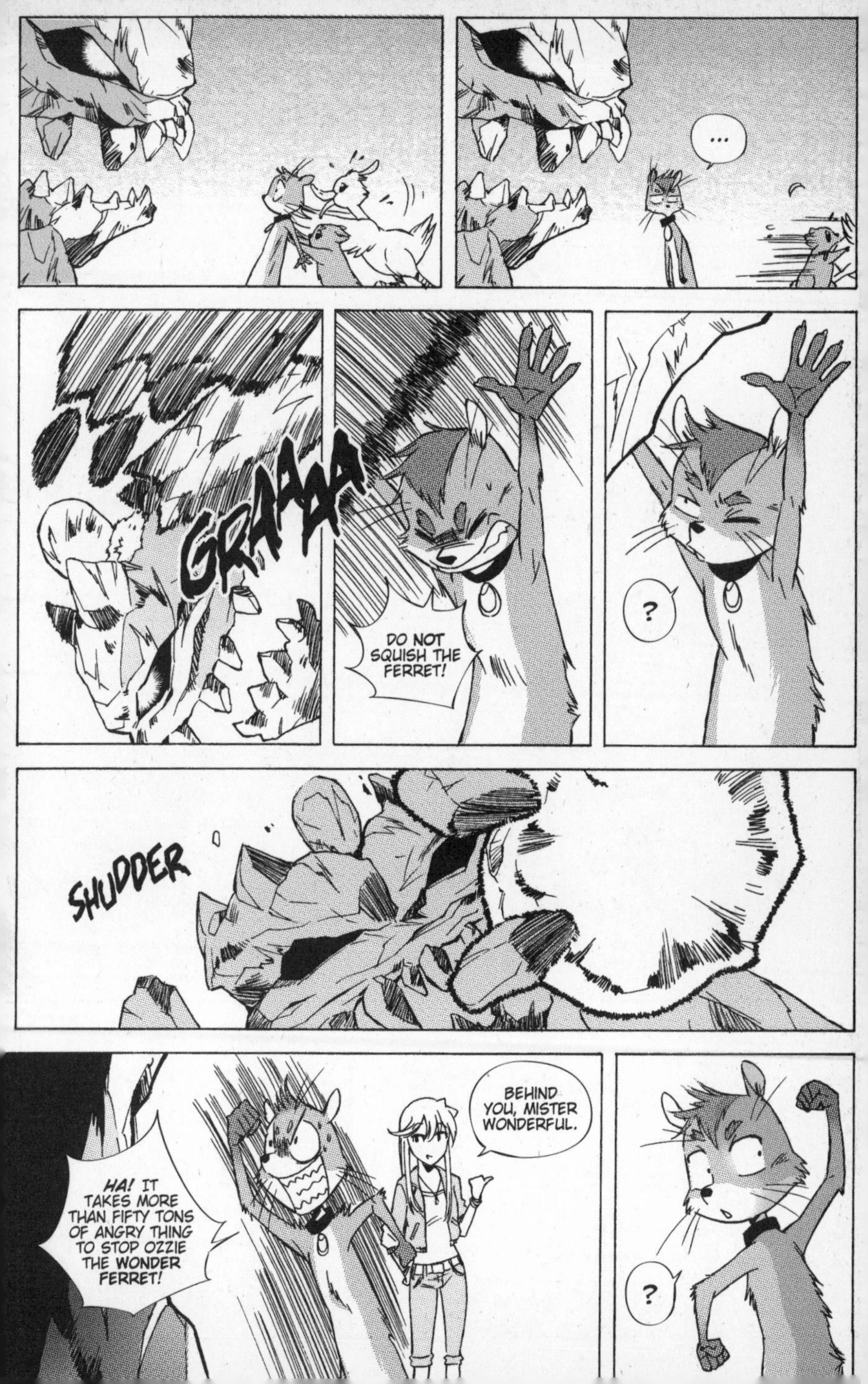
...
GRAAAA
DO NOT SQUISH THE FERRET!
?
SHUDDER
HA! IT TAKES MORE THAN FIFTY TONS OF ANGRY THING TO STOP OZZIE THE WONDER FERRET!
BEHIND YOU, MISTER WONDERFUL.
?

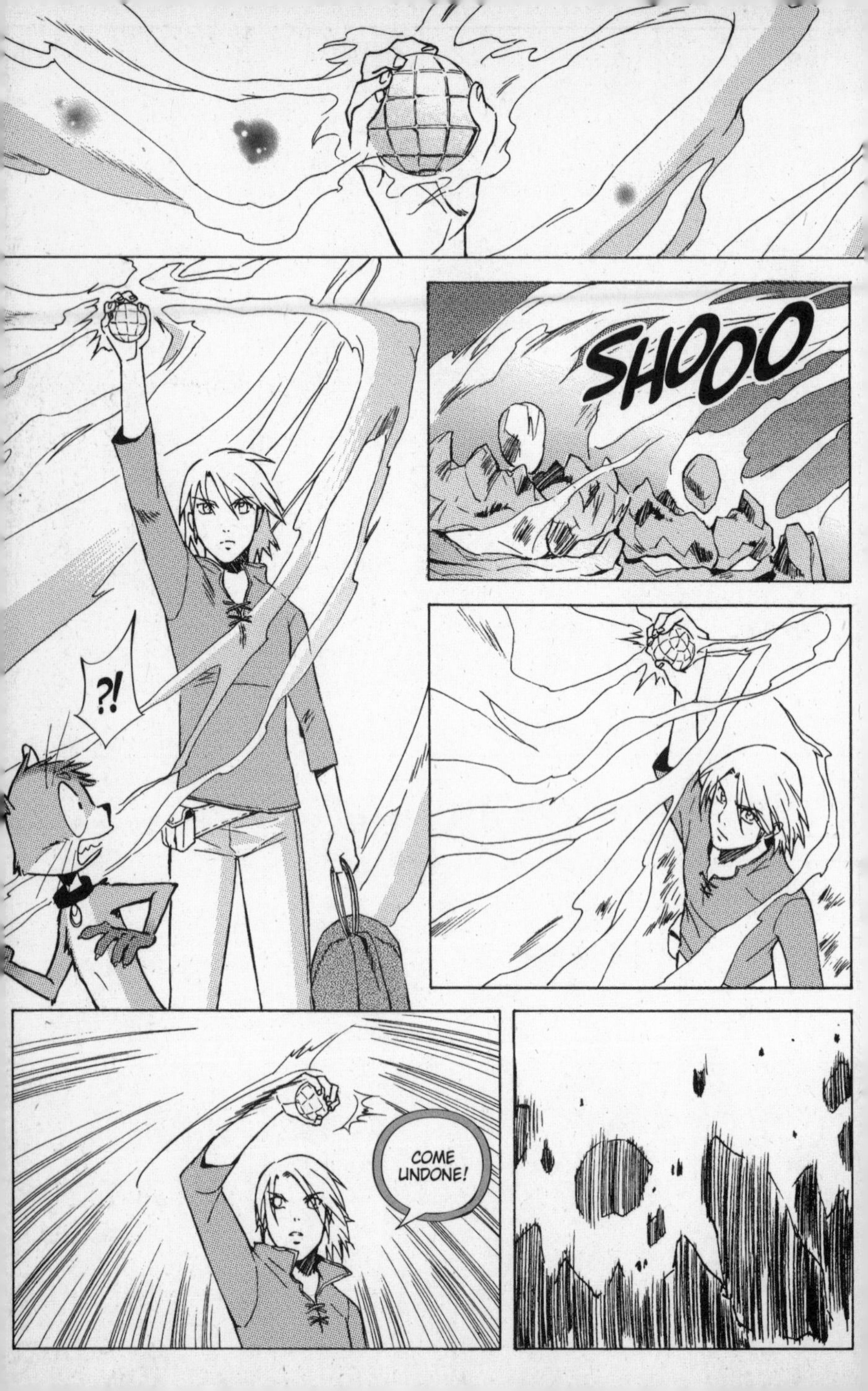
?!
SHOOO
COME UNDONE!

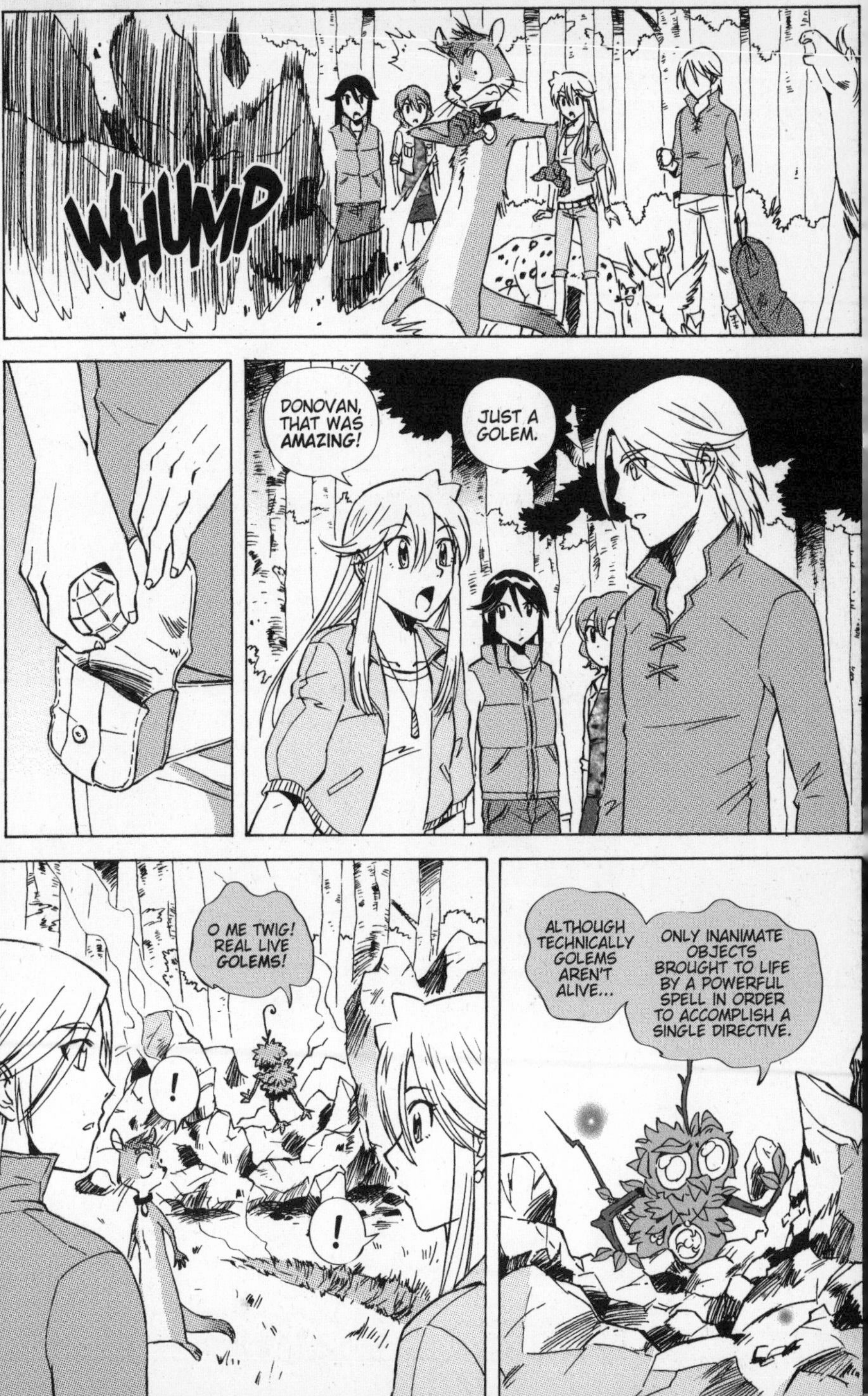
WHUMP
DONOVAN, THAT WAS AMAZING!
JUST A GOLEM.
O ME TWIG! REAL LIVE GOLEMS!
!
!
ALTHOUGH TECHNICALLY GOLEMS AREN'T ALIVE...
ONLY INANIMATE OBJECTS BROUGHT TO LIFE BY A POWERFUL SPELL IN ORDER TO ACCOMPLISH A SINGLE DIRECTIVE.

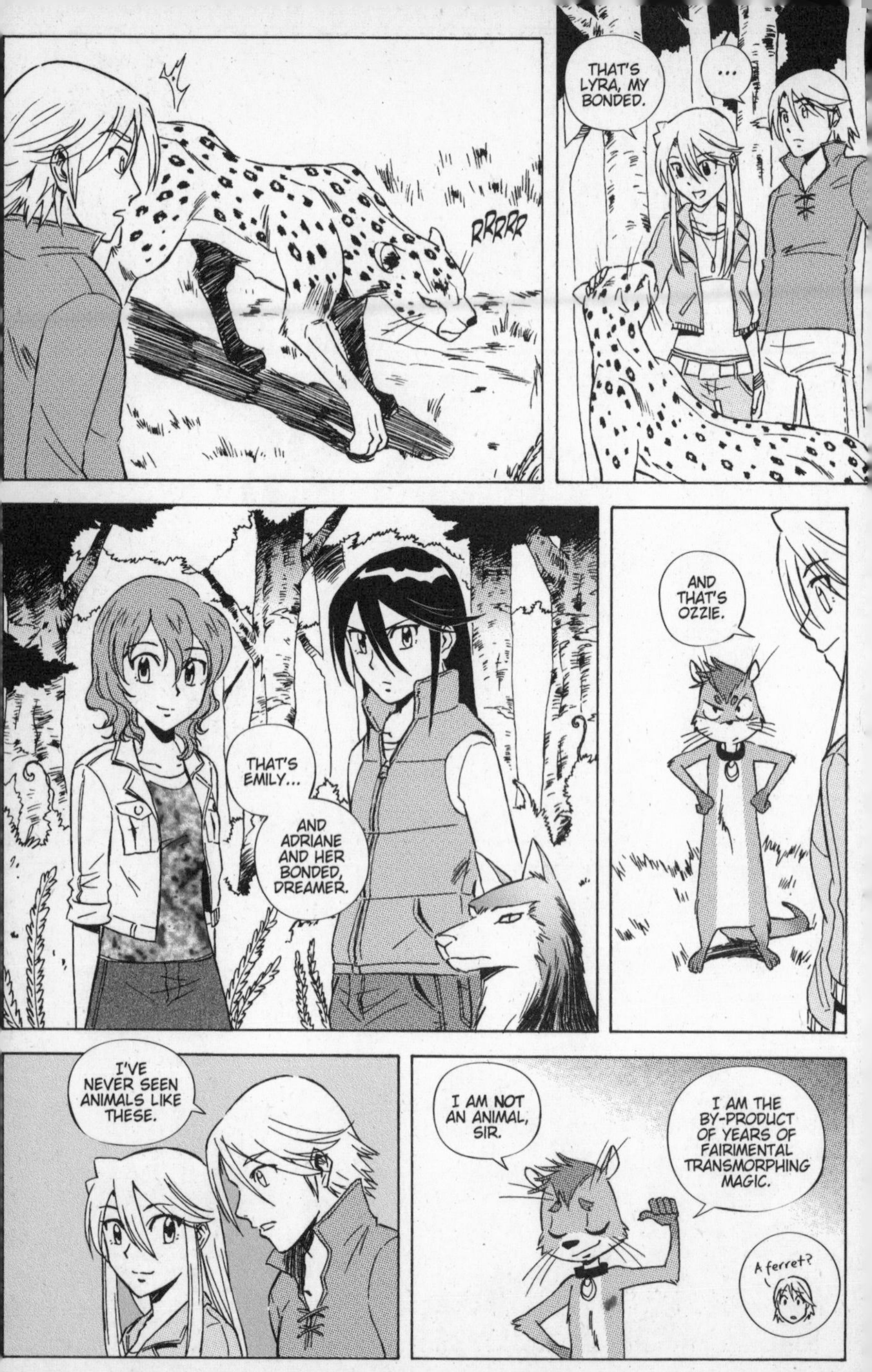
RRRRR
THAT'S LYRA, MY BONDED.
...
THAT'S EMILY...
AND ADRIANE AND HER BONDED, DREAMER.
AND THAT'S OZZIE.
I'VE NEVER SEEN ANIMALS LIKE THESE.
I AM NOT AN ANIMAL, SIR.
I AM THE BY-PRODUCT OF YEARS OF FAIRIMENTAL TRANSMORPHING MAGIC.
A ferret?

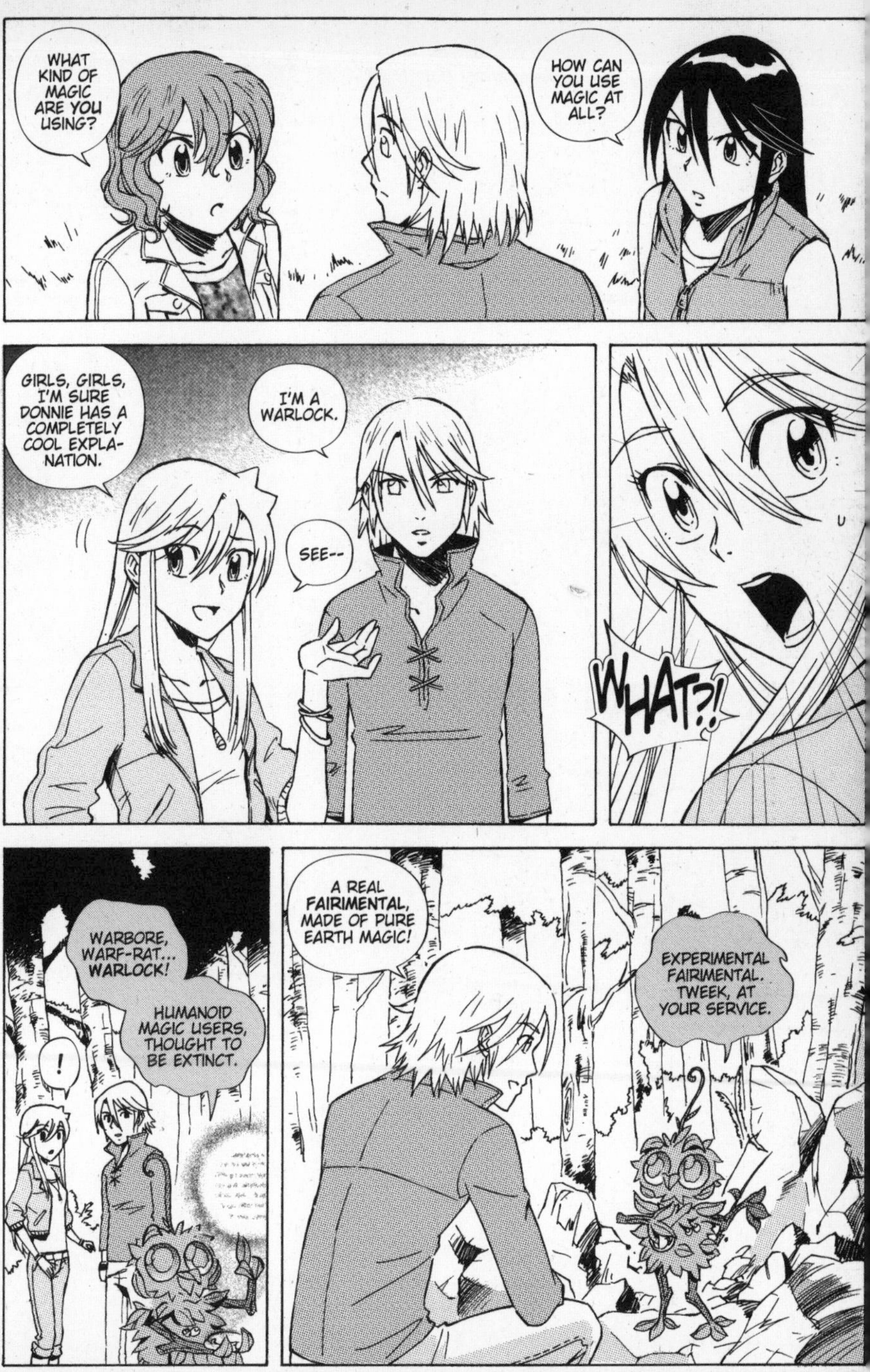
WHAT KIND OF MAGIC ARE YOU USING?
HOW CAN YOU USE MAGIC AT ALL?
GIRLS, GIRLS, I'M SURE DONNIE HAS A COMPLETELY COOL EXPLA-NATION.
I'M A WARLOCK.
SEE--
WHAT?!
WARBORE, WARF-RAT... WARLOCK!
HUMANOID MAGIC USERS, THOUGHT TO BE EXTINCT.
!
A REAL FAIRIMENTAL, MADE OF PURE EARTH MAGIC!
EXPERIMENTAL FAIRIMENTAL. TWEEK, AT YOUR SERVICE.

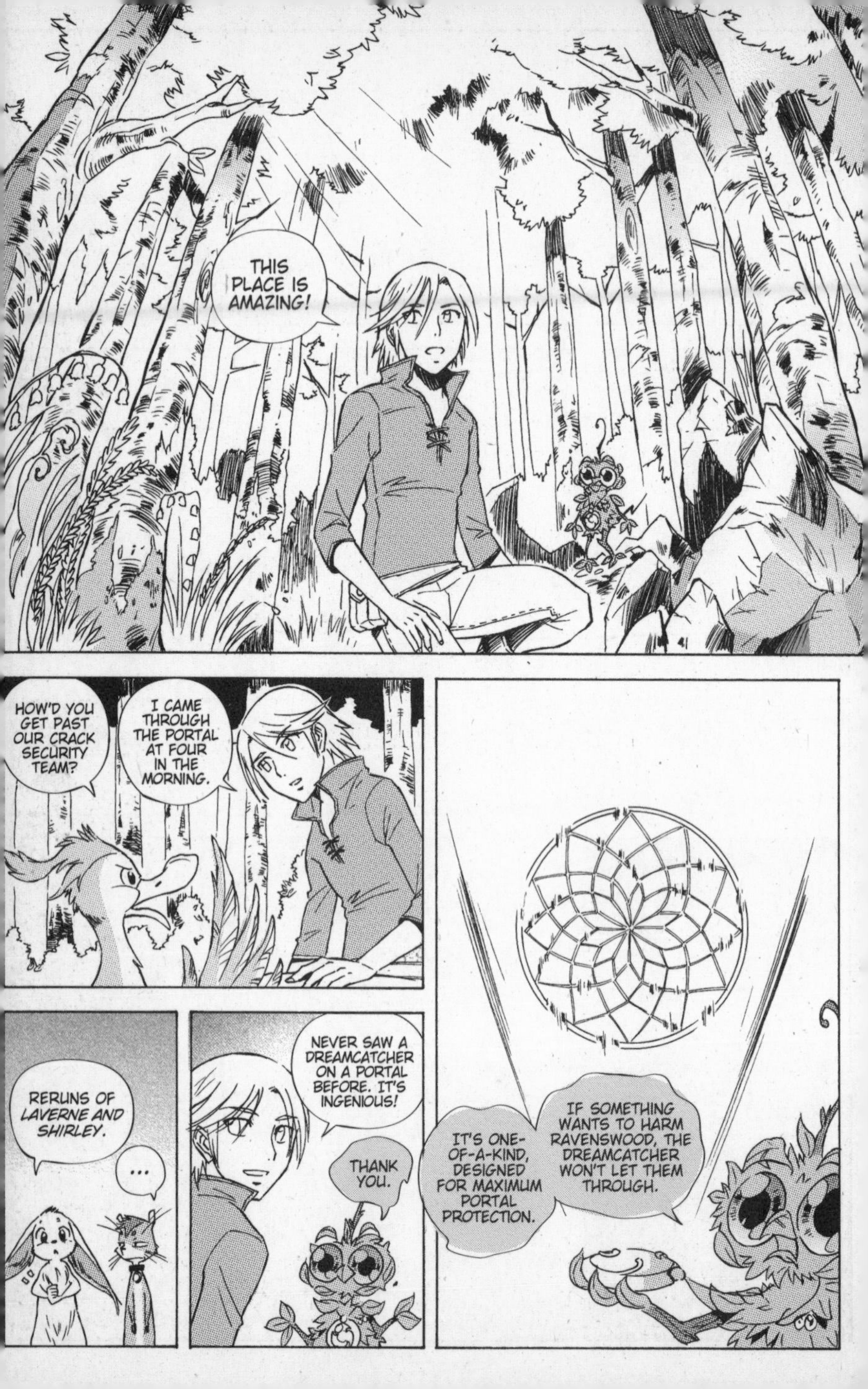
THIS PLACE IS AMAZING!
HOW'D YOU GET PAST OUR CRACK SECURITY TEAM?
I CAME THROUGH THE PORTAL AT FOUR IN THE MORNING.
RERUNS OF *LAVERNE AND SHIRLEY*.
...
NEVER SAW A DREAMCATCHER ON A PORTAL BEFORE. IT'S INGENIOUS!
THANK YOU.
IT'S ONE-OF-A-KIND, DESIGNED FOR MAXIMUM PORTAL PROTECTION.
IF SOMETHING WANTS TO HARM RAVENSWOOD, THE DREAMCATCHER WON'T LET THEM THROUGH.

THEN HOW DID HIS ROCK COLLECTION GET HERE?

I WILL ANALYZE SOME RESIDUE.

TWIGTASTIC! THE COMPLETE OPPOSITE OF MAGE MAGIC!

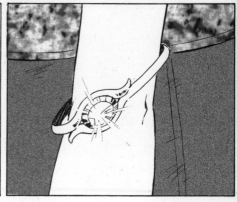

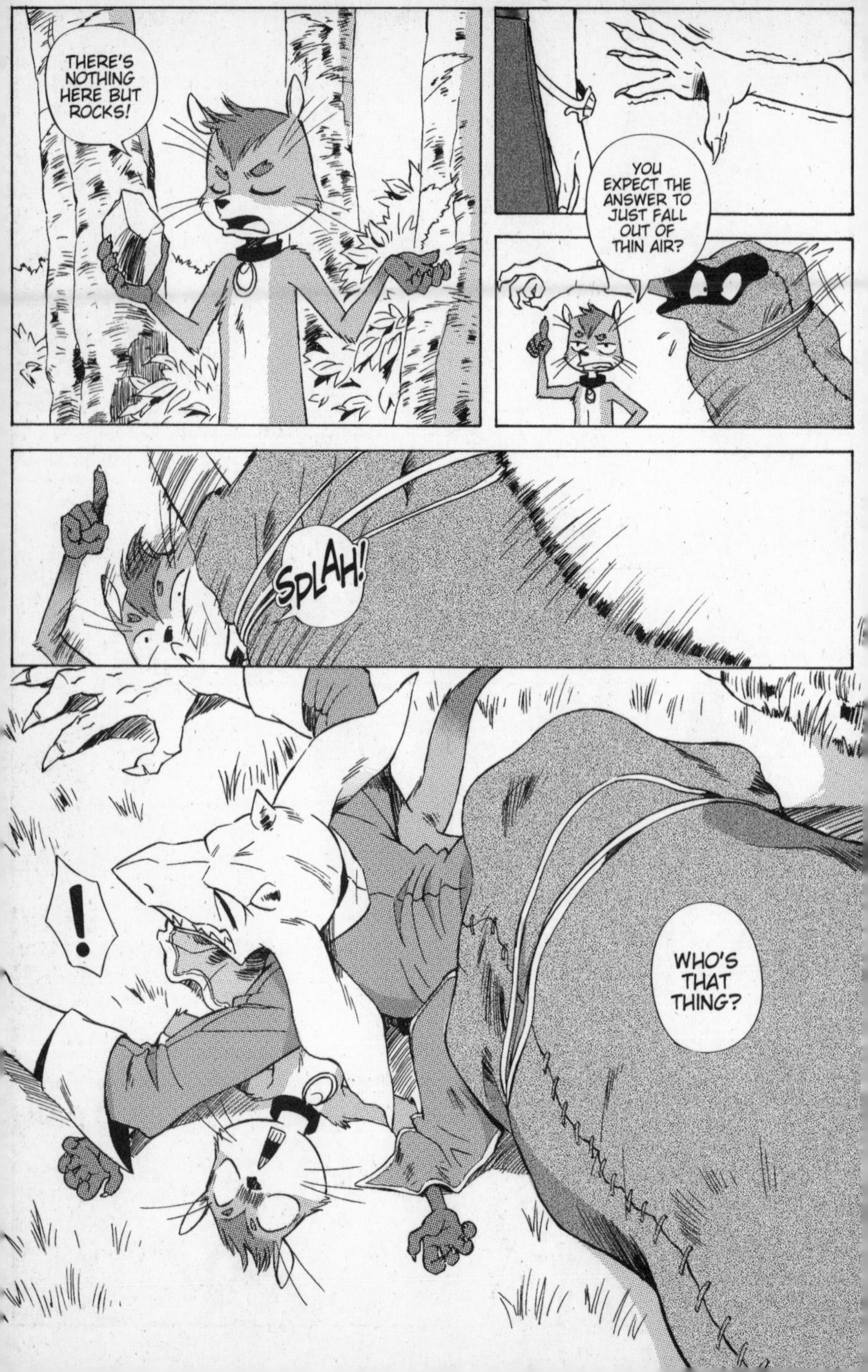
THERE'S NOTHING HERE BUT ROCKS!
YOU EXPECT THE ANSWER TO JUST FALL OUT OF THIN AIR?
SPLAH!
!
WHO'S THAT THING?

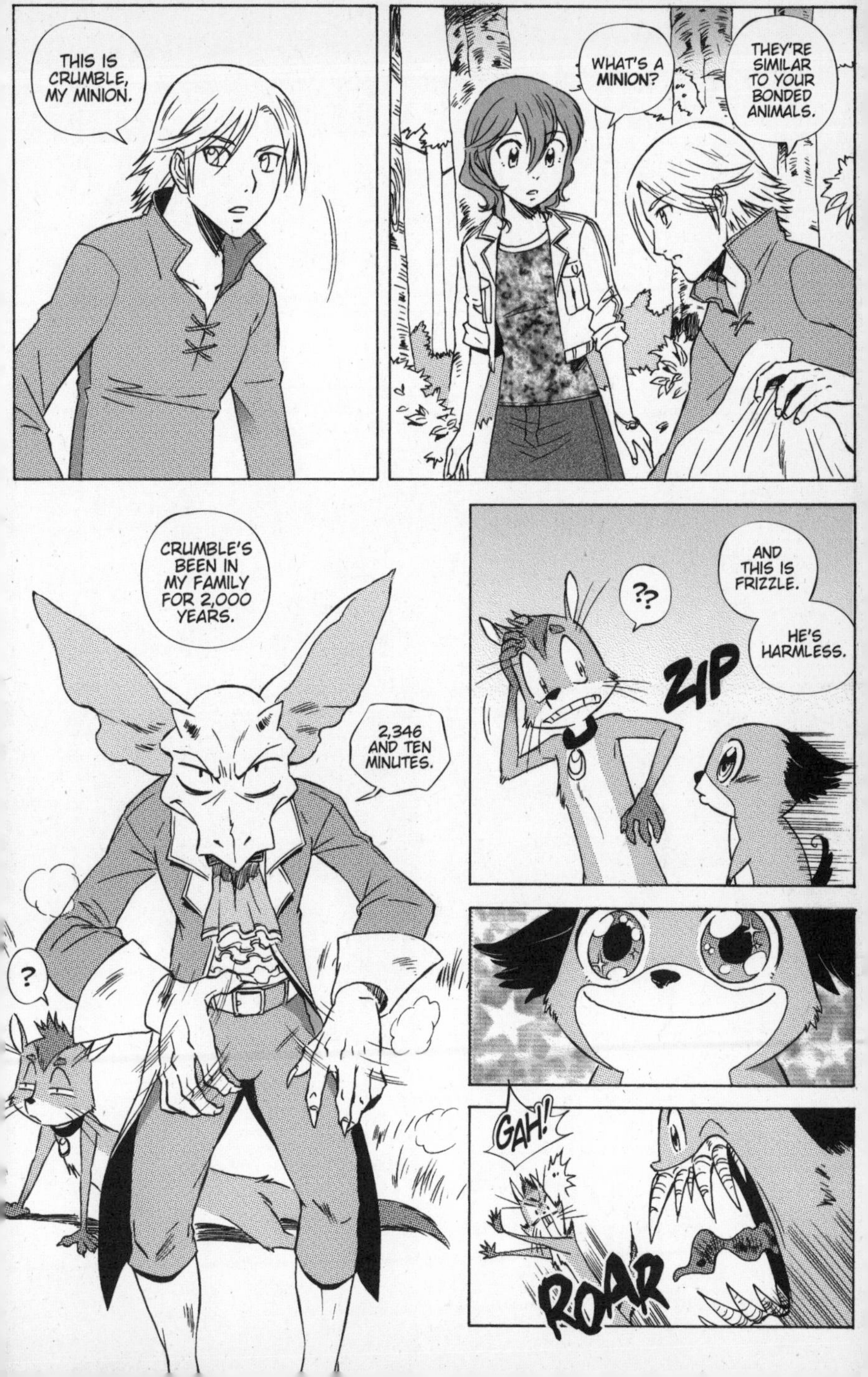
THIS IS CRUMBLE, MY MINION.
WHAT'S A MINION?
THEY'RE SIMILAR TO YOUR BONDED ANIMALS.
CRUMBLE'S BEEN IN MY FAMILY FOR 2,000 YEARS.
2,346 AND TEN MINUTES.
?
??
AND THIS IS FRIZZLE.
HE'S HARMLESS.
ZIP
GAH!
ROAR

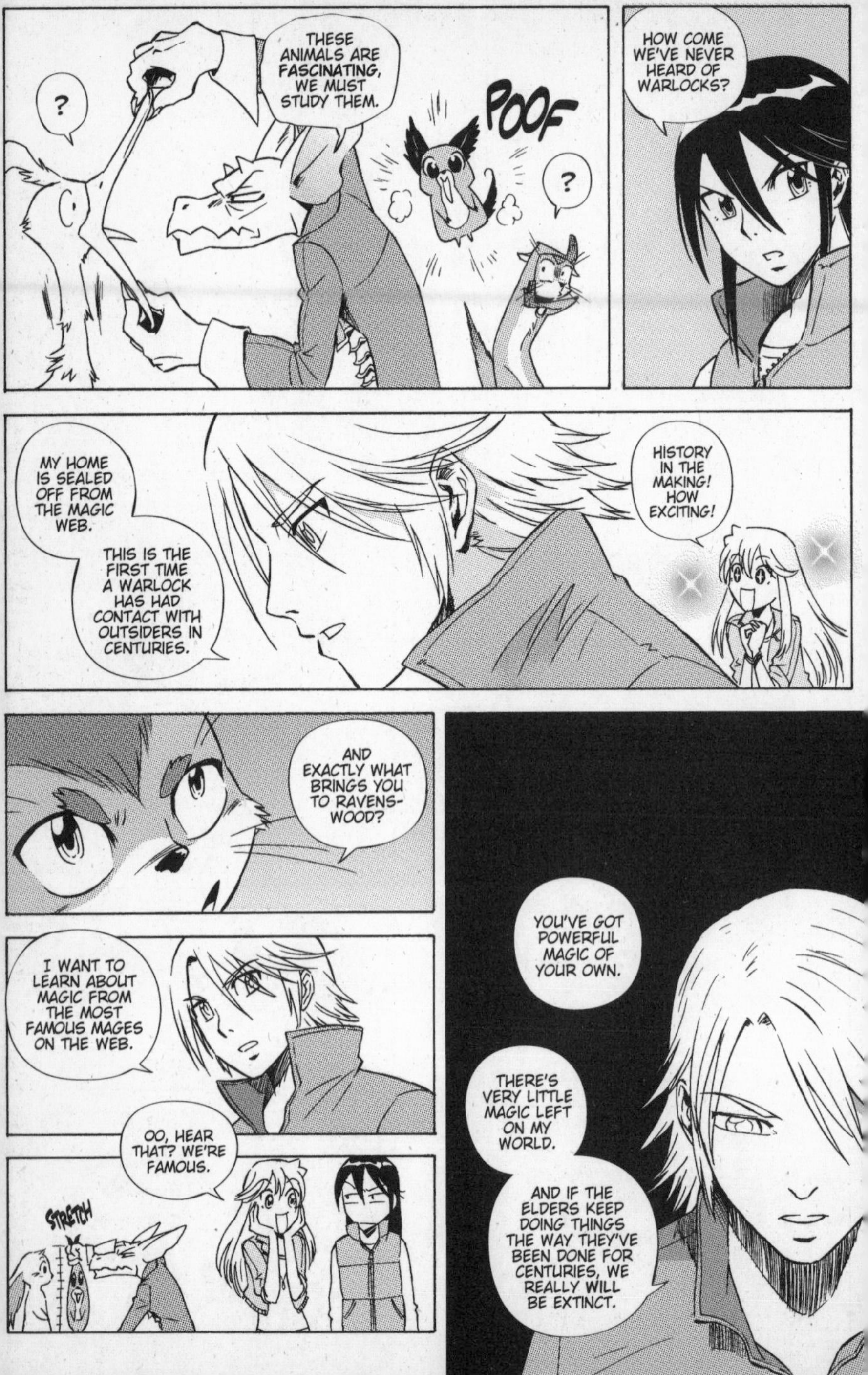
?
THESE ANIMALS ARE FASCINATING, WE MUST STUDY THEM.
POOF
?
HOW COME WE'VE NEVER HEARD OF WARLOCKS?
MY HOME IS SEALED OFF FROM THE MAGIC WEB.
THIS IS THE FIRST TIME A WARLOCK HAS HAD CONTACT WITH OUTSIDERS IN CENTURIES.
HISTORY IN THE MAKING! HOW EXCITING!
AND EXACTLY WHAT BRINGS YOU TO RAVENS-WOOD?
I WANT TO LEARN ABOUT MAGIC FROM THE MOST FAMOUS MAGES ON THE WEB.
OO, HEAR THAT? WE'RE FAMOUS.
STRETCH
YOU'VE GOT POWERFUL MAGIC OF YOUR OWN.
THERE'S VERY LITTLE MAGIC LEFT ON MY WORLD.
AND IF THE ELDERS KEEP DOING THINGS THE WAY THEY'VE BEEN DONE FOR CENTURIES, WE REALLY WILL BE EXTINCT.

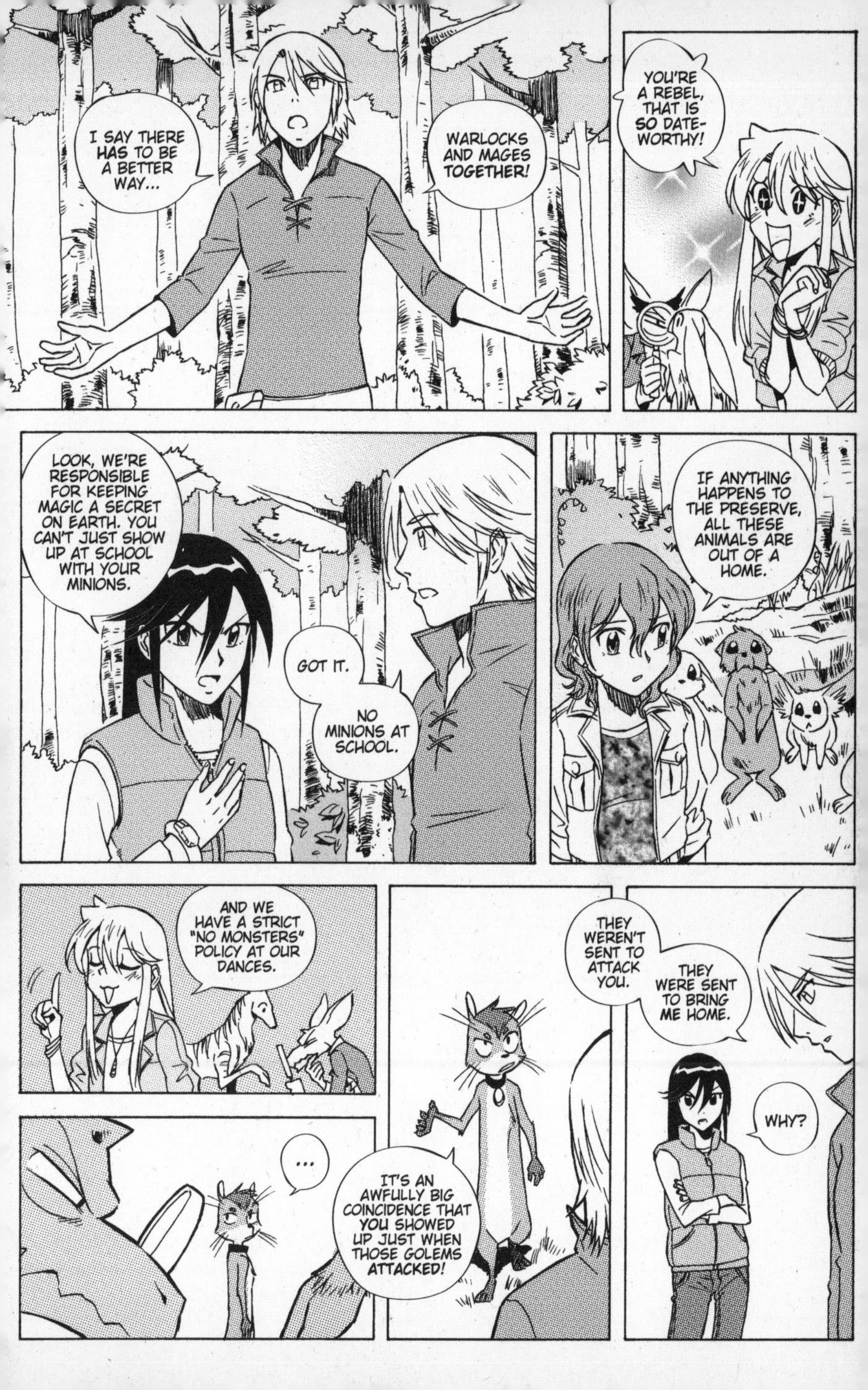
I SAY THERE HAS TO BE A BETTER WAY...
WARLOCKS AND MAGES TOGETHER!
YOU'RE A REBEL, THAT IS SO DATE-WORTHY!
LOOK, WE'RE RESPONSIBLE FOR KEEPING MAGIC A SECRET ON EARTH. YOU CAN'T JUST SHOW UP AT SCHOOL WITH YOUR MINIONS.
GOT IT.
NO MINIONS AT SCHOOL.
IF ANYTHING HAPPENS TO THE PRESERVE, ALL THESE ANIMALS ARE OUT OF A HOME.
AND WE HAVE A STRICT "NO MONSTERS" POLICY AT OUR DANCES.
...
IT'S AN AWFULLY BIG COINCIDENCE THAT YOU SHOWED UP JUST WHEN THOSE GOLEMS ATTACKED!
THEY WEREN'T SENT TO ATTACK YOU.
THEY WERE SENT TO BRING ME HOME.
WHY?

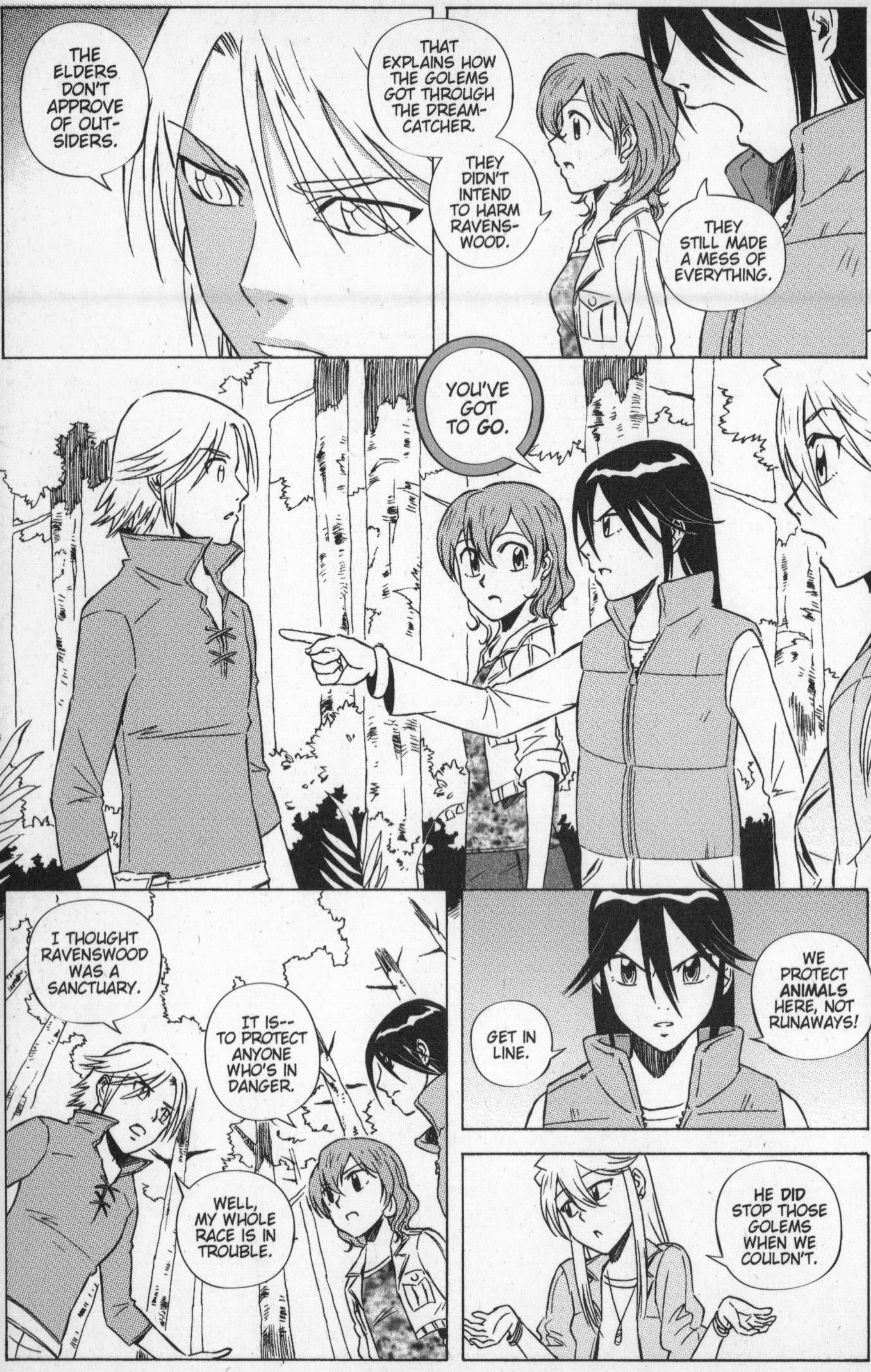
THE ELDERS DON'T APPROVE OF OUT-SIDERS.
THAT EXPLAINS HOW THE GOLEMS GOT THROUGH THE DREAM-CATCHER.
THEY DIDN'T INTEND TO HARM RAVENS-WOOD.
THEY STILL MADE A MESS OF EVERYTHING.
YOU'VE GOT TO GO.
I THOUGHT RAVENSWOOD WAS A SANCTUARY.
IT IS-- TO PROTECT ANYONE WHO'S IN DANGER.
WELL, MY WHOLE RACE IS IN TROUBLE.
GET IN LINE.
WE PROTECT ANIMALS HERE, NOT RUNAWAYS!
HE DID STOP THOSE GOLEMS WHEN WE COULDN'T.

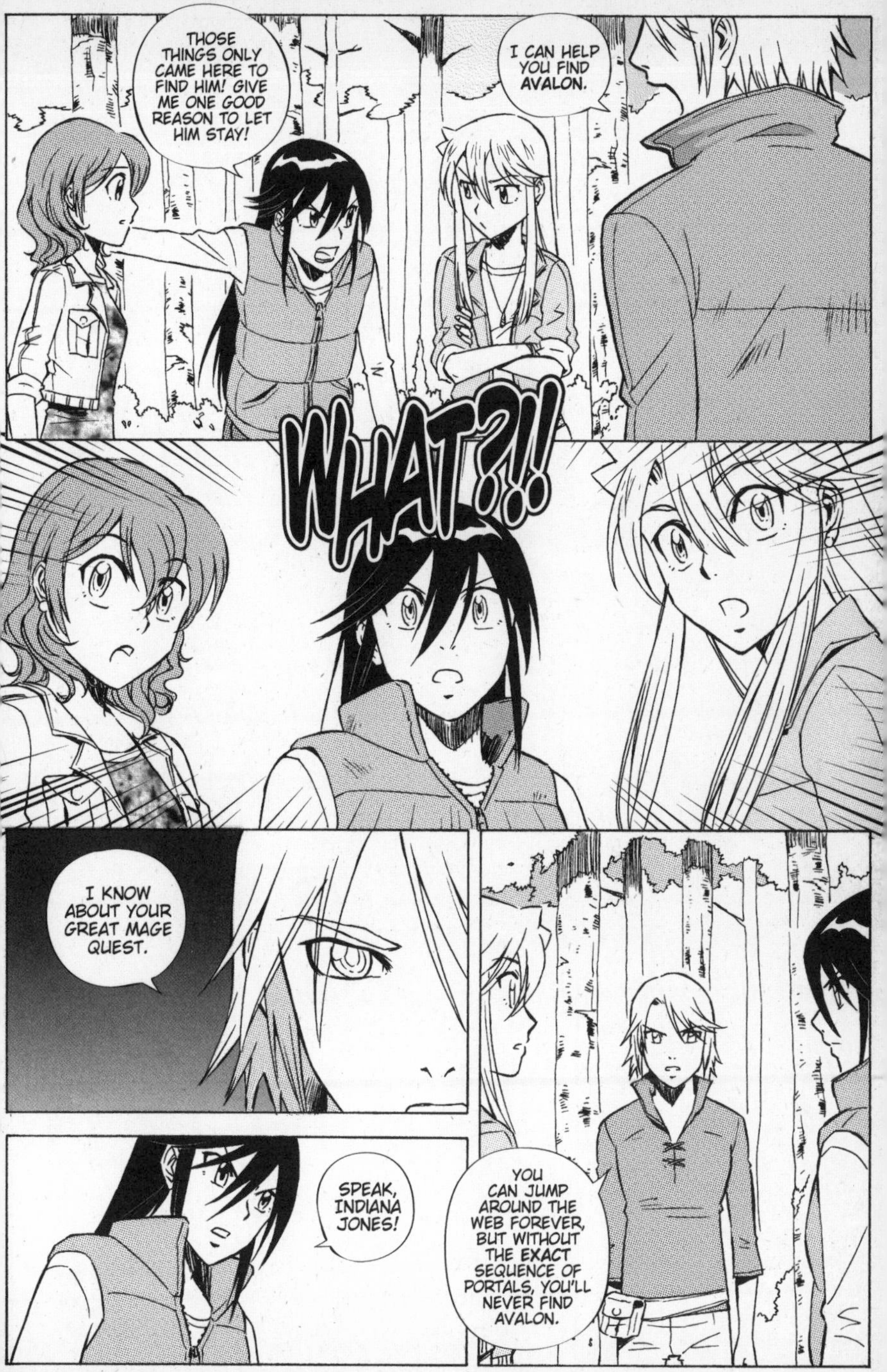
THOSE THINGS ONLY CAME HERE TO FIND HIM! GIVE ME ONE GOOD REASON TO LET HIM STAY!
I CAN HELP YOU FIND AVALON.
WHAT?!!
I KNOW ABOUT YOUR GREAT MAGE QUEST.
YOU CAN JUMP AROUND THE WEB FOREVER, BUT WITHOUT THE EXACT SEQUENCE OF PORTALS, YOU'LL NEVER FIND AVALON.
SPEAK, INDIANA JONES!

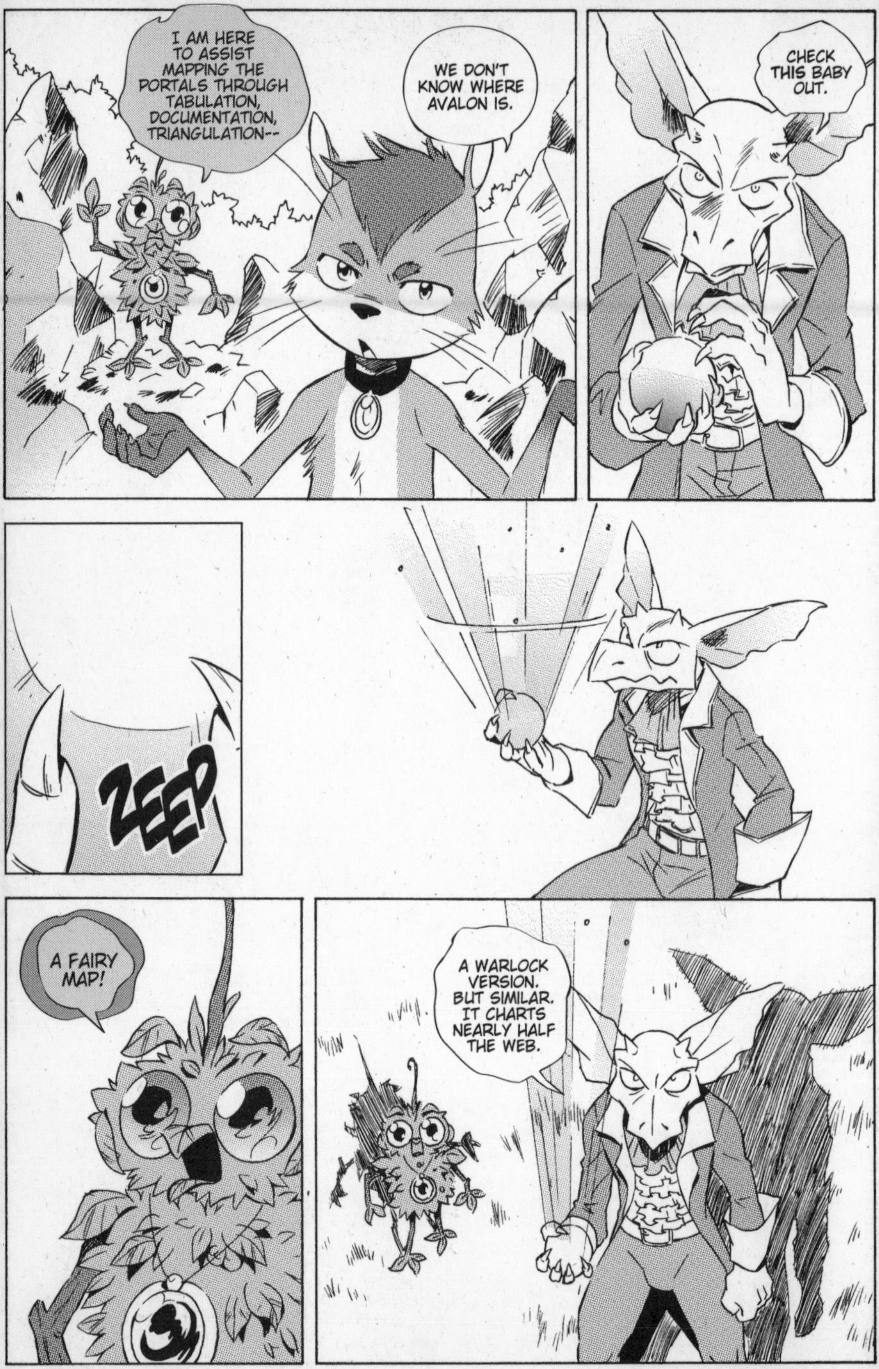
I AM HERE TO ASSIST MAPPING THE PORTALS THROUGH TABULATION, DOCUMENTATION, TRIANGULATION--
WE DON'T KNOW WHERE AVALON IS.
CHECK THIS BABY OUT.
ZEEP
A FAIRY MAP!
A WARLOCK VERSION. BUT SIMILAR. IT CHARTS NEARLY HALF THE WEB.

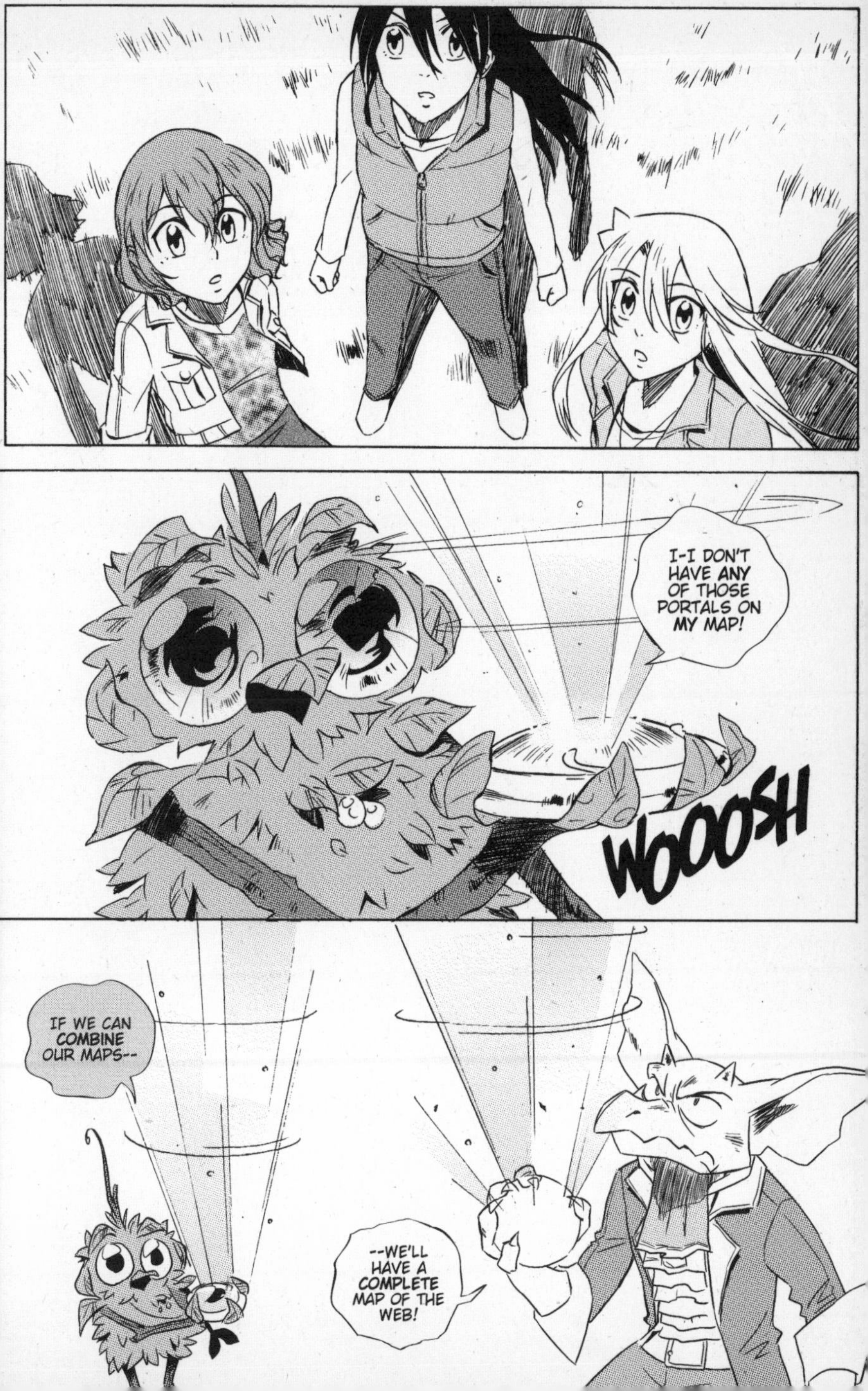
I-I DON'T HAVE ANY OF THOSE PORTALS ON MY MAP!
WOOOSH
IF WE CAN COMBINE OUR MAPS--
--WE'LL HAVE A COMPLETE MAP OF THE WEB!

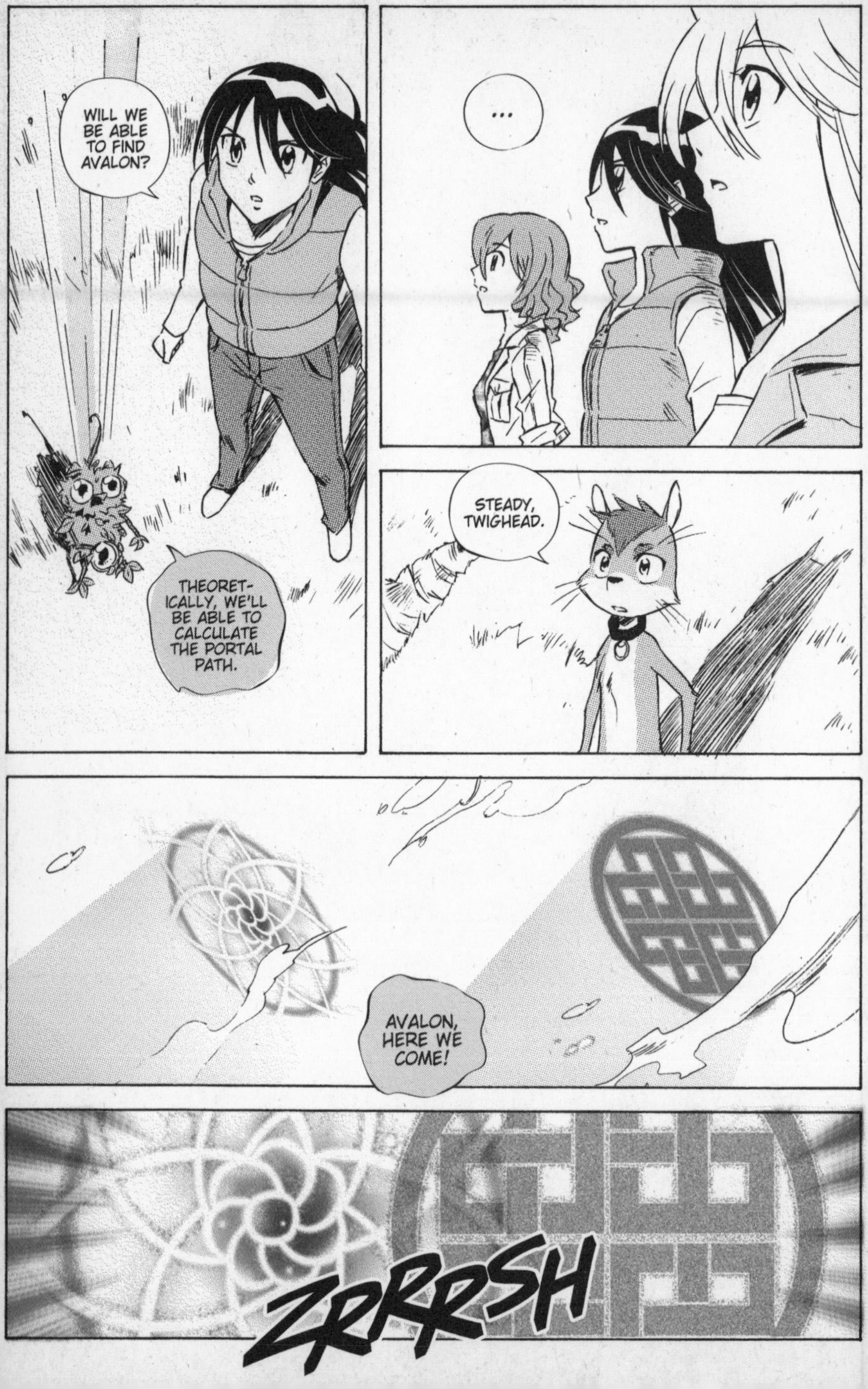
WILL WE BE ABLE TO FIND AVALON?
THEORET-ICALLY, WE'LL BE ABLE TO CALCULATE THE PORTAL PATH.
...
STEADY, TWIGHEAD.
AVALON, HERE WE COME!
ZRRRSH

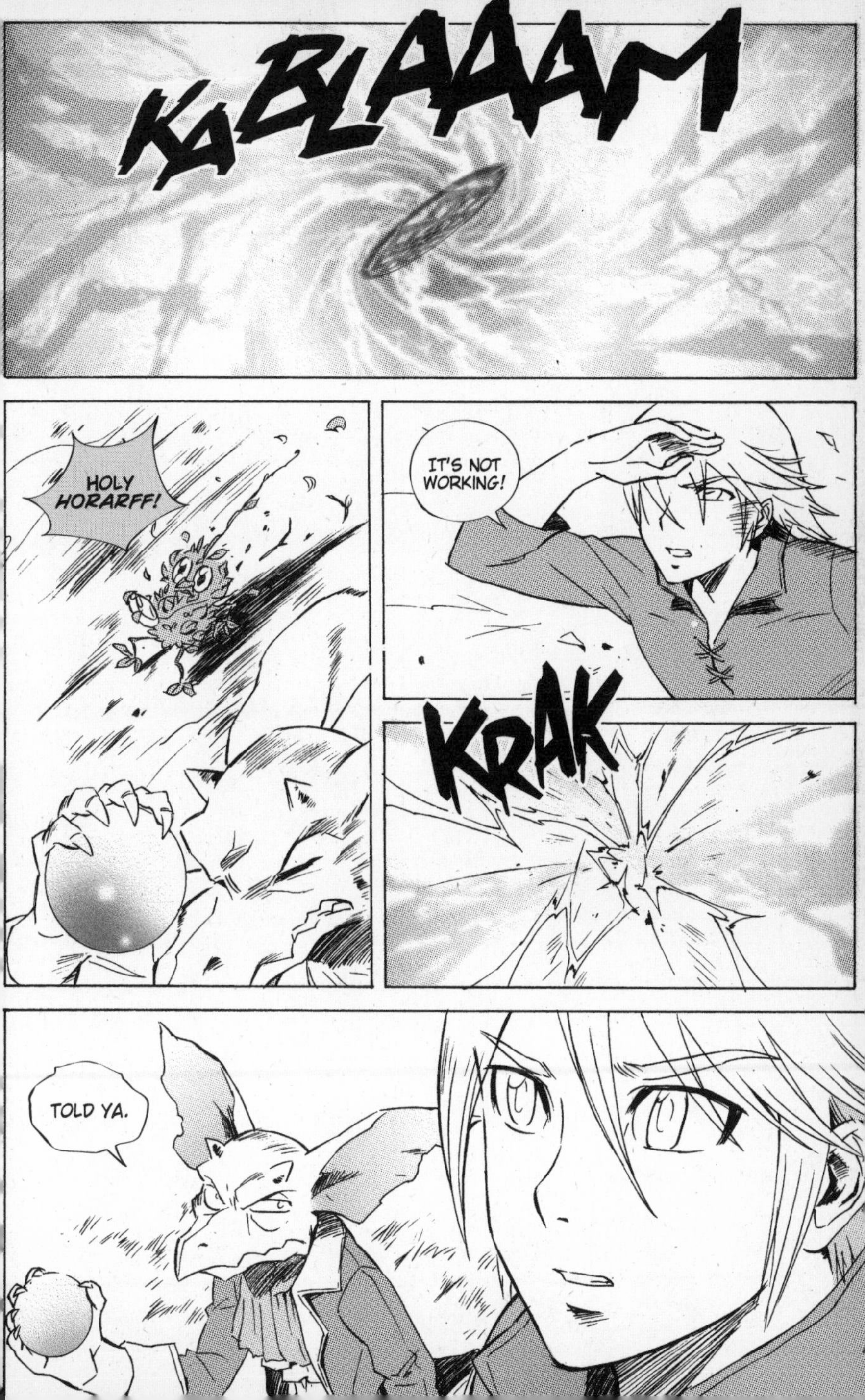
KA BLAAAM
HOLY HORARFF!
IT'S NOT WORKING!
KRAK
TOLD YA.

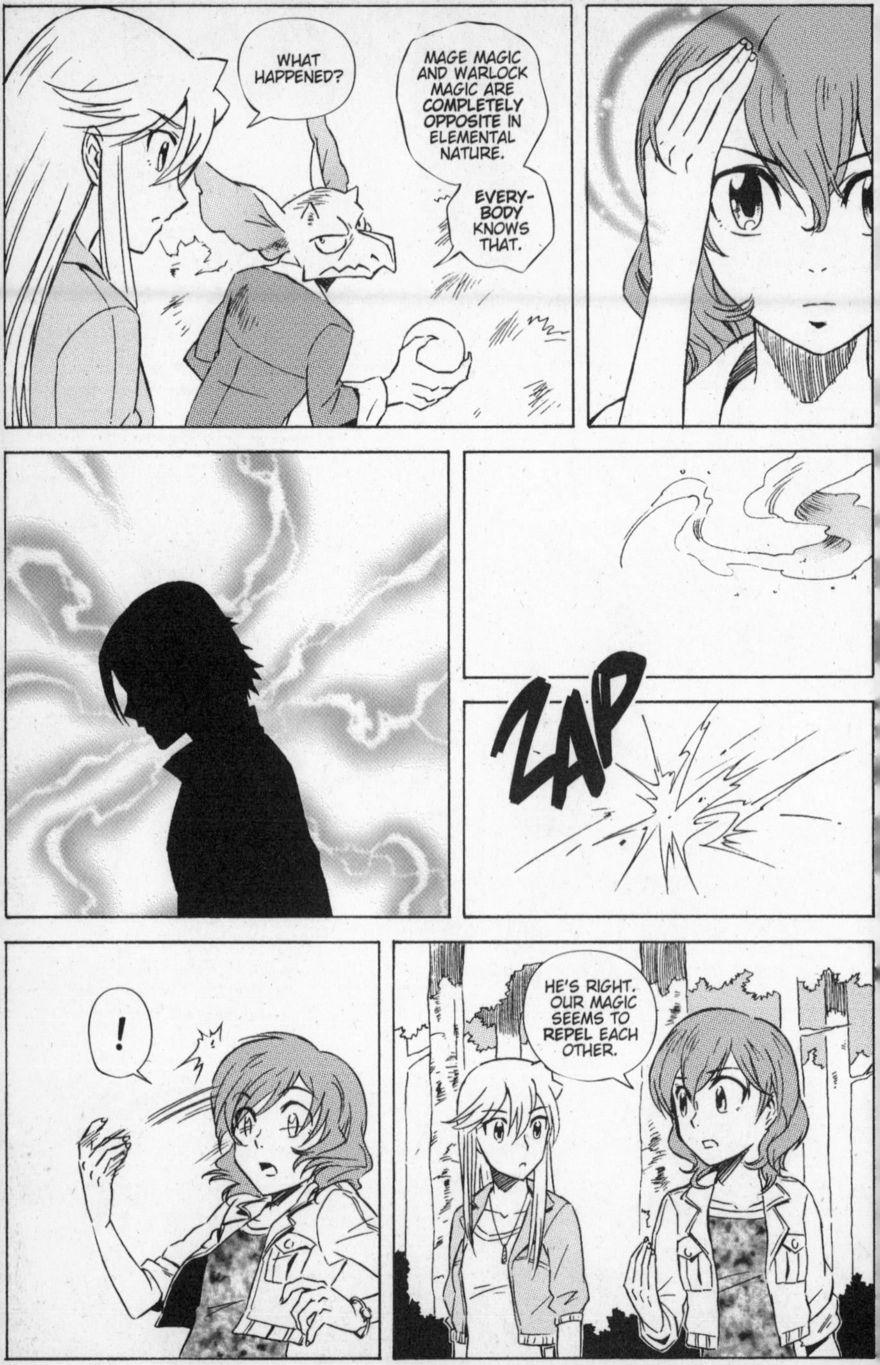
WHAT HAPPENED?
MAGE MAGIC AND WARLOCK MAGIC ARE COMPLETELY OPPOSITE IN ELEMENTAL NATURE.
EVERY-BODY KNOWS THAT.
ZAP
!
HE'S RIGHT. OUR MAGIC SEEMS TO REPEL EACH OTHER.

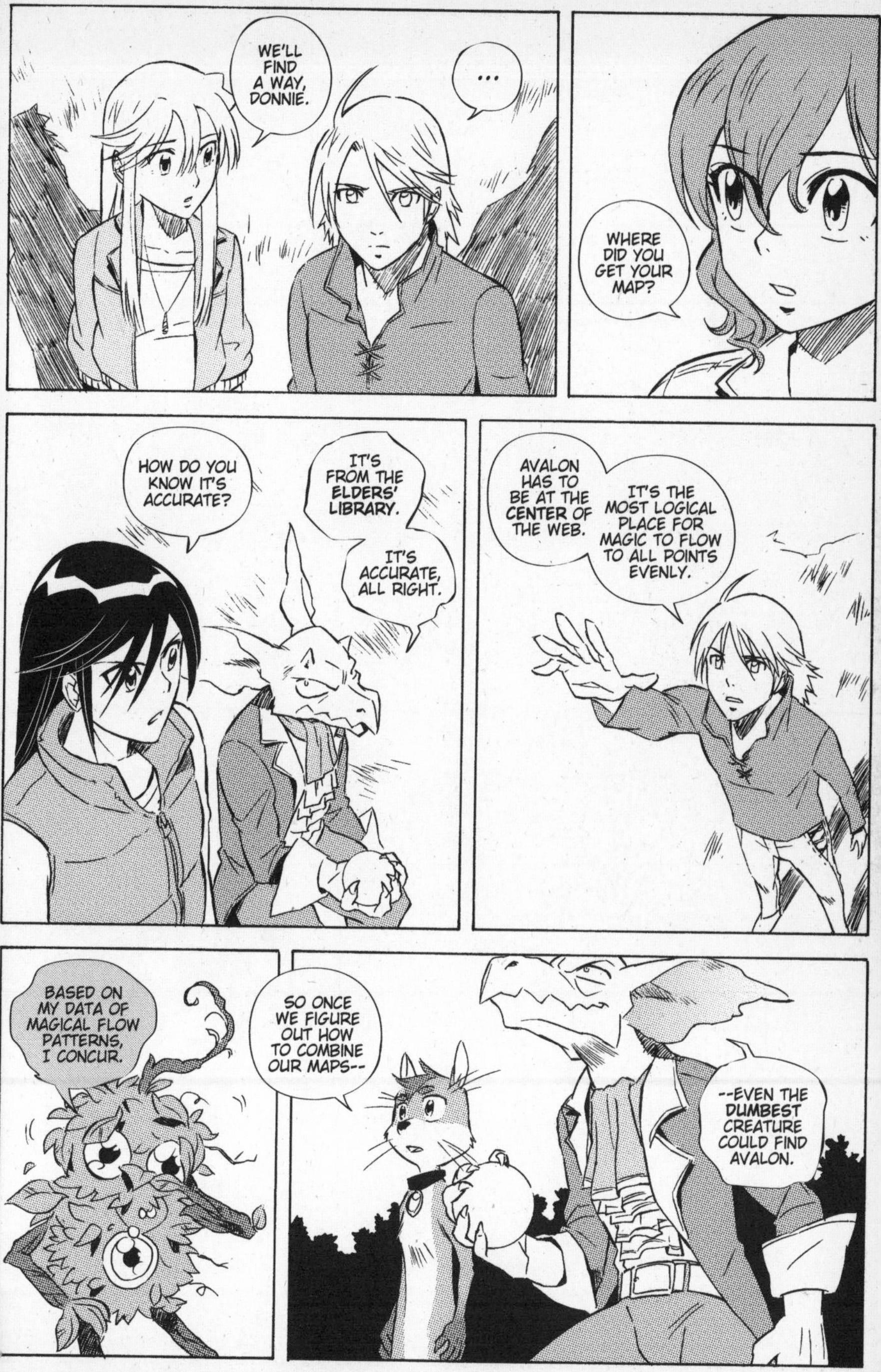
WE'LL FIND A WAY, DONNIE.
...
WHERE DID YOU GET YOUR MAP?
HOW DO YOU KNOW IT'S ACCURATE?
IT'S FROM THE ELDERS' LIBRARY.
IT'S ACCURATE, ALL RIGHT.
AVALON HAS TO BE AT THE CENTER OF THE WEB.
IT'S THE MOST LOGICAL PLACE FOR MAGIC TO FLOW TO ALL POINTS EVENLY.
BASED ON MY DATA OF MAGICAL FLOW PATTERNS, I CONCUR.
SO ONCE WE FIGURE OUT HOW TO COMBINE OUR MAPS--
--EVEN THE DUMBEST CREATURE COULD FIND AVALON.

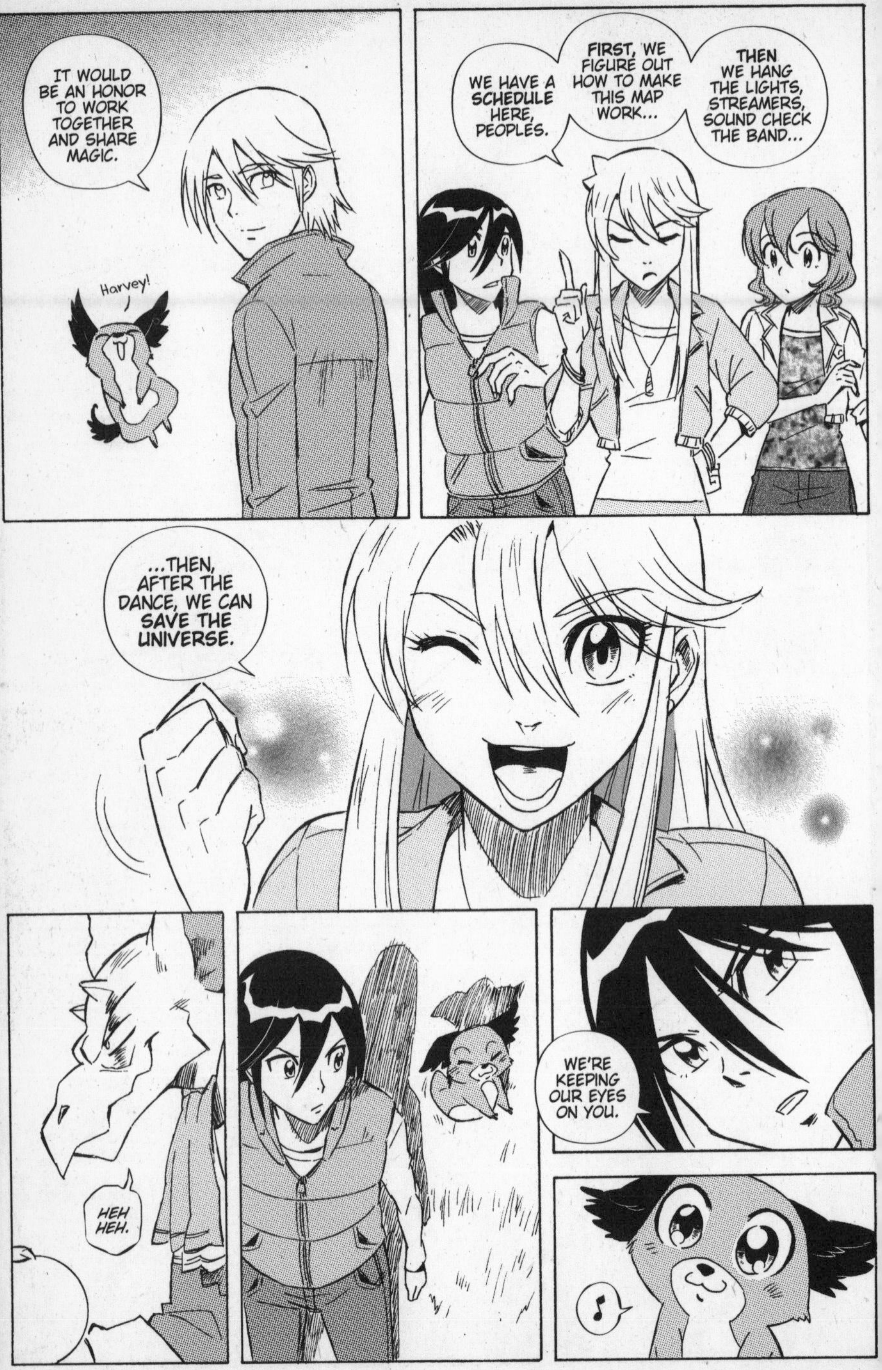
IT WOULD BE AN HONOR TO WORK TOGETHER AND SHARE MAGIC.
Harvey!
WE HAVE A SCHEDULE HERE, PEOPLES.
FIRST, WE FIGURE OUT HOW TO MAKE THIS MAP WORK...
THEN WE HANG THE LIGHTS, STREAMERS, SOUND CHECK THE BAND...
...THEN, AFTER THE DANCE, WE CAN SAVE THE UNIVERSE.
HEH HEH.
WE'RE KEEPING OUR EYES ON YOU.
♪

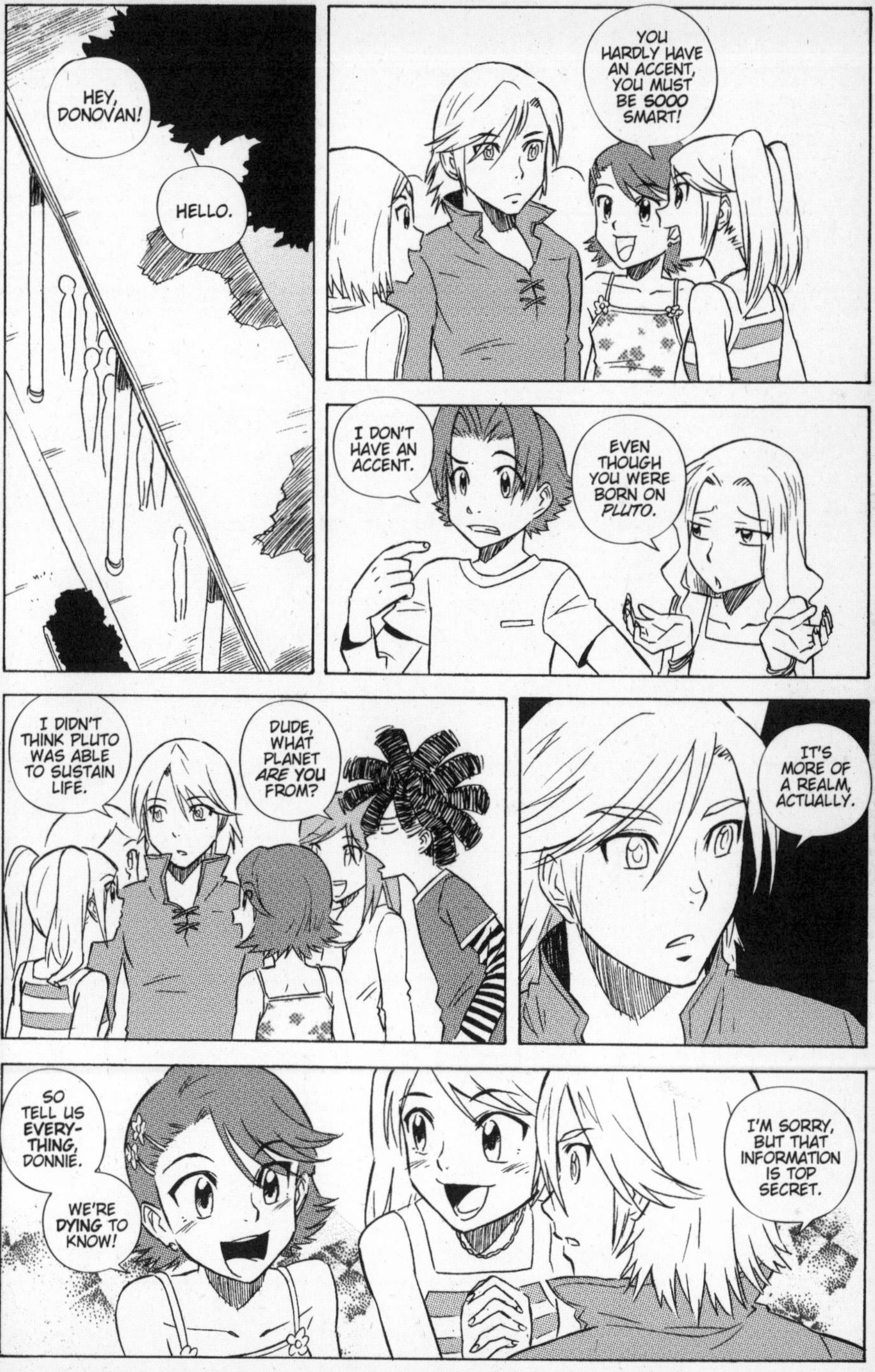
HEY, DONOVAN!
HELLO.
YOU HARDLY HAVE AN ACCENT, YOU MUST BE SOOO SMART!
I DON'T HAVE AN ACCENT.
EVEN THOUGH YOU WERE BORN ON *PLUTO*.
I DIDN'T THINK PLUTO WAS ABLE TO SUSTAIN LIFE.
DUDE, WHAT PLANET *ARE* YOU FROM?
IT'S MORE OF A REALM, ACTUALLY.
SO TELL US EVERY-THING, DONNIE.
WE'RE DYING TO KNOW!
I'M SORRY, BUT THAT INFORMATION IS TOP SECRET.

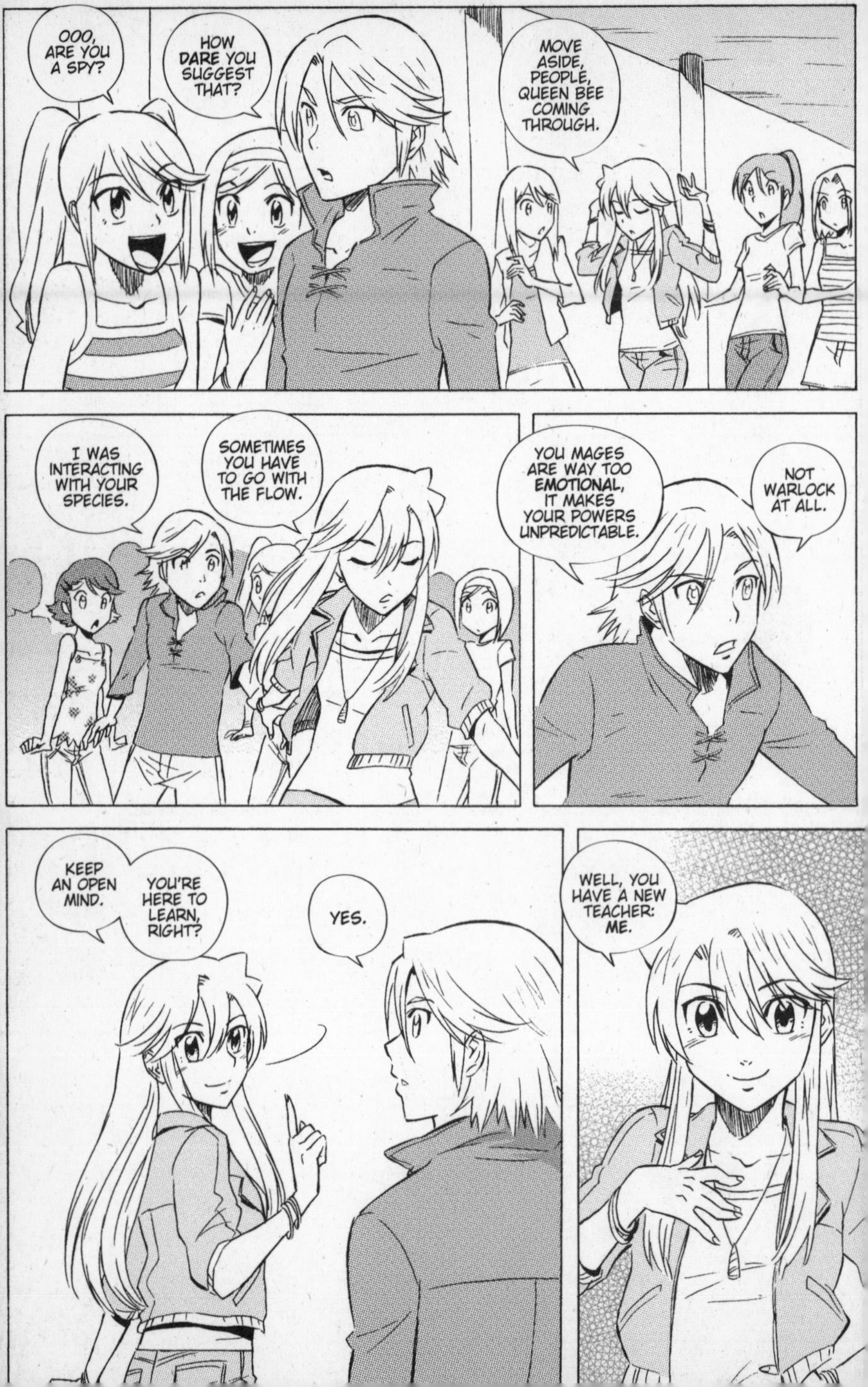
OOO, ARE YOU A SPY?
HOW DARE YOU SUGGEST THAT?
MOVE ASIDE, PEOPLE, QUEEN BEE COMING THROUGH.
I WAS INTERACTING WITH YOUR SPECIES.
SOMETIMES YOU HAVE TO GO WITH THE FLOW.
YOU MAGES ARE WAY TOO EMOTIONAL, IT MAKES YOUR POWERS UNPREDICTABLE.
NOT WARLOCK AT ALL.
KEEP AN OPEN MIND.
YOU'RE HERE TO LEARN, RIGHT?
YES.
WELL, YOU HAVE A NEW TEACHER: ME.

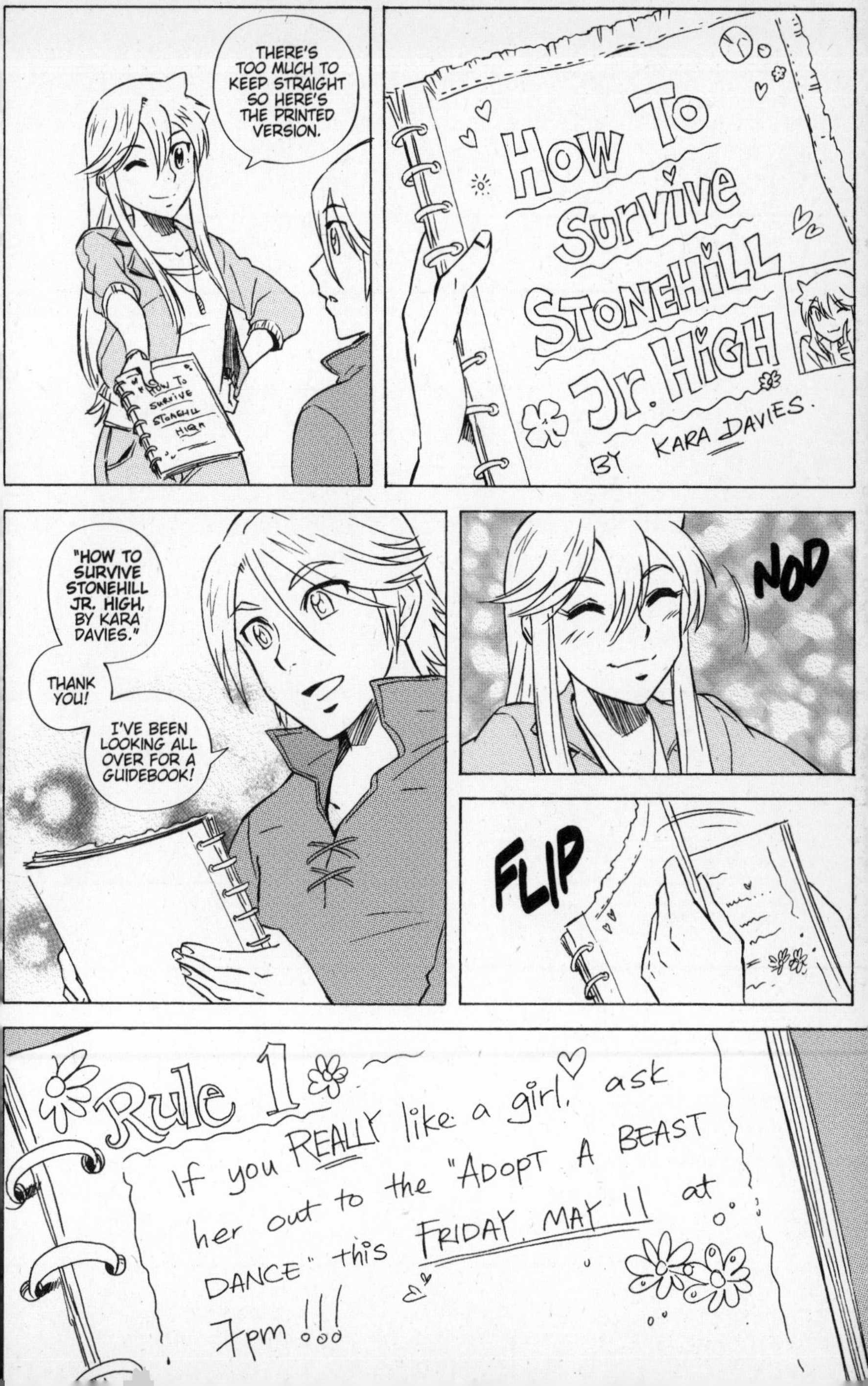
THERE'S TOO MUCH TO KEEP STRAIGHT SO HERE'S THE PRINTED VERSION.
HOW TO SURVIVE STONEHILL HIGH
How To Survive Stonehill Jr. High
BY KARA DAVIES.
"HOW TO SURVIVE STONEHILL JR. HIGH, BY KARA DAVIES."
THANK YOU!
I'VE BEEN LOOKING ALL OVER FOR A GUIDEBOOK!
NOD
FLIP
Rule 1
If you REALLY like a girl, ask her out to the "ADOPT A BEAST DANCE" this FRIDAY, MAY 11 at 7pm!!!

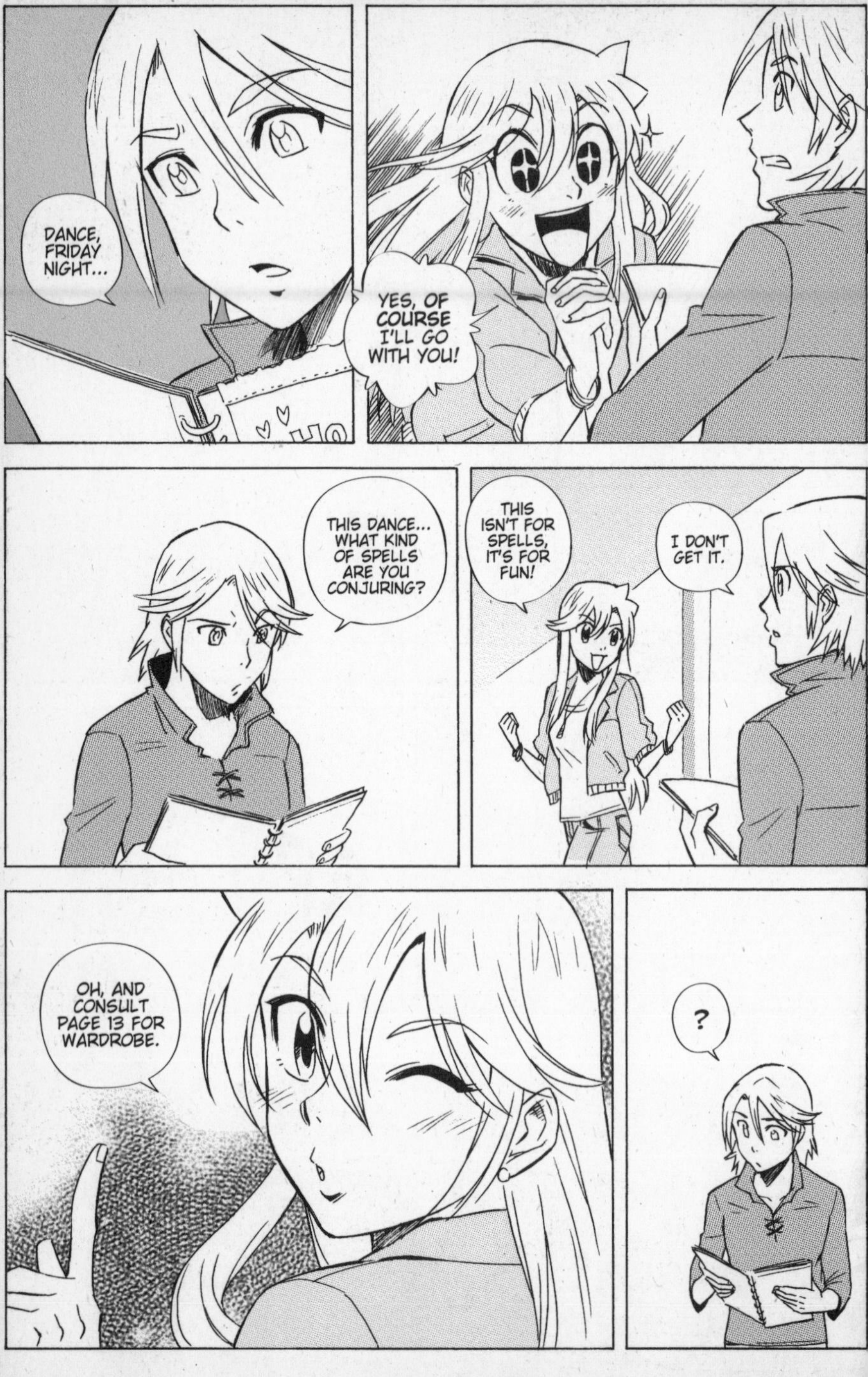
DANCE, FRIDAY NIGHT...
YES, OF COURSE I'LL GO WITH YOU!
THIS DANCE... WHAT KIND OF SPELLS ARE YOU CONJURING?
THIS ISN'T FOR SPELLS, IT'S FOR FUN!
I DON'T GET IT.
OH, AND CONSULT PAGE 13 FOR WARDROBE.
?

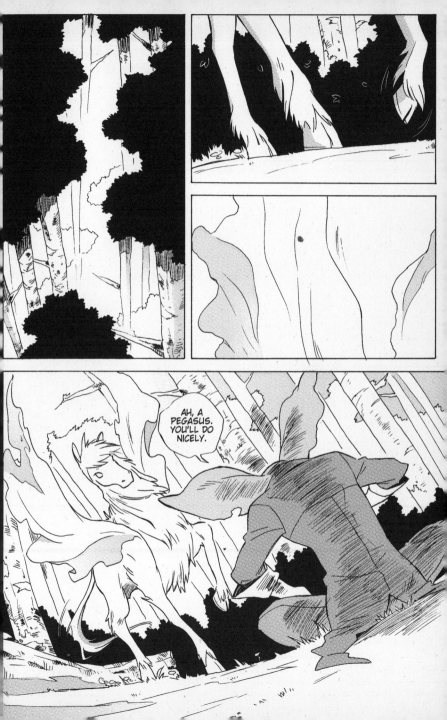

AH, A
PEGASUS.
YOU'LL DO
NICELY.

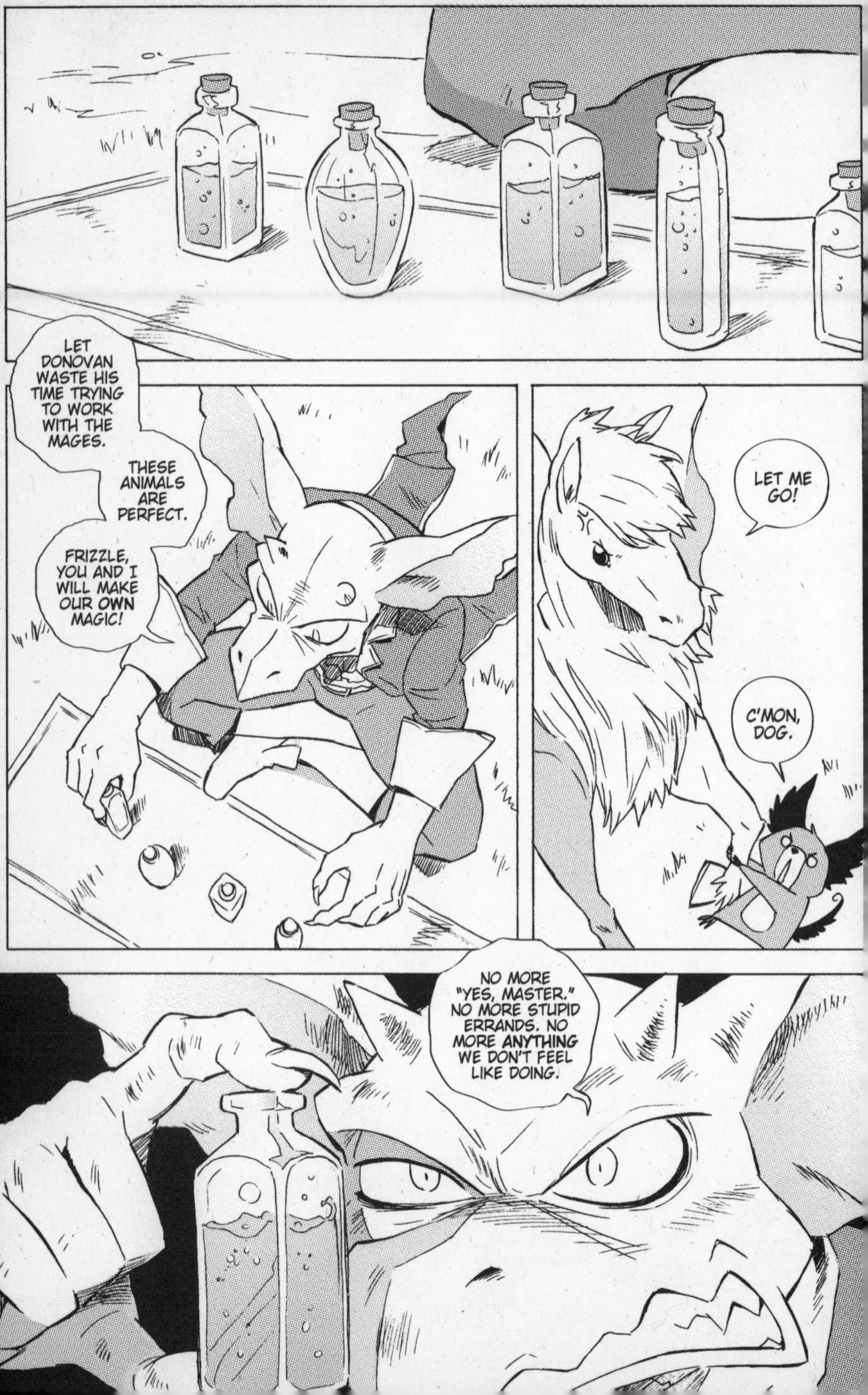
LET DONOVAN WASTE HIS TIME TRYING TO WORK WITH THE MAGES.
THESE ANIMALS ARE PERFECT.
FRIZZLE, YOU AND I WILL MAKE OUR OWN MAGIC!
LET ME GO!
C'MON, DOG.
NO MORE "YES, MASTER." NO MORE STUPID ERRANDS. NO MORE ANYTHING WE DON'T FEEL LIKE DOING.

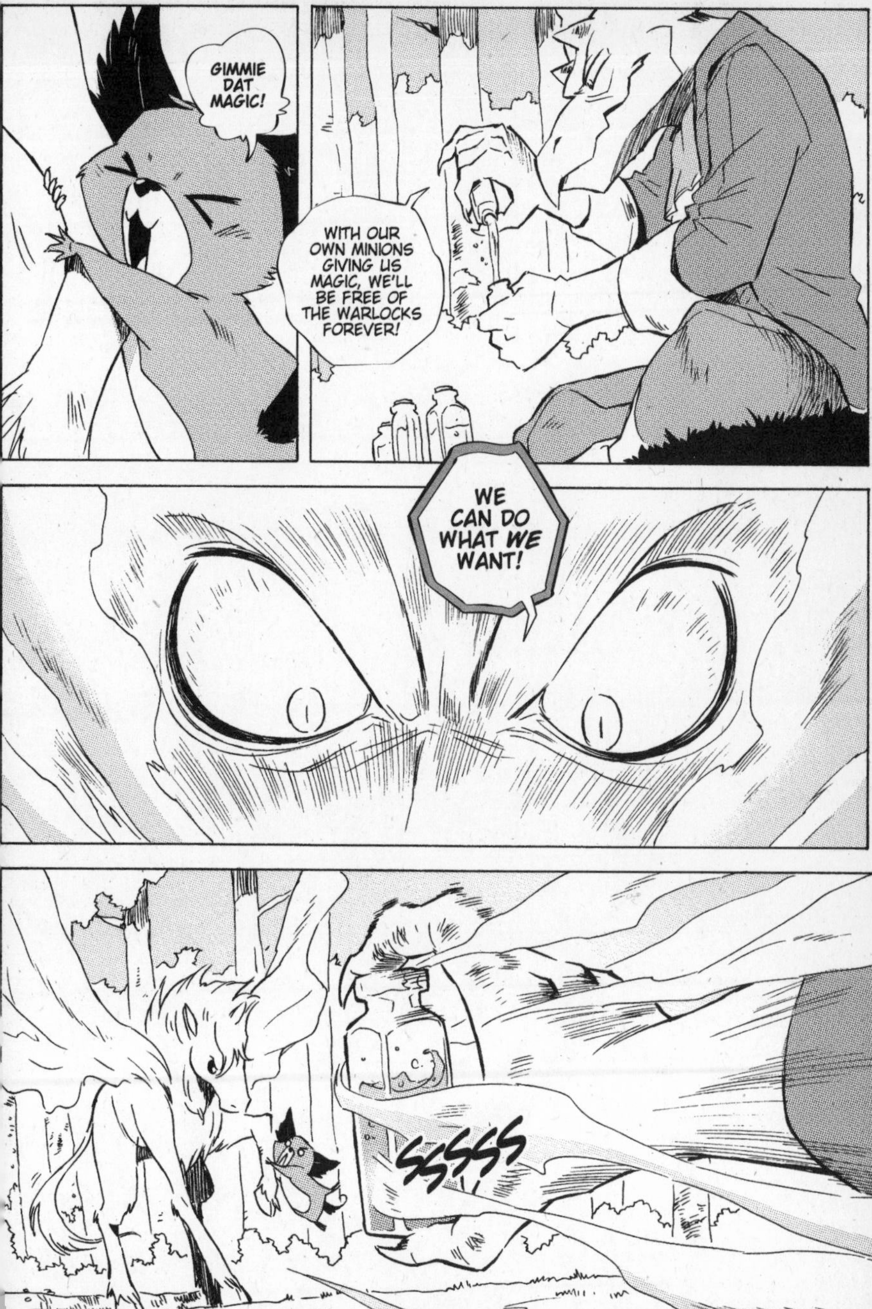
GIMMIE DAT MAGIC!
WITH OUR OWN MINIONS GIVING US MAGIC, WE'LL BE FREE OF THE WARLOCKS FOREVER!
WE CAN DO WHAT WE WANT!
SSSSS

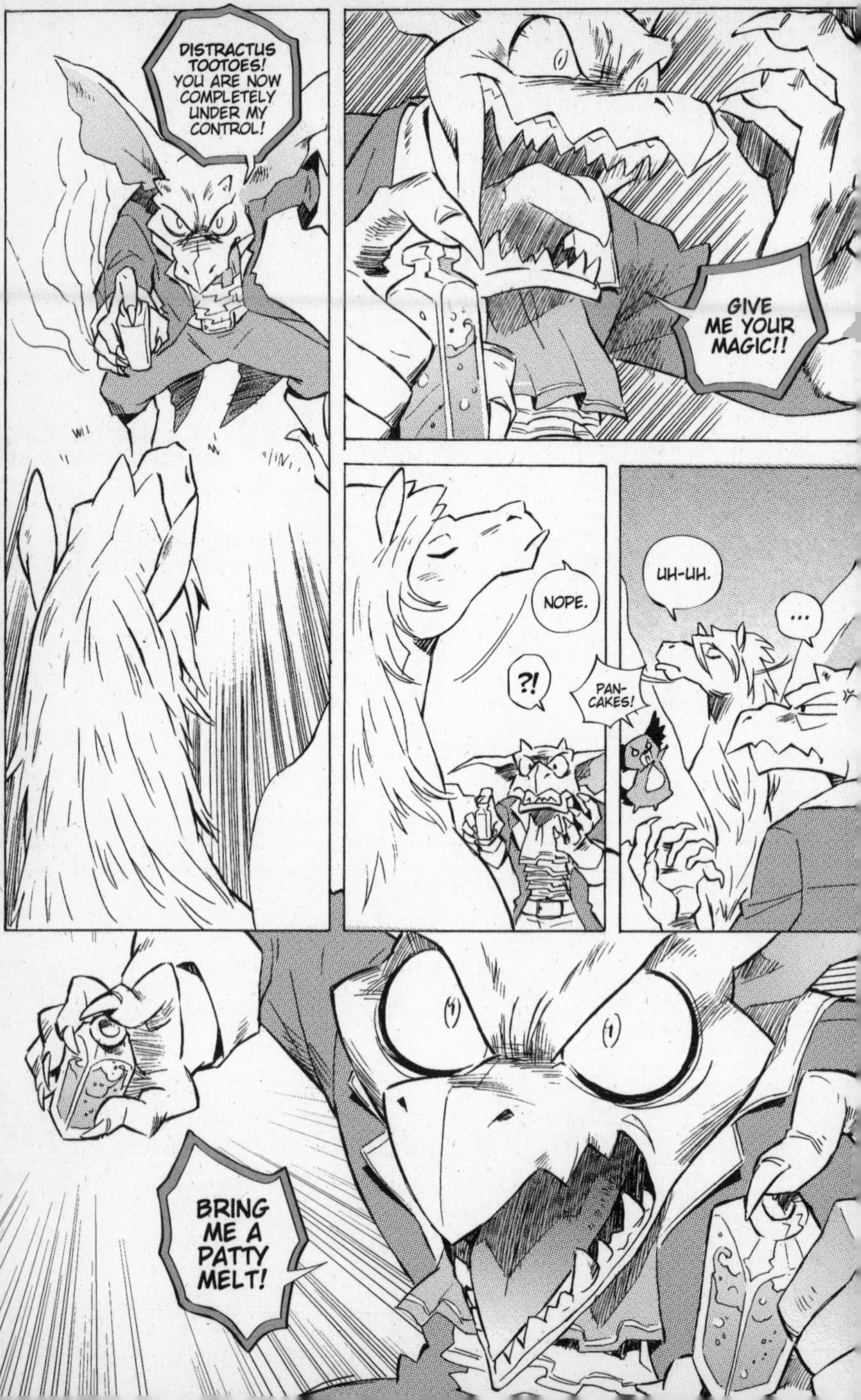
DISTRACTUS TOOTOES! YOU ARE NOW COMPLETELY UNDER MY CONTROL!
GIVE ME YOUR MAGIC!!
NOPE.
?!
PAN-CAKES!
UH-UH.
...
BRING ME A PATTY MELT!

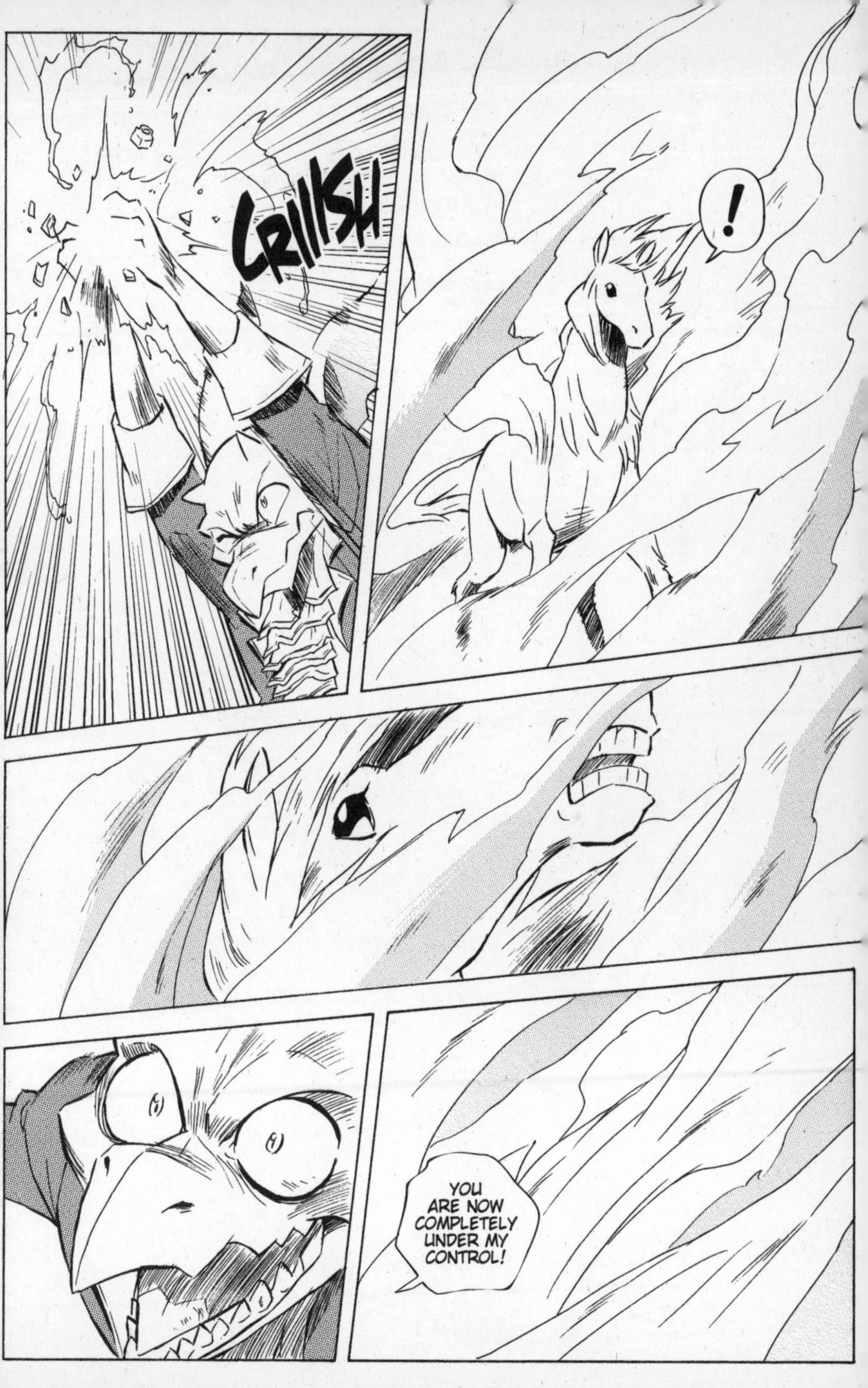
CRIIISH
!
YOU ARE NOW COMPLETELY UNDER MY CONTROL!

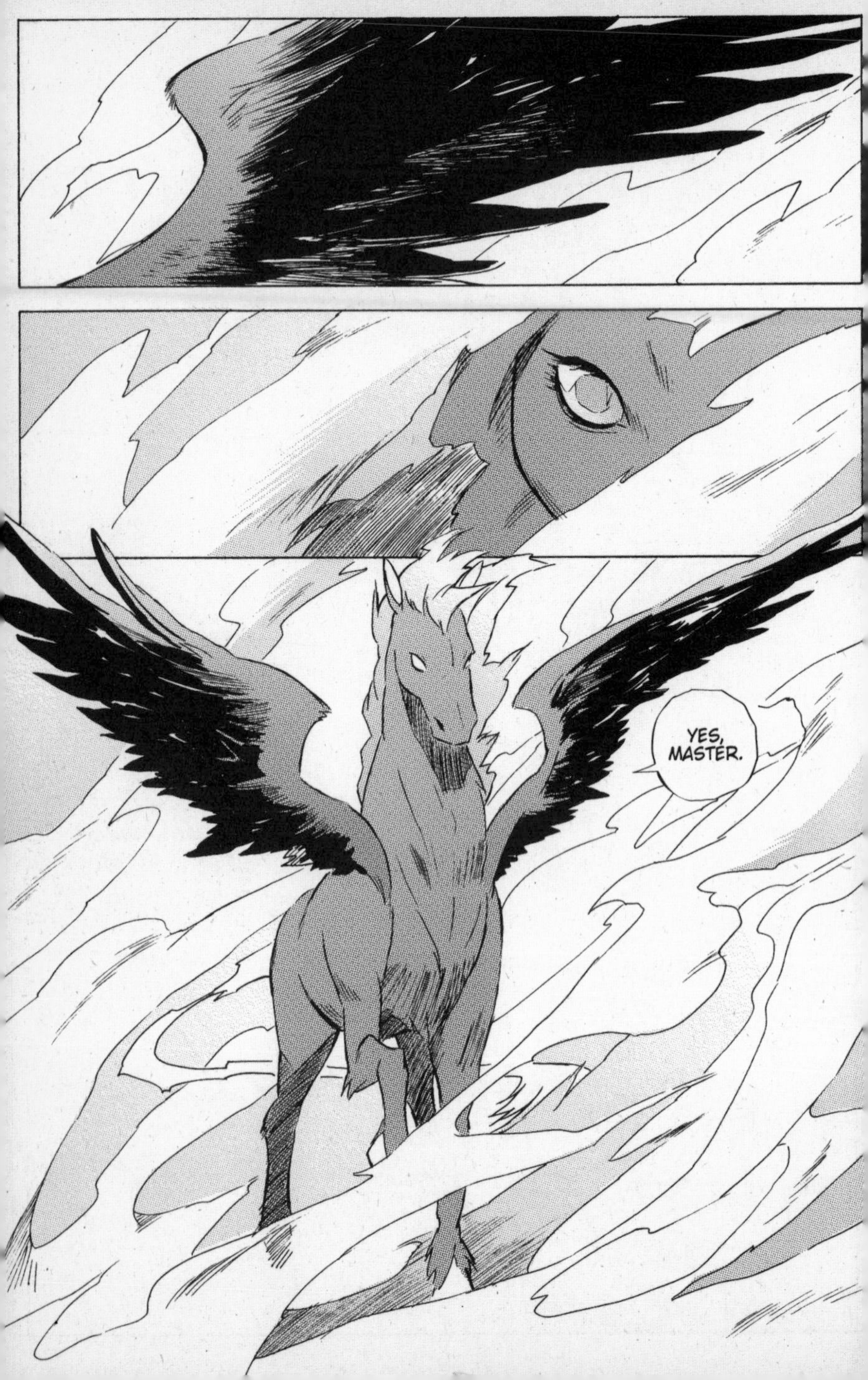
YES, MASTER.

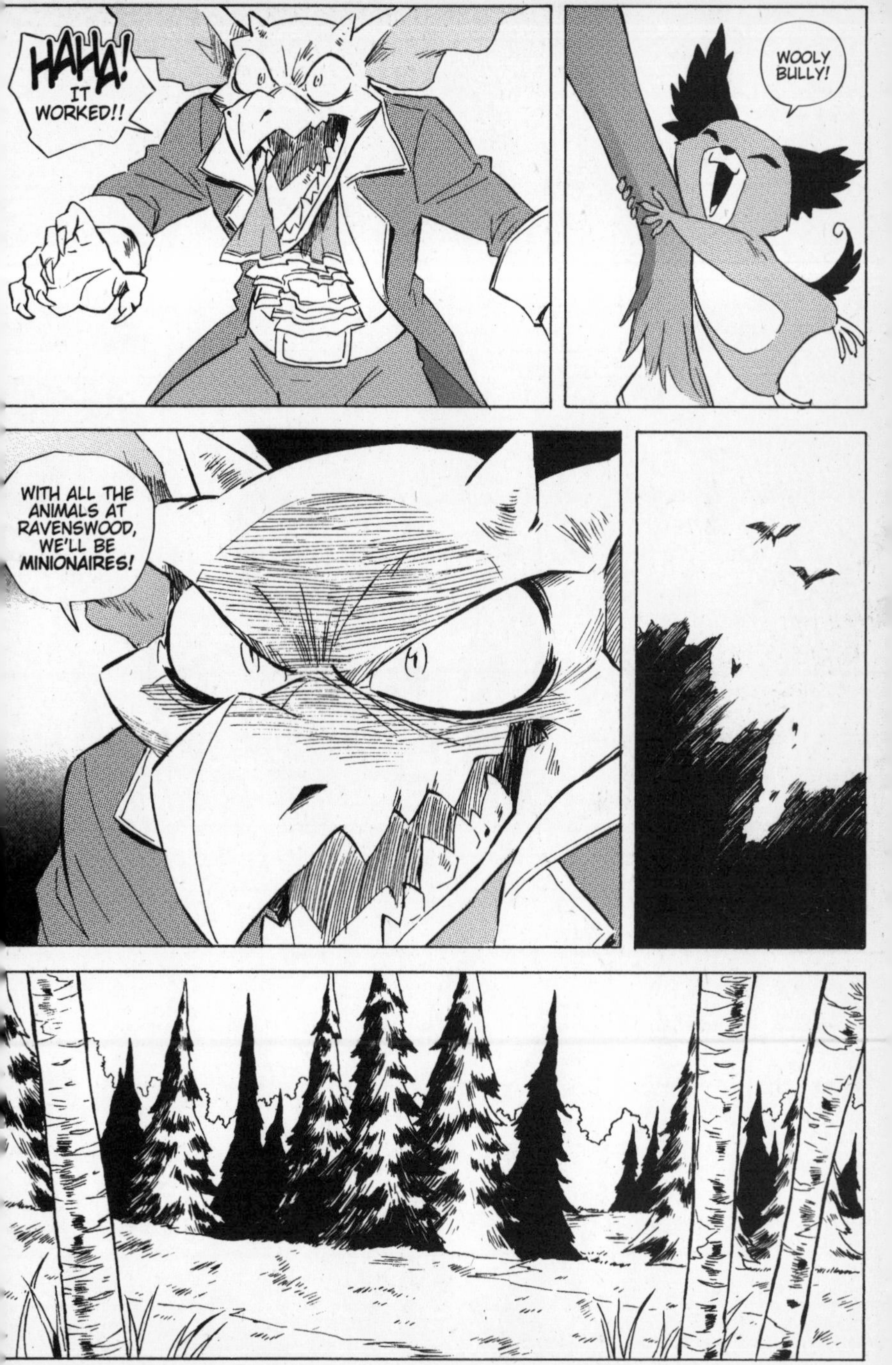
HAHA! IT WORKED!!
WOOLY BULLY!
WITH ALL THE ANIMALS AT RAVENSWOOD, WE'LL BE MINIONAIRES!

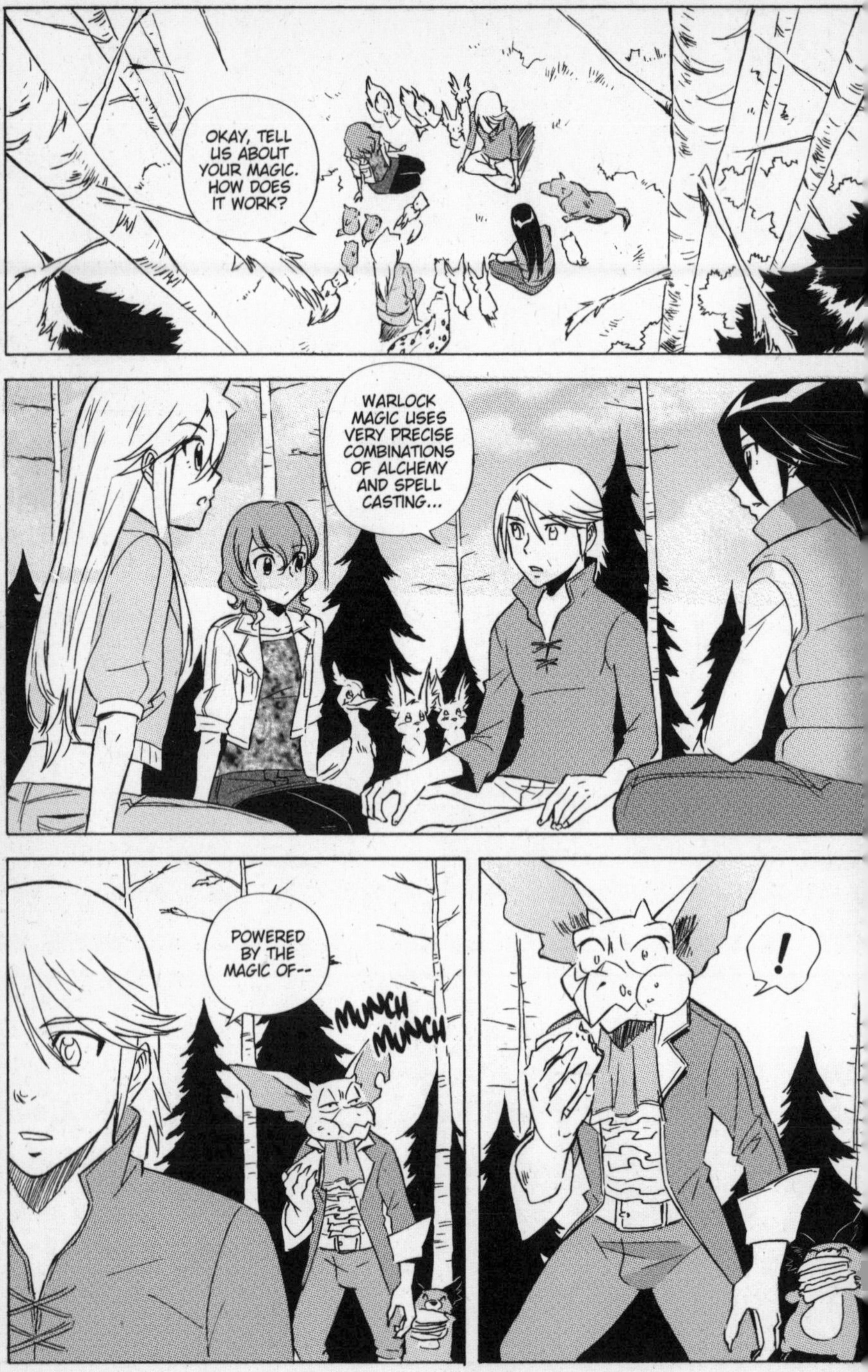
OKAY, TELL US ABOUT YOUR MAGIC. HOW DOES IT WORK?
WARLOCK MAGIC USES VERY PRECISE COMBINATIONS OF ALCHEMY AND SPELL CASTING...
POWERED BY THE MAGIC OF--
MUNCH MUNCH
!

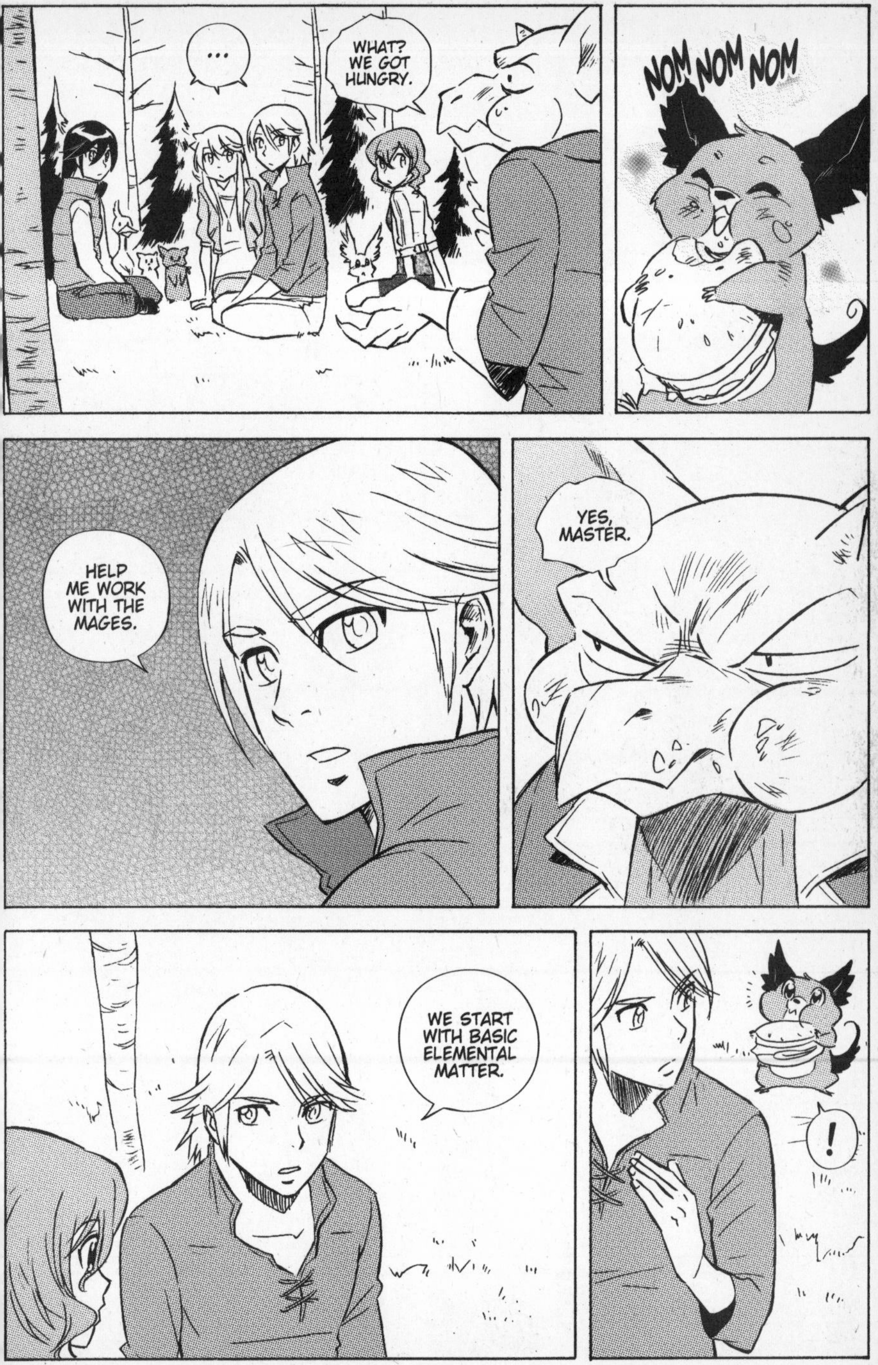
...
WHAT? WE GOT HUNGRY.
NOM NOM NOM
HELP ME WORK WITH THE MAGES.
YES, MASTER.
WE START WITH BASIC ELEMENTAL MATTER.
!

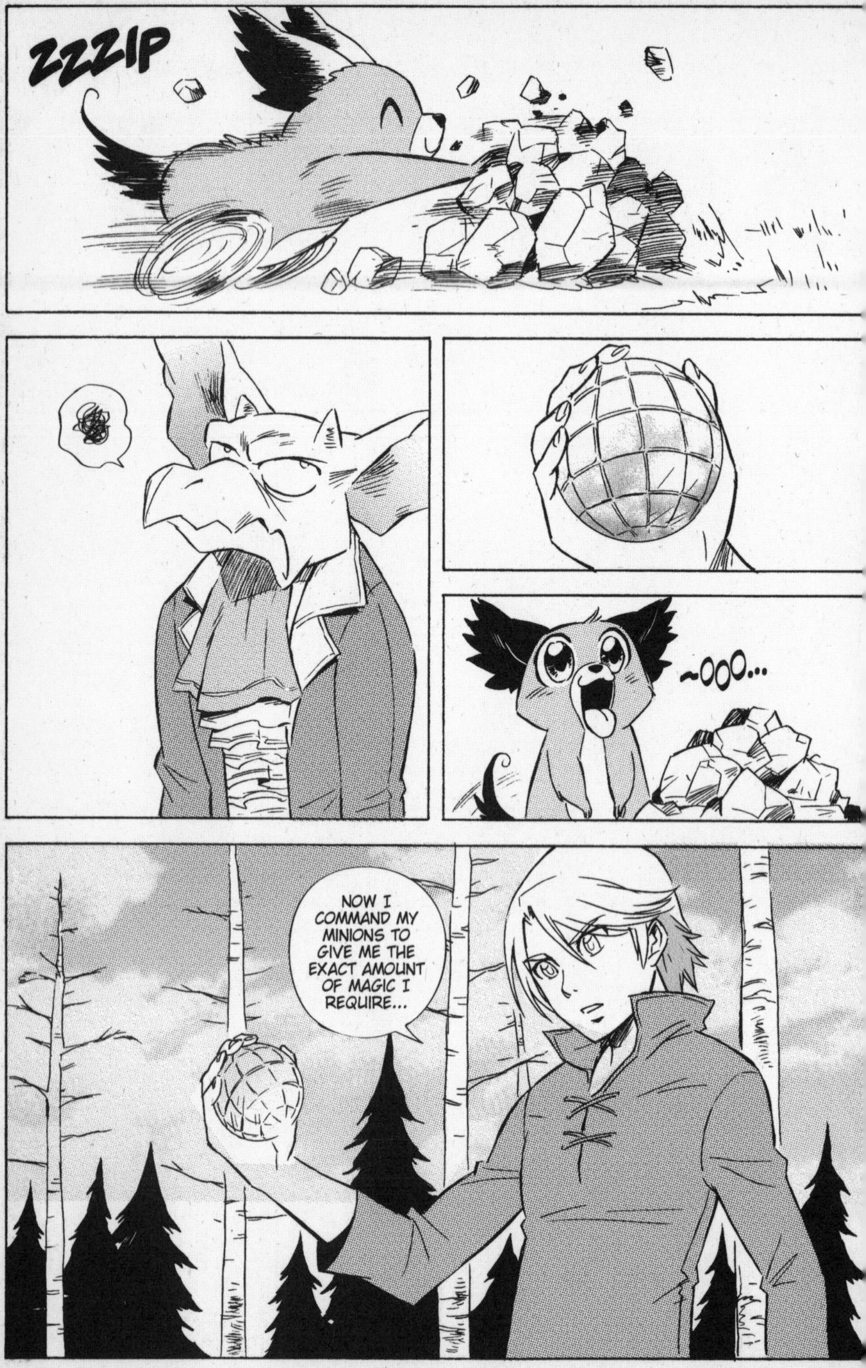
ZZZIP
~OOO...
NOW I COMMAND MY MINIONS TO GIVE ME THE EXACT AMOUNT OF MAGIC I REQUIRE...

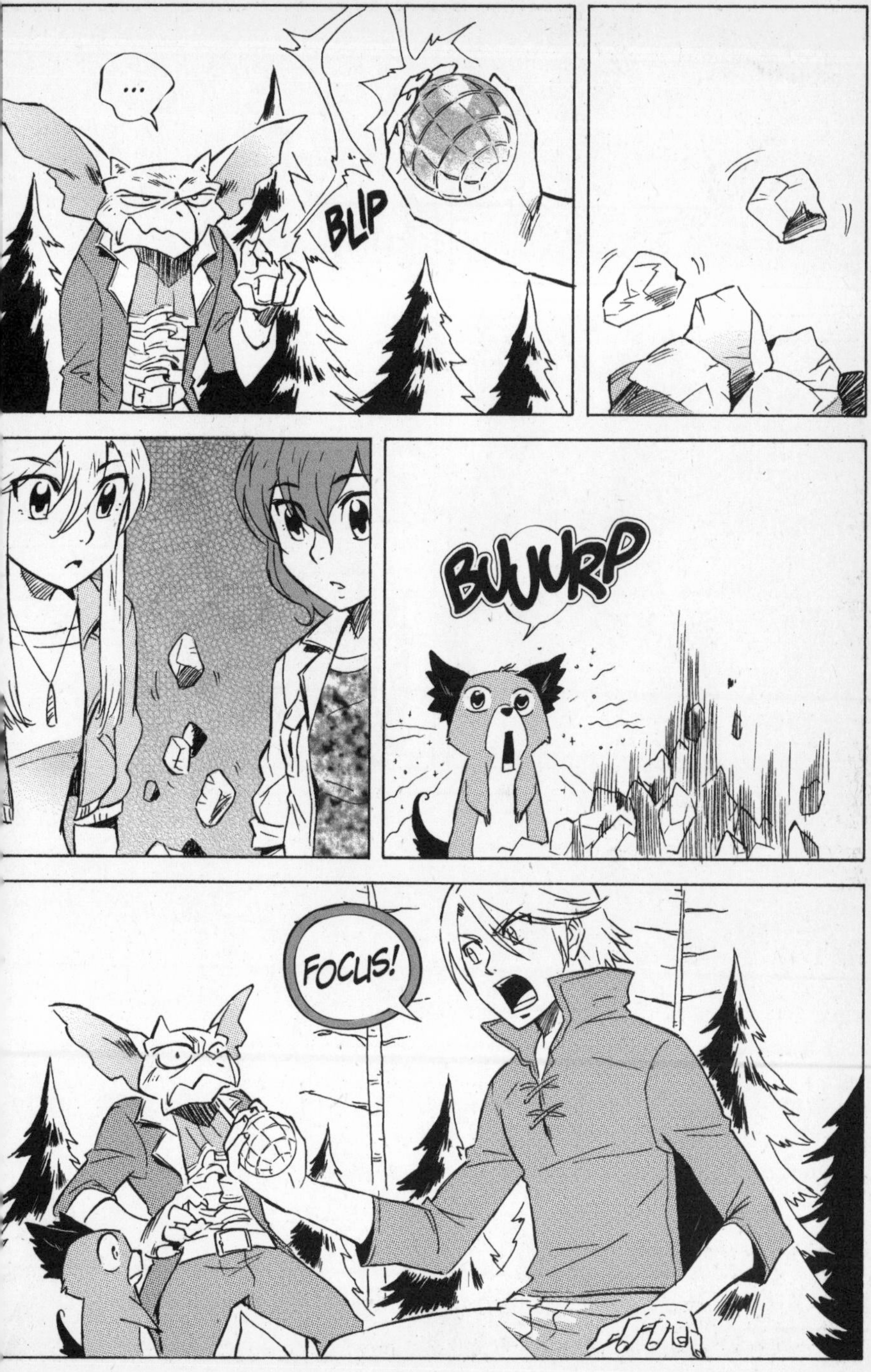
...
BLIP
BUUURP
FOCUS!

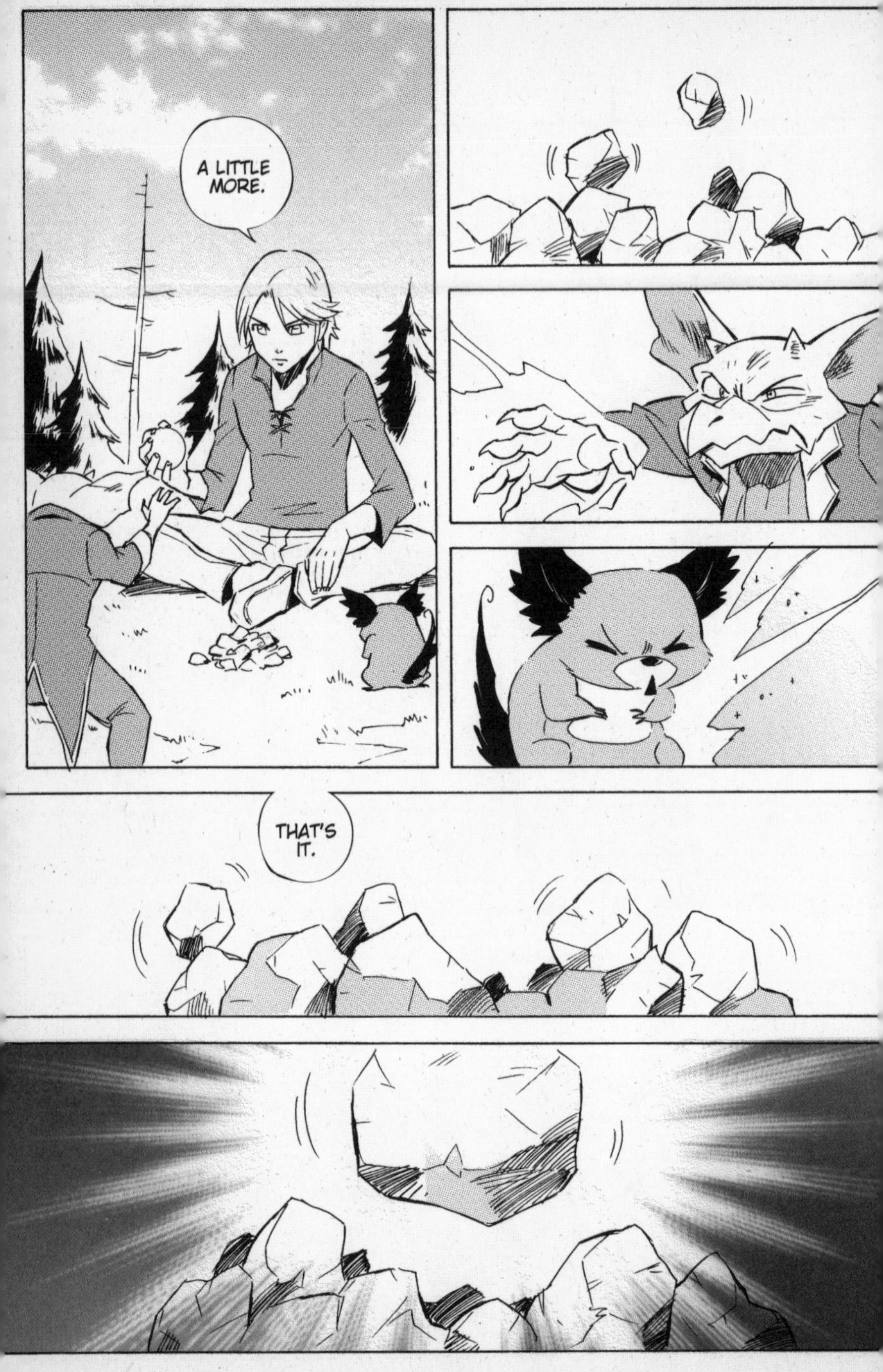
A LITTLE MORE.
THAT'S IT.

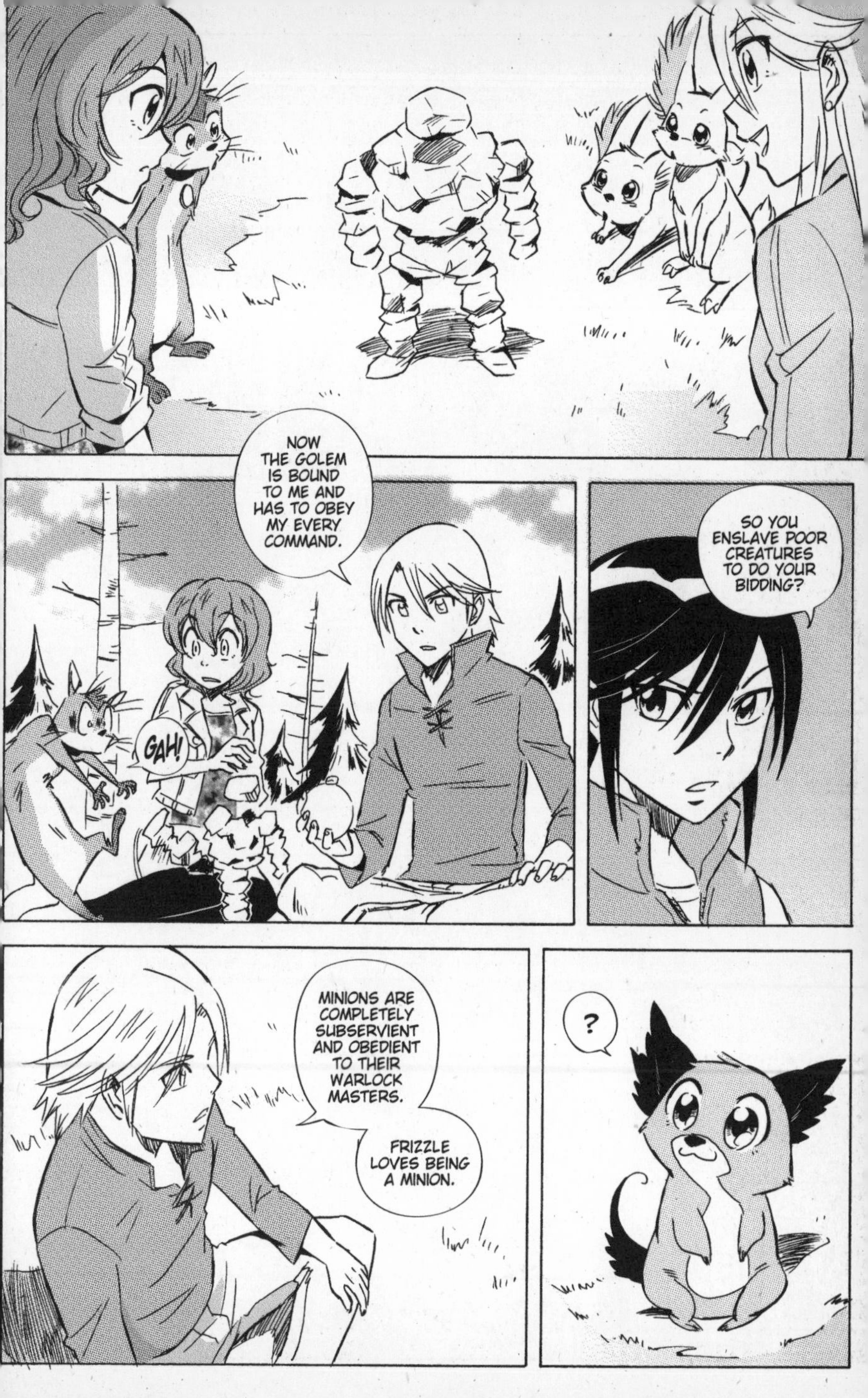
NOW THE GOLEM IS BOUND TO ME AND HAS TO OBEY MY EVERY COMMAND.
GAH!
SO YOU ENSLAVE POOR CREATURES TO DO YOUR BIDDING?
MINIONS ARE COMPLETELY SUBSERVIENT AND OBEDIENT TO THEIR WARLOCK MASTERS.
FRIZZLE LOVES BEING A MINION.
?

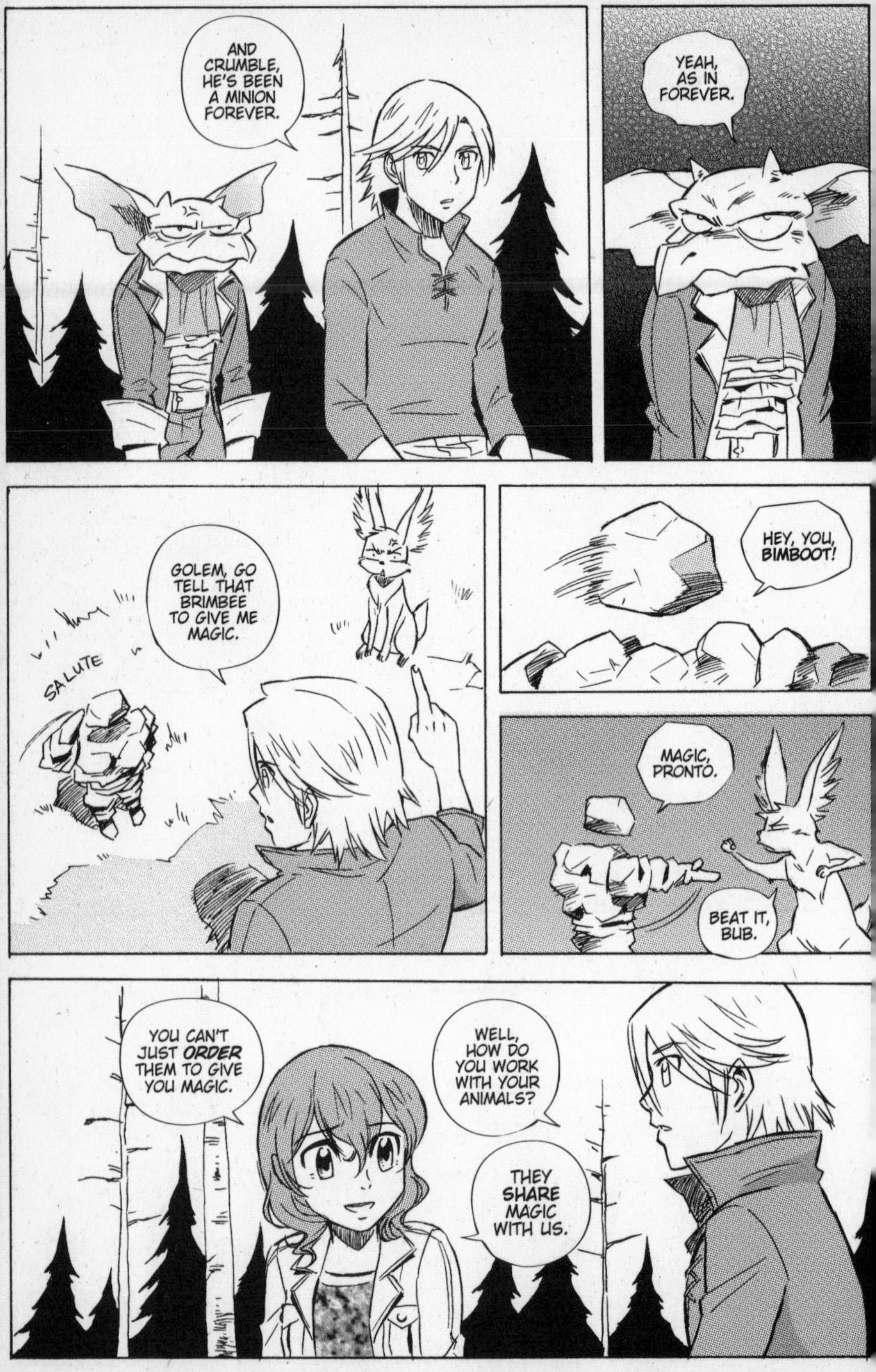
AND CRUMBLE, HE'S BEEN A MINION FOREVER.
YEAH, AS IN FOREVER.
GOLEM, GO TELL THAT BRIMBEE TO GIVE ME MAGIC.
SALUTE
HEY, YOU, BIMBOOT!
MAGIC, PRONTO.
BEAT IT, BUB.
YOU CAN'T JUST ORDER THEM TO GIVE YOU MAGIC.
WELL, HOW DO YOU WORK WITH YOUR ANIMALS?
THEY SHARE MAGIC WITH US.

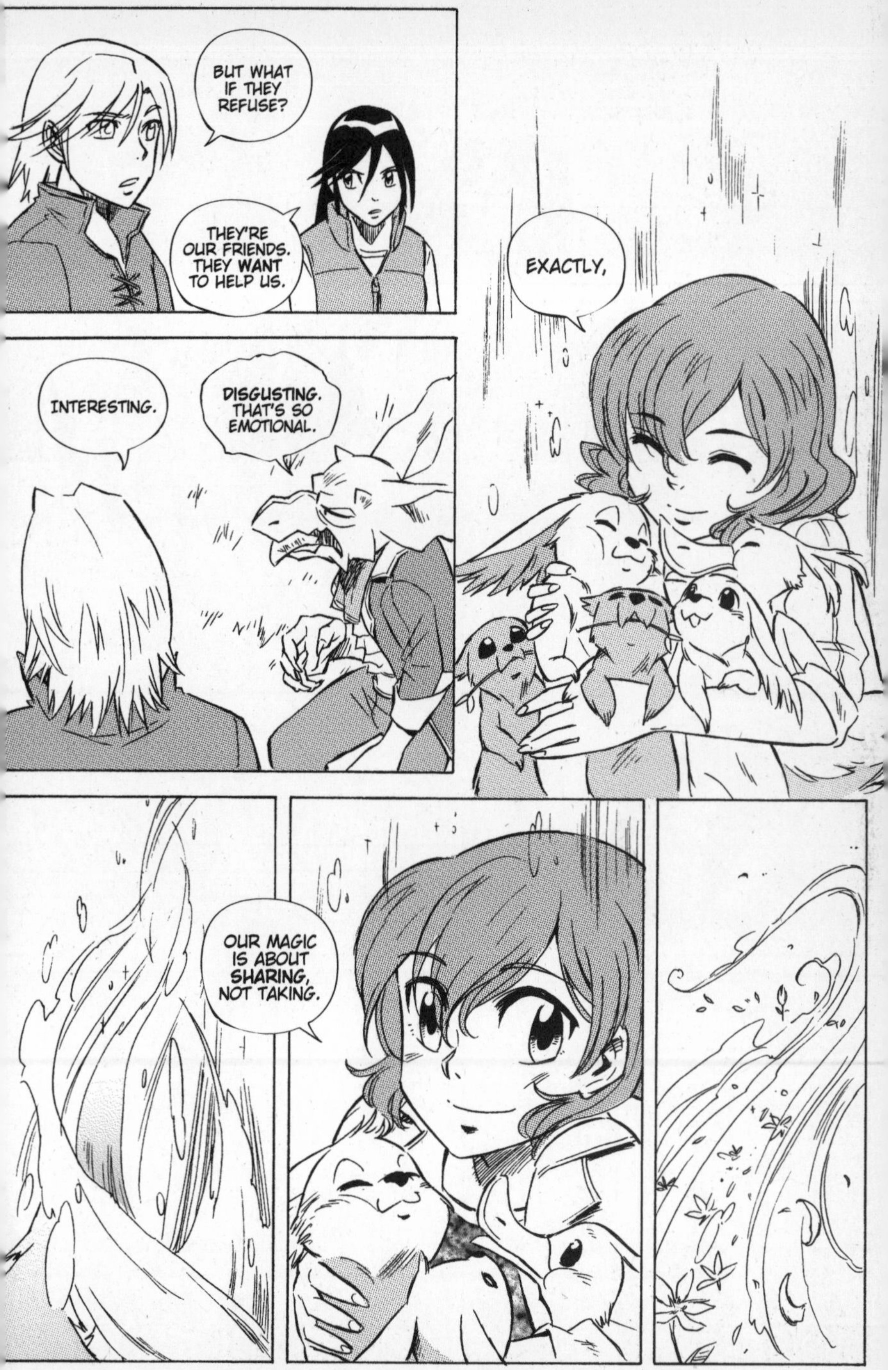
BUT WHAT IF THEY REFUSE?
THEY'RE OUR FRIENDS. THEY WANT TO HELP US.
EXACTLY,
INTERESTING.
DISGUSTING. THAT'S SO EMOTIONAL.
OUR MAGIC IS ABOUT SHARING, NOT TAKING.

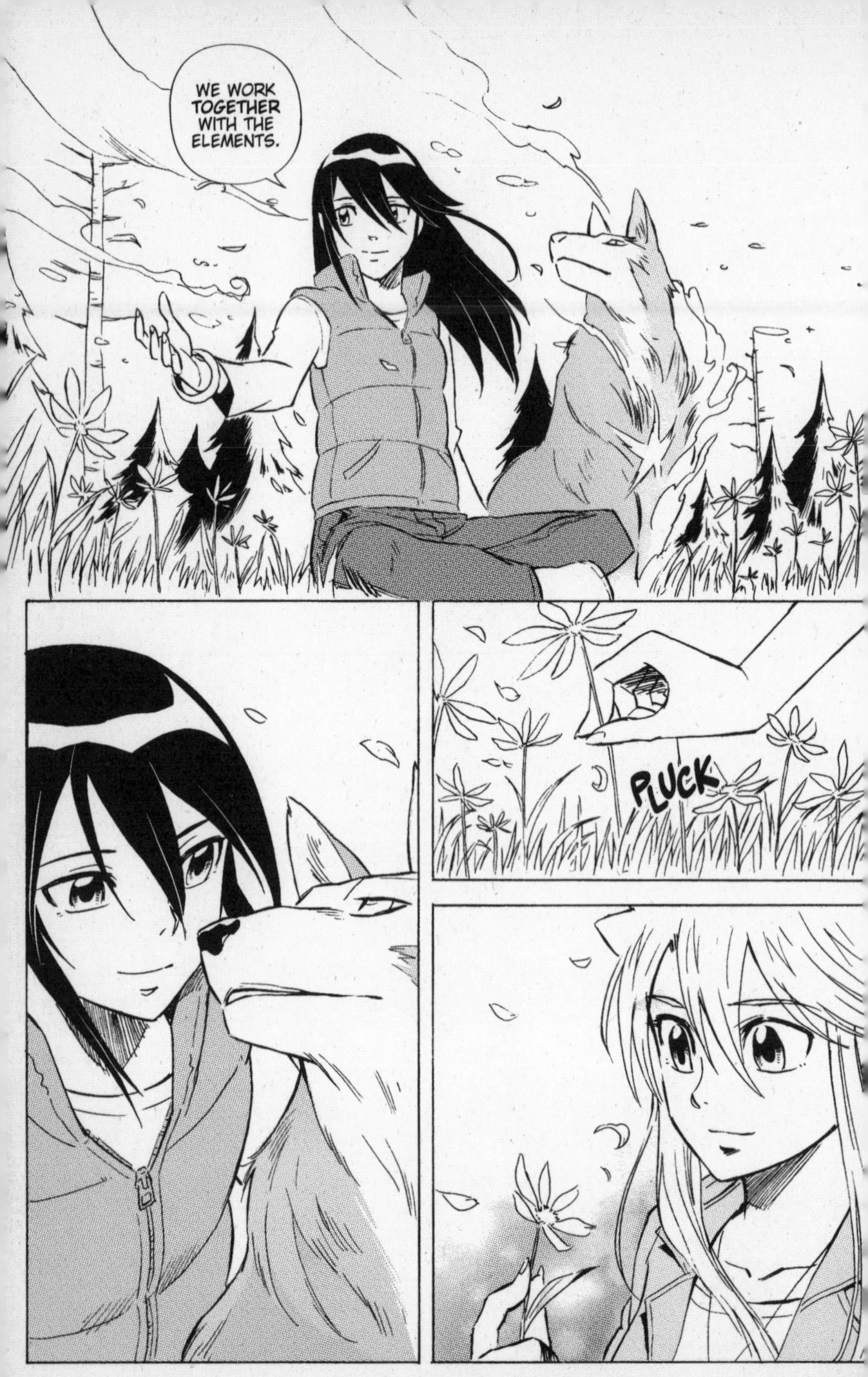
WE WORK TOGETHER WITH THE ELEMENTS.
PLUCK

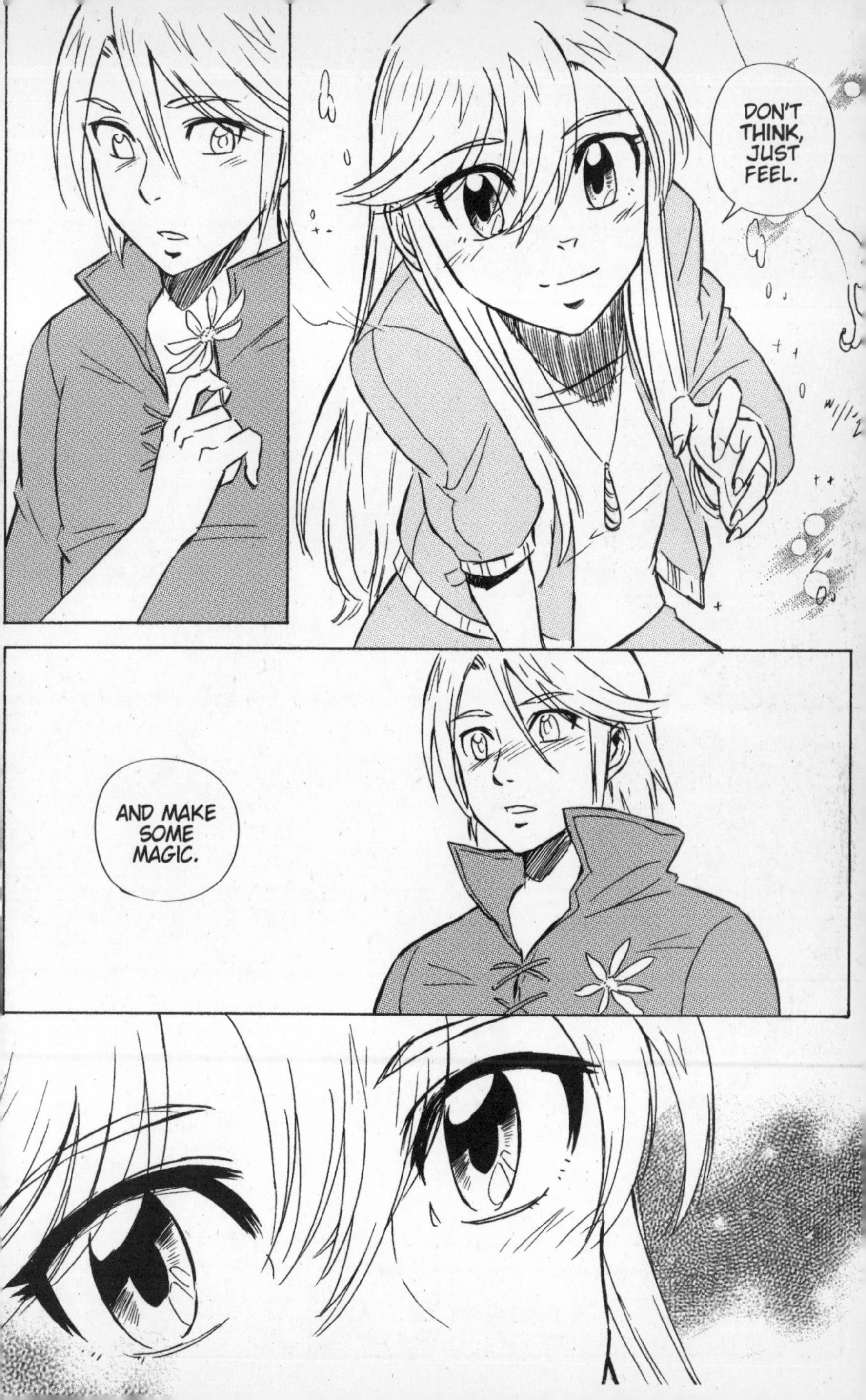
DON'T THINK, JUST FEEL.
AND MAKE SOME MAGIC.

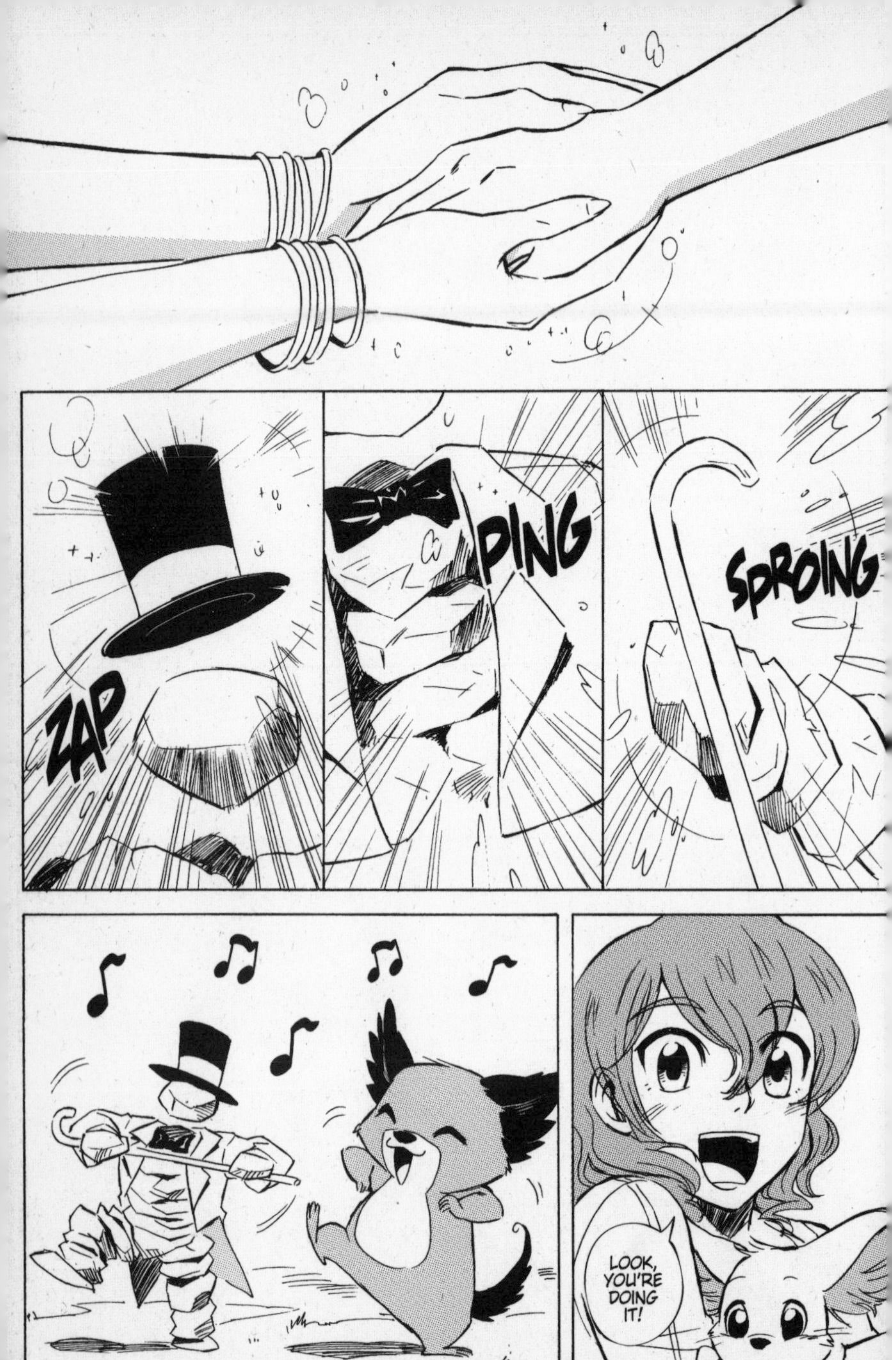
ZAP
PING
SPROING
LOOK, YOU'RE DOING IT!

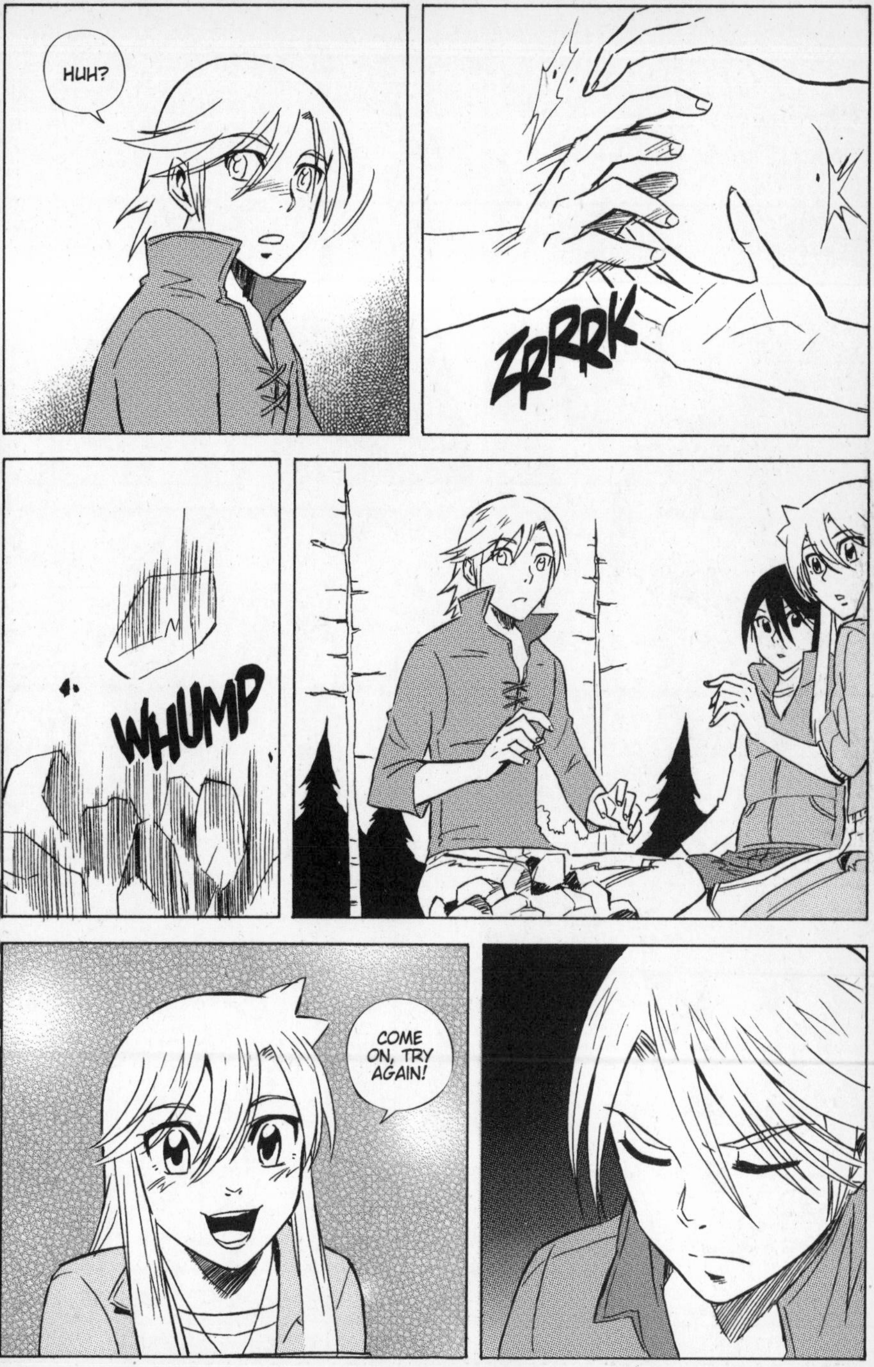
HUH?
ZRRRK
WHUMP
COME ON, TRY AGAIN!

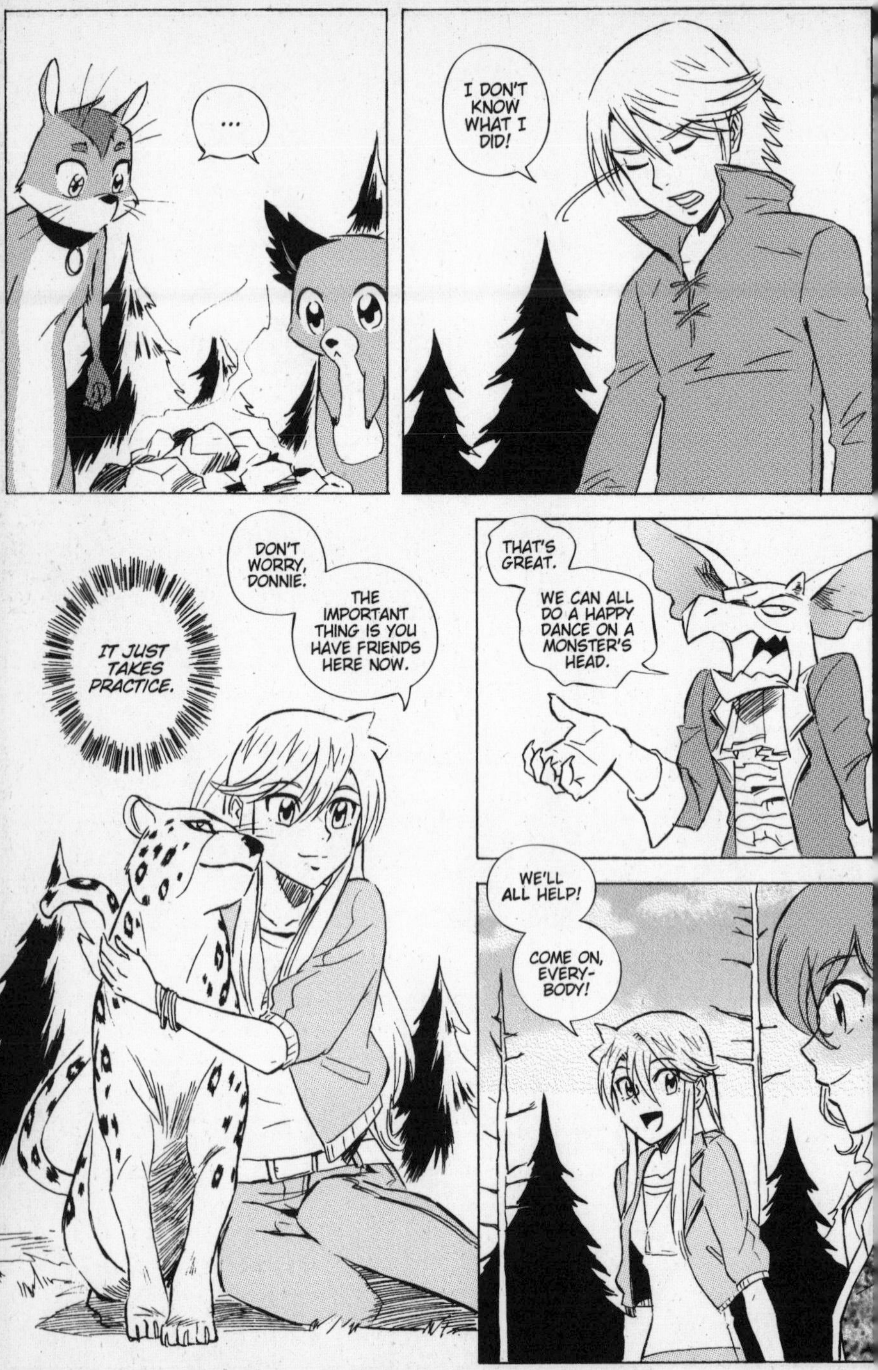
...
I DON'T KNOW WHAT I DID!
IT JUST TAKES PRACTICE.
DON'T WORRY, DONNIE.
THE IMPORTANT THING IS YOU HAVE FRIENDS HERE NOW.
THAT'S GREAT.
WE CAN ALL DO A HAPPY DANCE ON A MONSTER'S HEAD.
WE'LL ALL HELP!
COME ON, EVERY-BODY!

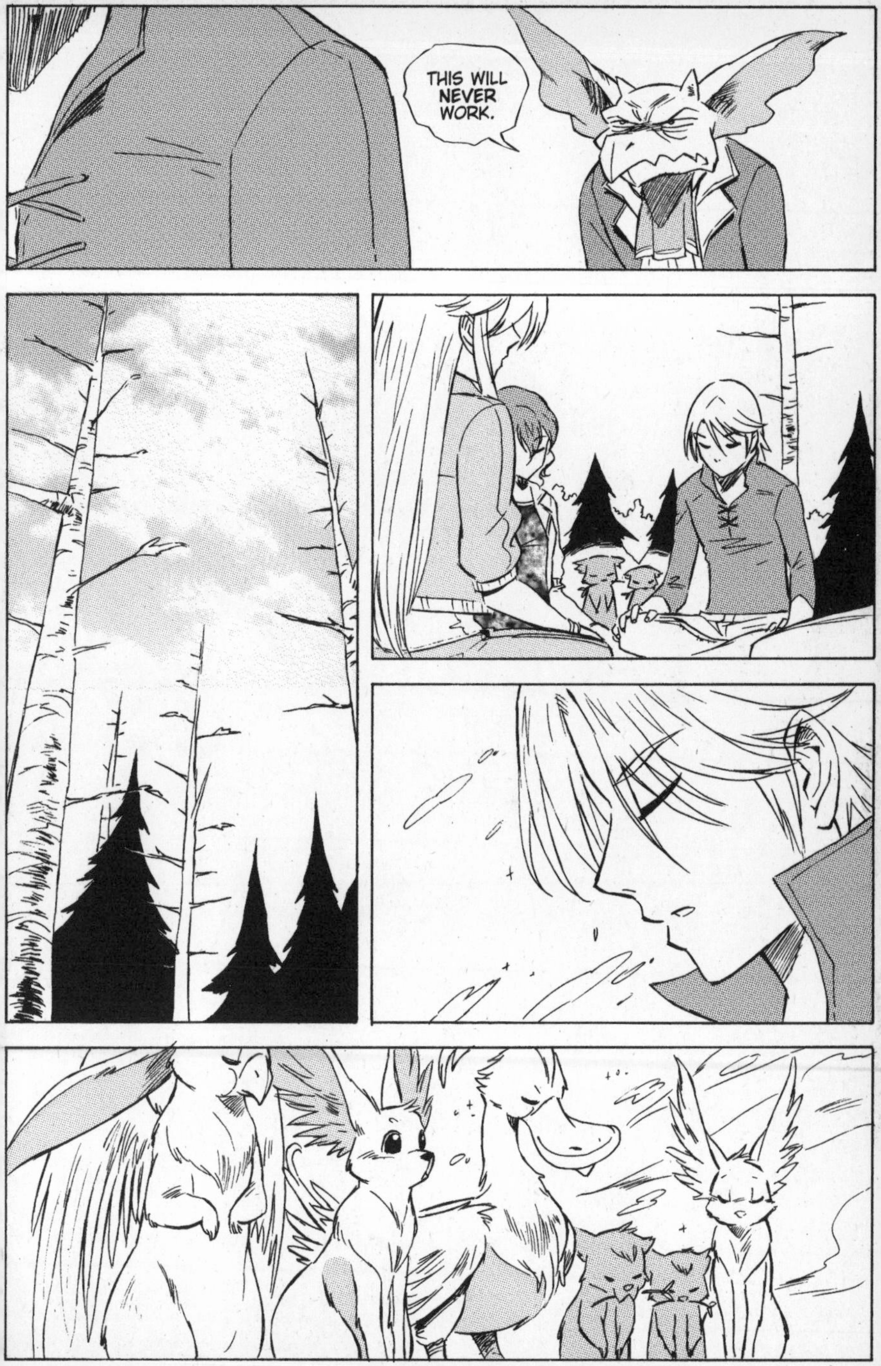
THIS WILL NEVER WORK.

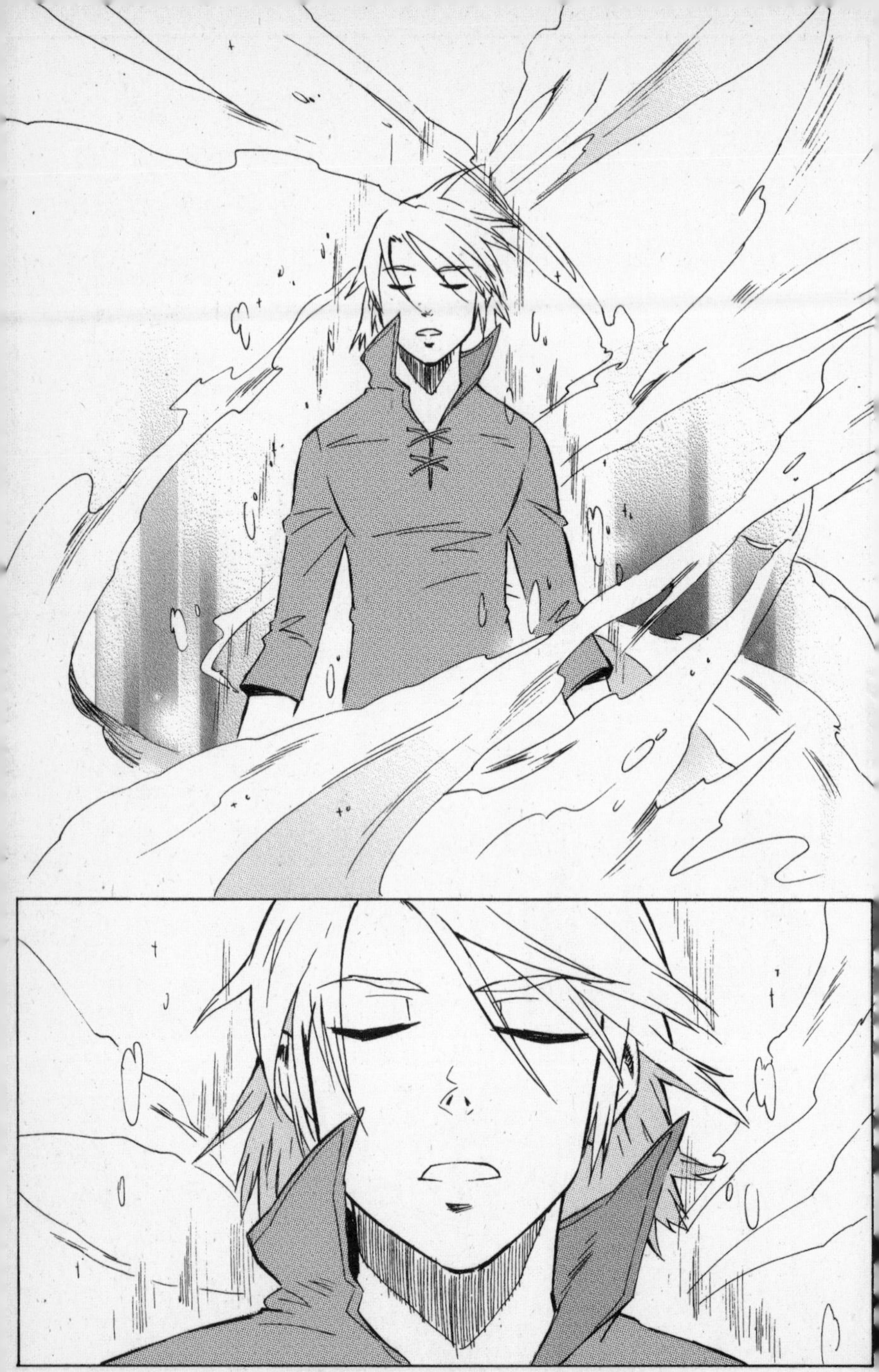

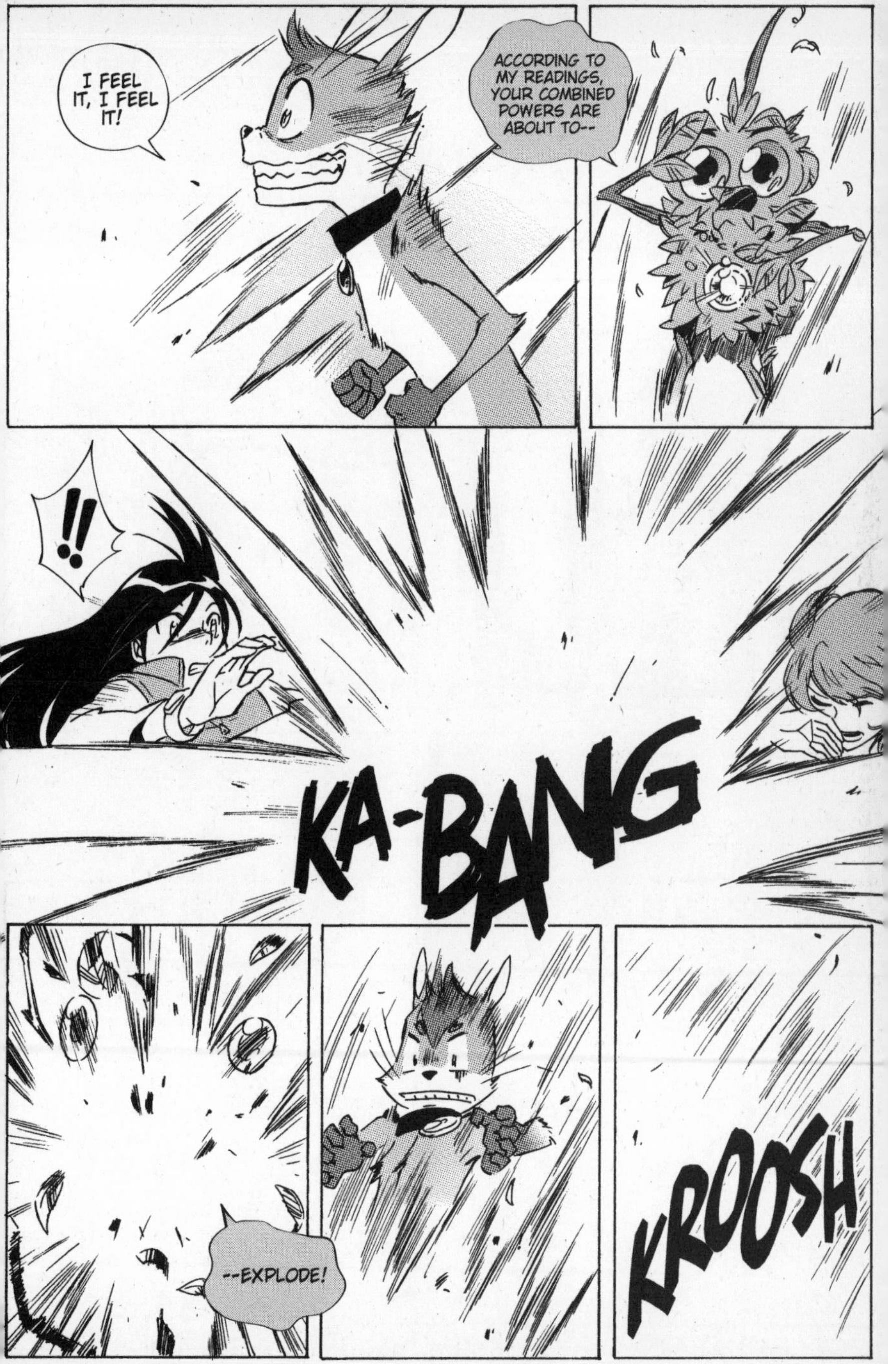
I FEEL IT, I FEEL IT!
ACCORDING TO MY READINGS, YOUR COMBINED POWERS ARE ABOUT TO--
!!
KA-BANG
BA
--EXPLODE!
KROOSH

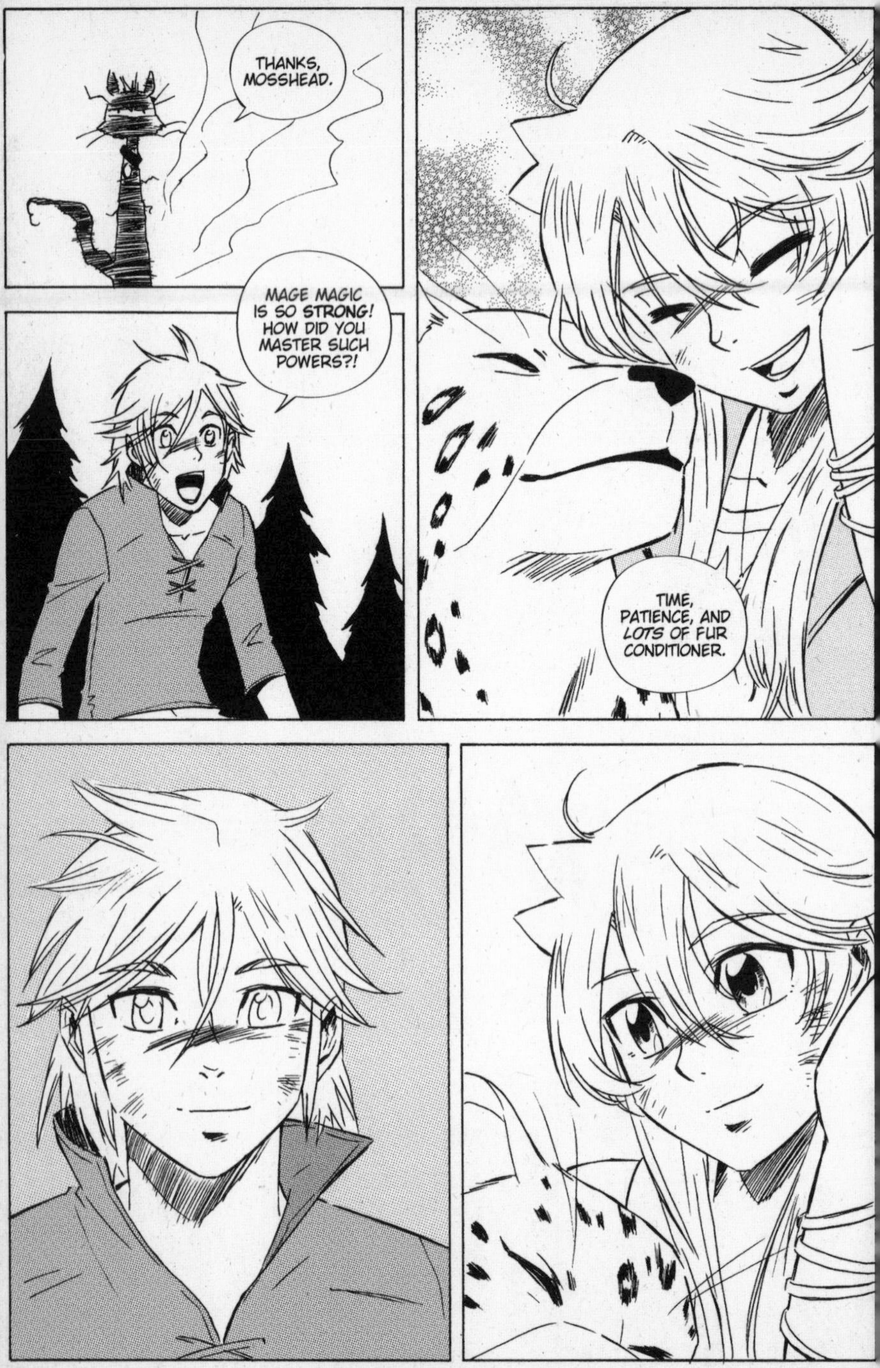
THANKS, MOSSHEAD.
MAGE MAGIC IS SO **STRONG**! HOW DID YOU MASTER SUCH POWERS?!
TIME, PATIENCE, AND *LOTS* OF FUR CONDITIONER.

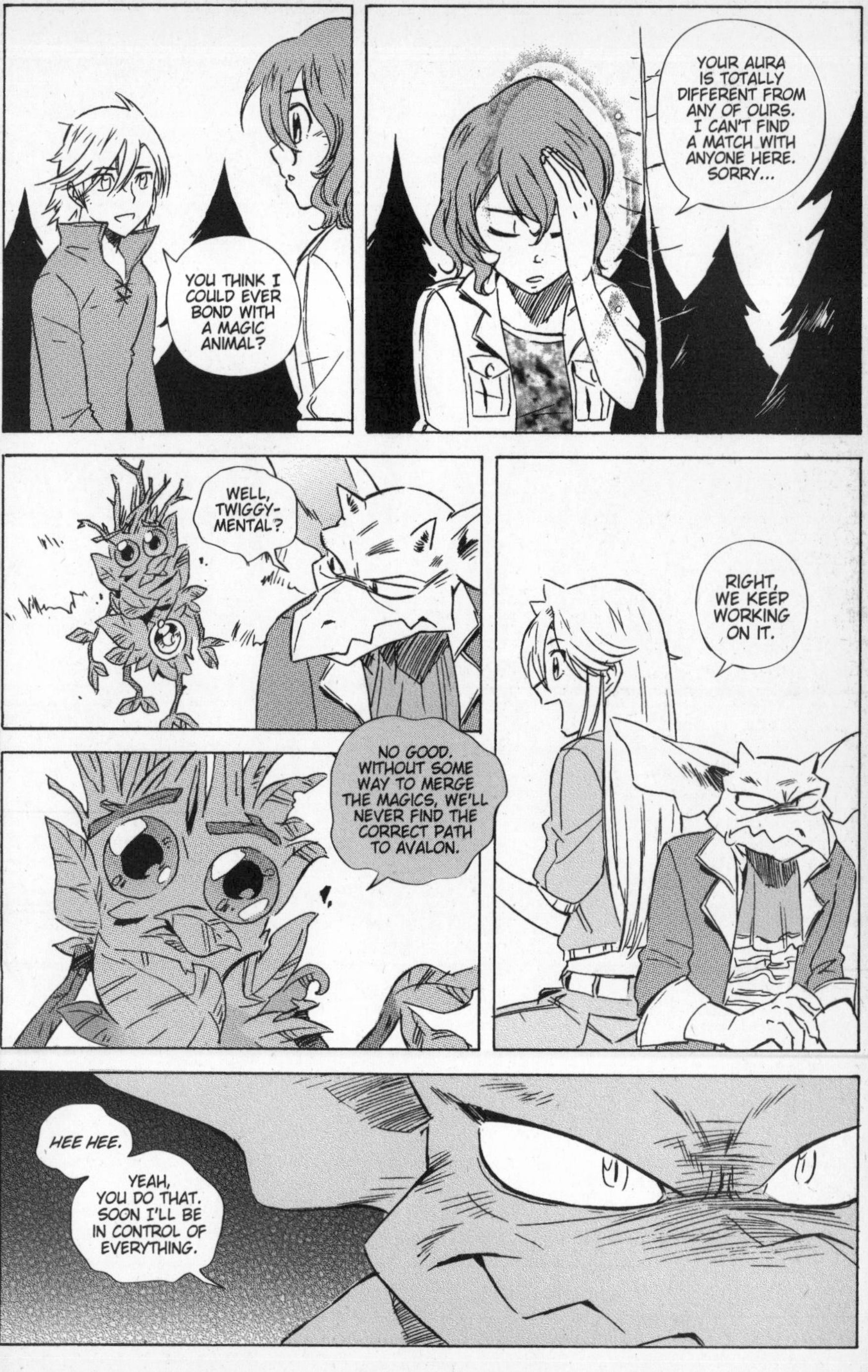
YOU THINK I COULD EVER BOND WITH A MAGIC ANIMAL?
YOUR AURA IS TOTALLY DIFFERENT FROM ANY OF OURS. I CAN'T FIND A MATCH WITH ANYONE HERE. SORRY...
WELL, TWIGGY-MENTAL?
RIGHT, WE KEEP WORKING ON IT.
NO GOOD. WITHOUT SOME WAY TO MERGE THE MAGICS, WE'LL NEVER FIND THE CORRECT PATH TO AVALON.
HEE HEE.
YEAH, YOU DO THAT. SOON I'LL BE IN CONTROL OF EVERYTHING.

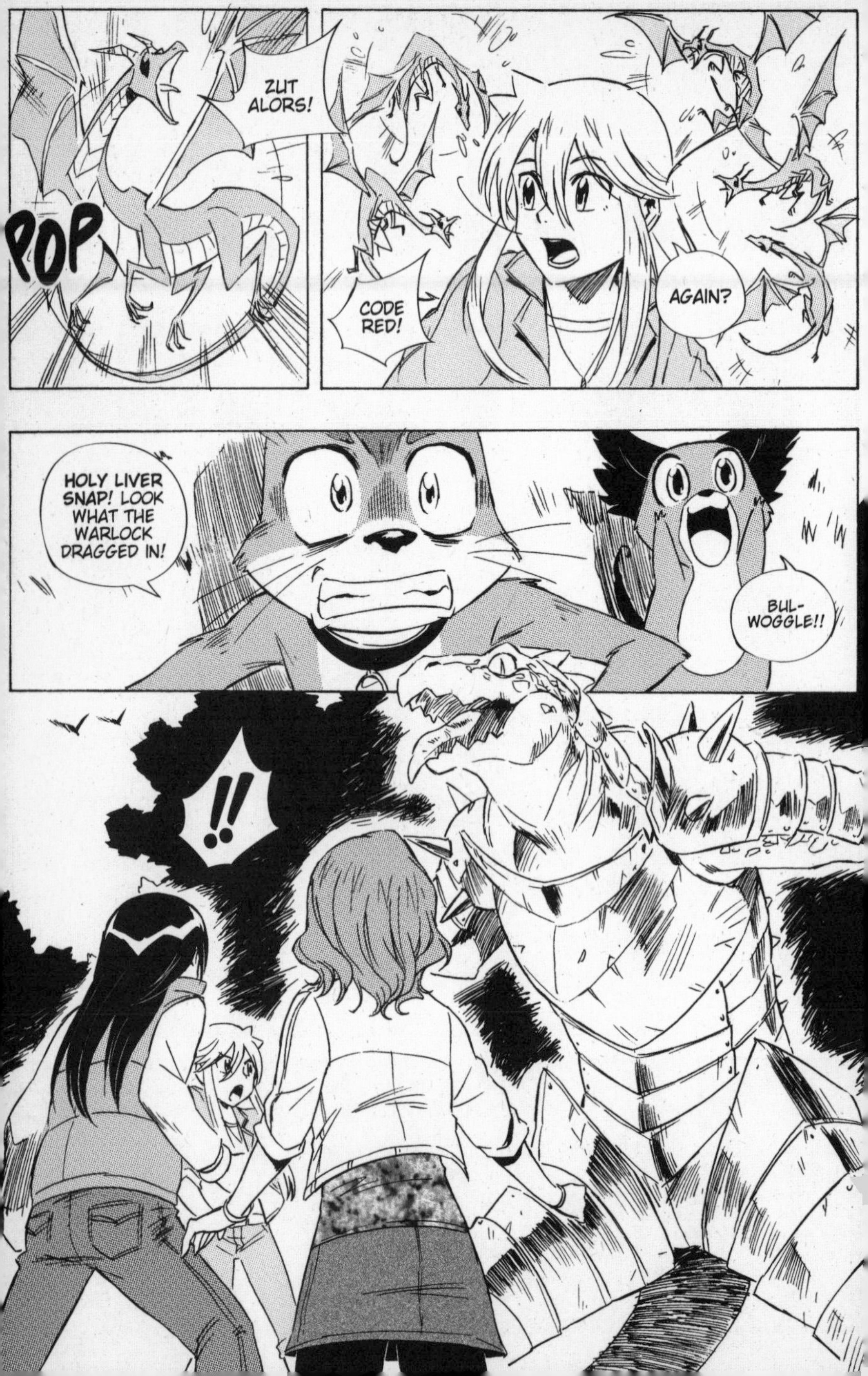
ZUT ALORS!
POP
CODE RED!
AGAIN?
HOLY LIVER SNAP! LOOK WHAT THE WARLOCK DRAGGED IN!
BUL-WOGGLE!!
!!

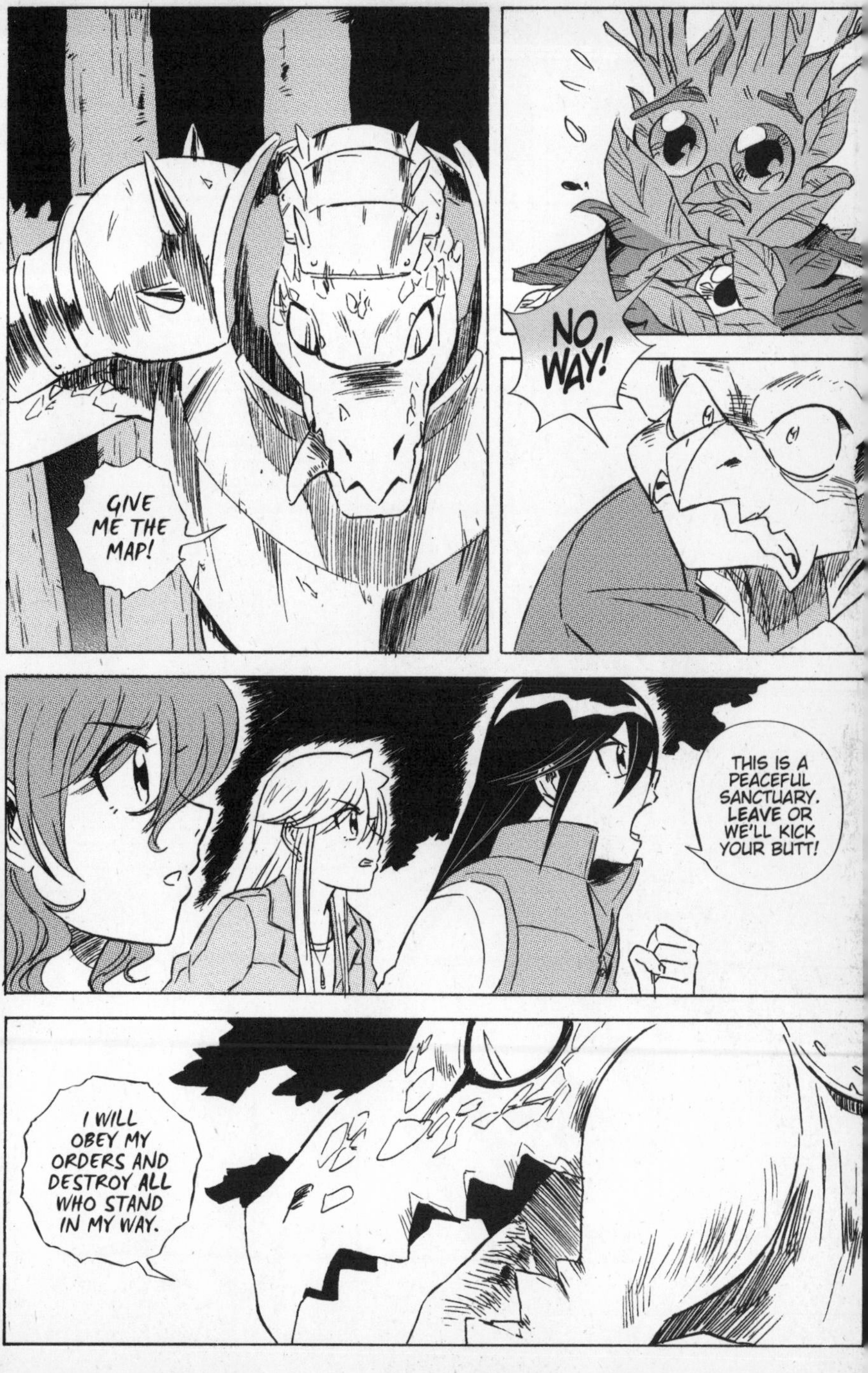
GIVE ME THE MAP!
NO WAY!
THIS IS A PEACEFUL SANCTUARY. LEAVE OR WE'LL KICK YOUR BUTT!
I WILL OBEY MY ORDERS AND DESTROY ALL WHO STAND IN MY WAY.

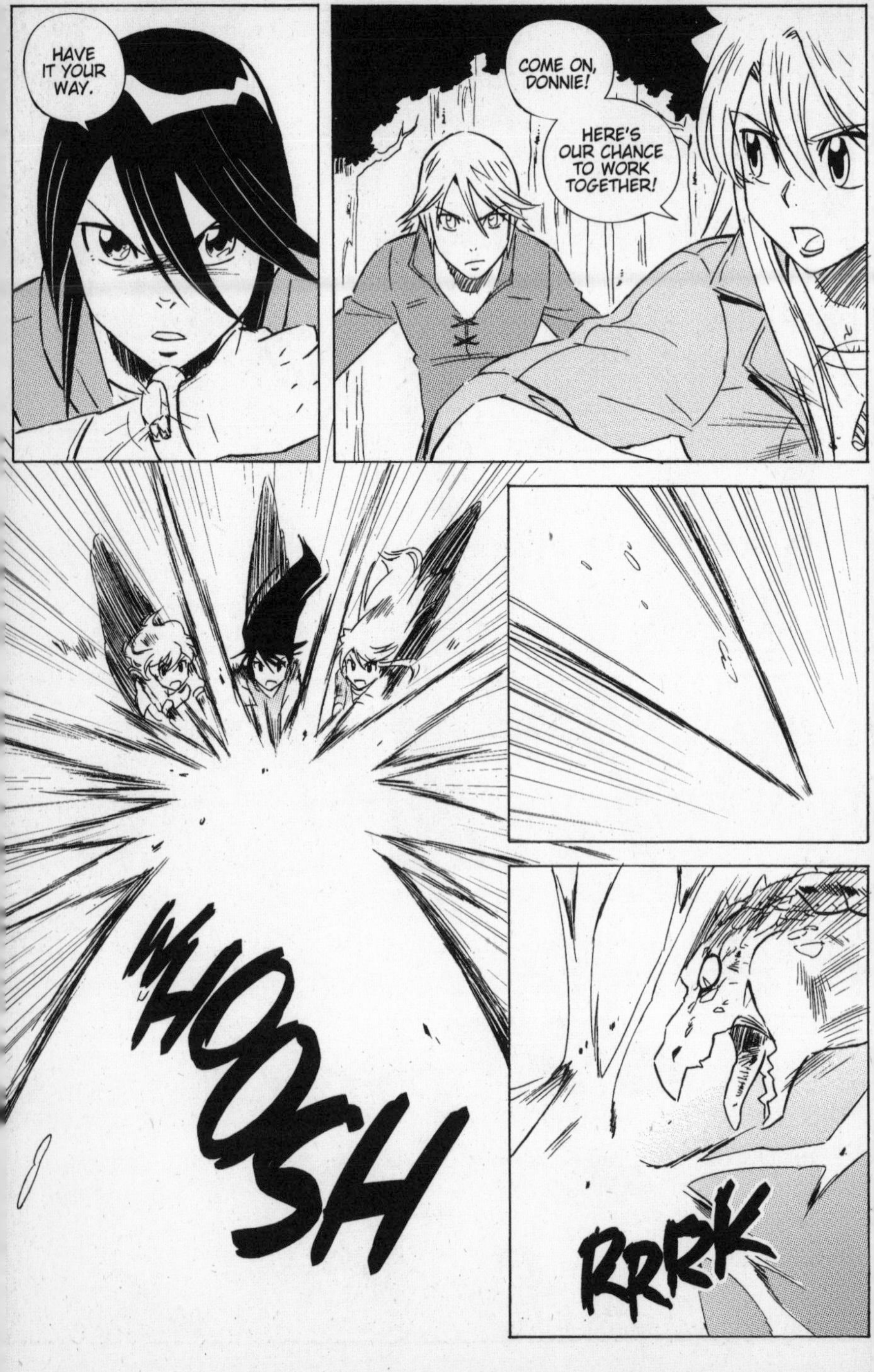
HAVE IT YOUR WAY.
COME ON, DONNIE!
HERE'S OUR CHANCE TO WORK TOGETHER!
WHOOSH
RRRK

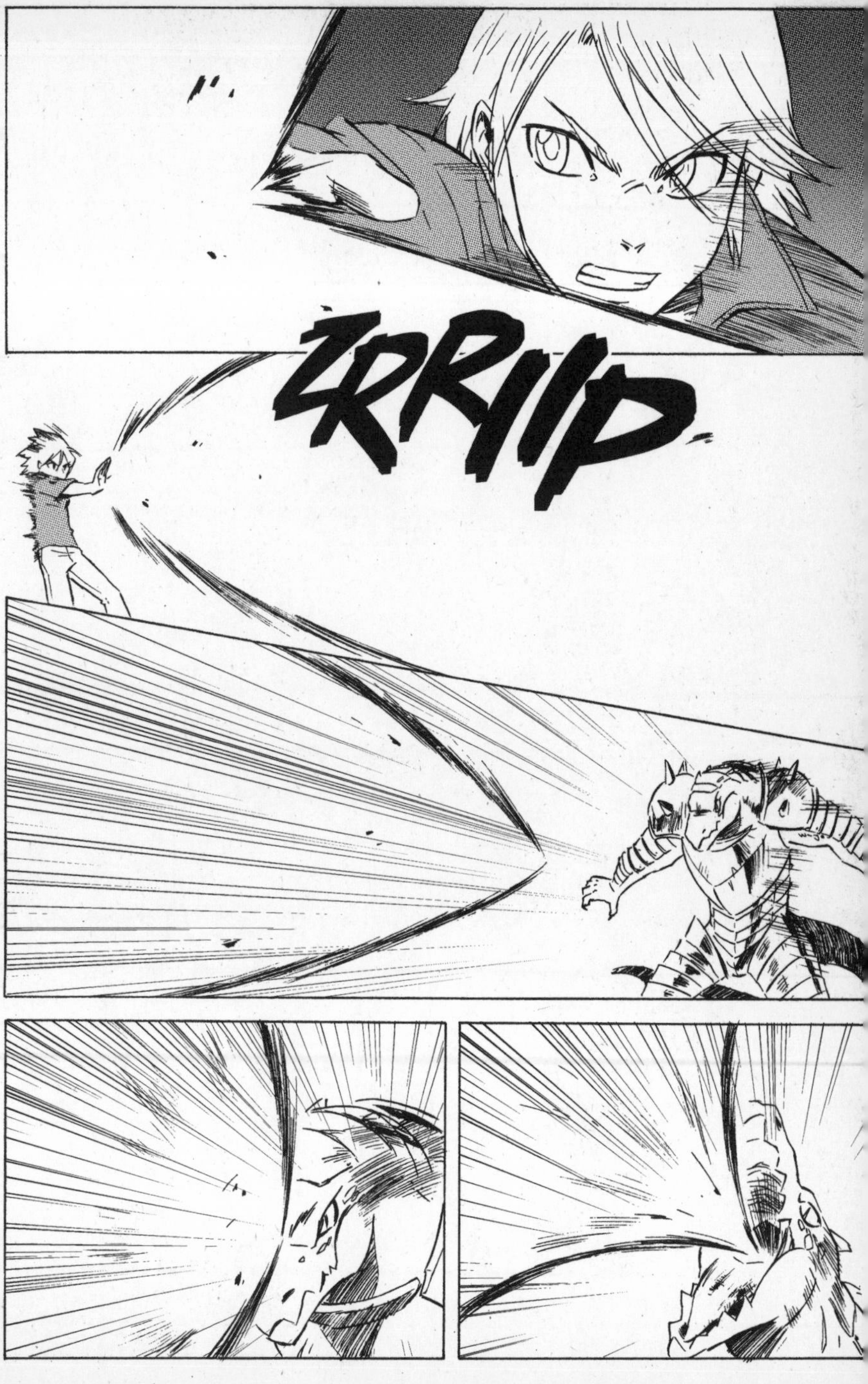
ZRRIIP

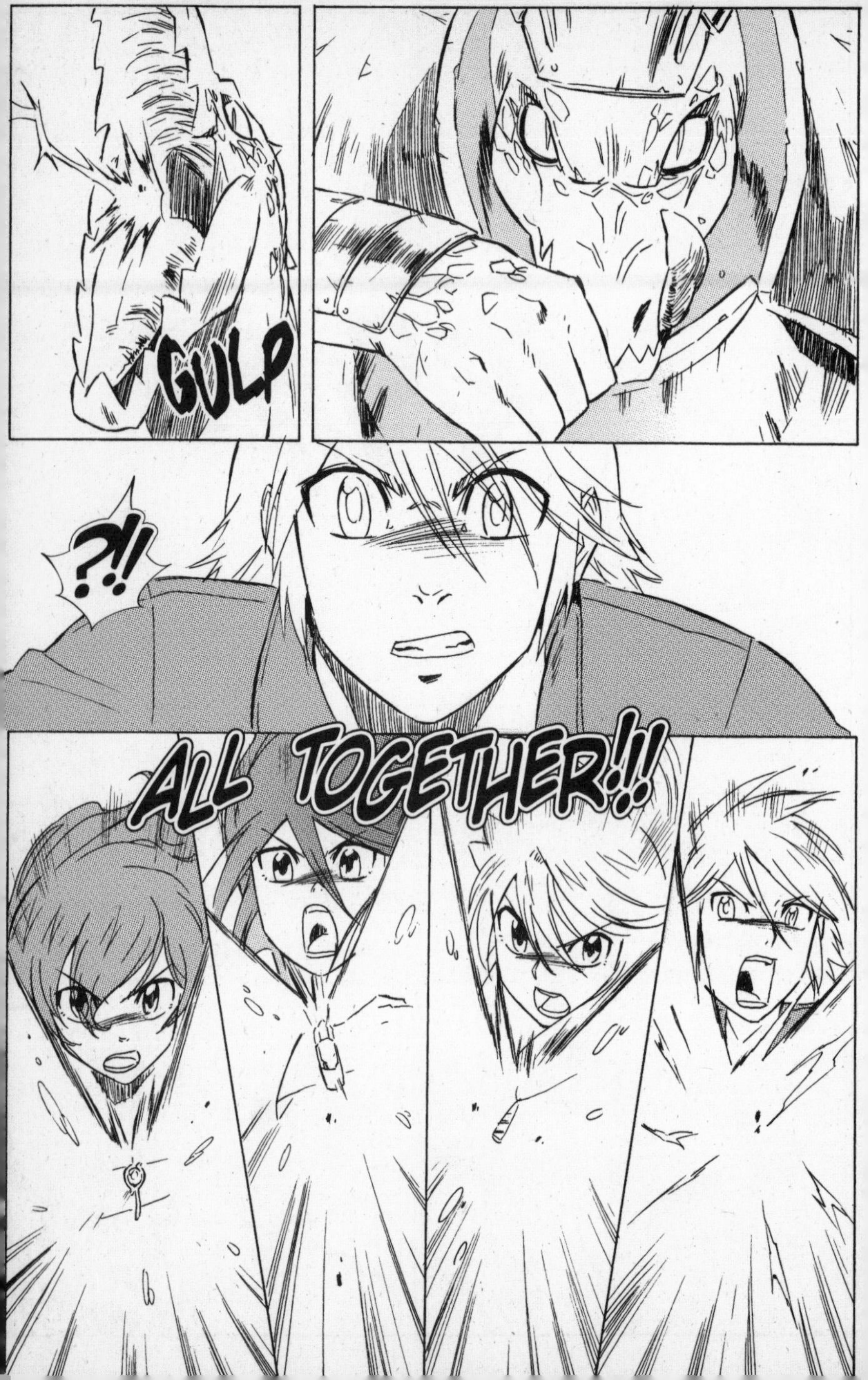
GULP
?!!
ALL TOGETHER!!!

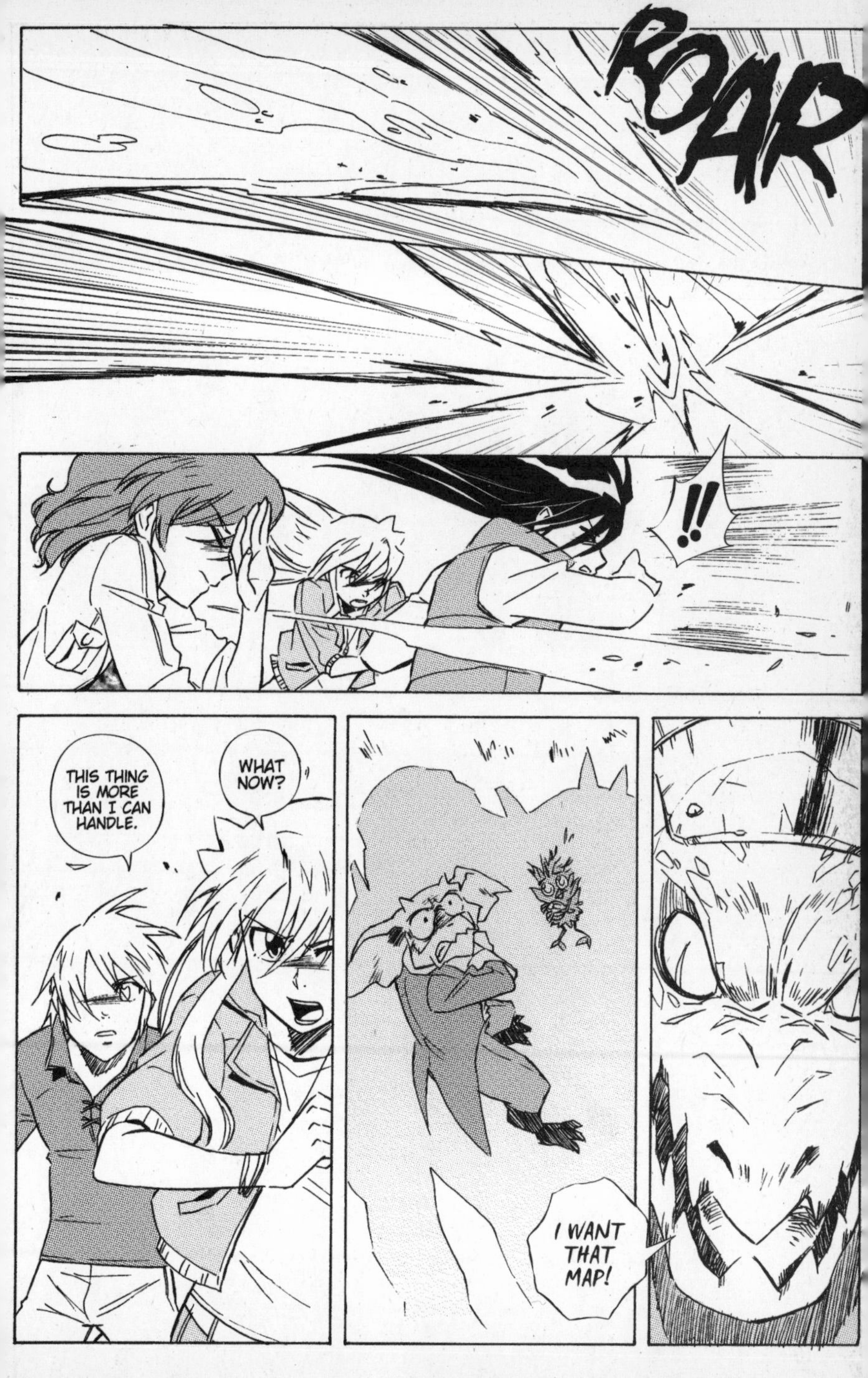
ROAR
!!
THIS THING IS MORE THAN I CAN HANDLE.
WHAT NOW?
I WANT THAT MAP!

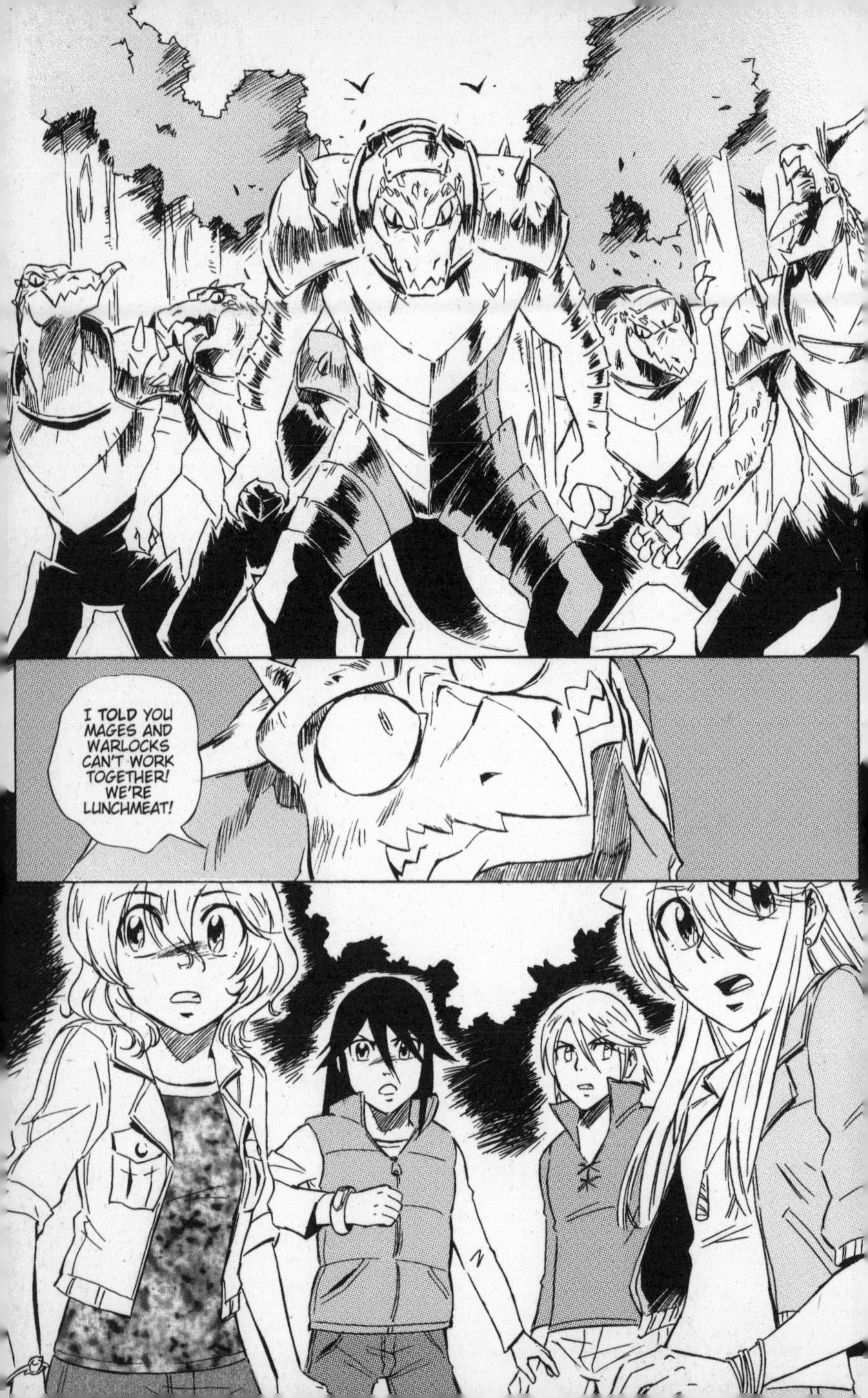
I TOLD YOU MAGES AND WARLOCKS CAN'T WORK TOGETHER! WE'RE LUNCHMEAT!

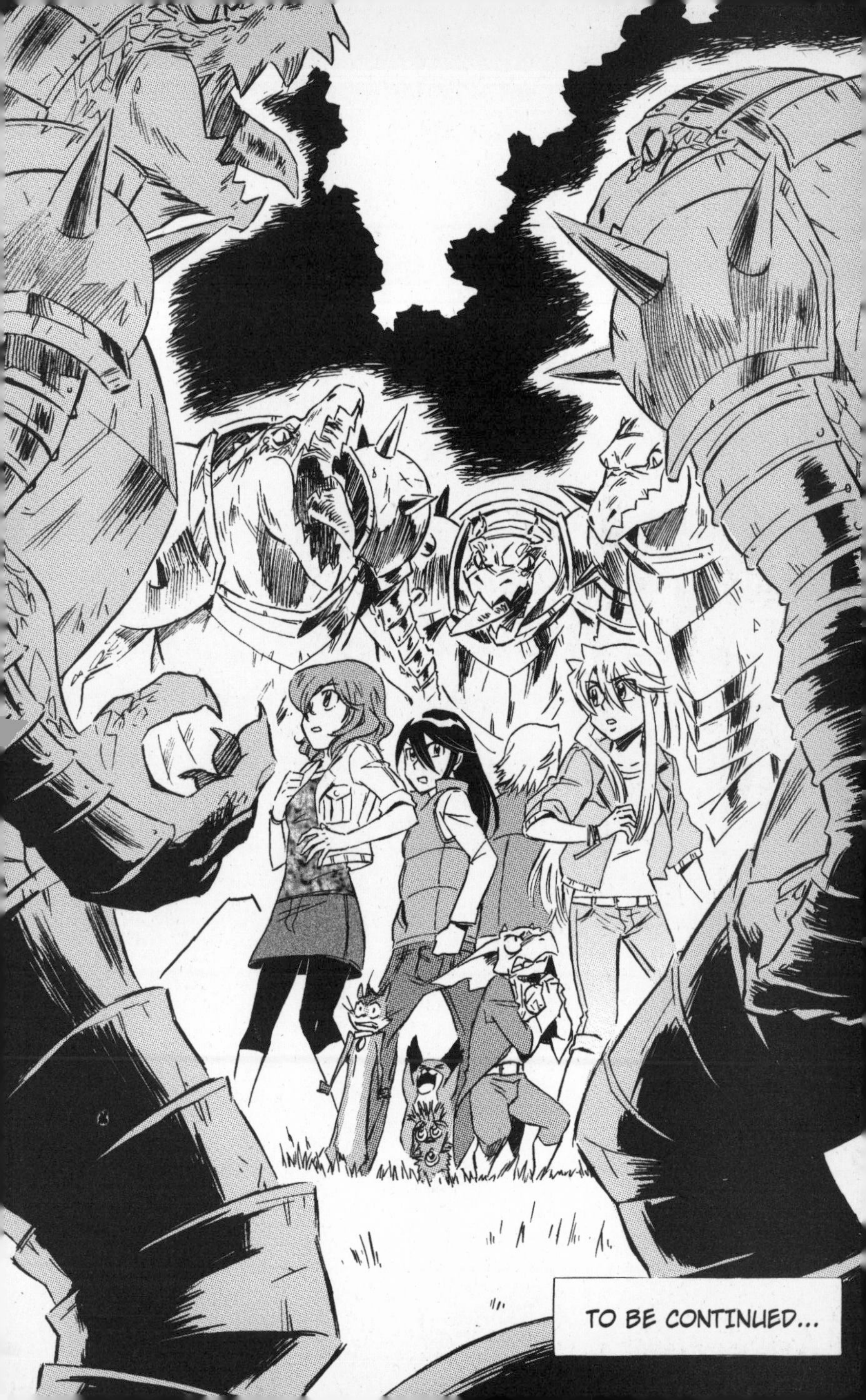
TO BE CONTINUED...

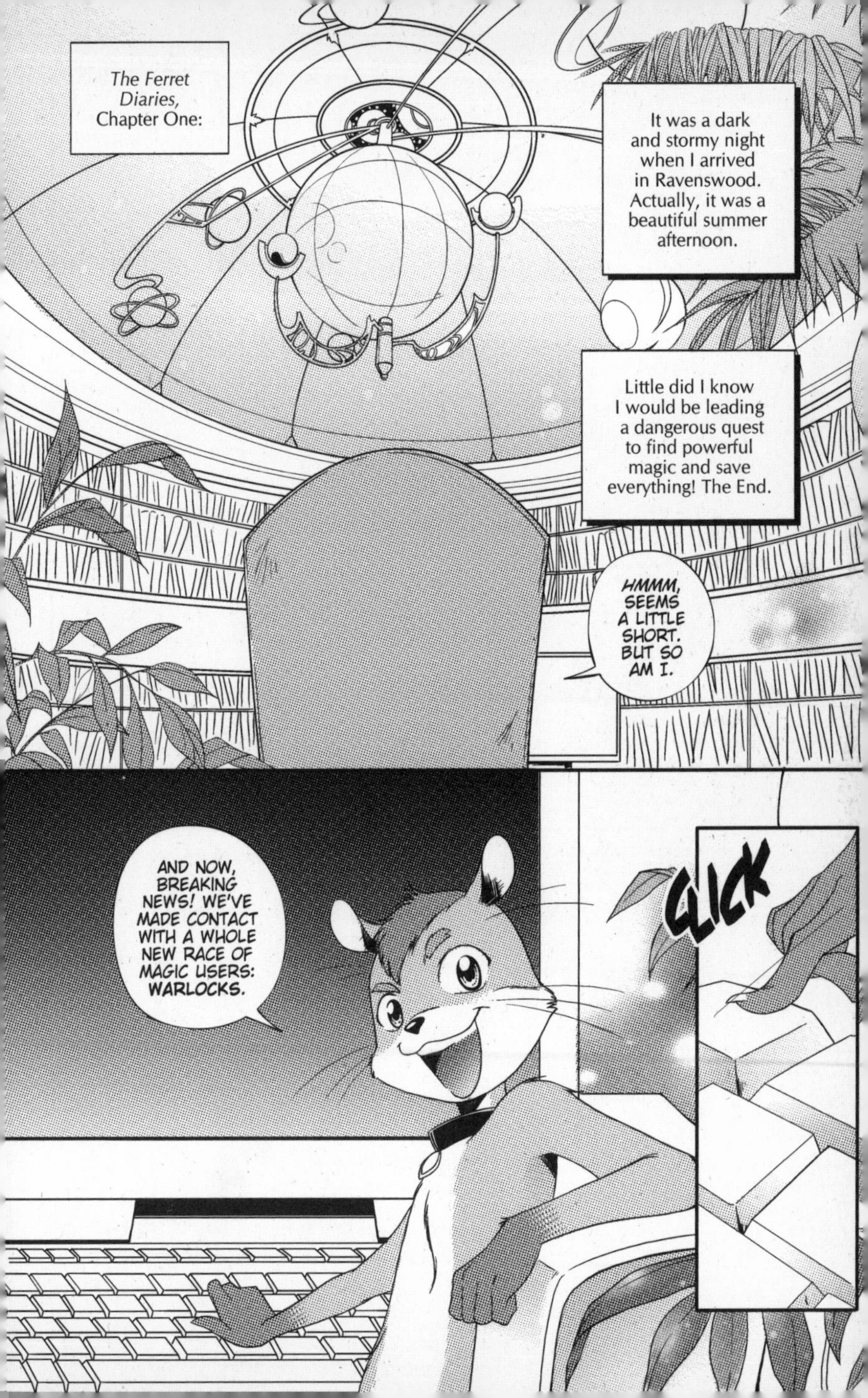
The Ferret Diaries, Chapter One:
It was a dark and stormy night when I arrived in Ravenswood. Actually, it was a beautiful summer afternoon.
Little did I know I would be leading a dangerous quest to find powerful magic and save everything! The End.
HMMM, SEEMS A LITTLE SHORT. BUT SO AM I.
AND NOW, BREAKING NEWS! WE'VE MADE CONTACT WITH A WHOLE NEW RACE OF MAGIC USERS: WARLOCKS.
CLICK

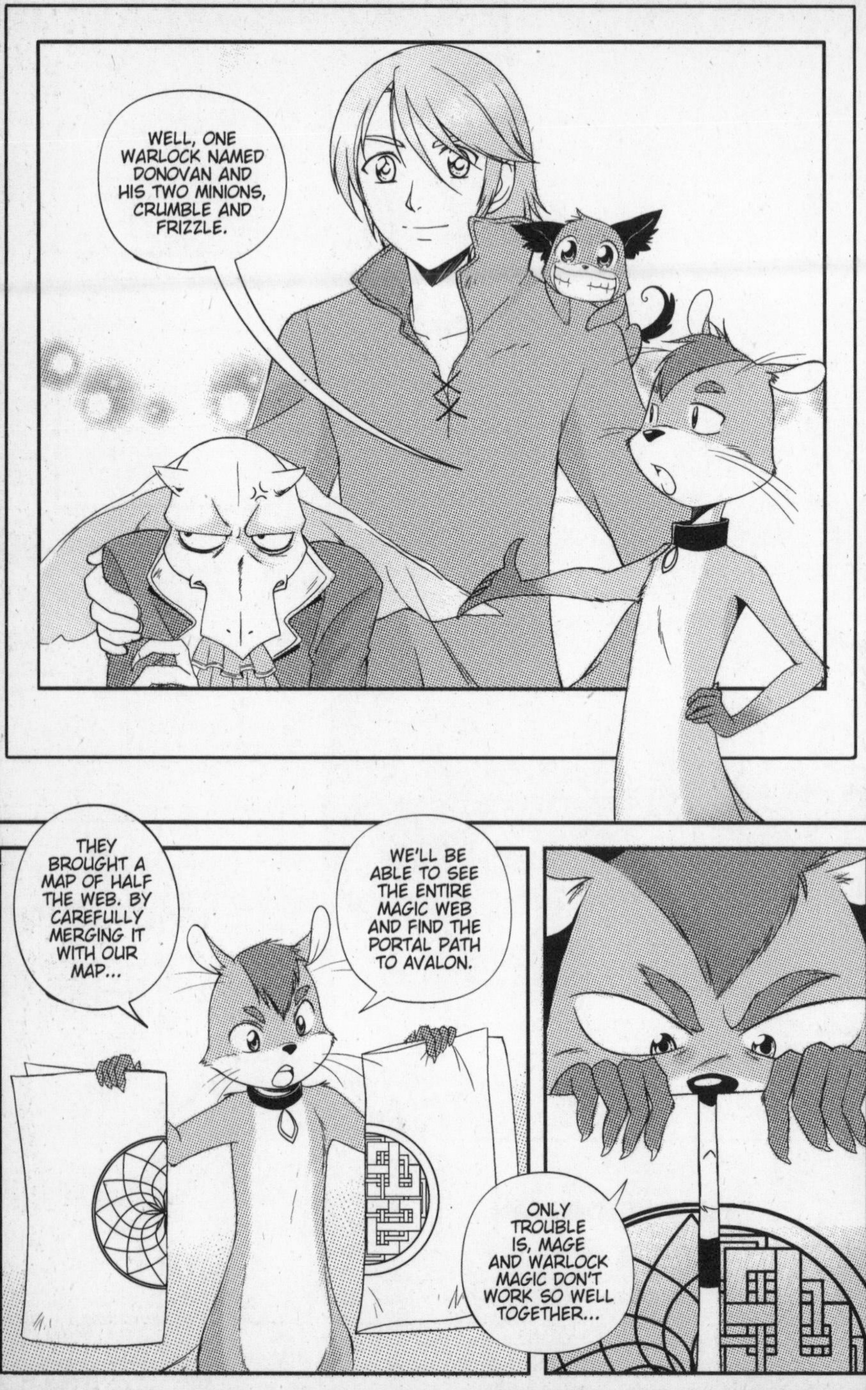
WELL, ONE WARLOCK NAMED DONOVAN AND HIS TWO MINIONS, CRUMBLE AND FRIZZLE.
THEY BROUGHT A MAP OF HALF THE WEB. BY CAREFULLY MERGING IT WITH OUR MAP...
WE'LL BE ABLE TO SEE THE ENTIRE MAGIC WEB AND FIND THE PORTAL PATH TO AVALON.
ONLY TROUBLE IS, MAGE AND WARLOCK MAGIC DON'T WORK SO WELL TOGETHER...

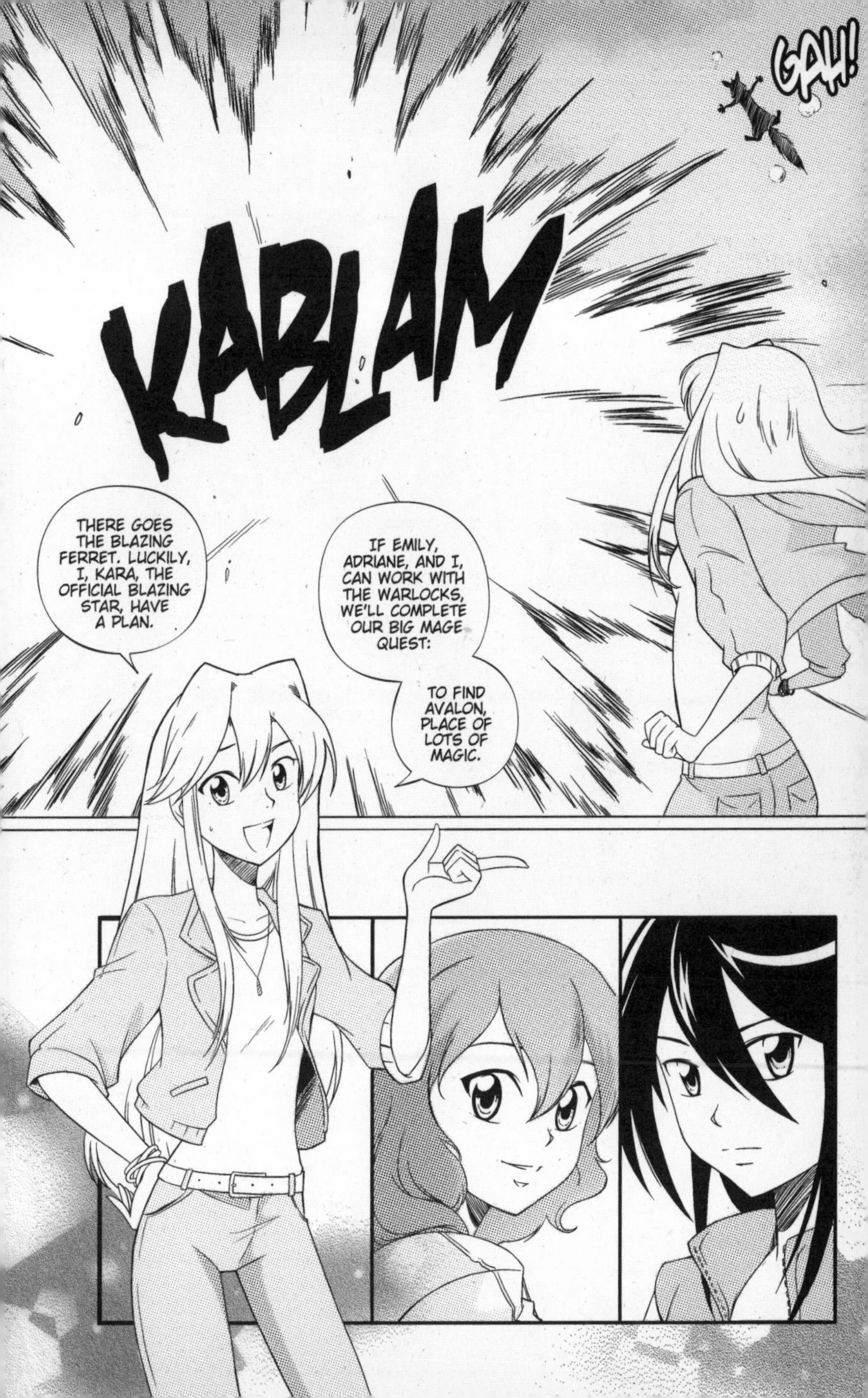
GAH!
KABLAM
THERE GOES THE BLAZING FERRET. LUCKILY, I, KARA, THE OFFICIAL BLAZING STAR, HAVE A PLAN.
IF EMILY, ADRIANE, AND I, CAN WORK WITH THE WARLOCKS, WE'LL COMPLETE OUR BIG MAGE QUEST:
TO FIND AVALON, PLACE OF LOTS OF MAGIC.

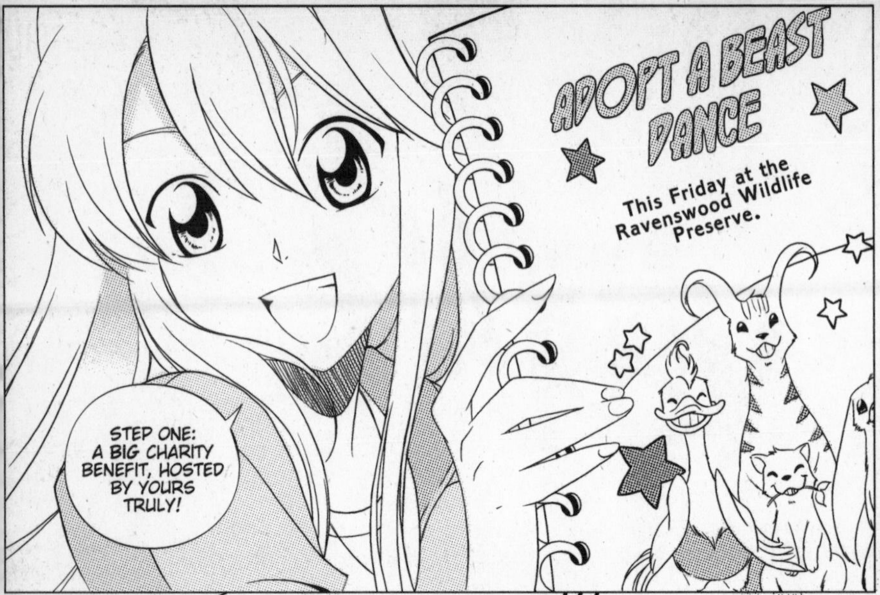
STEP ONE: A BIG CHARITY BENEFIT, HOSTED BY YOURS TRULY!
ADOPT A BEAST DANCE
This Friday at the Ravenswood Wildlife Preserve.

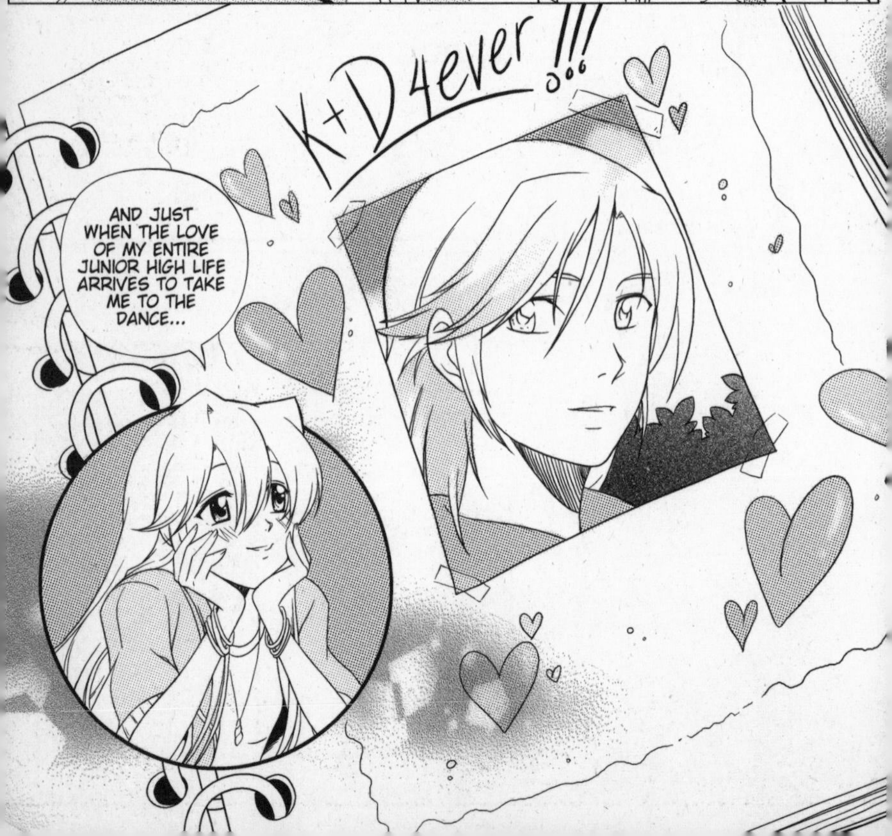
K+D 4ever!!!
AND JUST WHEN THE LOVE OF MY ENTIRE JUNIOR HIGH LIFE ARRIVES TO TAKE ME TO THE DANCE...

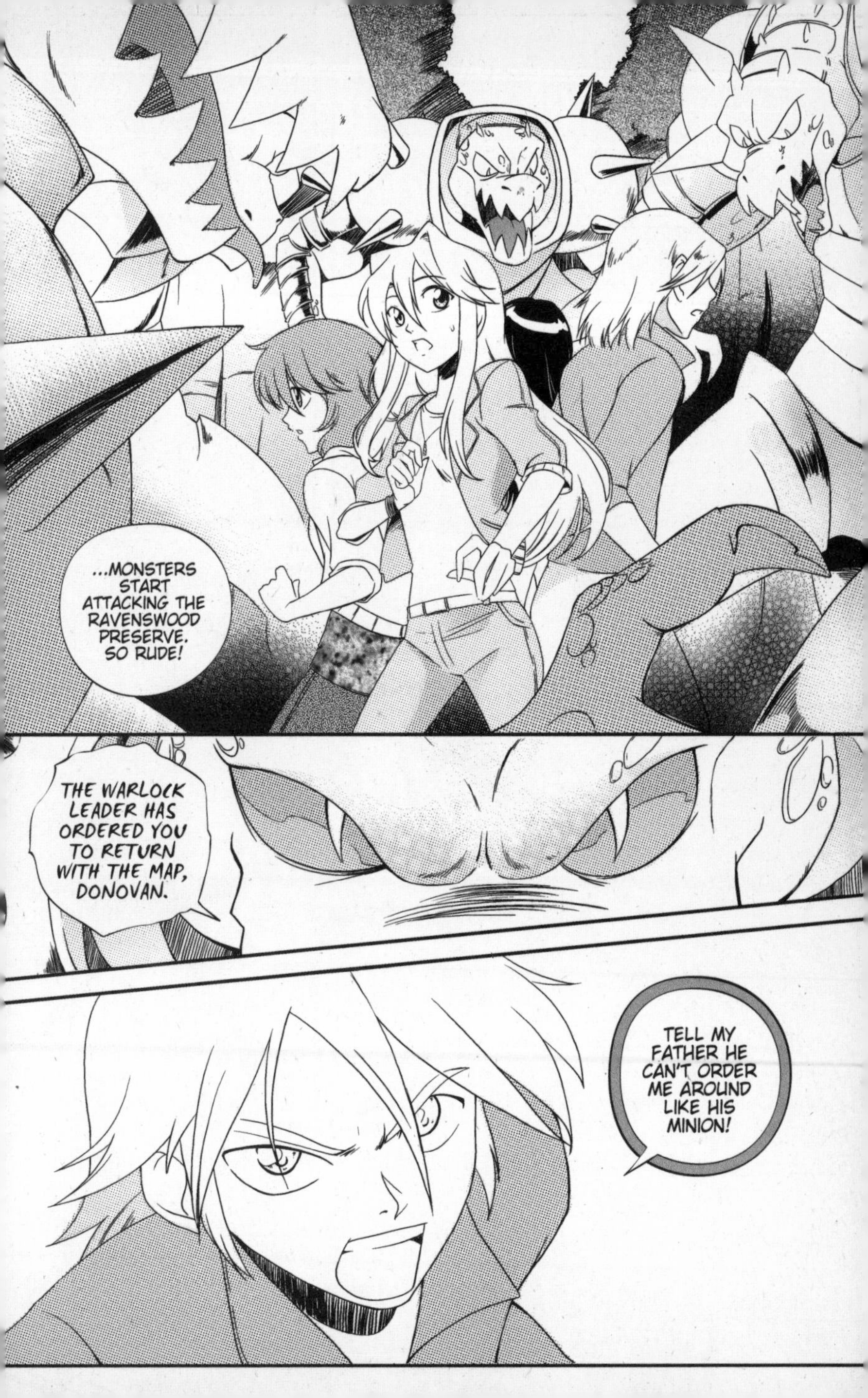
...MONSTERS START ATTACKING THE RAVENSWOOD PRESERVE. SO RUDE!
THE WARLOCK LEADER HAS ORDERED YOU TO RETURN WITH THE MAP, DONOVAN.
TELL MY FATHER HE CAN'T ORDER ME AROUND LIKE HIS MINION!

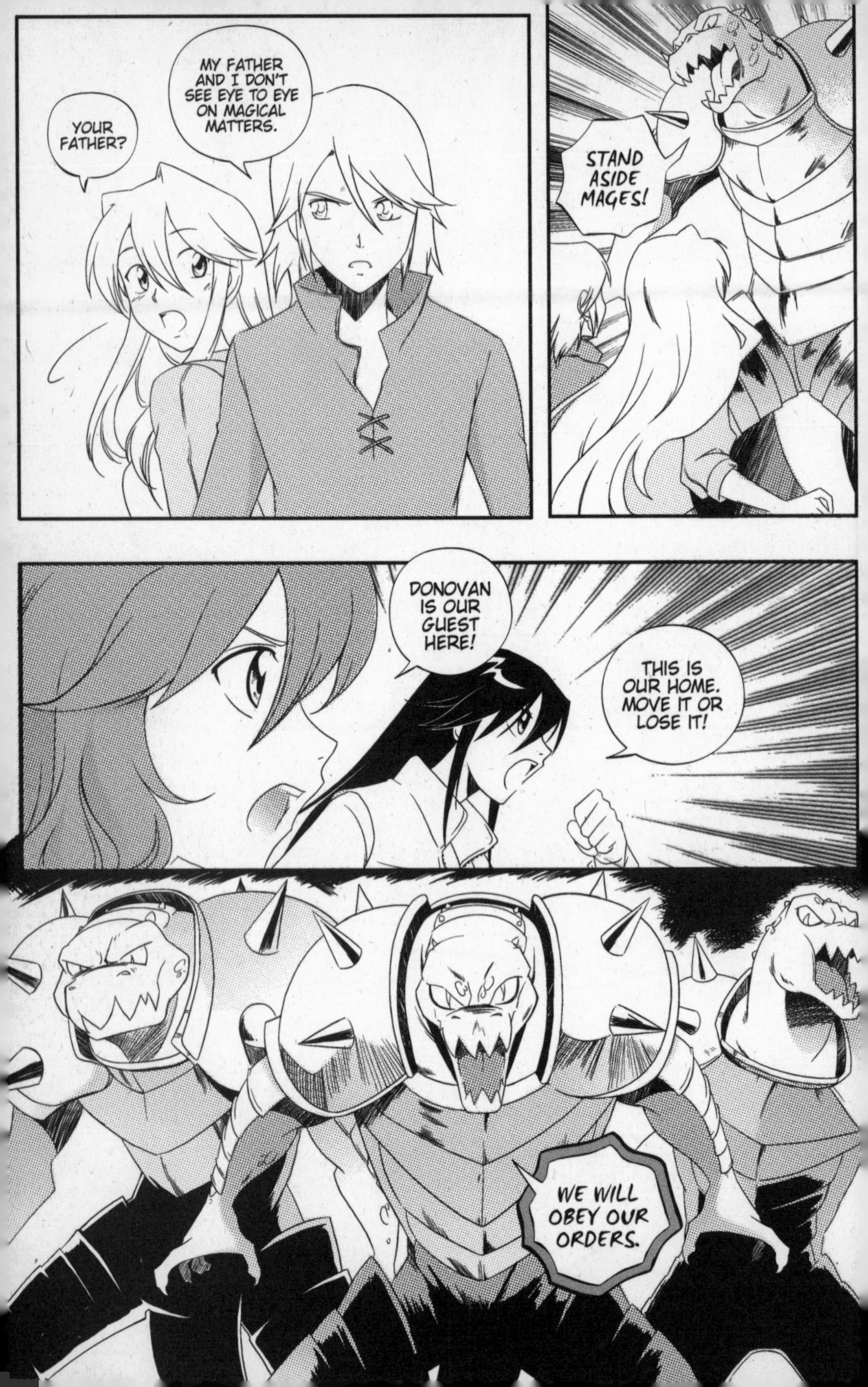
YOUR FATHER?
MY FATHER AND I DON'T SEE EYE TO EYE ON MAGICAL MATTERS.
STAND ASIDE MAGES!
DONOVAN IS OUR GUEST HERE!
THIS IS OUR HOME. MOVE IT OR LOSE IT!
WE WILL OBEY OUR ORDERS.

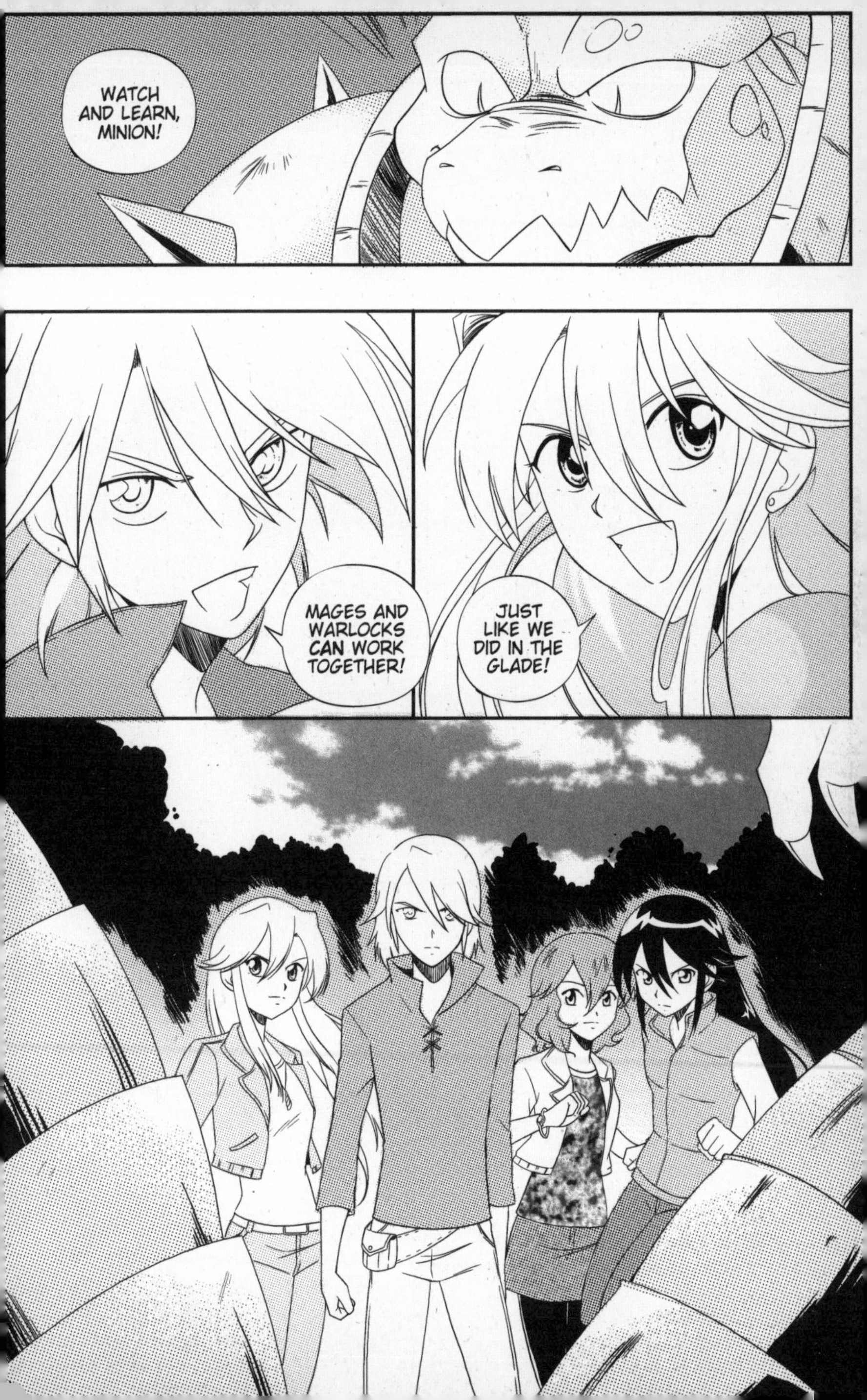
WATCH AND LEARN, MINION!
MAGES AND WARLOCKS CAN WORK TOGETHER!
JUST LIKE WE DID IN THE GLADE!

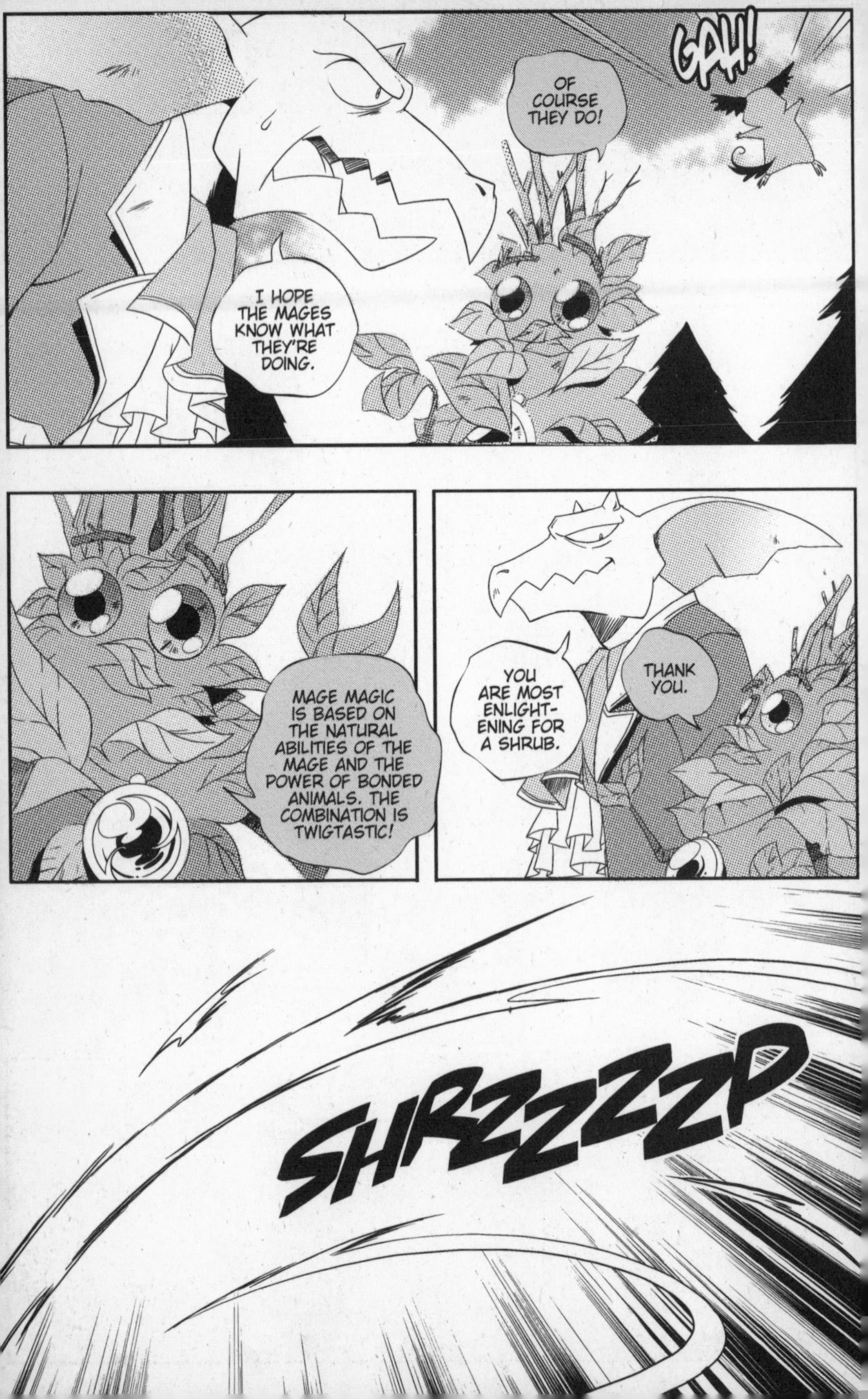
GAH!
OF COURSE THEY DO!
I HOPE THE MAGES KNOW WHAT THEY'RE DOING.
MAGE MAGIC IS BASED ON THE NATURAL ABILITIES OF THE MAGE AND THE POWER OF BONDED ANIMALS. THE COMBINATION IS TWIGTASTIC!
YOU ARE MOST ENLIGHT-ENING FOR A SHRUB.
THANK YOU.
SHRZZZZP

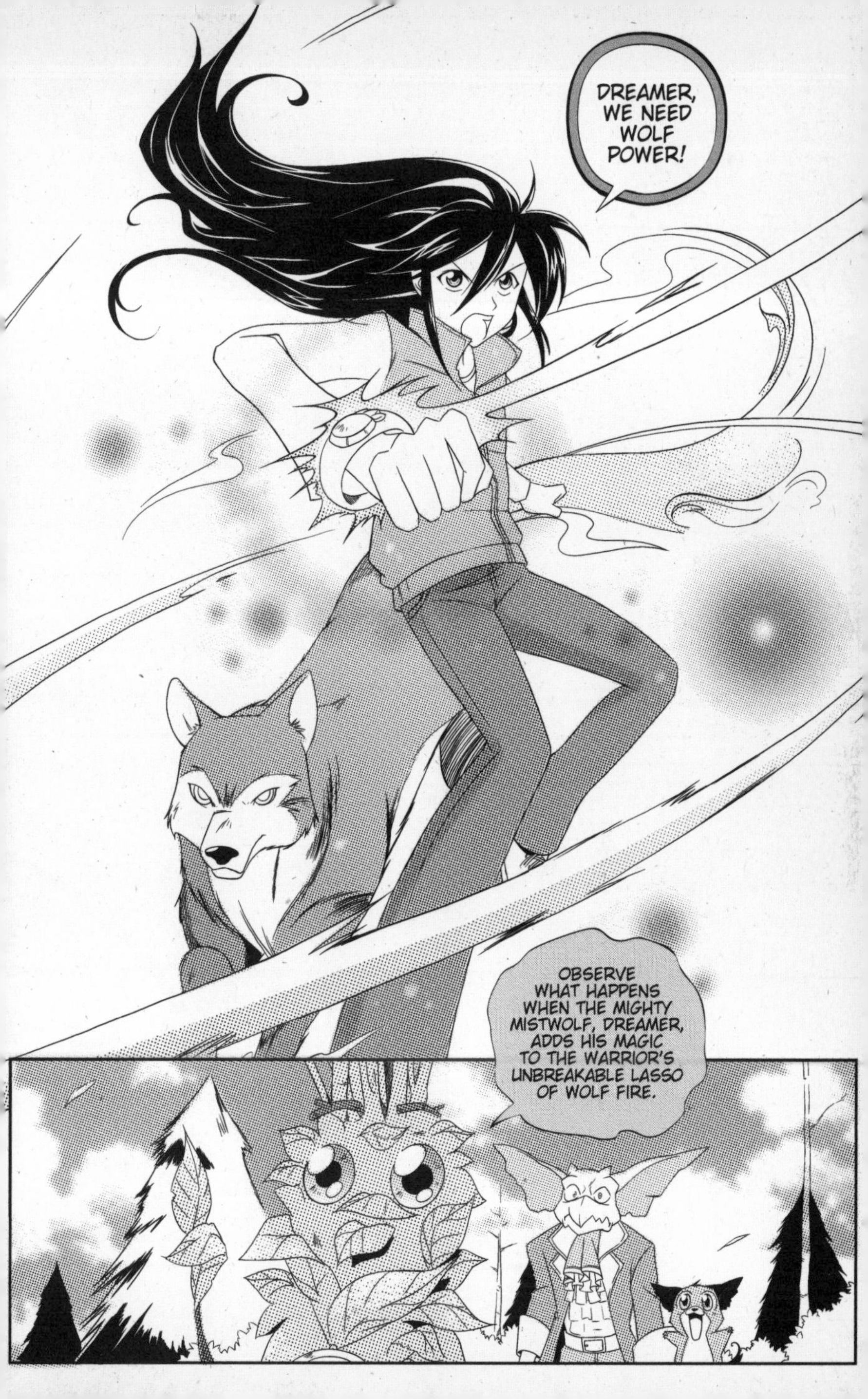
DREAMER, WE NEED WOLF POWER!
OBSERVE WHAT HAPPENS WHEN THE MIGHTY MISTWOLF, DREAMER, ADDS HIS MAGIC TO THE WARRIOR'S UNBREAKABLE LASSO OF WOLF FIRE.

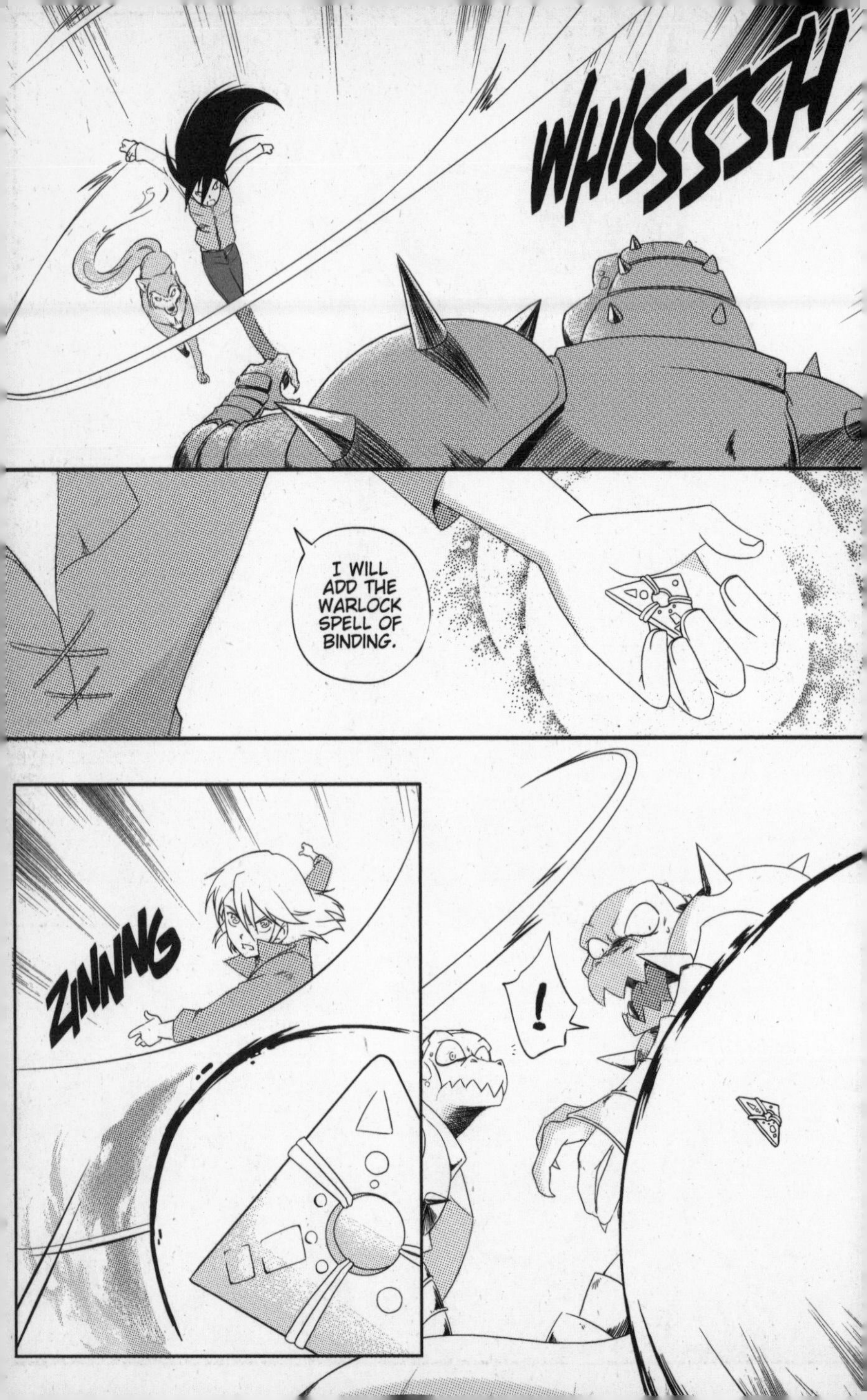
WHISSSSH
I WILL ADD THE WARLOCK SPELL OF BINDING.
ZINNNG
!

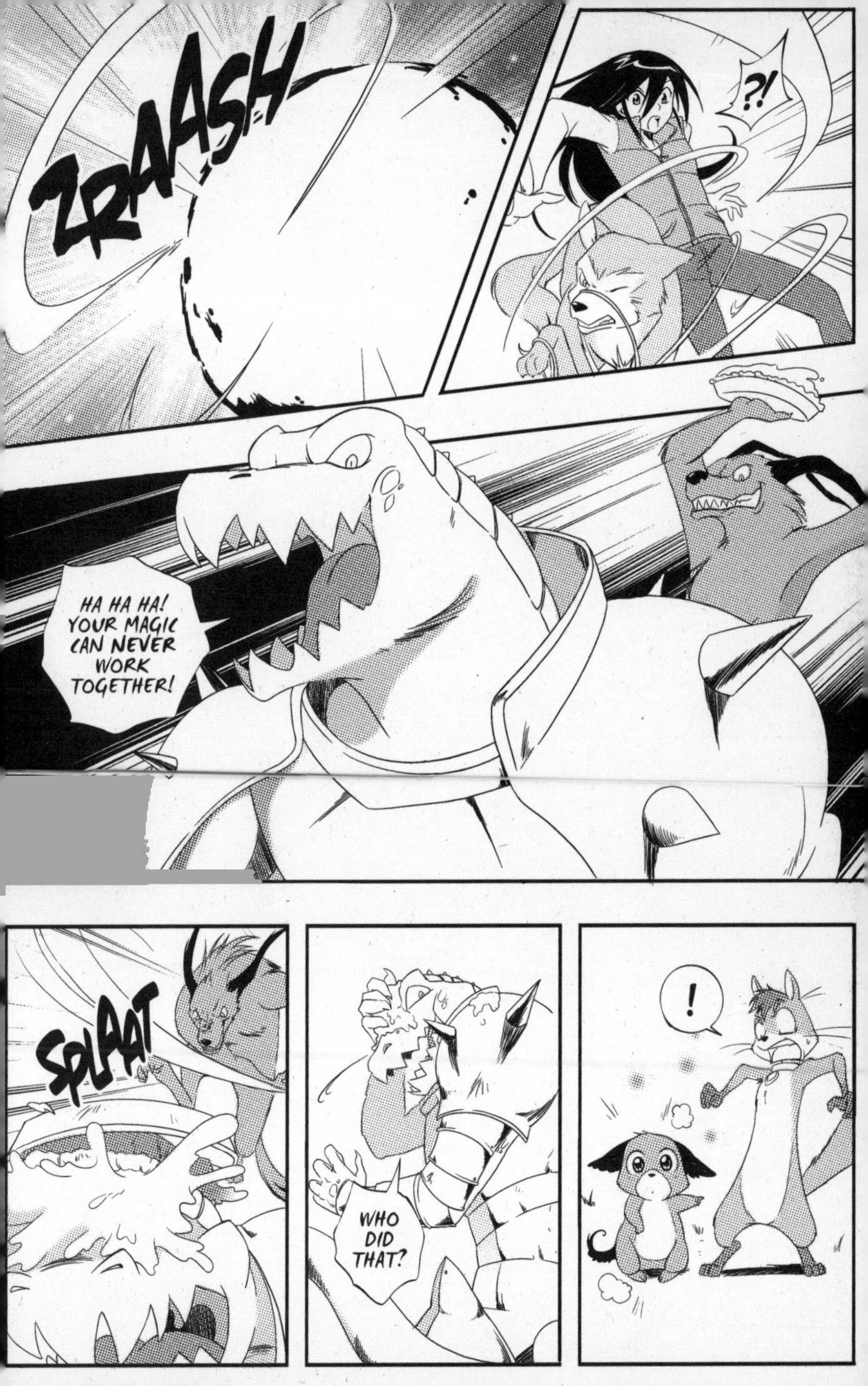
ZRAASH
?!
HA HA HA! YOUR MAGIC CAN NEVER WORK TOGETHER!
SPLAAT
WHO DID THAT?
!

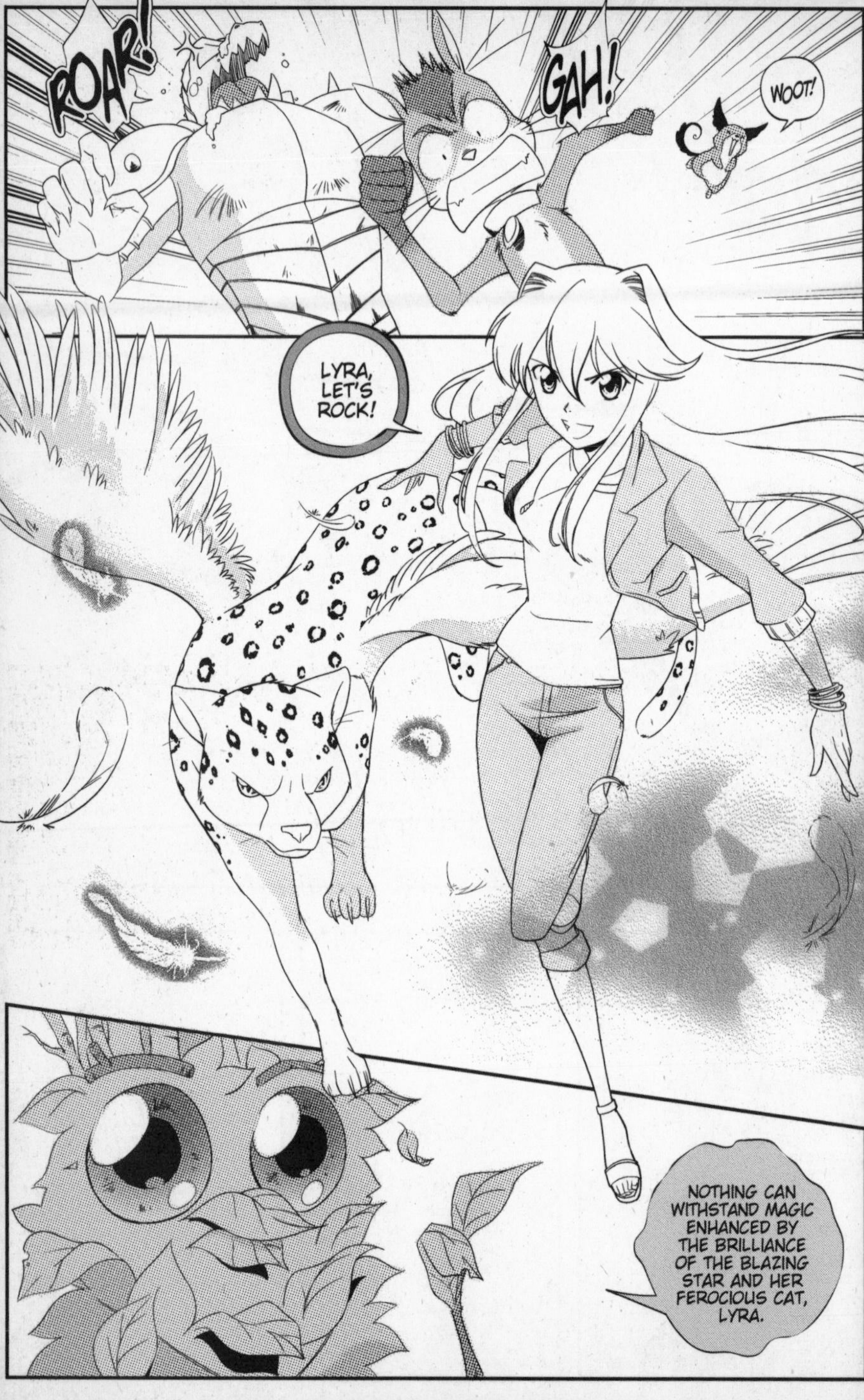
ROAR!
GAH!
WOOT!
LYRA, LET'S ROCK!
NOTHING CAN WITHSTAND MAGIC ENHANCED BY THE BRILLIANCE OF THE BLAZING STAR AND HER FEROCIOUS CAT, LYRA.

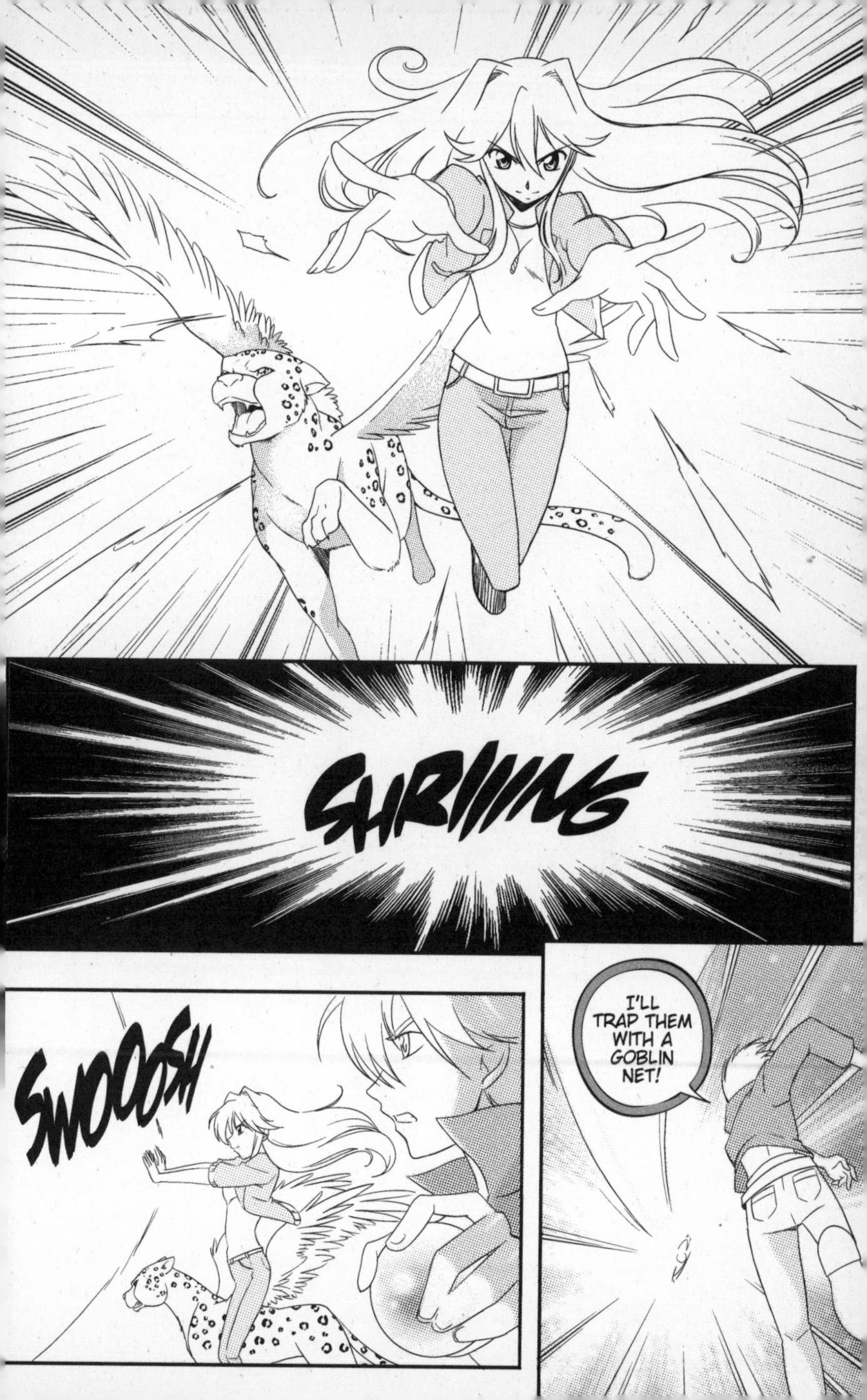
SHRIIING
SWOOOSH
I'LL TRAP THEM WITH A GOBLIN NET!

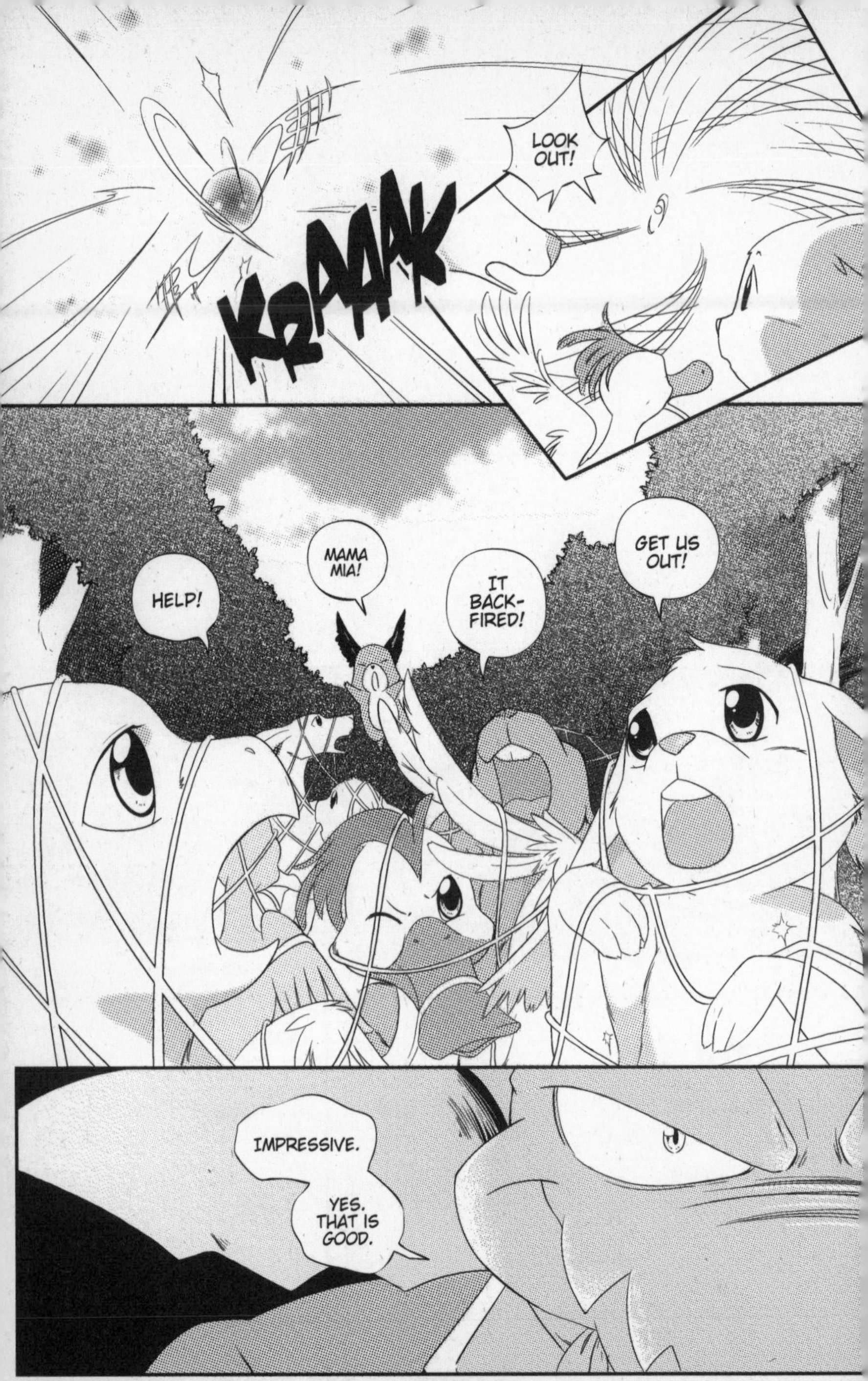
KRAAAK
LOOK OUT!
HELP!
MAMA MIA!
IT BACK-FIRED!
GET US OUT!
IMPRESSIVE.
YES. THAT IS GOOD.

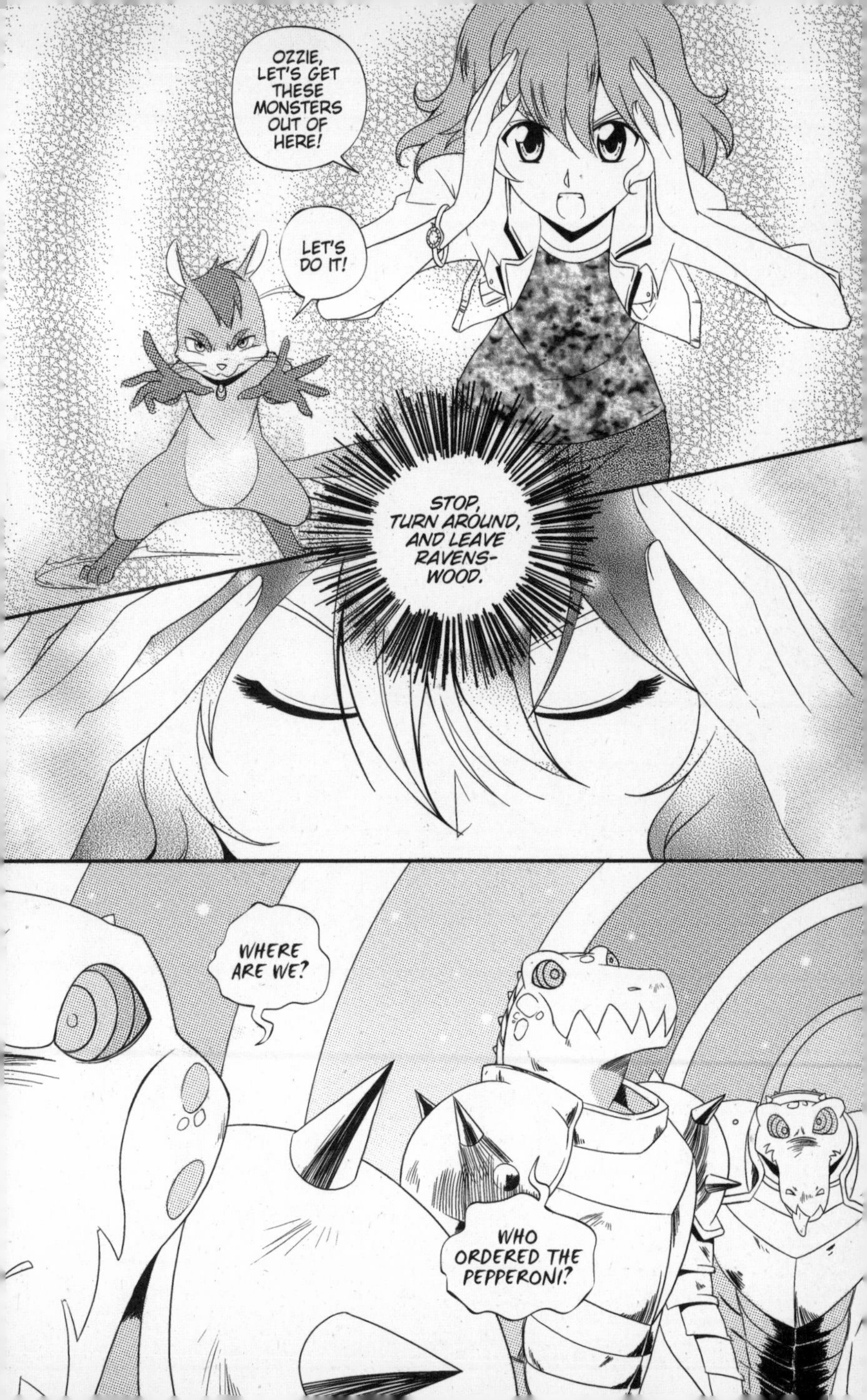
OZZIE, LET'S GET THESE MONSTERS OUT OF HERE!
LET'S DO IT!
STOP, TURN AROUND, AND LEAVE RAVENS-WOOD.
WHERE ARE WE?
WHO ORDERED THE PEPPERONI?

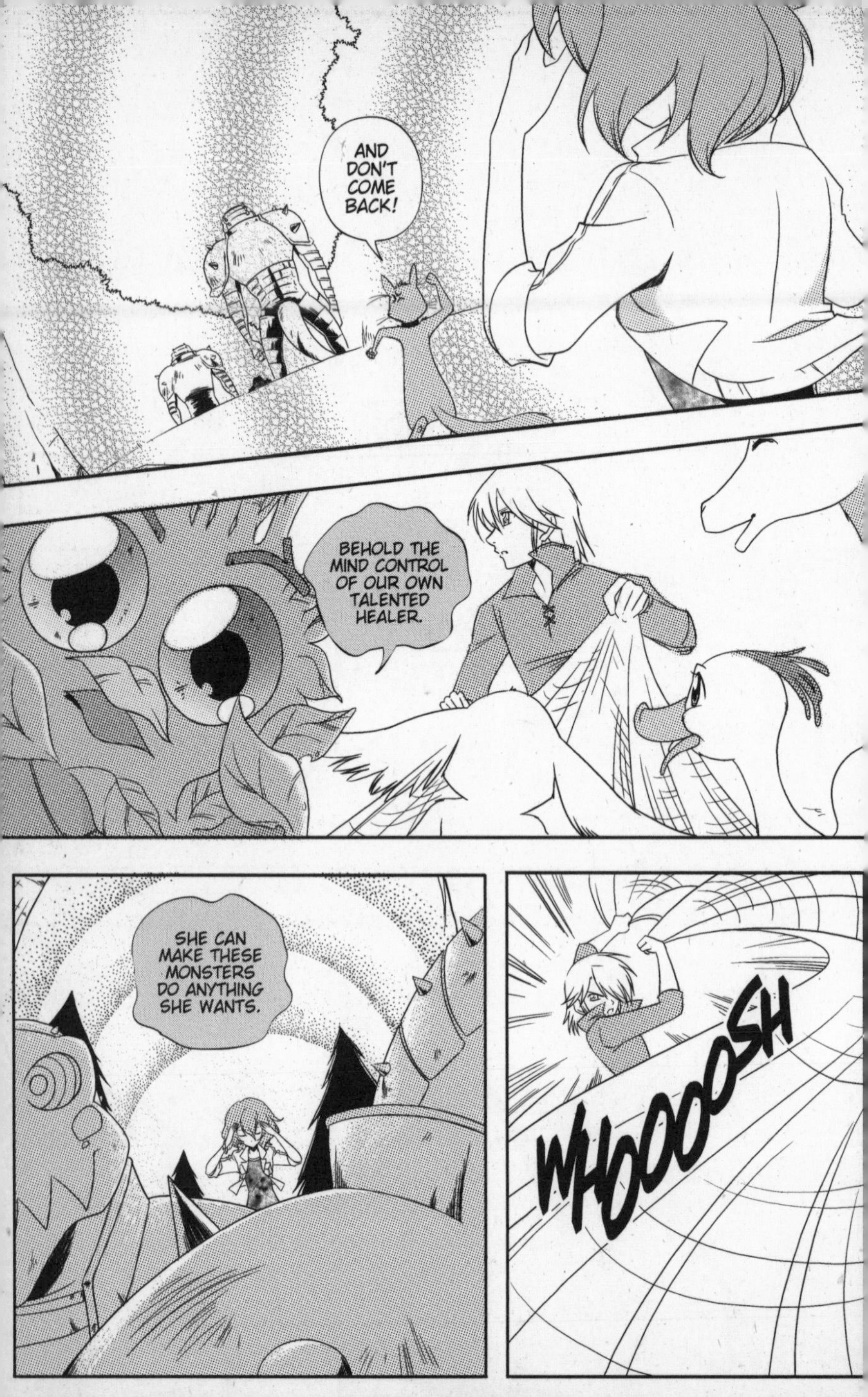
AND DON'T COME BACK!
BEHOLD THE MIND CONTROL OF OUR OWN TALENTED HEALER.
SHE CAN MAKE THESE MONSTERS DO ANYTHING SHE WANTS.
WHOOOOSH

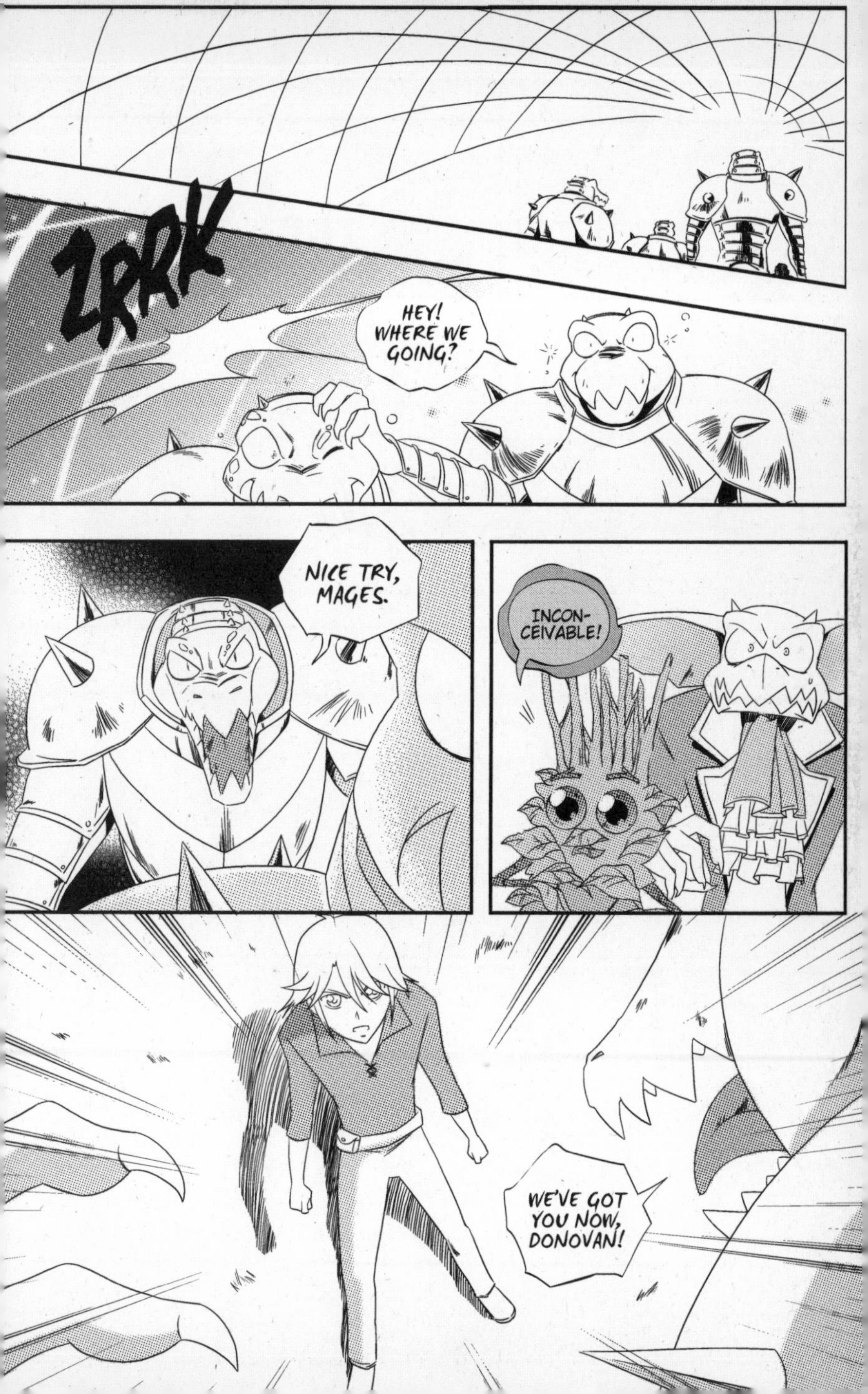
ZRRK
HEY! WHERE WE GOING?
NICE TRY, MAGES.
INCON-CEIVABLE!
WE'VE GOT YOU NOW, DONOVAN!

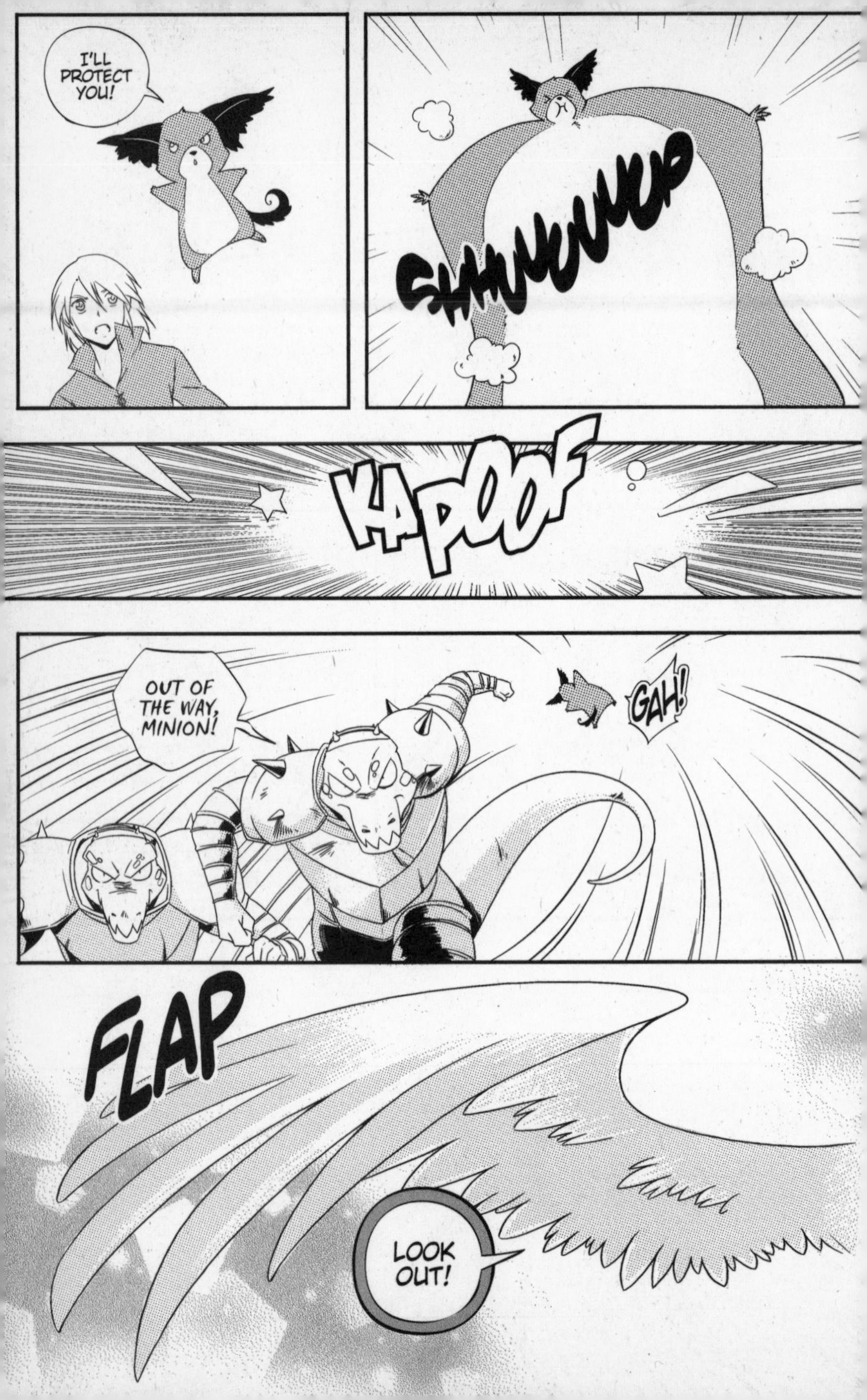
I'LL PROTECT YOU!
SHWUUUUP
KAPOOF
OUT OF THE WAY, MINION!
GAH!
FLAP
LOOK OUT!

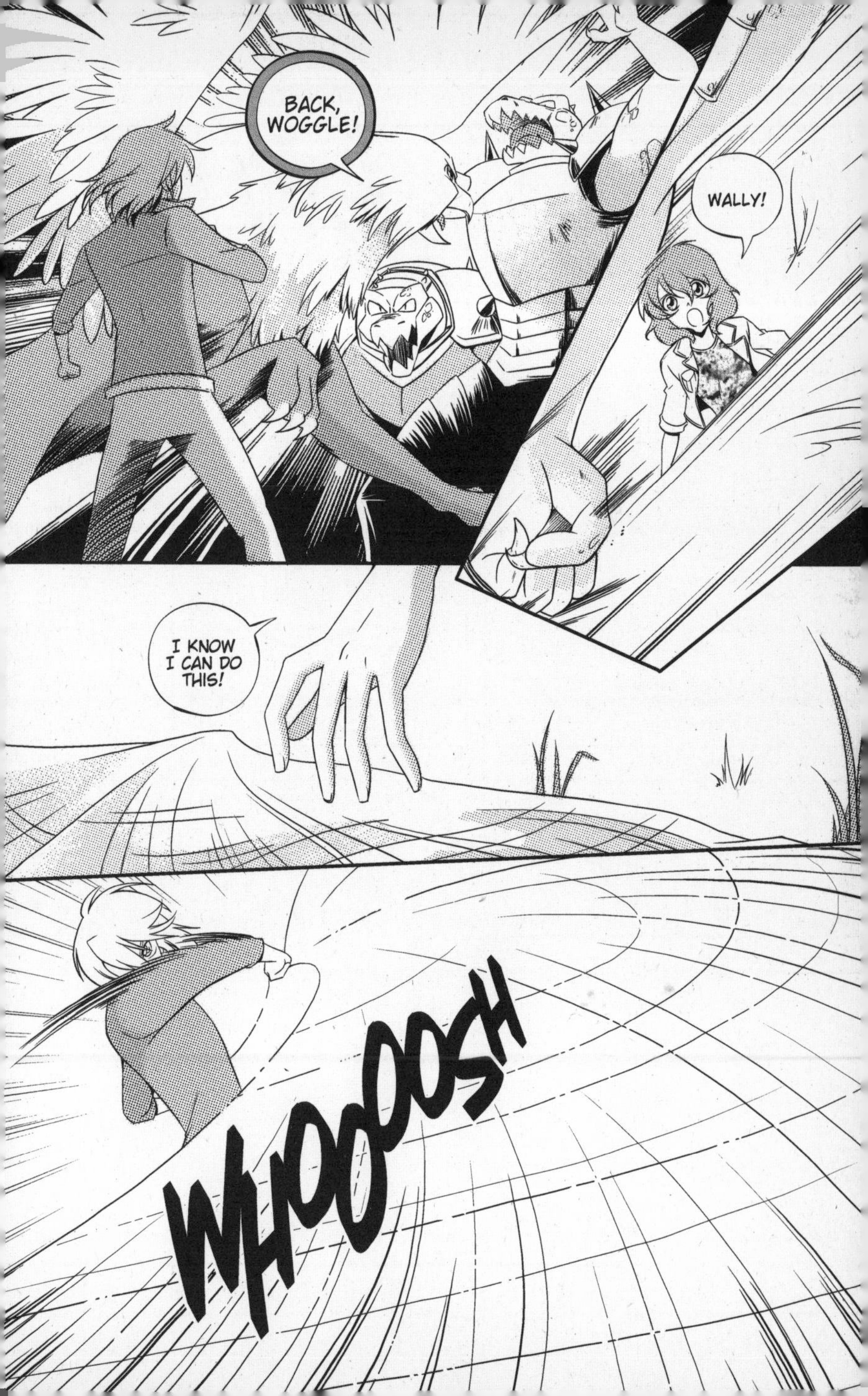
BACK, WOGGLE!
WALLY!
I KNOW I CAN DO THIS!
WHOOOOSH

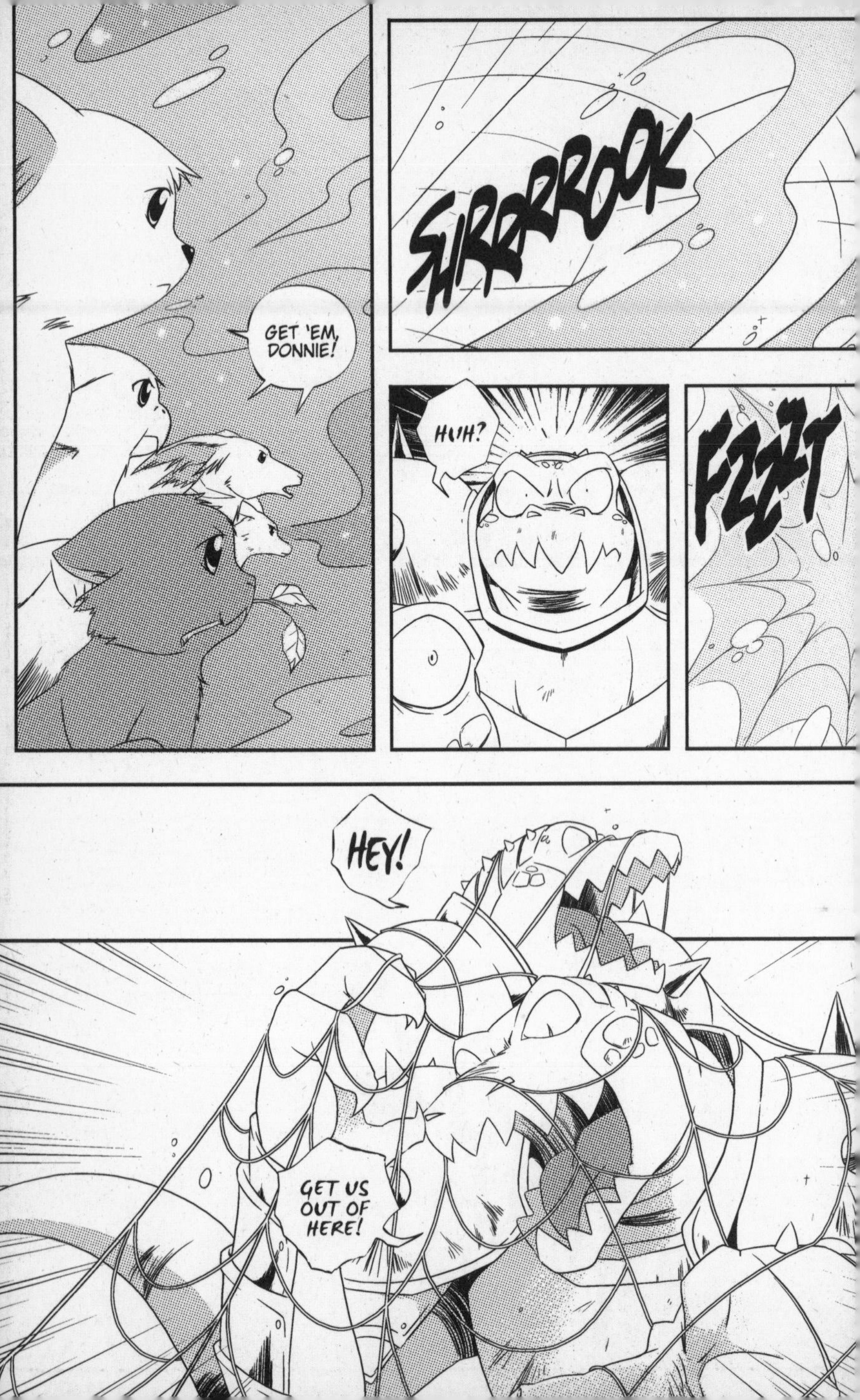
GET 'EM, DONNIE!
SHRRRROOK
HUH?
FZZZT
HEY!
GET US OUT OF HERE!

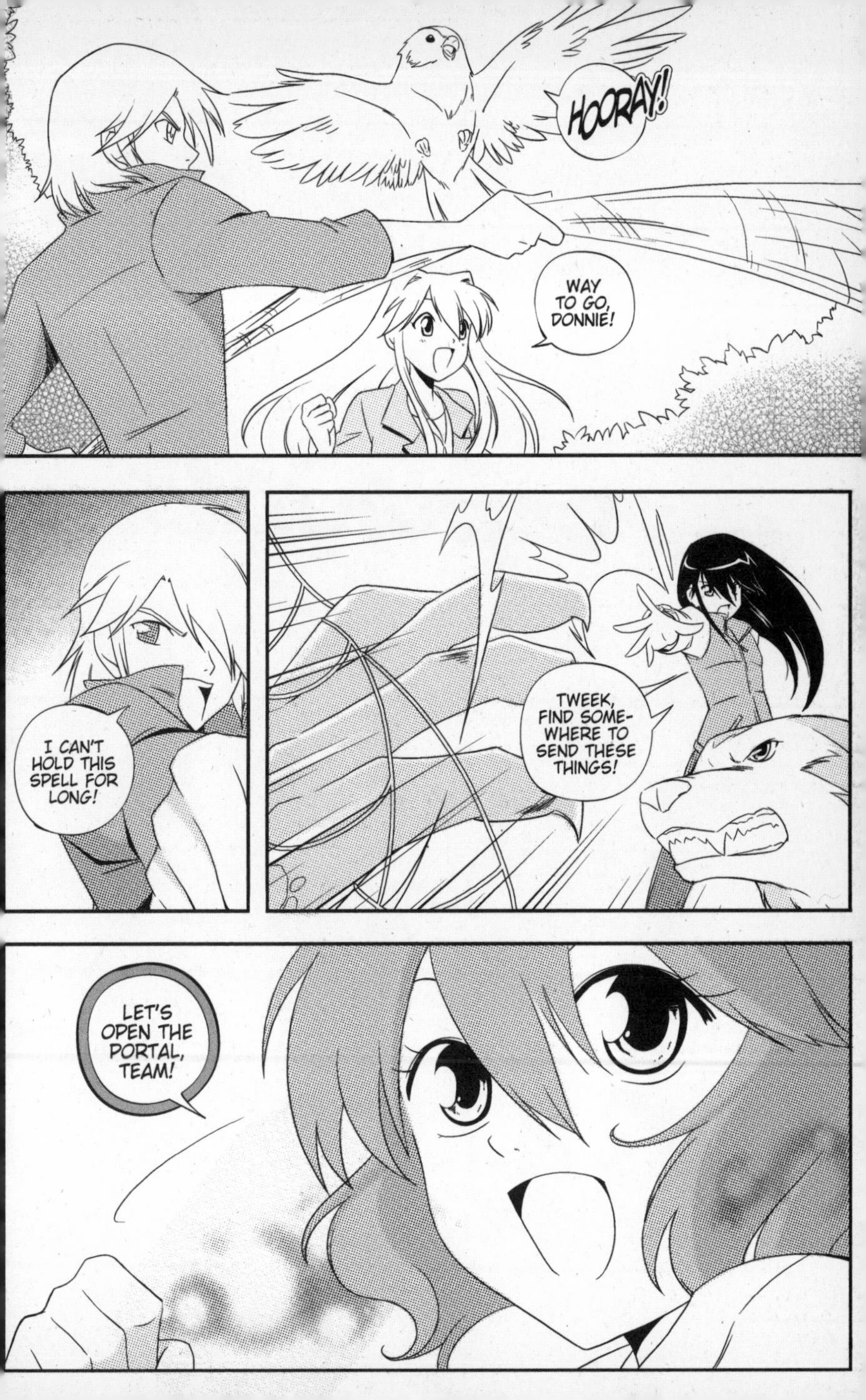
HOORAY!
WAY TO GO, DONNIE!
I CAN'T HOLD THIS SPELL FOR LONG!
TWEEK, FIND SOME-WHERE TO SEND THESE THINGS!
LET'S OPEN THE PORTAL, TEAM!

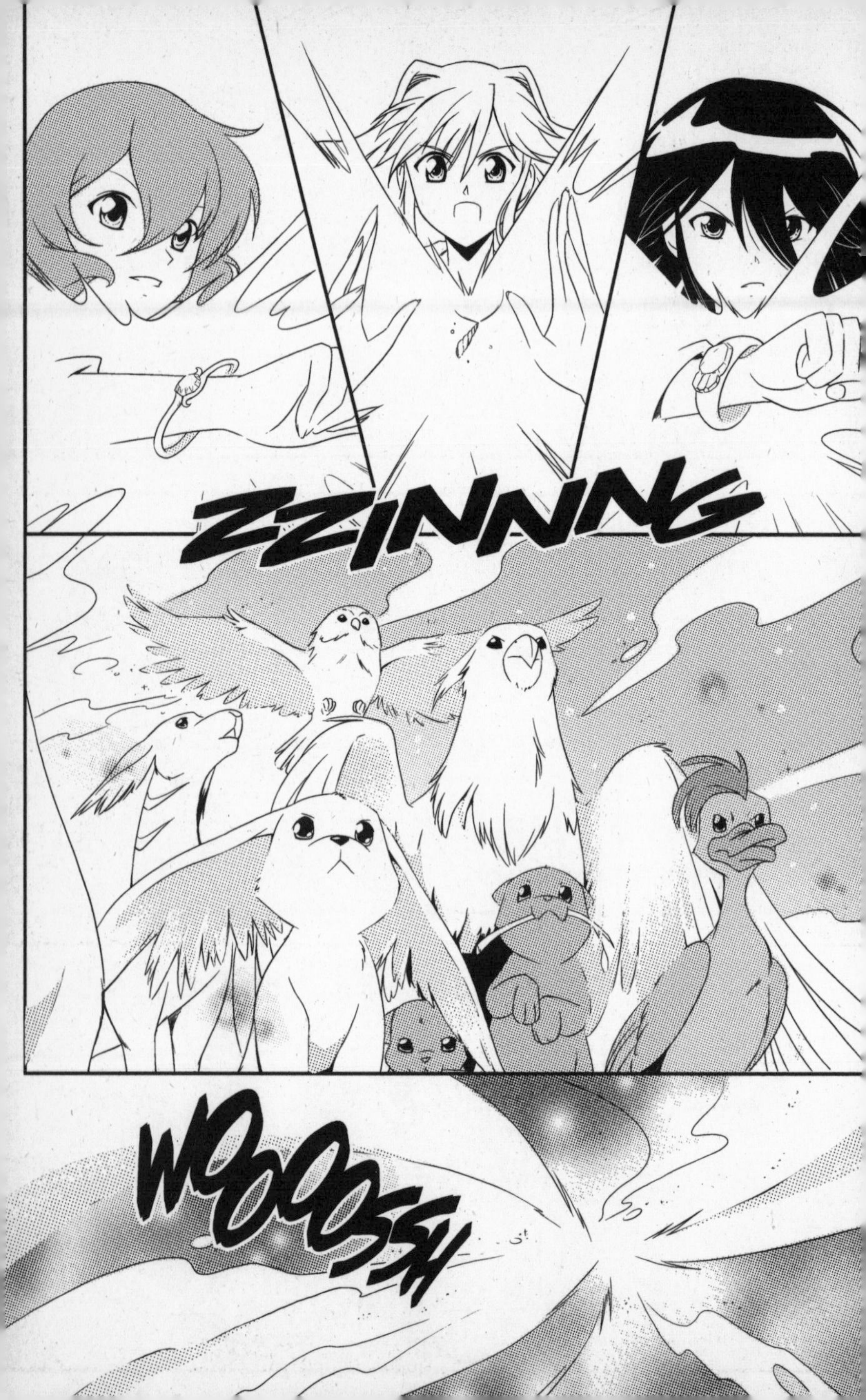
ZZINNNG
WOOOOSH

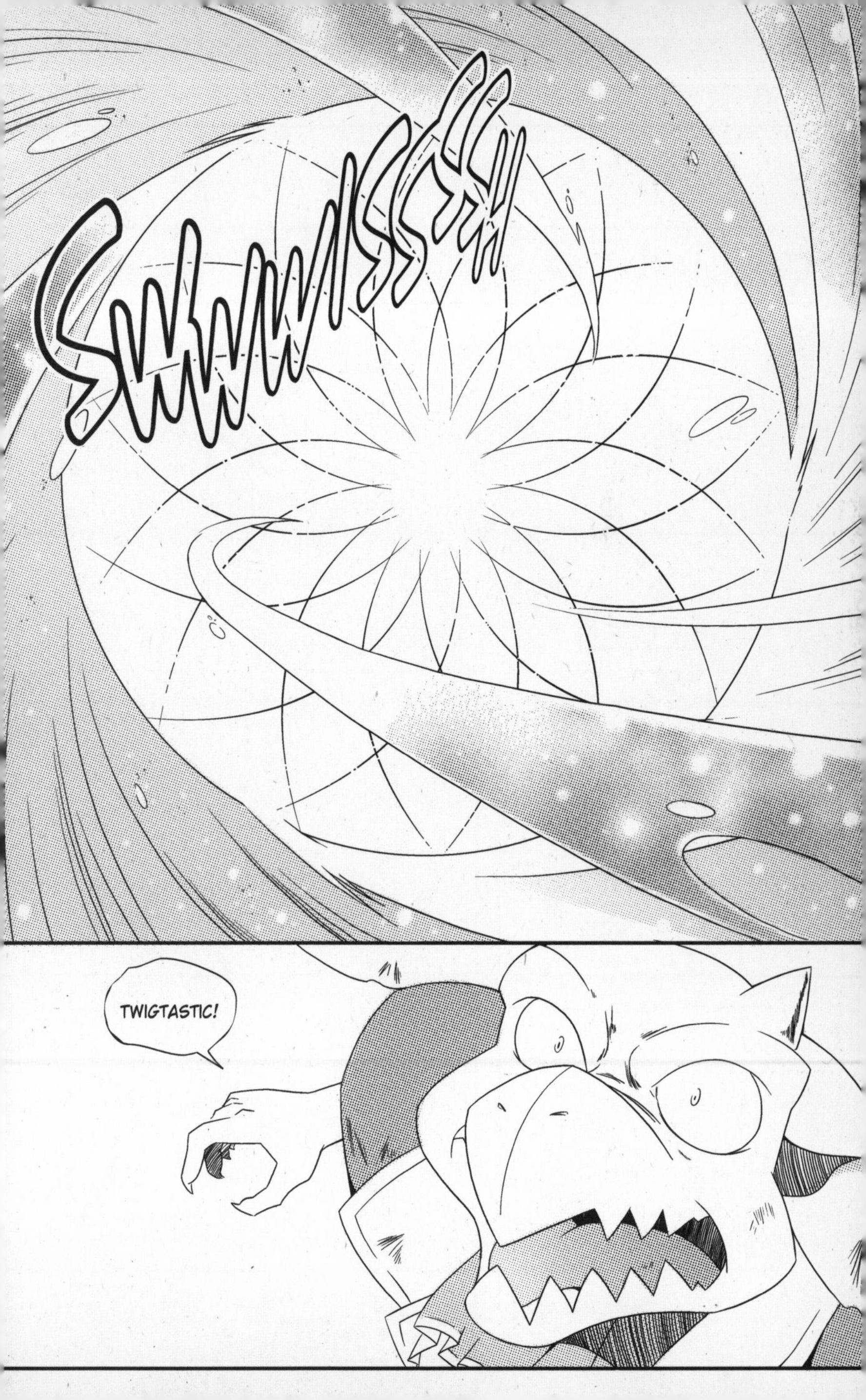
TWIGTASTIC!

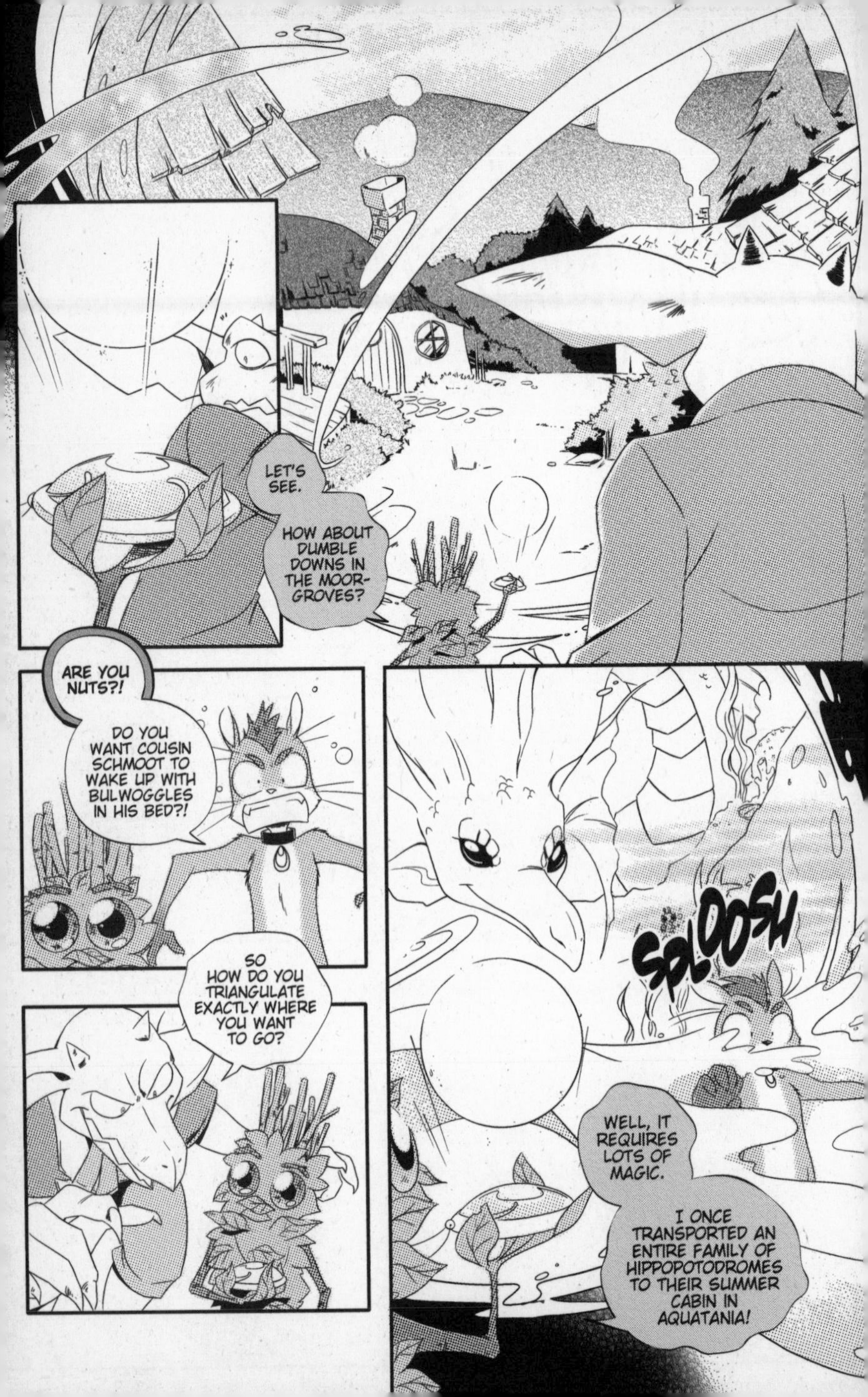
LET'S SEE.
HOW ABOUT DUMBLE DOWNS IN THE MOOR-GROVES?
ARE YOU NUTS?!
DO YOU WANT COUSIN SCHMOOT TO WAKE UP WITH BULWOGGLES IN HIS BED?!
SPLOOSH
SO HOW DO YOU TRIANGULATE EXACTLY WHERE YOU WANT TO GO?
WELL, IT REQUIRES LOTS OF MAGIC.
I ONCE TRANSPORTED AN ENTIRE FAMILY OF HIPPOPOTODROMES TO THEIR SUMMER CABIN IN AQUATANIA!

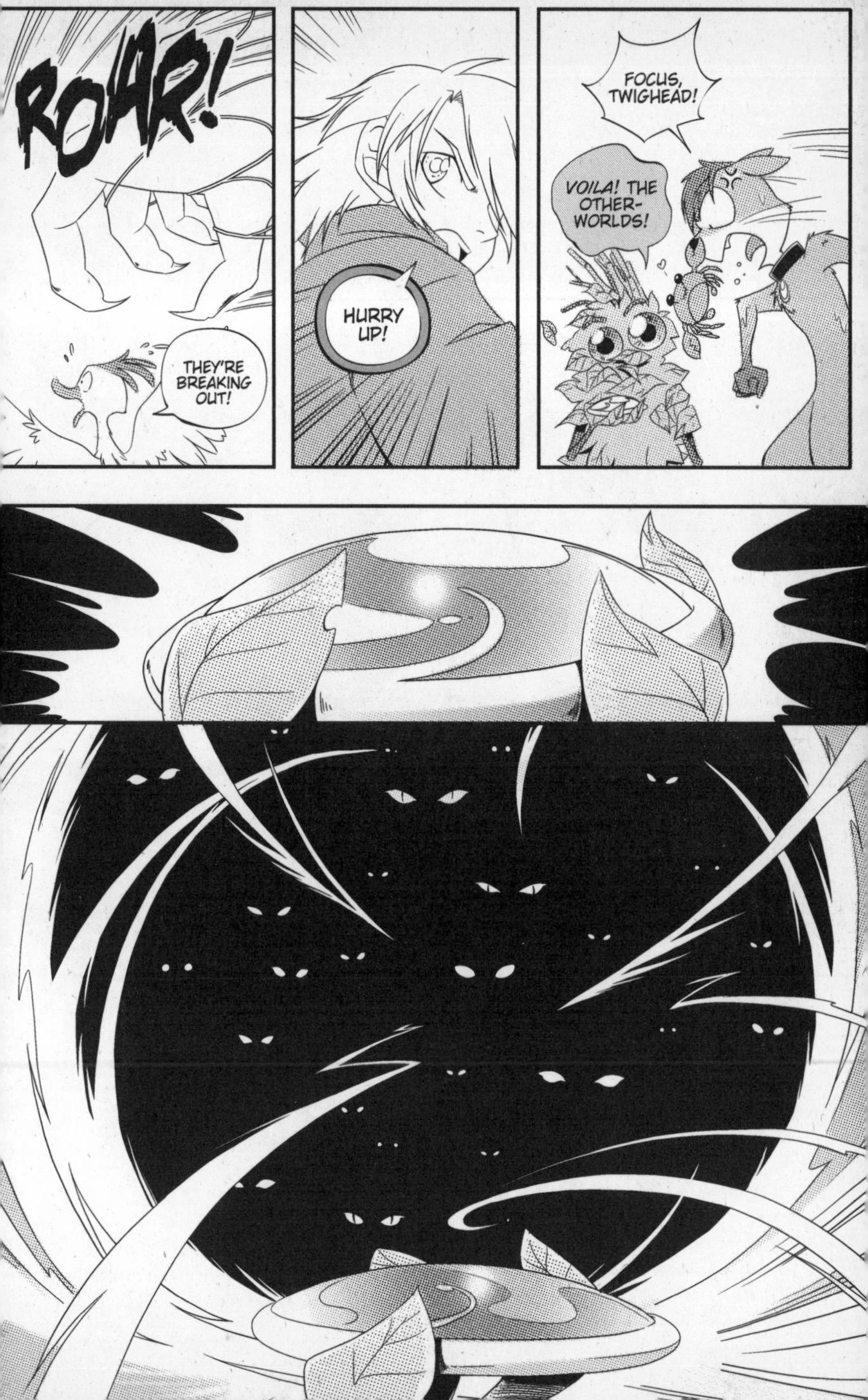
ROAR!
THEY'RE BREAKING OUT!
HURRY UP!
FOCUS, TWIGHEAD!
VOILA! THE OTHER-WORLDS!

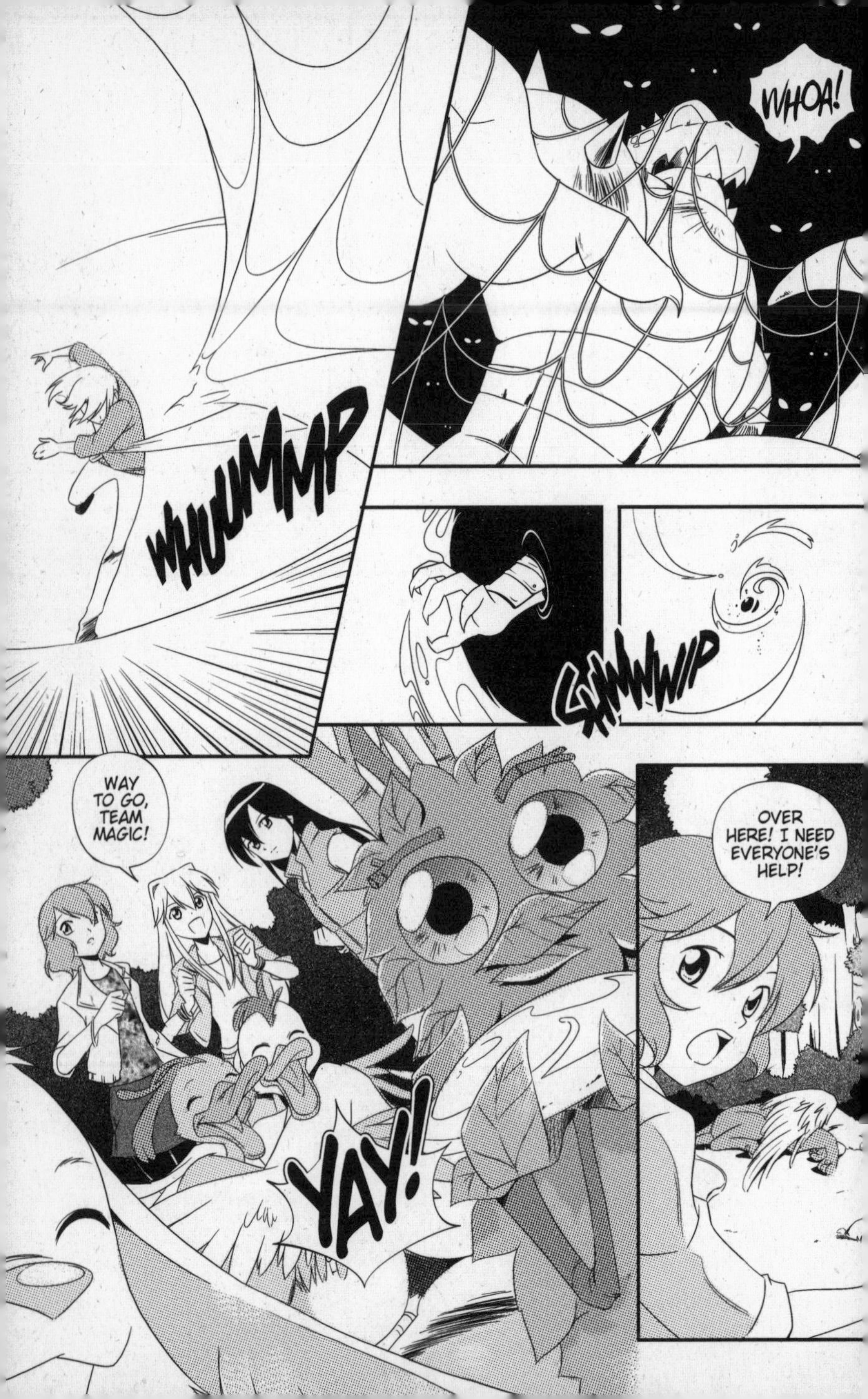
WHUUMMP
WHOA!
SHWWWIP
WAY TO GO, TEAM MAGIC!
YAY!
OVER HERE! I NEED EVERYONE'S HELP!

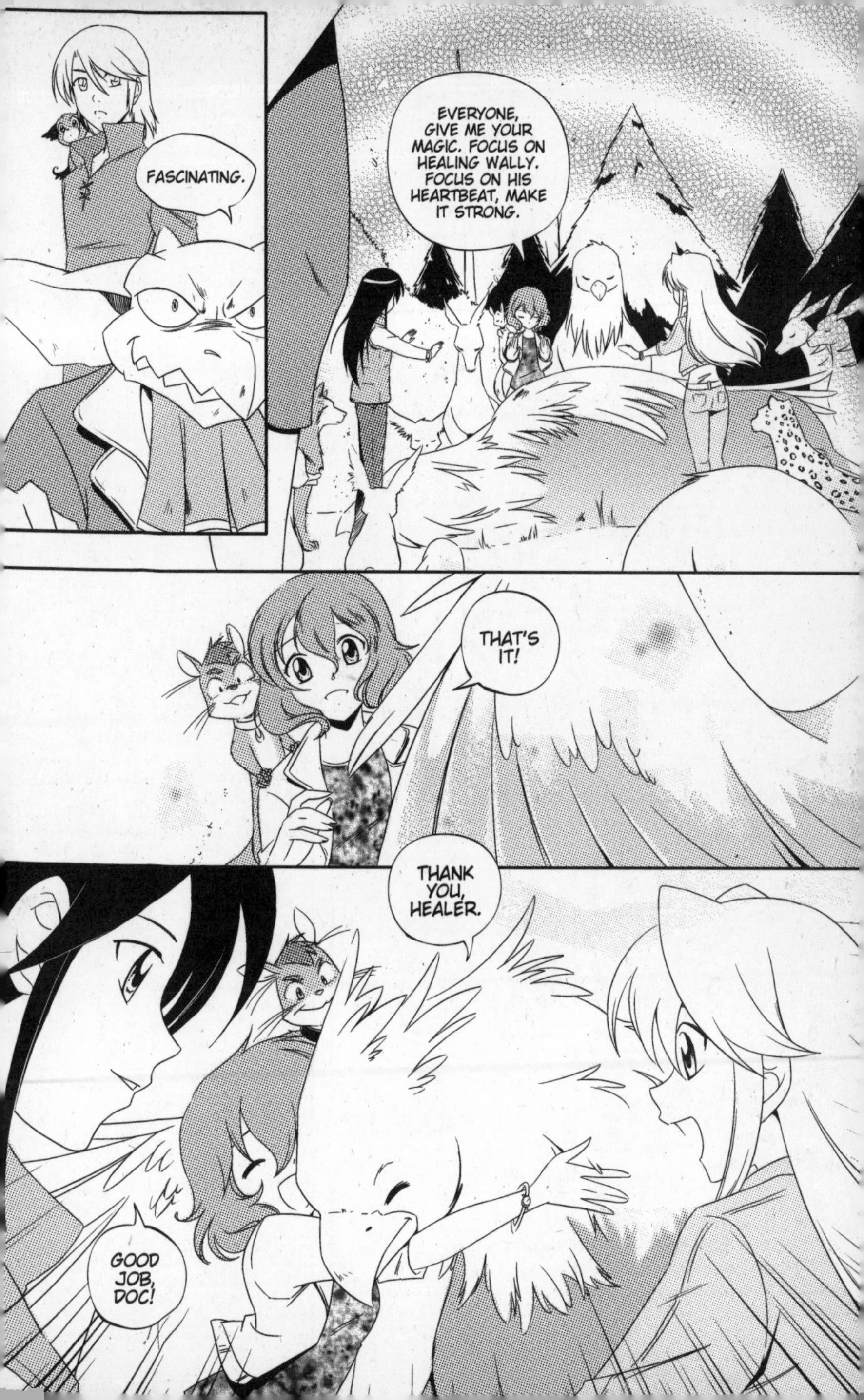
FASCINATING.
EVERYONE, GIVE ME YOUR MAGIC. FOCUS ON HEALING WALLY. FOCUS ON HIS HEARTBEAT, MAKE IT STRONG.
THAT'S IT!
THANK YOU, HEALER.
GOOD JOB, DOC!

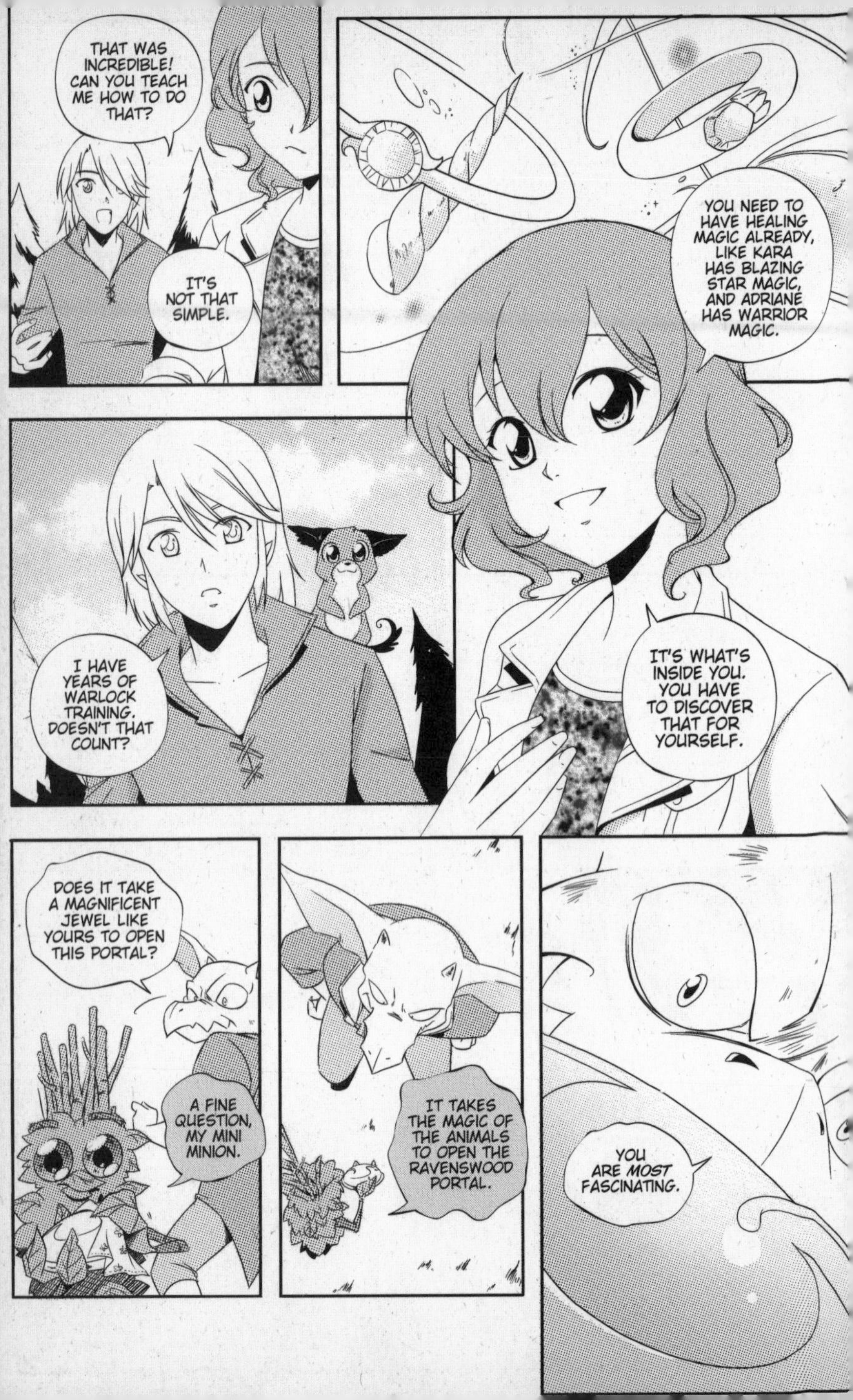
THAT WAS INCREDIBLE! CAN YOU TEACH ME HOW TO DO THAT?
IT'S NOT THAT SIMPLE.
YOU NEED TO HAVE HEALING MAGIC ALREADY, LIKE KARA HAS BLAZING STAR MAGIC, AND ADRIANE HAS WARRIOR MAGIC.
I HAVE YEARS OF WARLOCK TRAINING. DOESN'T THAT COUNT?
IT'S WHAT'S INSIDE YOU. YOU HAVE TO DISCOVER THAT FOR YOURSELF.
DOES IT TAKE A MAGNIFICENT JEWEL LIKE YOURS TO OPEN THIS PORTAL?
A FINE QUESTION, MY MINI MINION.
IT TAKES THE MAGIC OF THE ANIMALS TO OPEN THE RAVENSWOOD PORTAL.
YOU ARE MOST FASCINATING.

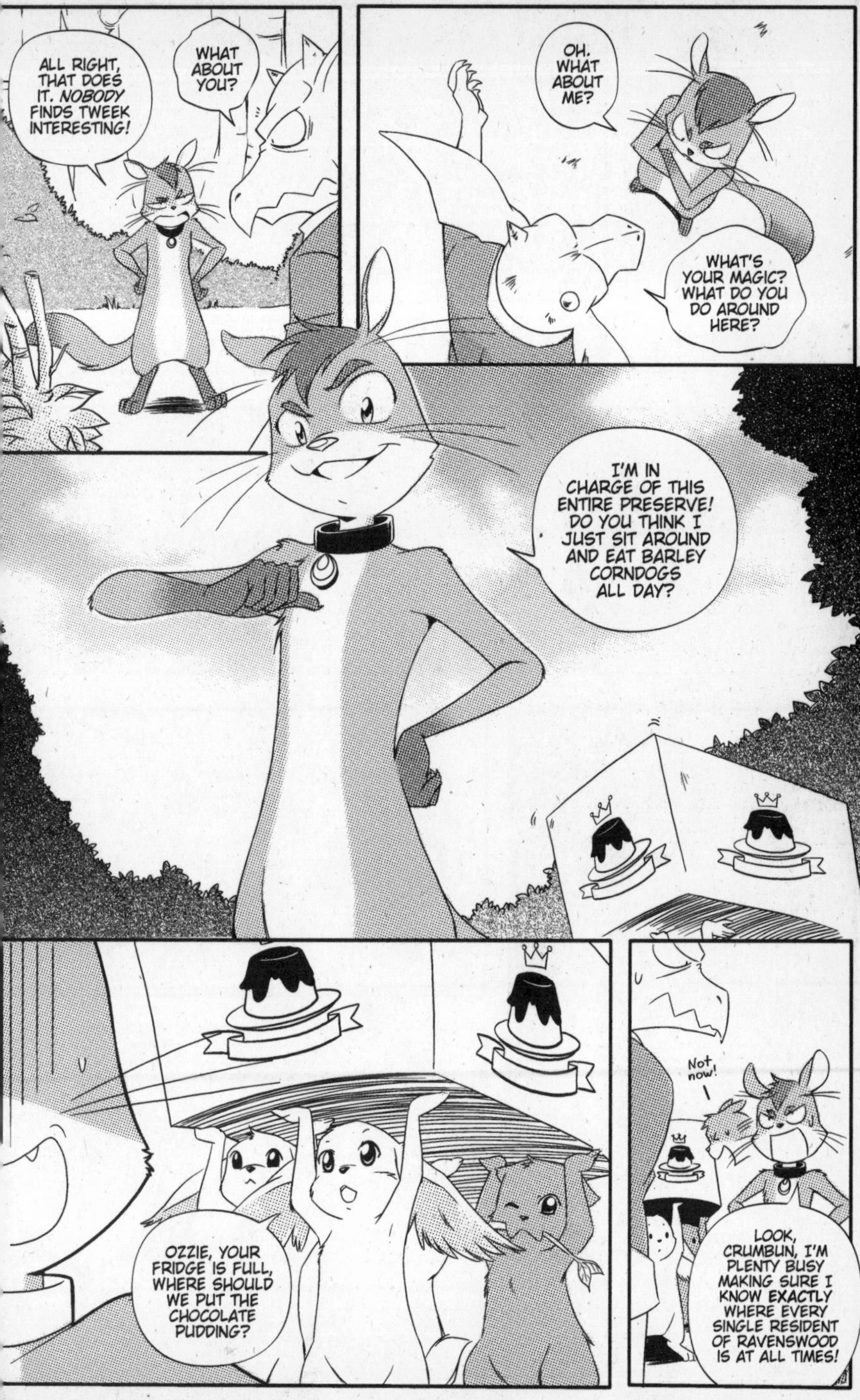
ALL RIGHT, THAT DOES IT. *NOBODY* FINDS TWEEK INTERESTING!
WHAT ABOUT YOU?
OH. WHAT ABOUT ME?
WHAT'S YOUR MAGIC? WHAT DO YOU DO AROUND HERE?
I'M IN CHARGE OF THIS ENTIRE PRESERVE! DO YOU THINK I JUST SIT AROUND AND EAT BARLEY CORNDOGS ALL DAY?
OZZIE, YOUR FRIDGE IS FULL, WHERE SHOULD WE PUT THE CHOCOLATE PUDDING?
Not now!
LOOK, CRUMBUN, I'M PLENTY BUSY MAKING SURE I KNOW EXACTLY WHERE EVERY SINGLE RESIDENT OF RAVENSWOOD IS AT ALL TIMES!

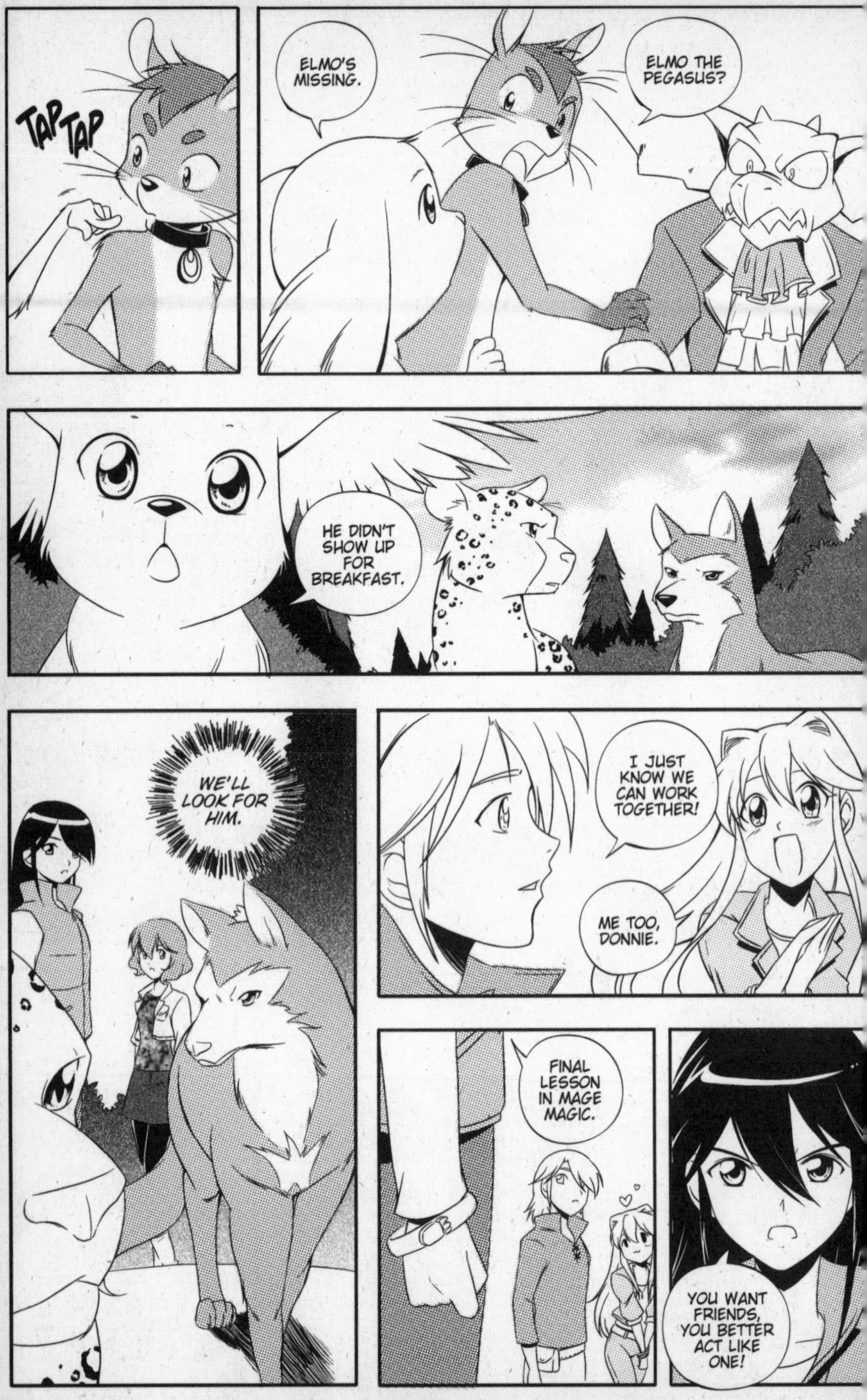
TAP TAP
ELMO'S MISSING.
ELMO THE PEGASUS?
HE DIDN'T SHOW UP FOR BREAKFAST.
WE'LL LOOK FOR HIM.
I JUST KNOW WE CAN WORK TOGETHER!
ME TOO, DONNIE.
FINAL LESSON IN MAGE MAGIC.
YOU WANT FRIENDS, YOU BETTER ACT LIKE ONE!

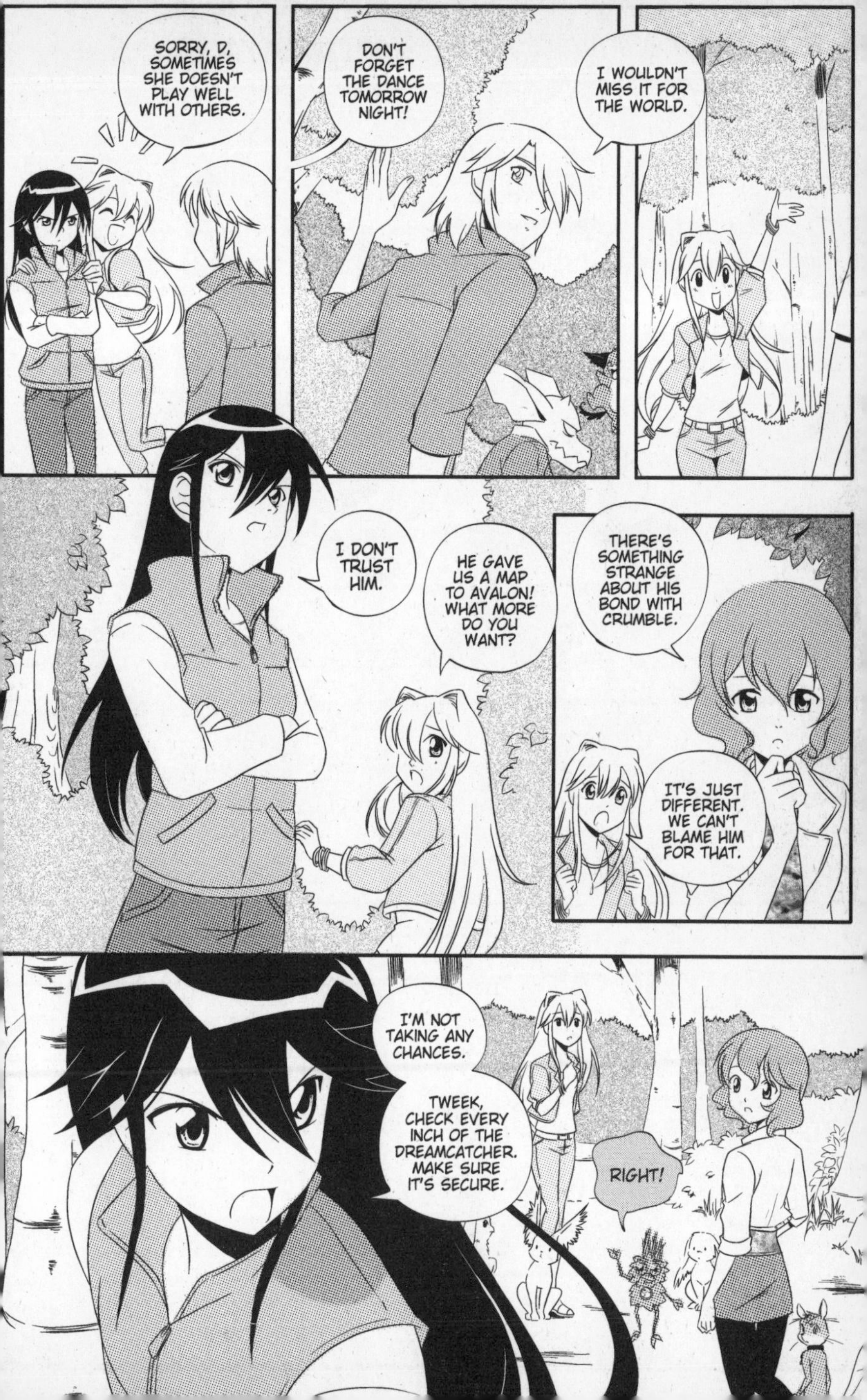
SORRY, D, SOMETIMES SHE DOESN'T PLAY WELL WITH OTHERS.
DON'T FORGET THE DANCE TOMORROW NIGHT!
I WOULDN'T MISS IT FOR THE WORLD.
I DON'T TRUST HIM.
HE GAVE US A MAP TO AVALON! WHAT MORE DO YOU WANT?
THERE'S SOMETHING STRANGE ABOUT HIS BOND WITH CRUMBLE.
IT'S JUST DIFFERENT. WE CAN'T BLAME HIM FOR THAT.
I'M NOT TAKING ANY CHANCES.
TWEEK, CHECK EVERY INCH OF THE DREAMCATCHER. MAKE SURE IT'S SECURE.
RIGHT!

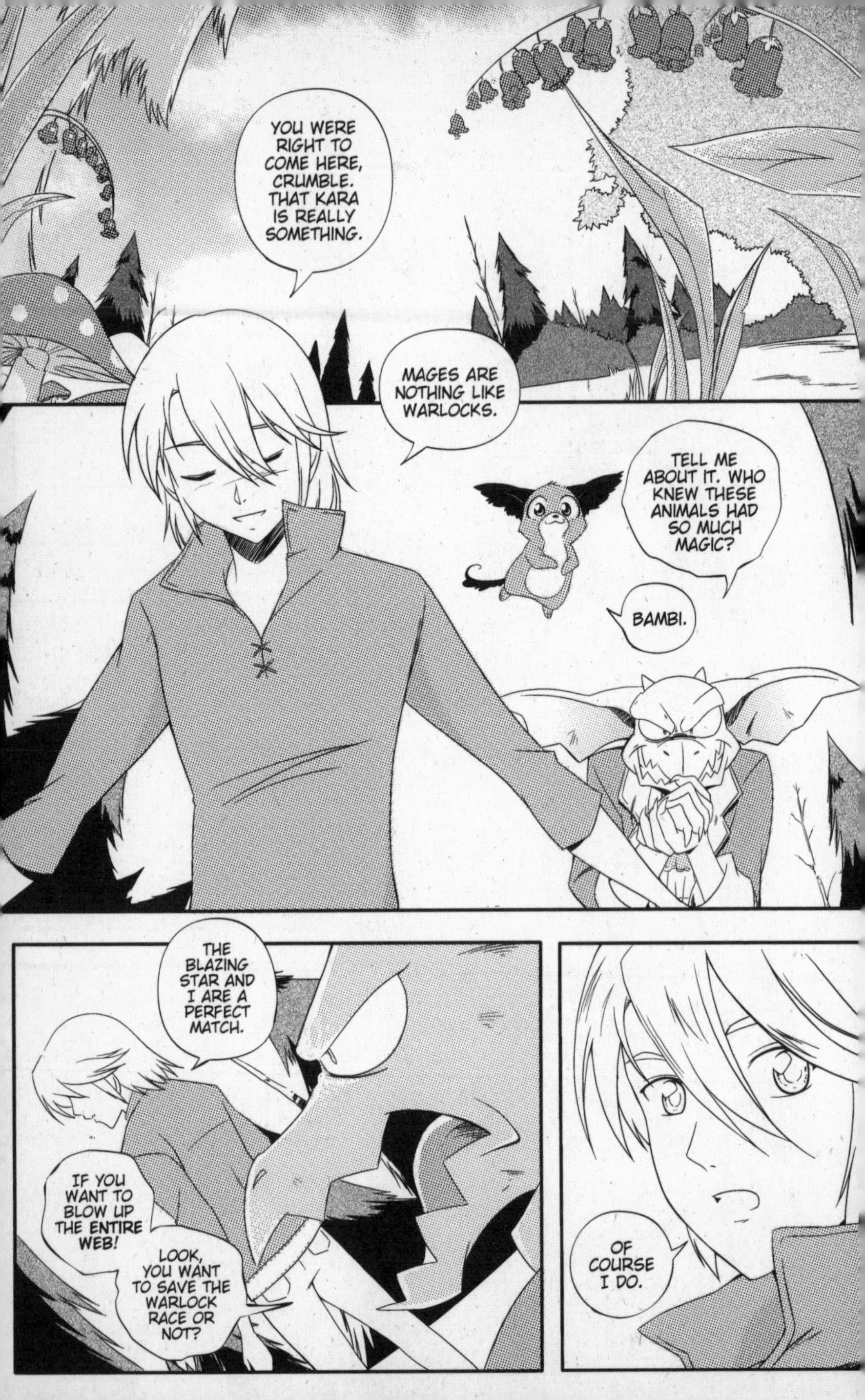
YOU WERE RIGHT TO COME HERE, CRUMBLE. THAT KARA IS REALLY SOMETHING.
MAGES ARE NOTHING LIKE WARLOCKS.
TELL ME ABOUT IT. WHO KNEW THESE ANIMALS HAD SO MUCH MAGIC?
BAMBI.
THE BLAZING STAR AND I ARE A PERFECT MATCH.
IF YOU WANT TO BLOW UP THE ENTIRE WEB!
LOOK, YOU WANT TO SAVE THE WARLOCK RACE OR NOT?
OF COURSE I DO.

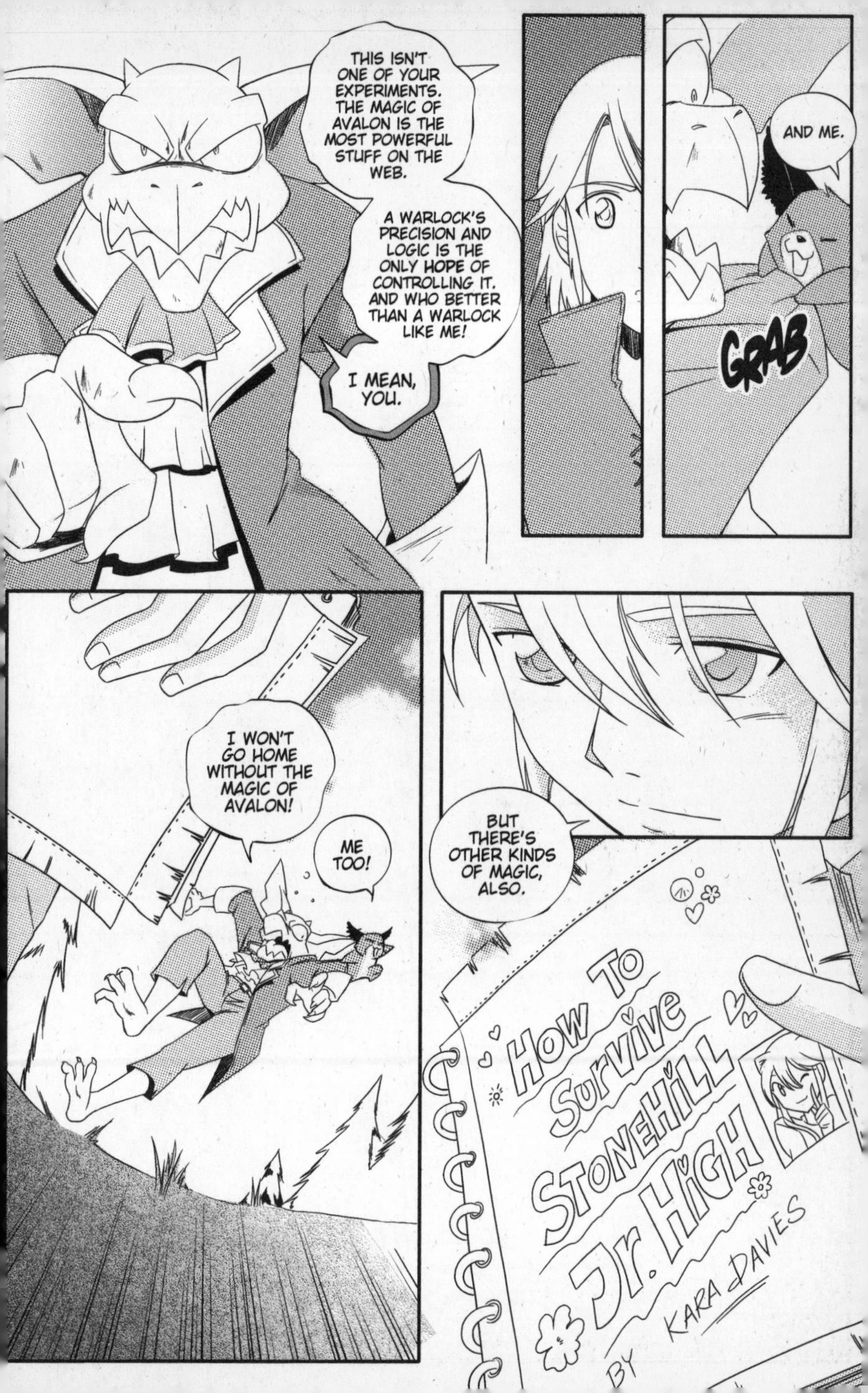
THIS ISN'T ONE OF YOUR EXPERIMENTS. THE MAGIC OF AVALON IS THE MOST POWERFUL STUFF ON THE WEB.
A WARLOCK'S PRECISION AND LOGIC IS THE ONLY HOPE OF CONTROLLING IT. AND WHO BETTER THAN A WARLOCK LIKE ME!
I MEAN, YOU.
AND ME.
GRAB
I WON'T GO HOME WITHOUT THE MAGIC OF AVALON!
ME TOO!
BUT THERE'S OTHER KINDS OF MAGIC, ALSO.
How To Survive StoneHill Jr. High
BY KARA DAVIES

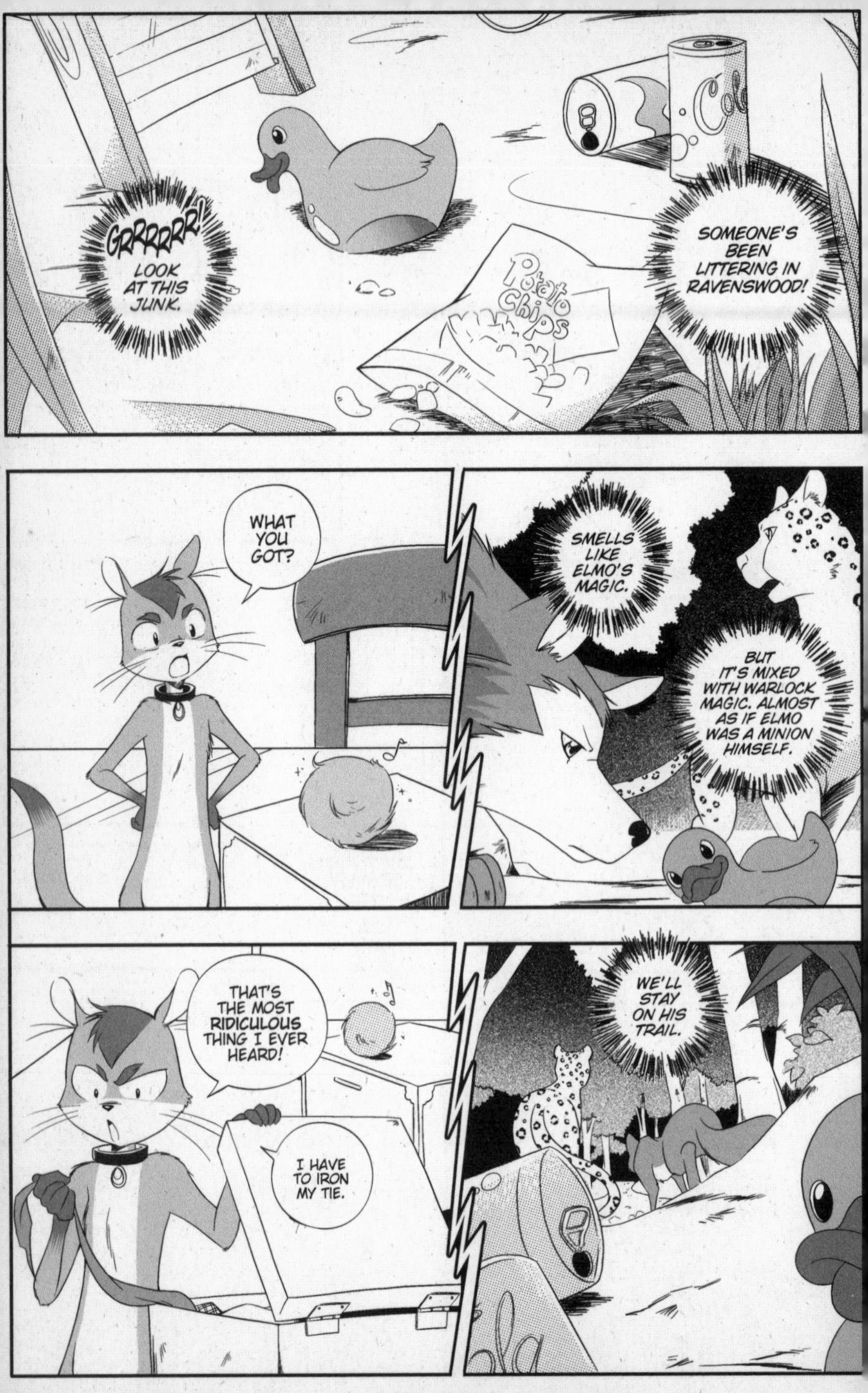
GRRRRRR!
LOOK AT THIS JUNK.
Cola
Potato Chips
SOMEONE'S BEEN LITTERING IN RAVENSWOOD!
WHAT YOU GOT?
SMELLS LIKE ELMO'S MAGIC.
BUT IT'S MIXED WITH WARLOCK MAGIC. ALMOST AS IF ELMO WAS A MINION HIMSELF.
THAT'S THE MOST RIDICULOUS THING I EVER HEARD!
I HAVE TO IRON MY TIE.
WE'LL STAY ON HIS TRAIL.

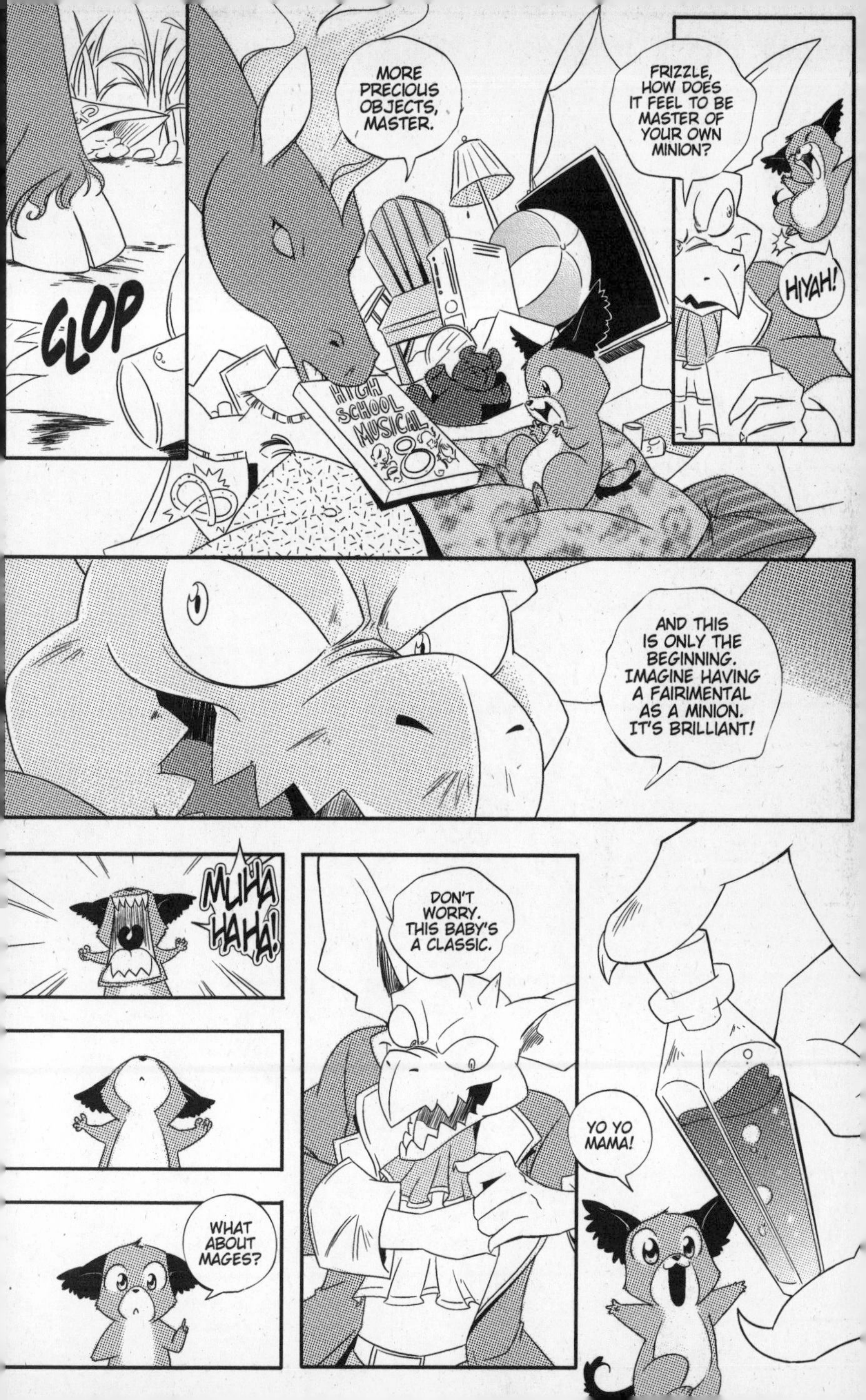
CLOP
MORE PRECIOUS OBJECTS, MASTER.
HIGH SCHOOL MUSICAL 8
FRIZZLE, HOW DOES IT FEEL TO BE MASTER OF YOUR OWN MINION?
HIYAH!
AND THIS IS ONLY THE BEGINNING. IMAGINE HAVING A FAIRIMENTAL AS A MINION. IT'S BRILLIANT!
MUHAHAHA!
WHAT ABOUT MAGES?
DON'T WORRY. THIS BABY'S A CLASSIC.
YO YO MAMA!

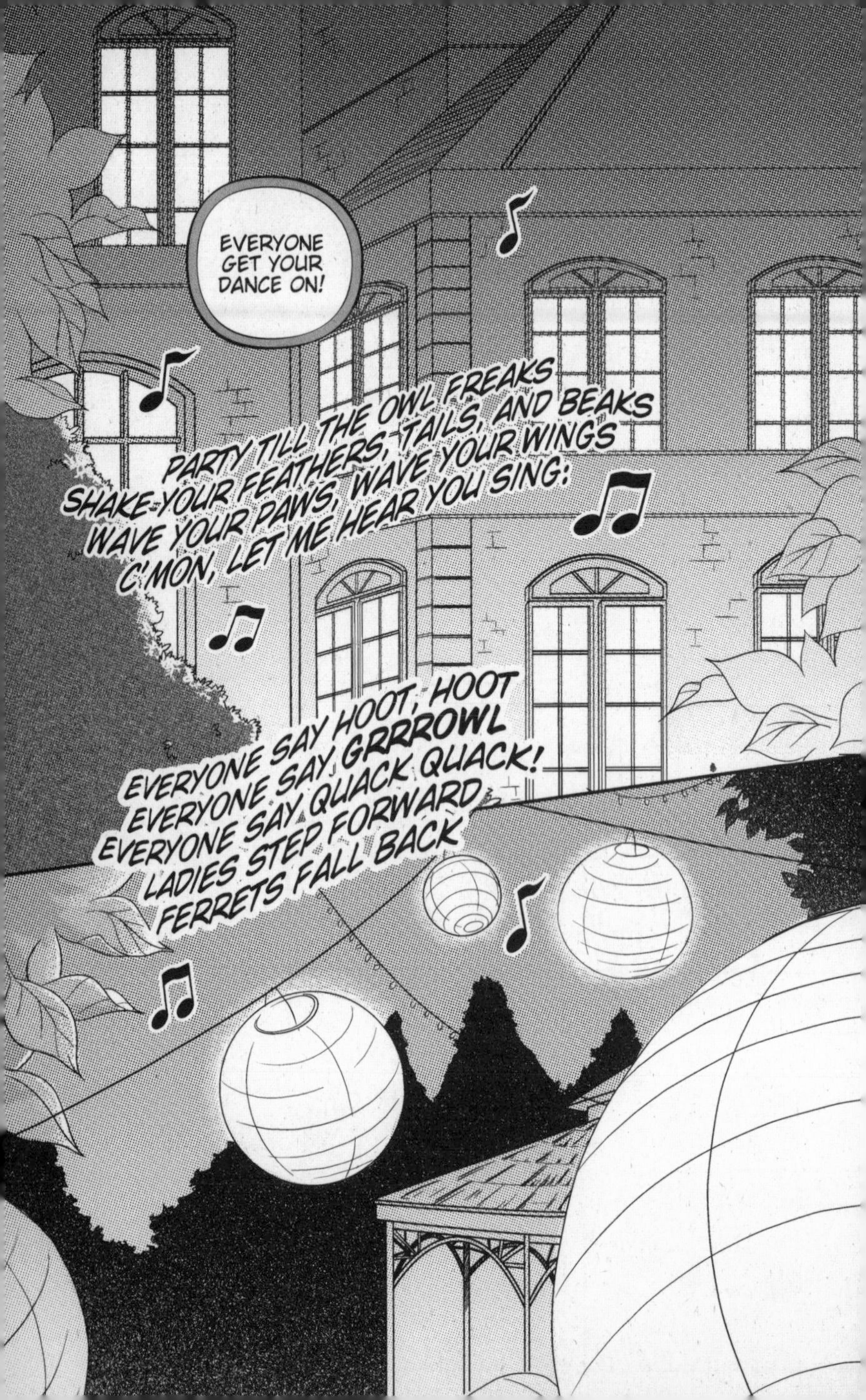
EVERYONE GET YOUR DANCE ON!
PARTY TILL THE OWL FREAKS
SHAKE YOUR FEATHERS, TAILS, AND BEAKS
WAVE YOUR PAWS, WAVE YOUR WINGS
C'MON, LET ME HEAR YOU SING:
EVERYONE SAY HOOT, HOOT
EVERYONE SAY GRRROWL
EVERYONE SAY QUACK QUACK!
LADIES STEP FORWARD
FERRETS FALL BACK

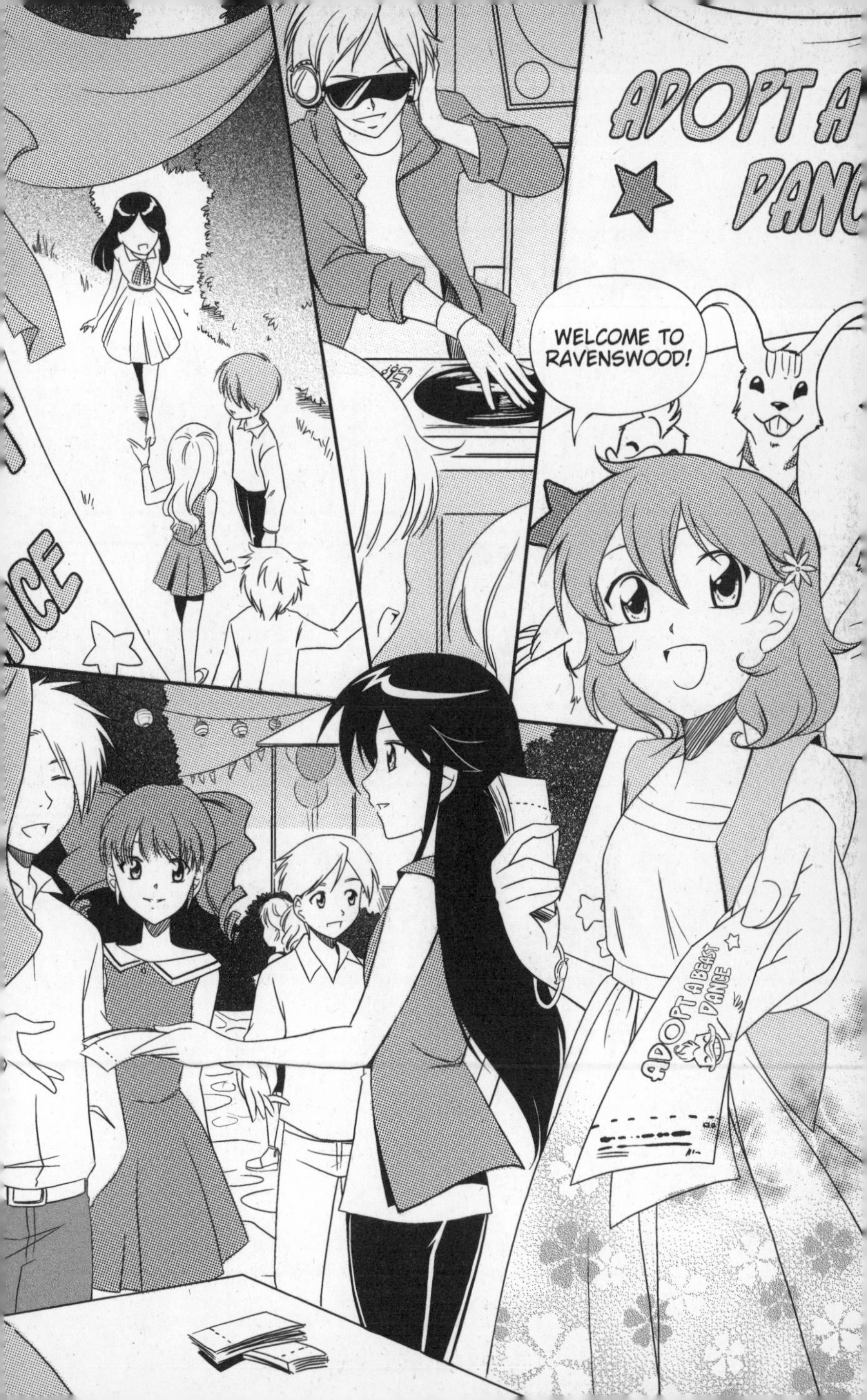
ADOPT A
WELCOME TO RAVENSWOOD!
ADOPT A BEAST DANCE

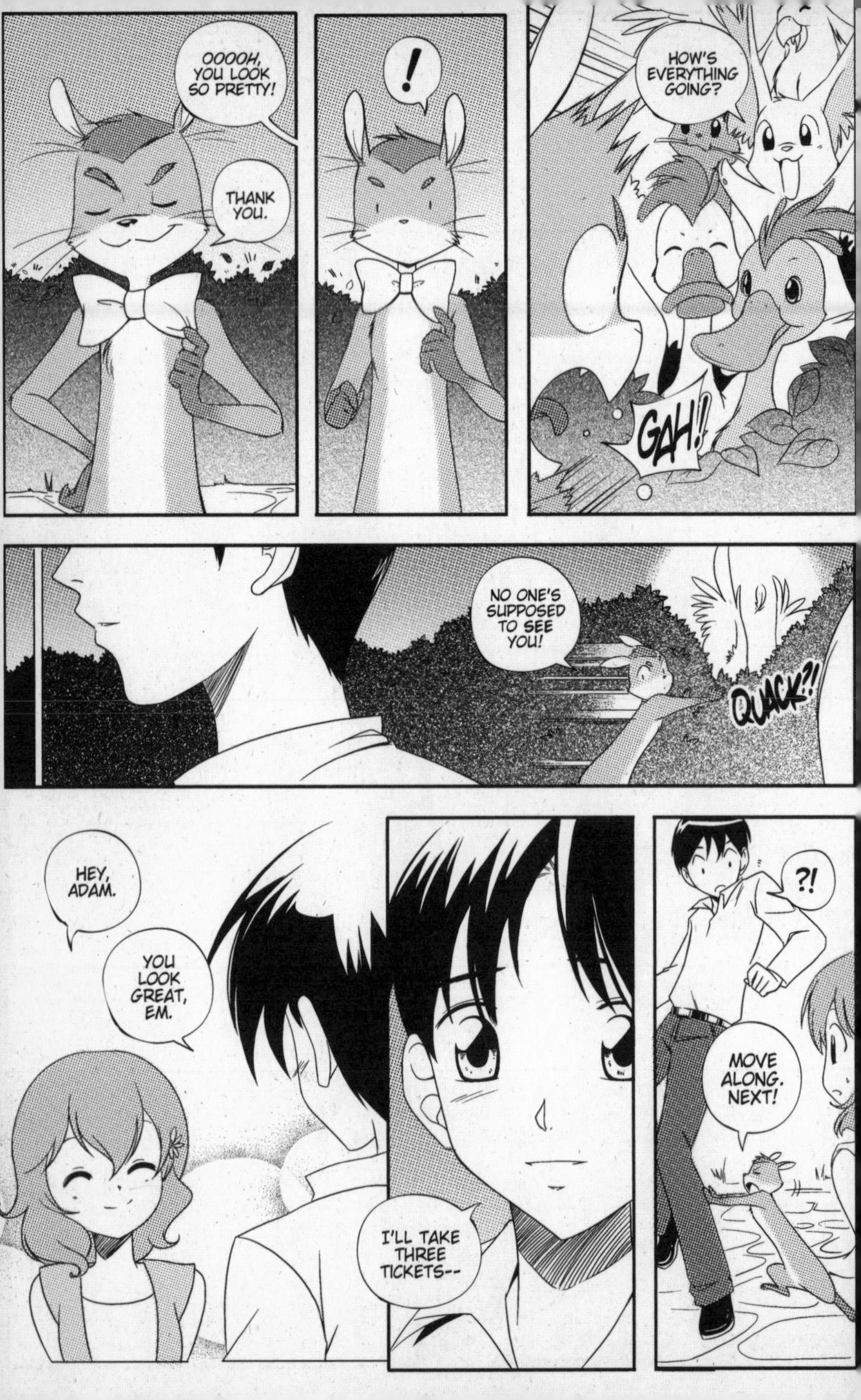
OOOOH, YOU LOOK SO PRETTY!
THANK YOU.
!
HOW'S EVERYTHING GOING?
GAH!!
NO ONE'S SUPPOSED TO SEE YOU!
QUACK?!
HEY, ADAM.
YOU LOOK GREAT, EM.
I'LL TAKE THREE TICKETS--
?!
MOVE ALONG. NEXT!

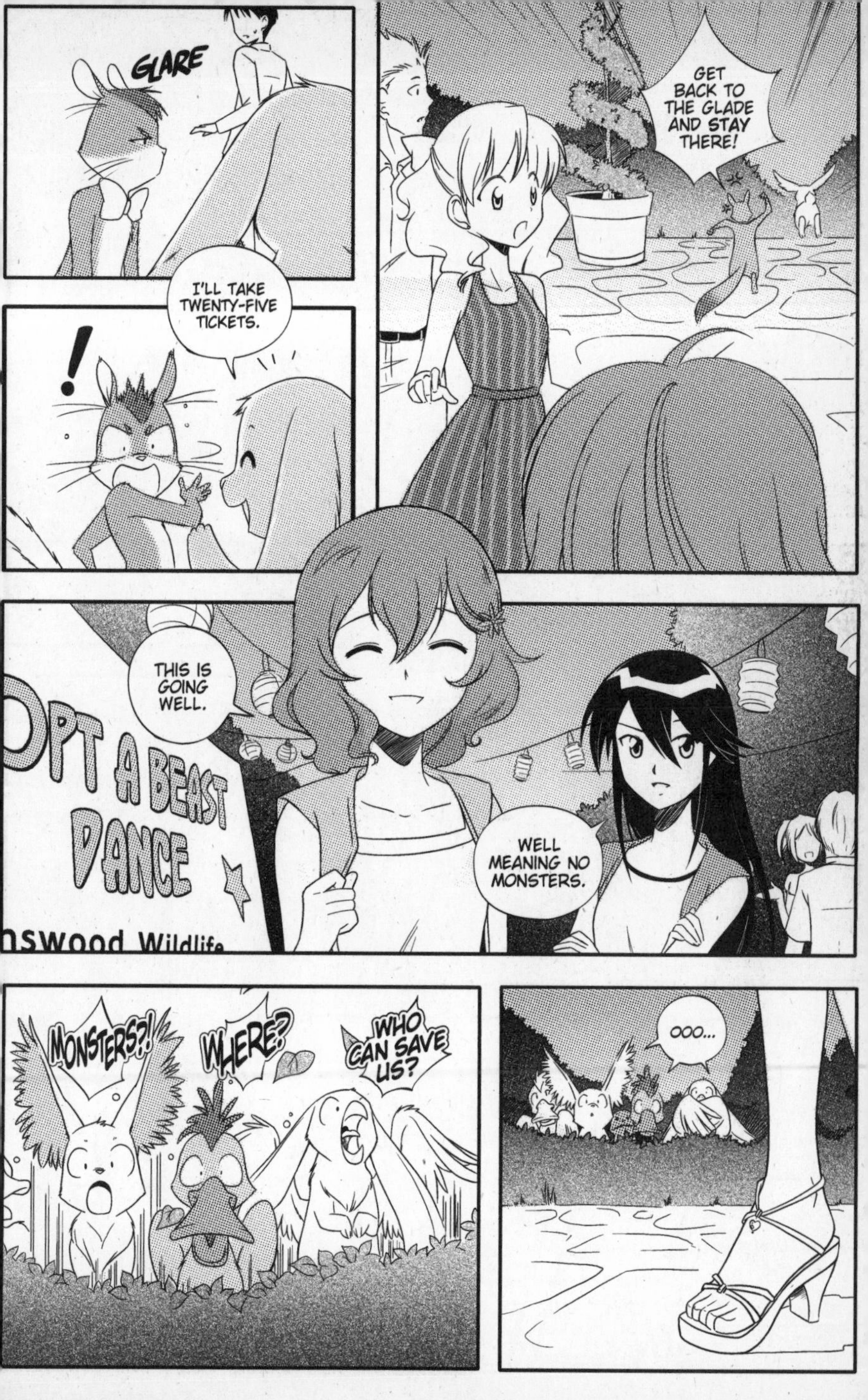
GLARE
I'LL TAKE TWENTY-FIVE TICKETS.
!
GET BACK TO THE GLADE AND STAY THERE!
THIS IS GOING WELL.
OPT A BEAST DANCE
nswood Wildlife
WELL MEANING NO MONSTERS.
MONSTERS?!
WHERE?
WHO CAN SAVE US?
OOO...

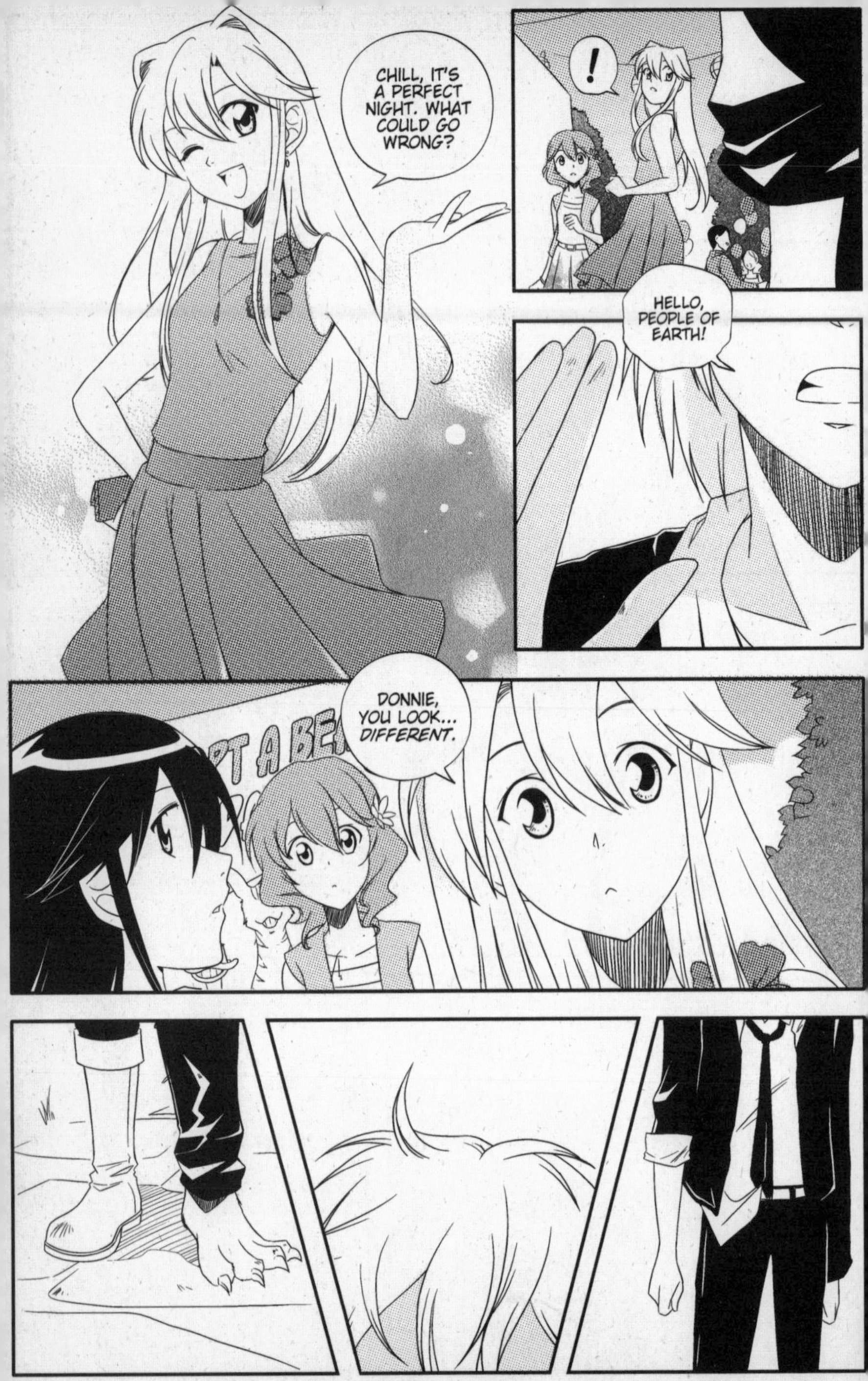
CHILL, IT'S A PERFECT NIGHT. WHAT COULD GO WRONG?
!
HELLO, PEOPLE OF EARTH!
DONNIE, YOU LOOK... *DIFFERENT*.

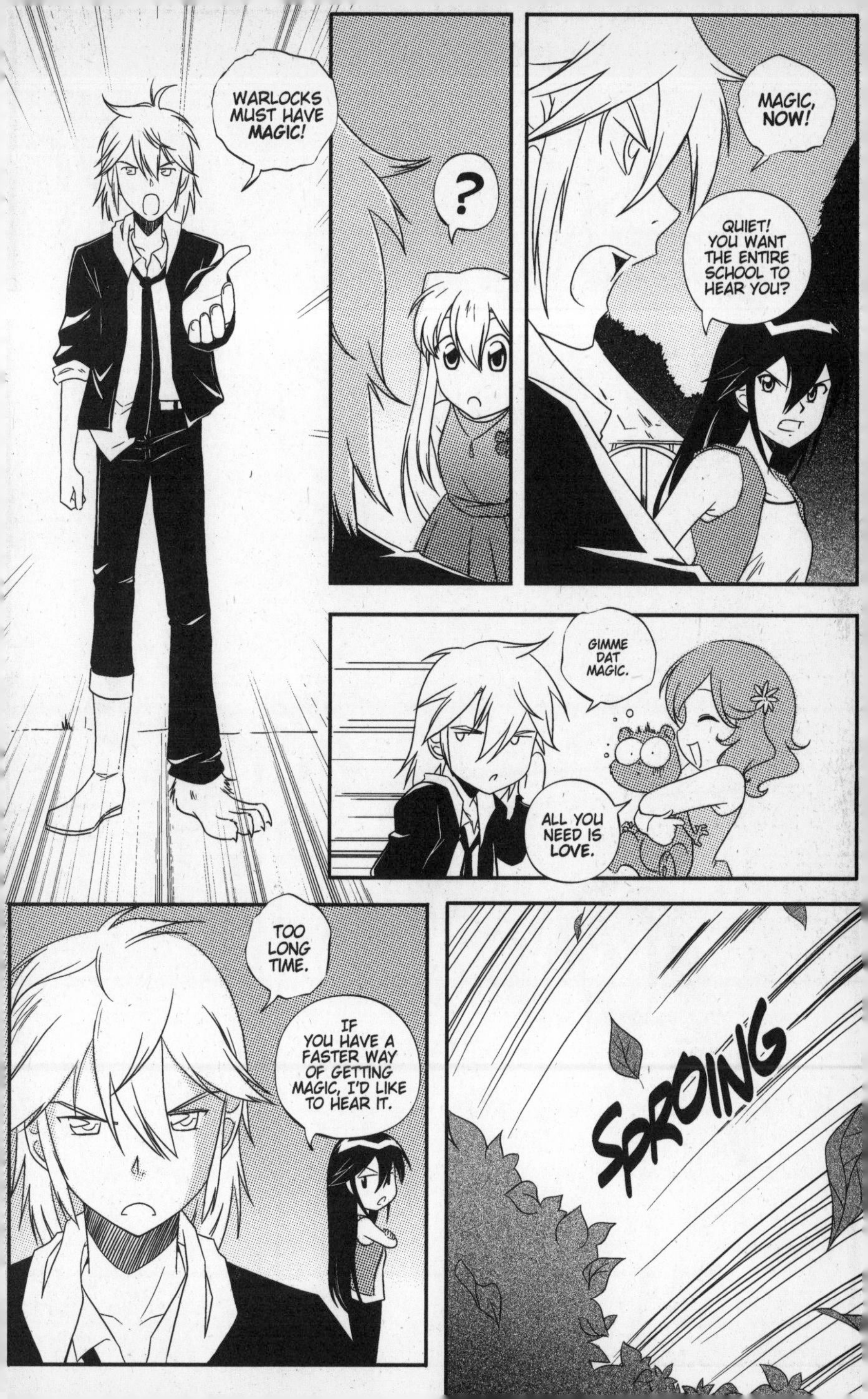
WARLOCKS MUST HAVE MAGIC!
?
MAGIC, NOW!
QUIET! YOU WANT THE ENTIRE SCHOOL TO HEAR YOU?
GIMME DAT MAGIC.
ALL YOU NEED IS LOVE.
TOO LONG TIME.
IF YOU HAVE A FASTER WAY OF GETTING MAGIC, I'D LIKE TO HEAR IT.
SPROING

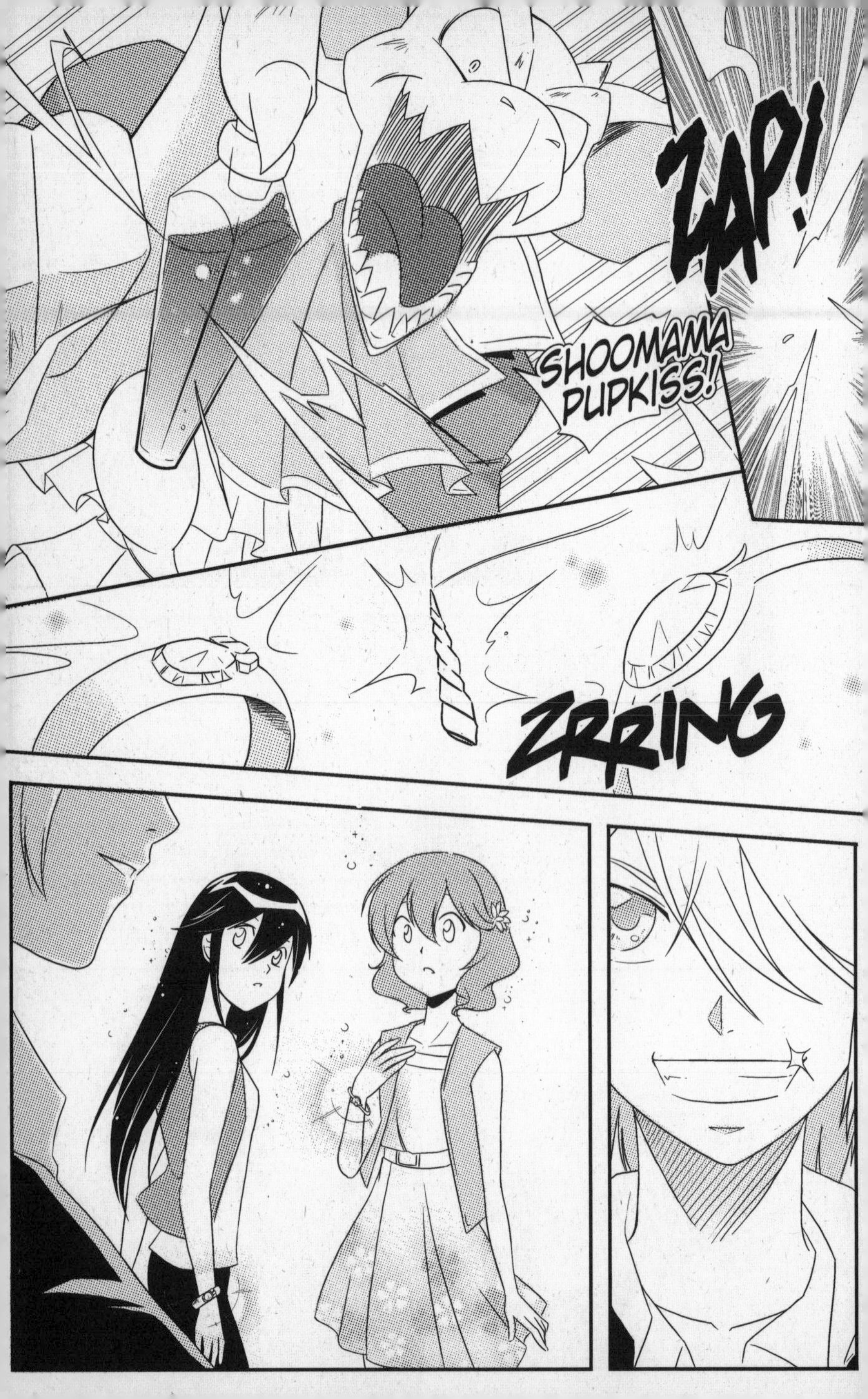
ZAP!
SHOOMAMA PUPKISS!
ZRRING

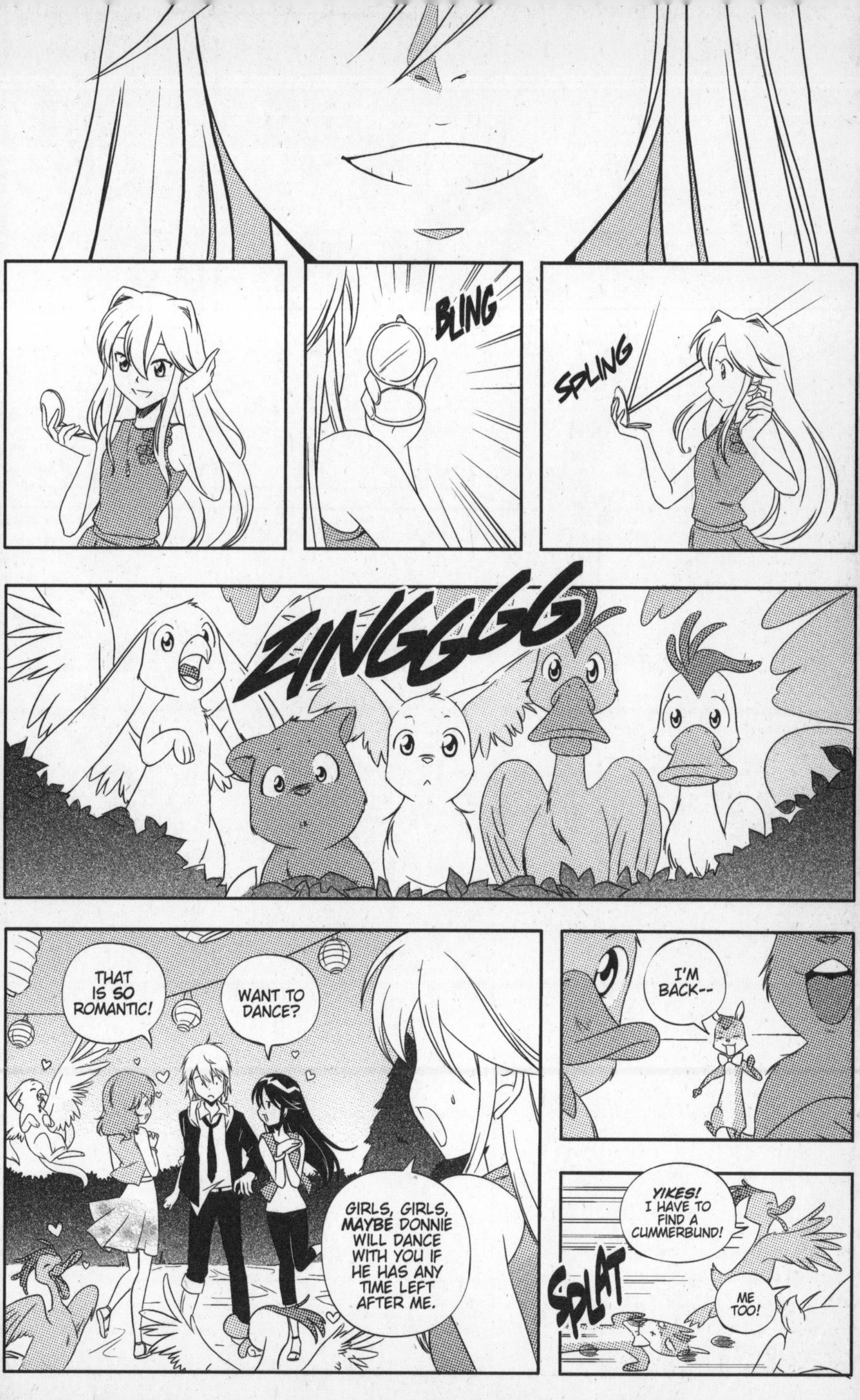
BLING
SPLING
ZINGGGG
THAT IS SO ROMANTIC!
WANT TO DANCE?
GIRLS, GIRLS, MAYBE DONNIE WILL DANCE WITH YOU IF HE HAS ANY TIME LEFT AFTER ME.
I'M BACK--
YIKES! I HAVE TO FIND A CUMMERBUND!
SPLAT
ME TOO!

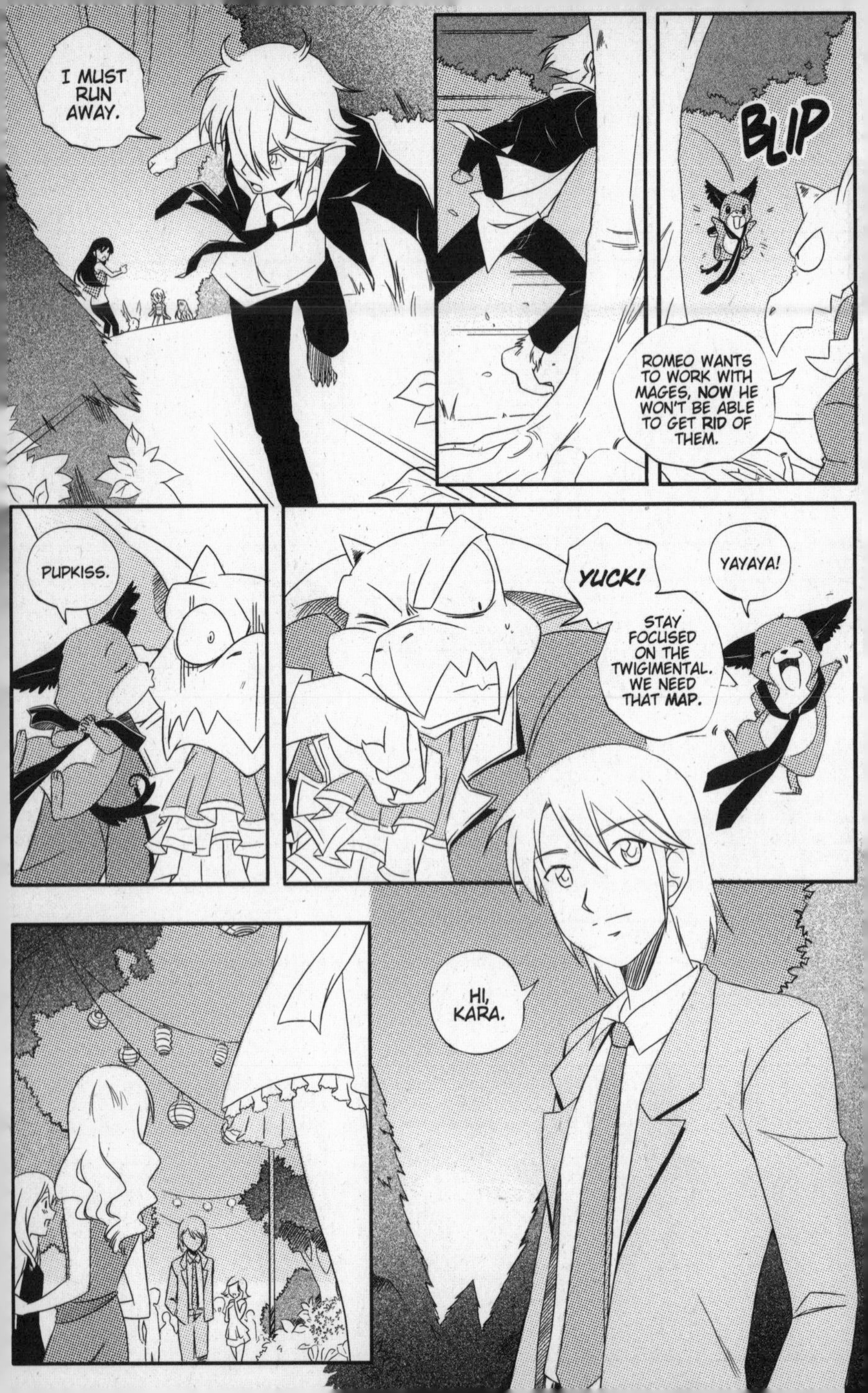
I MUST RUN AWAY.
BLIP
ROMEO WANTS TO WORK WITH MAGES, NOW HE WON'T BE ABLE TO GET RID OF THEM.
PUPKISS.
YUCK!
STAY FOCUSED ON THE TWIGIMENTAL. WE NEED THAT MAP.
YAYAYA!
HI, KARA.

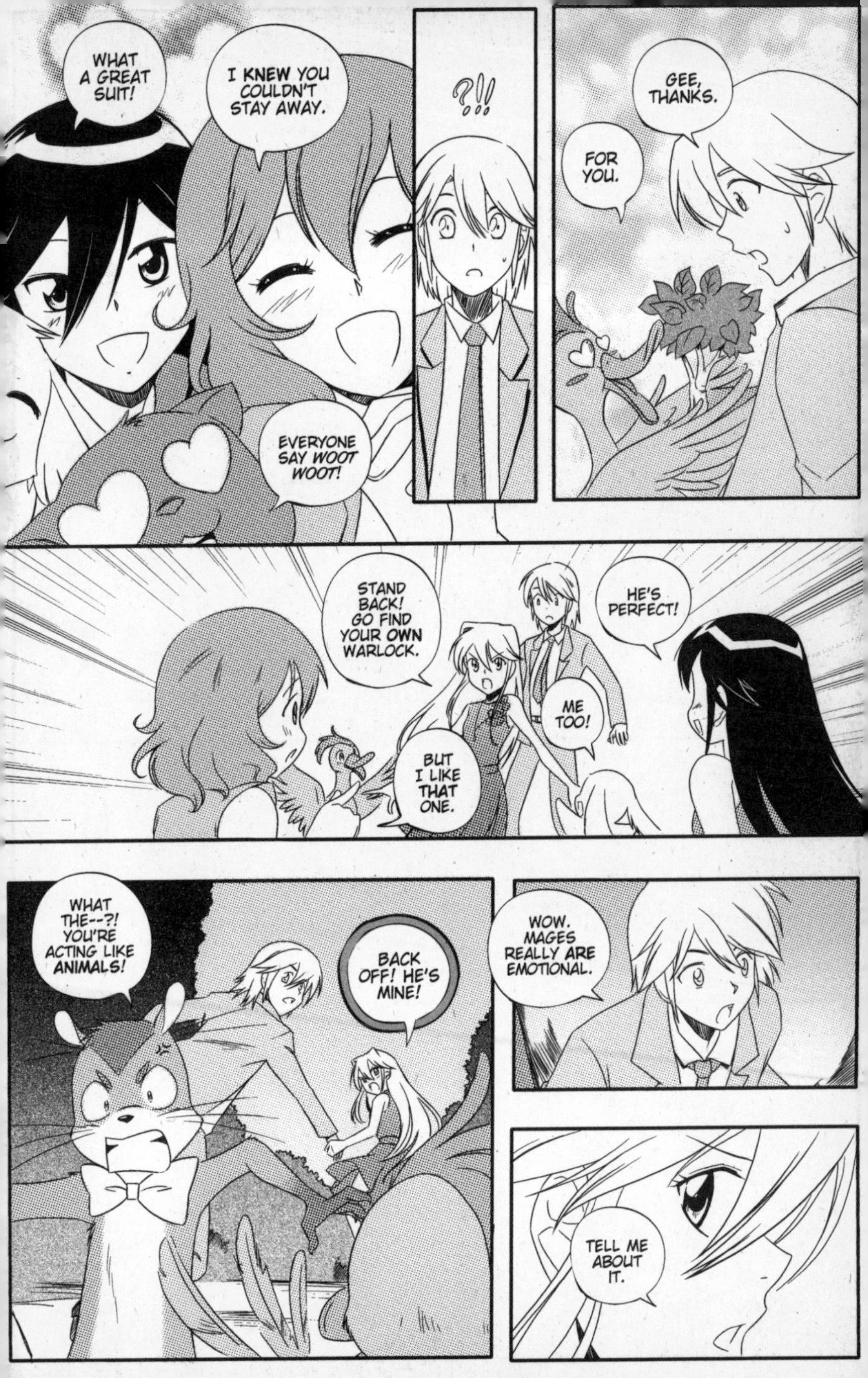
WHAT A GREAT SUIT!
I KNEW YOU COULDN'T STAY AWAY.
EVERYONE SAY WOOT WOOT!
?!!
GEE, THANKS.
FOR YOU.
STAND BACK! GO FIND YOUR OWN WARLOCK.
BUT I LIKE THAT ONE.
ME TOO!
HE'S PERFECT!
WHAT THE--?! YOU'RE ACTING LIKE ANIMALS!
BACK OFF! HE'S MINE!
WOW. MAGES REALLY ARE EMOTIONAL.
TELL ME ABOUT IT.

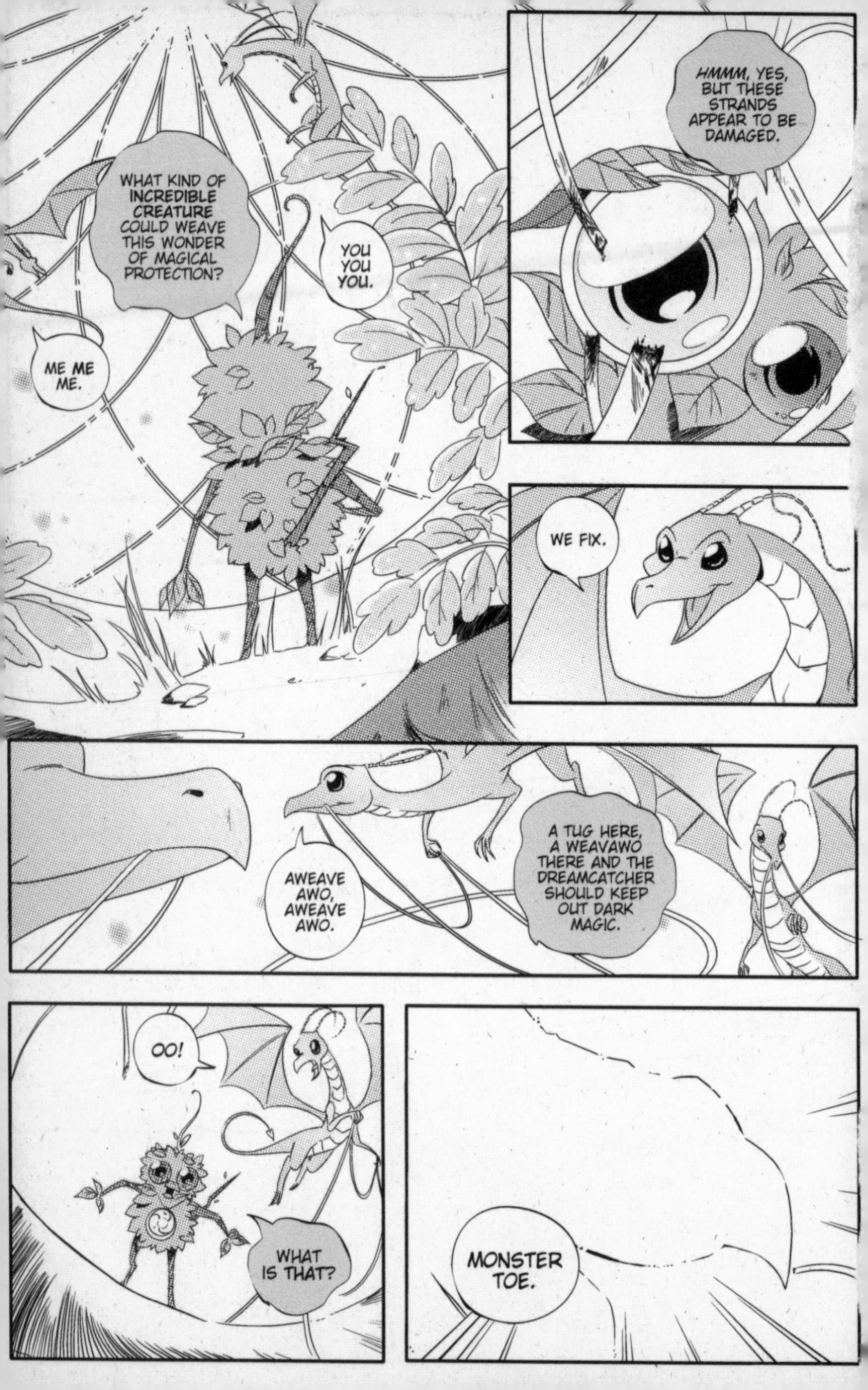
WHAT KIND OF INCREDIBLE CREATURE COULD WEAVE THIS WONDER OF MAGICAL PROTECTION?
YOU YOU YOU.
ME ME ME.
HMMM, YES, BUT THESE STRANDS APPEAR TO BE DAMAGED.
WE FIX.
AWEAVE AWO, AWEAVE AWO.
A TUG HERE, A WEAVAWO THERE AND THE DREAMCATCHER SHOULD KEEP OUT DARK MAGIC.
OO!
WHAT IS THAT?
MONSTER TOE.

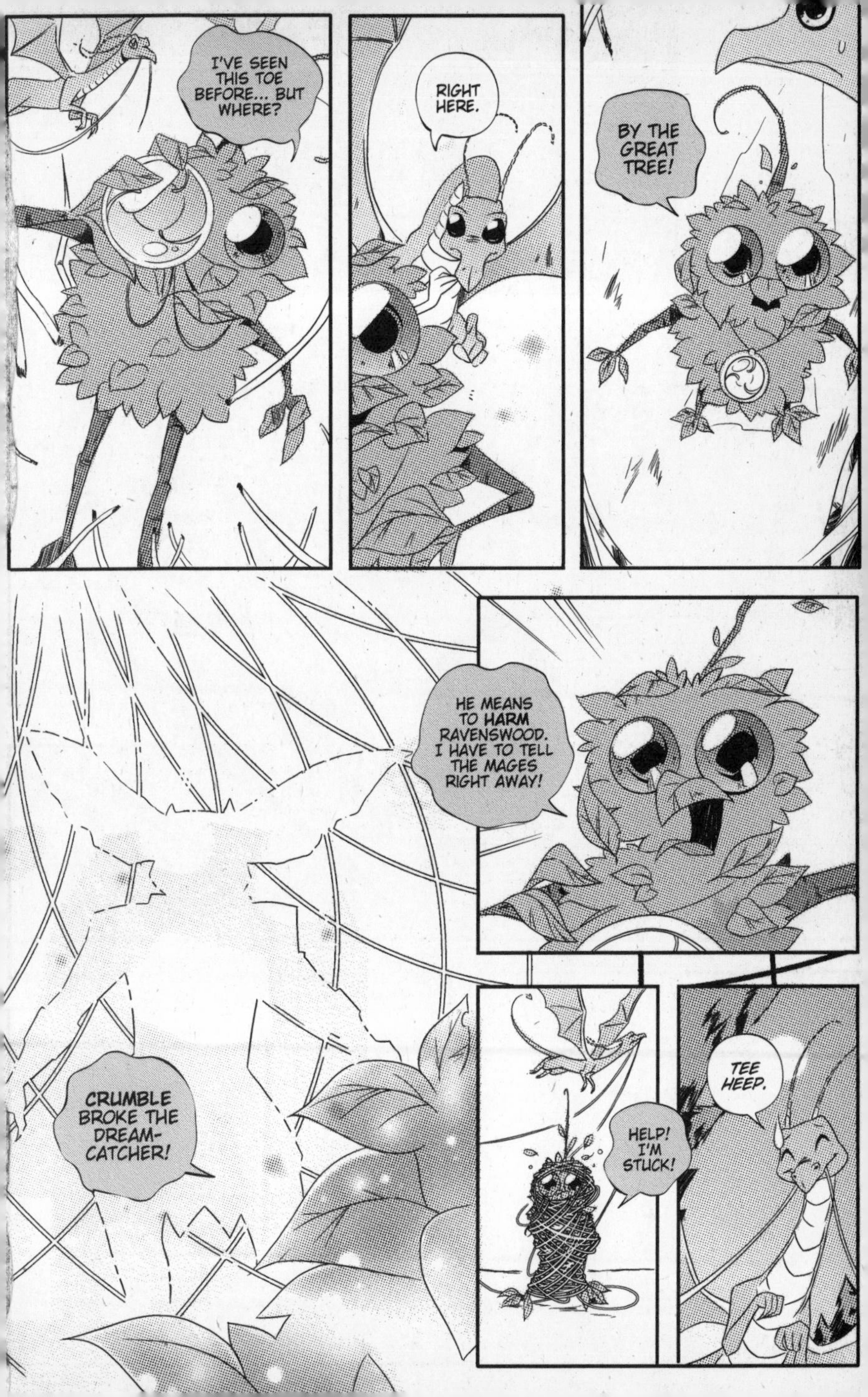
I'VE SEEN THIS TOE BEFORE... BUT WHERE?
RIGHT HERE.
BY THE GREAT TREE!
CRUMBLE BROKE THE DREAM-CATCHER!
HE MEANS TO HARM RAVENSWOOD. I HAVE TO TELL THE MAGES RIGHT AWAY!
HELP! I'M STUCK!
TEE HEEP.

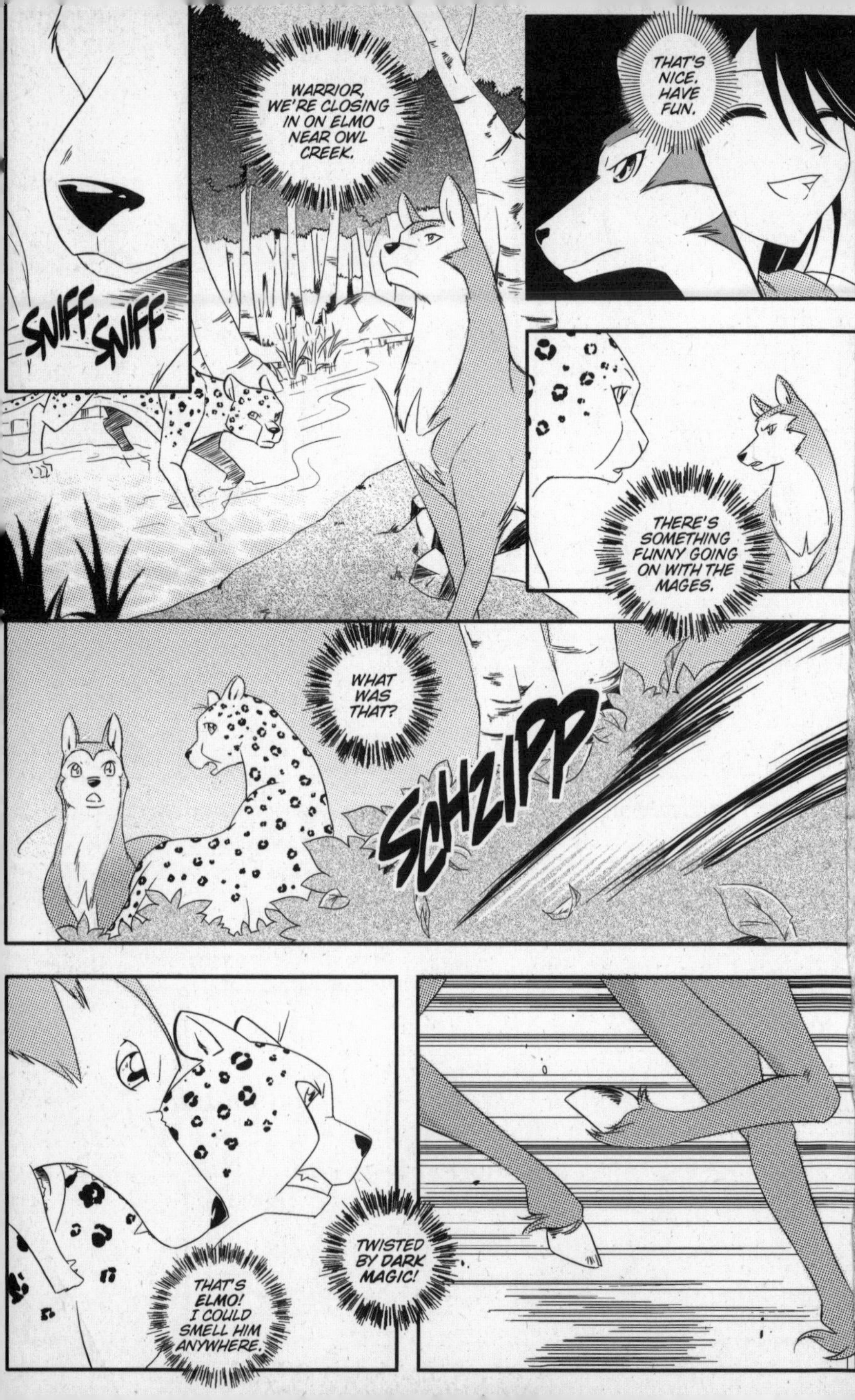
SNIFF SNIFF
WARRIOR, WE'RE CLOSING IN ON ELMO NEAR OWL CREEK.
THAT'S NICE. HAVE FUN.
THERE'S SOMETHING FUNNY GOING ON WITH THE MAGES.
WHAT WAS THAT?
SCHZIPP
THAT'S ELMO! I COULD SMELL HIM ANYWHERE.
TWISTED BY DARK MAGIC!

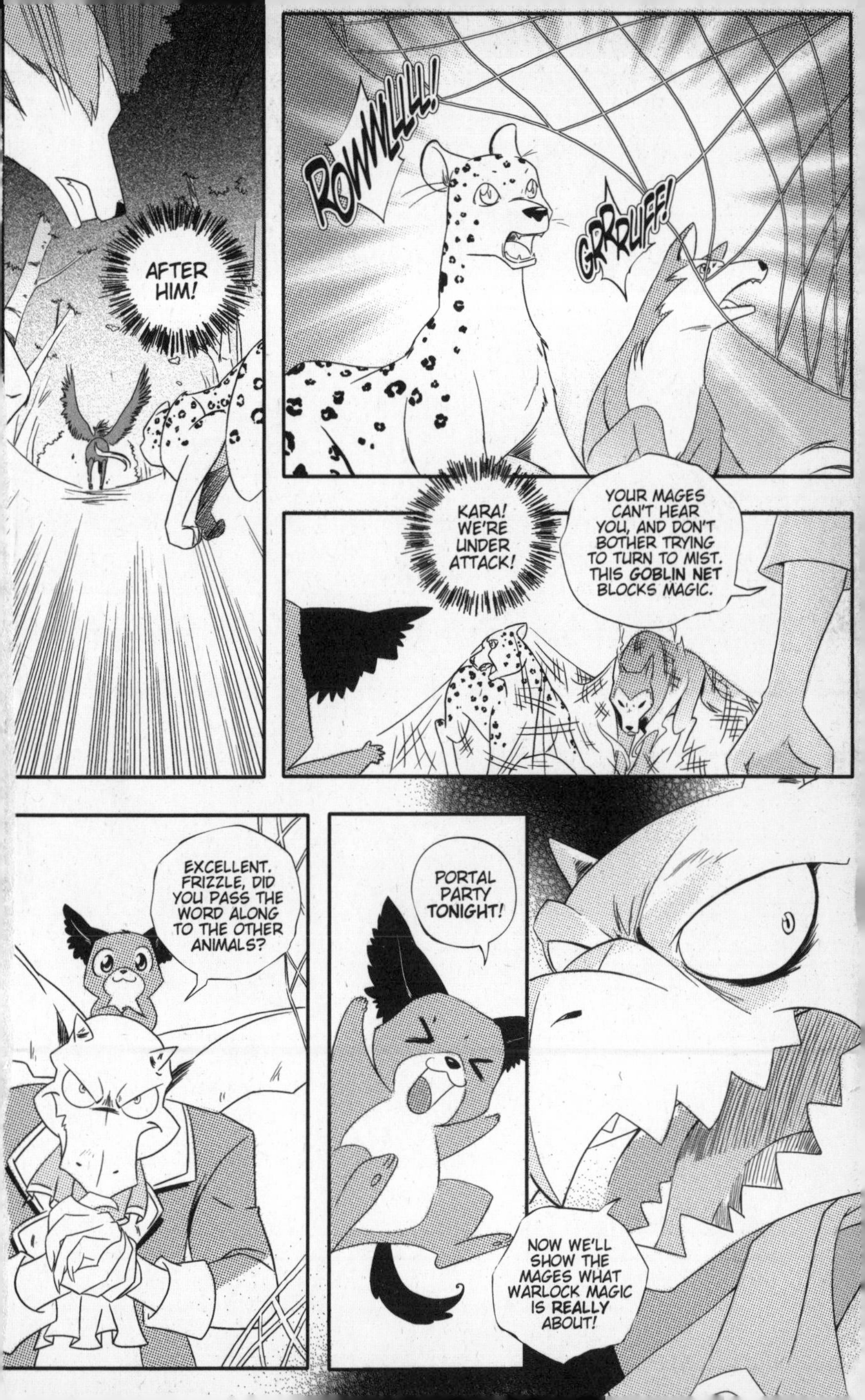
AFTER HIM!
ROWWLLLL!
GRRRUFF!
KARA! WE'RE UNDER ATTACK!
YOUR MAGES CAN'T HEAR YOU, AND DON'T BOTHER TRYING TO TURN TO MIST. THIS GOBLIN NET BLOCKS MAGIC.
EXCELLENT. FRIZZLE, DID YOU PASS THE WORD ALONG TO THE OTHER ANIMALS?
PORTAL PARTY TONIGHT!
NOW WE'LL SHOW THE MAGES WHAT WARLOCK MAGIC IS REALLY ABOUT!

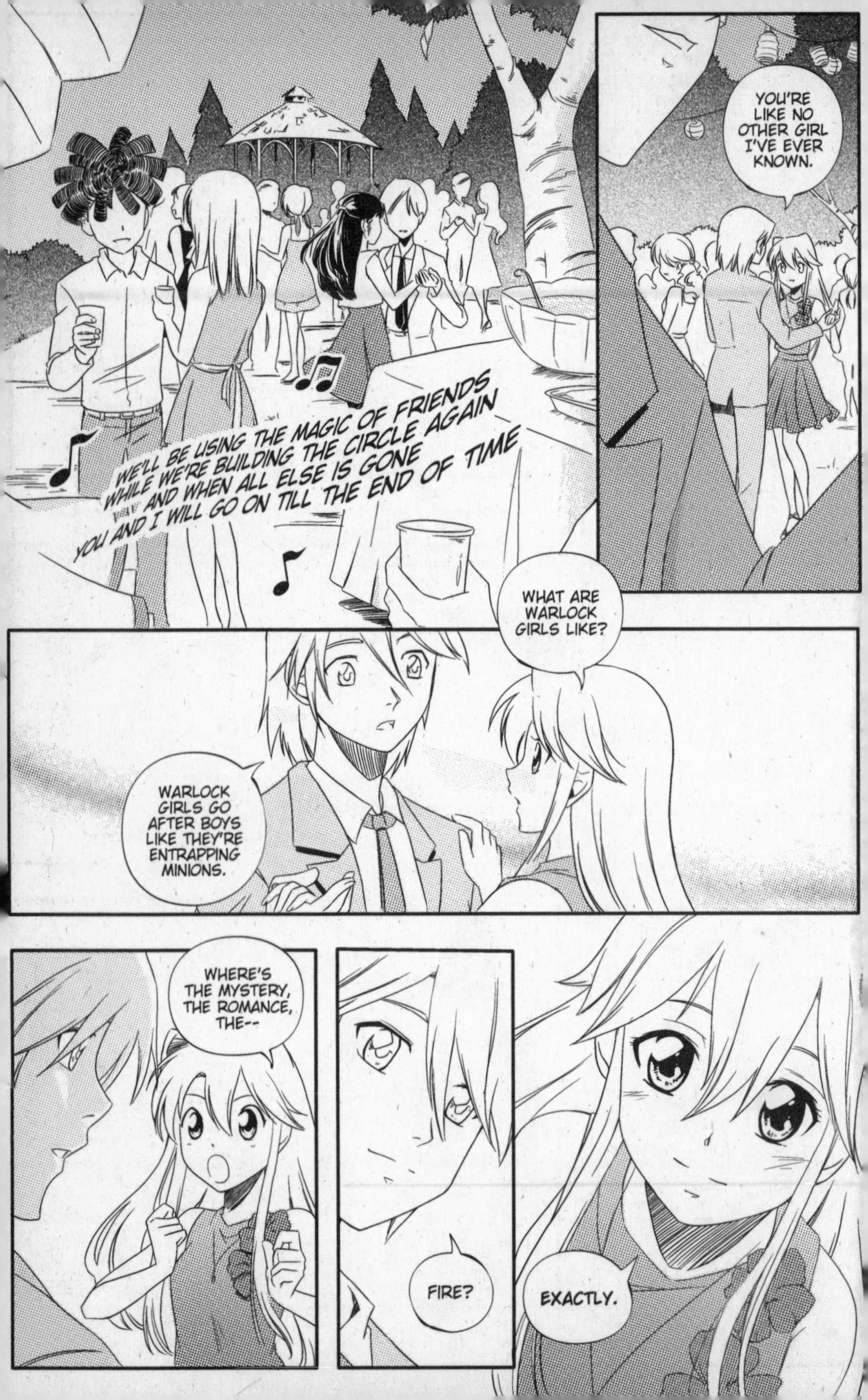
WE'LL BE USING THE MAGIC OF FRIENDS
WHILE WE'RE BUILDING THE CIRCLE AGAIN
AND WHEN ALL ELSE IS GONE
YOU AND I WILL GO ON TILL THE END OF TIME
YOU'RE LIKE NO OTHER GIRL I'VE EVER KNOWN.
WHAT ARE WARLOCK GIRLS LIKE?
WARLOCK GIRLS GO AFTER BOYS LIKE THEY'RE ENTRAPPING MINIONS.
WHERE'S THE MYSTERY, THE ROMANCE, THE--
FIRE?
EXACTLY.

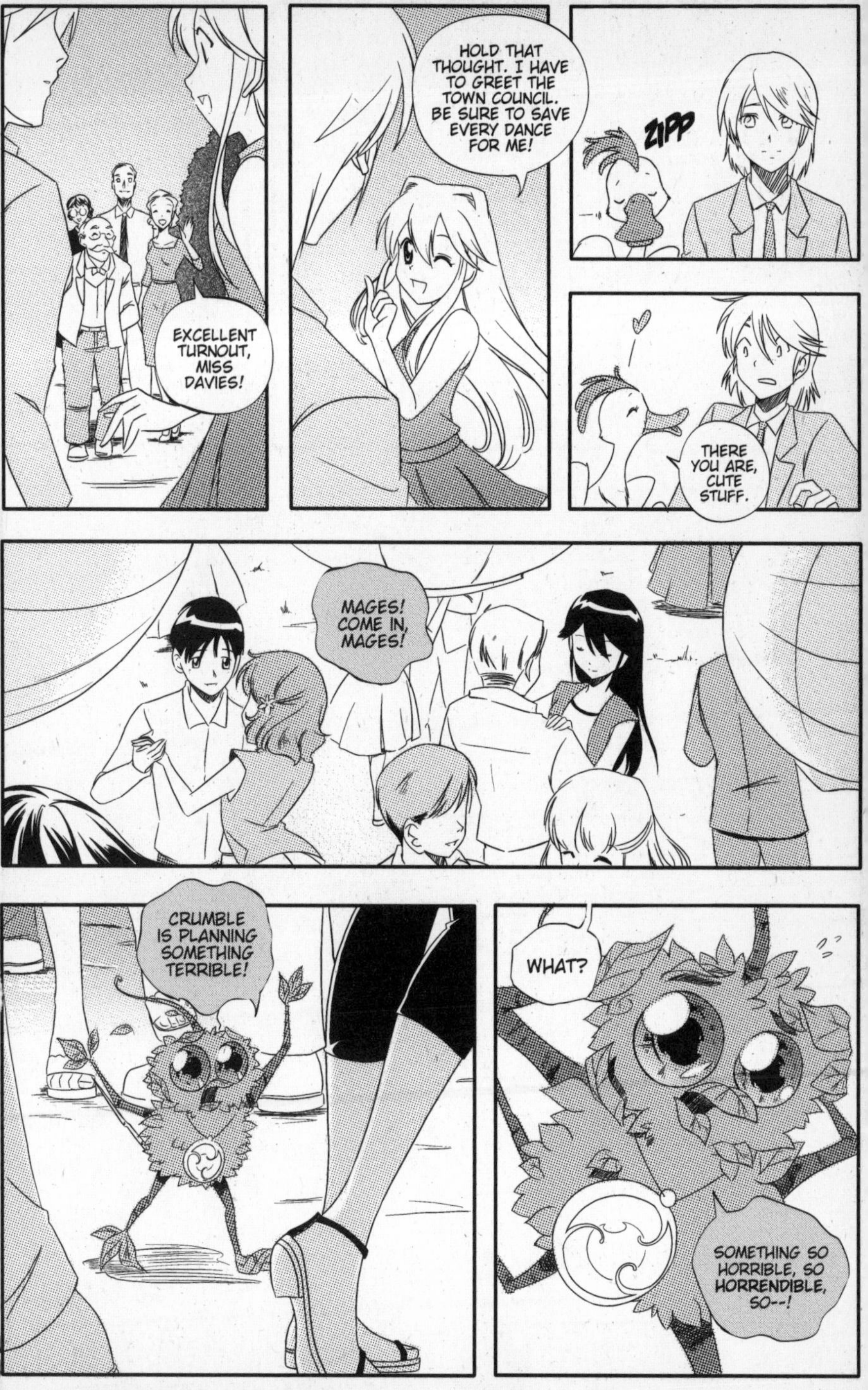
EXCELLENT TURNOUT, MISS DAVIES!
HOLD THAT THOUGHT. I HAVE TO GREET THE TOWN COUNCIL. BE SURE TO SAVE EVERY DANCE FOR ME!
ZIPP
THERE YOU ARE, CUTE STUFF.
MAGES! COME IN, MAGES!
CRUMBLE IS PLANNING SOMETHING TERRIBLE!
WHAT?
SOMETHING SO HORRIBLE, SO HORRENDIBLE, SO--!

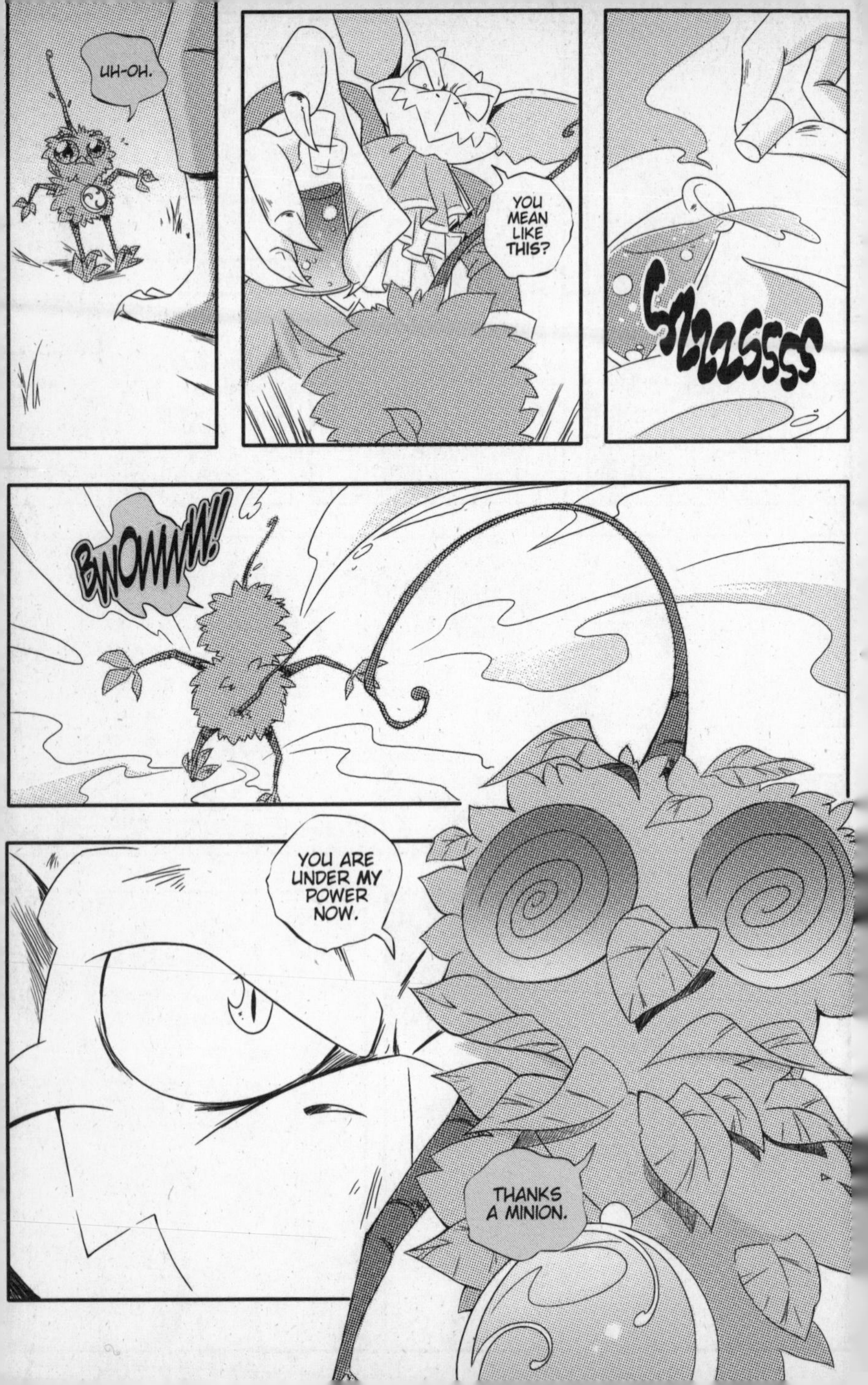
UH-OH.
YOU MEAN LIKE THIS?
SZZZSSSS
BWOWWW!!
YOU ARE UNDER MY POWER NOW.
THANKS A MINION.

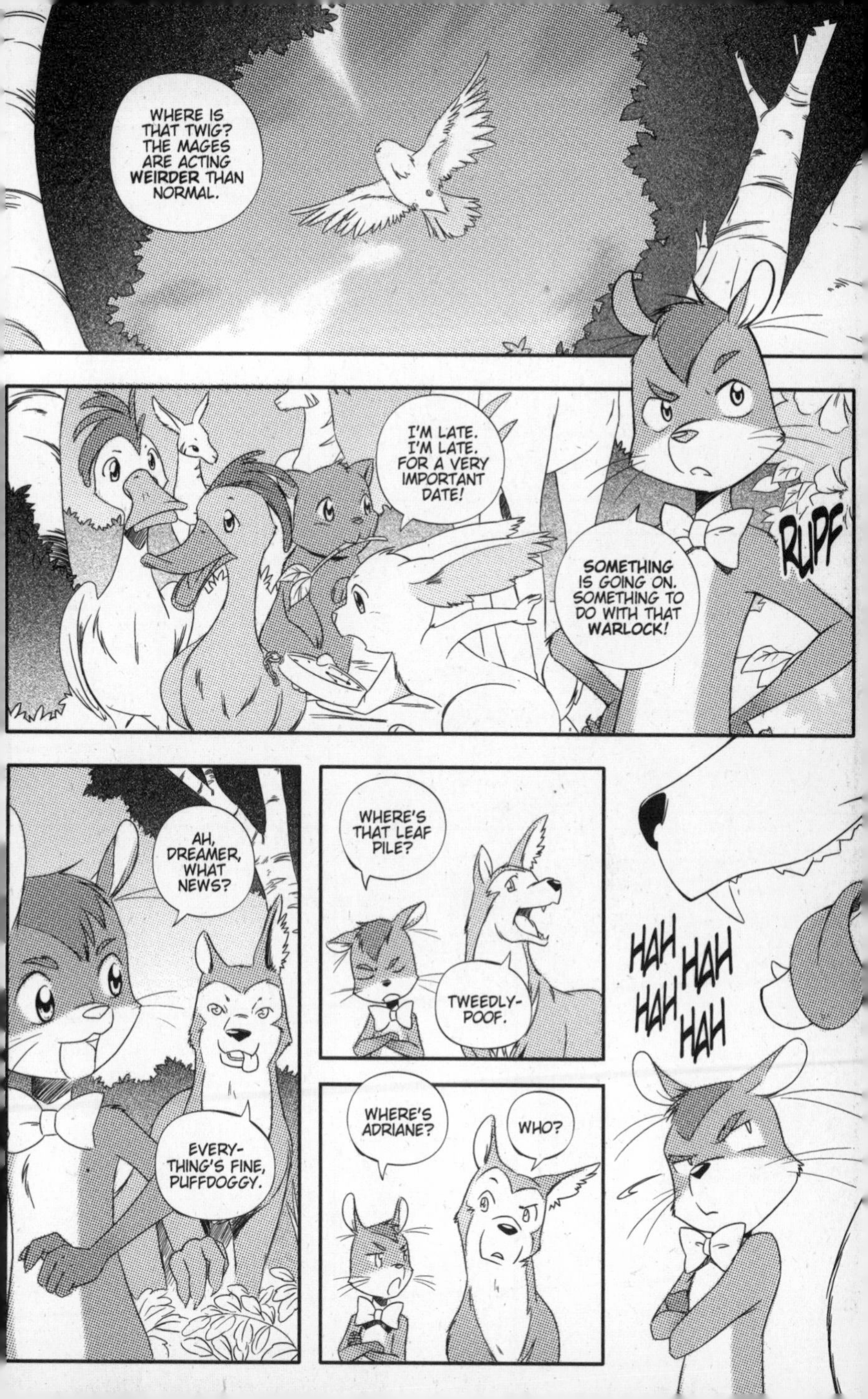
WHERE IS THAT TWIG? THE MAGES ARE ACTING WEIRDER THAN NORMAL.
I'M LATE. I'M LATE. FOR A VERY IMPORTANT DATE!
SOMETHING IS GOING ON. SOMETHING TO DO WITH THAT WARLOCK!
RUFF
AH, DREAMER, WHAT NEWS?
EVERY-THING'S FINE, PUFFDOGGY.
WHERE'S THAT LEAF PILE?
TWEEDLY-POOF.
HAH HAH HAH HAH
WHERE'S ADRIANE?
WHO?

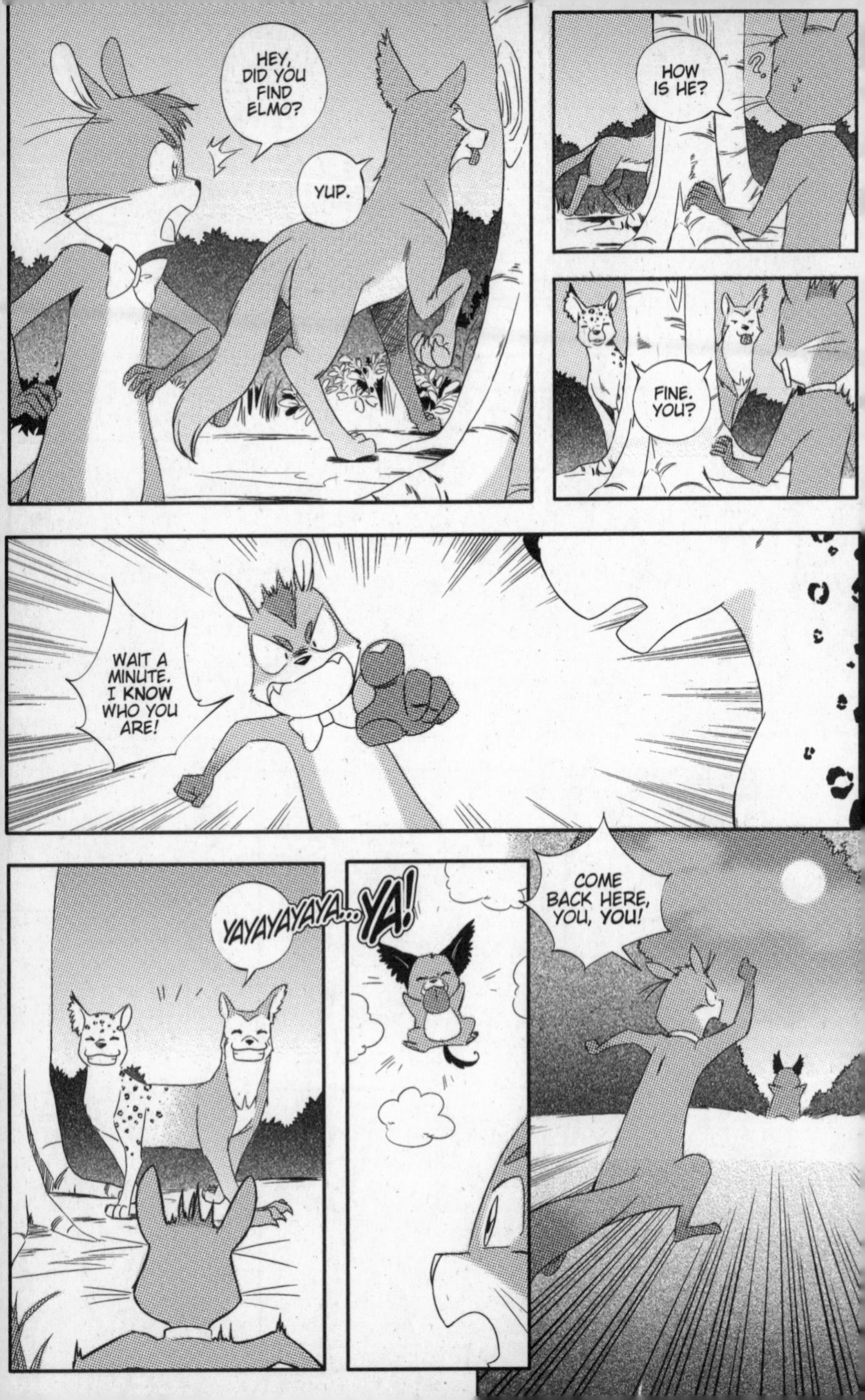
HEY, DID YOU FIND ELMO?
YUP.
HOW IS HE?
FINE. YOU?
WAIT A MINUTE. I KNOW WHO YOU ARE!
YAYAYAYAYA...YA!
COME BACK HERE, YOU, YOU!

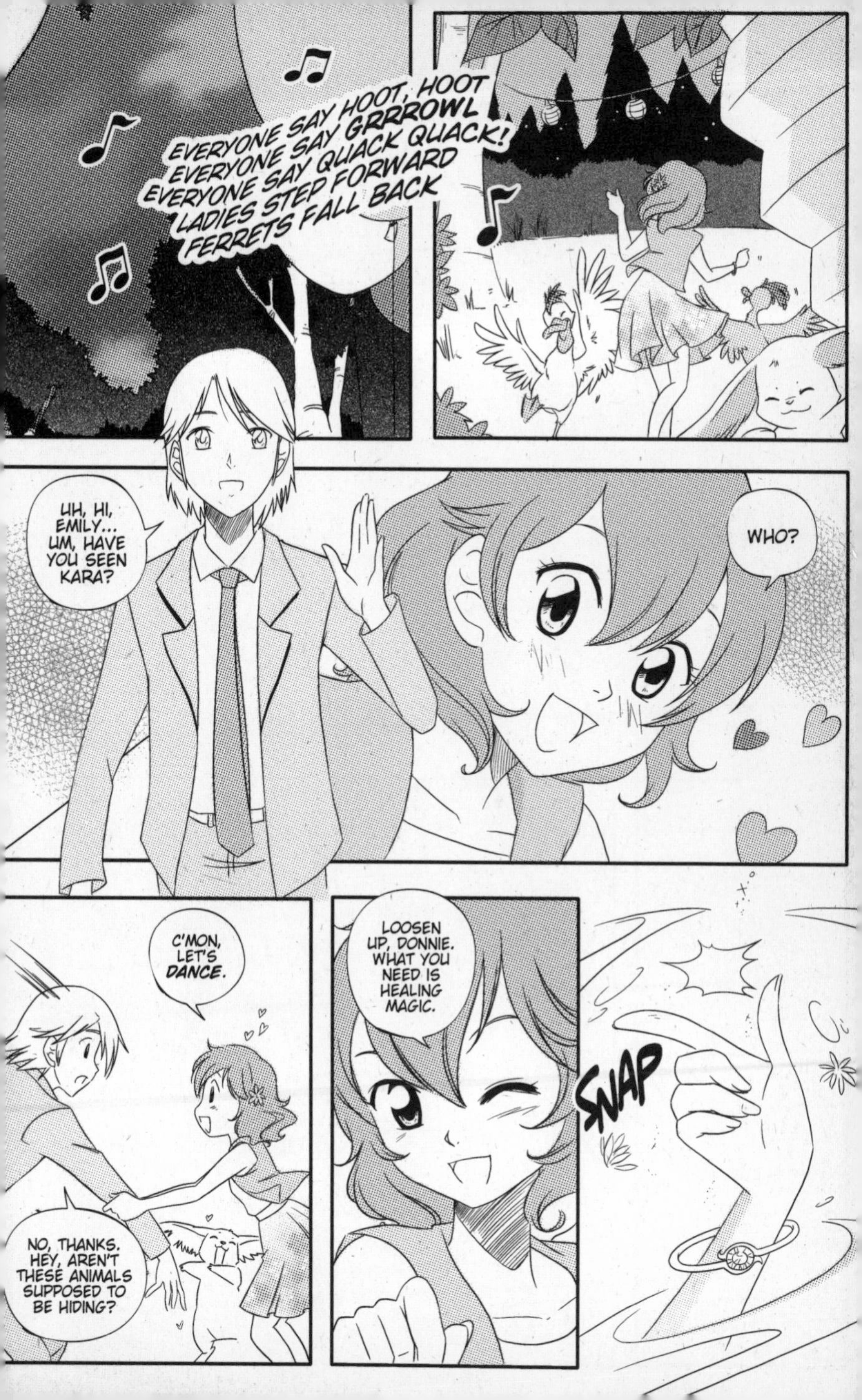
EVERYONE SAY HOOT, HOOT
EVERYONE SAY GRRROWL
EVERYONE SAY QUACK QUACK!
LADIES STEP FORWARD
FERRETS FALL BACK
UH, HI, EMILY... UM, HAVE YOU SEEN KARA?
WHO?
C'MON, LET'S DANCE.
NO, THANKS. HEY, AREN'T THESE ANIMALS SUPPOSED TO BE HIDING?
LOOSEN UP, DONNIE. WHAT YOU NEED IS HEALING MAGIC.
SNAP

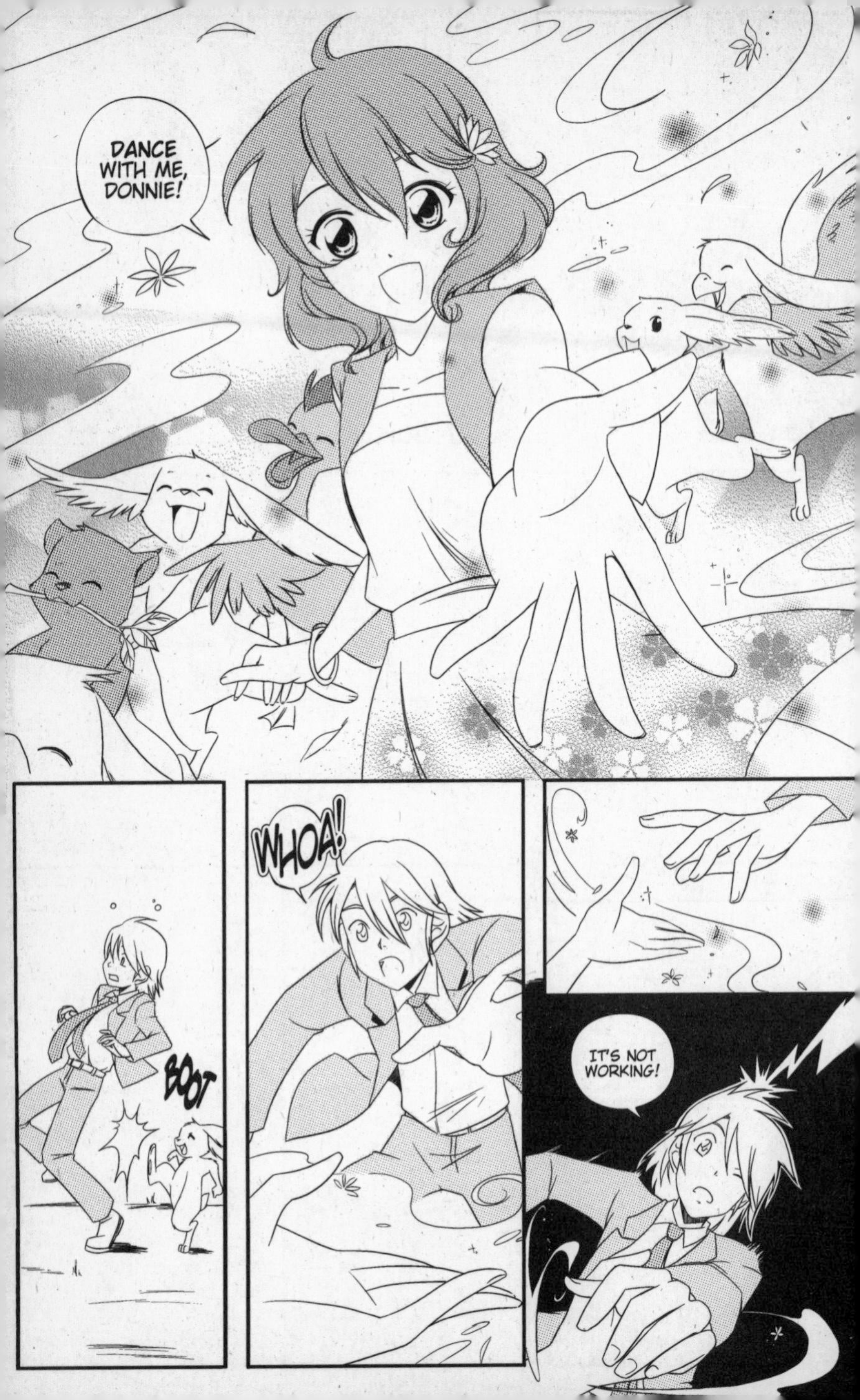
DANCE WITH ME, DONNIE!
BOOT
WHOA!
IT'S NOT WORKING!

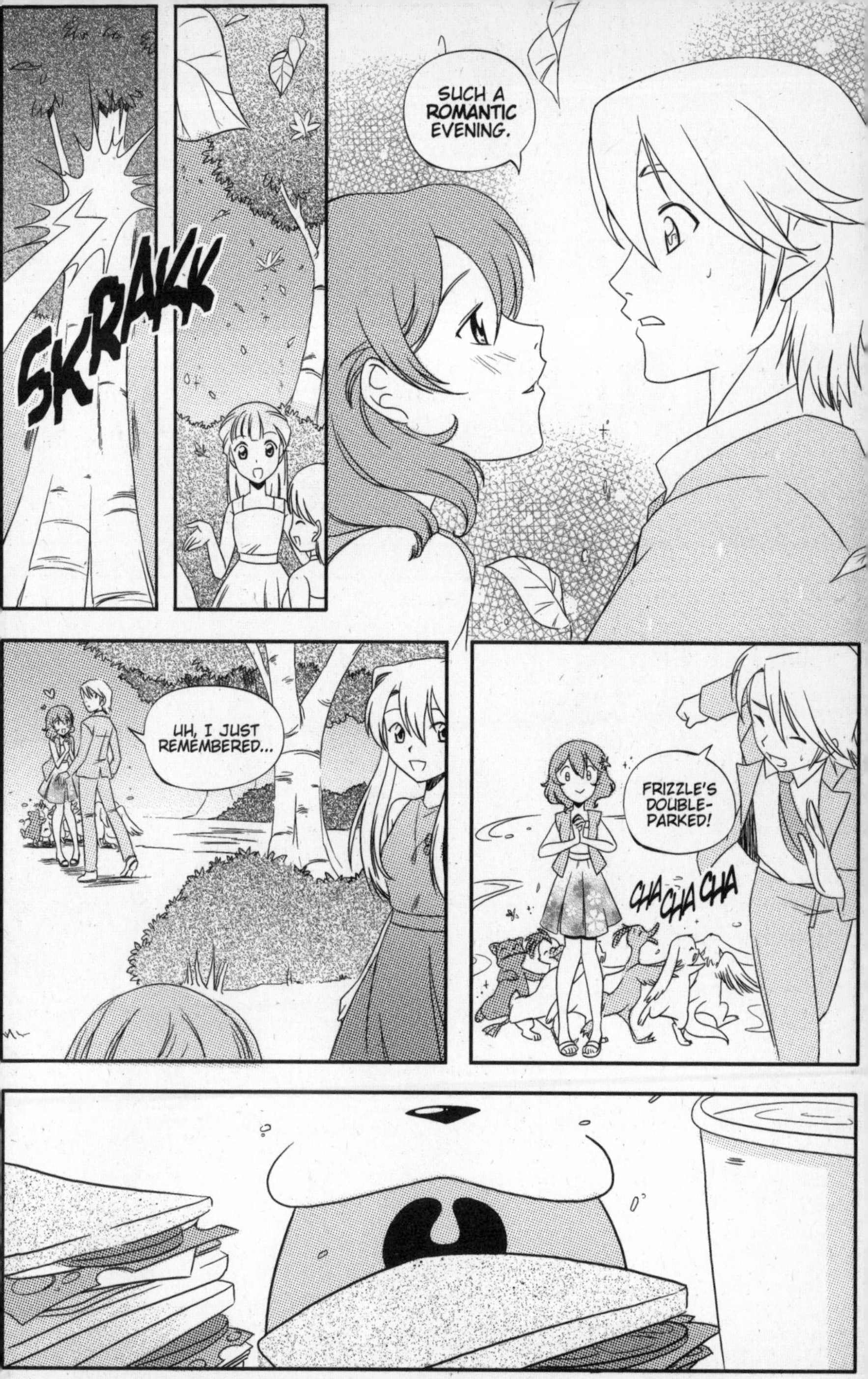
SKRAKK
SUCH A ROMANTIC EVENING.
UH, I JUST REMEMBERED...
FRIZZLE'S DOUBLE-PARKED!
CHA CHA CHA

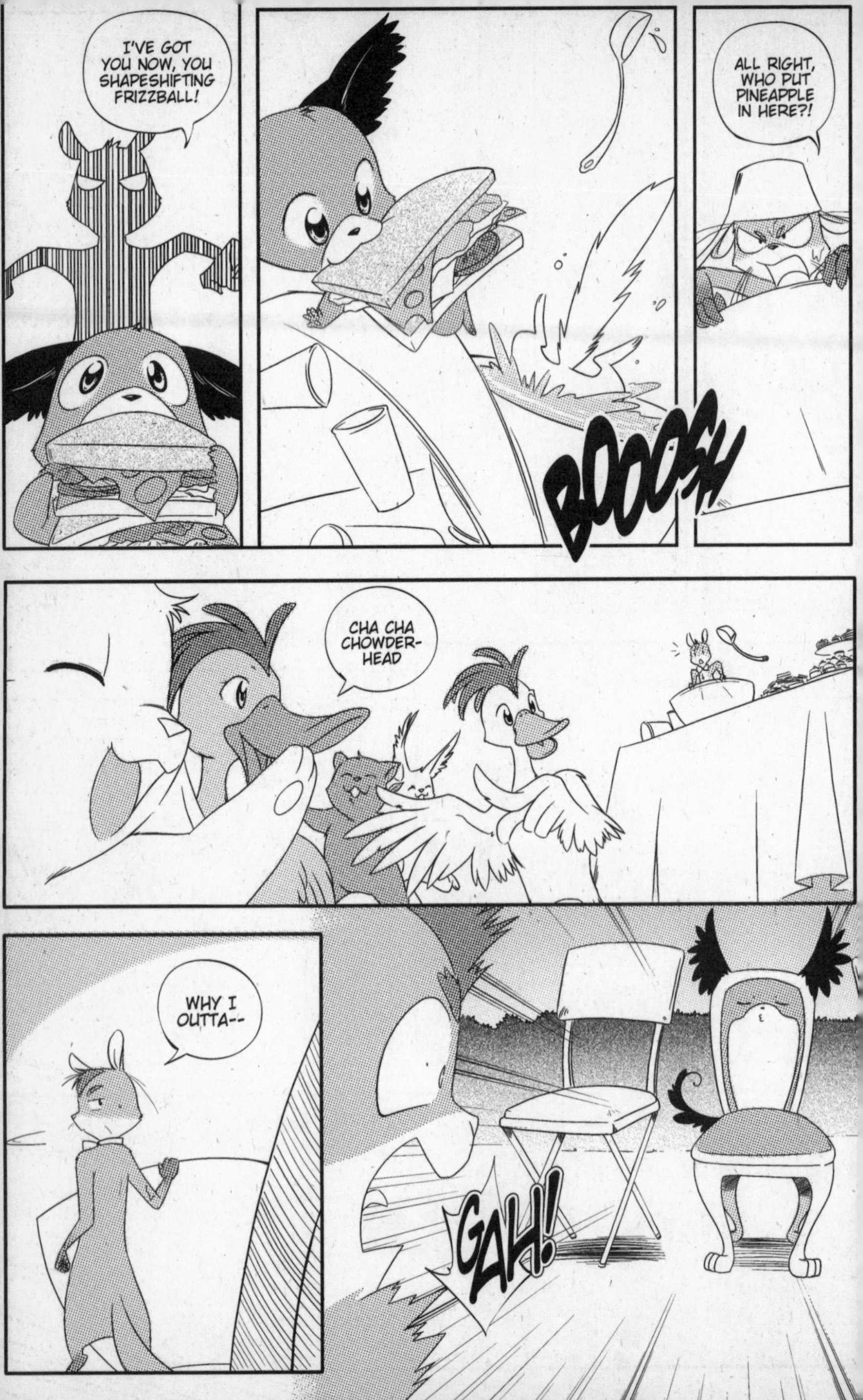
I'VE GOT YOU NOW, YOU SHAPESHIFTING FRIZZBALL!
BOOOSH
ALL RIGHT, WHO PUT PINEAPPLE IN HERE?!
CHA CHA CHOWDER-HEAD
WHY I OUTTA--
GAH!

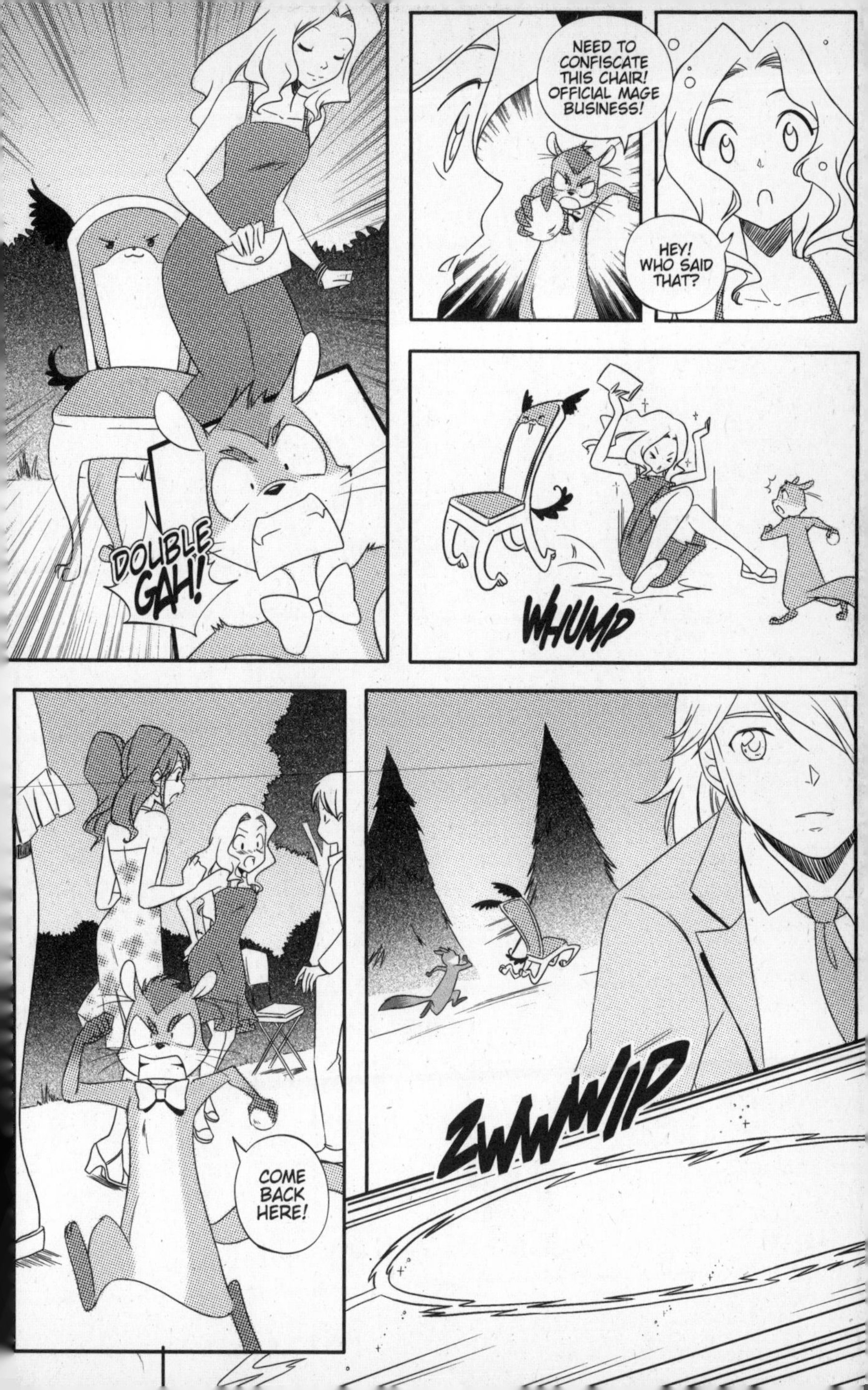
DOUBLE GAH!
NEED TO CONFISCATE THIS CHAIR! OFFICIAL MAGE BUSINESS!
HEY! WHO SAID THAT?
WHUMP
COME BACK HERE!
ZWWWIP

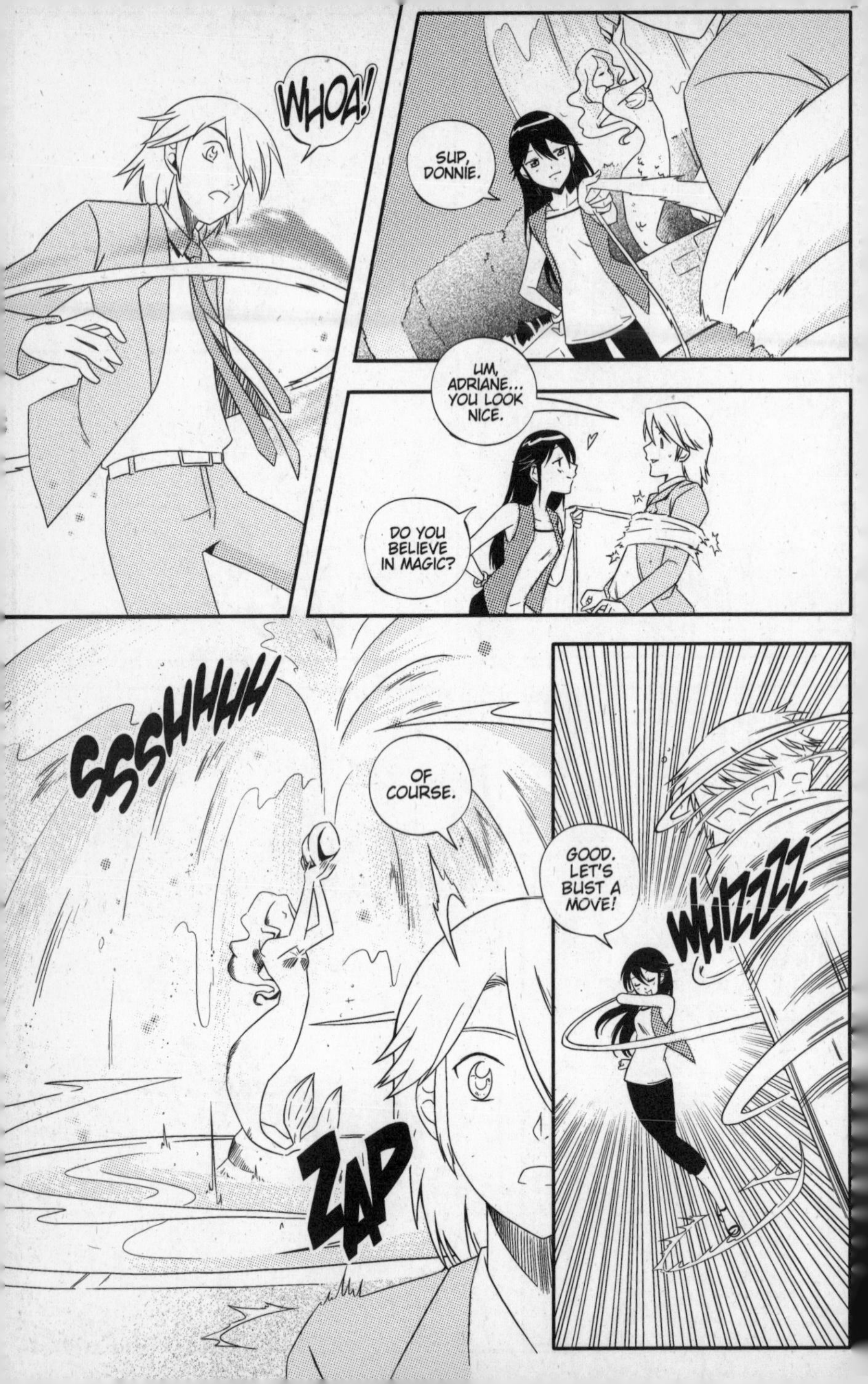
WHOA!
SUP, DONNIE.
UM, ADRIANE... YOU LOOK NICE.
DO YOU BELIEVE IN MAGIC?
SSSHHHH
OF COURSE.
ZAP
GOOD. LET'S BUST A MOVE!
WHIZZZZ

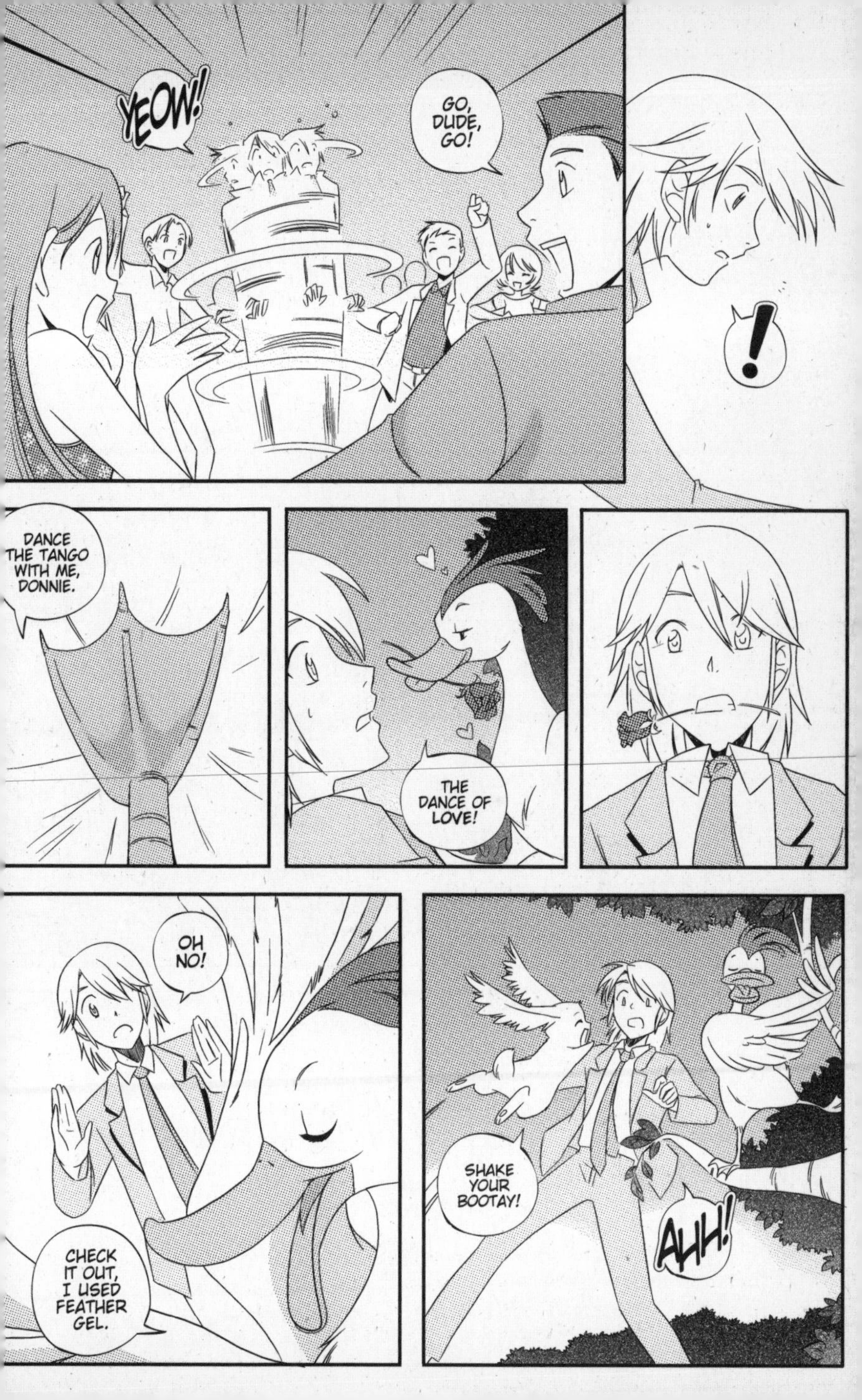
YEOW!
GO, DUDE, GO!
!
DANCE THE TANGO WITH ME, DONNIE.
THE DANCE OF LOVE!
OH NO!
CHECK IT OUT, I USED FEATHER GEL.
SHAKE YOUR BOOTAY!
AHH!

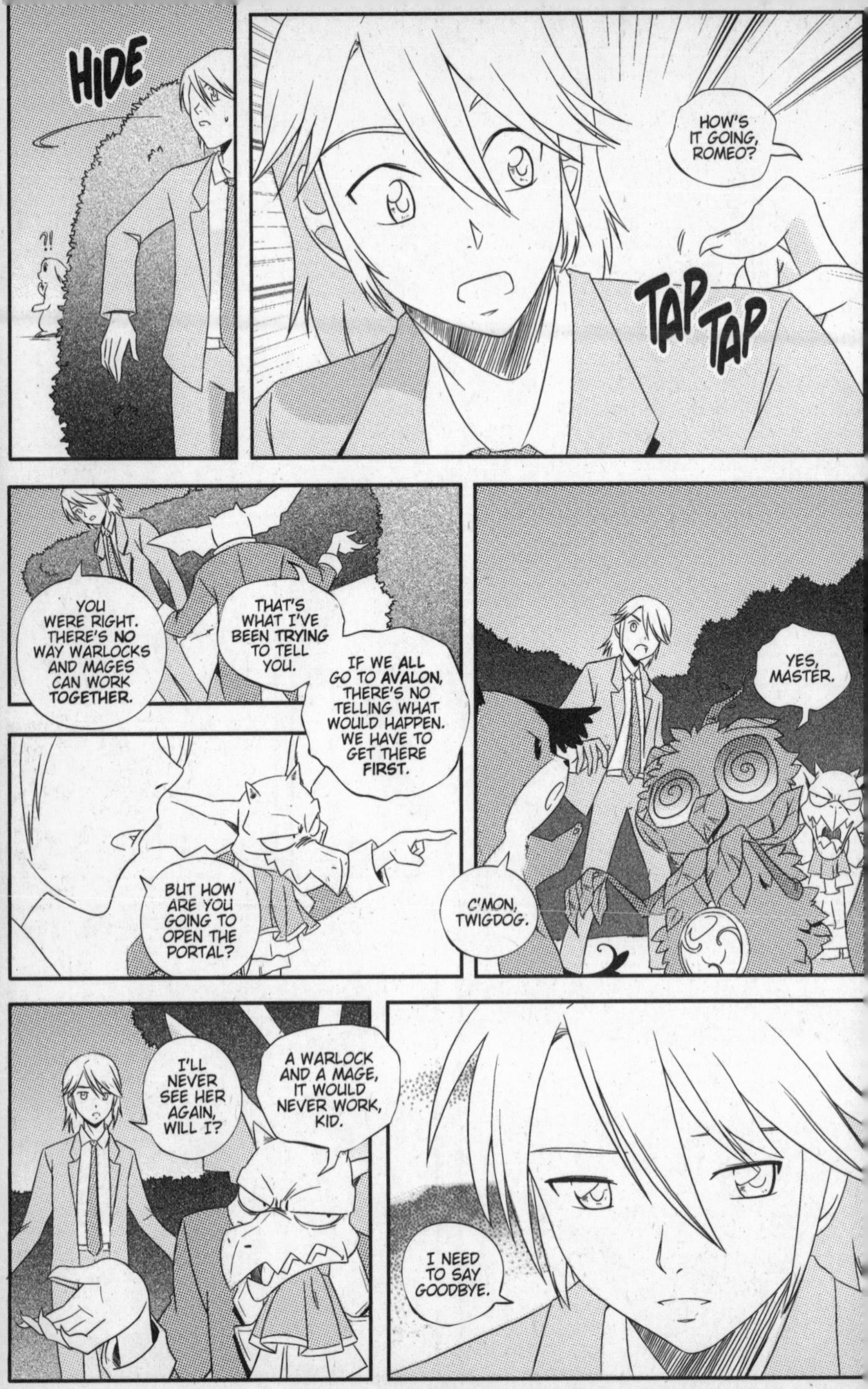
HIDE
?!
HOW'S IT GOING, ROMEO?
TAP TAP
YOU WERE RIGHT. THERE'S NO WAY WARLOCKS AND MAGES CAN WORK TOGETHER.
THAT'S WHAT I'VE BEEN TRYING TO TELL YOU.
IF WE ALL GO TO AVALON, THERE'S NO TELLING WHAT WOULD HAPPEN. WE HAVE TO GET THERE FIRST.
BUT HOW ARE YOU GOING TO OPEN THE PORTAL?
YES, MASTER.
C'MON, TWIGDOG.
I'LL NEVER SEE HER AGAIN, WILL I?
A WARLOCK AND A MAGE, IT WOULD NEVER WORK, KID.
I NEED TO SAY GOODBYE.

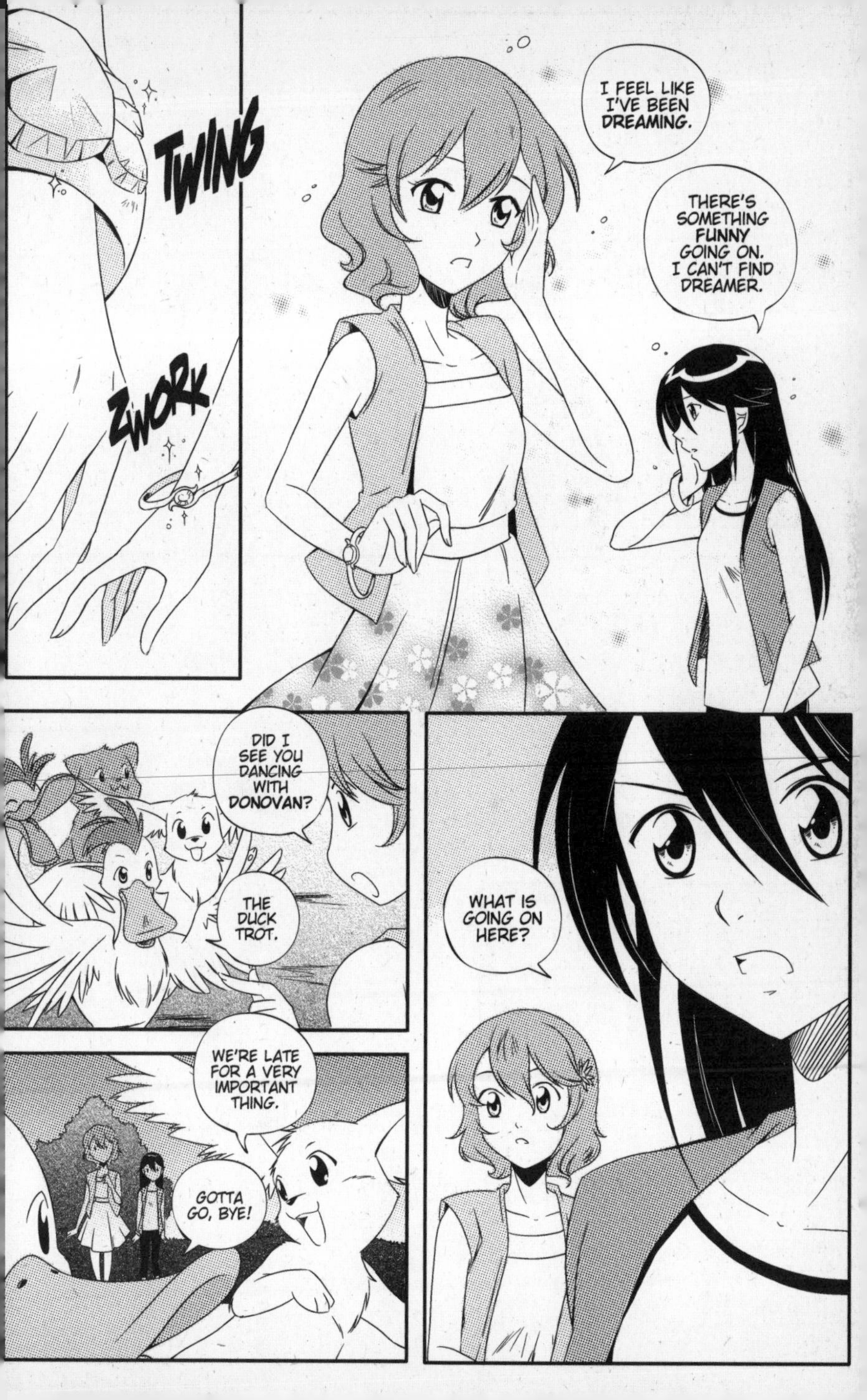
TWING
ZWORK
I FEEL LIKE I'VE BEEN DREAMING.
THERE'S SOMETHING FUNNY GOING ON. I CAN'T FIND DREAMER.
DID I SEE YOU DANCING WITH DONOVAN?
THE DUCK TROT.
WHAT IS GOING ON HERE?
WE'RE LATE FOR A VERY IMPORTANT THING.
GOTTA GO, BYE!

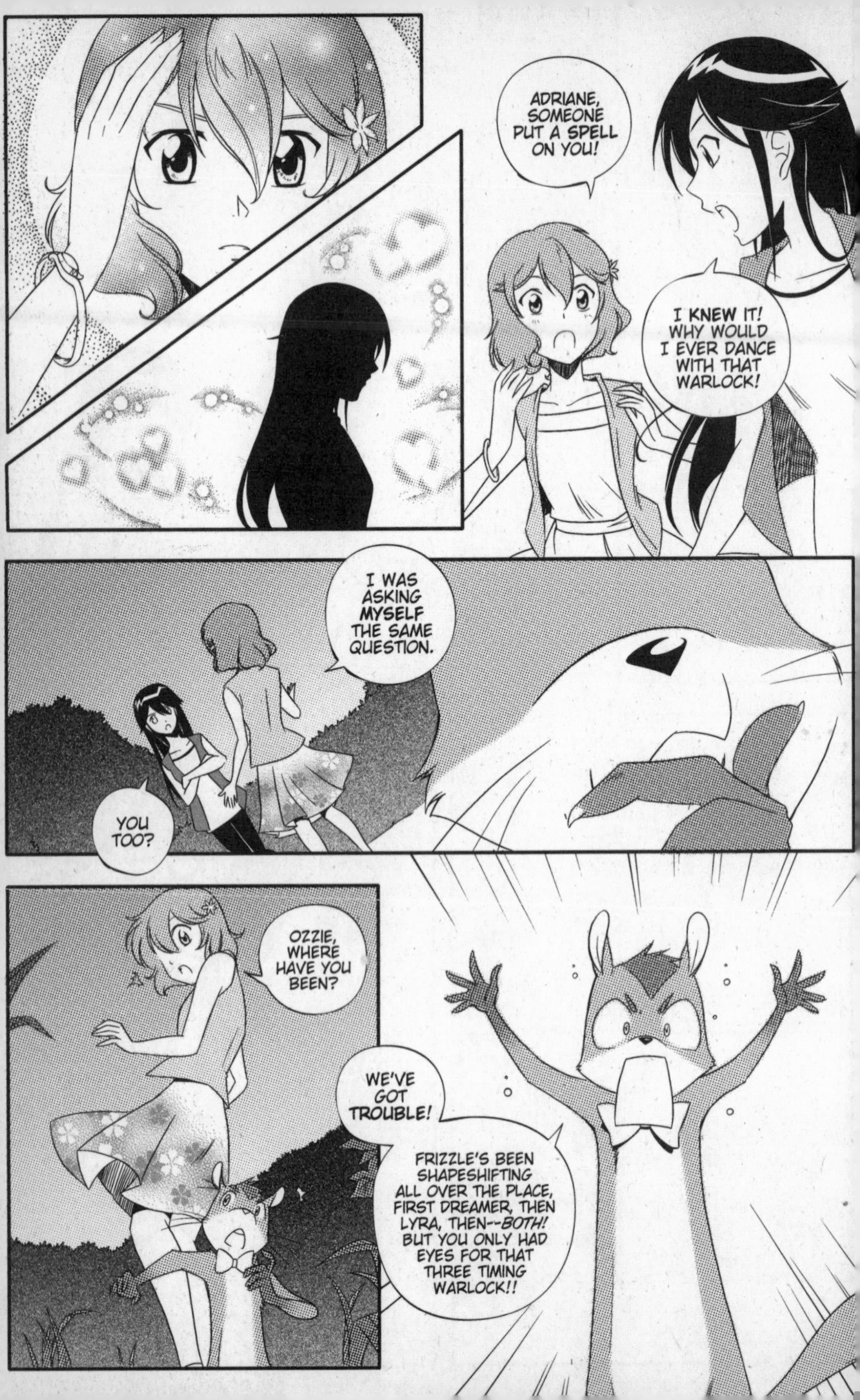
ADRIANE, SOMEONE PUT A SPELL ON YOU!
I KNEW IT! WHY WOULD I EVER DANCE WITH THAT WARLOCK!
YOU TOO?
I WAS ASKING MYSELF THE SAME QUESTION.
OZZIE, WHERE HAVE YOU BEEN?
WE'VE GOT TROUBLE!
FRIZZLE'S BEEN SHAPESHIFTING ALL OVER THE PLACE, FIRST DREAMER, THEN LYRA, THEN--*BOTH!* BUT YOU ONLY HAD EYES FOR THAT THREE TIMING WARLOCK!!

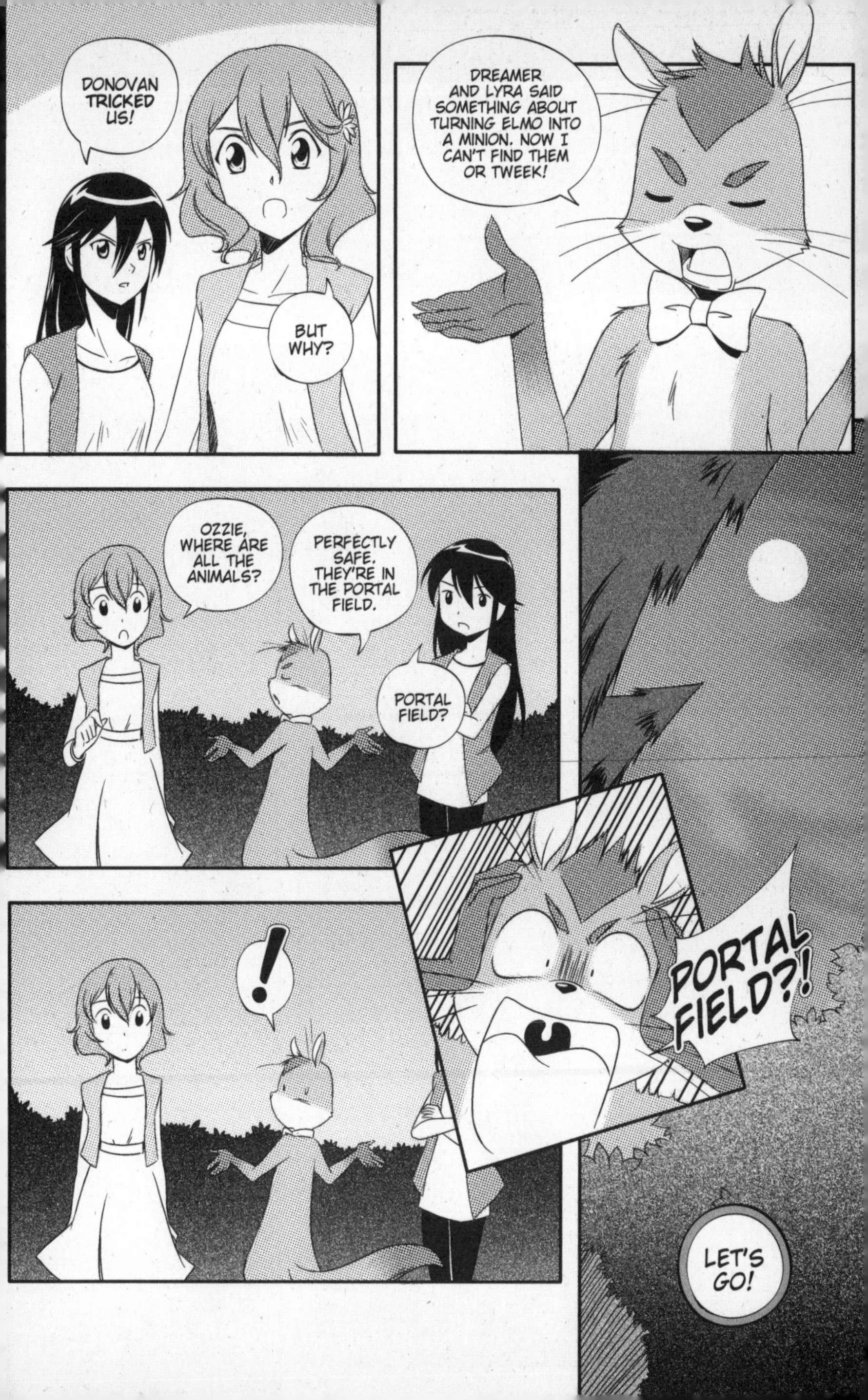
DONOVAN TRICKED US!
BUT WHY?
DREAMER AND LYRA SAID SOMETHING ABOUT TURNING ELMO INTO A MINION. NOW I CAN'T FIND THEM OR TWEEK!
OZZIE, WHERE ARE ALL THE ANIMALS?
PERFECTLY SAFE. THEY'RE IN THE PORTAL FIELD.
PORTAL FIELD?
!
PORTAL FIELD?!
LET'S GO!

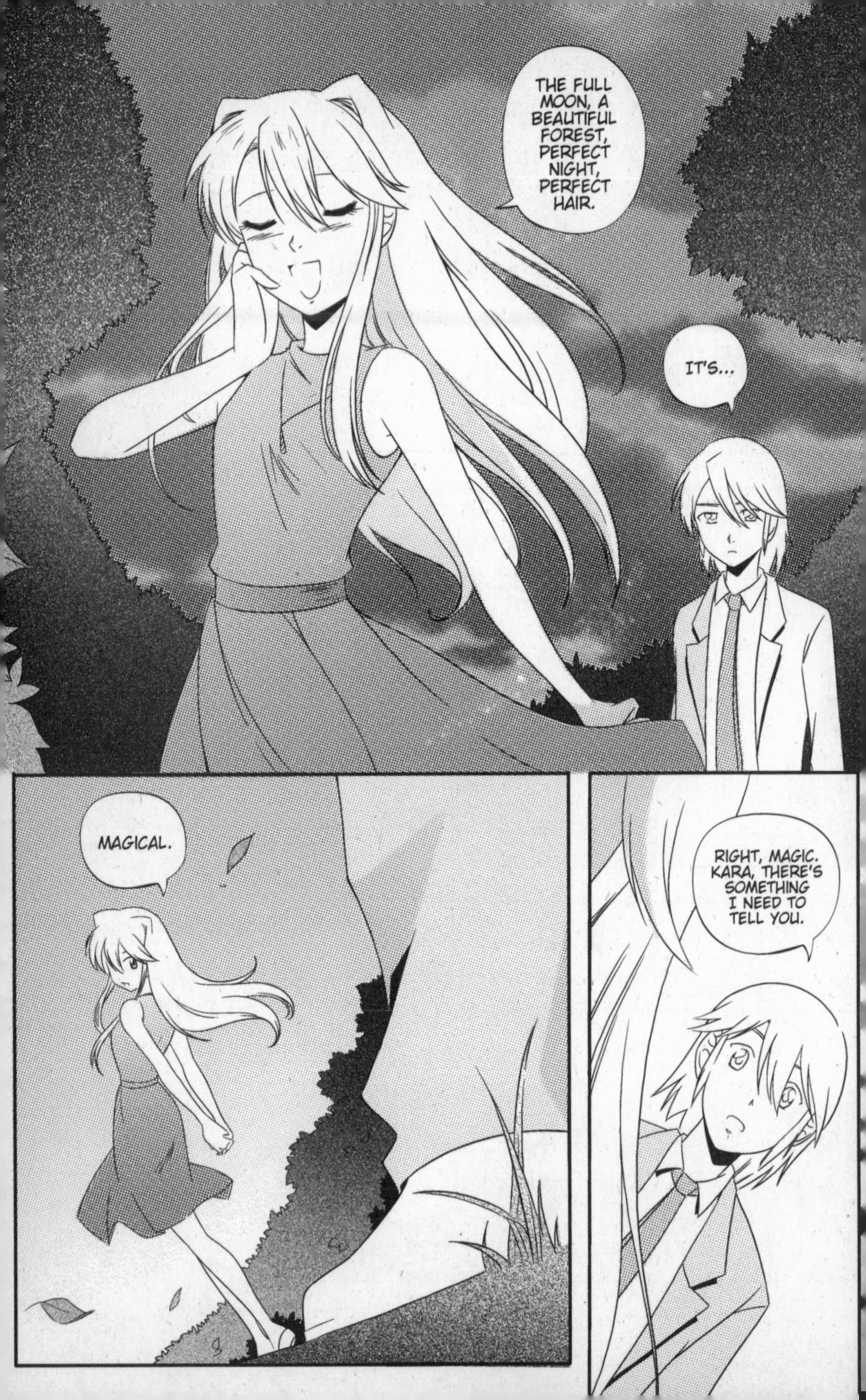
THE FULL MOON, A BEAUTIFUL FOREST, PERFECT NIGHT, PERFECT HAIR.
IT'S...
MAGICAL.
RIGHT, MAGIC. KARA, THERE'S SOMETHING I NEED TO TELL YOU.

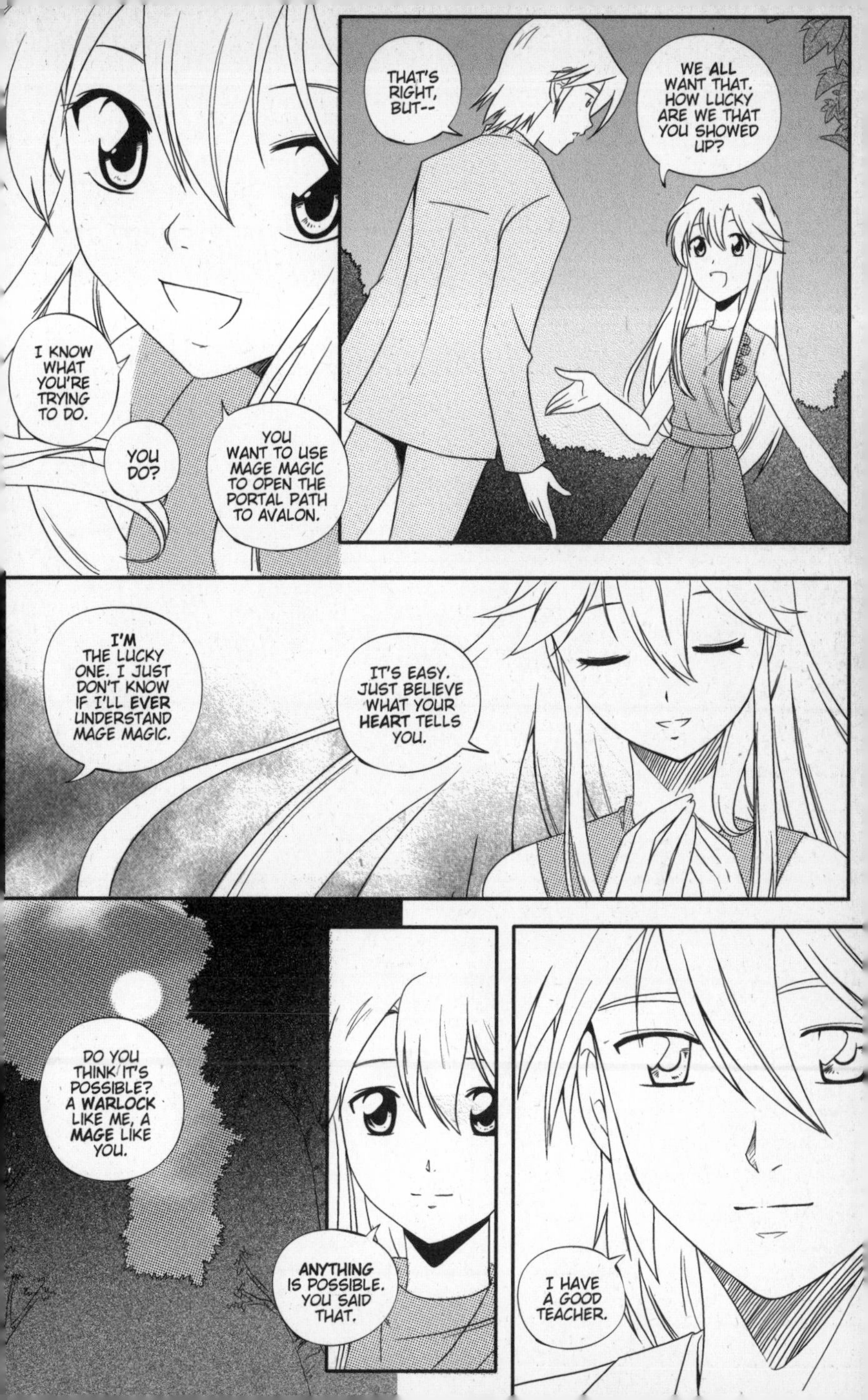
I KNOW WHAT YOU'RE TRYING TO DO.
YOU DO?
YOU WANT TO USE MAGE MAGIC TO OPEN THE PORTAL PATH TO AVALON.
THAT'S RIGHT, BUT--
WE **ALL** WANT THAT. HOW LUCKY ARE WE THAT YOU SHOWED UP?
I'M THE LUCKY ONE. I JUST DON'T KNOW IF I'LL **EVER** UNDERSTAND MAGE MAGIC.
IT'S EASY. JUST BELIEVE WHAT YOUR **HEART** TELLS YOU.
DO YOU THINK IT'S POSSIBLE? A **WARLOCK** LIKE ME, A **MAGE** LIKE YOU.
ANYTHING IS POSSIBLE. YOU SAID THAT.
I HAVE A GOOD TEACHER.

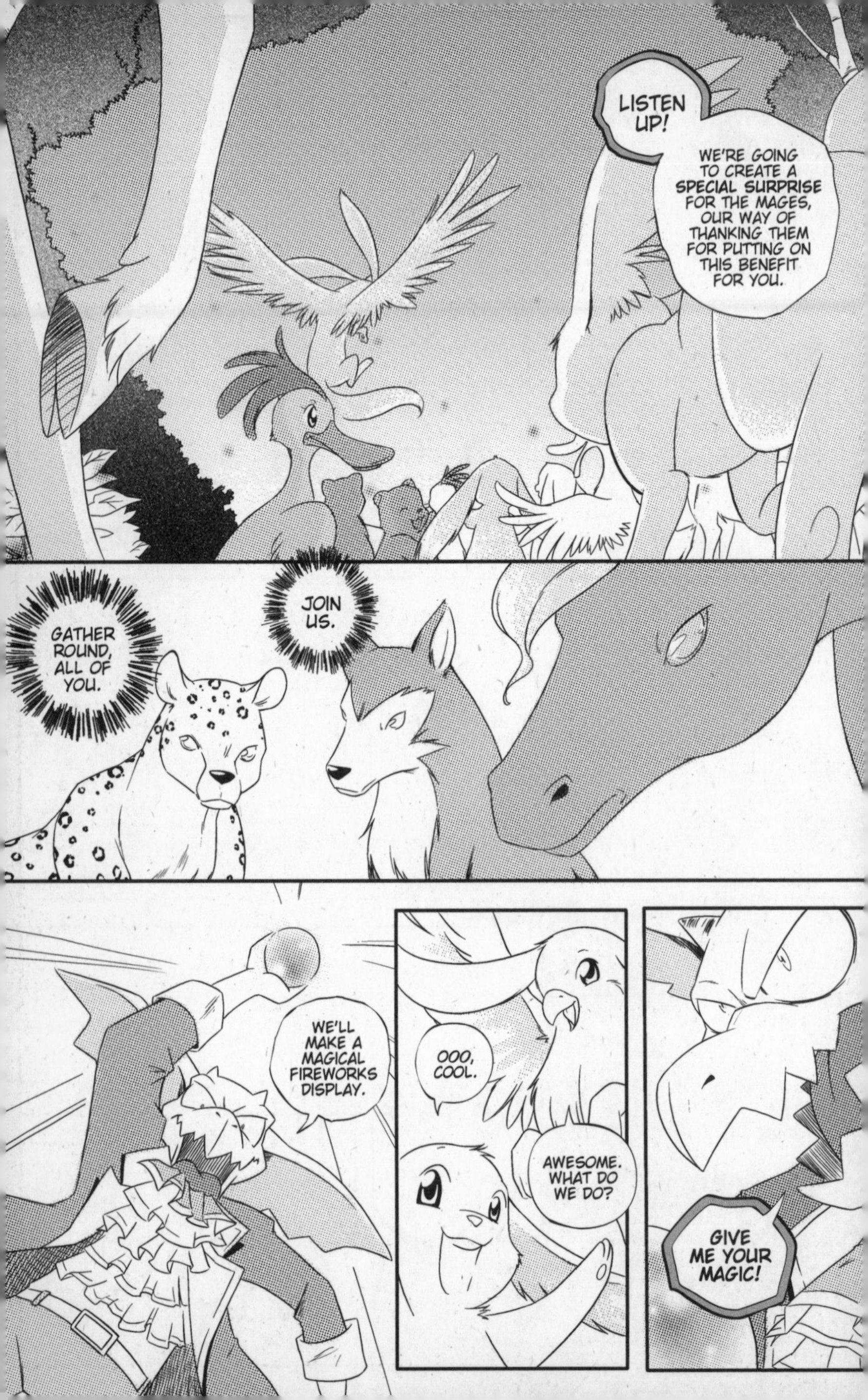
LISTEN UP!
WE'RE GOING TO CREATE A SPECIAL SURPRISE FOR THE MAGES, OUR WAY OF THANKING THEM FOR PUTTING ON THIS BENEFIT FOR YOU.
GATHER ROUND, ALL OF YOU.
JOIN US.
WE'LL MAKE A MAGICAL FIREWORKS DISPLAY.
OOO, COOL.
AWESOME. WHAT DO WE DO?
GIVE ME YOUR MAGIC!

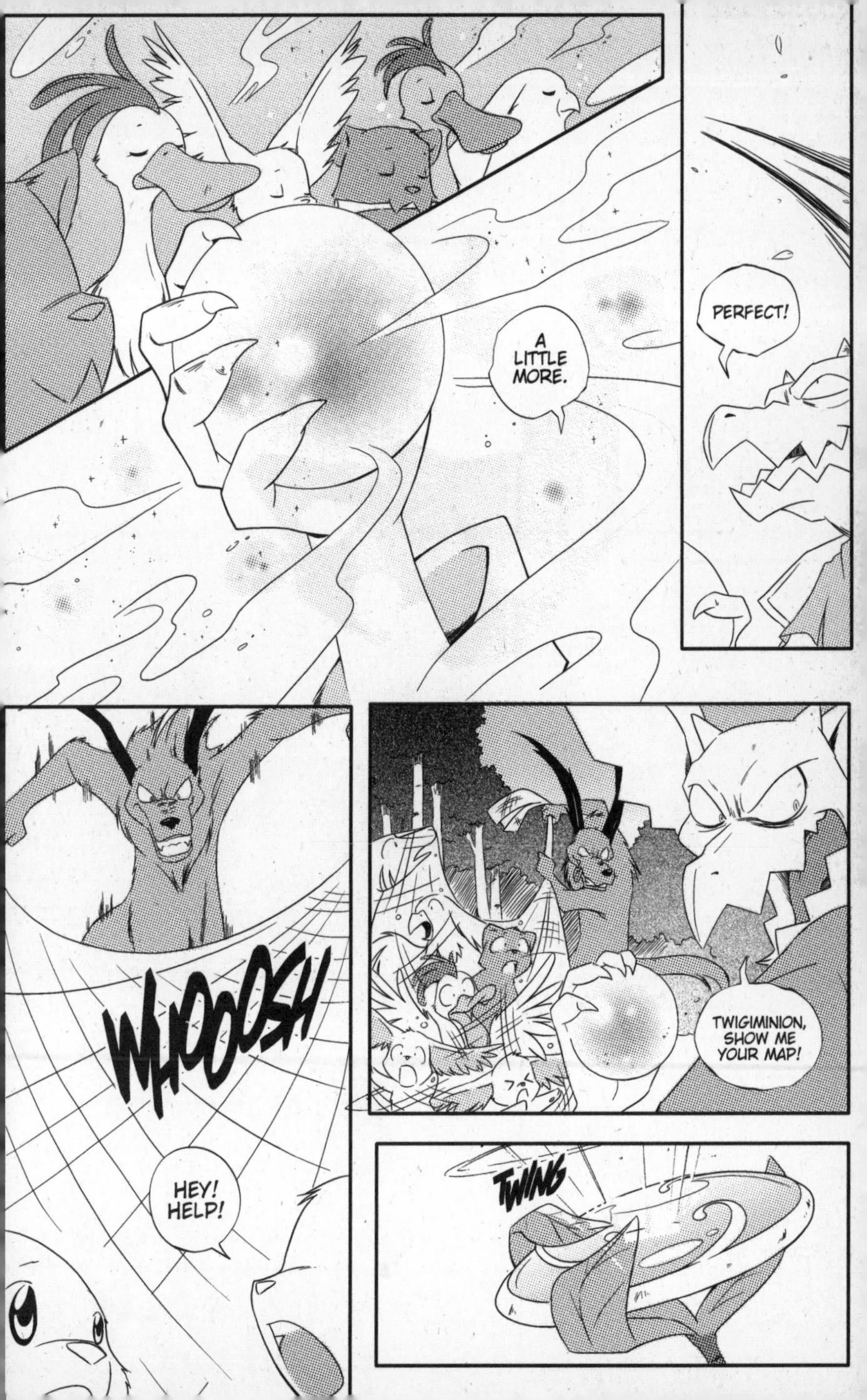
A LITTLE MORE.
PERFECT!
WHOOOSH
HEY! HELP!
TWIGIMINION, SHOW ME YOUR MAP!
TWING

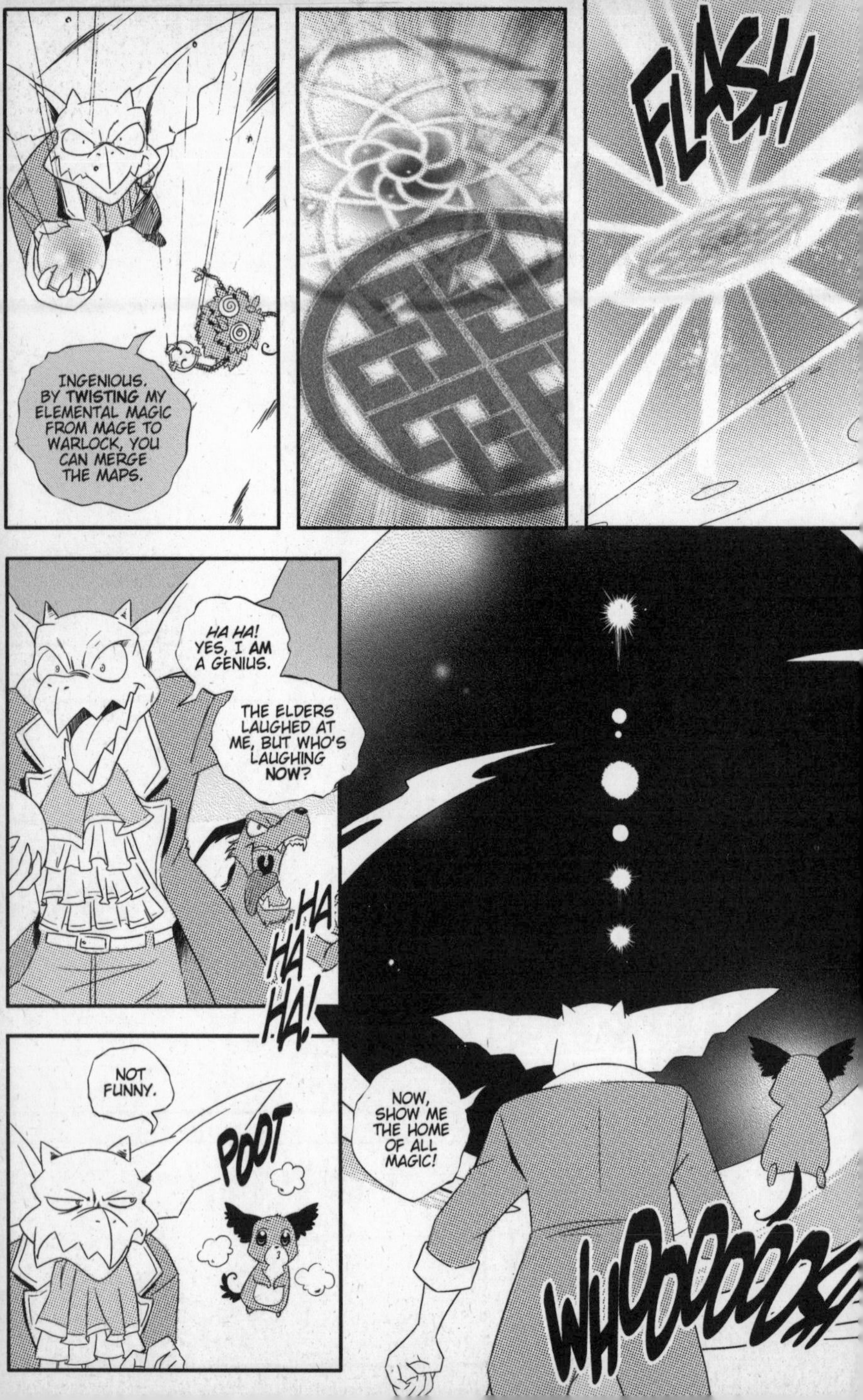

INGENIOUS. BY TWISTING MY ELEMENTAL MAGIC FROM MAGE TO WARLOCK, YOU CAN MERGE THE MAPS.
FLASH
HA HA! YES, I AM A GENIUS.
THE ELDERS LAUGHED AT ME, BUT WHO'S LAUGHING NOW?
HA HA HA!
NOT FUNNY.
POOT
NOW, SHOW ME THE HOME OF ALL MAGIC!
WHOOOOOSH

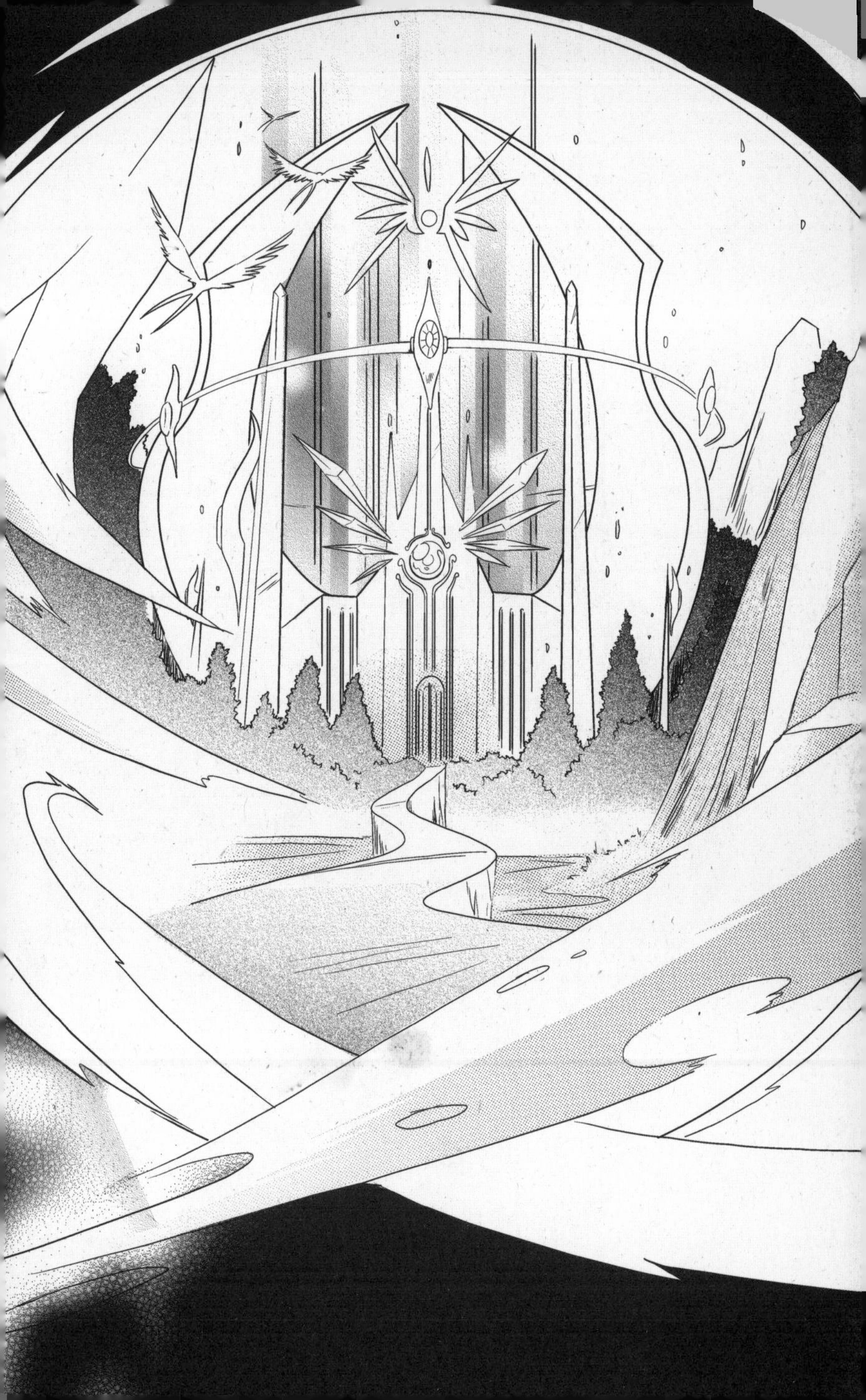

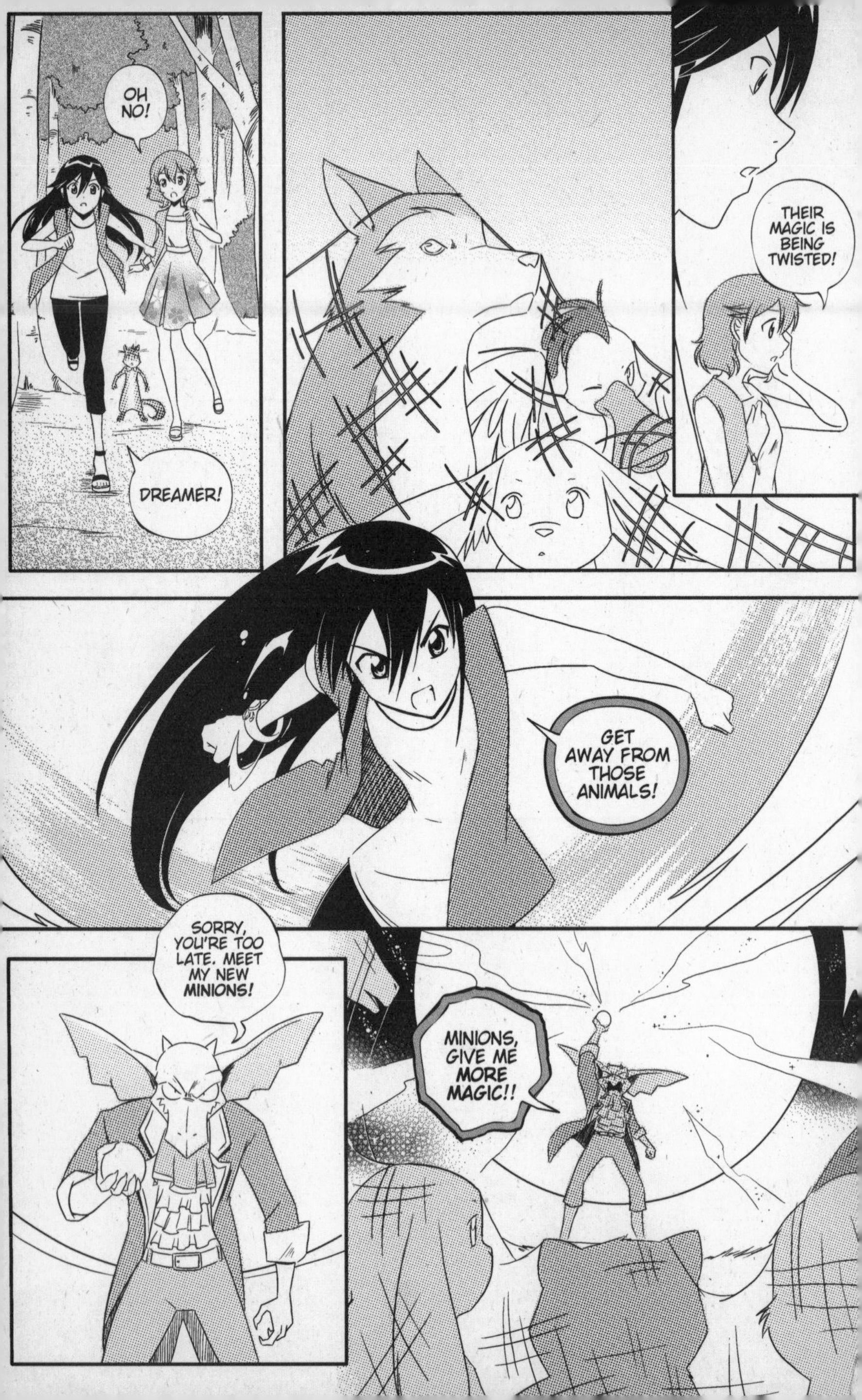
OH NO!
DREAMER!
THEIR MAGIC IS BEING TWISTED!
GET AWAY FROM THOSE ANIMALS!
SORRY, YOU'RE TOO LATE. MEET MY NEW MINIONS!
MINIONS, GIVE ME MORE MAGIC!!

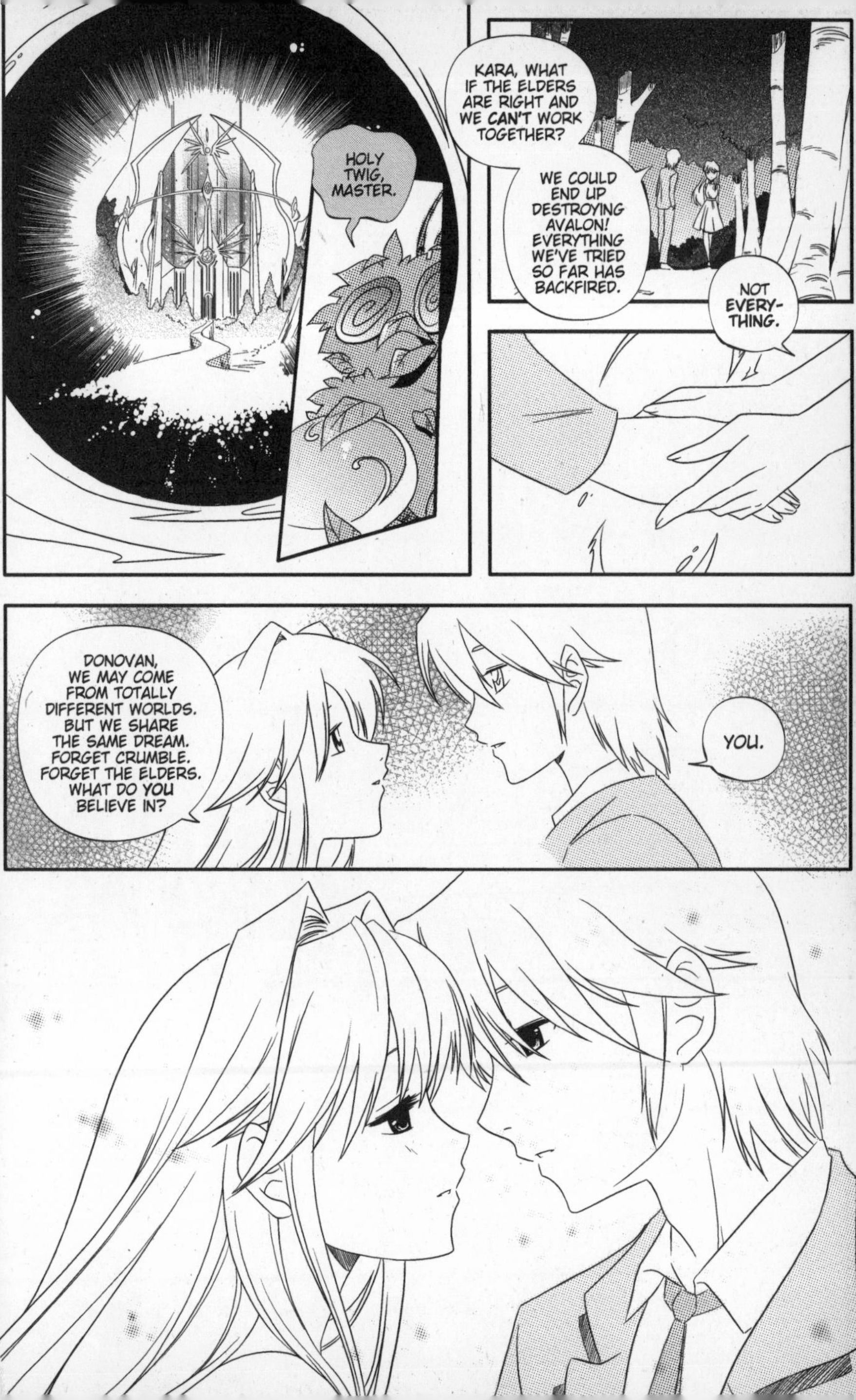
HOLY TWIG, MASTER.
KARA, WHAT IF THE ELDERS ARE RIGHT AND WE CAN'T WORK TOGETHER?
WE COULD END UP DESTROYING AVALON! EVERYTHING WE'VE TRIED SO FAR HAS BACKFIRED.
NOT EVERYTHING.
DONOVAN, WE MAY COME FROM TOTALLY DIFFERENT WORLDS. BUT WE SHARE THE SAME DREAM. FORGET CRUMBLE. FORGET THE ELDERS. WHAT DO YOU BELIEVE IN?
YOU.

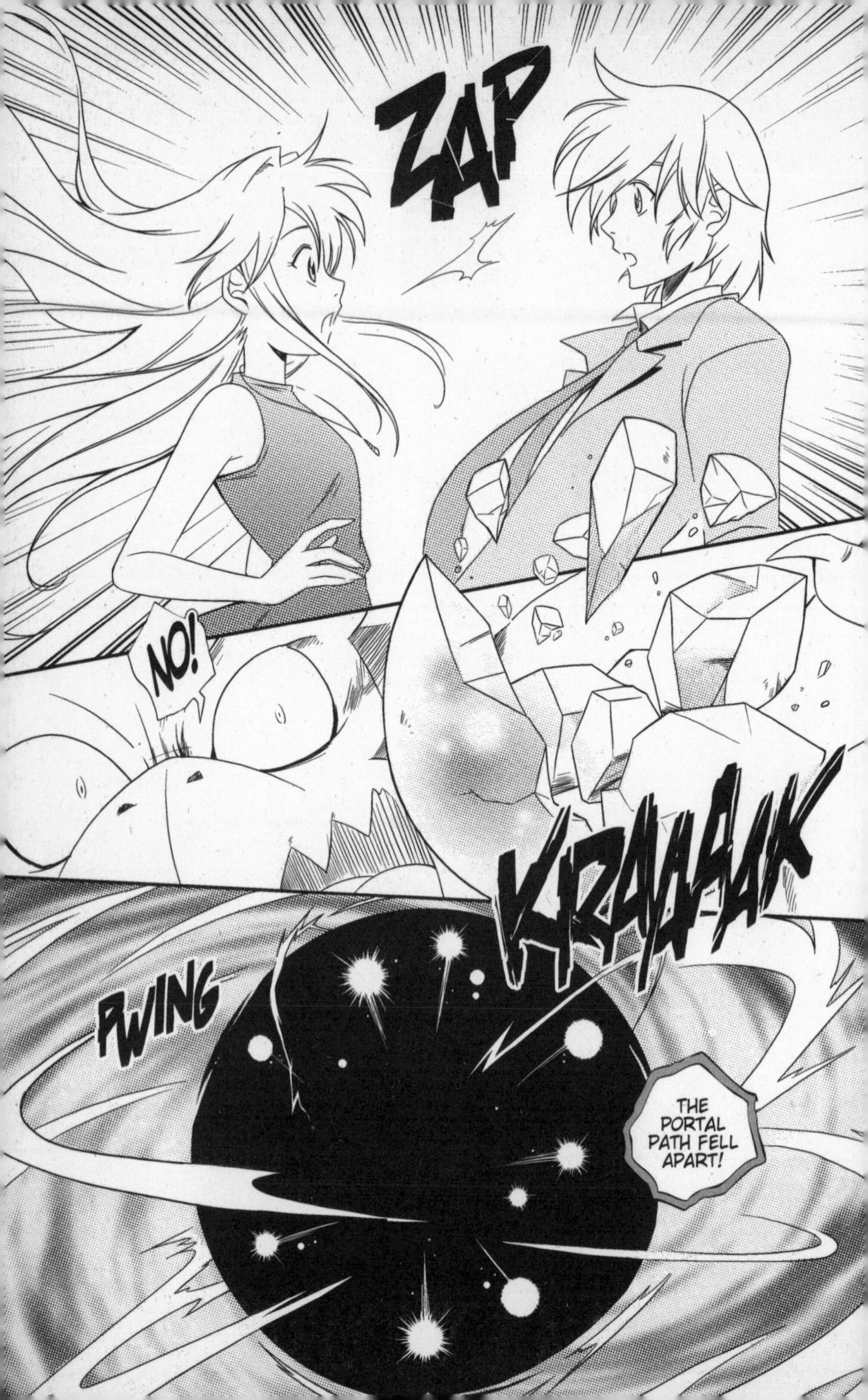
ZAP
NO!
KRAAAAK
PWING
THE PORTAL PATH FELL APART!

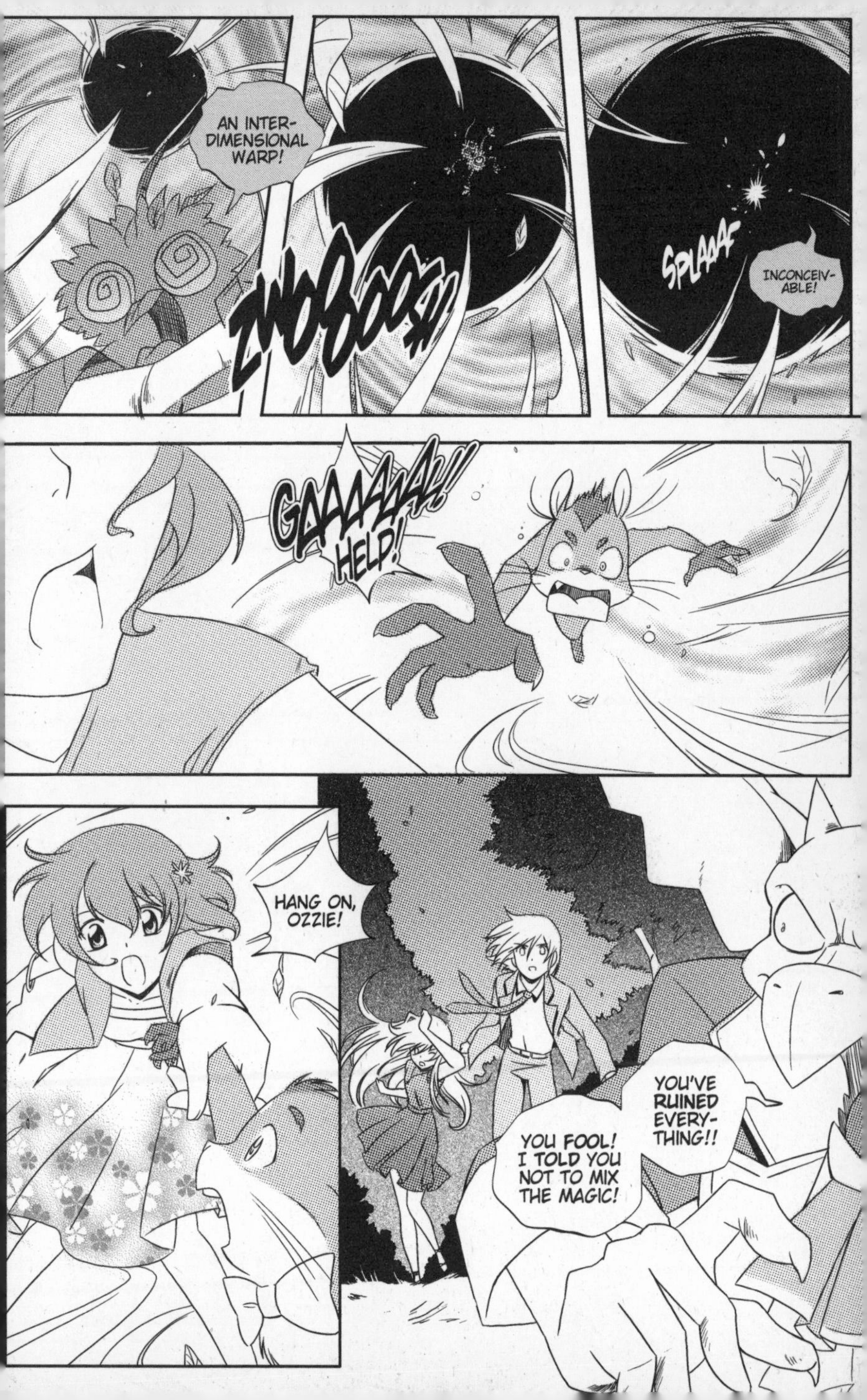
AN INTER-DIMENSIONAL WARP!
ZWOBOOSH
SPLAAAF
INCONCEIV-ABLE!
GAAAAAH!! HELP!
HANG ON, OZZIE!
YOU'VE RUINED EVERY-THING!!
YOU FOOL! I TOLD YOU NOT TO MIX THE MAGIC!

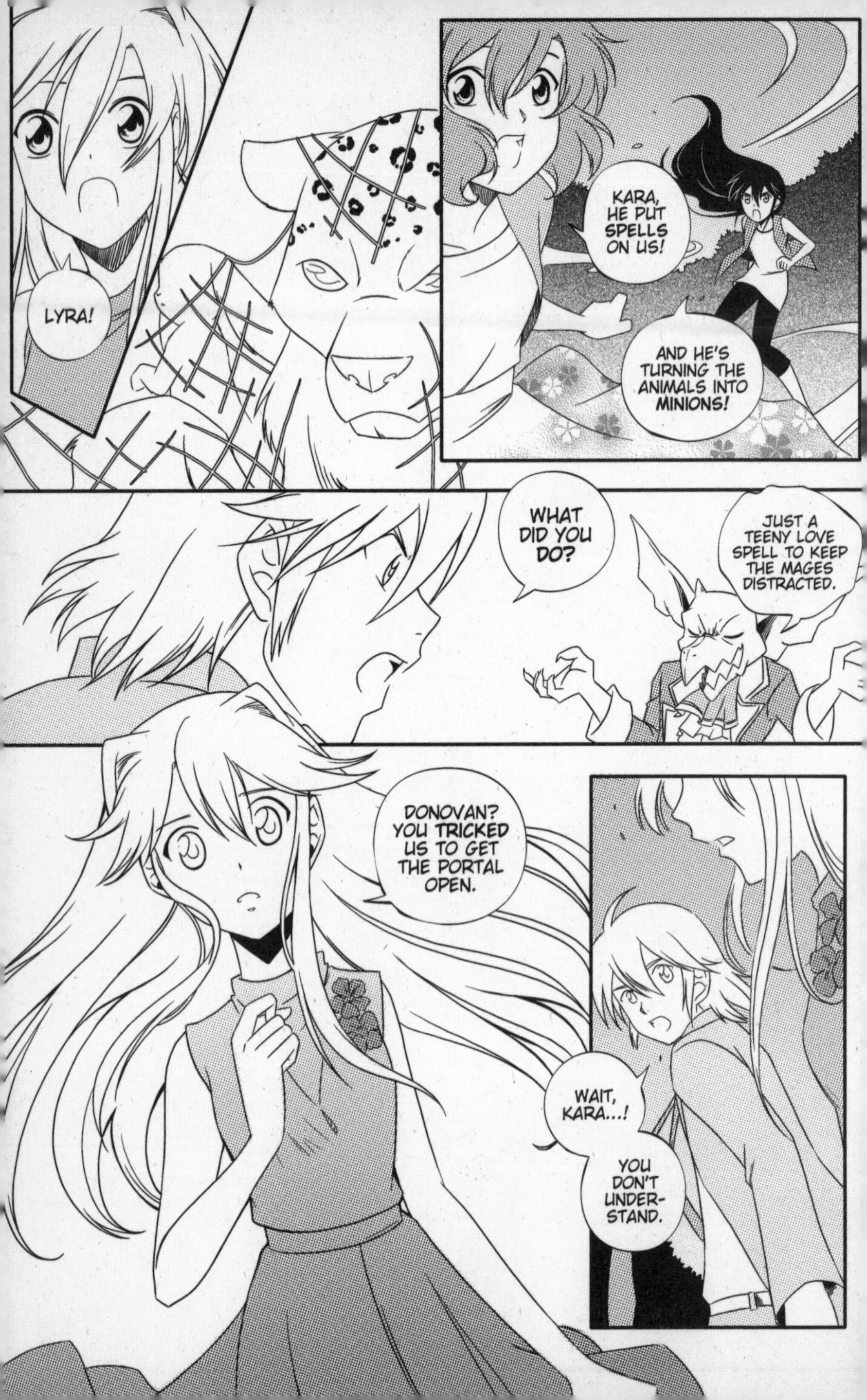
LYRA!
KARA, HE PUT SPELLS ON US!
AND HE'S TURNING THE ANIMALS INTO MINIONS!
WHAT DID YOU DO?
JUST A TEENY LOVE SPELL TO KEEP THE MAGES DISTRACTED.
DONOVAN? YOU TRICKED US TO GET THE PORTAL OPEN.
WAIT, KARA...!
YOU DON'T UNDER-STAND.

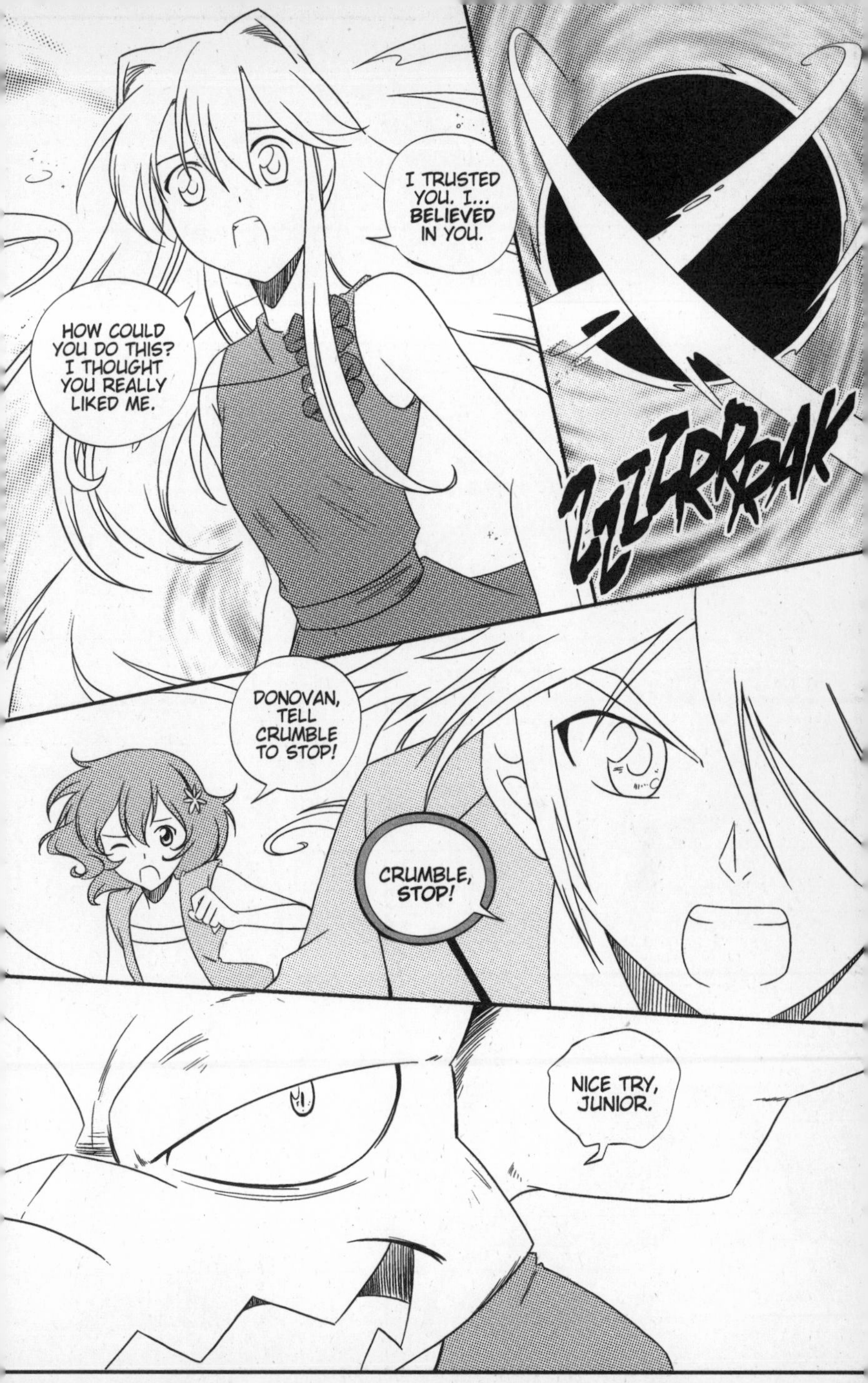
I TRUSTED YOU. I... BELIEVED IN YOU.
HOW COULD YOU DO THIS? I THOUGHT YOU REALLY LIKED ME.
ZZZZRRRAK
DONOVAN, TELL CRUMBLE TO STOP!
CRUMBLE, STOP!
NICE TRY, JUNIOR.

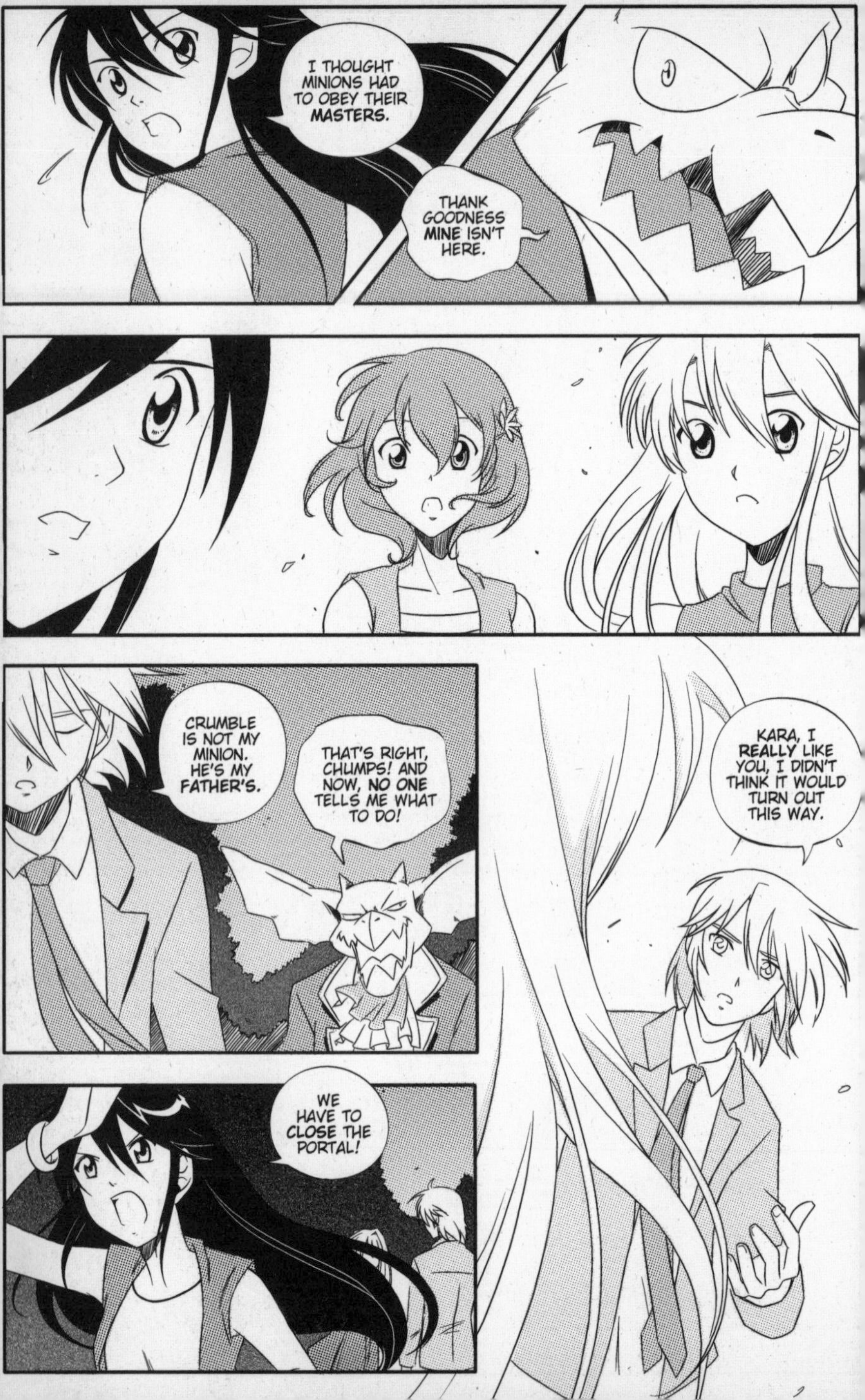
I THOUGHT MINIONS HAD TO OBEY THEIR MASTERS.
THANK GOODNESS MINE ISN'T HERE.
CRUMBLE IS NOT MY MINION. HE'S MY FATHER'S.
THAT'S RIGHT, CHUMPS! AND NOW, NO ONE TELLS ME WHAT TO DO!
WE HAVE TO CLOSE THE PORTAL!
KARA, I REALLY LIKE YOU, I DIDN'T THINK IT WOULD TURN OUT THIS WAY.

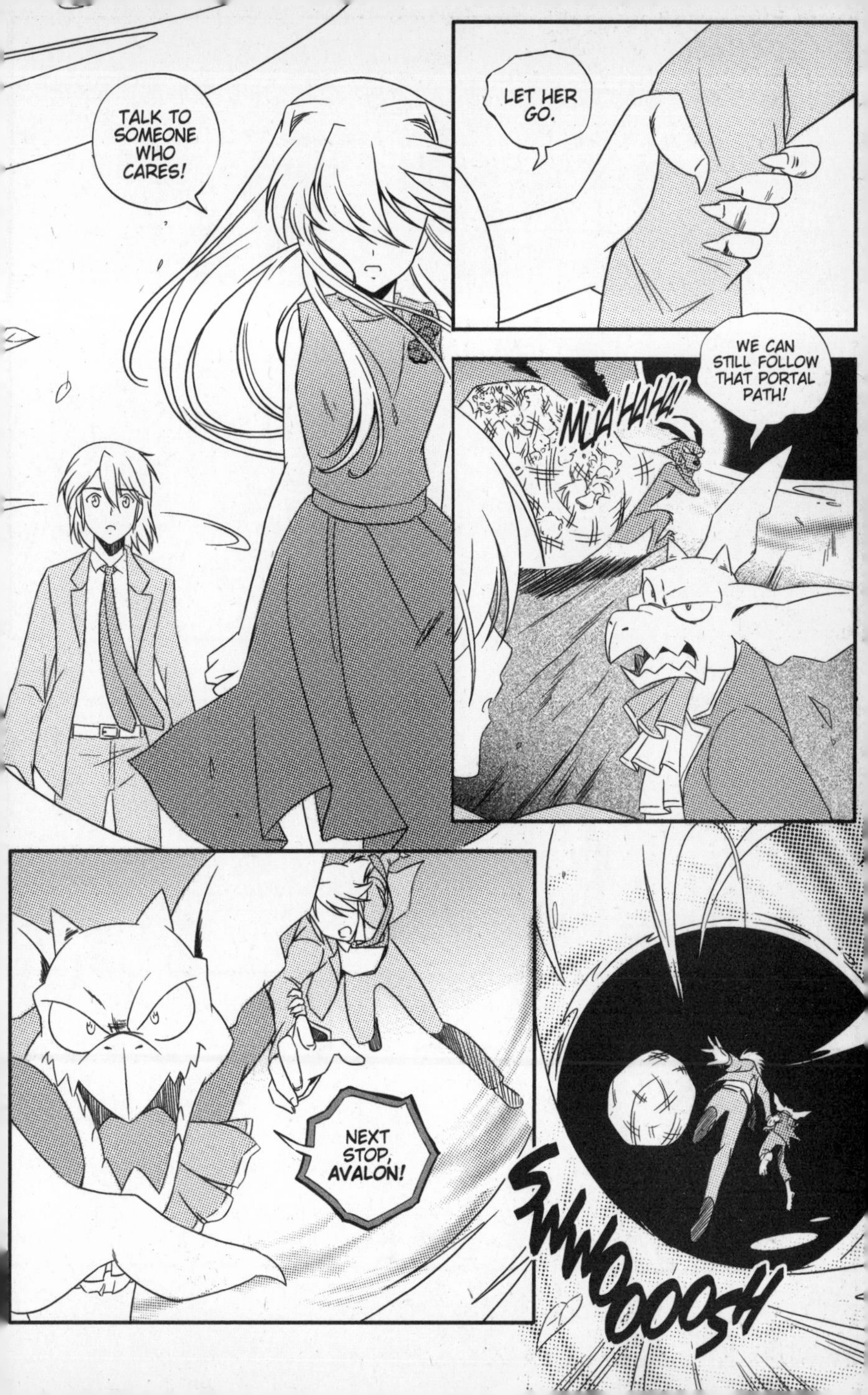
TALK TO SOMEONE WHO CARES!
LET HER GO.
MUA HAHA!
WE CAN STILL FOLLOW THAT PORTAL PATH!
NEXT STOP, AVALON!
SWWOOOOSH

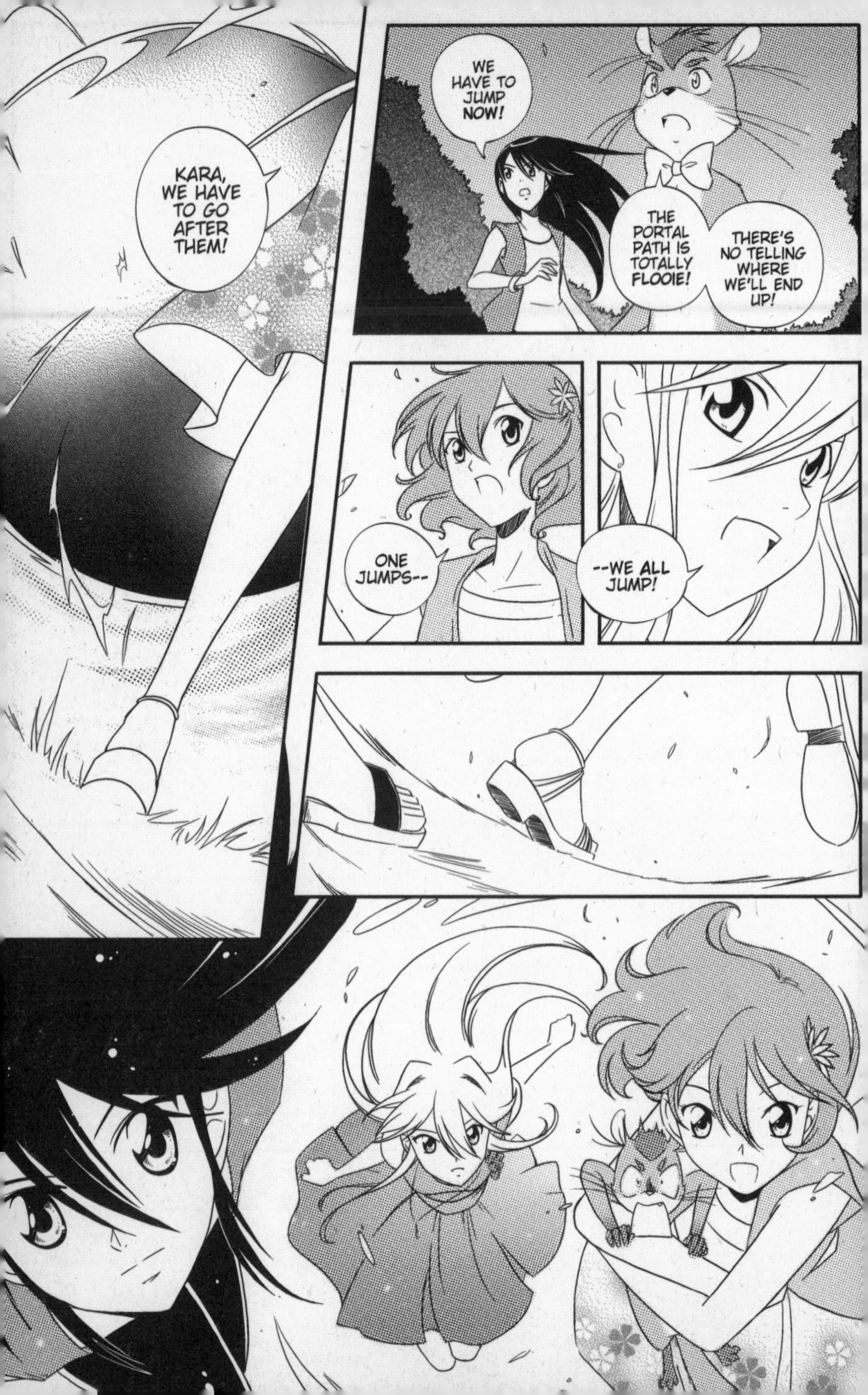
KARA, WE HAVE TO GO AFTER THEM!
WE HAVE TO JUMP NOW!
THE PORTAL PATH IS TOTALLY FLOOIE!
THERE'S NO TELLING WHERE WE'LL END UP!
ONE JUMPS--
--WE ALL JUMP!

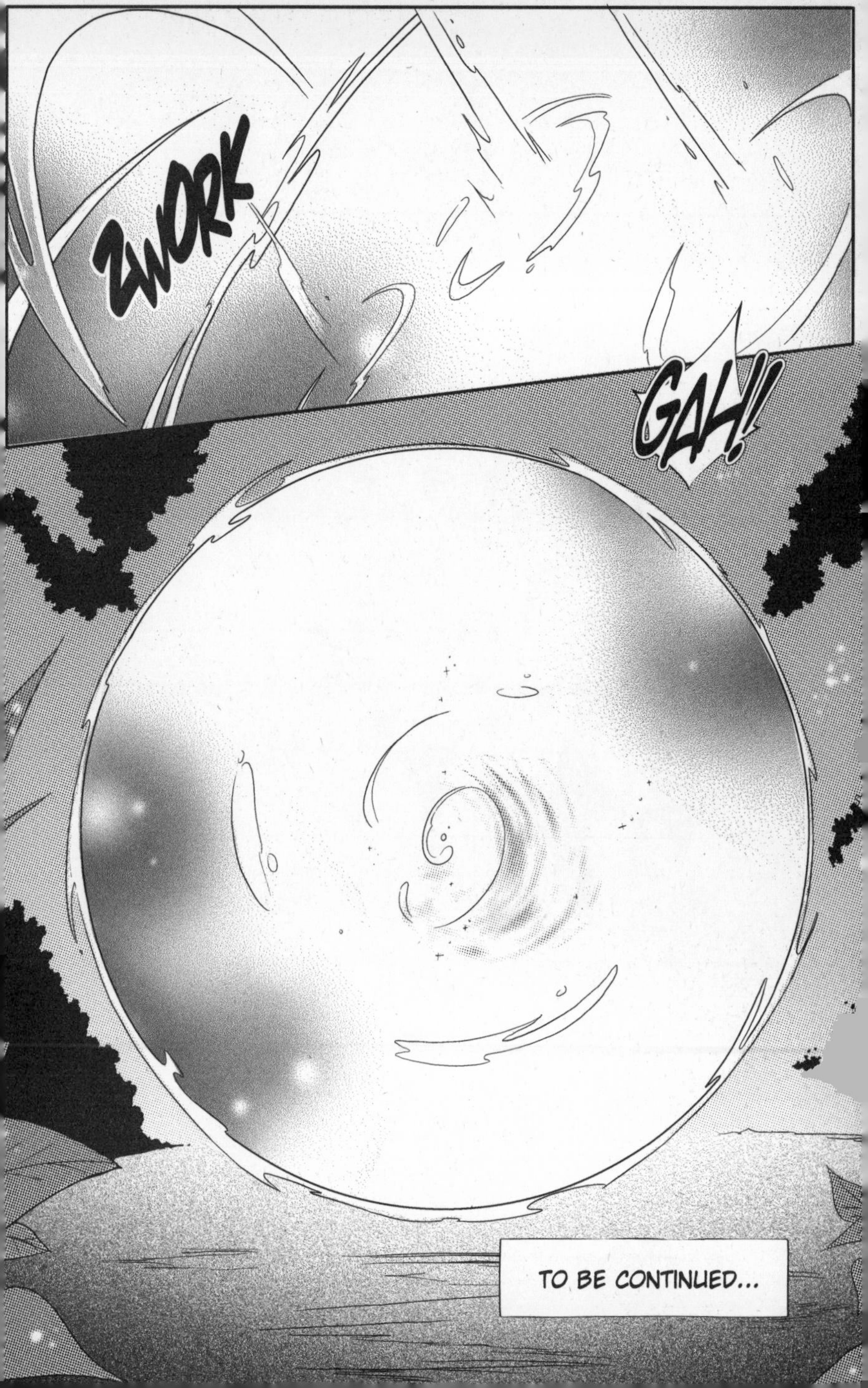
ZWORK
GAH!
TO BE CONTINUED...

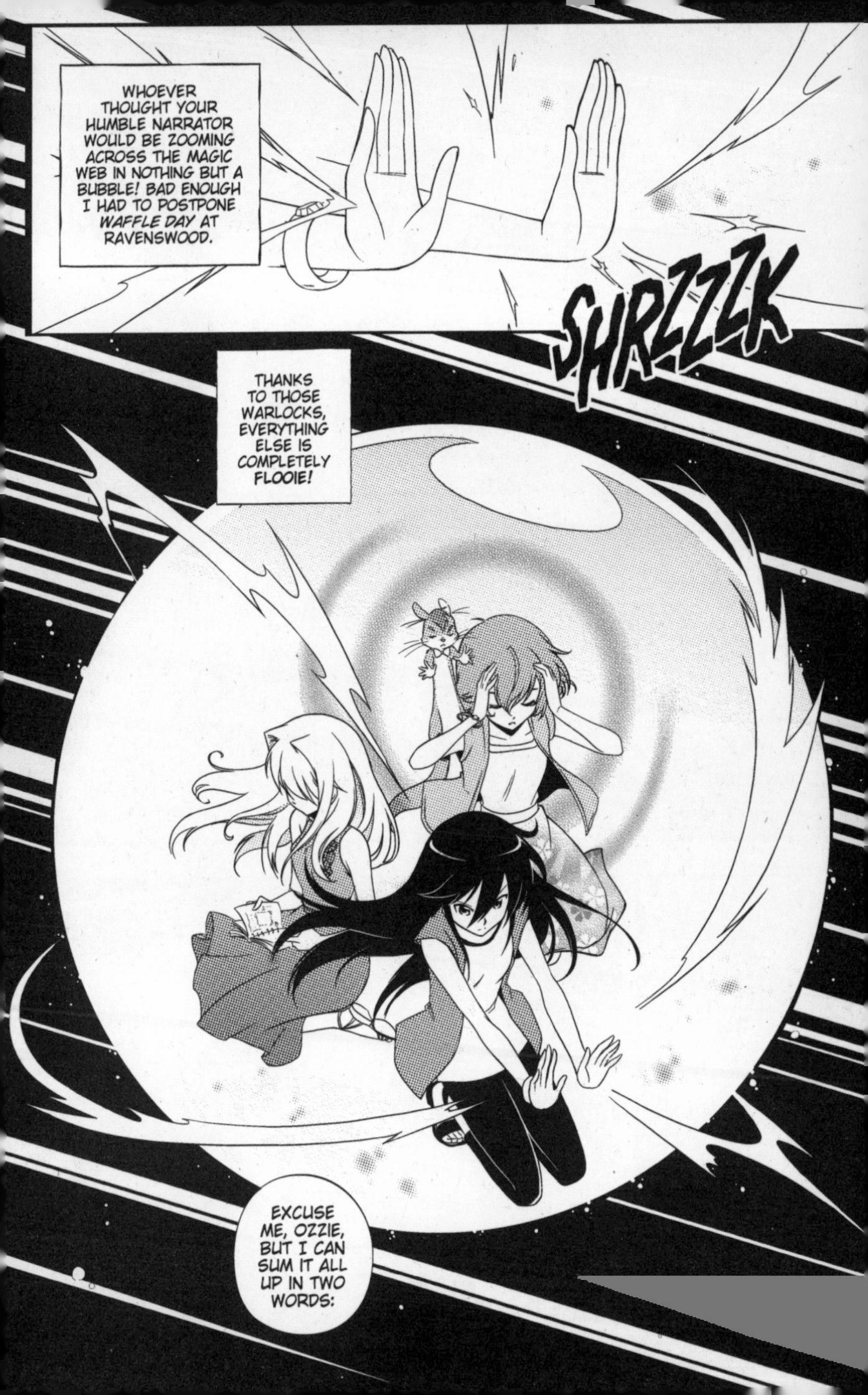
WHOEVER THOUGHT YOUR HUMBLE NARRATOR WOULD BE ZOOMING ACROSS THE MAGIC WEB IN NOTHING BUT A BUBBLE! BAD ENOUGH I HAD TO POSTPONE *WAFFLE DAY* AT RAVENSWOOD.
SHRZZZK
THANKS TO THOSE WARLOCKS, EVERYTHING ELSE IS COMPLETELY FLOOIE!
EXCUSE ME, OZZIE, BUT I CAN SUM IT ALL UP IN TWO WORDS:

LOVE STINKS!

RIP

ONE MINUTE YOU'RE ON THE PERFECT DATE WITH A *GORGEOUS WARLOCK* FROM ANOTHER DIMENSION.

THE NEXT HE'S TOTALLY BETRAYED YOU, STOLEN YOUR BONDED ANIMAL, AND TAKEN OVER YOUR MAGE QUEST TO FIND AVALON!

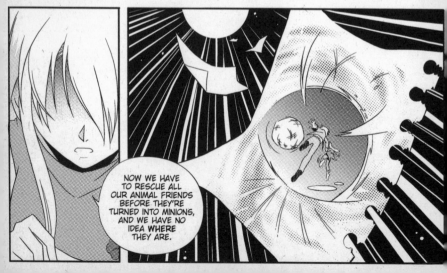

NOW WE HAVE TO RESCUE ALL OUR ANIMAL FRIENDS BEFORE THEY'RE TURNED INTO MINIONS, AND WE HAVE NO IDEA WHERE THEY ARE.

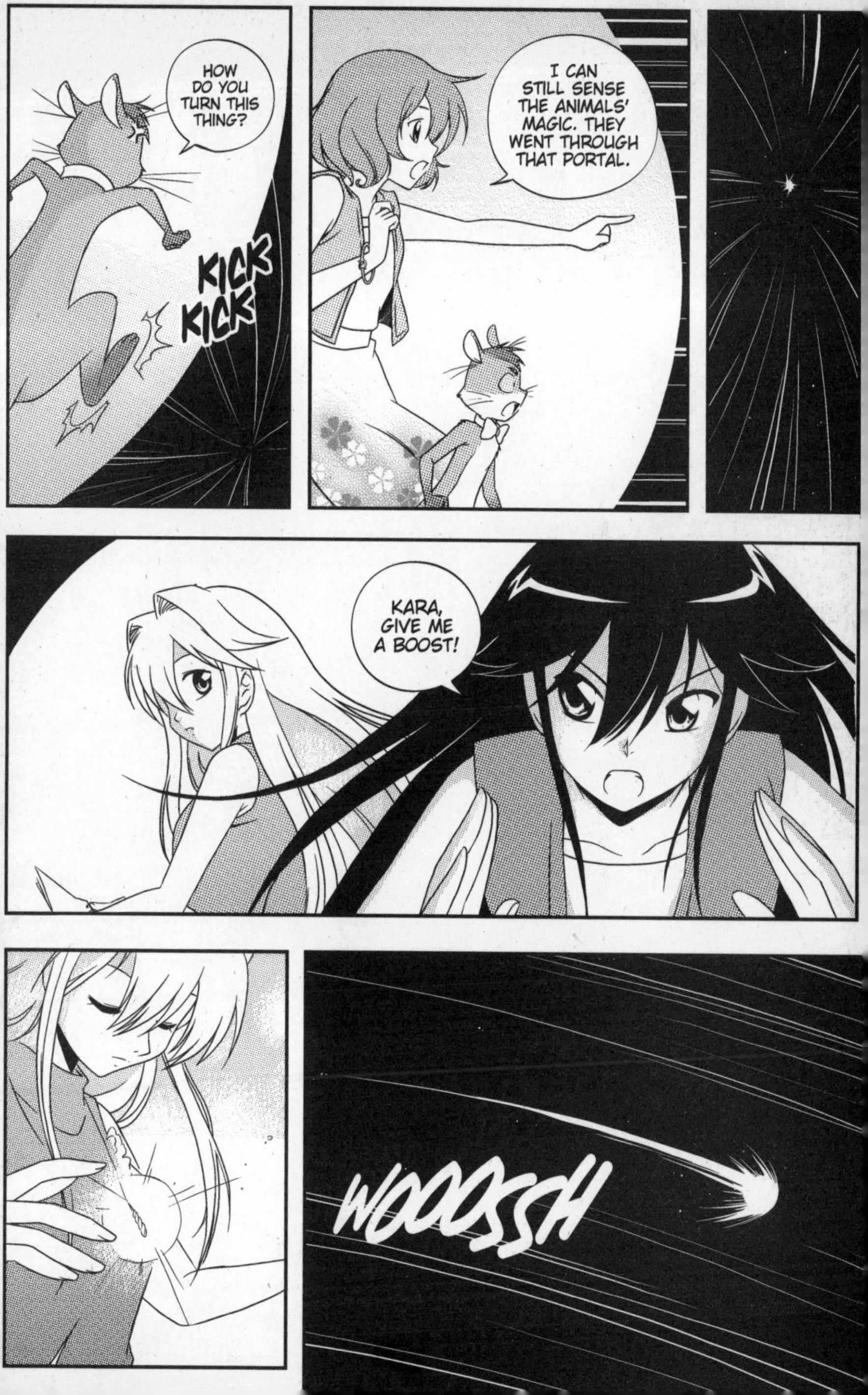
HOW DO YOU TURN THIS THING?
KICK KICK
I CAN STILL SENSE THE ANIMALS' MAGIC. THEY WENT THROUGH THAT PORTAL.
KARA, GIVE ME A BOOST!
WOOOSSH

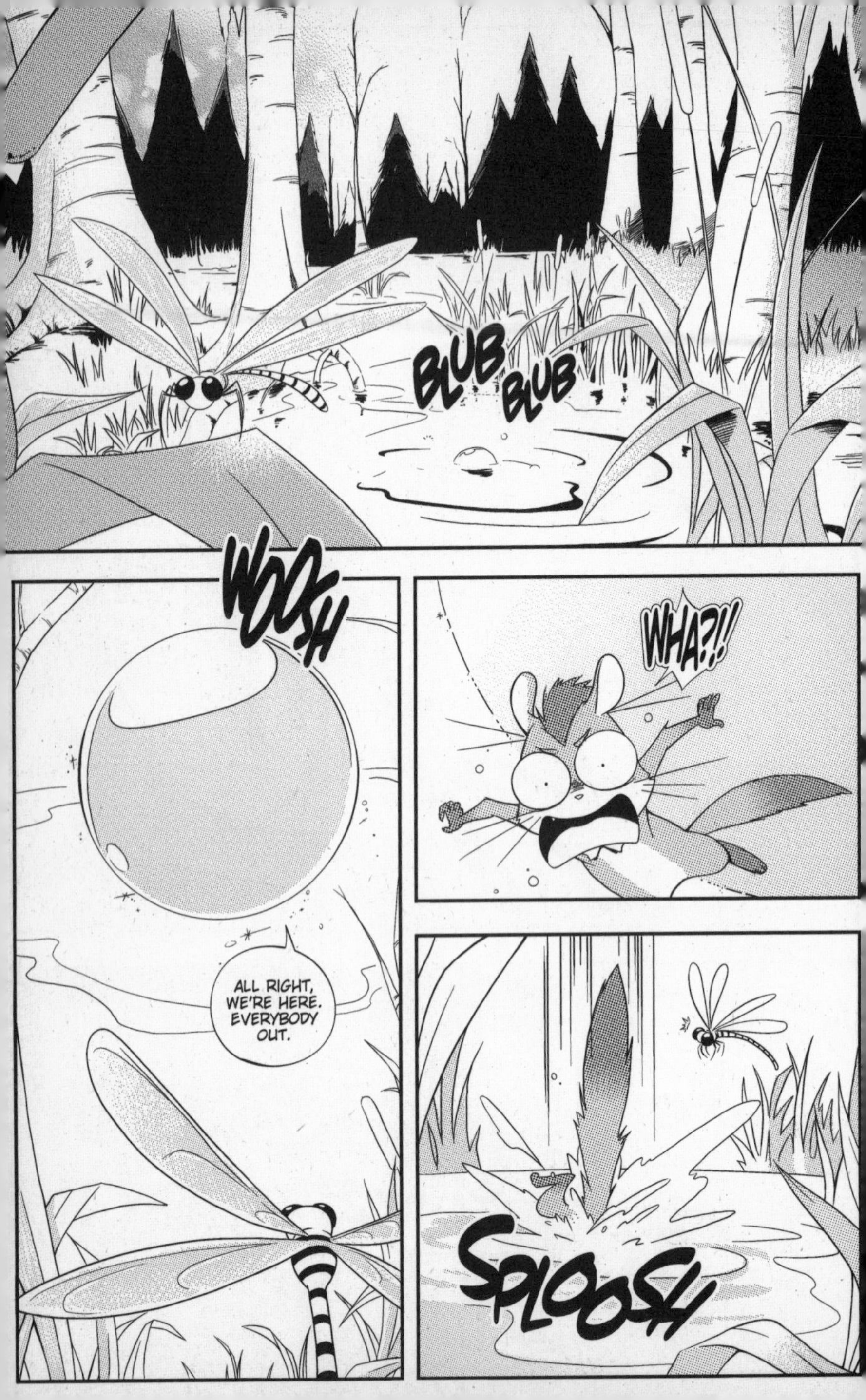
BLUB
BLUB
WOOSH
ALL RIGHT, WE'RE HERE. EVERYBODY OUT.
WHA?!!
SPLOOSH

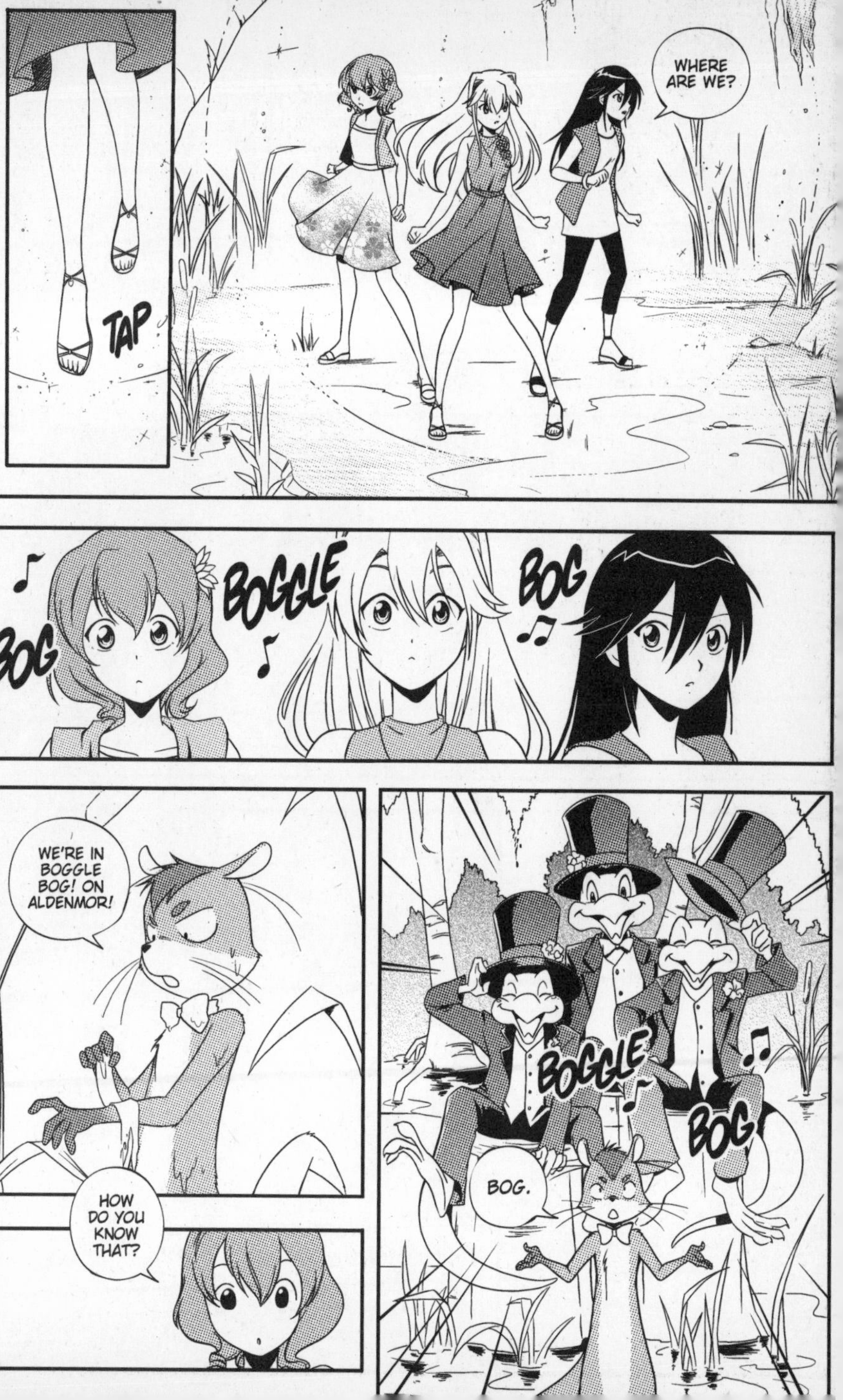
TAP
WHERE ARE WE?
BOG
BOGGLE
BOG
WE'RE IN BOGGLE BOG! ON ALDENMOR!
HOW DO YOU KNOW THAT?
BOGGLE
BOG
BOG.

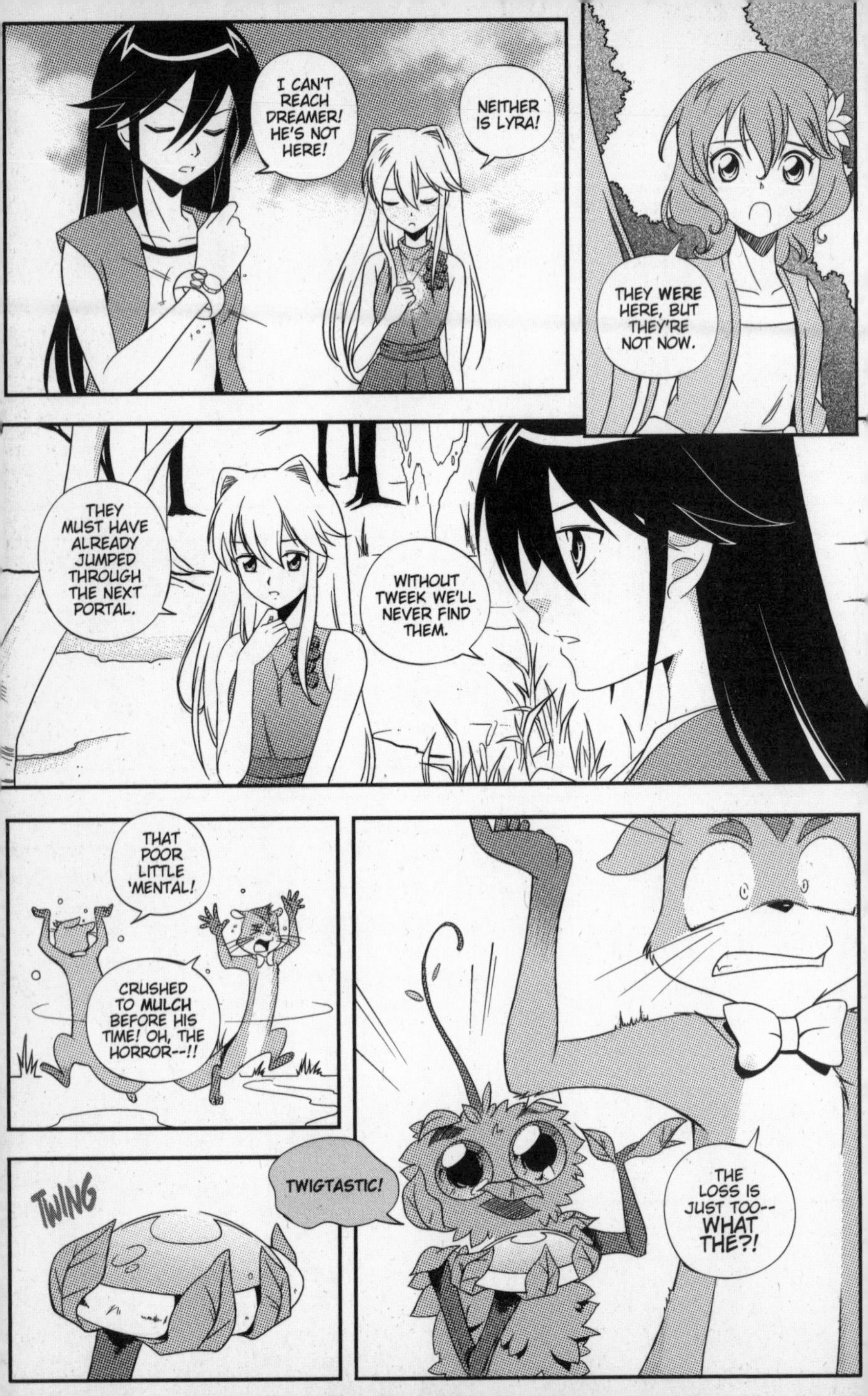
I CAN'T REACH DREAMER! HE'S NOT HERE!
NEITHER IS LYRA!
THEY WERE HERE, BUT THEY'RE NOT NOW.
THEY MUST HAVE ALREADY JUMPED THROUGH THE NEXT PORTAL.
WITHOUT TWEEK WE'LL NEVER FIND THEM.
THAT POOR LITTLE 'MENTAL!
CRUSHED TO MULCH BEFORE HIS TIME! OH, THE HORROR--!!
THE LOSS IS JUST TOO-- WHAT THE?!
TWING
TWIGTASTIC!

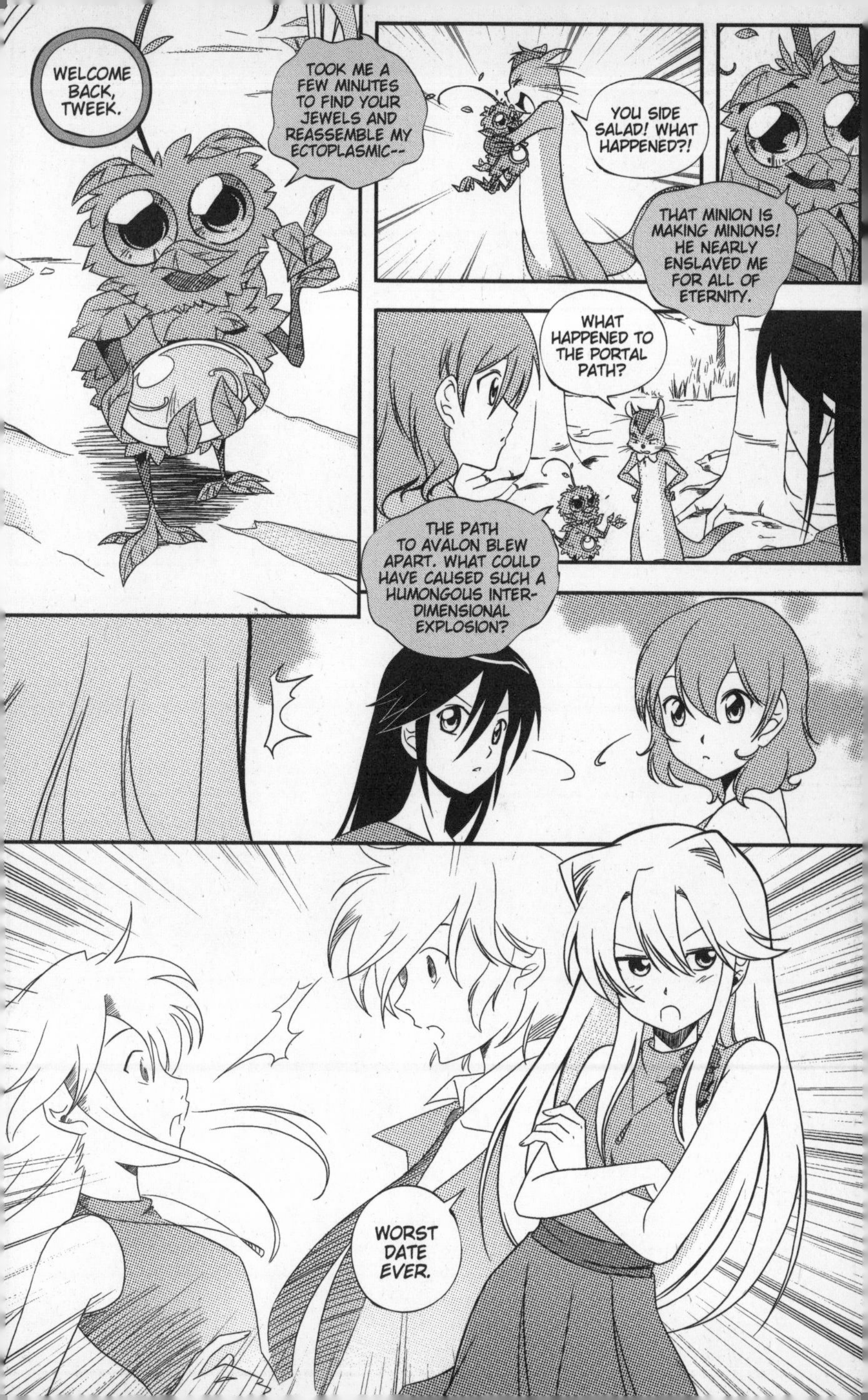
WELCOME BACK, TWEEK.
TOOK ME A FEW MINUTES TO FIND YOUR JEWELS AND REASSEMBLE MY ECTOPLASMIC--
YOU SIDE SALAD! WHAT HAPPENED?!
THAT MINION IS MAKING MINIONS! HE NEARLY ENSLAVED ME FOR ALL OF ETERNITY.
WHAT HAPPENED TO THE PORTAL PATH?
THE PATH TO AVALON BLEW APART. WHAT COULD HAVE CAUSED SUCH A HUMONGOUS INTER-DIMENSIONAL EXPLOSION?
WORST DATE EVER.

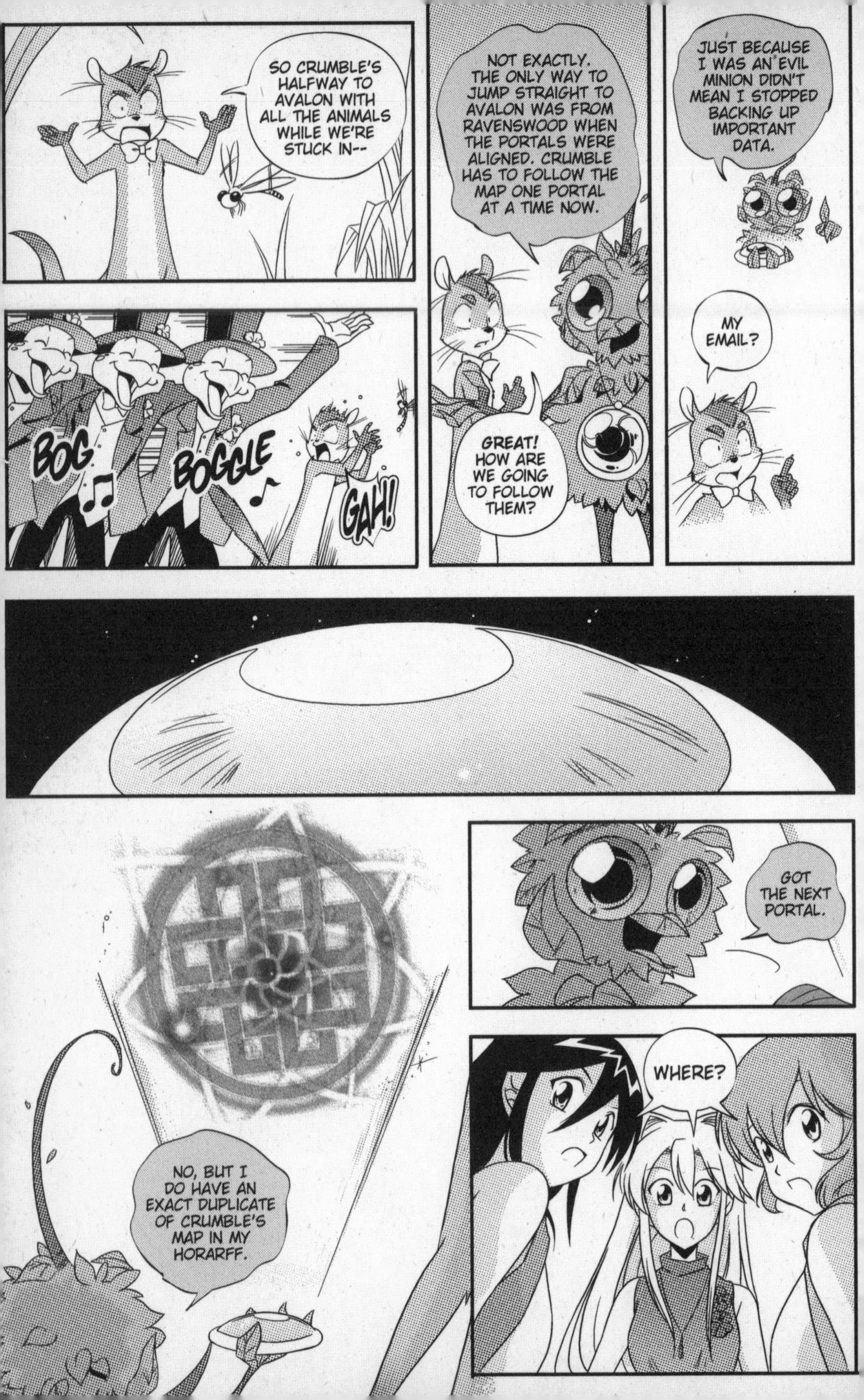
SO CRUMBLE'S HALFWAY TO AVALON WITH ALL THE ANIMALS WHILE WE'RE STUCK IN--
BOG
BOGGLE
GAH!
NOT EXACTLY. THE ONLY WAY TO JUMP STRAIGHT TO AVALON WAS FROM RAVENSWOOD WHEN THE PORTALS WERE ALIGNED. CRUMBLE HAS TO FOLLOW THE MAP ONE PORTAL AT A TIME NOW.
GREAT! HOW ARE WE GOING TO FOLLOW THEM?
JUST BECAUSE I WAS AN EVIL MINION DIDN'T MEAN I STOPPED BACKING UP IMPORTANT DATA.
MY EMAIL?
NO, BUT I DO HAVE AN EXACT DUPLICATE OF CRUMBLE'S MAP IN MY HORARFF.
GOT THE NEXT PORTAL.
WHERE?

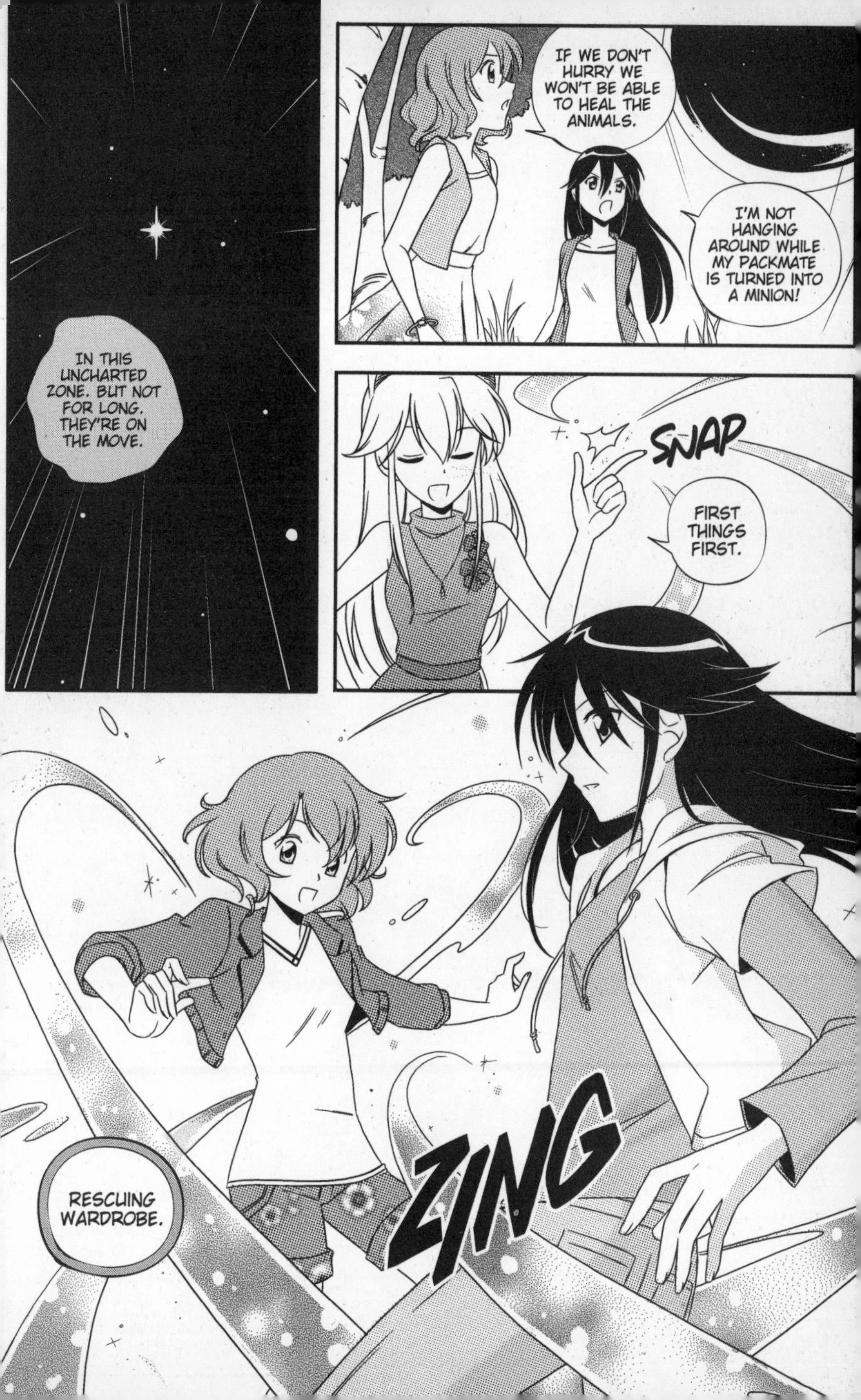
IN THIS UNCHARTED ZONE. BUT NOT FOR LONG. THEY'RE ON THE MOVE.
IF WE DON'T HURRY WE WON'T BE ABLE TO HEAL THE ANIMALS.
I'M NOT HANGING AROUND WHILE MY PACKMATE IS TURNED INTO A MINION!
SNAP
FIRST THINGS FIRST.
RESCUING WARDROBE.
ZING

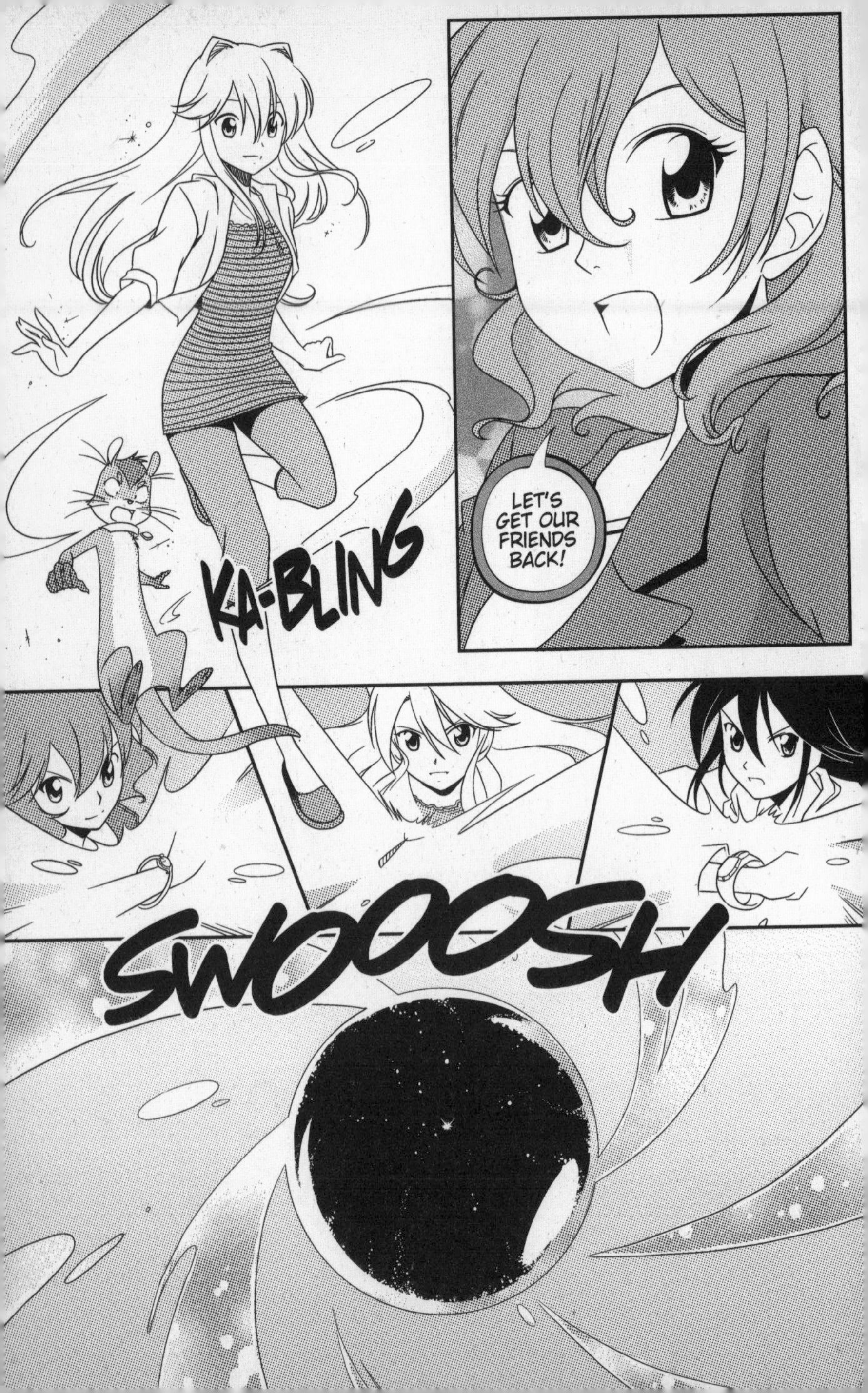
LET'S GET OUR FRIENDS BACK!
KA-BLING
SWOOOSH

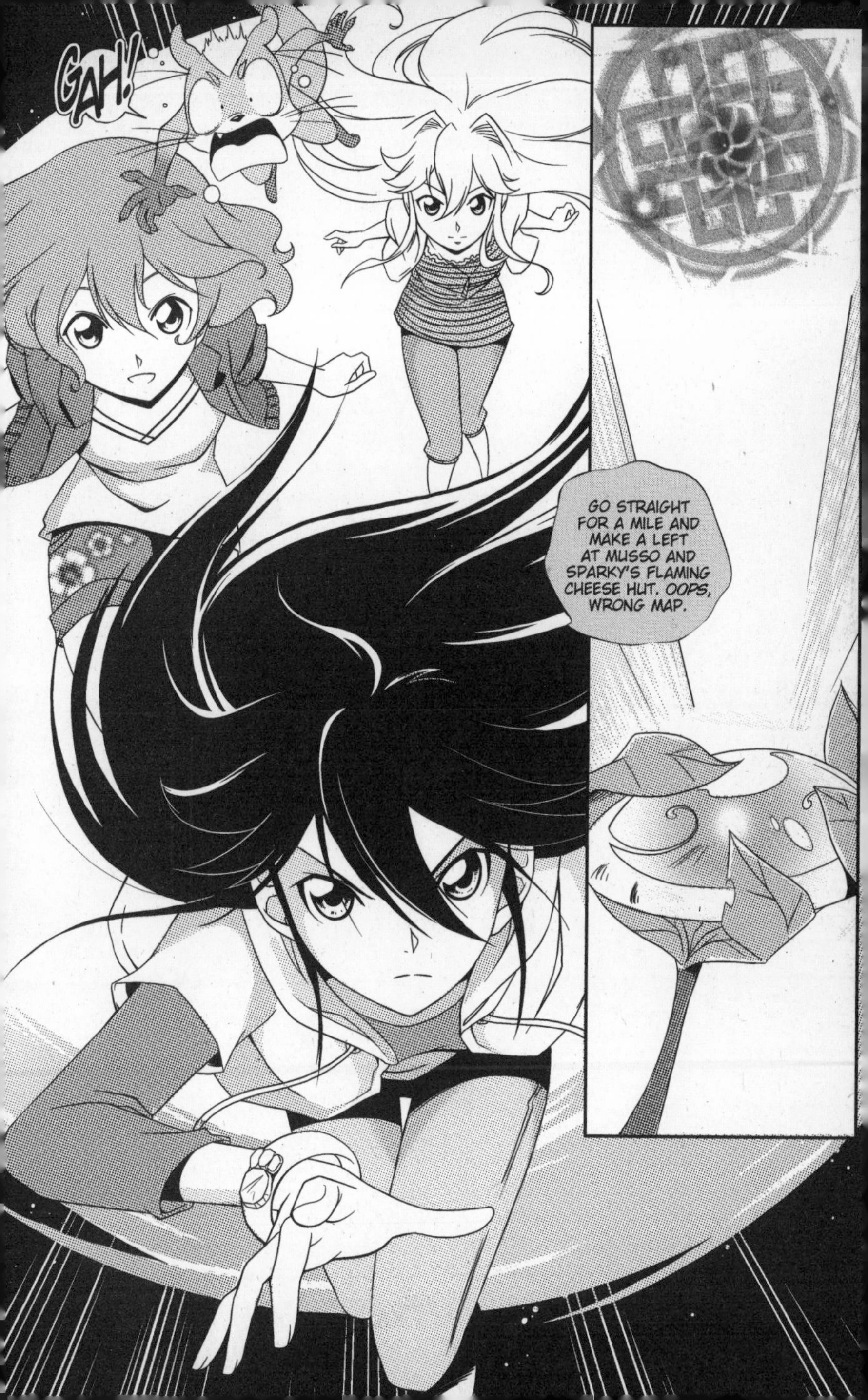
GAH!
GO STRAIGHT FOR A MILE AND MAKE A LEFT AT MUSSO AND SPARKY'S FLAMING CHEESE HUT. OOPS, WRONG MAP.

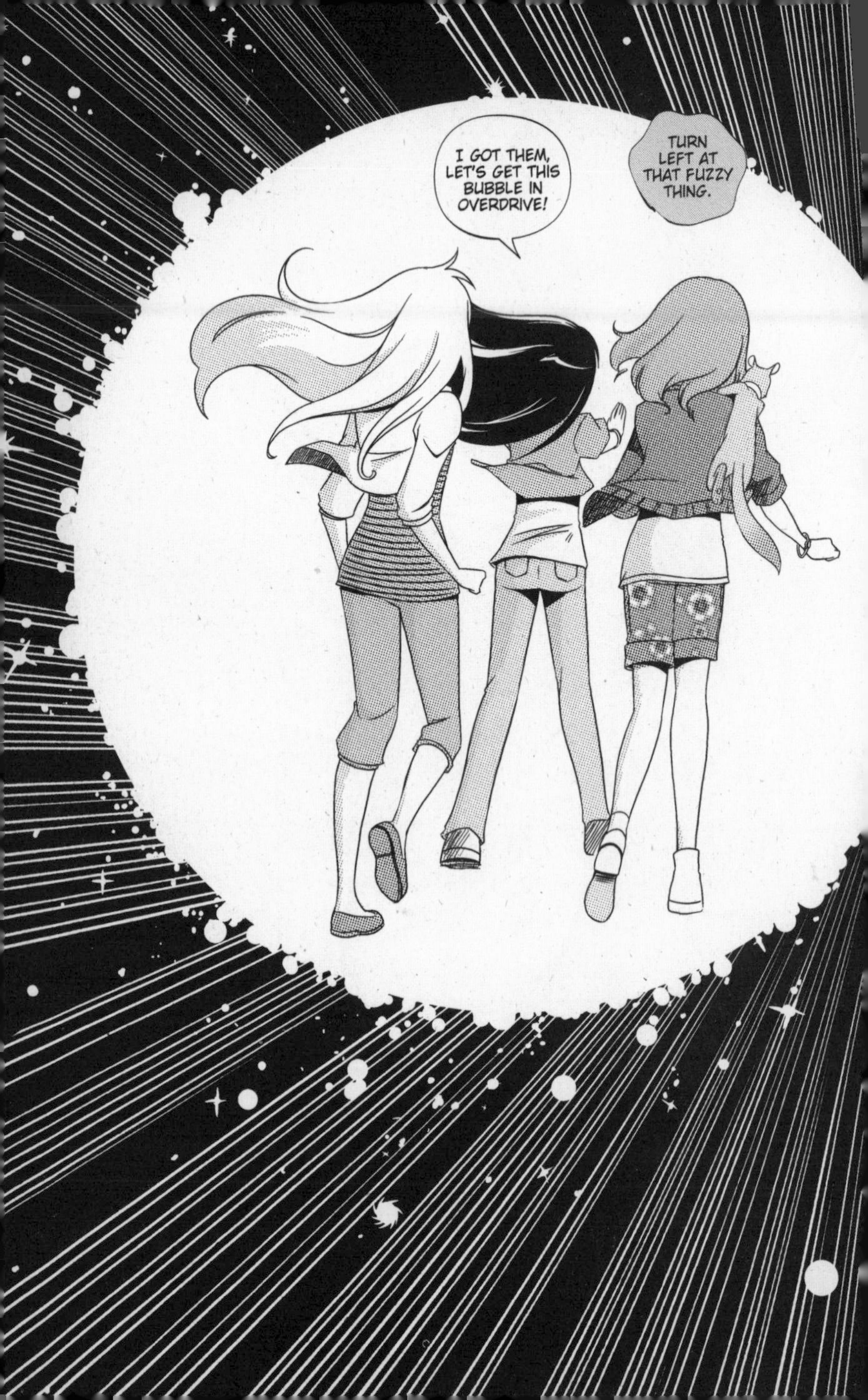
I GOT THEM, LET'S GET THIS BUBBLE IN OVERDRIVE!
TURN LEFT AT THAT FUZZY THING.

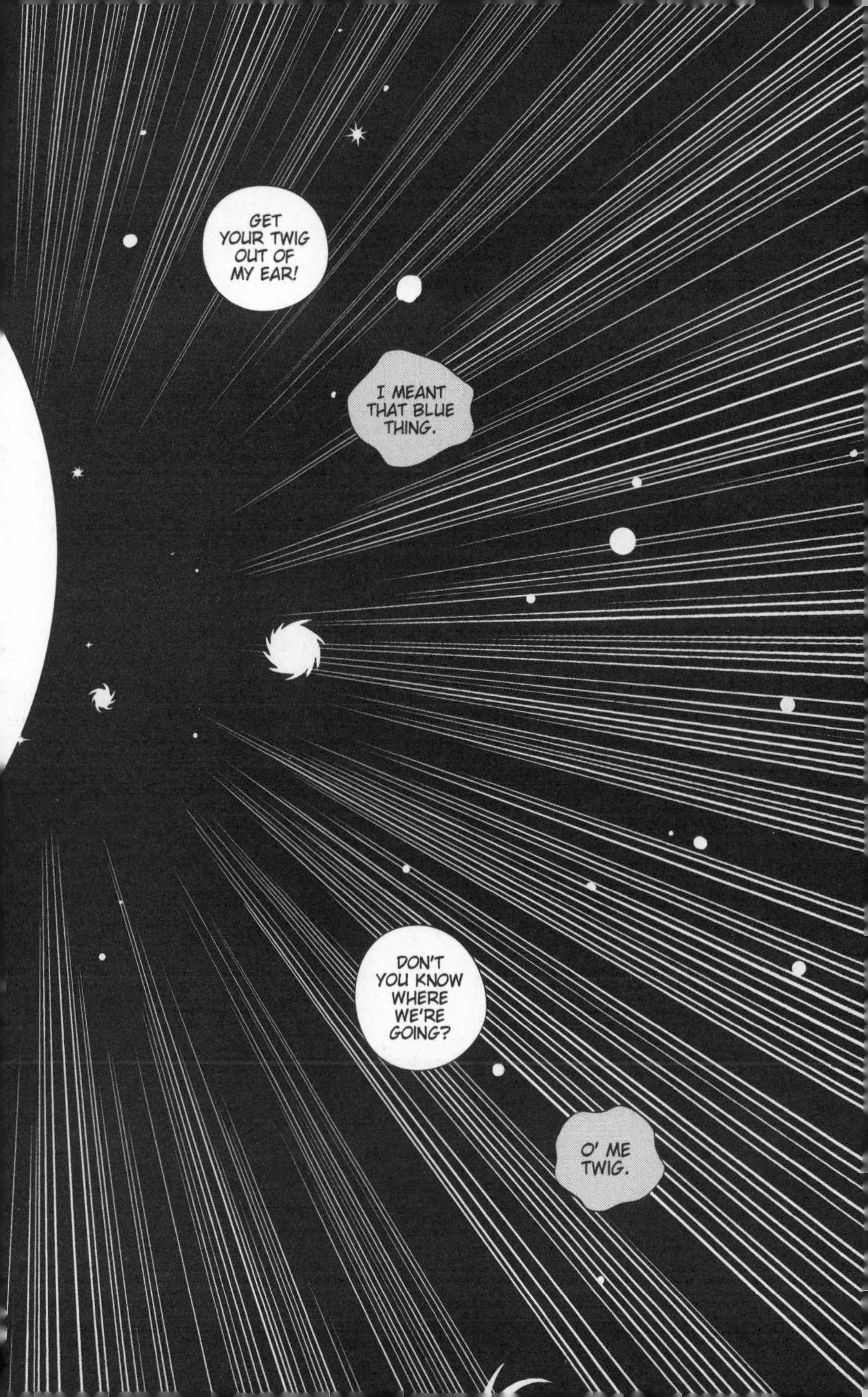
GET YOUR TWIG OUT OF MY EAR!
I MEANT THAT BLUE THING.
DON'T YOU KNOW WHERE WE'RE GOING?
O' ME TWIG.

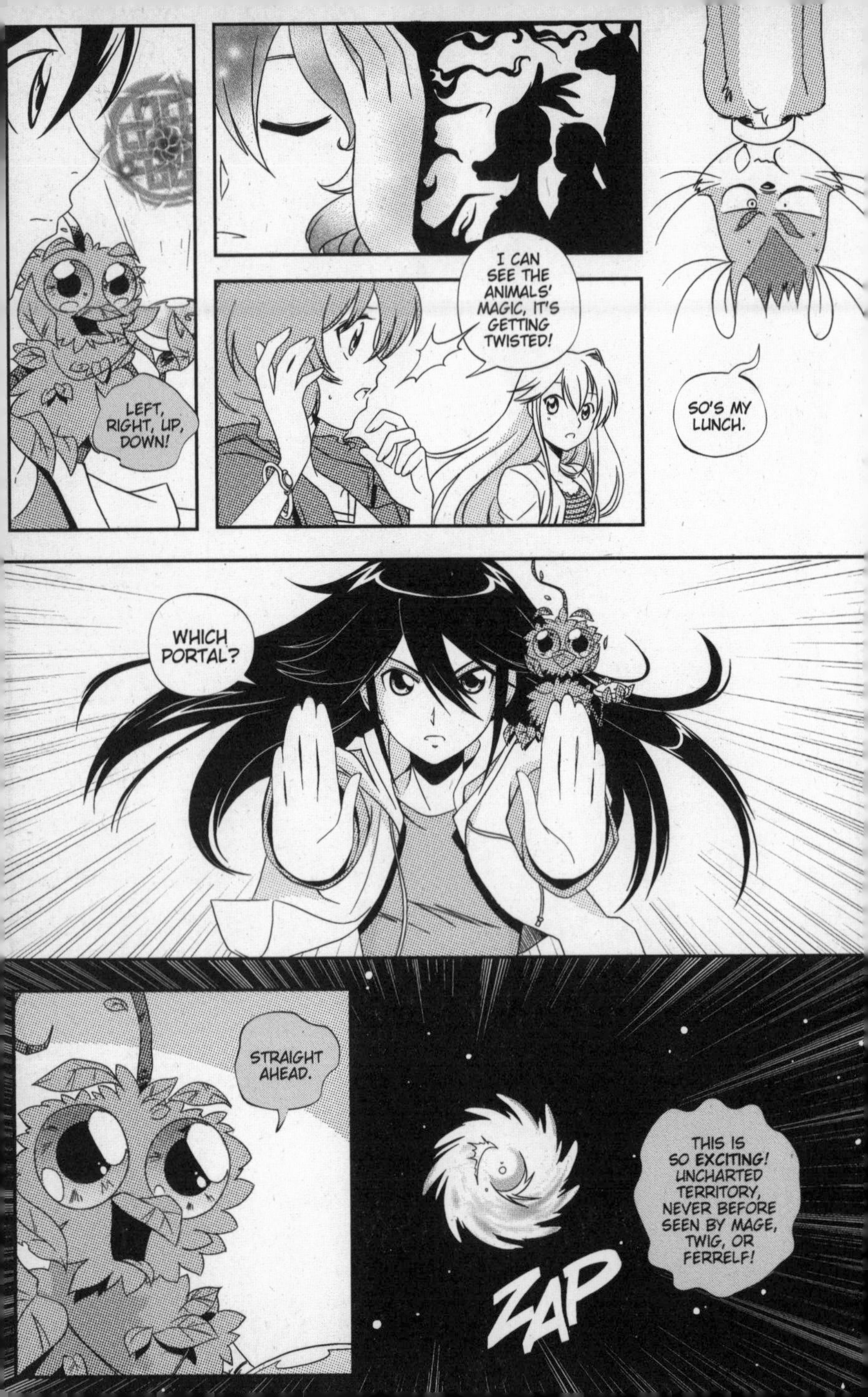
LEFT, RIGHT, UP, DOWN!
I CAN SEE THE ANIMALS' MAGIC, IT'S GETTING TWISTED!
SO'S MY LUNCH.
WHICH PORTAL?
STRAIGHT AHEAD.
THIS IS SO EXCITING! UNCHARTED TERRITORY, NEVER BEFORE SEEN BY MAGE, TWIG, OR FERRELF!
ZAP

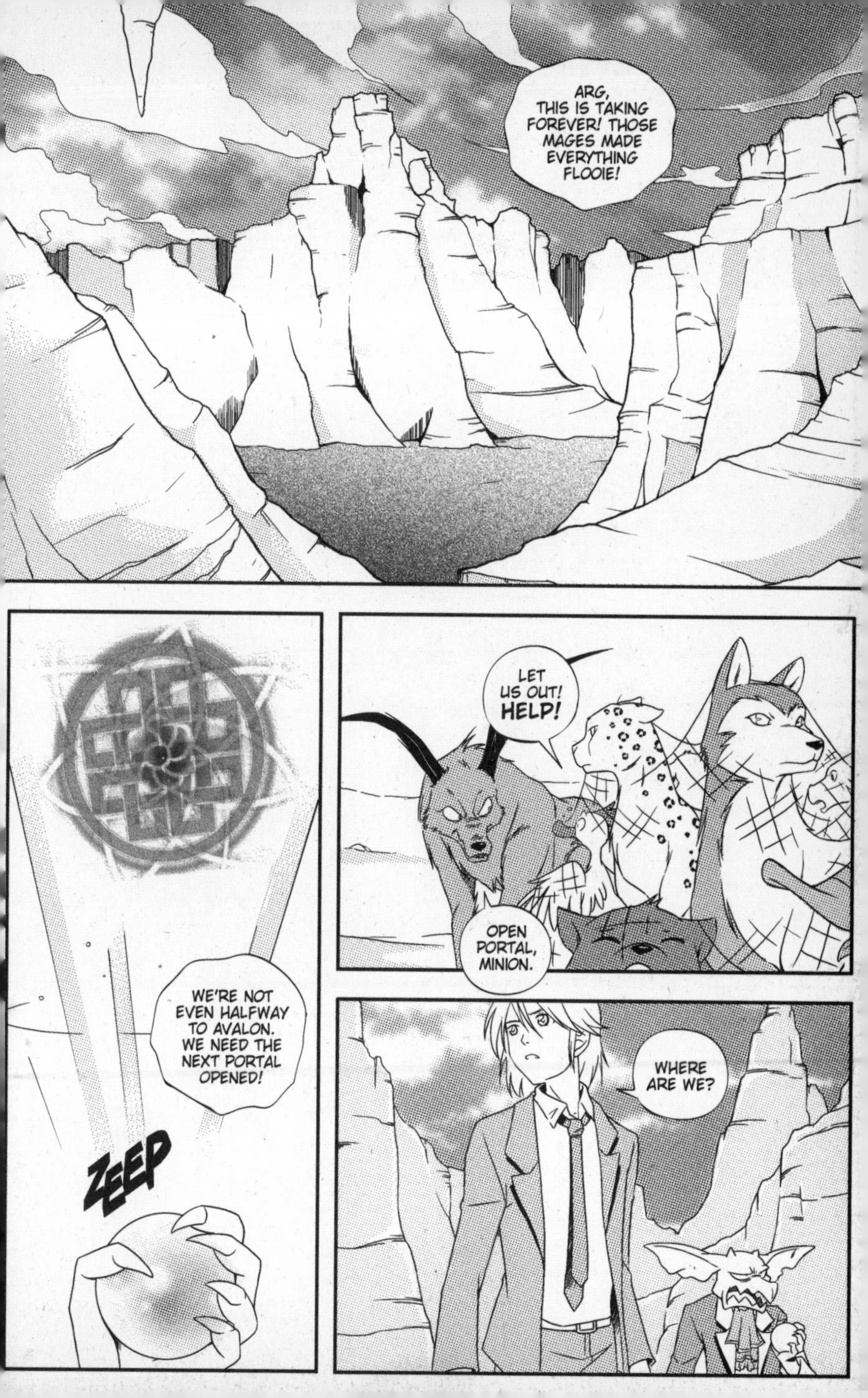
ARG, THIS IS TAKING FOREVER! THOSE MAGES MADE EVERYTHING FLOOIE!
WE'RE NOT EVEN HALFWAY TO AVALON. WE NEED THE NEXT PORTAL OPENED!
ZEEP
LET US OUT! HELP!
OPEN PORTAL, MINION.
WHERE ARE WE?

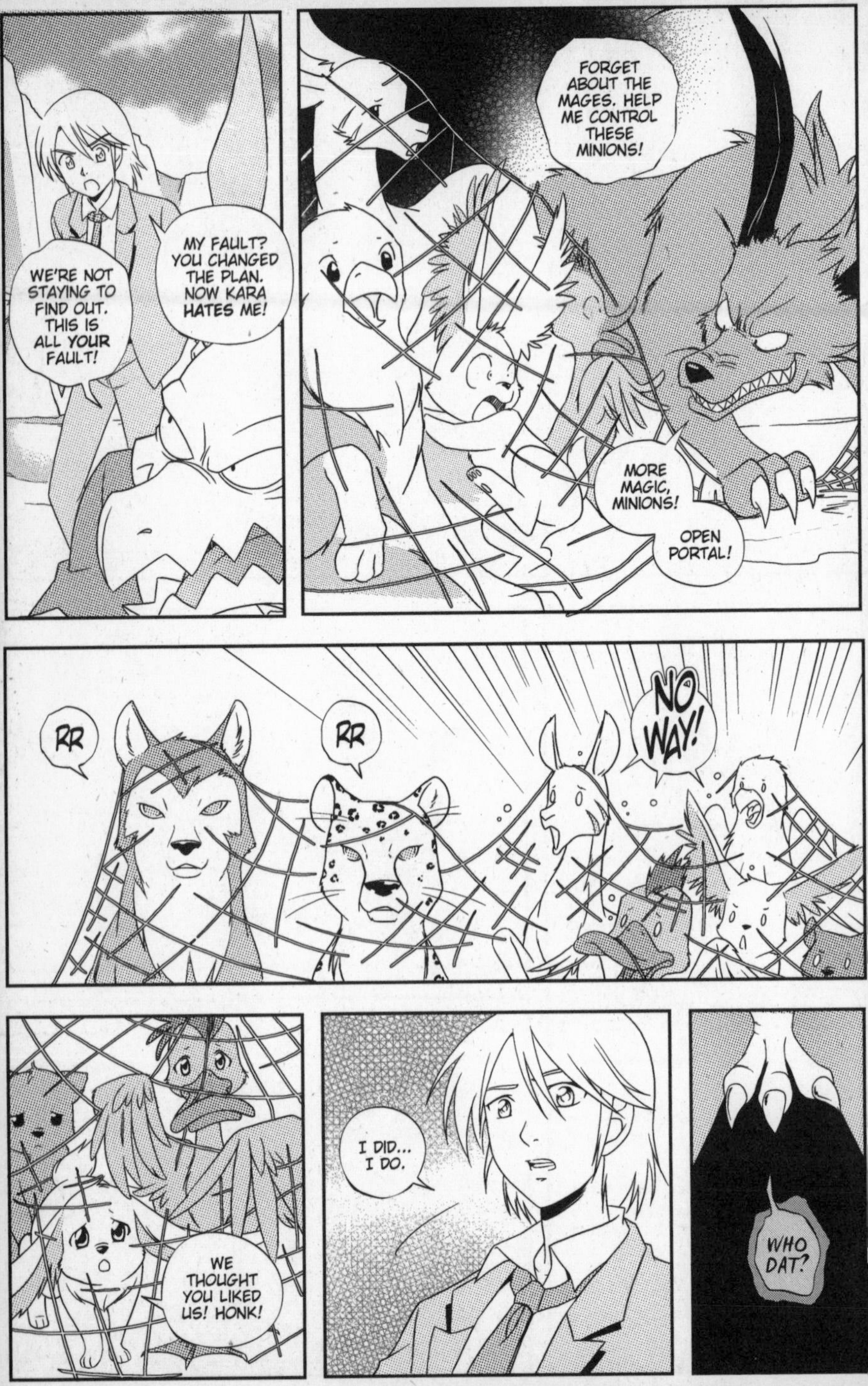
MY FAULT? YOU CHANGED THE PLAN. NOW KARA HATES ME!
WE'RE NOT STAYING TO FIND OUT. THIS IS ALL YOUR FAULT!
FORGET ABOUT THE MAGES. HELP ME CONTROL THESE MINIONS!
MORE MAGIC, MINIONS!
OPEN PORTAL!
RR
RR
NO WAY!
WE THOUGHT YOU LIKED US! HONK!
I DID... I DO.
WHO DAT?

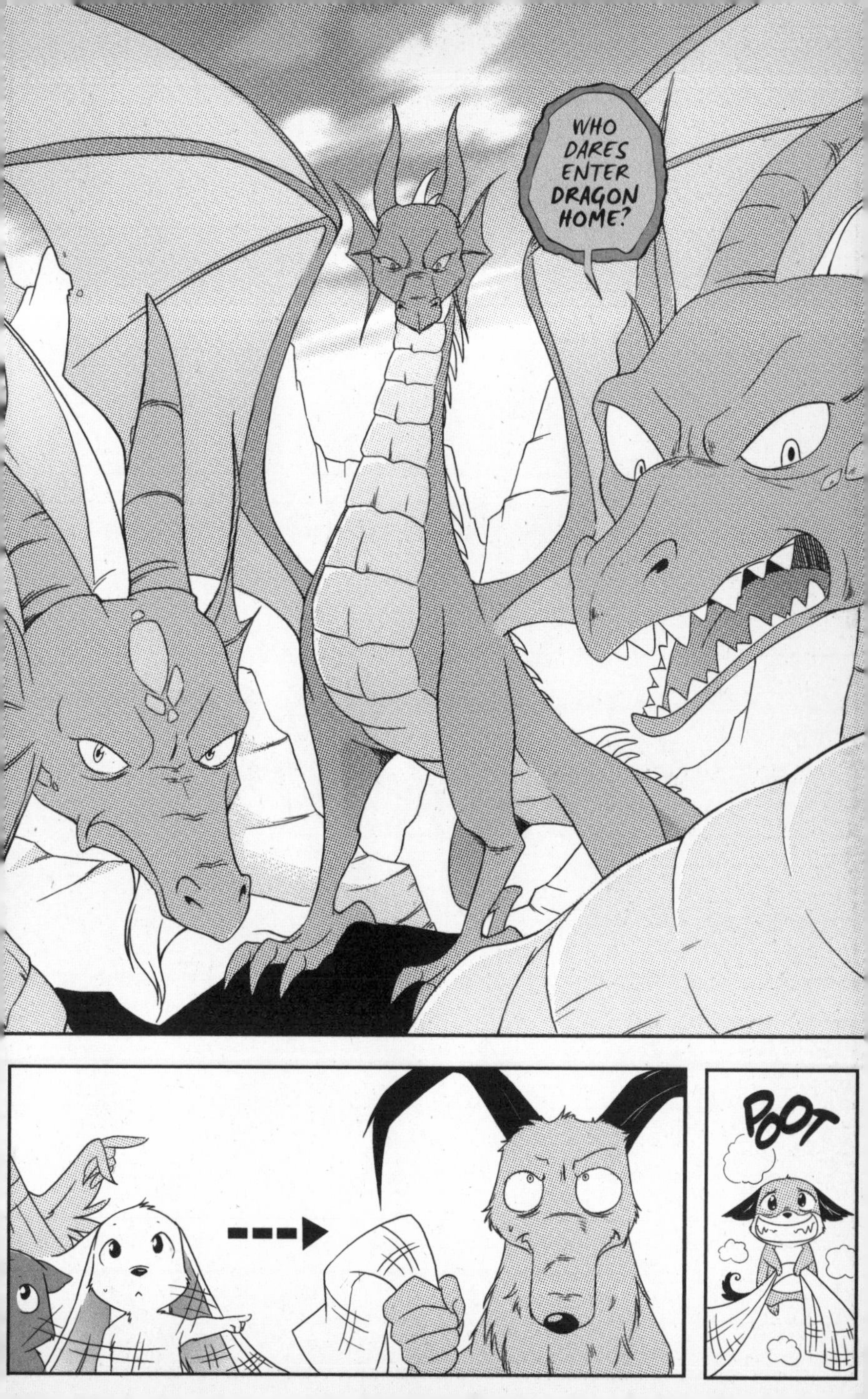
WHO DARES ENTER DRAGON HOME?
POOT

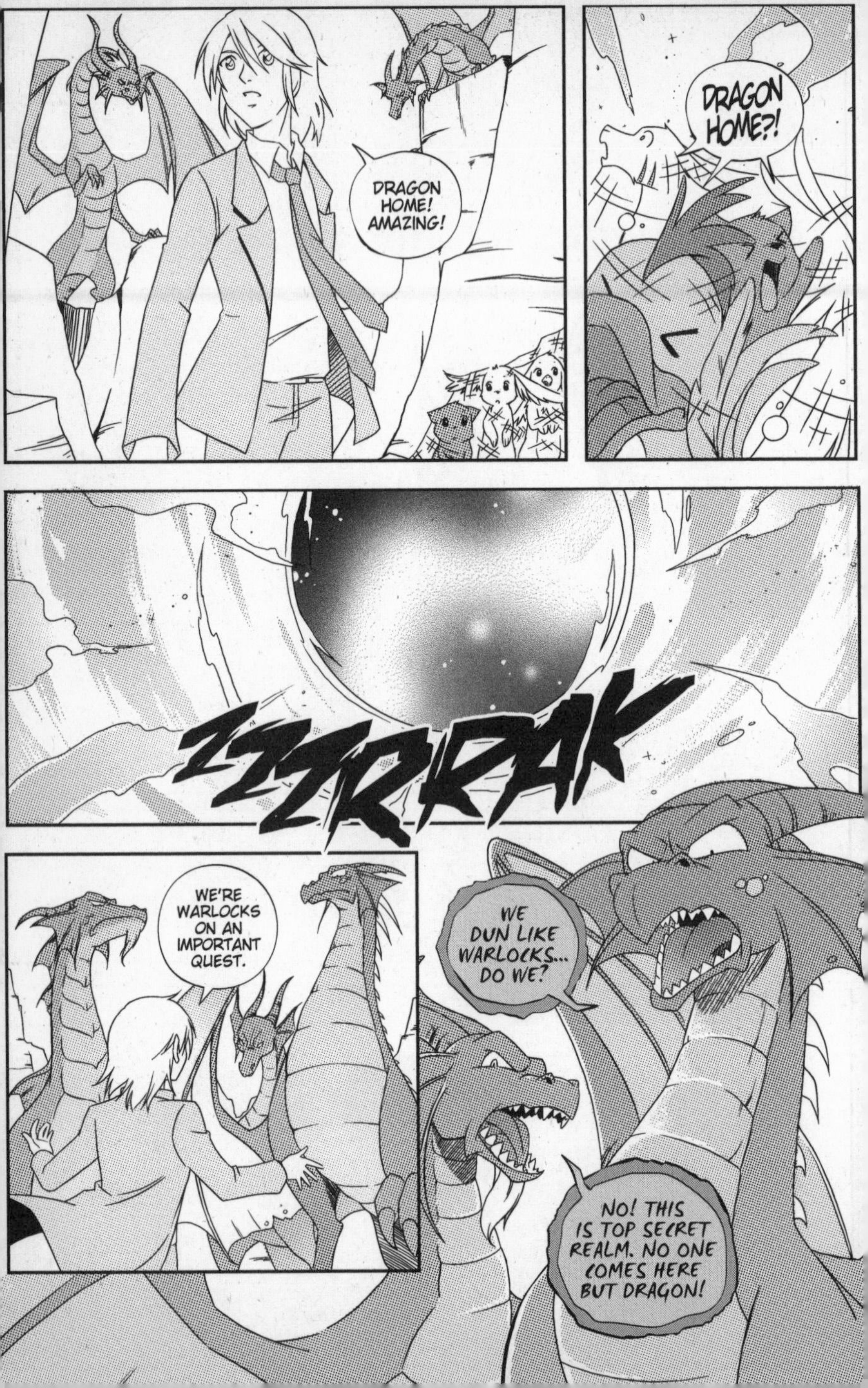
DRAGON HOME! AMAZING!
DRAGON HOME?!
ZZZRRAK
WE'RE WARLOCKS ON AN IMPORTANT QUEST.
WE DUN LIKE WARLOCKS... DO WE?
NO! THIS IS TOP SECRET REALM. NO ONE COMES HERE BUT DRAGON!

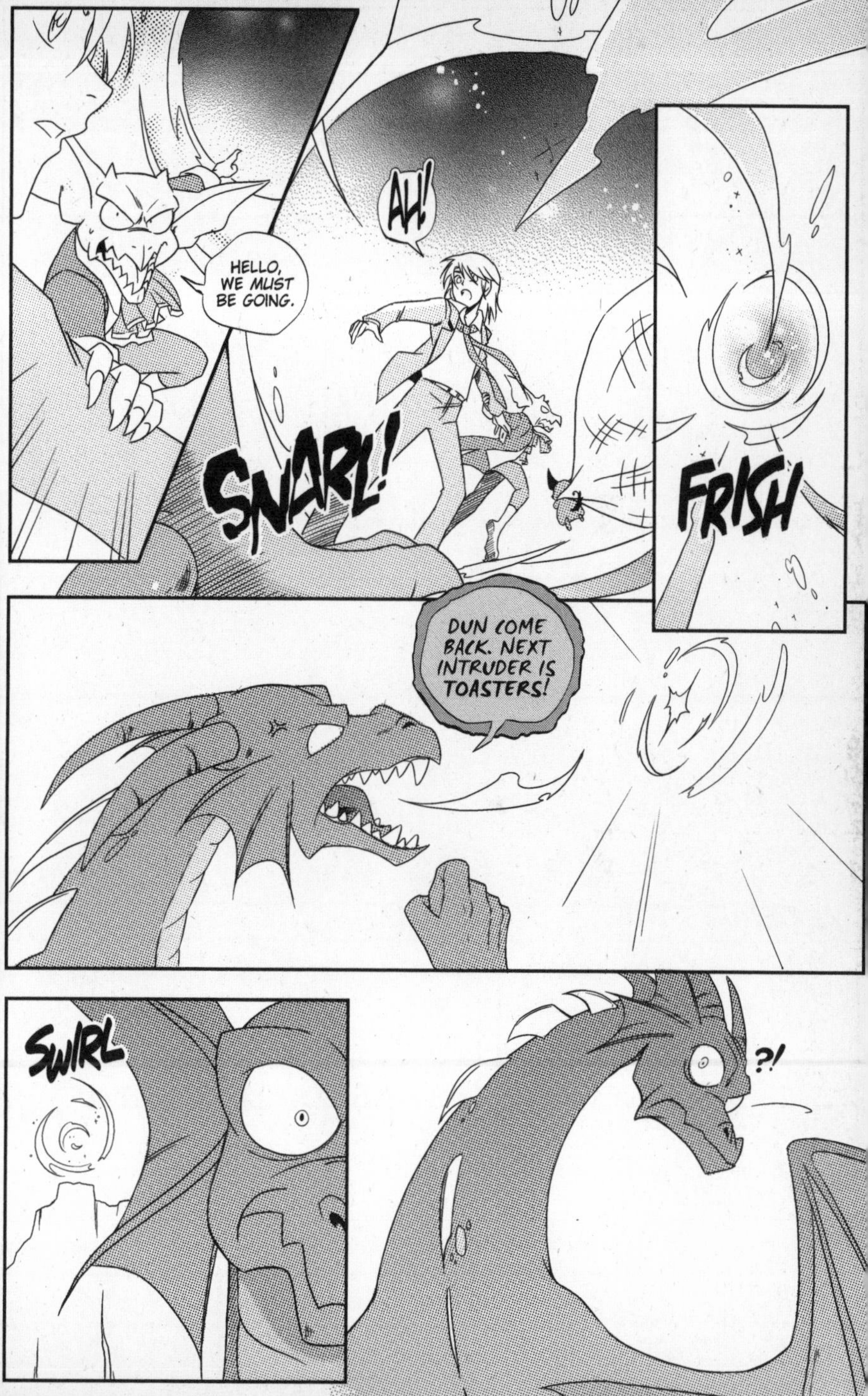
AH!
HELLO, WE MUST BE GOING.
SNARL!
FRISH
DUN COME BACK. NEXT INTRUDER IS TOASTERS!
SWIRL
?!

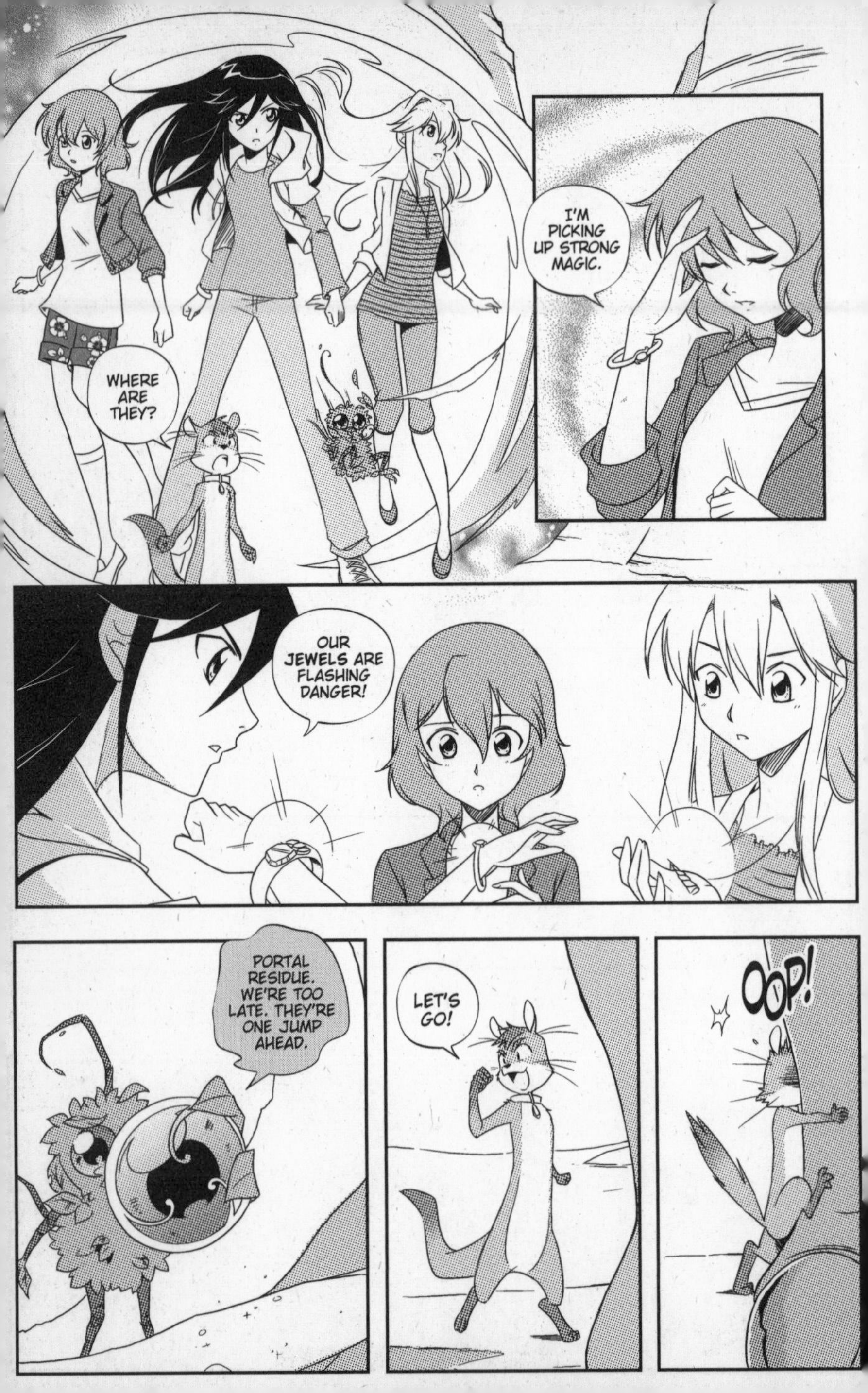
WHERE ARE THEY?
I'M PICKING UP STRONG MAGIC.
OUR JEWELS ARE FLASHING DANGER!
PORTAL RESIDUE. WE'RE TOO LATE. THEY'RE ONE JUMP AHEAD.
LET'S GO!
OOP!

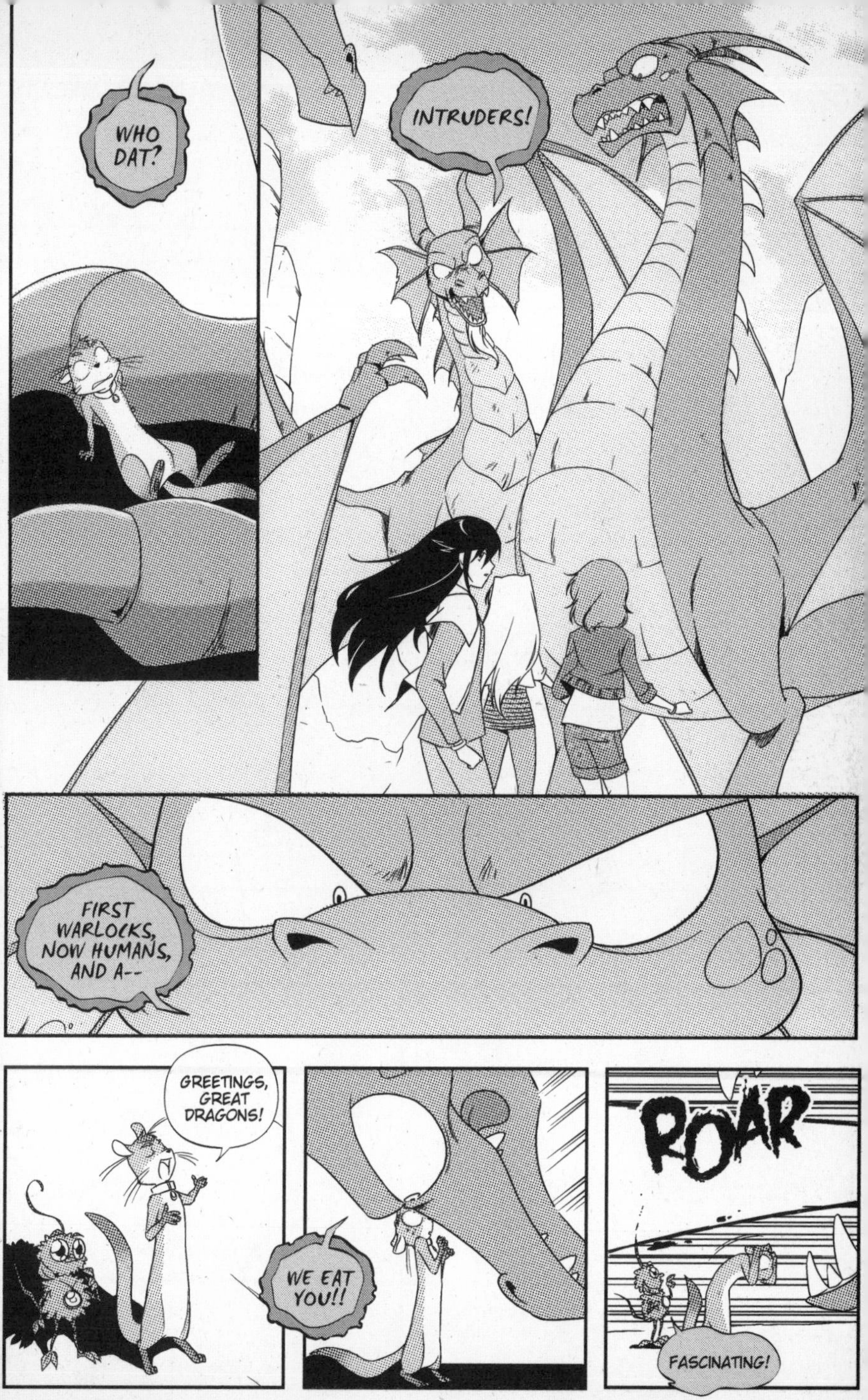
WHO DAT?
INTRUDERS!
FIRST WARLOCKS, NOW HUMANS, AND A--
GREETINGS, GREAT DRAGONS!
WE EAT YOU!!
ROAR
FASCINATING!

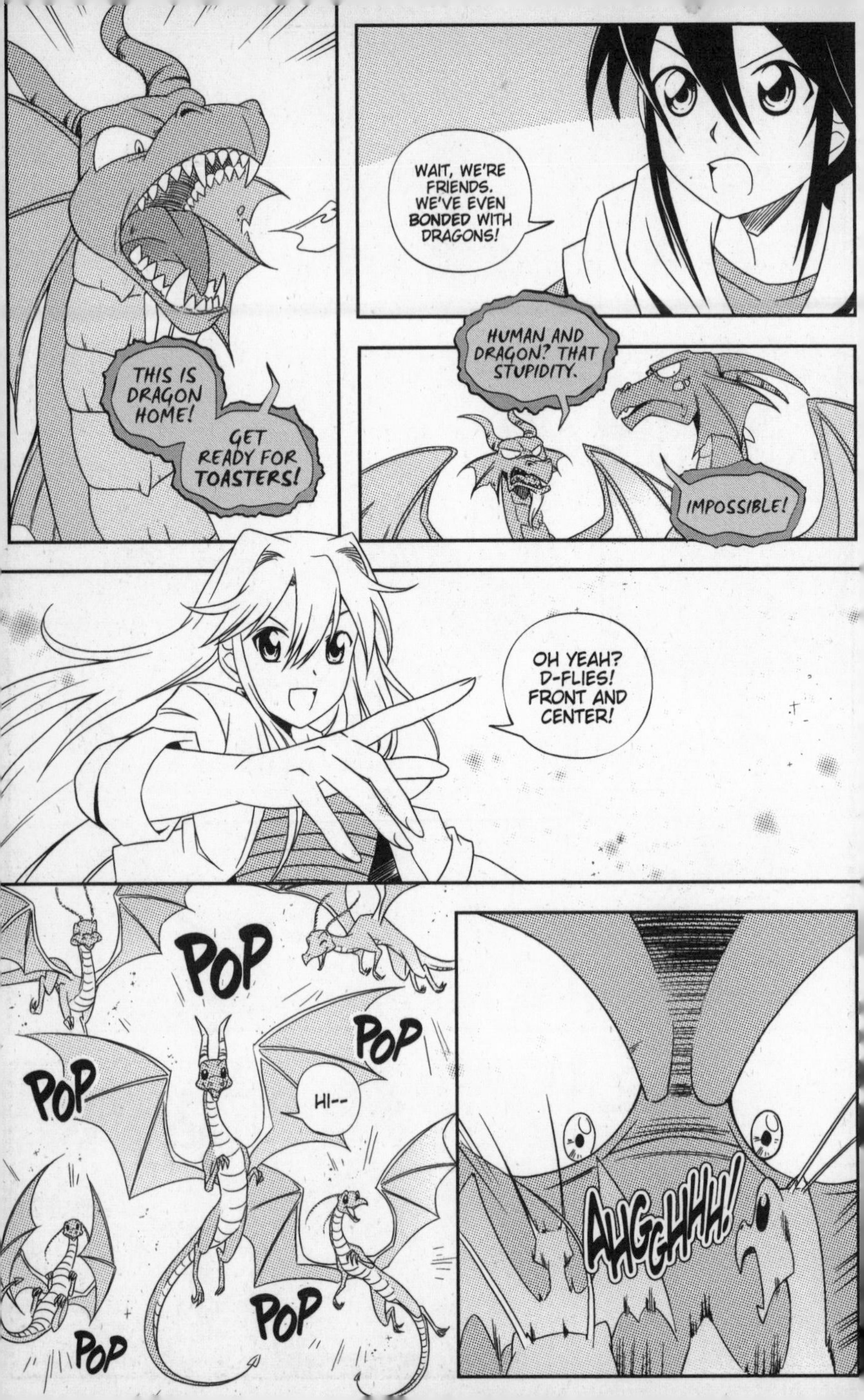
THIS IS DRAGON HOME!
GET READY FOR TOASTERS!
WAIT, WE'RE FRIENDS. WE'VE EVEN BONDED WITH DRAGONS!
HUMAN AND DRAGON? THAT STUPIDITY.
IMPOSSIBLE!
OH YEAH? D-FLIES! FRONT AND CENTER!
POP
POP
POP
HI--
POP
POP
AUGHHH!

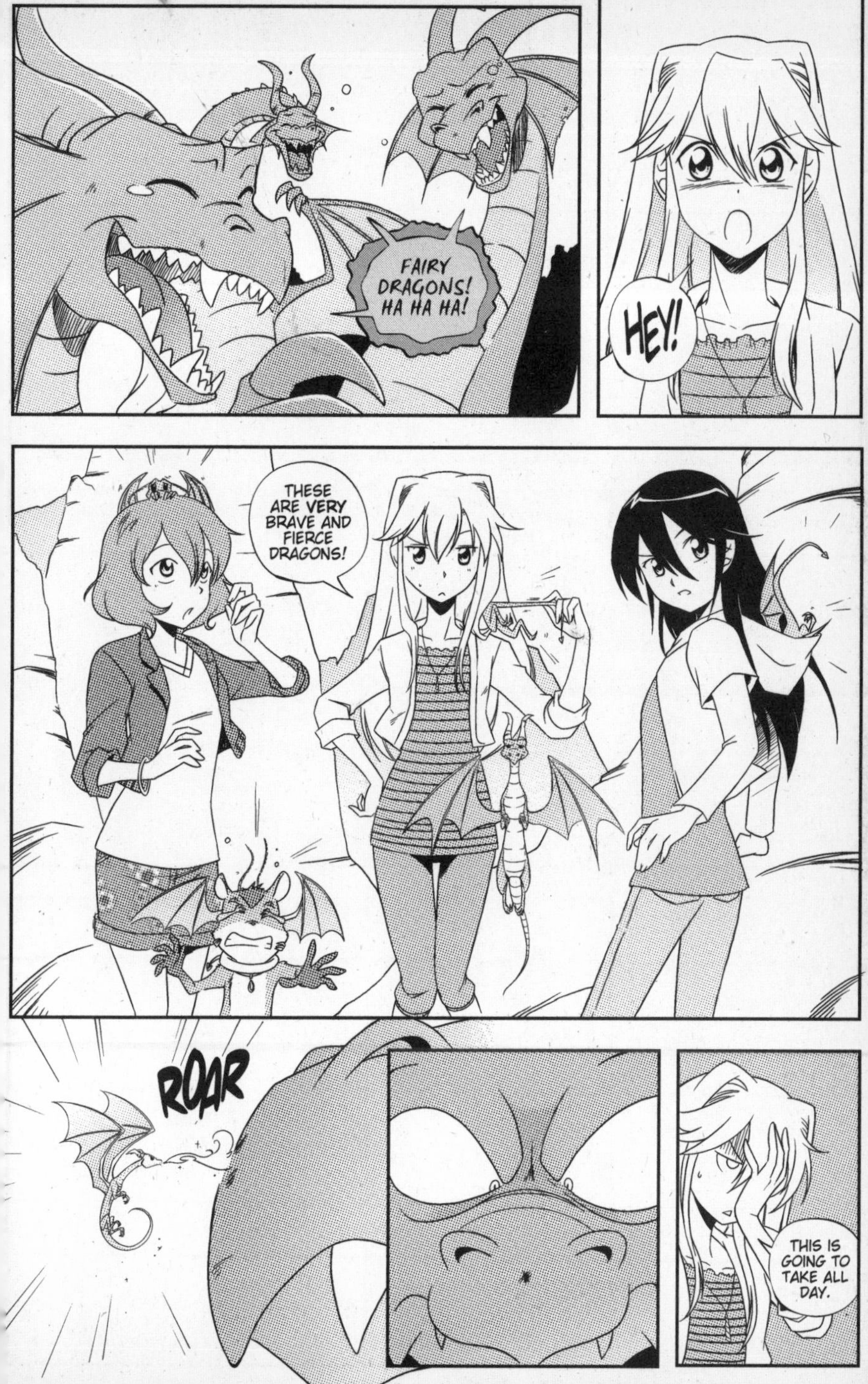
FAIRY DRAGONS! HA HA HA!
HEY!
THESE ARE VERY BRAVE AND FIERCE DRAGONS!
ROAR
THIS IS GOING TO TAKE ALL DAY.

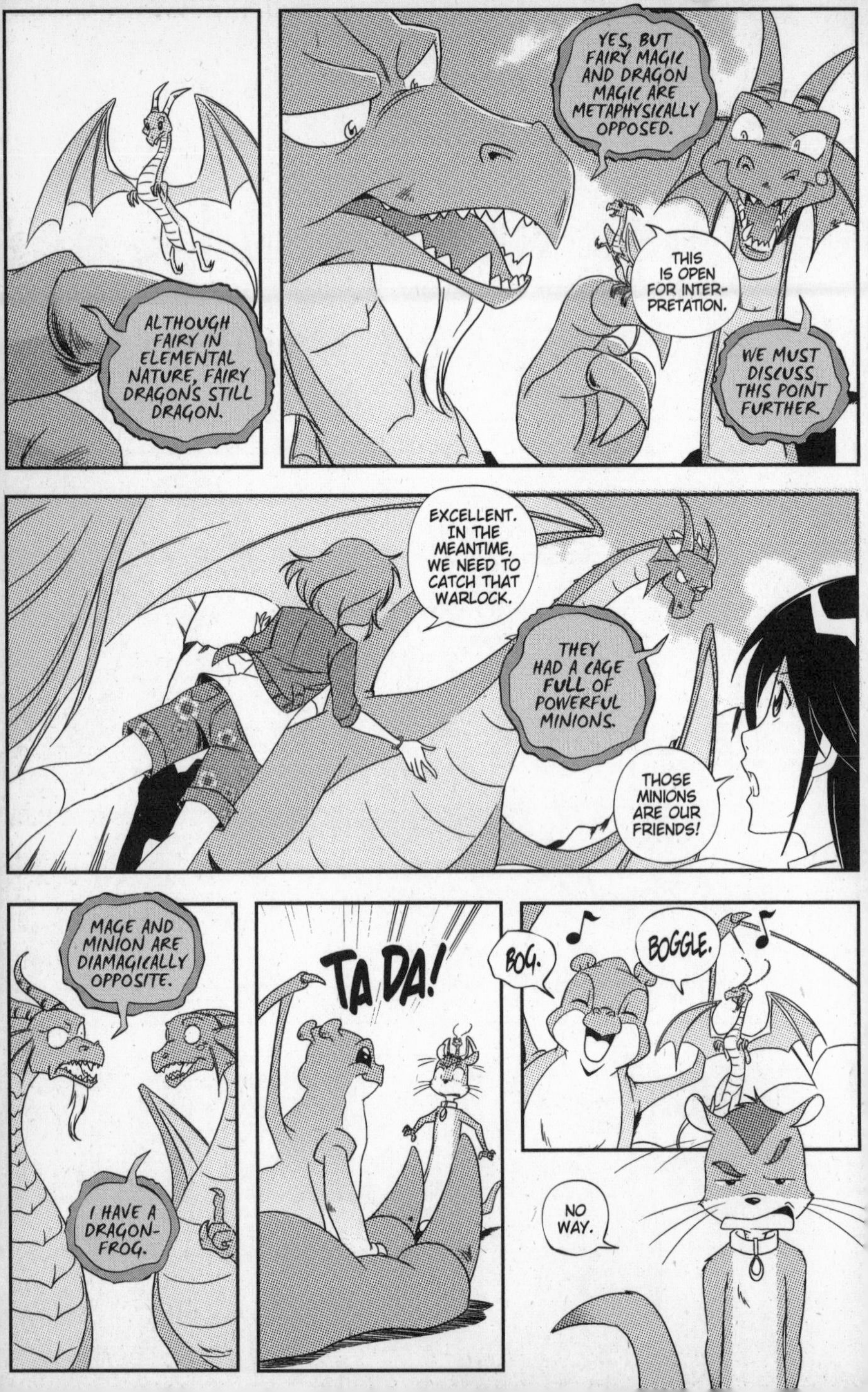
ALTHOUGH FAIRY IN ELEMENTAL NATURE, FAIRY DRAGON'S STILL DRAGON.
YES, BUT FAIRY MAGIC AND DRAGON MAGIC ARE METAPHYSICALLY OPPOSED.
THIS IS OPEN FOR INTER-PRETATION.
WE MUST DISCUSS THIS POINT FURTHER.
EXCELLENT. IN THE MEANTIME, WE NEED TO CATCH THAT WARLOCK.
THEY HAD A CAGE FULL OF POWERFUL MINIONS.
THOSE MINIONS ARE OUR FRIENDS!
MAGE AND MINION ARE DIAMAGICALLY OPPOSITE.
I HAVE A DRAGON-FROG.
TA DA!
BOG.
BOGGLE.
NO WAY.

I FOUND THE NEXT PORTAL!

IF WE HURRY WE CAN CATCH THEM.

LET'S GO.

MAGIC SYMPOSIUM ON DRAGON BONDING TOMORROW AT NOON. BRING YOUR DRAGONFROG.

BAWOW!! I MUST EXTRA-POLATE.

CALL US SOMETIME. WE'RE IN THE BOOK.

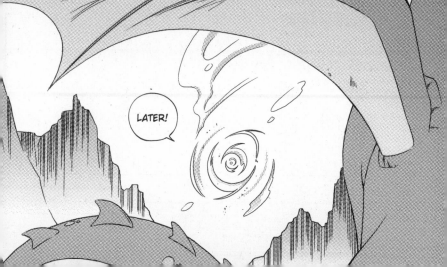

LATER!

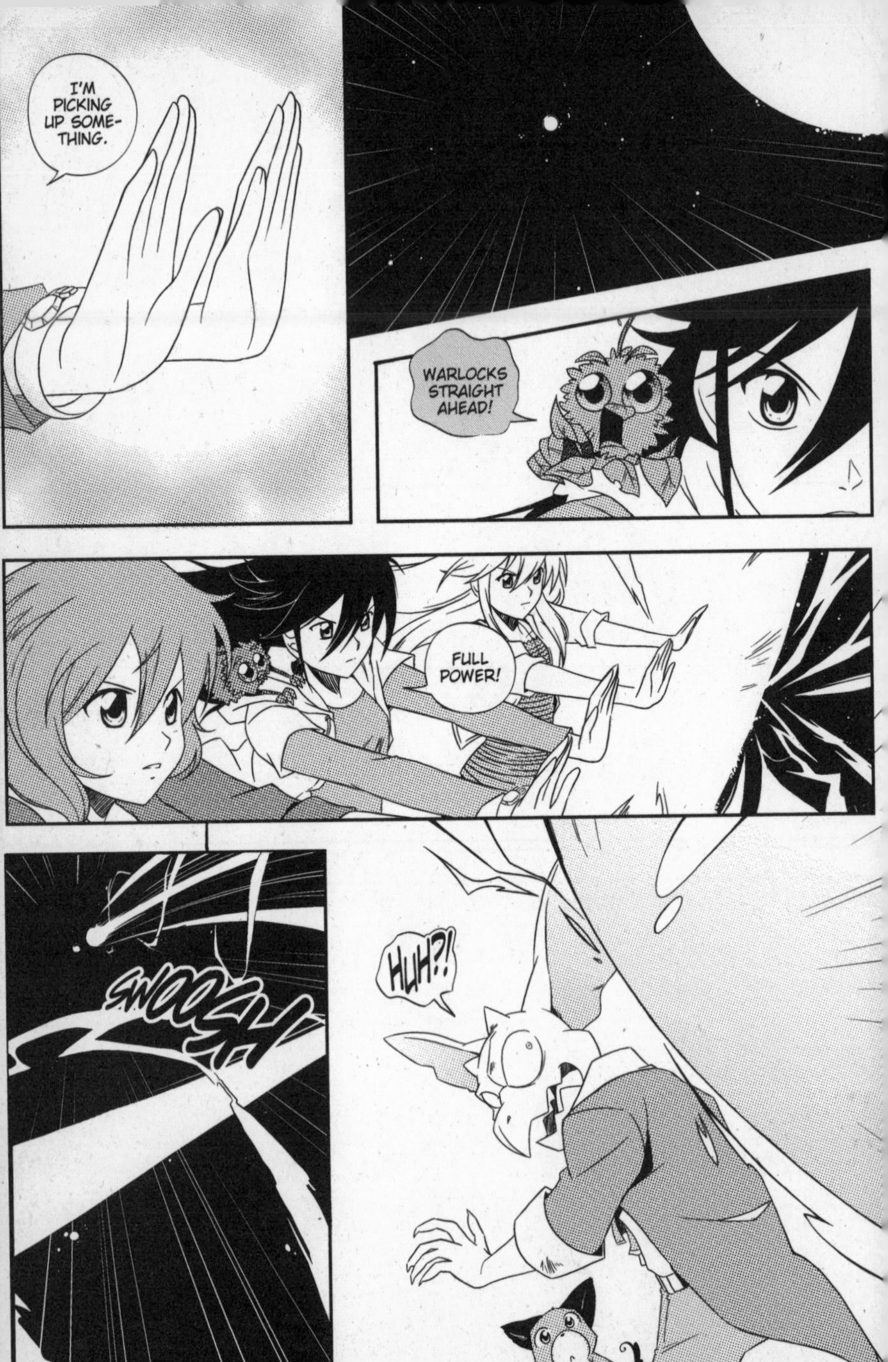
I'M PICKING UP SOME-THING.
WARLOCKS STRAIGHT AHEAD!
FULL POWER!
SWOOSH
HUH?!

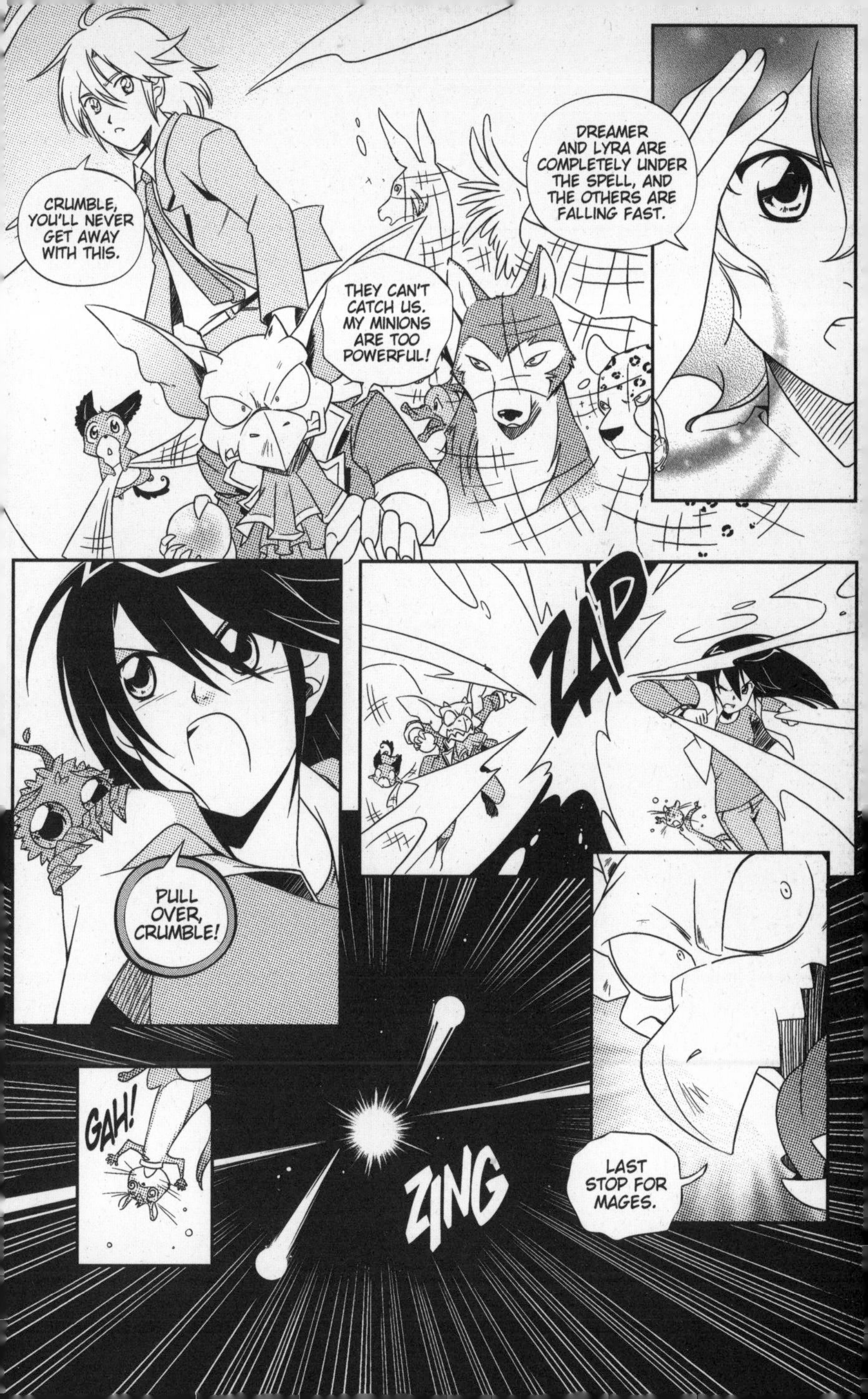
CRUMBLE, YOU'LL NEVER GET AWAY WITH THIS.
THEY CAN'T CATCH US. MY MINIONS ARE TOO POWERFUL!
DREAMER AND LYRA ARE COMPLETELY UNDER THE SPELL, AND THE OTHERS ARE FALLING FAST.
PULL OVER, CRUMBLE!
ZAP
GAH!
ZING
LAST STOP FOR MAGES.

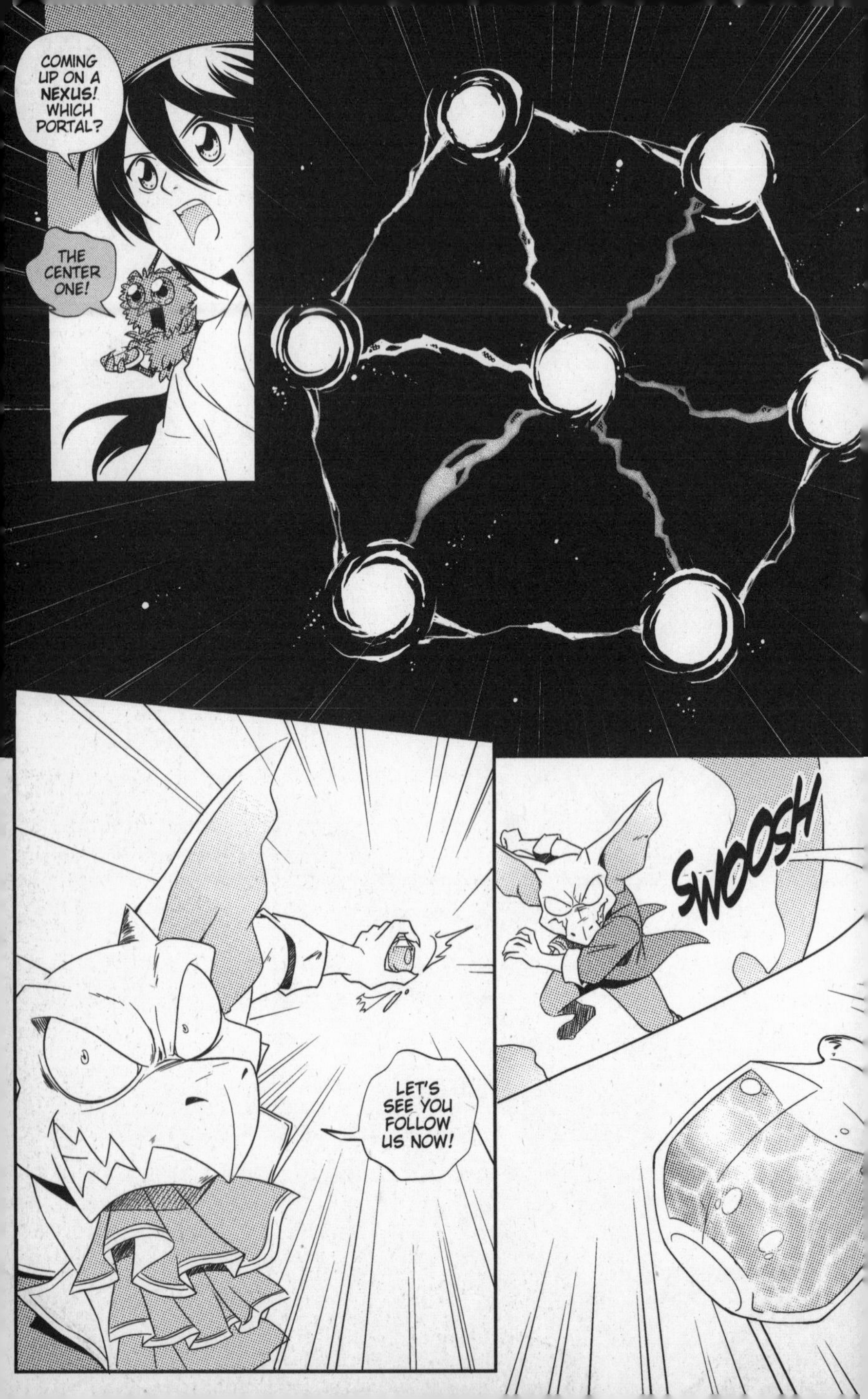
COMING UP ON A NEXUS! WHICH PORTAL?
THE CENTER ONE!
LET'S SEE YOU FOLLOW US NOW!
SWOOSH

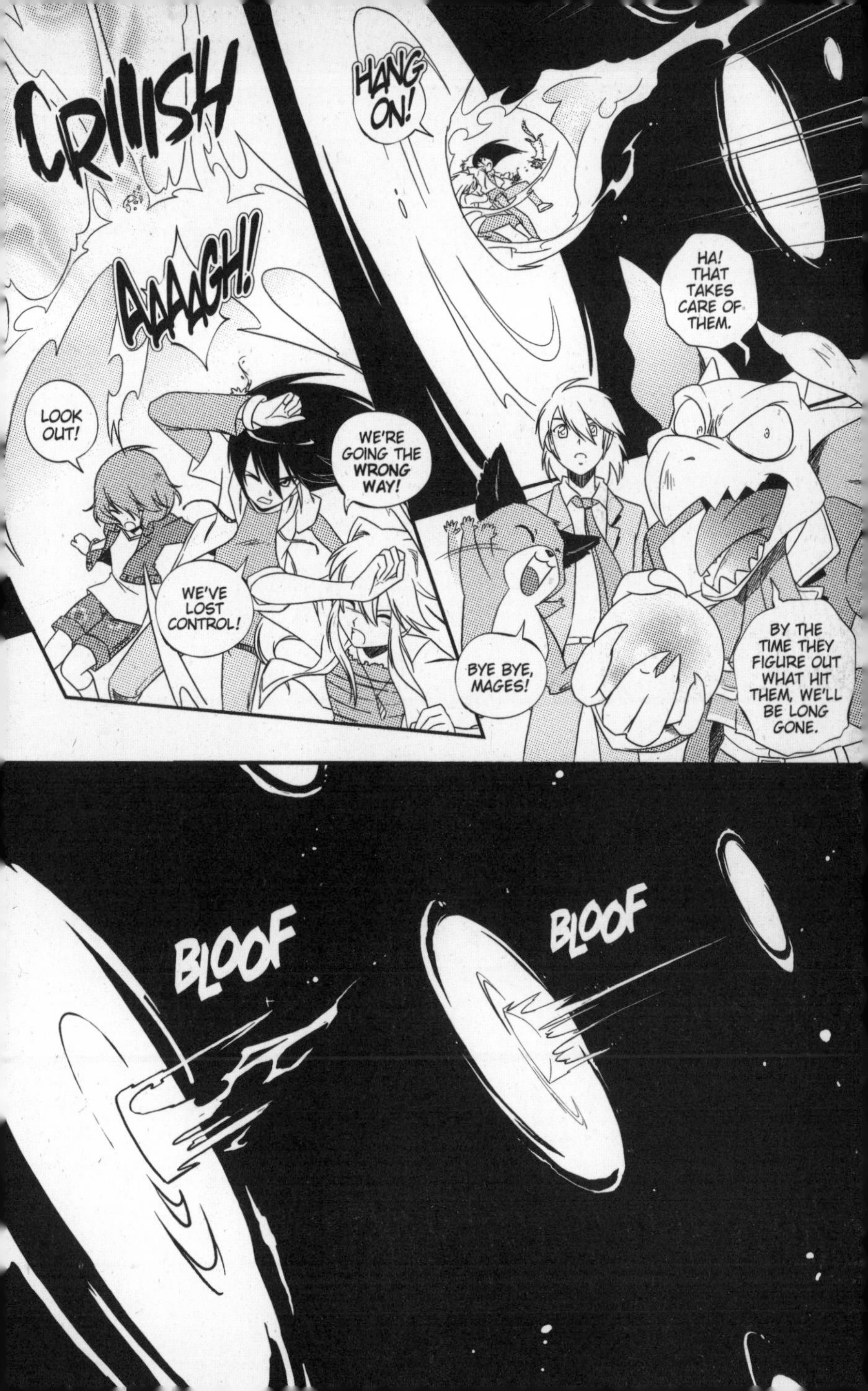
CRIIISH
AAAAGH!
LOOK OUT!
WE'RE GOING THE WRONG WAY!
WE'VE LOST CONTROL!
HANG ON!
HA! THAT TAKES CARE OF THEM.
BYE BYE, MAGES!
BY THE TIME THEY FIGURE OUT WHAT HIT THEM, WE'LL BE LONG GONE.
BLOOF
BLOOF

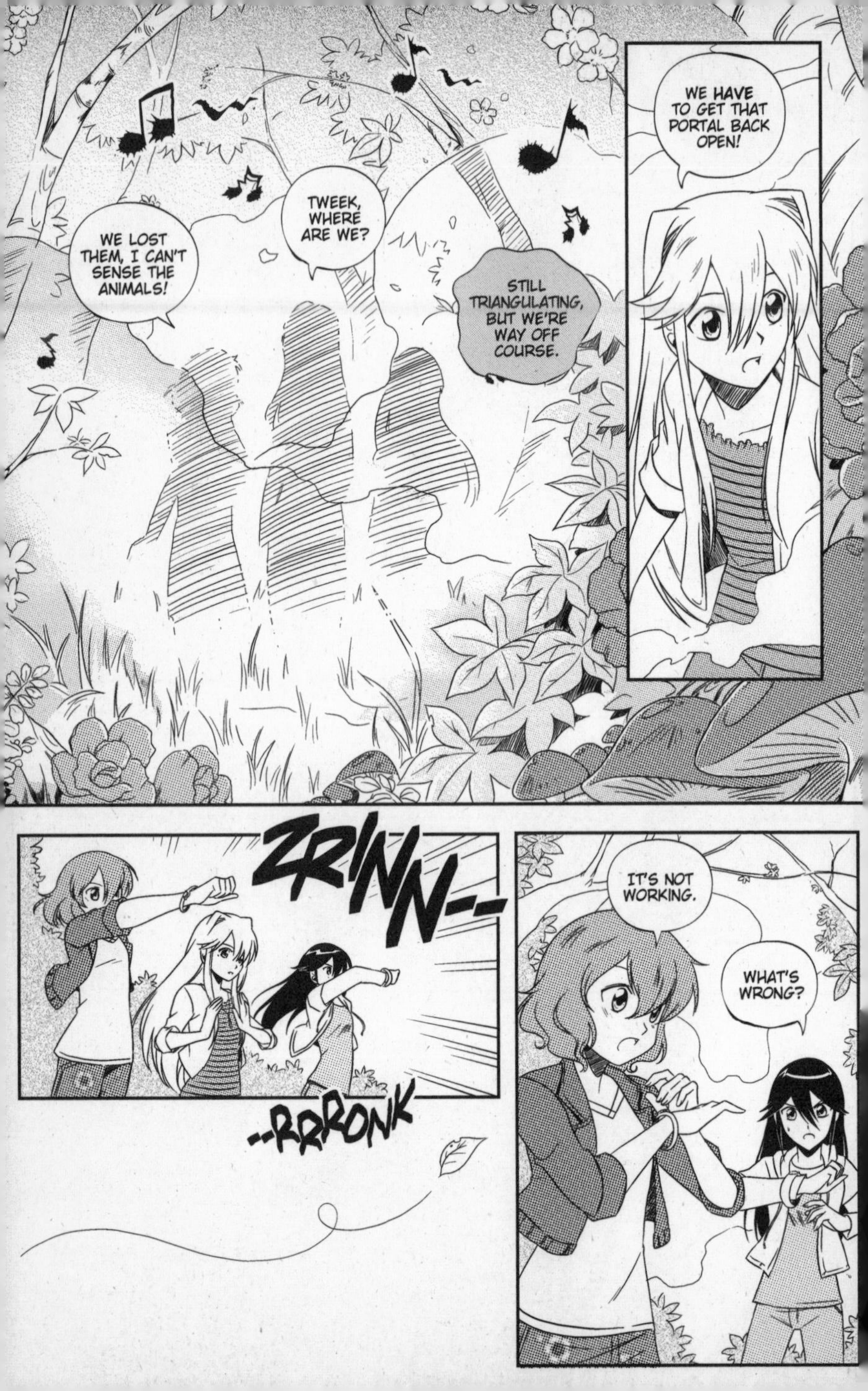
WE LOST THEM, I CAN'T SENSE THE ANIMALS!
TWEEK, WHERE ARE WE?
STILL TRIANGULATING, BUT WE'RE WAY OFF COURSE.
WE HAVE TO GET THAT PORTAL BACK OPEN!
ZRINNN--
--RRRONK
IT'S NOT WORKING.
WHAT'S WRONG?

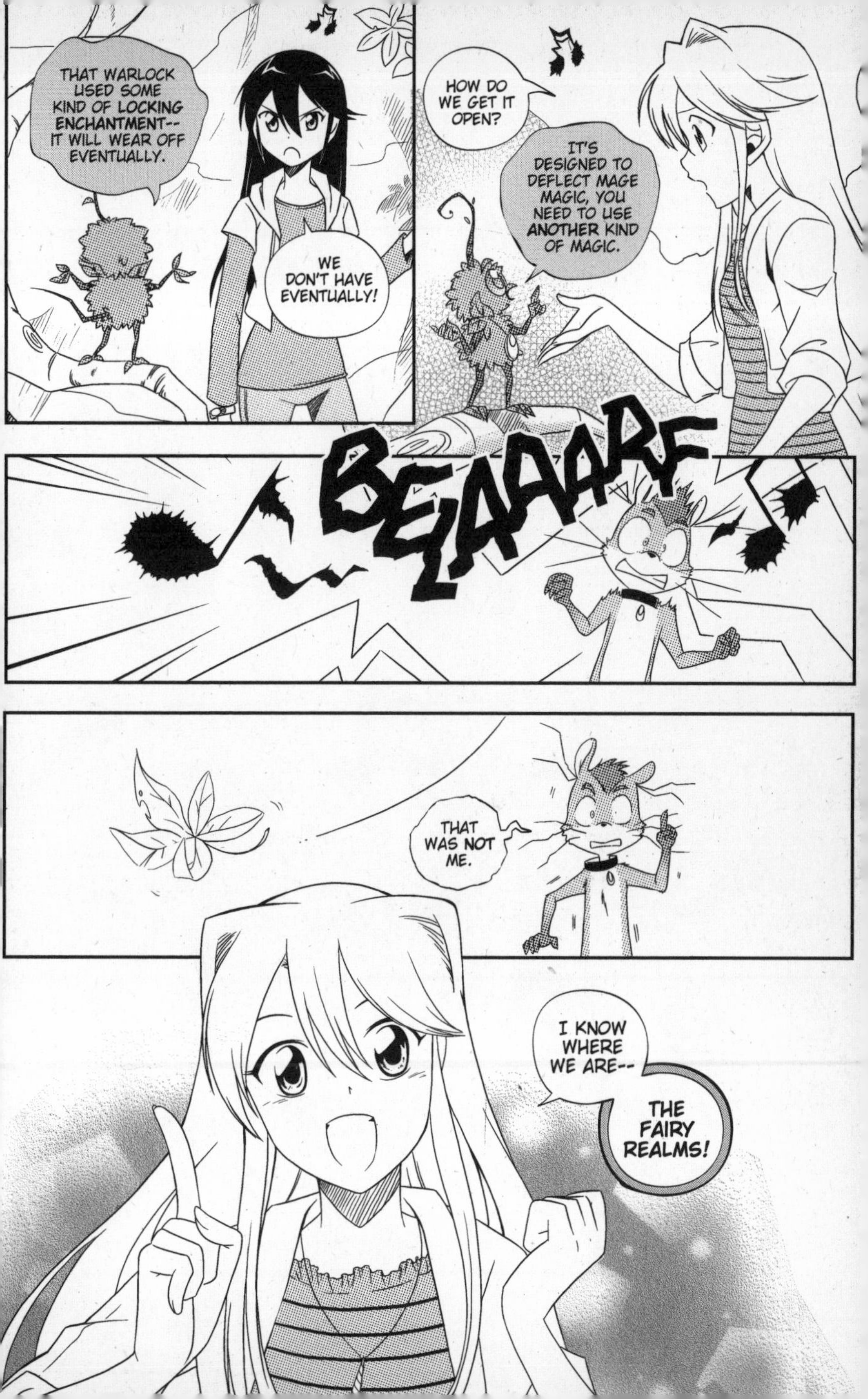
THAT WARLOCK USED SOME KIND OF LOCKING ENCHANTMENT-- IT WILL WEAR OFF EVENTUALLY.
WE DON'T HAVE EVENTUALLY!
HOW DO WE GET IT OPEN?
IT'S DESIGNED TO DEFLECT MAGE MAGIC, YOU NEED TO USE ANOTHER KIND OF MAGIC.
BELAAARF
THAT WAS NOT ME.
I KNOW WHERE WE ARE--
THE FAIRY REALMS!

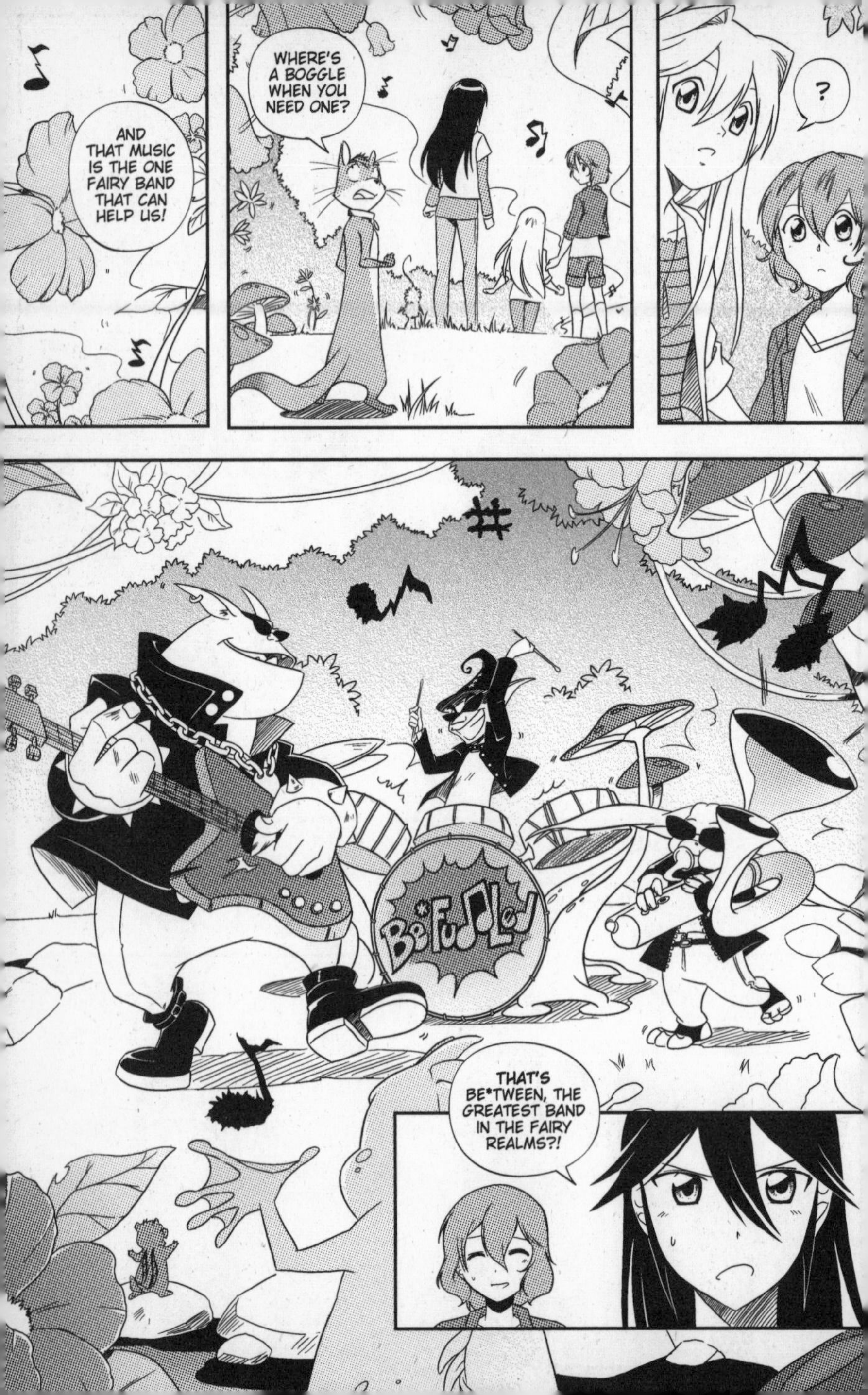
AND THAT MUSIC IS THE ONE FAIRY BAND THAT CAN HELP US!
WHERE'S A BOGGLE WHEN YOU NEED ONE?
?
Be*FuDDLeD
THAT'S BE*TWEEN, THE GREATEST BAND IN THE FAIRY REALMS?!

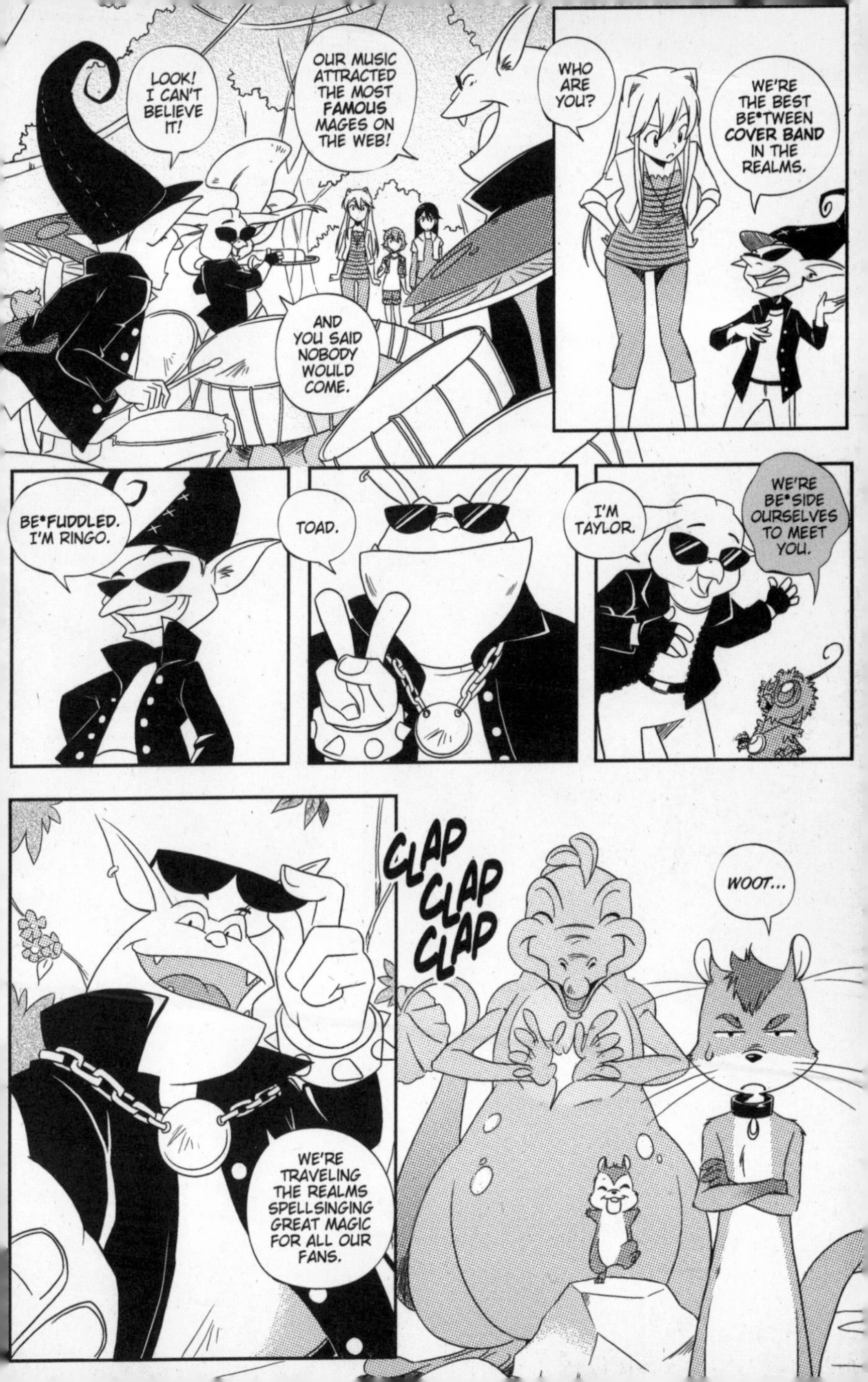
LOOK! I CAN'T BELIEVE IT!
OUR MUSIC ATTRACTED THE MOST FAMOUS MAGES ON THE WEB!
AND YOU SAID NOBODY WOULD COME.
WHO ARE YOU?
WE'RE THE BEST BE*TWEEN COVER BAND IN THE REALMS.
BE*FUDDLED. I'M RINGO.
TOAD.
I'M TAYLOR.
WE'RE BE*SIDE OURSELVES TO MEET YOU.
CLAP CLAP CLAP
WOOT...
WE'RE TRAVELING THE REALMS SPELLSINGING GREAT MAGIC FOR ALL OUR FANS.

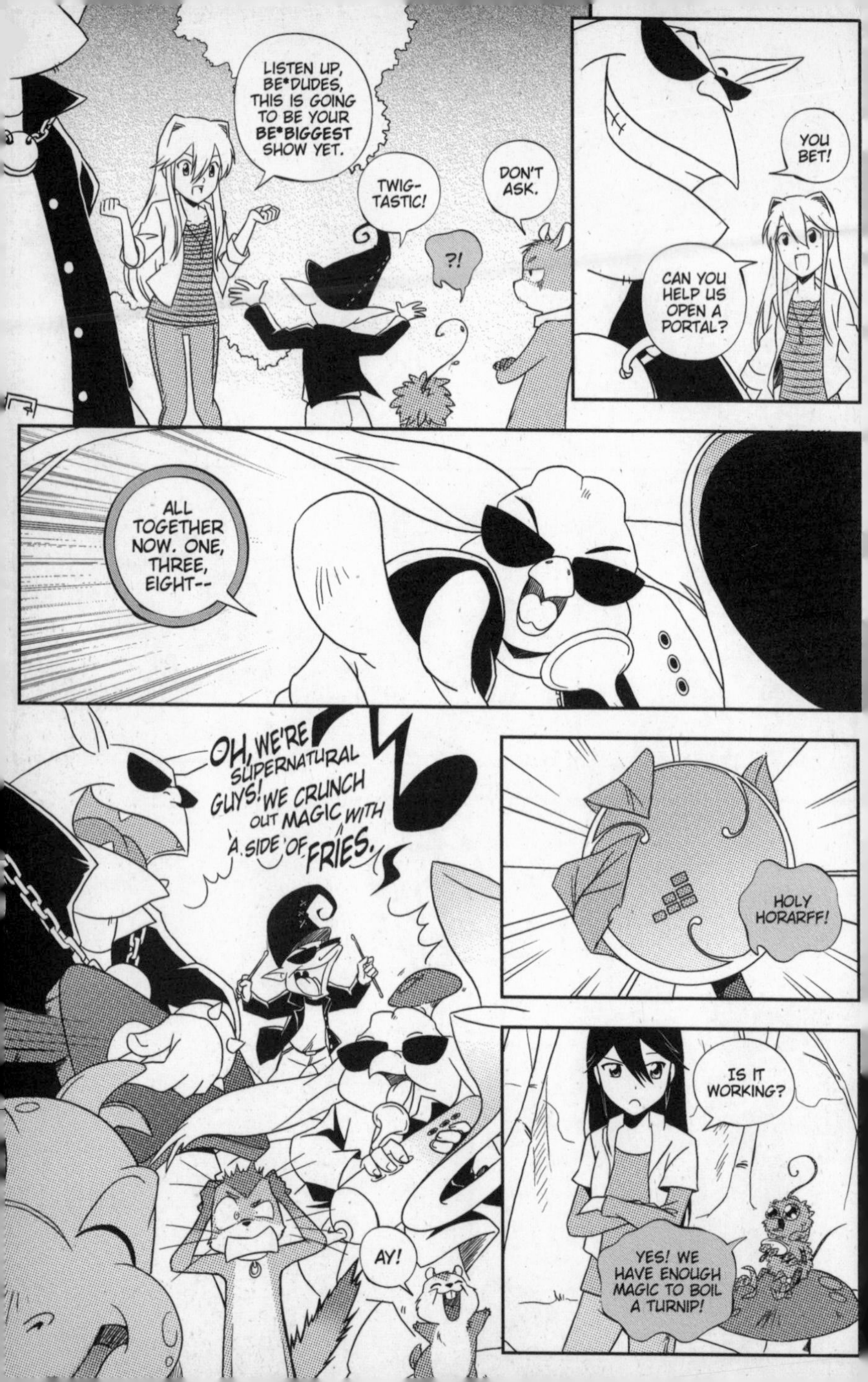
LISTEN UP, BE*DUDES, THIS IS GOING TO BE YOUR BE*BIGGEST SHOW YET.
TWIG-TASTIC!
?!
DON'T ASK.
YOU BET!
CAN YOU HELP US OPEN A PORTAL?
ALL TOGETHER NOW. ONE, THREE, EIGHT--
OH, WE'RE SUPERNATURAL GUYS! WE CRUNCH OUT MAGIC WITH A SIDE OF FRIES.
AY!
HOLY HORARFF!
IS IT WORKING?
YES! WE HAVE ENOUGH MAGIC TO BOIL A TURNIP!

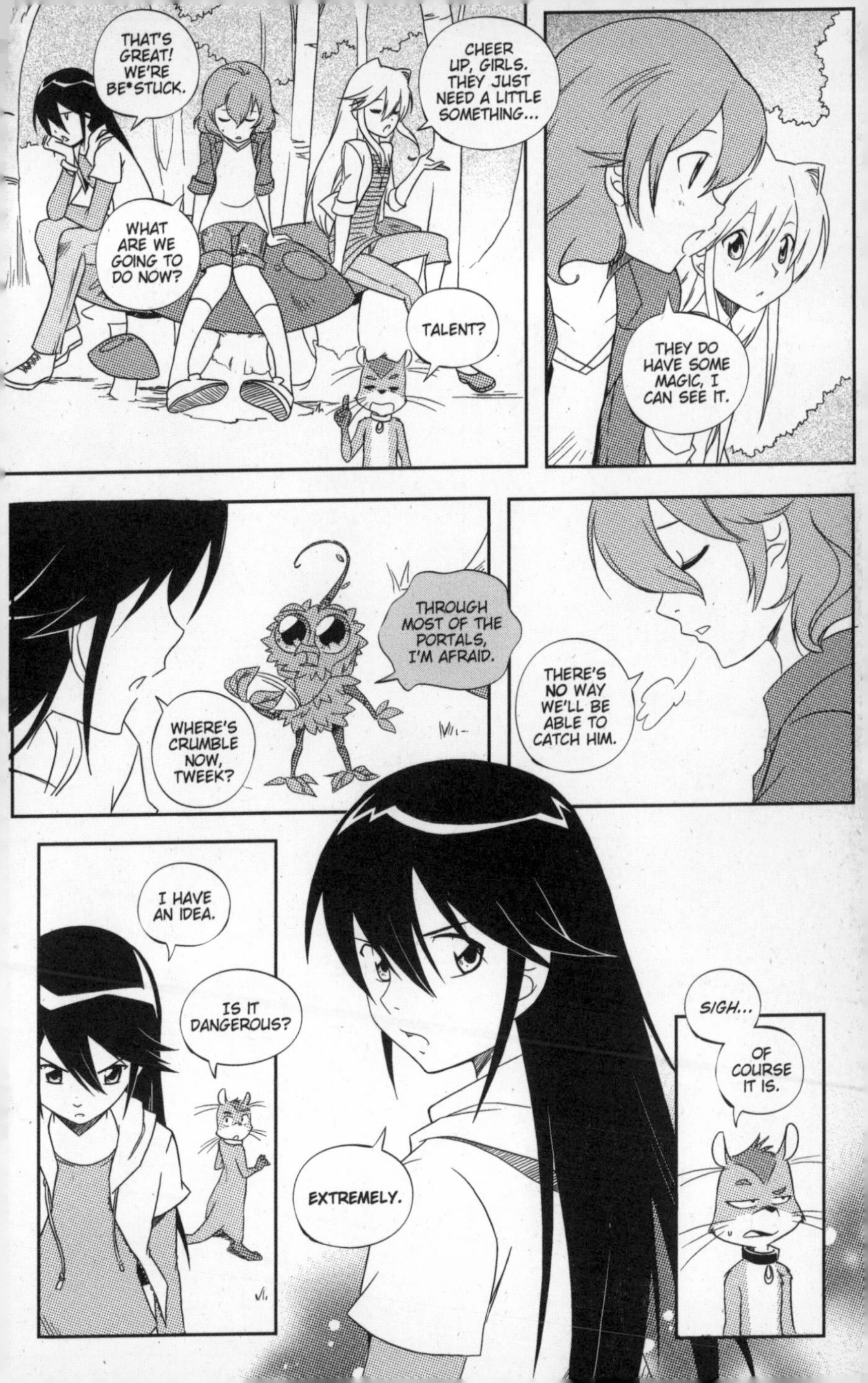
THAT'S GREAT! WE'RE BE*STUCK.
CHEER UP, GIRLS. THEY JUST NEED A LITTLE SOMETHING...
WHAT ARE WE GOING TO DO NOW?
TALENT?
THEY DO HAVE SOME MAGIC, I CAN SEE IT.
THROUGH MOST OF THE PORTALS, I'M AFRAID.
WHERE'S CRUMBLE NOW, TWEEK?
THERE'S NO WAY WE'LL BE ABLE TO CATCH HIM.
I HAVE AN IDEA.
IS IT DANGEROUS?
EXTREMELY.
SIGH...
OF COURSE IT IS.

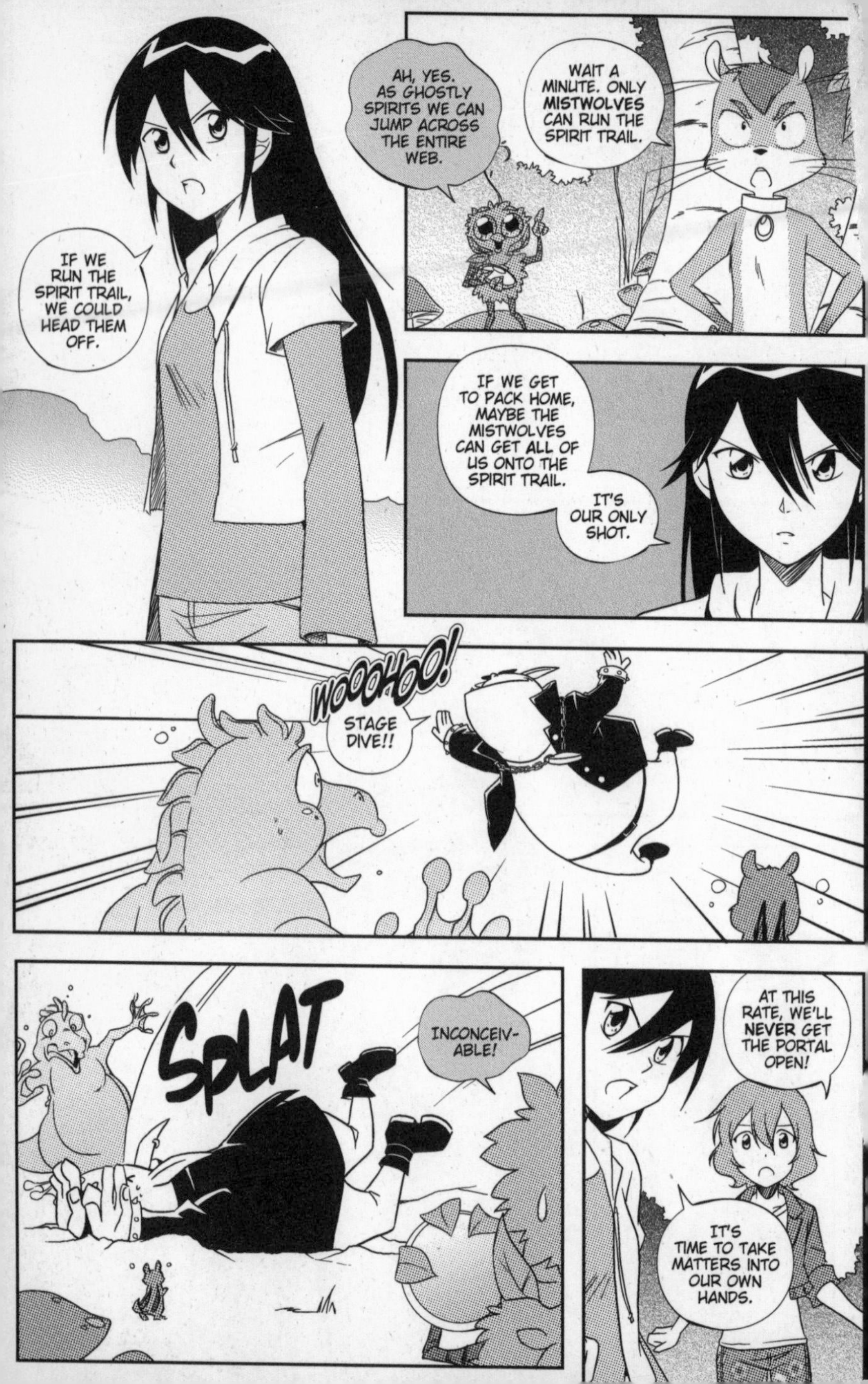
IF WE RUN THE SPIRIT TRAIL, WE COULD HEAD THEM OFF.
AH, YES. AS GHOSTLY SPIRITS WE CAN JUMP ACROSS THE ENTIRE WEB.
WAIT A MINUTE. ONLY MISTWOLVES CAN RUN THE SPIRIT TRAIL.
IF WE GET TO PACK HOME, MAYBE THE MISTWOLVES CAN GET ALL OF US ONTO THE SPIRIT TRAIL.
IT'S OUR ONLY SHOT.
WOOOHOO!
STAGE DIVE!!
SPLAT
INCONCEIV-ABLE!
AT THIS RATE, WE'LL NEVER GET THE PORTAL OPEN!
IT'S TIME TO TAKE MATTERS INTO OUR OWN HANDS.

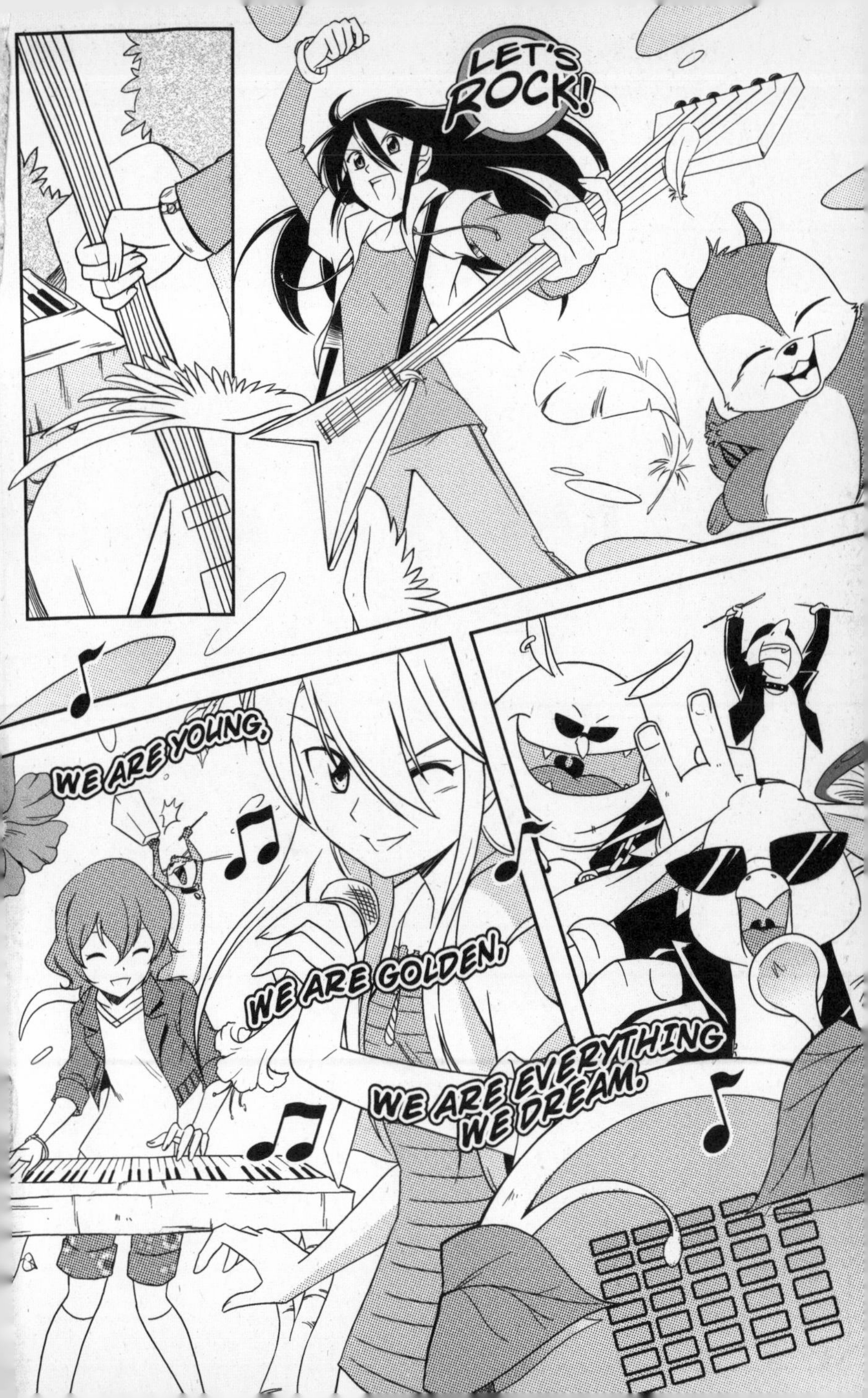
LET'S ROCK!
WE ARE YOUNG,
WE ARE GOLDEN,
WE ARE EVERYTHING WE DREAM.

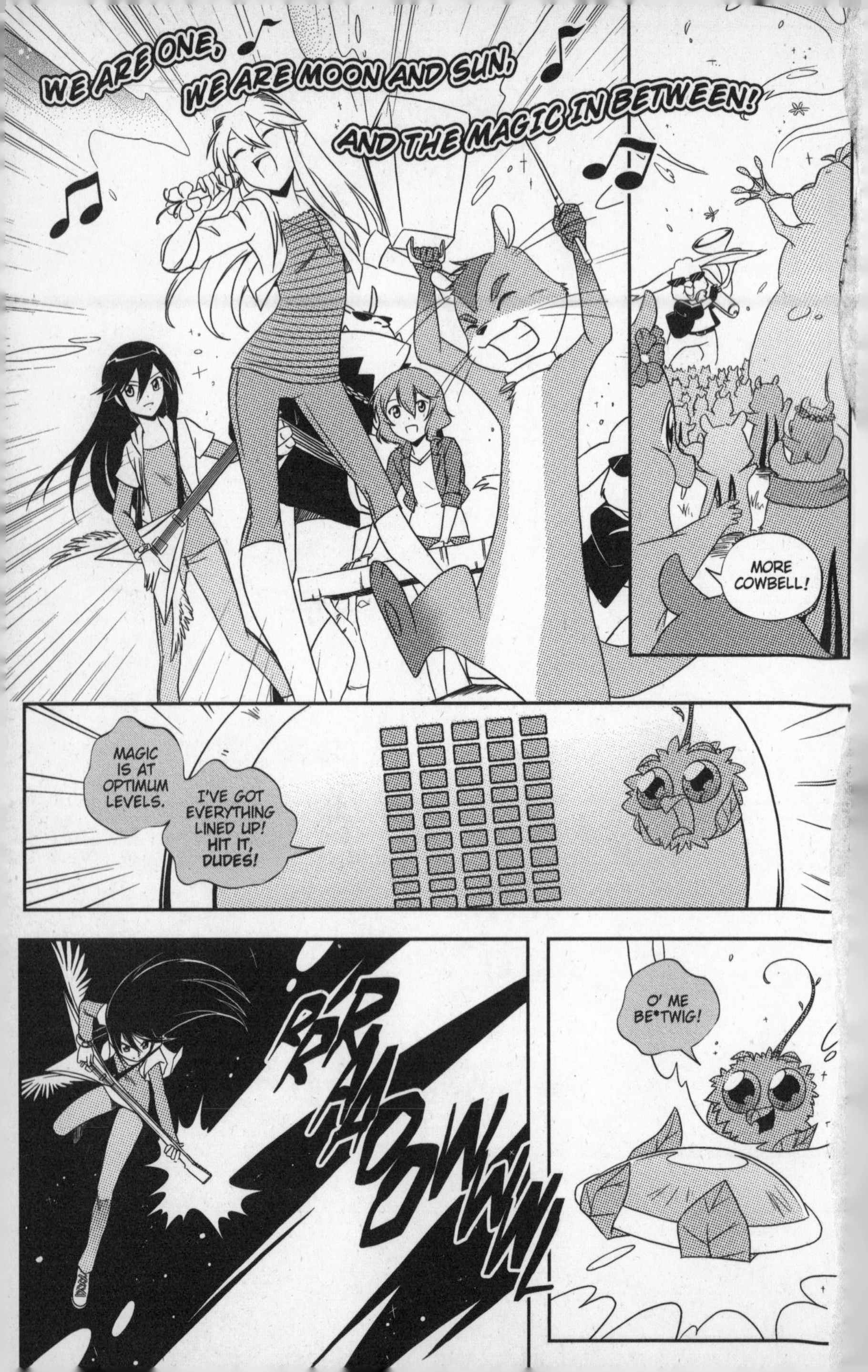
WE ARE ONE,
WE ARE MOON AND SUN,
AND THE MAGIC IN BETWEEN!
MORE COWBELL!
MAGIC IS AT OPTIMUM LEVELS.
I'VE GOT EVERYTHING LINED UP! HIT IT, DUDES!
RRRAAOWWWL
O' ME BE*TWIG!

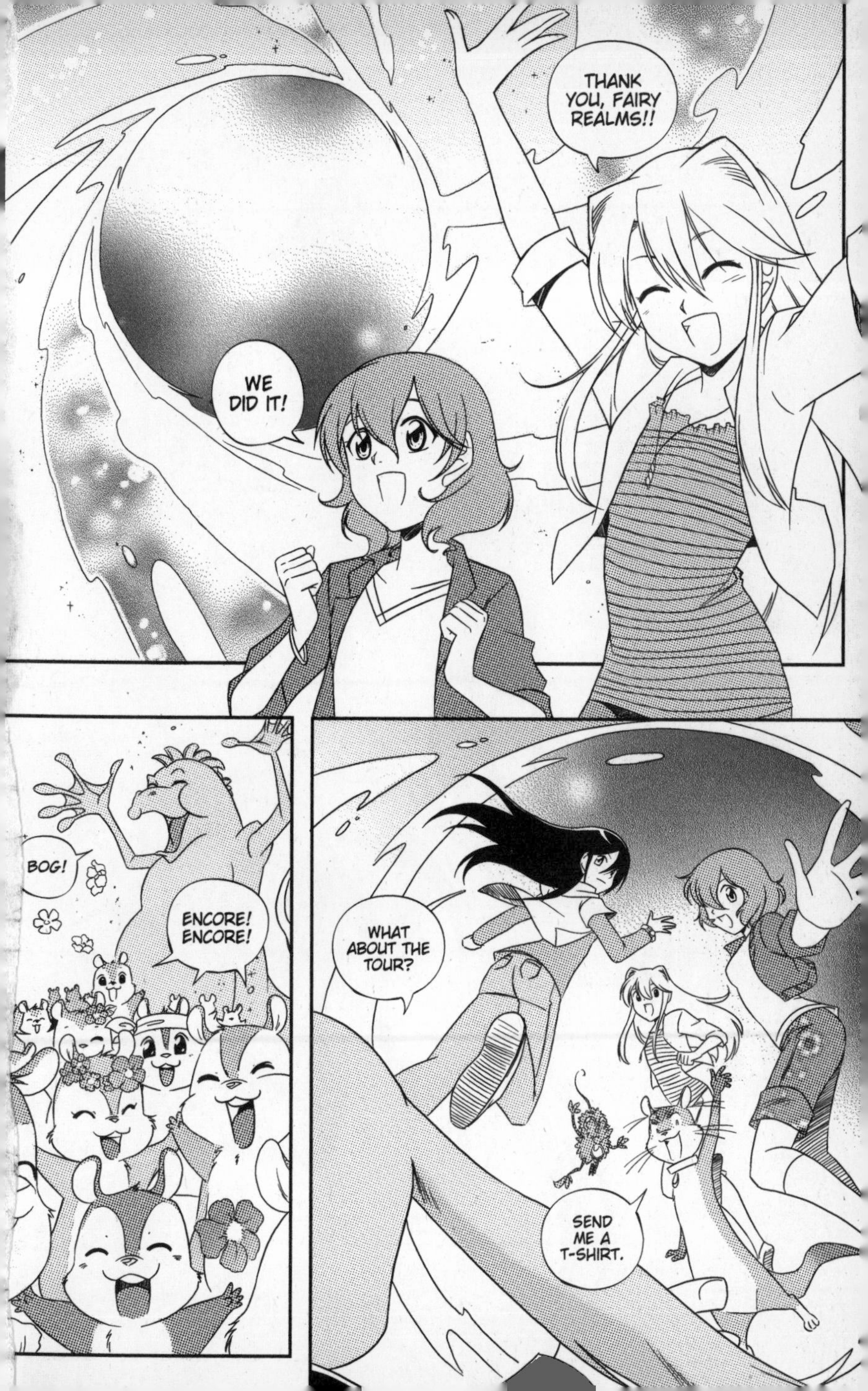
THANK YOU, FAIRY REALMS!!
WE DID IT!
BOG!
ENCORE! ENCORE!
WHAT ABOUT THE TOUR?
SEND ME A T-SHIRT.

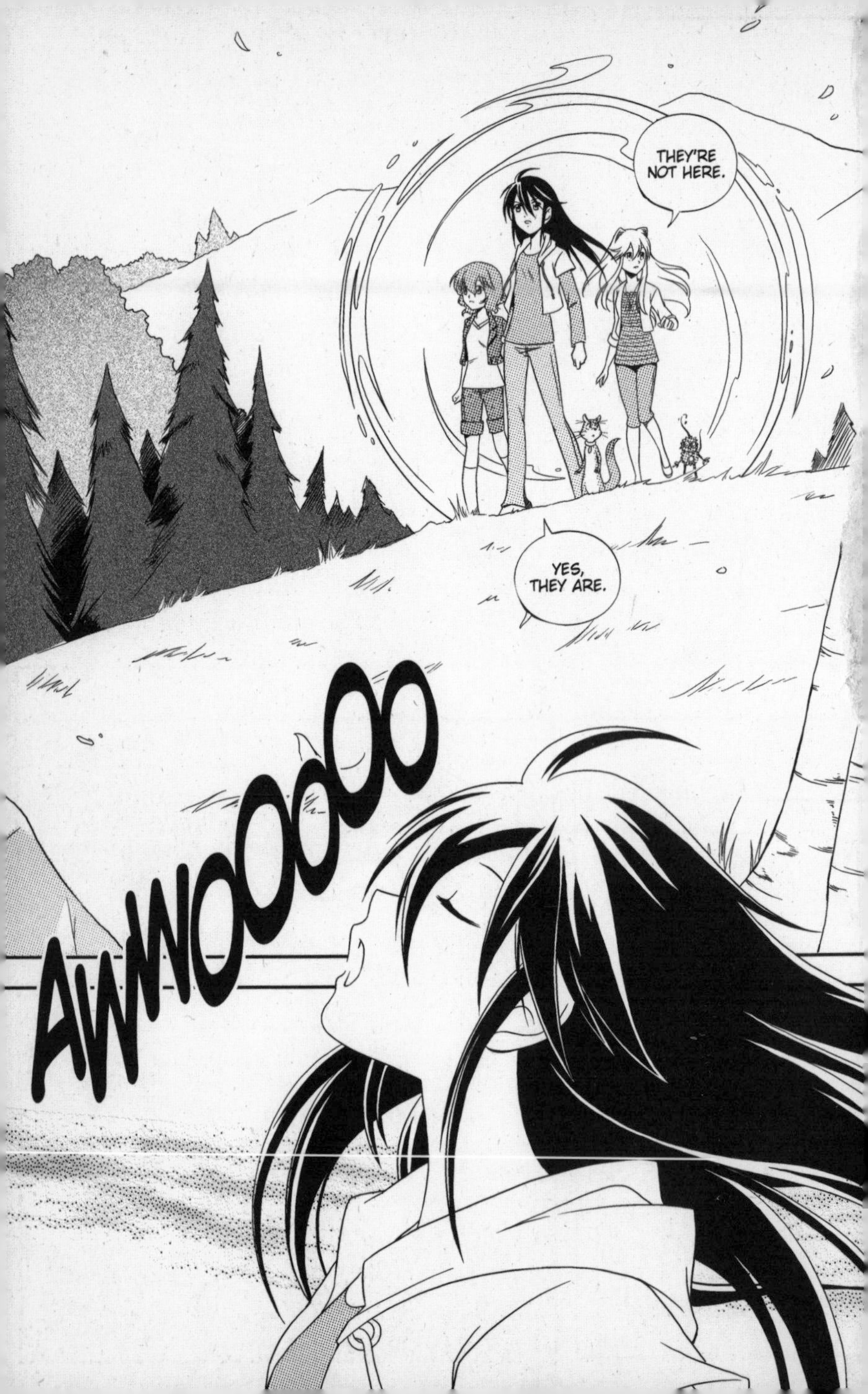
THEY'RE NOT HERE.
YES, THEY ARE.
AWWOOOOOO

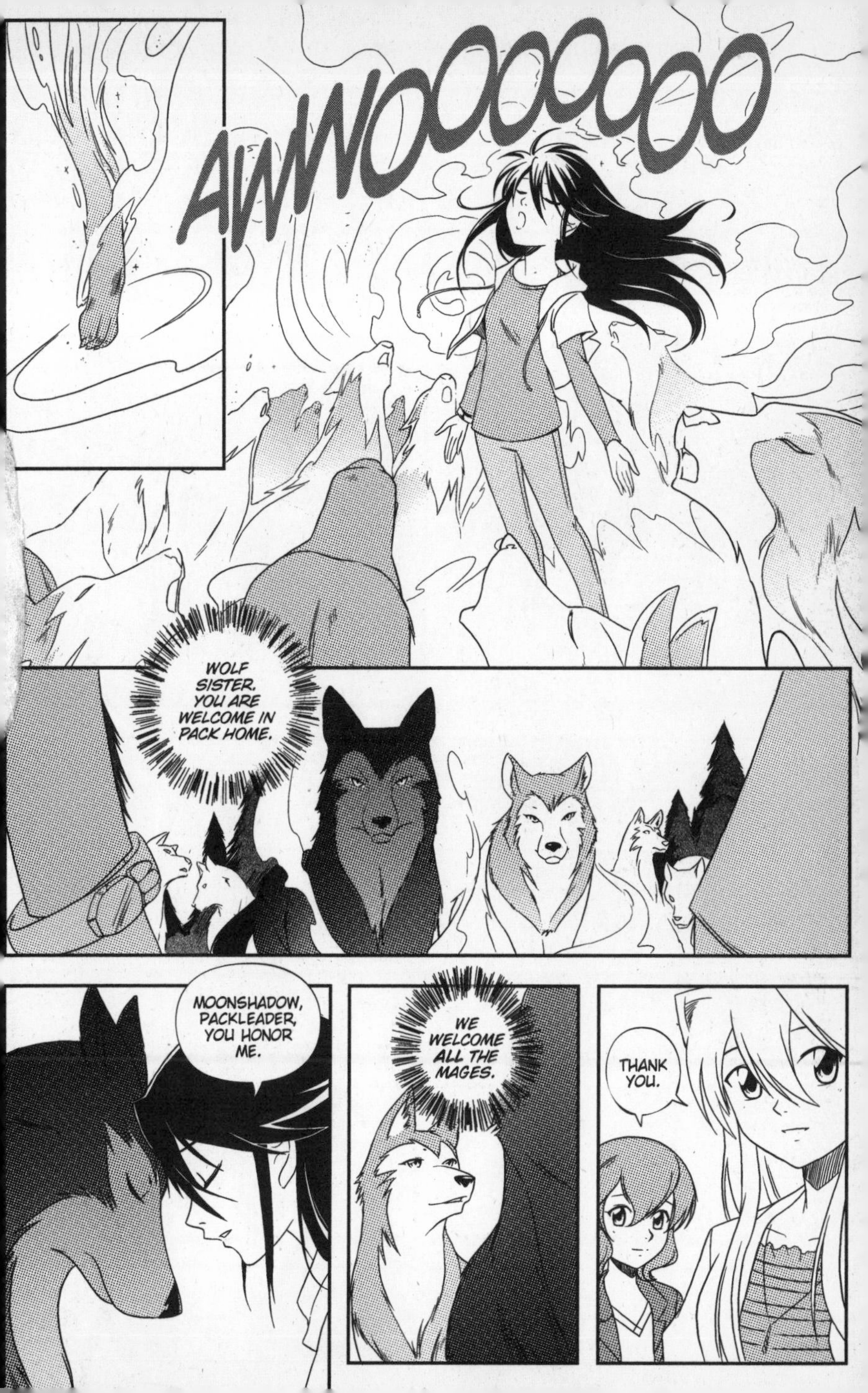
AWWOOOOOOO
WOLF SISTER. YOU ARE WELCOME IN PACK HOME.
MOONSHADOW, PACKLEADER, YOU HONOR ME.
WE WELCOME ALL THE MAGES.
THANK YOU.

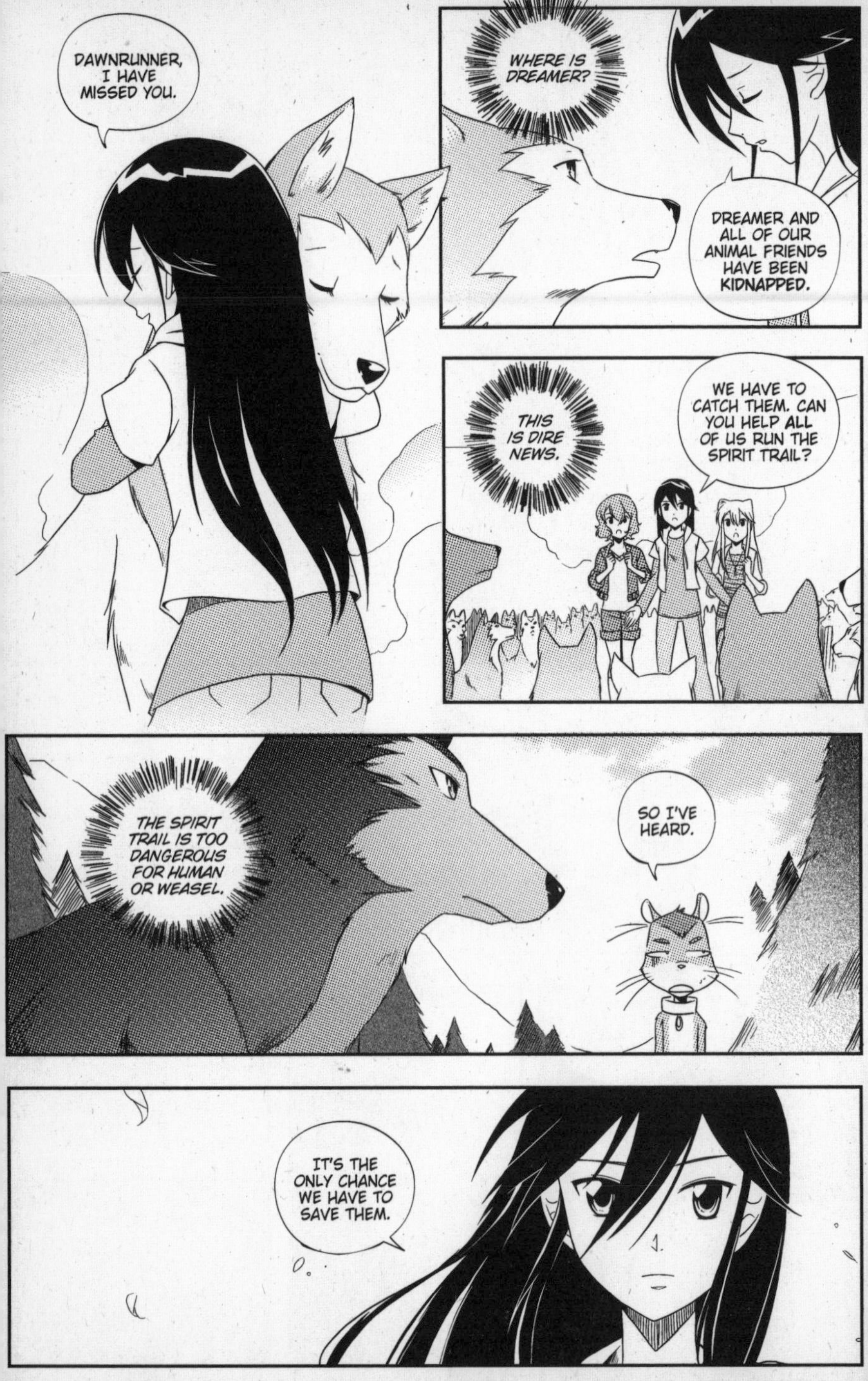
DAWNRUNNER, I HAVE MISSED YOU.
WHERE IS DREAMER?
DREAMER AND ALL OF OUR ANIMAL FRIENDS HAVE BEEN KIDNAPPED.
THIS IS DIRE NEWS.
WE HAVE TO CATCH THEM. CAN YOU HELP ALL OF US RUN THE SPIRIT TRAIL?
THE SPIRIT TRAIL IS TOO DANGEROUS FOR HUMAN OR WEASEL.
SO I'VE HEARD.
IT'S THE ONLY CHANCE WE HAVE TO SAVE THEM.

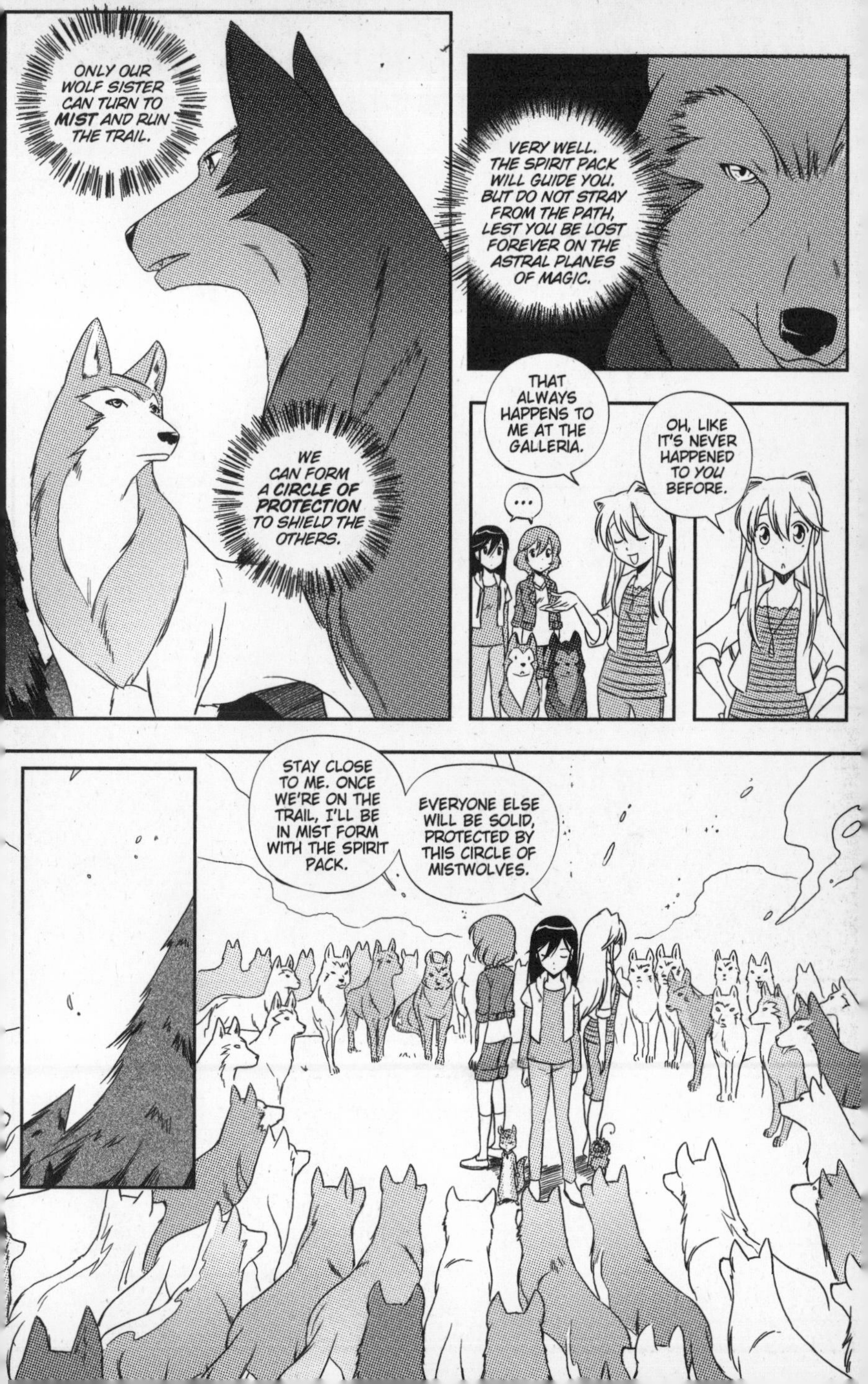
ONLY OUR WOLF SISTER CAN TURN TO MIST AND RUN THE TRAIL.
WE CAN FORM A CIRCLE OF PROTECTION TO SHIELD THE OTHERS.
VERY WELL. THE SPIRIT PACK WILL GUIDE YOU. BUT DO NOT STRAY FROM THE PATH, LEST YOU BE LOST FOREVER ON THE ASTRAL PLANES OF MAGIC.
THAT ALWAYS HAPPENS TO ME AT THE GALLERIA.
...
OH, LIKE IT'S NEVER HAPPENED TO YOU BEFORE.
STAY CLOSE TO ME. ONCE WE'RE ON THE TRAIL, I'LL BE IN MIST FORM WITH THE SPIRIT PACK.
EVERYONE ELSE WILL BE SOLID, PROTECTED BY THIS CIRCLE OF MISTWOLVES.

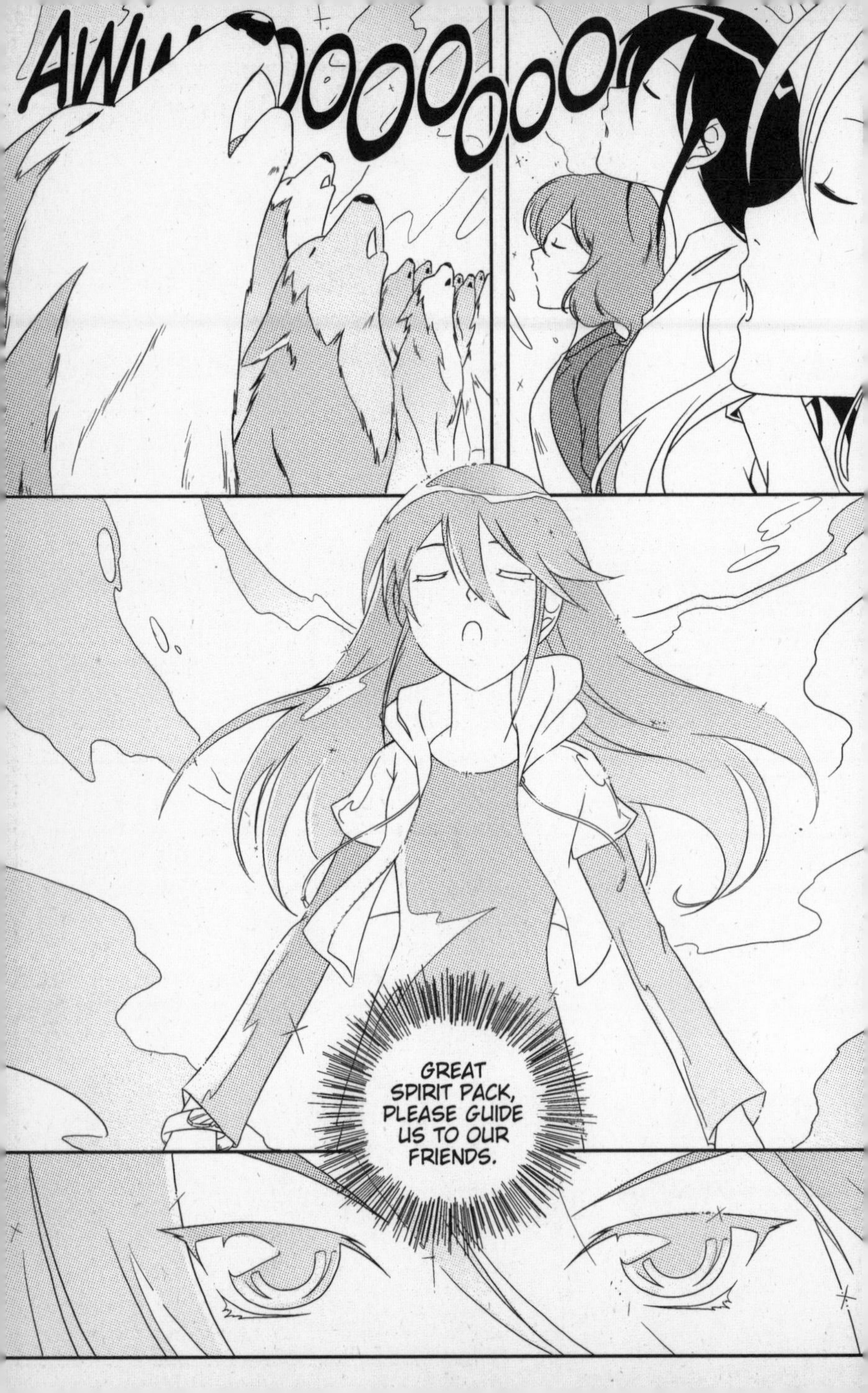
AWWOOOOOOOOO
GREAT SPIRIT PACK, PLEASE GUIDE US TO OUR FRIENDS.

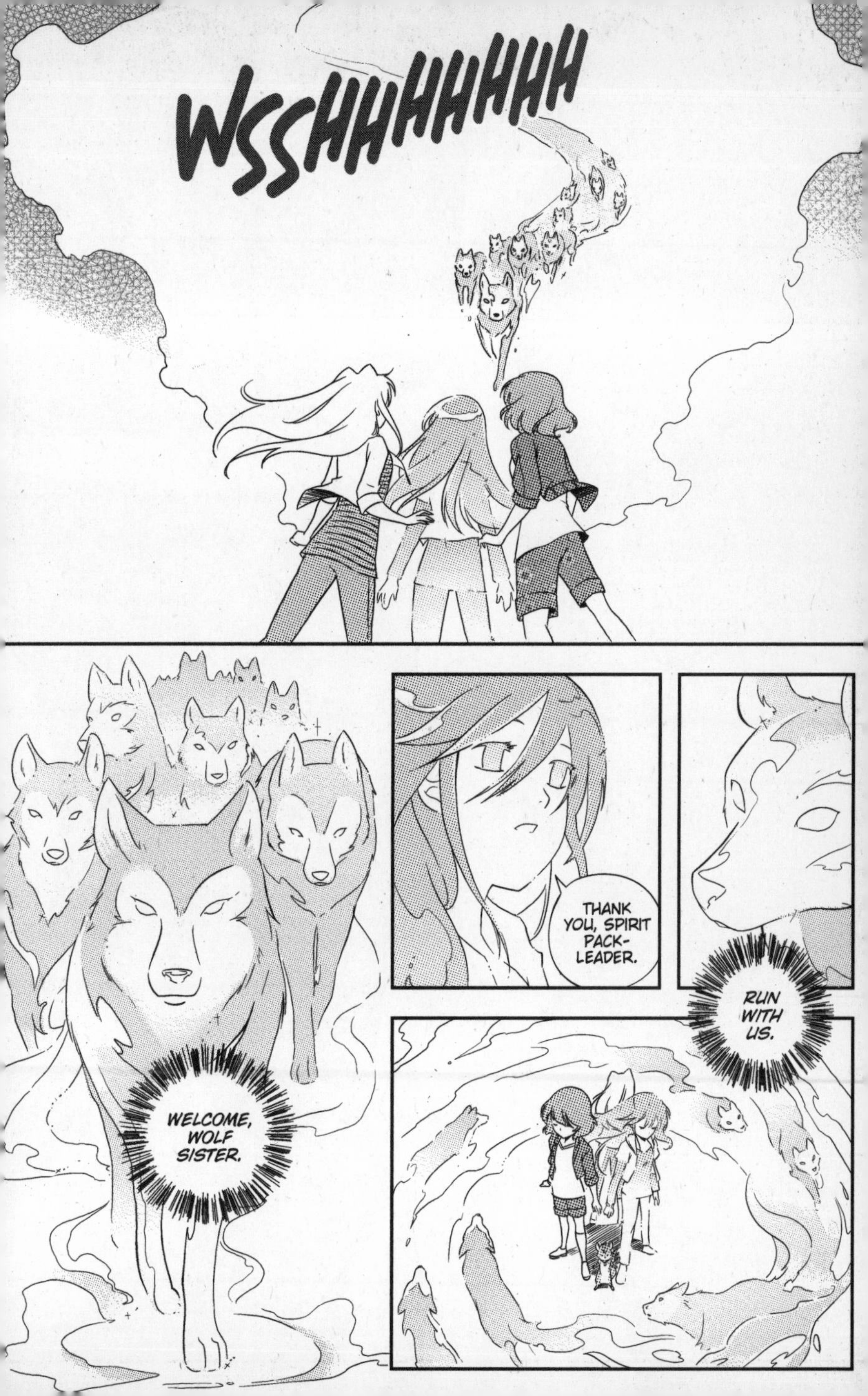
WSSHHHHHHH
WELCOME, WOLF SISTER.
THANK YOU, SPIRIT PACK-LEADER.
RUN WITH US.

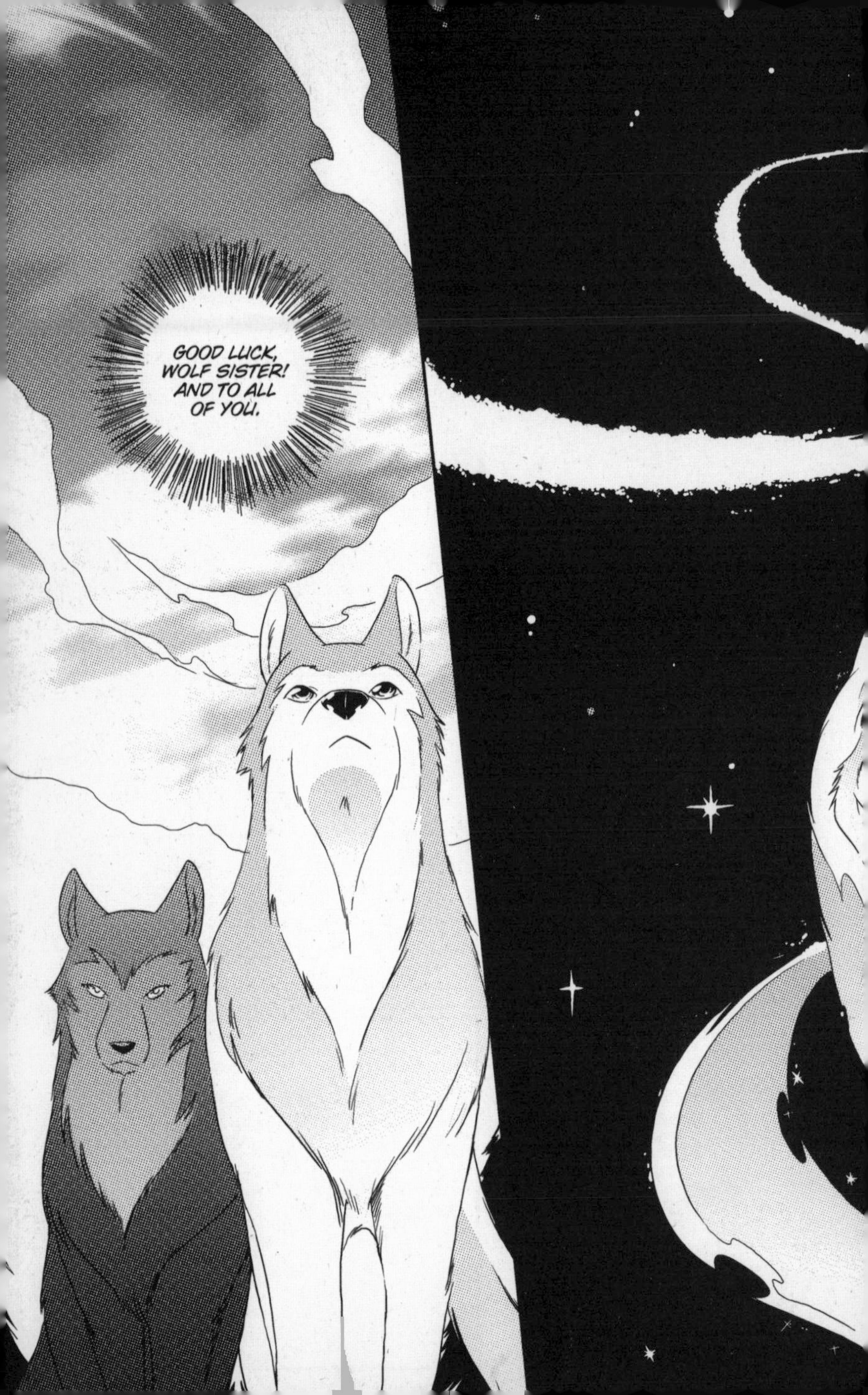
GOOD LUCK, WOLF SISTER! AND TO ALL OF YOU.

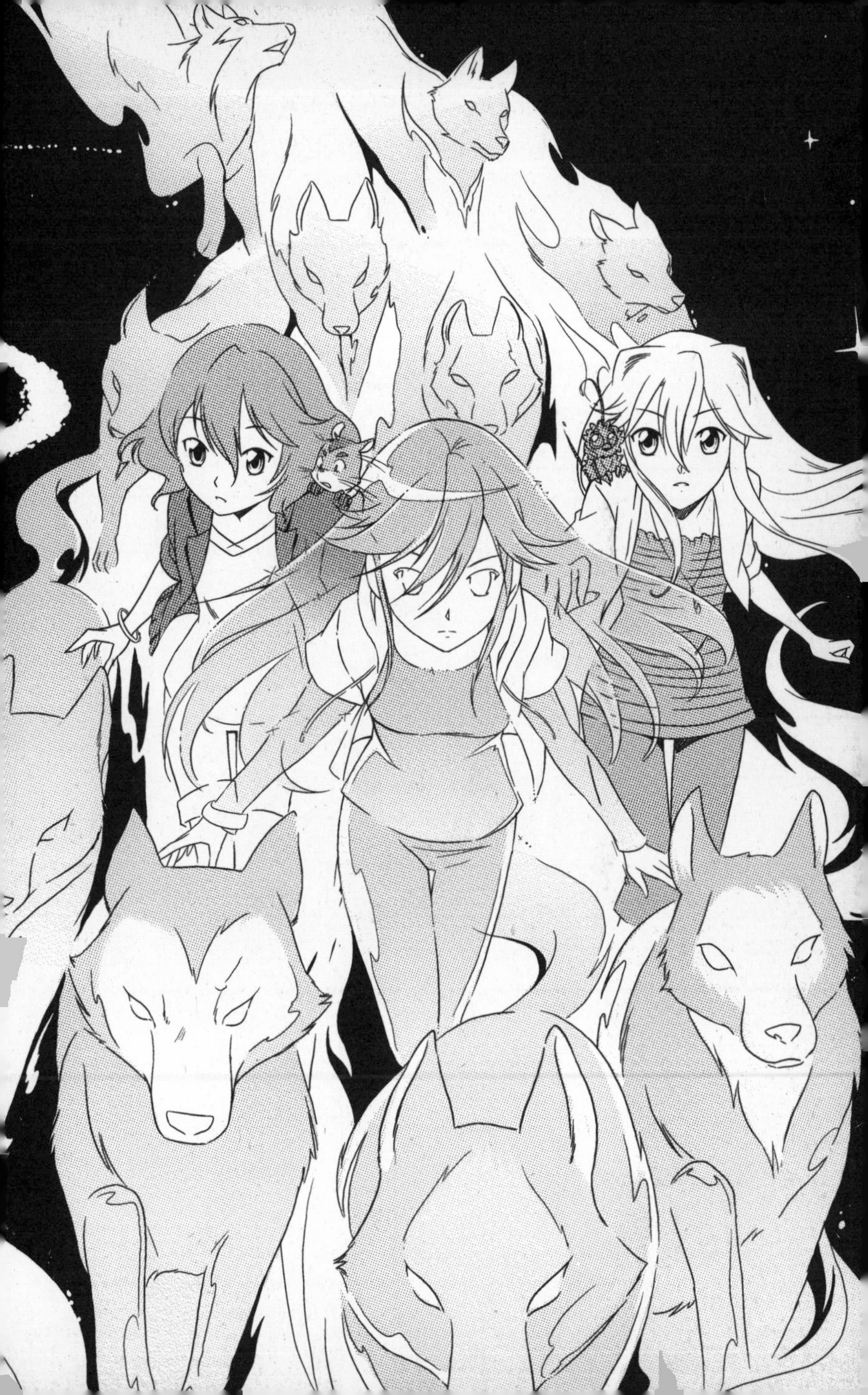

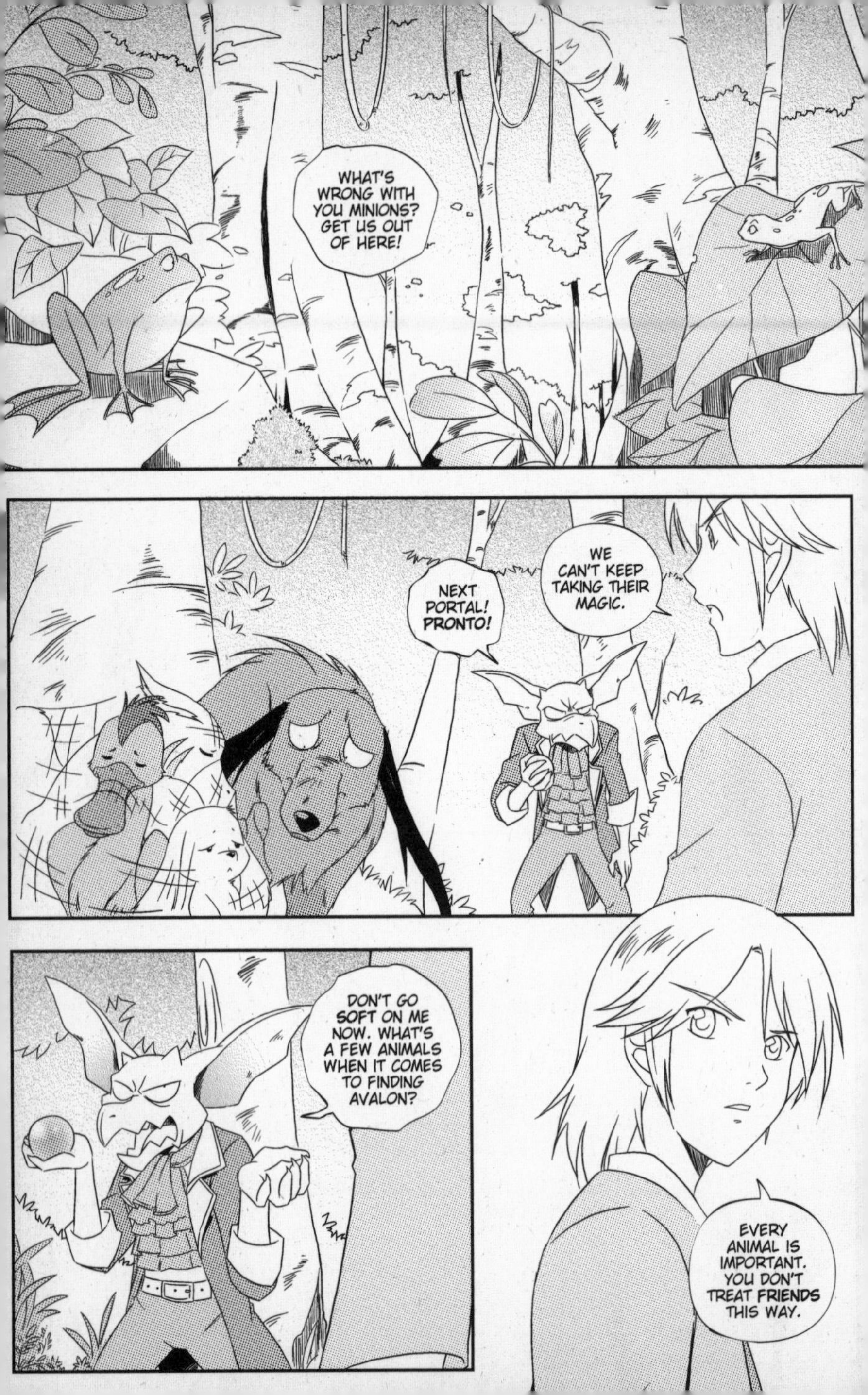
WHAT'S WRONG WITH YOU MINIONS? GET US OUT OF HERE!
NEXT PORTAL! PRONTO!
WE CAN'T KEEP TAKING THEIR MAGIC.
DON'T GO SOFT ON ME NOW. WHAT'S A FEW ANIMALS WHEN IT COMES TO FINDING AVALON?
EVERY ANIMAL IS IMPORTANT. YOU DON'T TREAT FRIENDS THIS WAY.

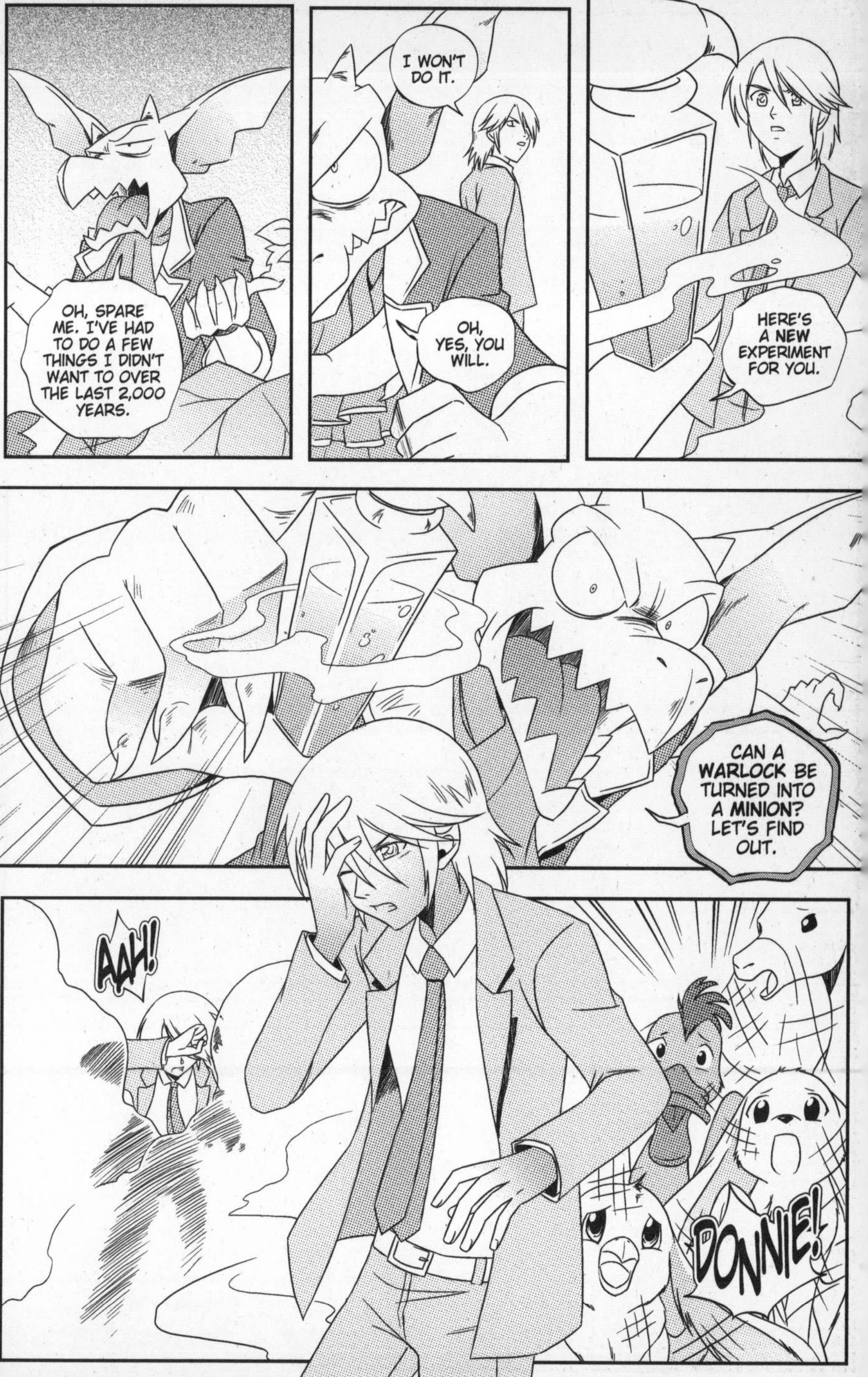
OH, SPARE ME. I'VE HAD TO DO A FEW THINGS I DIDN'T WANT TO OVER THE LAST 2,000 YEARS.
I WON'T DO IT.
OH, YES, YOU WILL.
HERE'S A NEW EXPERIMENT FOR YOU.
CAN A WARLOCK BE TURNED INTO A MINION? LET'S FIND OUT.
AAH!
DONNIE!

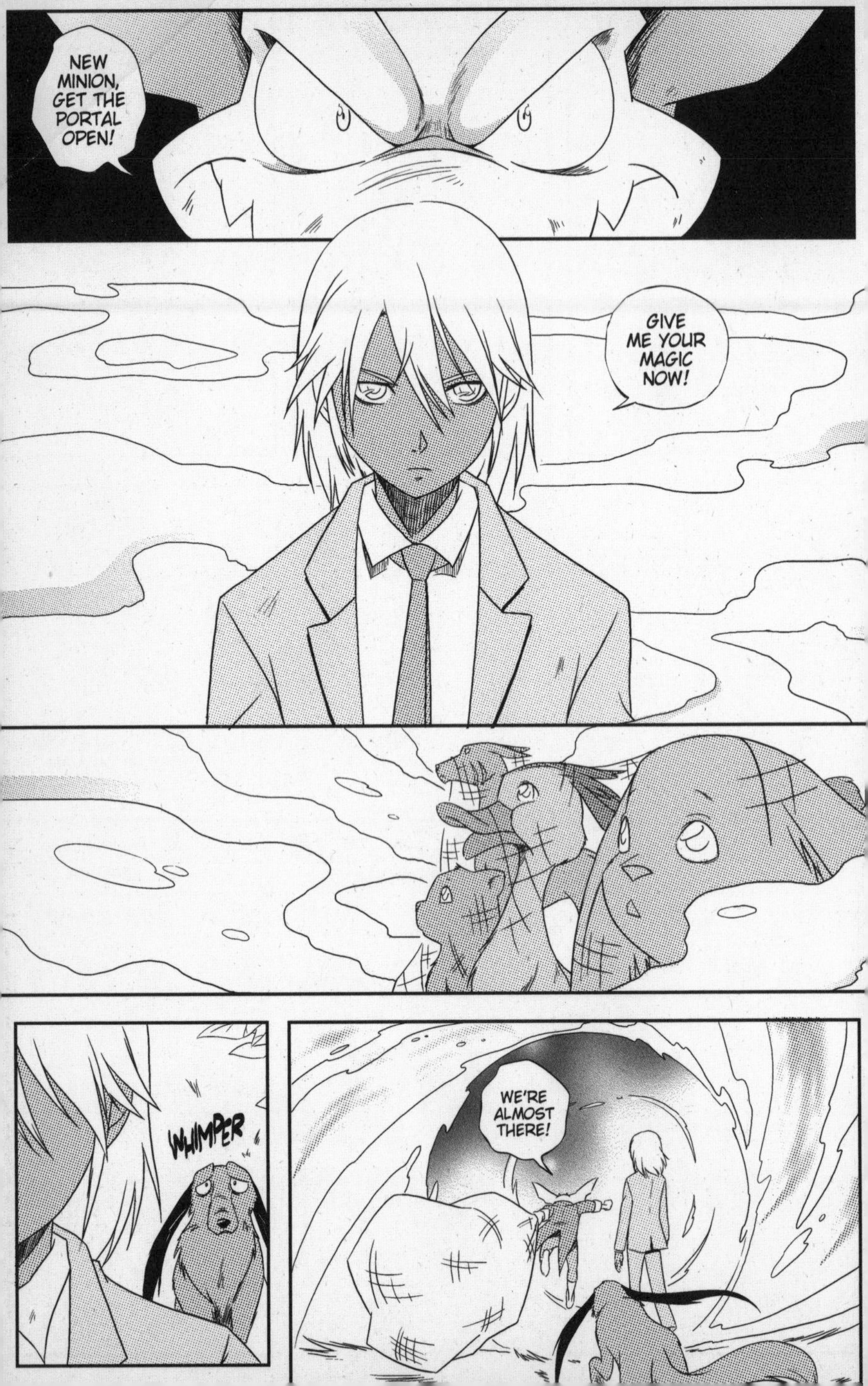
NEW MINION, GET THE PORTAL OPEN!
GIVE ME YOUR MAGIC NOW!
WHIMPER
WE'RE ALMOST THERE!

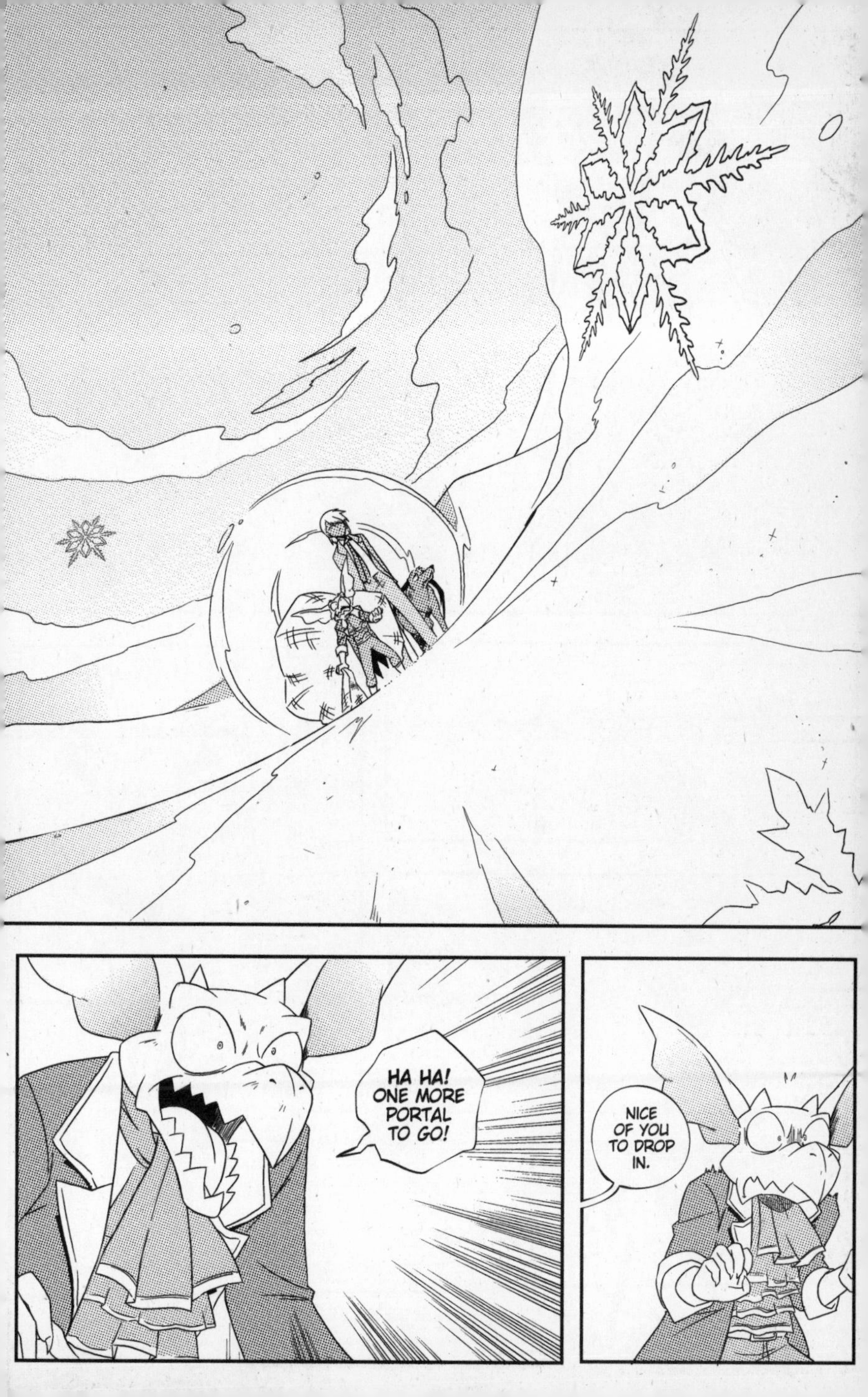
HA HA! ONE MORE PORTAL TO GO!
NICE OF YOU TO DROP IN.

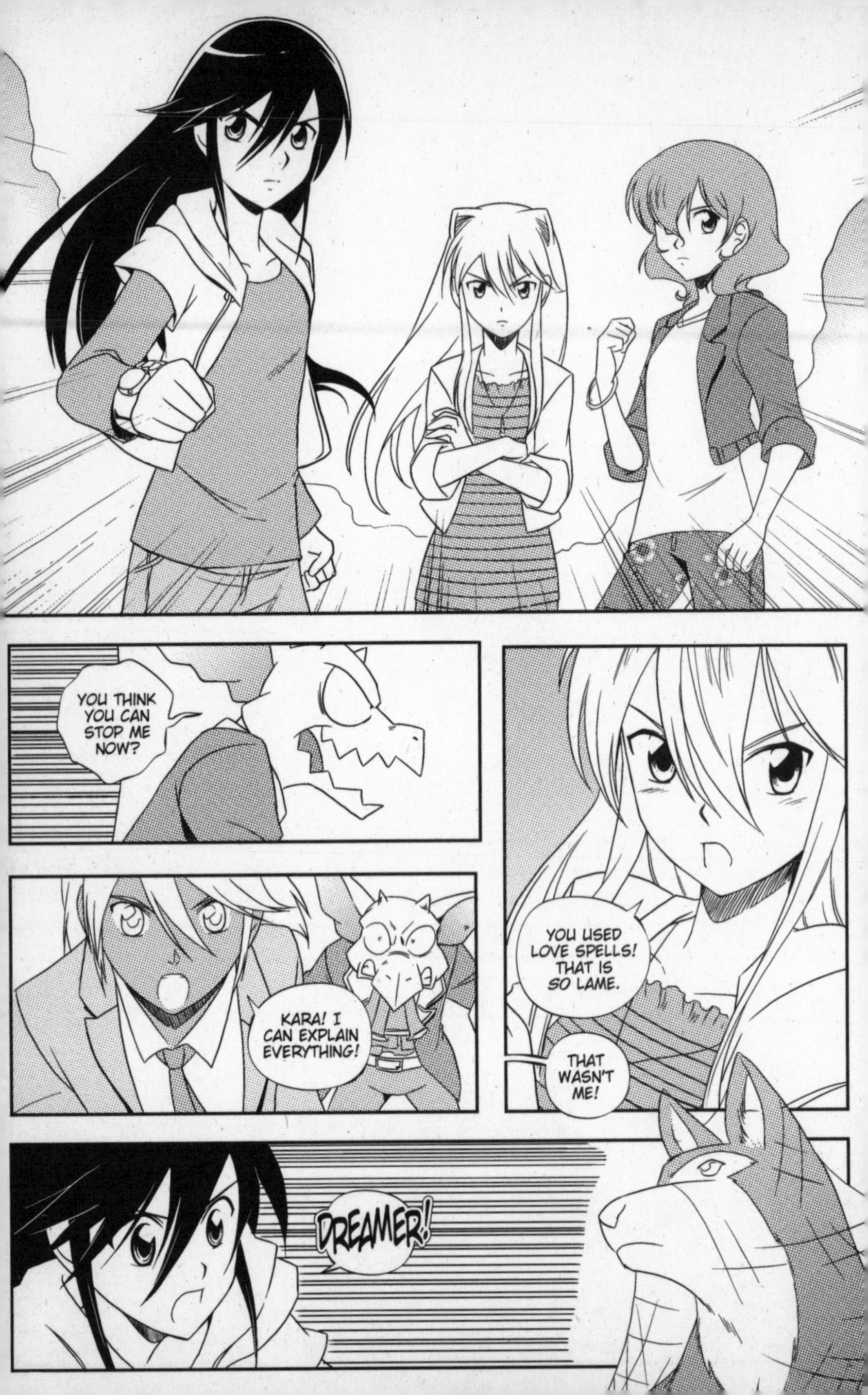
YOU THINK YOU CAN STOP ME NOW?
KARA! I CAN EXPLAIN EVERYTHING!
YOU USED LOVE SPELLS! THAT IS SO LAME.
THAT WASN'T ME!
DREAMER!

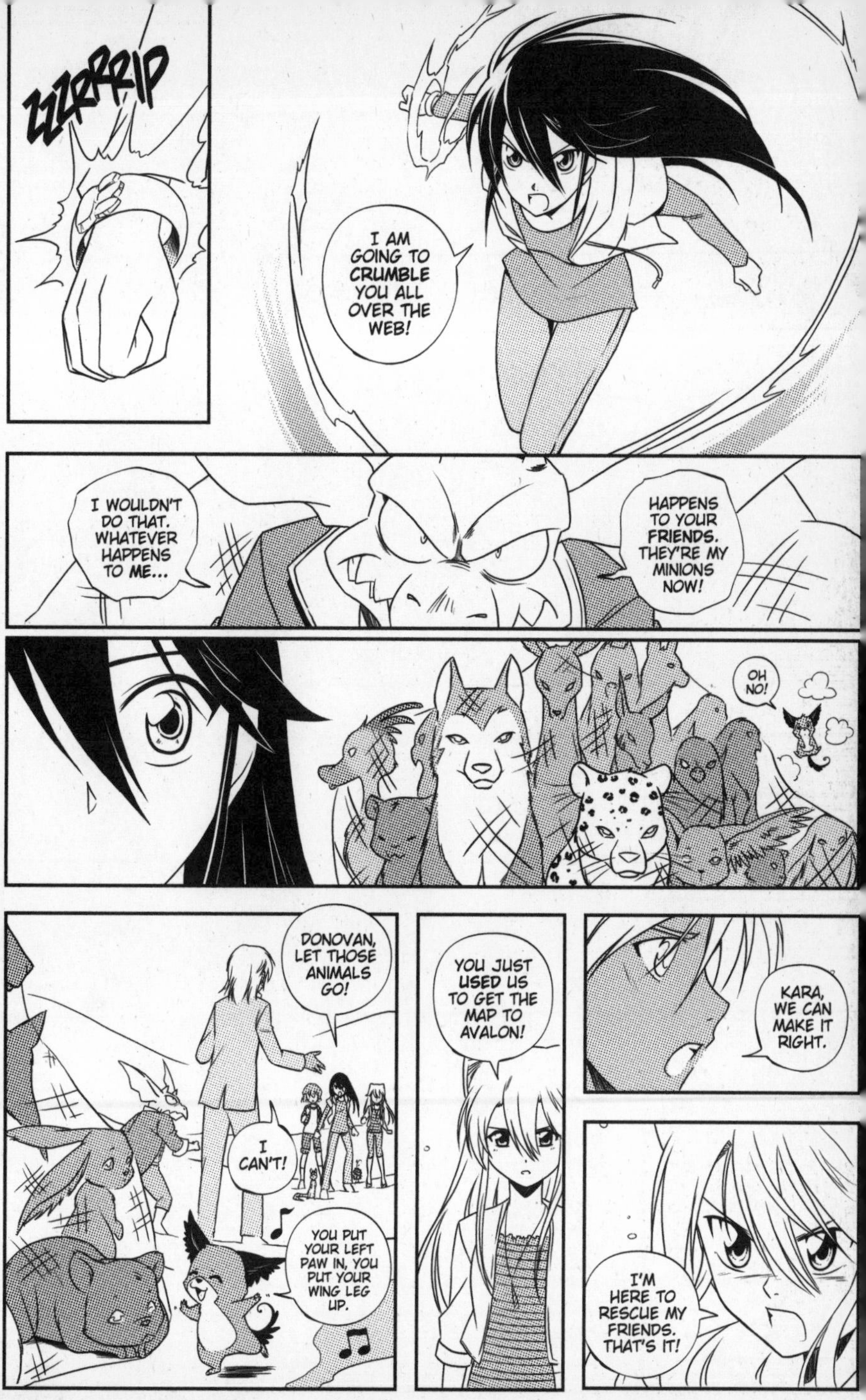
ZZZRRRIP
I AM GOING TO CRUMBLE YOU ALL OVER THE WEB!
I WOULDN'T DO THAT. WHATEVER HAPPENS TO ME...
HAPPENS TO YOUR FRIENDS. THEY'RE MY MINIONS NOW!
OH NO!
DONOVAN, LET THOSE ANIMALS GO!
I CAN'T!
YOU PUT YOUR LEFT PAW IN, YOU PUT YOUR WING LEG UP.
YOU JUST USED US TO GET THE MAP TO AVALON!
KARA, WE CAN MAKE IT RIGHT.
I'M HERE TO RESCUE MY FRIENDS. THAT'S IT!

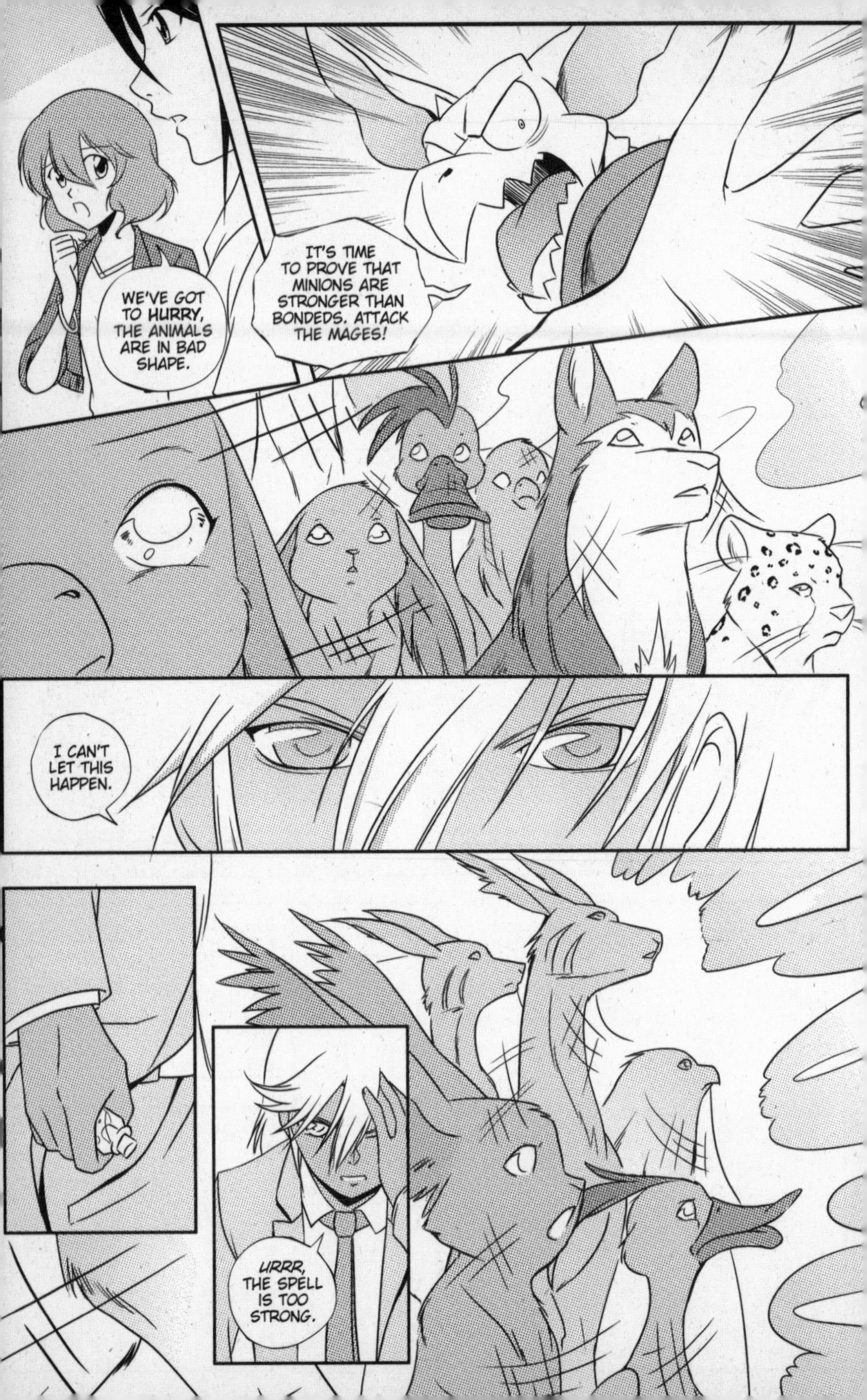
WE'VE GOT TO HURRY, THE ANIMALS ARE IN BAD SHAPE.
IT'S TIME TO PROVE THAT MINIONS ARE STRONGER THAN BONDEDS. ATTACK THE MAGES!
I CAN'T LET THIS HAPPEN.
URRR, THE SPELL IS TOO STRONG.

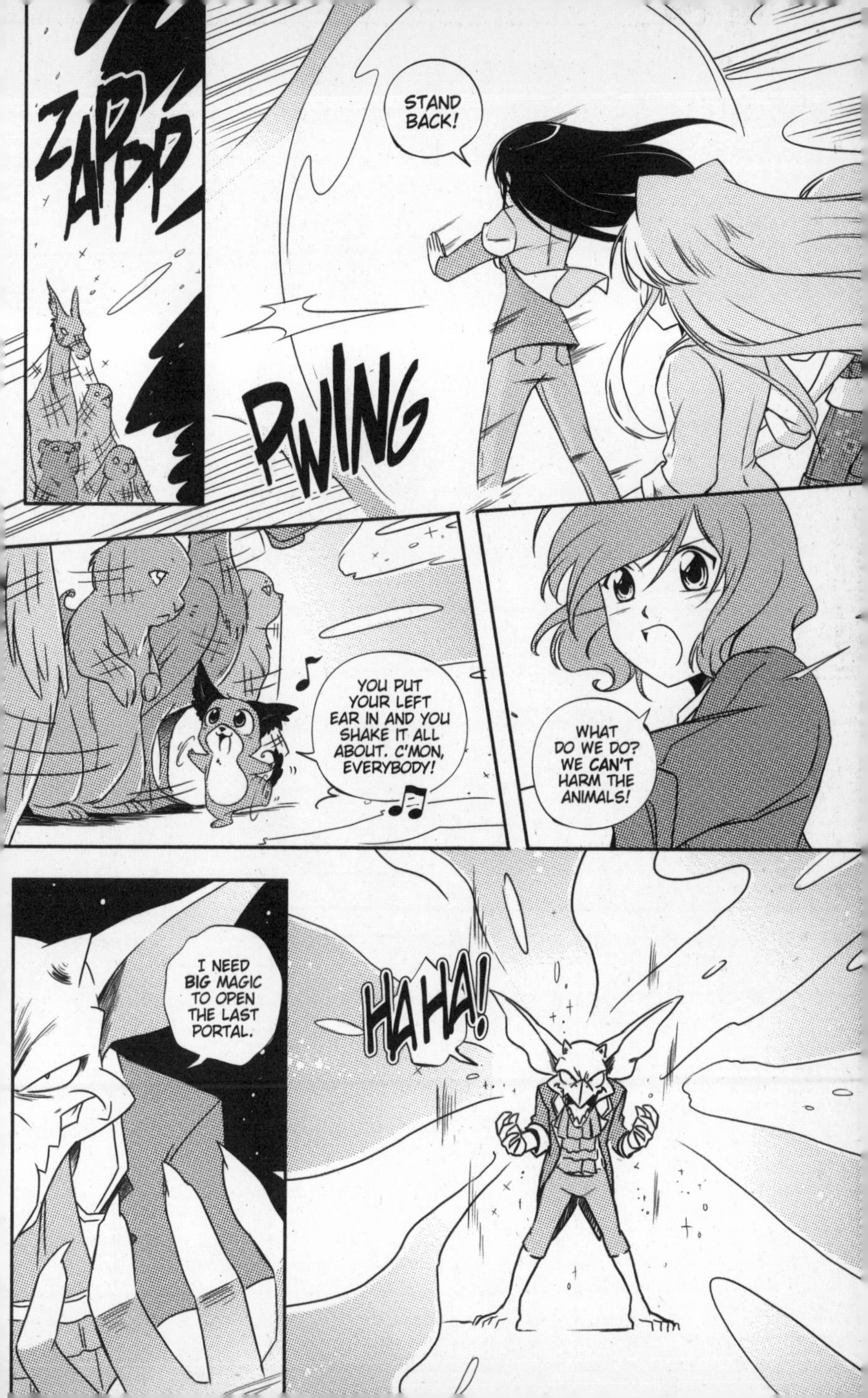
ZAPP
STAND BACK!
PWING
YOU PUT YOUR LEFT EAR IN AND YOU SHAKE IT ALL ABOUT. C'MON, EVERYBODY!
WHAT DO WE DO? WE CAN'T HARM THE ANIMALS!
I NEED BIG MAGIC TO OPEN THE LAST PORTAL.
HAHA!

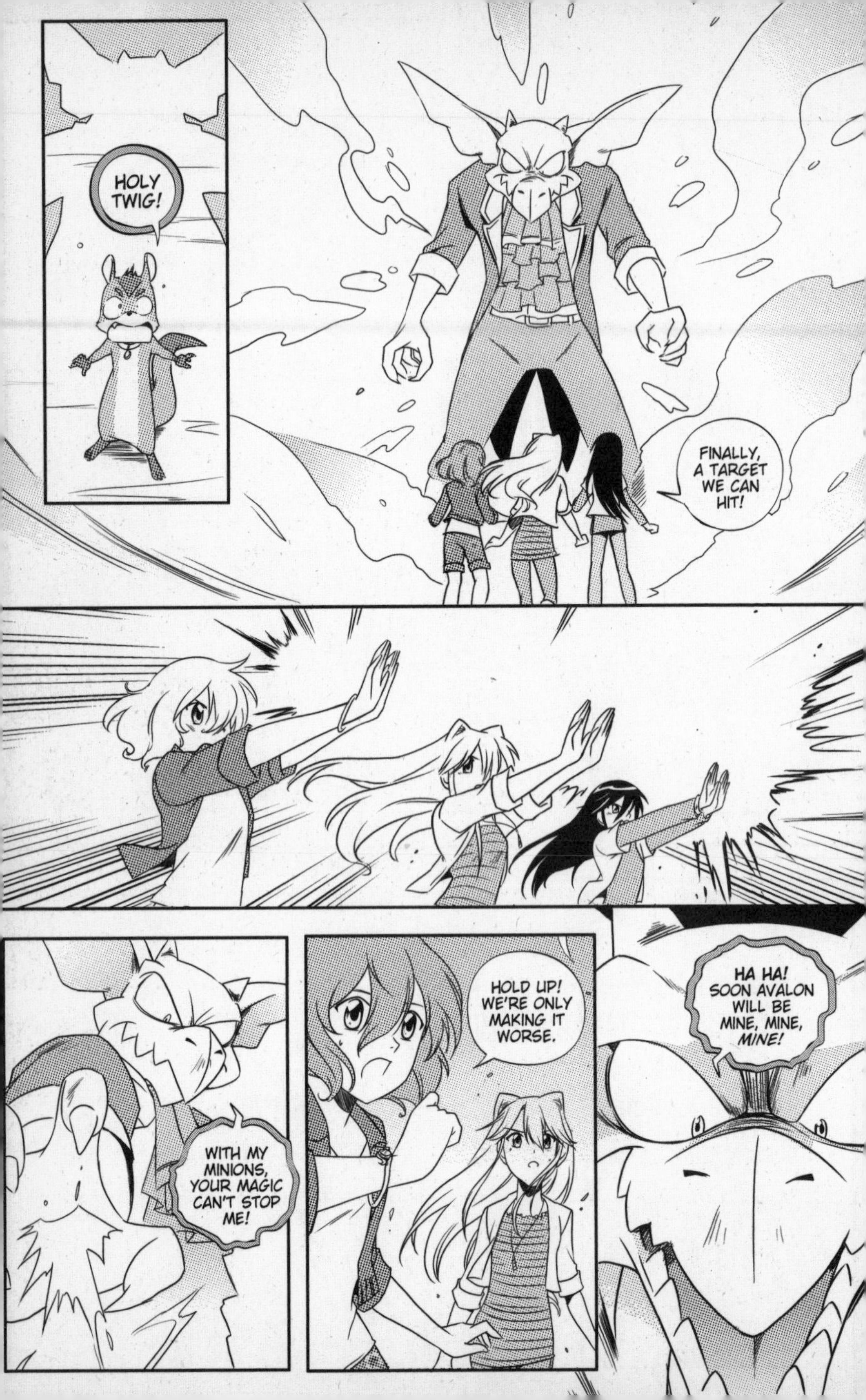
HOLY TWIG!
FINALLY, A TARGET WE CAN HIT!
WITH MY MINIONS, YOUR MAGIC CAN'T STOP ME!
HOLD UP! WE'RE ONLY MAKING IT WORSE.
HA HA! SOON AVALON WILL BE MINE, MINE, *MINE!*

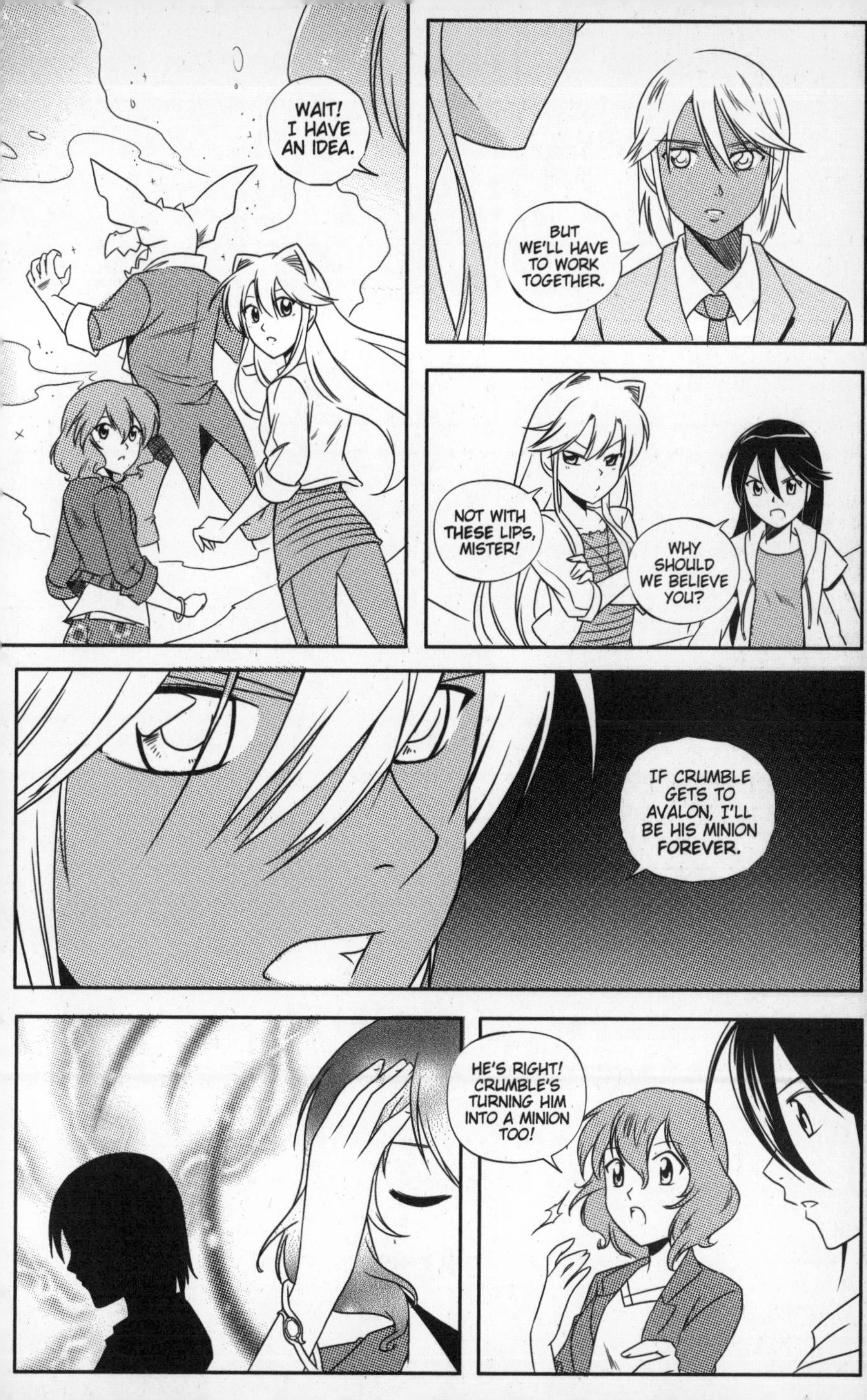
WAIT! I HAVE AN IDEA.
BUT WE'LL HAVE TO WORK TOGETHER.
NOT WITH THESE LIPS, MISTER!
WHY SHOULD WE BELIEVE YOU?
IF CRUMBLE GETS TO AVALON, I'LL BE HIS MINION FOREVER.
HE'S RIGHT! CRUMBLE'S TURNING HIM INTO A MINION TOO!

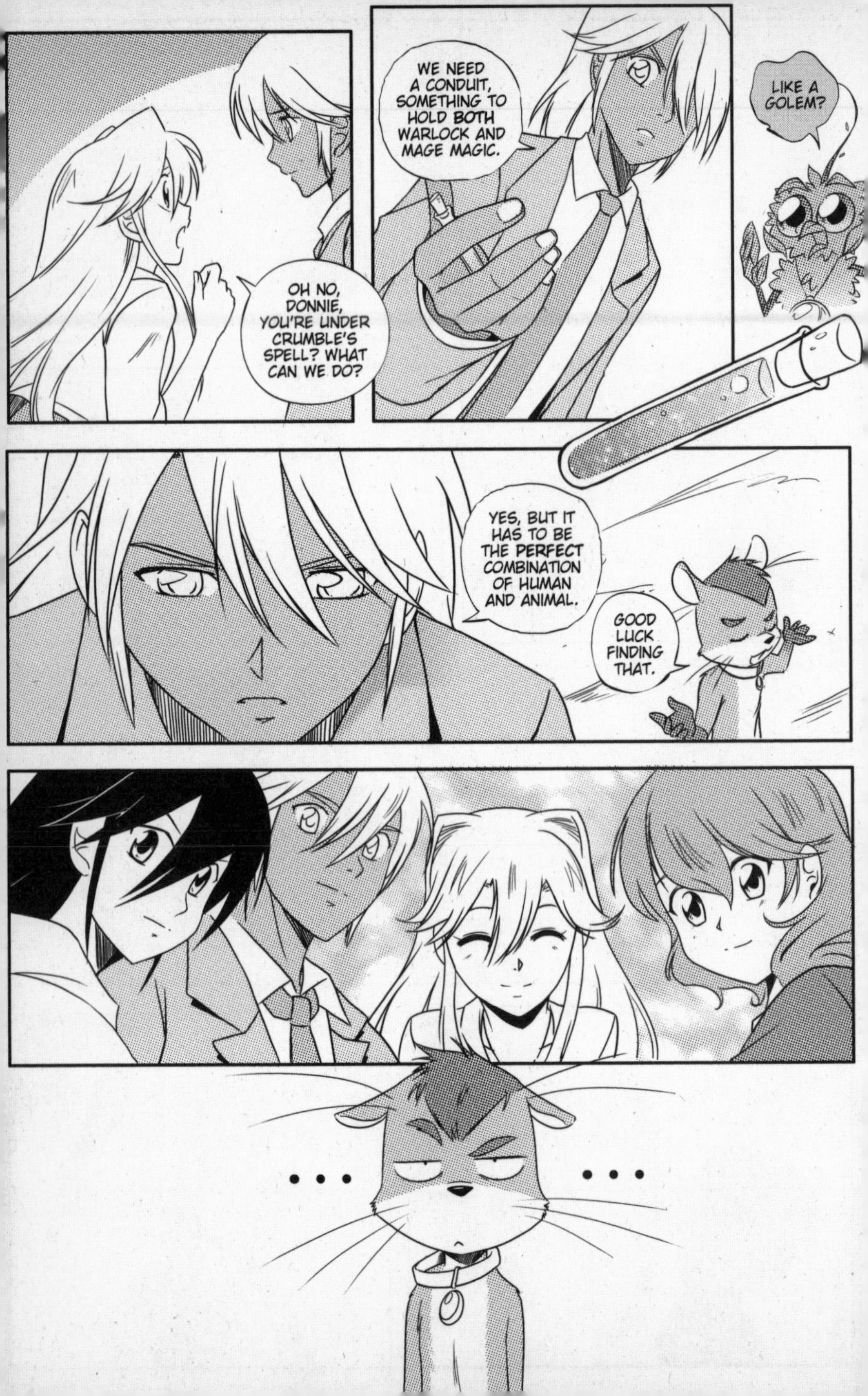
OH NO, DONNIE, YOU'RE UNDER CRUMBLE'S SPELL? WHAT CAN WE DO?
WE NEED A CONDUIT, SOMETHING TO HOLD BOTH WARLOCK AND MAGE MAGIC.
LIKE A GOLEM?
YES, BUT IT HAS TO BE THE PERFECT COMBINATION OF HUMAN AND ANIMAL.
GOOD LUCK FINDING THAT.
• • •
• • •

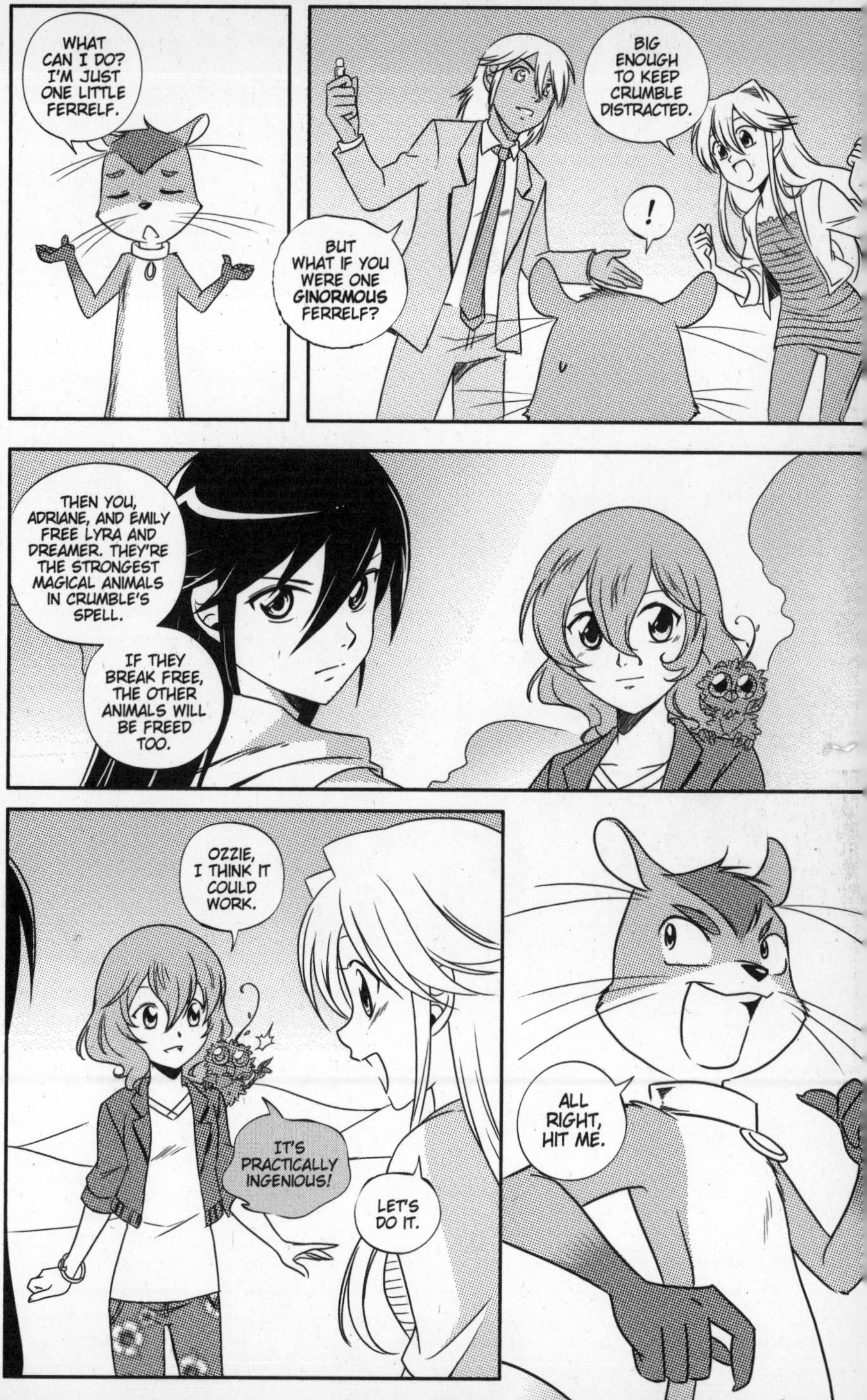
WHAT CAN I DO? I'M JUST ONE LITTLE FERRELF.
BIG ENOUGH TO KEEP CRUMBLE DISTRACTED.
!
BUT WHAT IF YOU WERE ONE GINORMOUS FERRELF?
THEN YOU, ADRIANE, AND EMILY FREE LYRA AND DREAMER. THEY'RE THE STRONGEST MAGICAL ANIMALS IN CRUMBLE'S SPELL.
IF THEY BREAK FREE, THE OTHER ANIMALS WILL BE FREED TOO.
OZZIE, I THINK IT COULD WORK.
IT'S PRACTICALLY INGENIOUS!
LET'S DO IT.
ALL RIGHT, HIT ME.

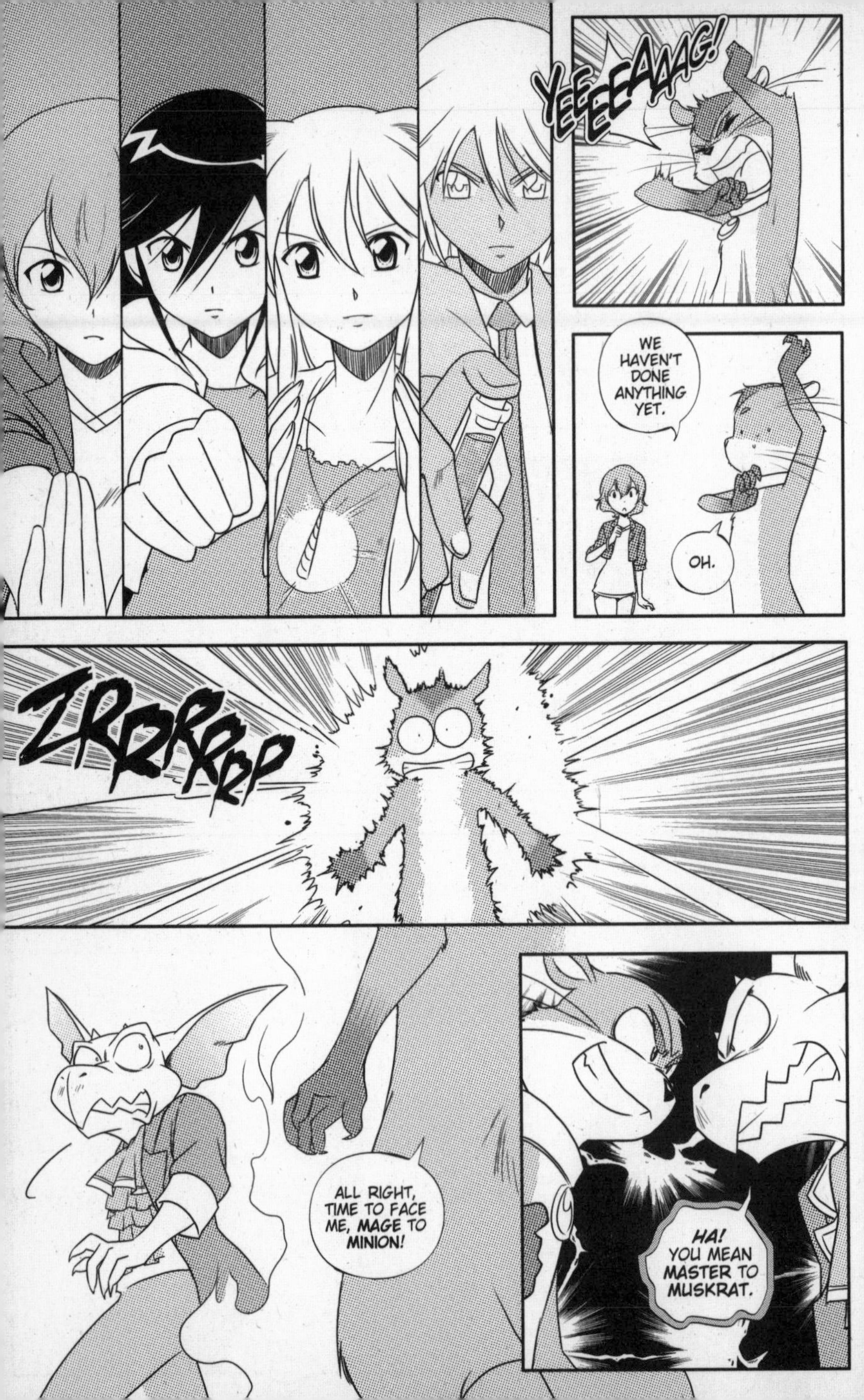
YEEEEAAAG!
WE HAVEN'T DONE ANYTHING YET.
OH.
ZRRRRRP
ALL RIGHT, TIME TO FACE ME, MAGE TO MINION!
HA! YOU MEAN MASTER TO MUSKRAT.

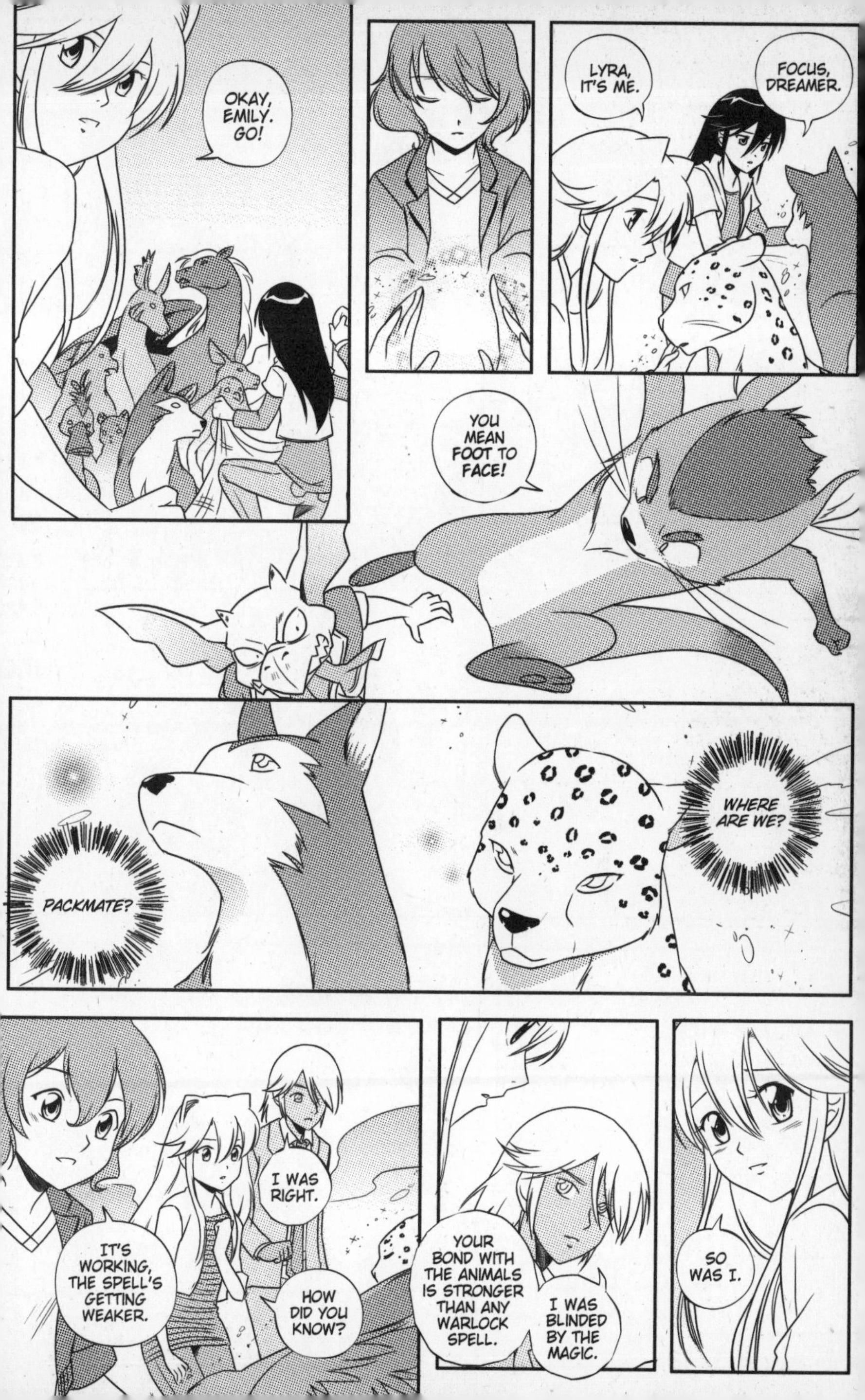
OKAY, EMILY. GO!
LYRA, IT'S ME.
FOCUS, DREAMER.
YOU MEAN FOOT TO FACE!
PACKMATE?
WHERE ARE WE?
IT'S WORKING, THE SPELL'S GETTING WEAKER.
I WAS RIGHT.
HOW DID YOU KNOW?
YOUR BOND WITH THE ANIMALS IS STRONGER THAN ANY WARLOCK SPELL.
I WAS BLINDED BY THE MAGIC.
SO WAS I.

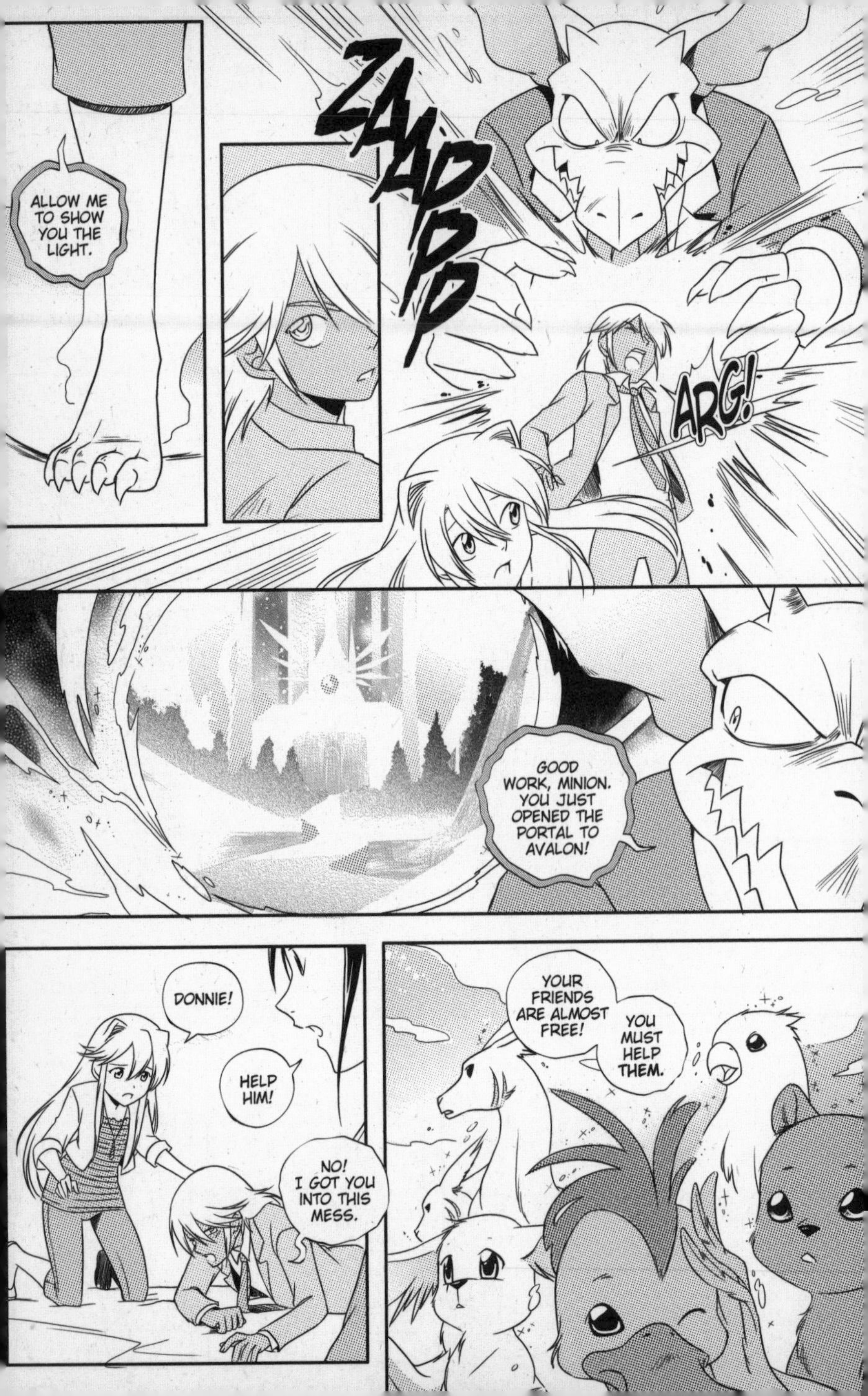
ALLOW ME TO SHOW YOU THE LIGHT.
ZAMPP
ARG!
GOOD WORK, MINION. YOU JUST OPENED THE PORTAL TO AVALON!
DONNIE!
HELP HIM!
NO! I GOT YOU INTO THIS MESS.
YOUR FRIENDS ARE ALMOST FREE!
YOU MUST HELP THEM.

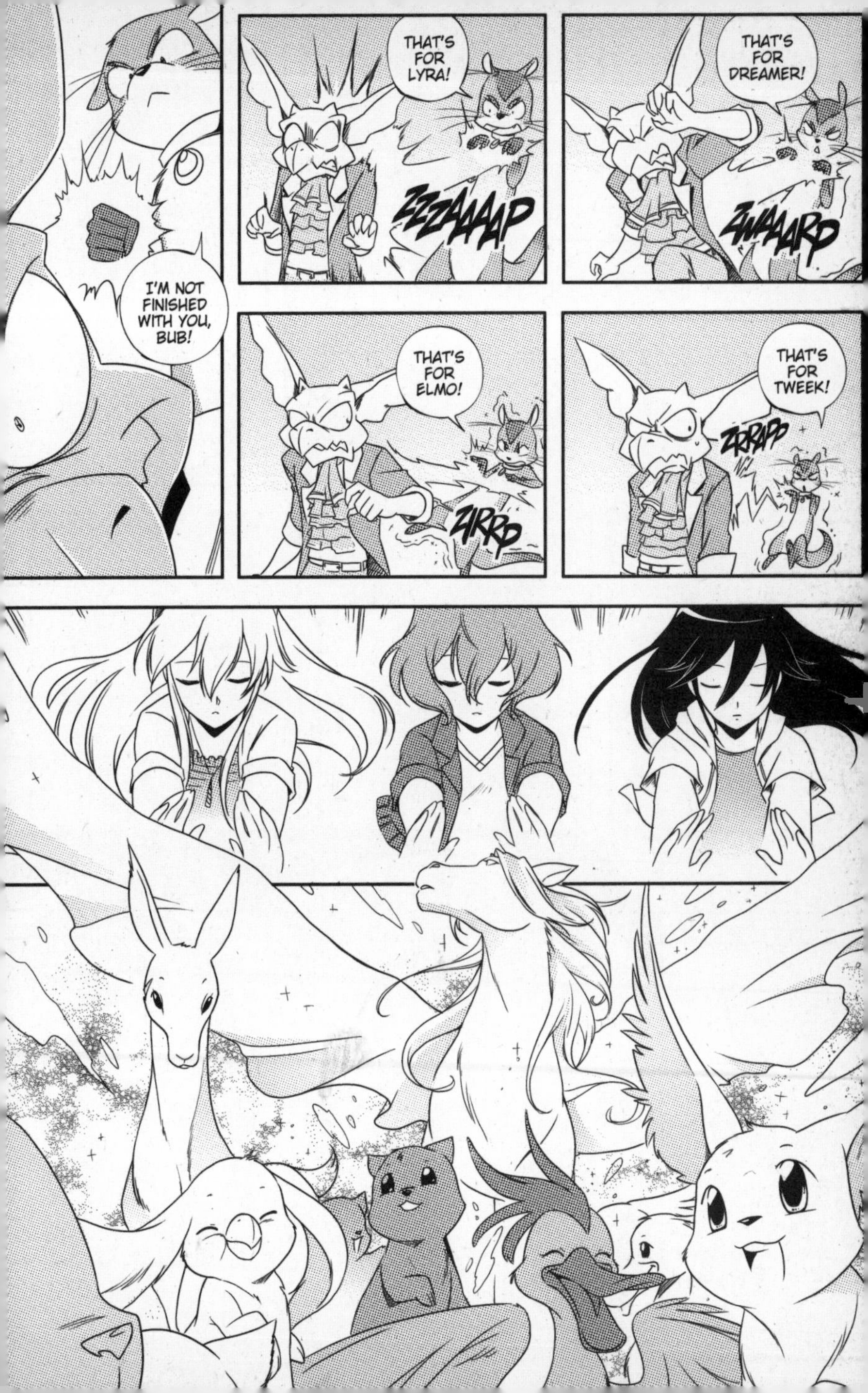
I'M NOT FINISHED WITH YOU, BUB!
THAT'S FOR LYRA!
ZZZZAAAAAP
THAT'S FOR DREAMER!
ZWAAARP
THAT'S FOR ELMO!
ZIRRP
THAT'S FOR TWEEK!
ZRRAPP

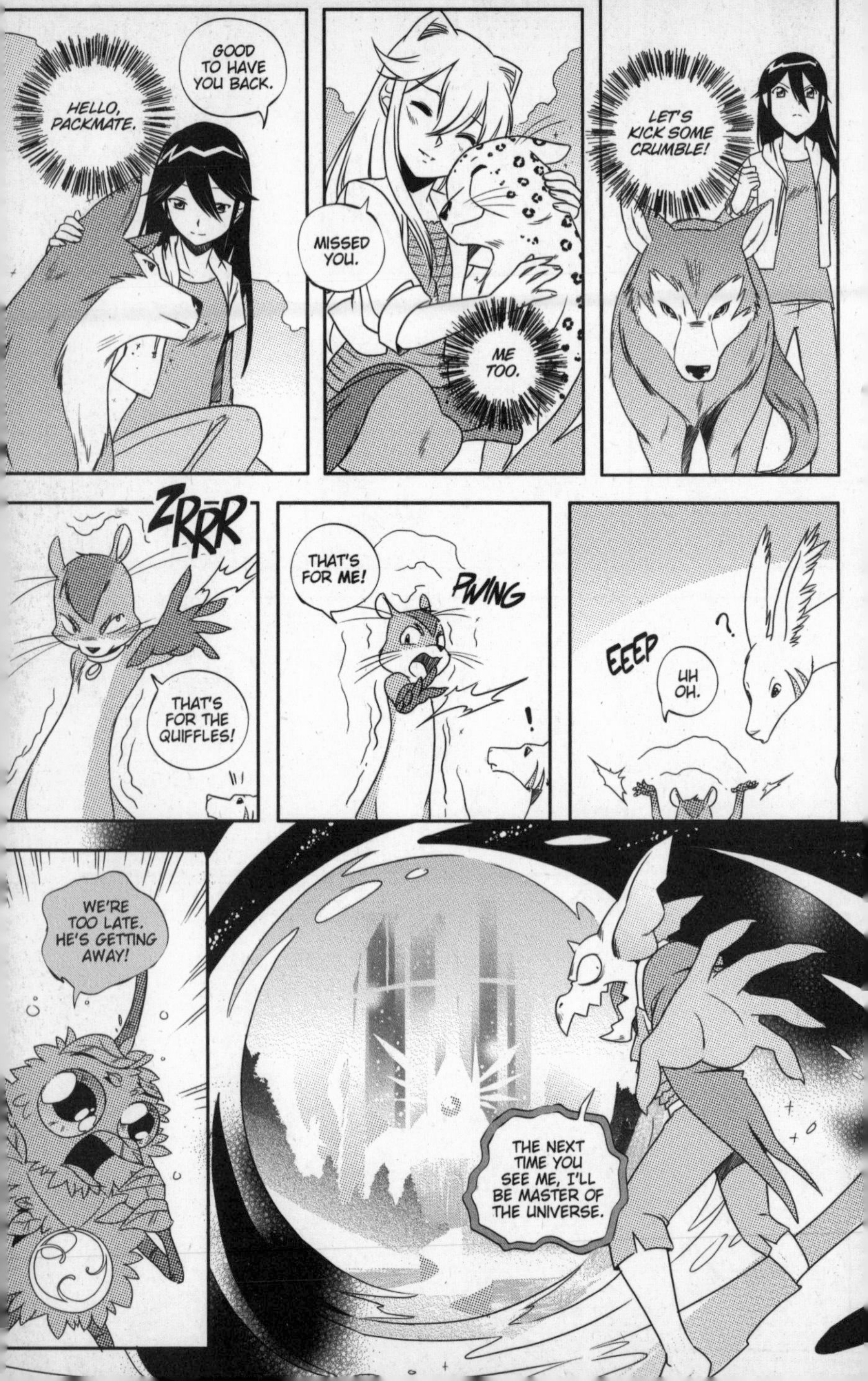
HELLO, PACKMATE.
GOOD TO HAVE YOU BACK.
MISSED YOU.
ME TOO.
LET'S KICK SOME CRUMBLE!
ZRRR
THAT'S FOR THE QUIFFLES!
THAT'S FOR ME!
PWING
!
EEEP
UH OH.
?
WE'RE TOO LATE. HE'S GETTING AWAY!
THE NEXT TIME YOU SEE ME, I'LL BE MASTER OF THE UNIVERSE.

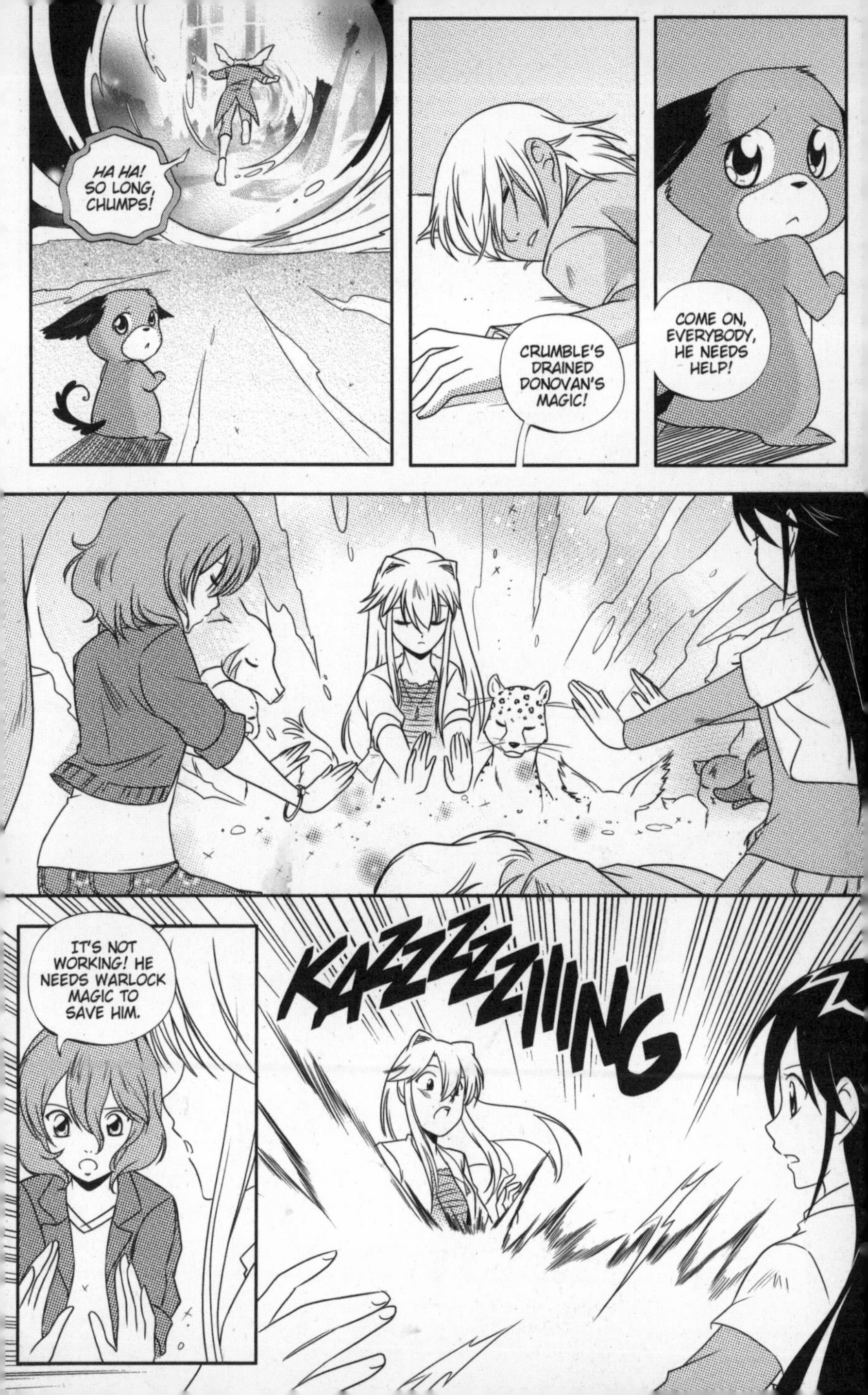
HA HA! SO LONG, CHUMPS!
CRUMBLE'S DRAINED DONOVAN'S MAGIC!
COME ON, EVERYBODY, HE NEEDS HELP!
IT'S NOT WORKING! HE NEEDS WARLOCK MAGIC TO SAVE HIM.
KAZZZZZIIING

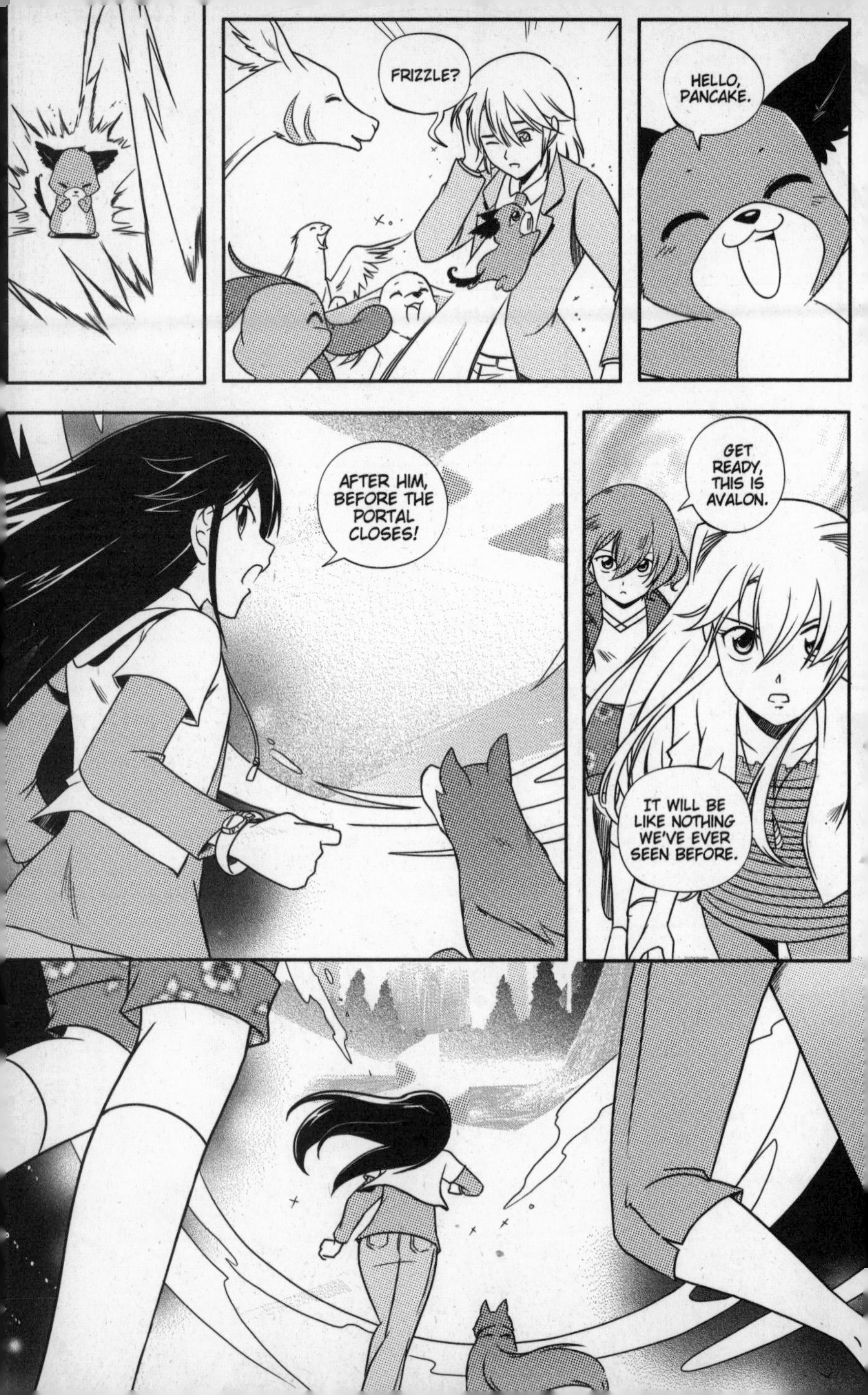
FRIZZLE?
HELLO, PANCAKE.
AFTER HIM, BEFORE THE PORTAL CLOSES!
GET READY, THIS IS AVALON.
IT WILL BE LIKE NOTHING WE'VE EVER SEEN BEFORE.

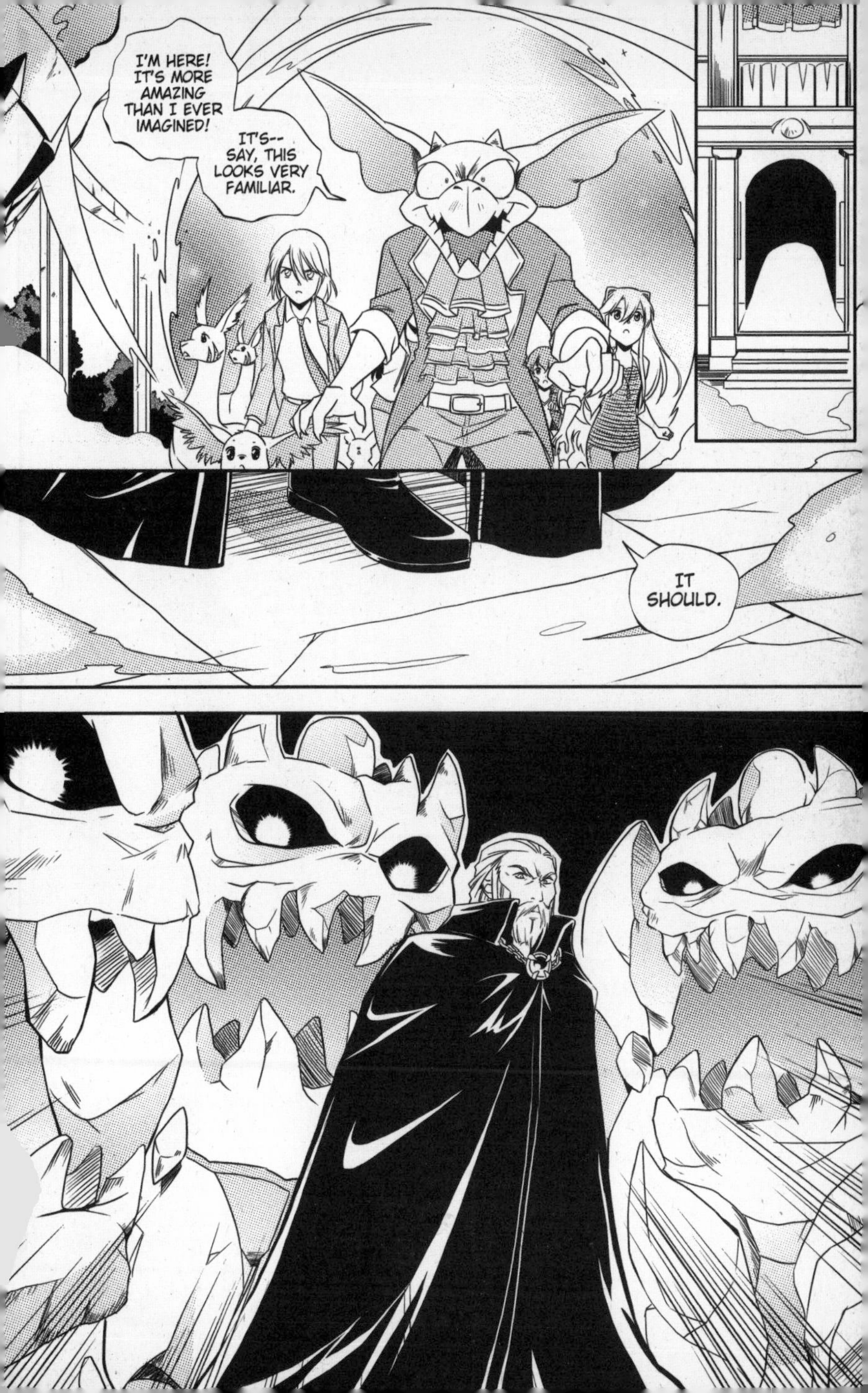
I'M HERE! IT'S MORE AMAZING THAN I EVER IMAGINED!
IT'S-- SAY, THIS LOOKS VERY FAMILIAR.
IT SHOULD.

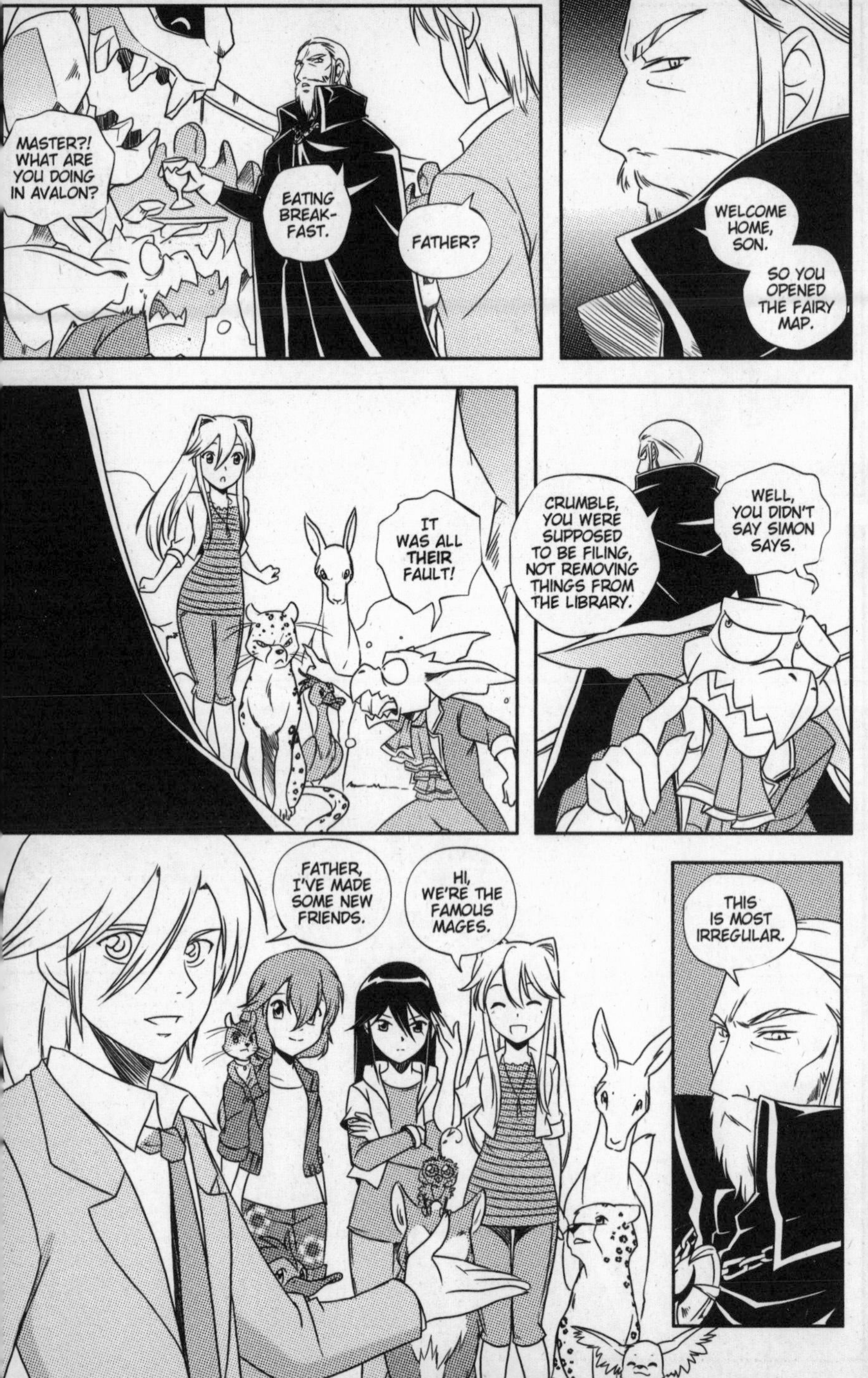
MASTER?! WHAT ARE YOU DOING IN AVALON?
EATING BREAK-FAST.
FATHER?
WELCOME HOME, SON.
SO YOU OPENED THE FAIRY MAP.
IT WAS ALL **THEIR** FAULT!
CRUMBLE, YOU WERE SUPPOSED TO BE FILING, NOT REMOVING THINGS FROM THE LIBRARY.
WELL, YOU DIDN'T SAY SIMON SAYS.
FATHER, I'VE MADE SOME NEW FRIENDS.
HI, WE'RE THE FAMOUS MAGES.
THIS IS MOST IRREGULAR.

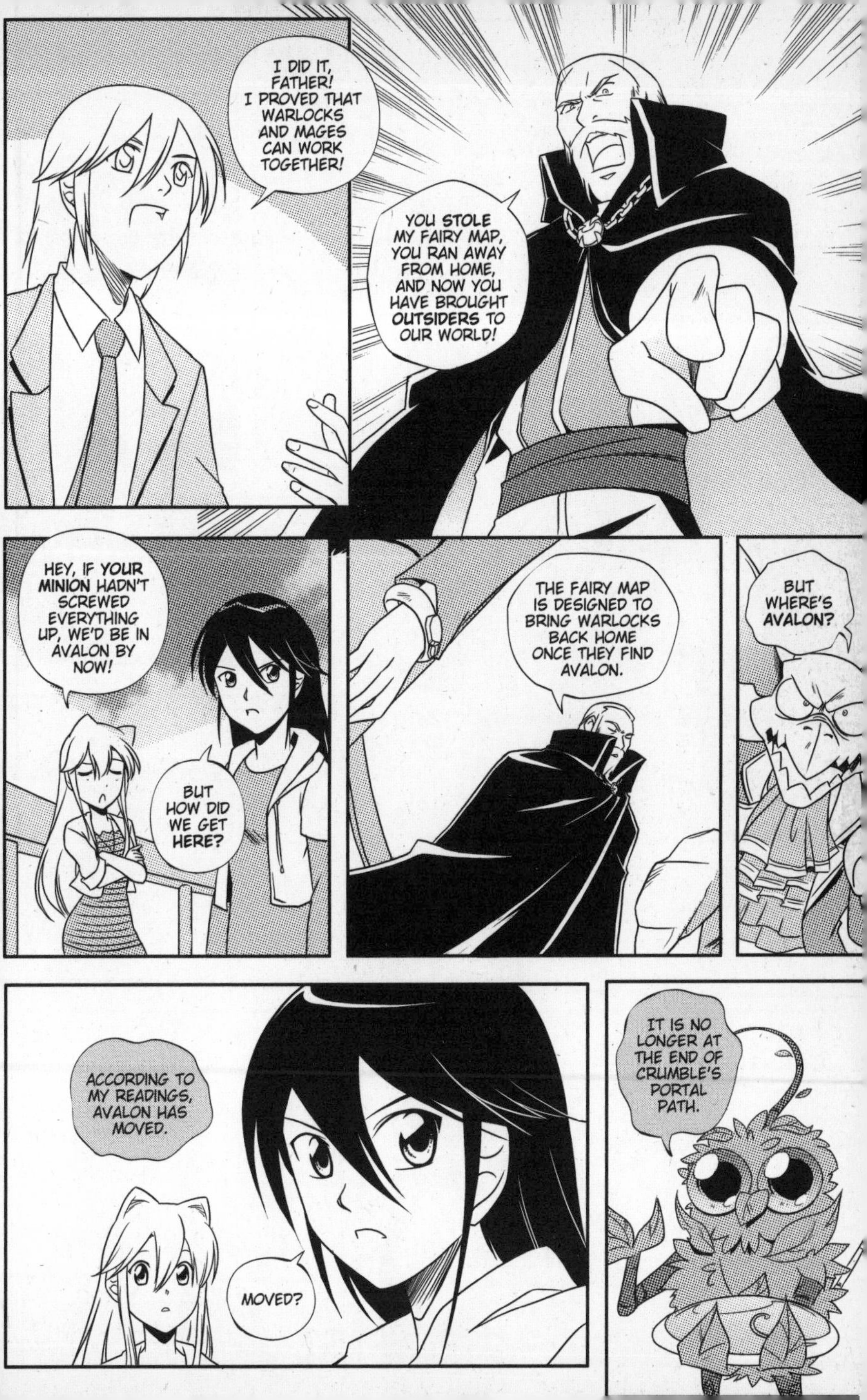
I DID IT, FATHER! I PROVED THAT WARLOCKS AND MAGES CAN WORK TOGETHER!
YOU STOLE MY FAIRY MAP, YOU RAN AWAY FROM HOME, AND NOW YOU HAVE BROUGHT OUTSIDERS TO OUR WORLD!
HEY, IF YOUR MINION HADN'T SCREWED EVERYTHING UP, WE'D BE IN AVALON BY NOW!
BUT HOW DID WE GET HERE?
THE FAIRY MAP IS DESIGNED TO BRING WARLOCKS BACK HOME ONCE THEY FIND AVALON.
BUT WHERE'S AVALON?
ACCORDING TO MY READINGS, AVALON HAS MOVED.
MOVED?
IT IS NO LONGER AT THE END OF CRUMBLE'S PORTAL PATH.

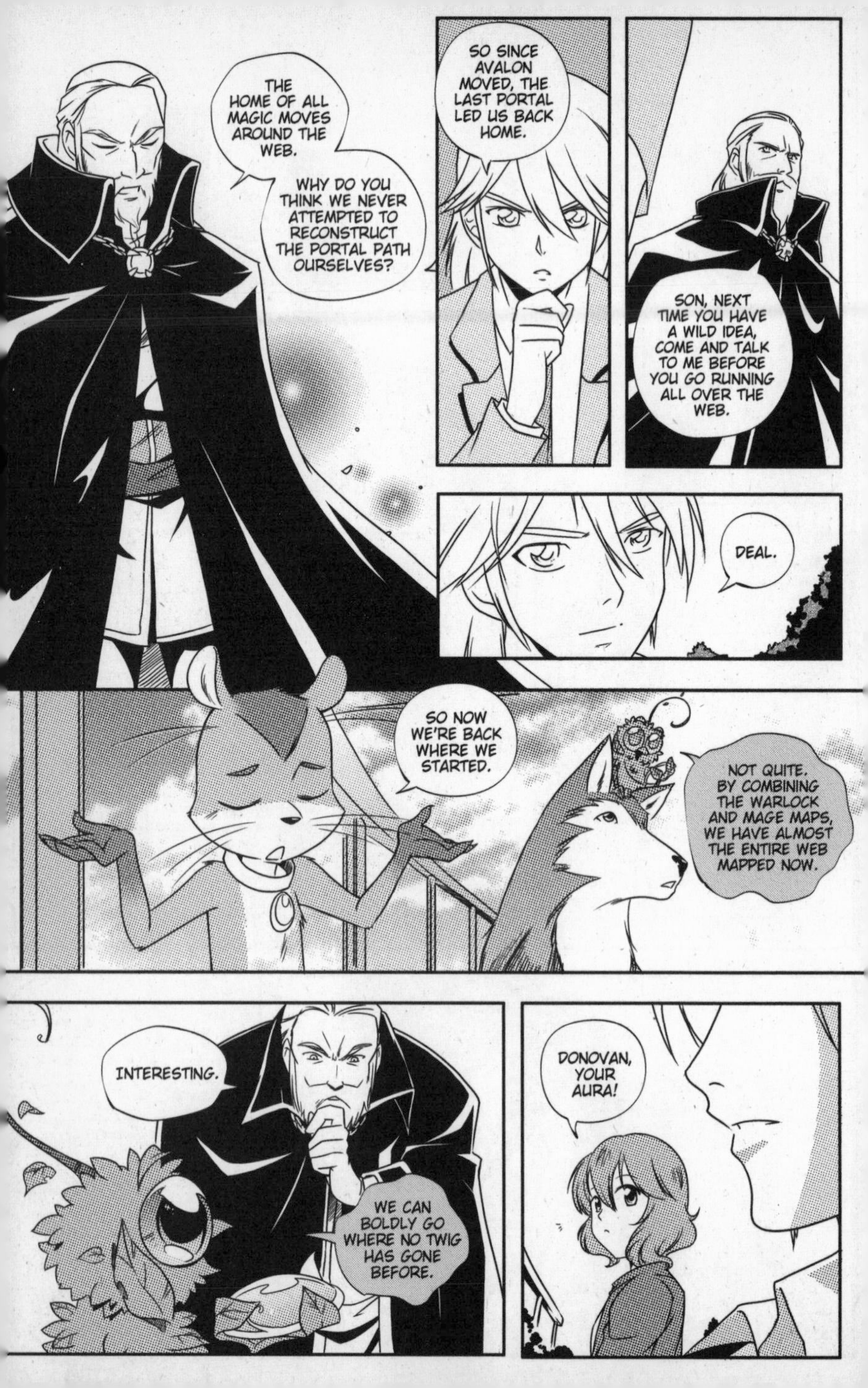
THE HOME OF ALL MAGIC MOVES AROUND THE WEB.
WHY DO YOU THINK WE NEVER ATTEMPTED TO RECONSTRUCT THE PORTAL PATH OURSELVES?
SO SINCE AVALON MOVED, THE LAST PORTAL LED US BACK HOME.
SON, NEXT TIME YOU HAVE A WILD IDEA, COME AND TALK TO ME BEFORE YOU GO RUNNING ALL OVER THE WEB.
DEAL.
SO NOW WE'RE BACK WHERE WE STARTED.
NOT QUITE. BY COMBINING THE WARLOCK AND MAGE MAPS, WE HAVE ALMOST THE ENTIRE WEB MAPPED NOW.
INTERESTING.
WE CAN BOLDLY GO WHERE NO TWIG HAS GONE BEFORE.
DONOVAN, YOUR AURA!

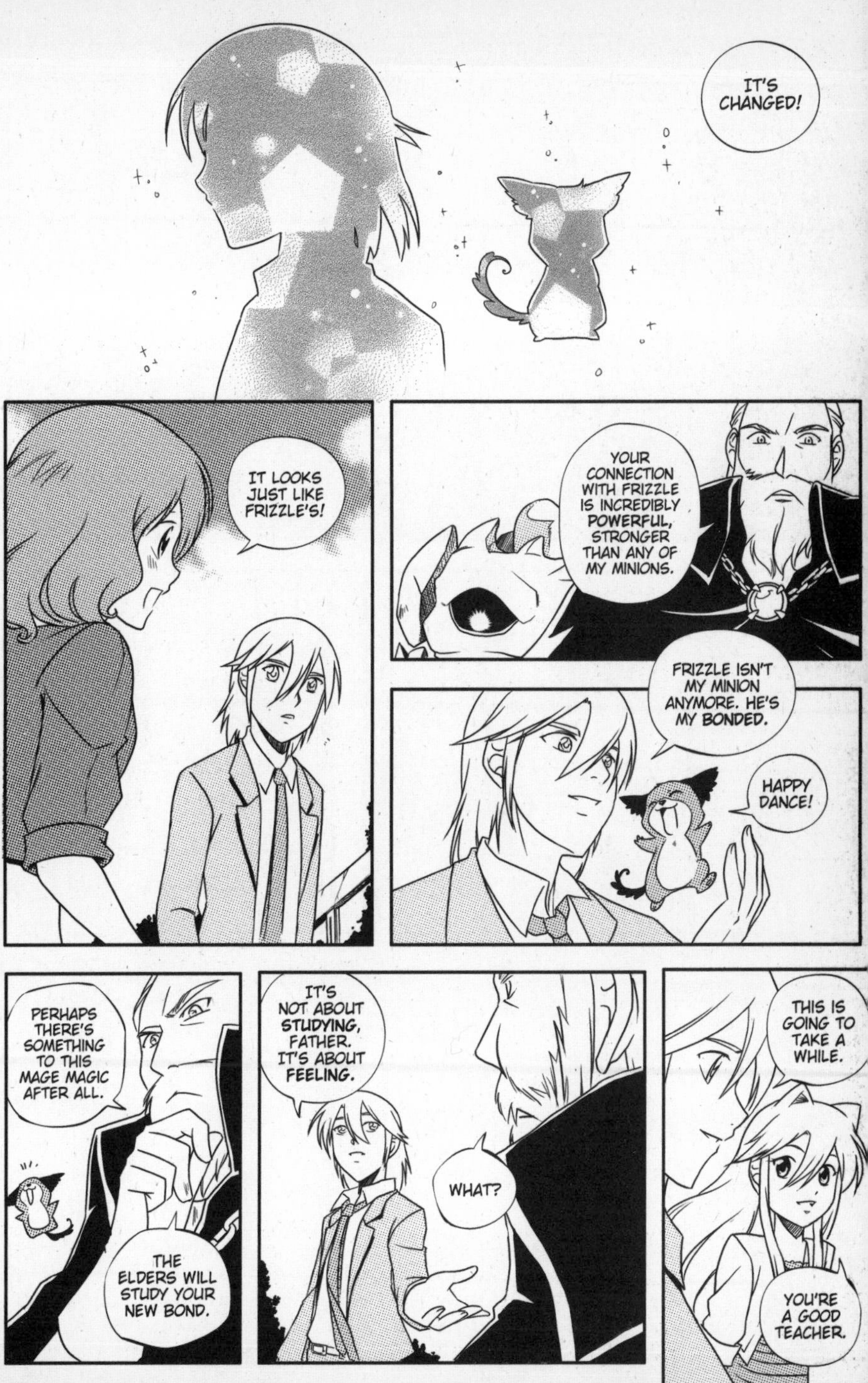
IT'S CHANGED!
IT LOOKS JUST LIKE FRIZZLE'S!
YOUR CONNECTION WITH FRIZZLE IS INCREDIBLY POWERFUL, STRONGER THAN ANY OF MY MINIONS.
FRIZZLE ISN'T MY MINION ANYMORE. HE'S MY **BONDED**.
HAPPY DANCE!
PERHAPS THERE'S SOMETHING TO THIS MAGE MAGIC AFTER ALL.
THE ELDERS WILL STUDY YOUR NEW BOND.
IT'S NOT ABOUT **STUDYING**, FATHER. IT'S ABOUT **FEELING**.
WHAT?
THIS IS GOING TO TAKE A WHILE.
YOU'RE A GOOD TEACHER.

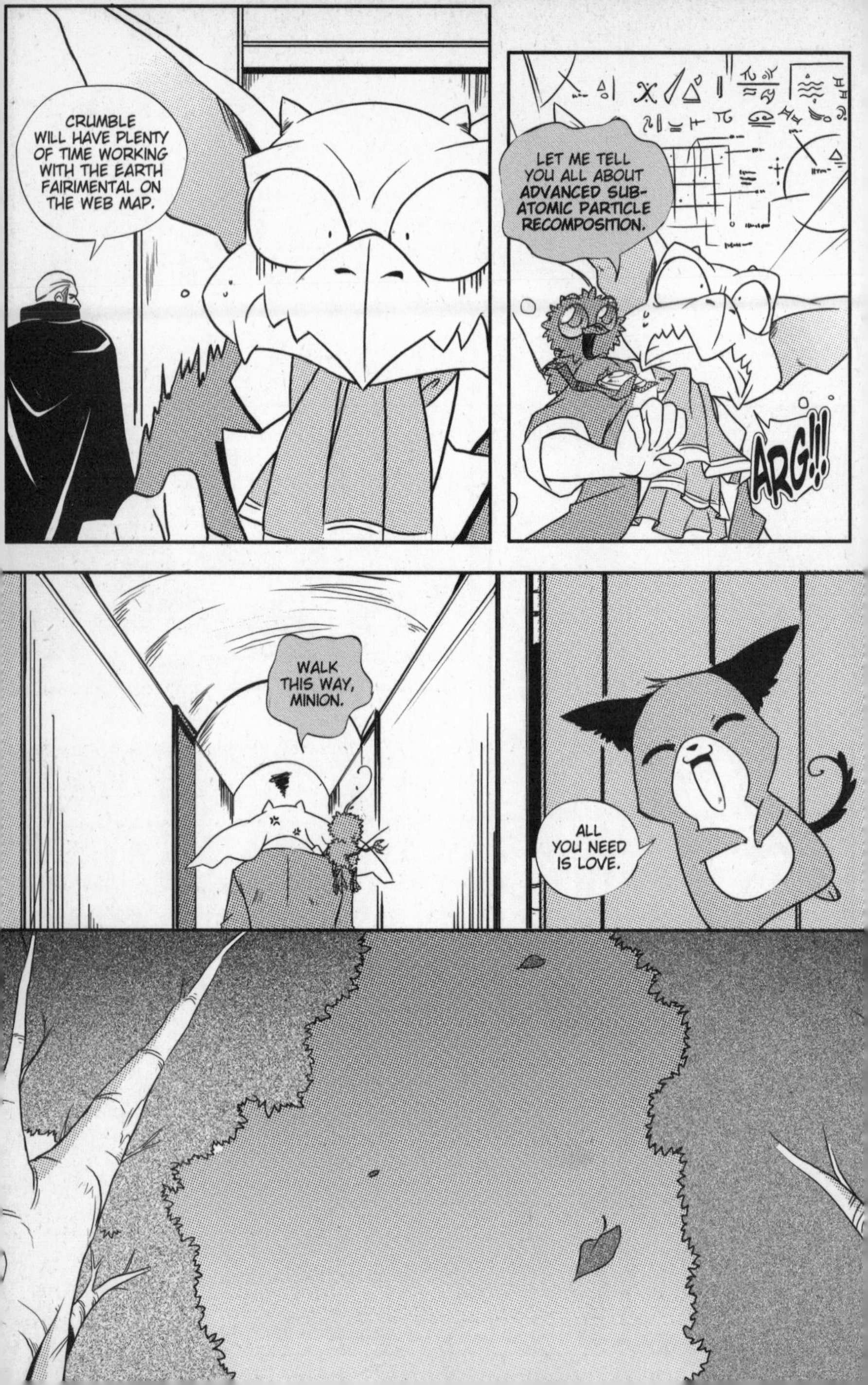
CRUMBLE WILL HAVE PLENTY OF TIME WORKING WITH THE EARTH FAIRIMENTAL ON THE WEB MAP.
LET ME TELL YOU ALL ABOUT ADVANCED SUB-ATOMIC PARTICLE RECOMPOSITION.
ARG!!!
WALK THIS WAY, MINION.
ALL YOU NEED IS LOVE.

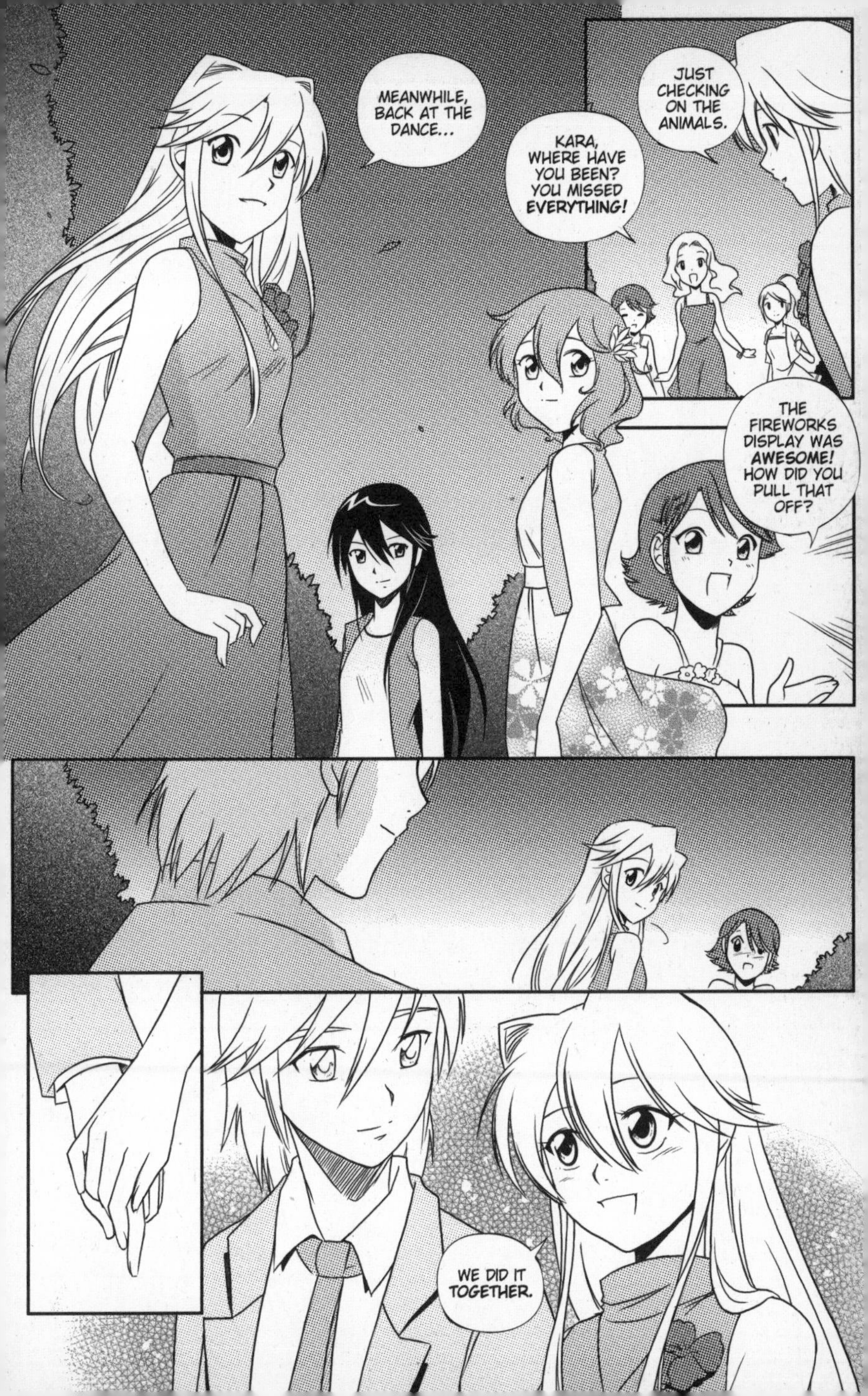
MEANWHILE, BACK AT THE DANCE...
KARA, WHERE HAVE YOU BEEN? YOU MISSED EVERYTHING!
JUST CHECKING ON THE ANIMALS.
THE FIREWORKS DISPLAY WAS AWESOME! HOW DID YOU PULL THAT OFF?
WE DID IT TOGETHER.

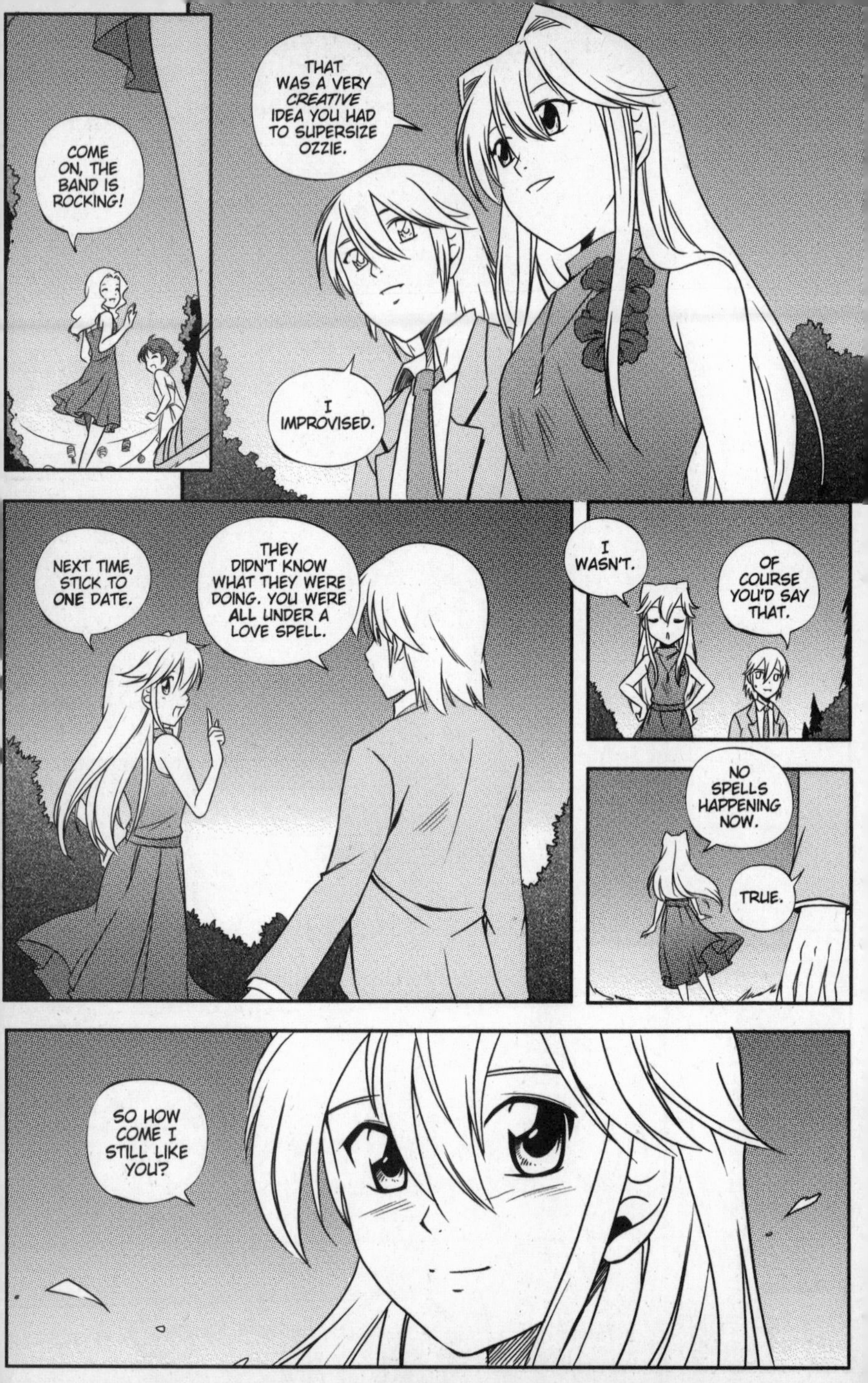
COME ON, THE BAND IS ROCKING!
THAT WAS A VERY *CREATIVE* IDEA YOU HAD TO SUPERSIZE OZZIE.
I IMPROVISED.
NEXT TIME, STICK TO ONE DATE.
THEY DIDN'T KNOW WHAT THEY WERE DOING. YOU WERE ALL UNDER A LOVE SPELL.
I WASN'T.
OF COURSE YOU'D SAY THAT.
NO SPELLS HAPPENING NOW.
TRUE.
SO HOW COME I STILL LIKE YOU?

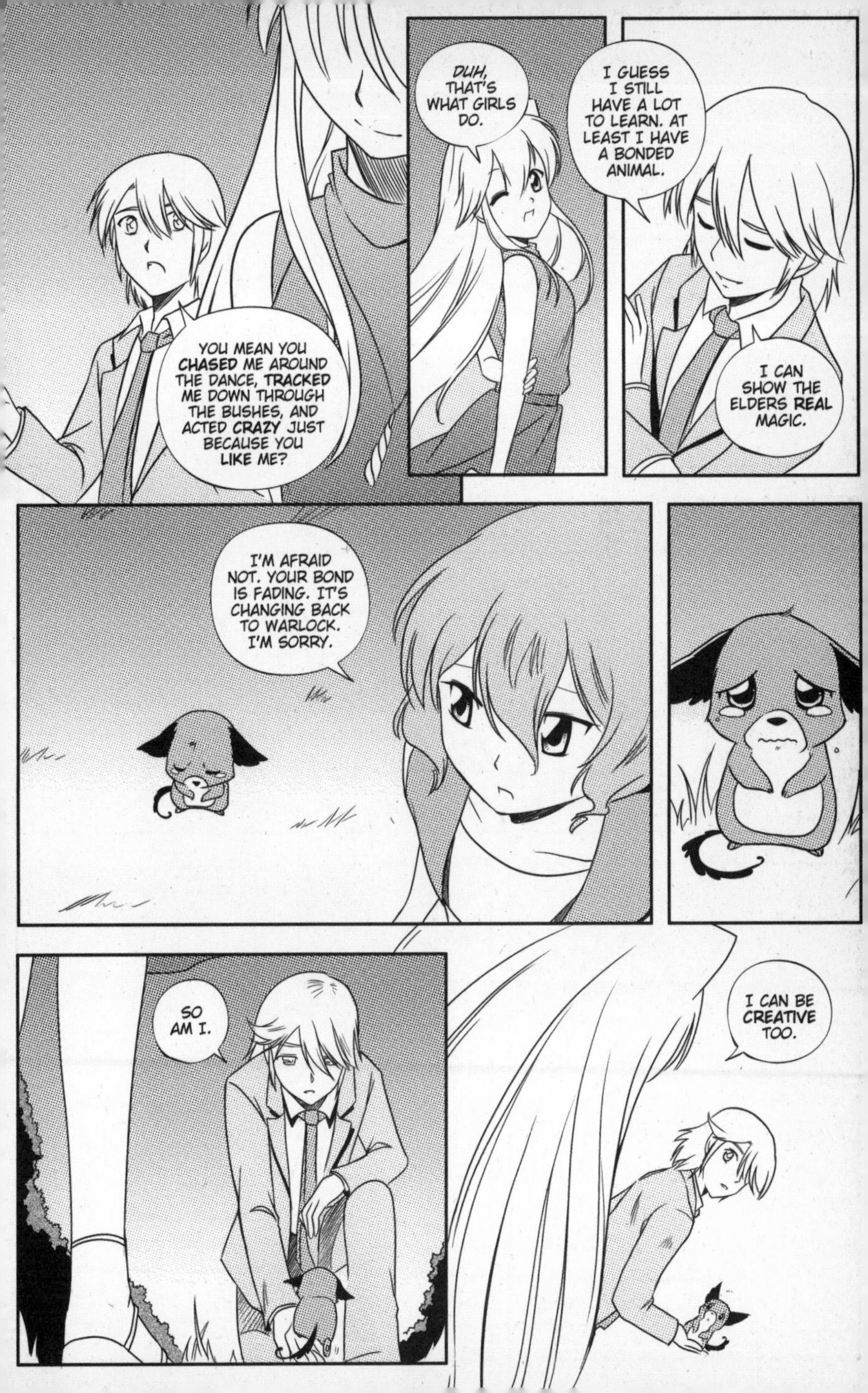
YOU MEAN YOU CHASED ME AROUND THE DANCE, TRACKED ME DOWN THROUGH THE BUSHES, AND ACTED CRAZY JUST BECAUSE YOU LIKE ME?
DUH, THAT'S WHAT GIRLS DO.
I GUESS I STILL HAVE A LOT TO LEARN. AT LEAST I HAVE A BONDED ANIMAL.
I CAN SHOW THE ELDERS REAL MAGIC.
I'M AFRAID NOT. YOUR BOND IS FADING. IT'S CHANGING BACK TO WARLOCK. I'M SORRY.
SO AM I.
I CAN BE CREATIVE TOO.

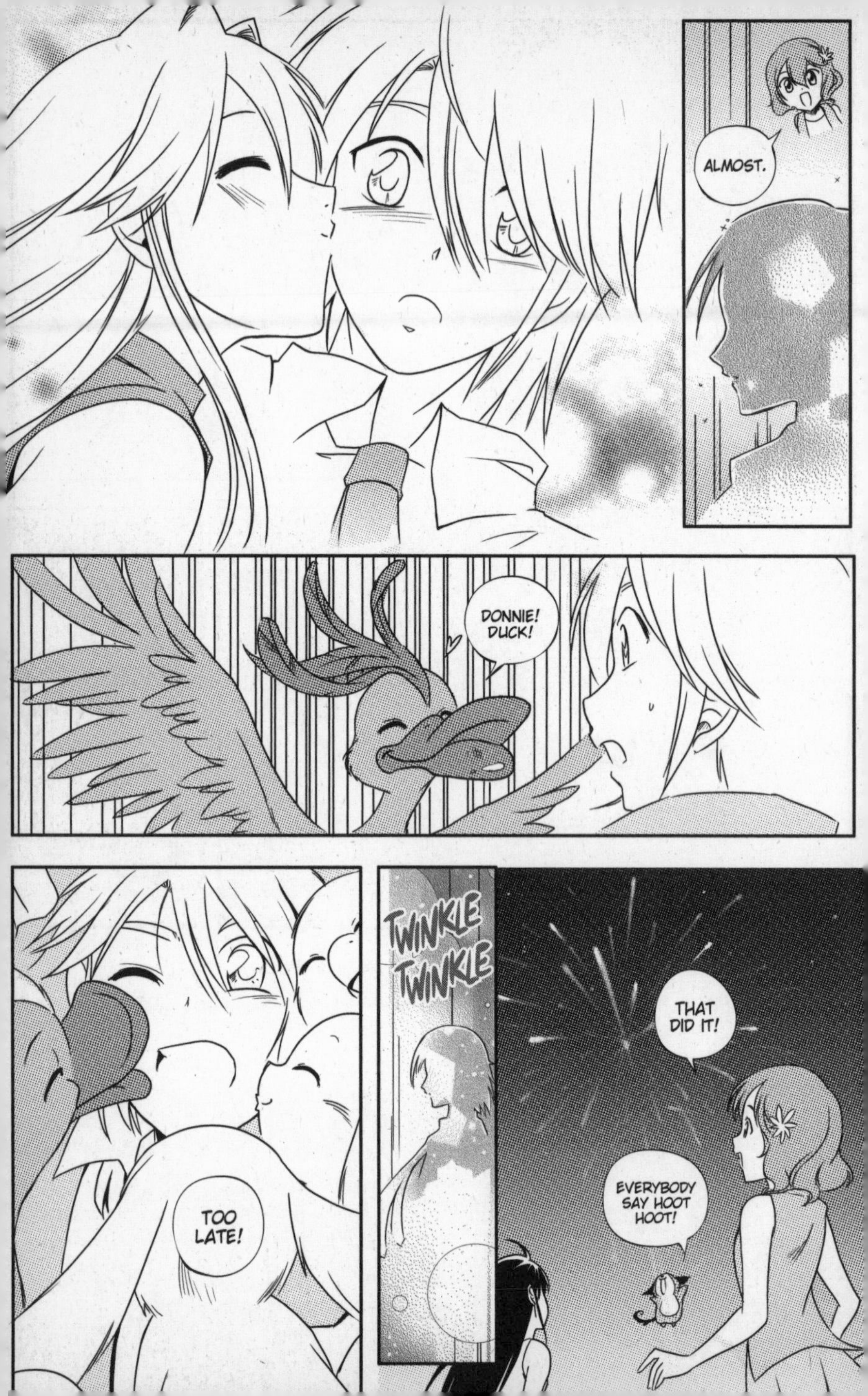
ALMOST.
DONNIE! DUCK!
TOO LATE!
TWINKLE TWINKLE
THAT DID IT!
EVERYBODY SAY HOOT HOOT!

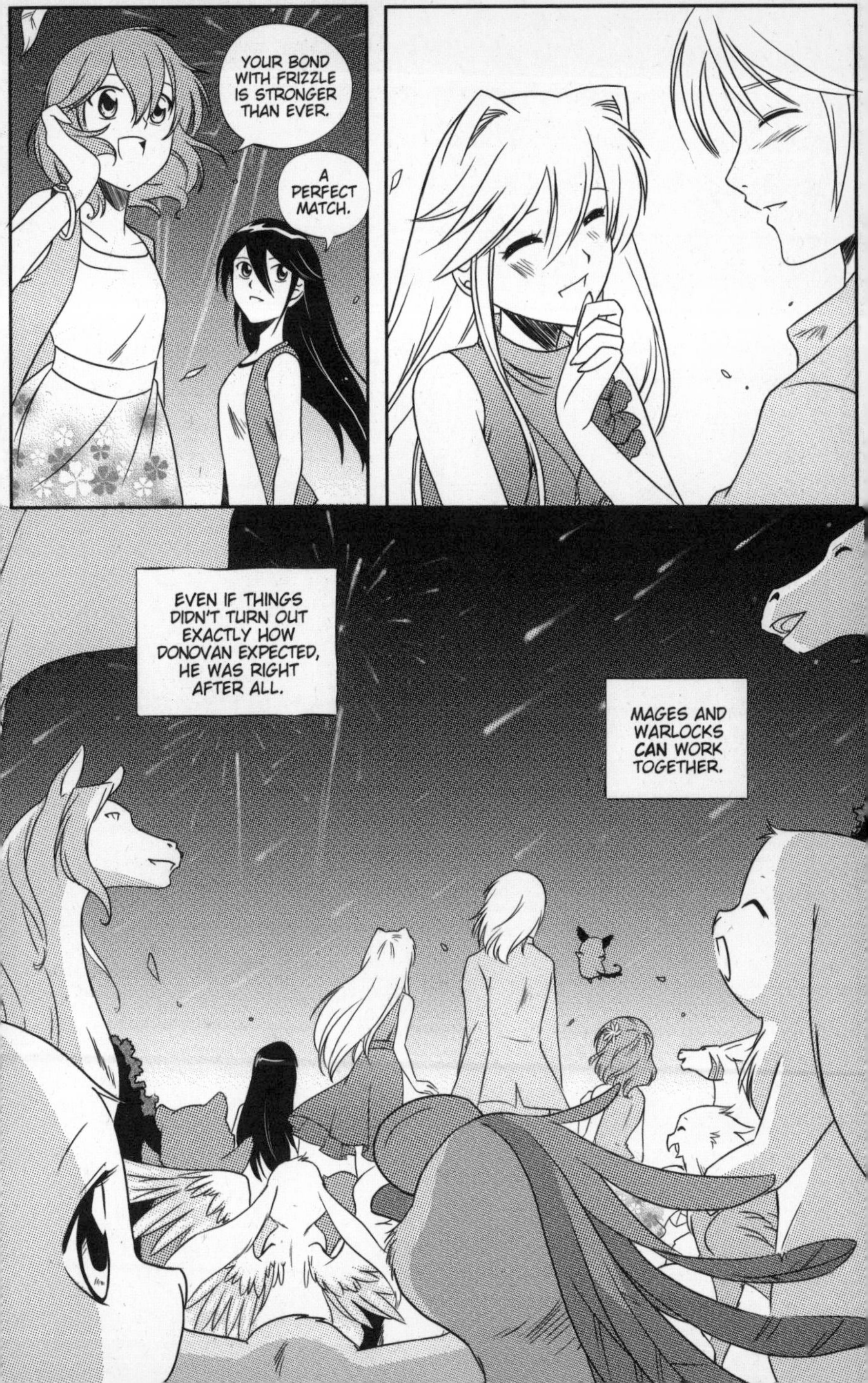
YOUR BOND WITH FRIZZLE IS STRONGER THAN EVER.
A PERFECT MATCH.
EVEN IF THINGS DIDN'T TURN OUT EXACTLY HOW DONOVAN EXPECTED, HE WAS RIGHT AFTER ALL.
MAGES AND WARLOCKS CAN WORK TOGETHER.

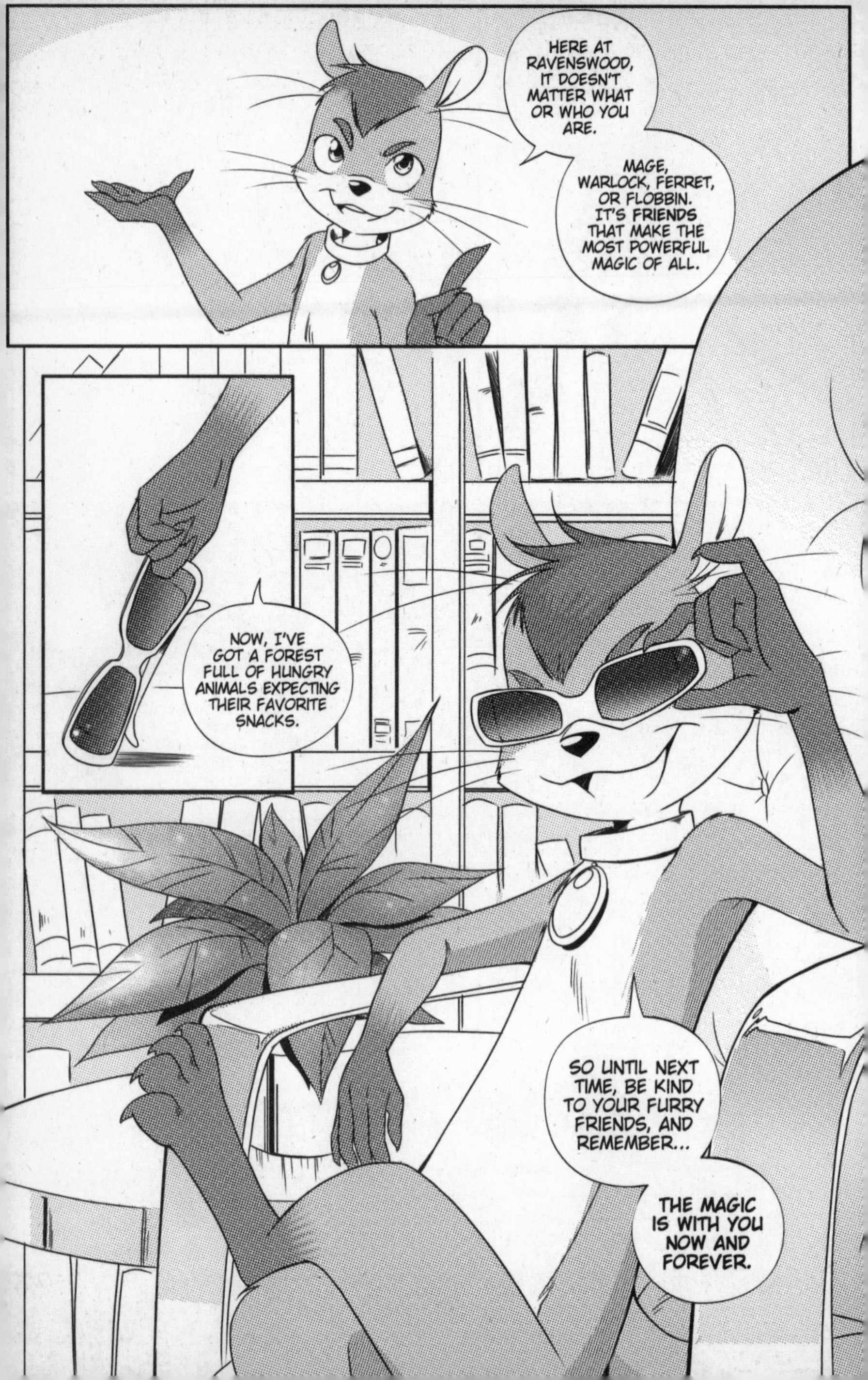
HERE AT RAVENSWOOD, IT DOESN'T MATTER WHAT OR WHO YOU ARE.
MAGE, WARLOCK, FERRET, OR FLOBBIN. IT'S FRIENDS THAT MAKE THE MOST POWERFUL MAGIC OF ALL.
NOW, I'VE GOT A FOREST FULL OF HUNGRY ANIMALS EXPECTING THEIR FAVORITE SNACKS.
SO UNTIL NEXT TIME, BE KIND TO YOUR FURRY FRIENDS, AND REMEMBER...
THE MAGIC IS WITH YOU NOW AND FOREVER.

AVALON

■ Art Gallery ■

ADRIANE   Emily   KARA

EMILY

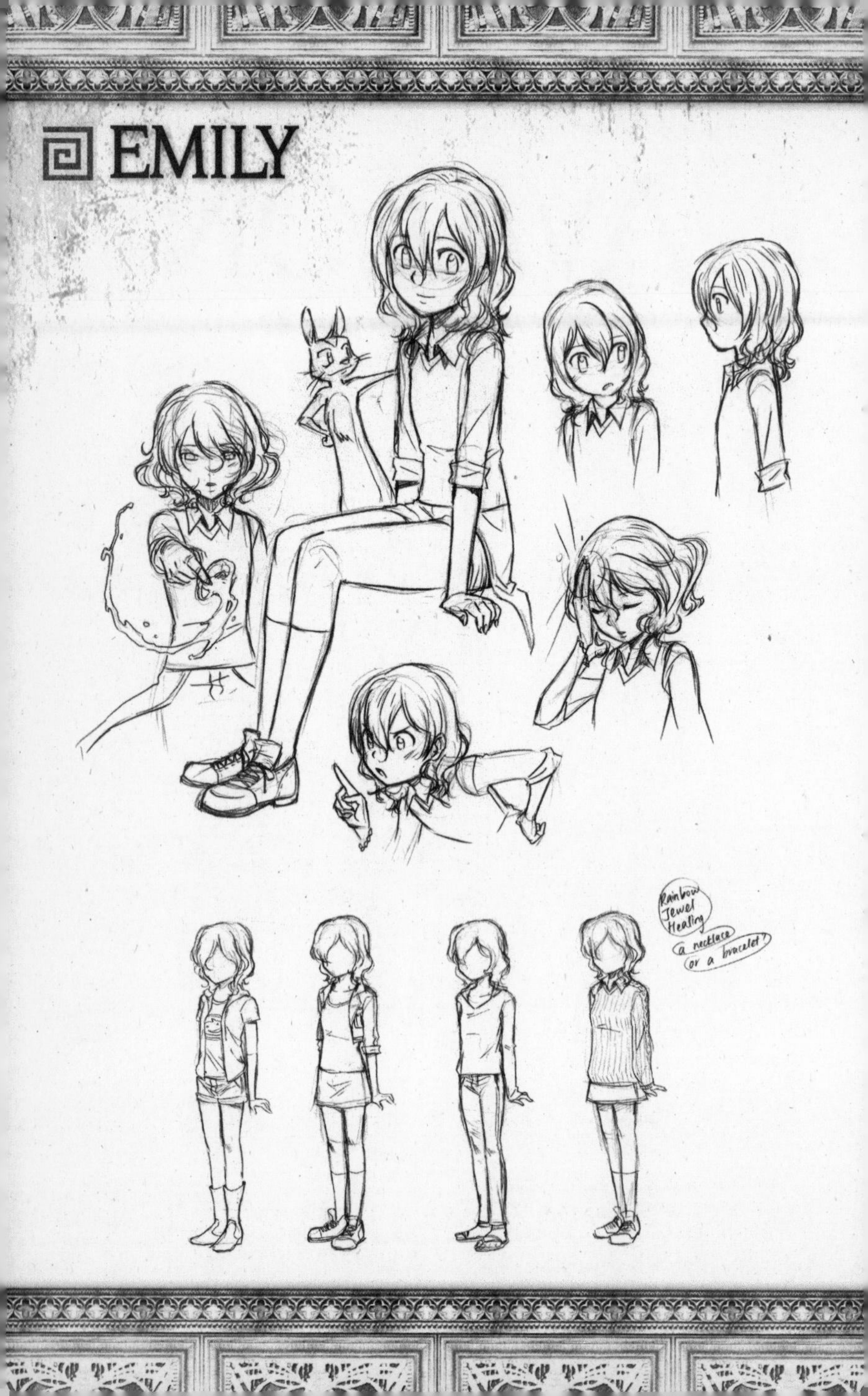
Rainbow Jewel Healing
a necklace or a bracelet?

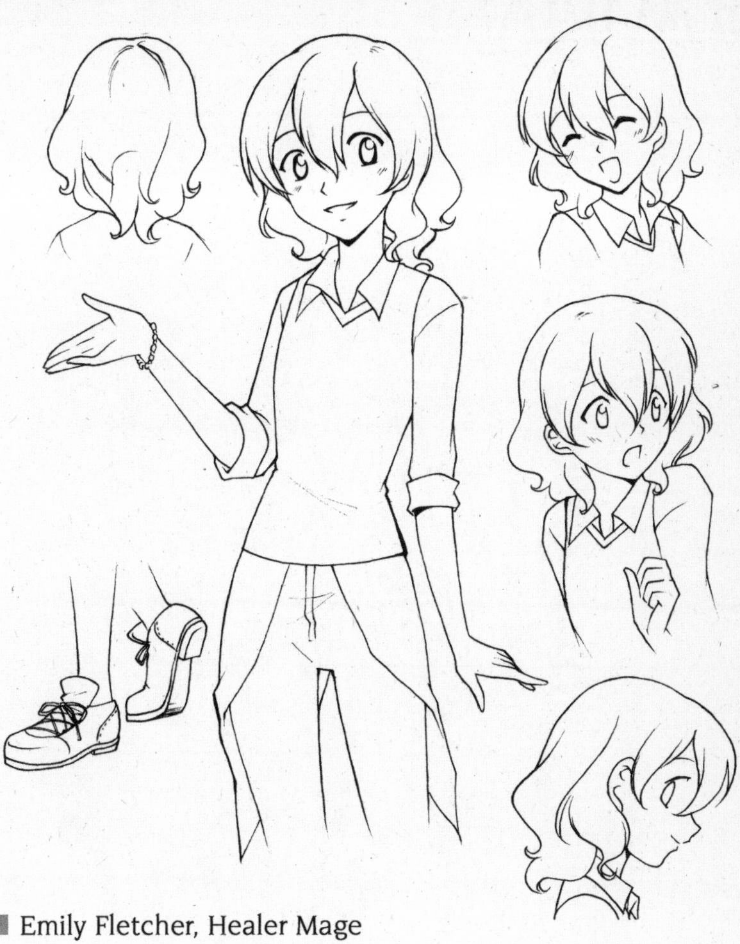

Emily Fletcher, Healer Mage

Emily has a natural affinity for animals, having grown up around critters all her life. Her single mom is a veterinarian. Emily uses a rainbow jewel that helps focus her healing magic. Her strong musical abilities also help focus magic. Her affinity for animals will manifest itself in a special way: in addition to the ability to communicate with magical animals, Emily's ability to sense the feelings and communicate with non-magical animals will be enhanced. Although technically not a real animal, the ferr-elf, Ozzie, has become Emily's self-appointed protector and best animal buddy.

ADRIANE

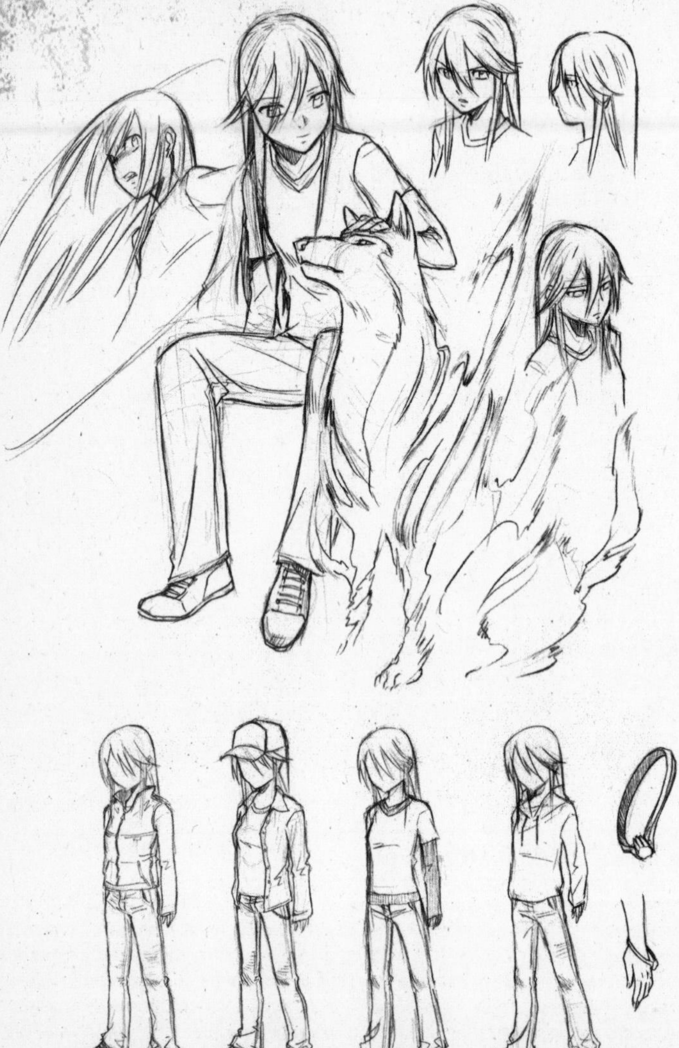

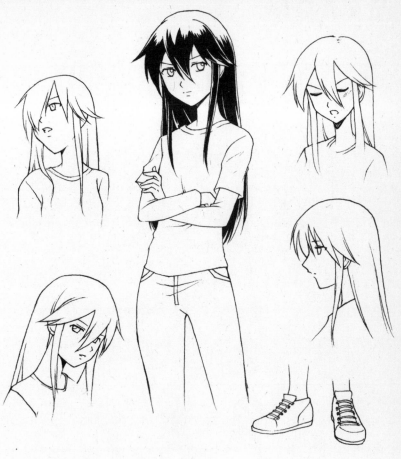

◼ Adriane Charday, Warrior Mage

Adriane lives with her grandmother at the Ravenswood Preserve while her artist parents travel the world. Her magical abilities manifest themselves in the ways of nature and of physical things: strength, jumping higher and running faster. Adriane has an extremely strong bond with her packmate, Dreamer. Using wolf senses that enhance her hearing, vision and reflexes, she seems to communicate with nature itself, feeling things around her that others cannot hear or see.

KARA

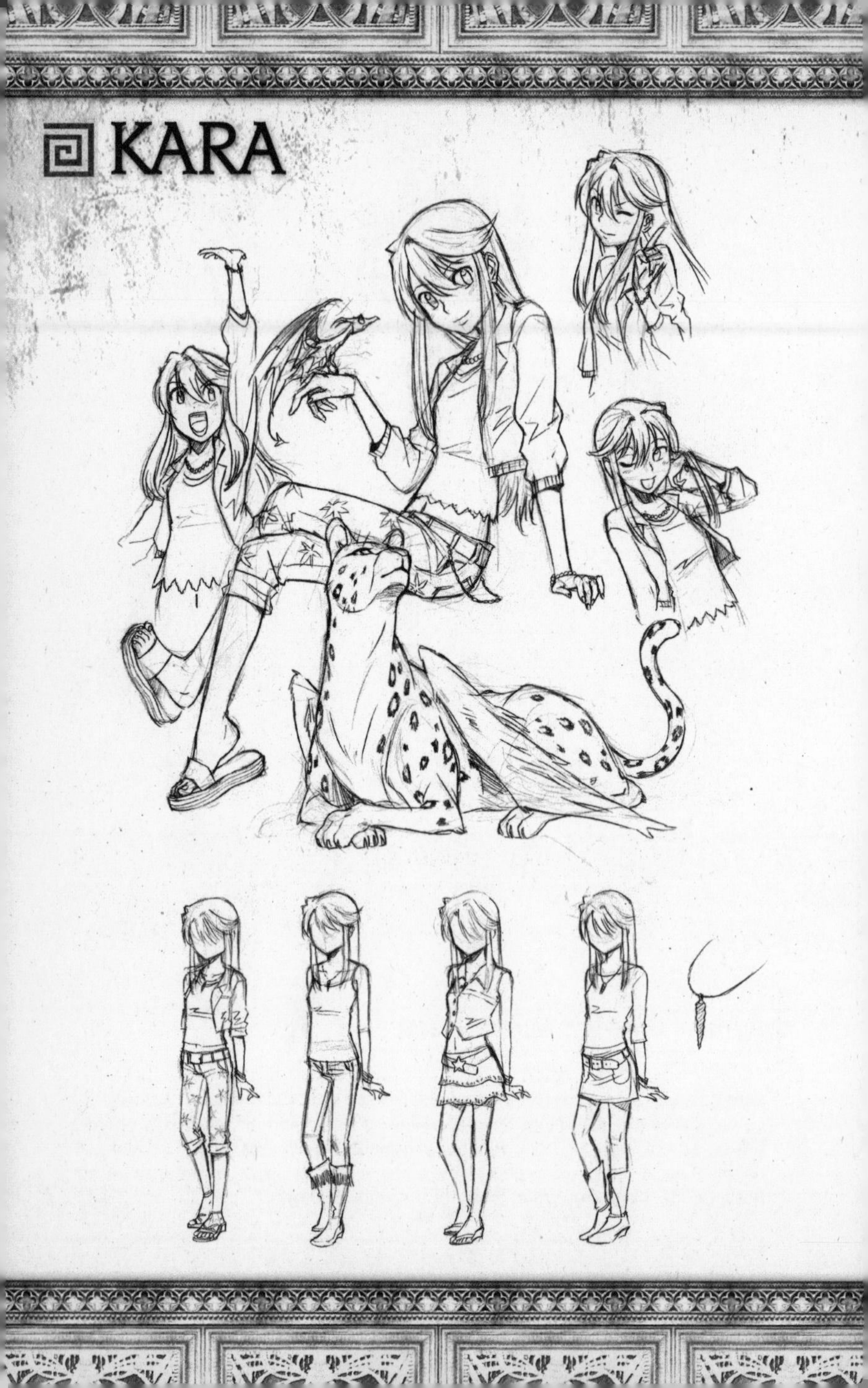

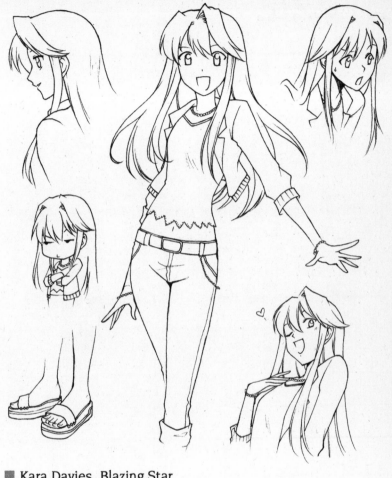

■ Kara Davies, Blazing Star

Kara is the daughter of the town mayor and a hotshot lawyer. She is a magnet for magic, and a natural magic amplifier. The magic likes her, and always works better when she is around. She has a strong bond with Lyra, a magical flying cat, as well as five dragonflies, half the unicorn population, and any other creature along the magic web who encounters her brilliant magic.

OZZIE

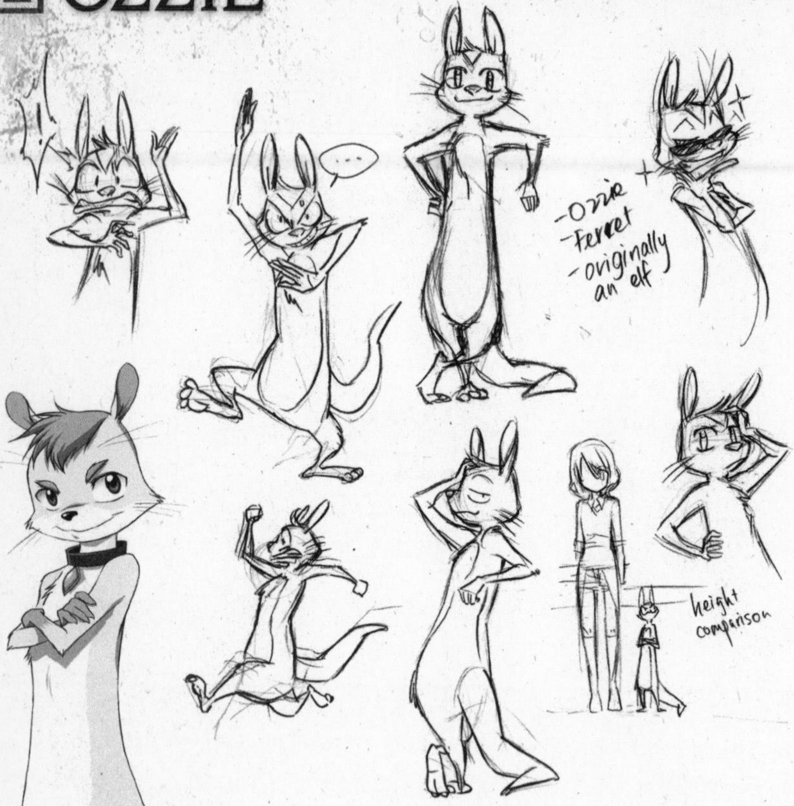

-Ozzie
-Ferret
-originally an elf
height comparison

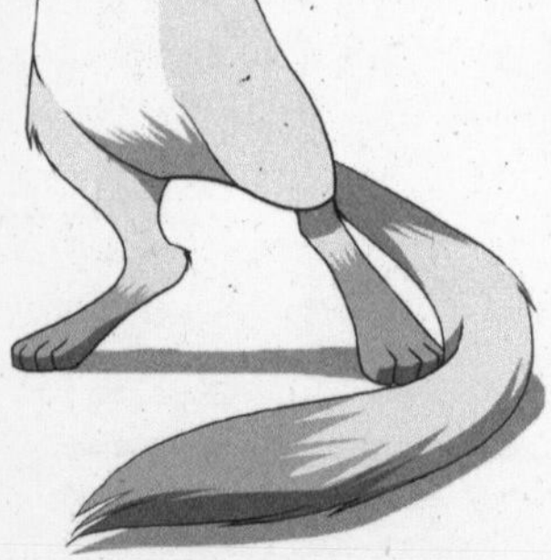

Ozzie, ferr-elf

Ozzie is an elf sent to Earth disguised as a ferret to find three mages. He is proud and confident and thinks he can handle anything, until he meets three teenage girls. His mission: help the girls become magic users. Ozzie is easily flustered and over-excitable. The Fairimentals chose him, but the true nature of his magic is a mystery.

TWEEK

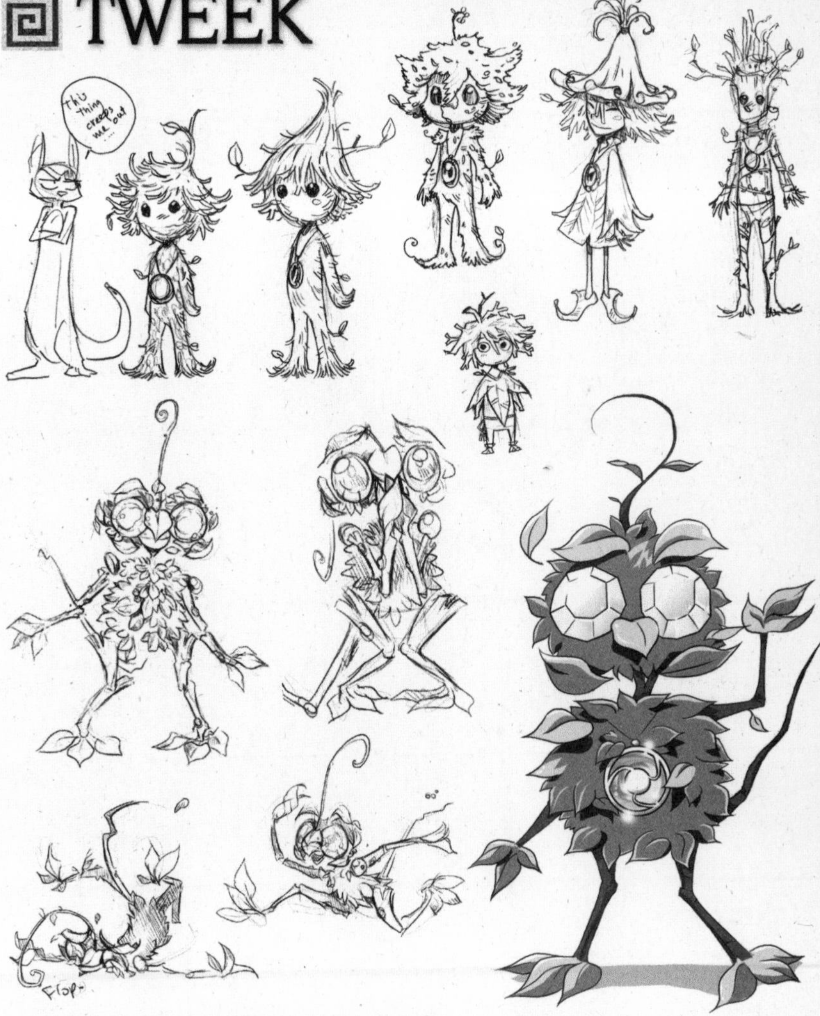
this thing creeps me out ....
Flop!

Tweek, Experimental Earth Fairimental

Created by the Fairimentals of Aldenmor to stay on Earth and aid the mages. Patrols Ravenswood riding on Ariel the snow owl. Wears a turquoise data crystal known as the HORARFF – Handbook of Rules and Regulations for Fairimentals.

DONOVAN

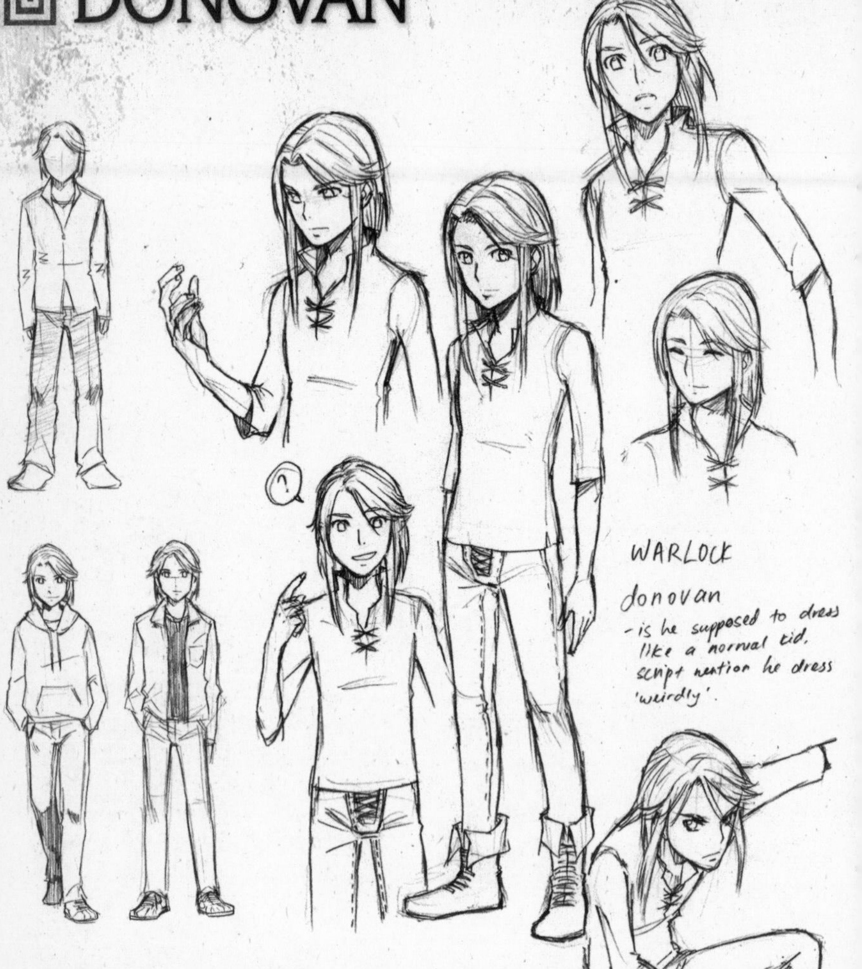

?
WARLOCK
donovan
- is he supposed to dress like a normal kid, script mention he dress 'weirdly'.

Donovan

Teenage warlock rebel who wants to prove to the Elders that warlocks and mages can work together to find Avalon and save the magic web. With the help of his minions, Donovan uses ancient spells and potions to make magic.

CRUMBLE

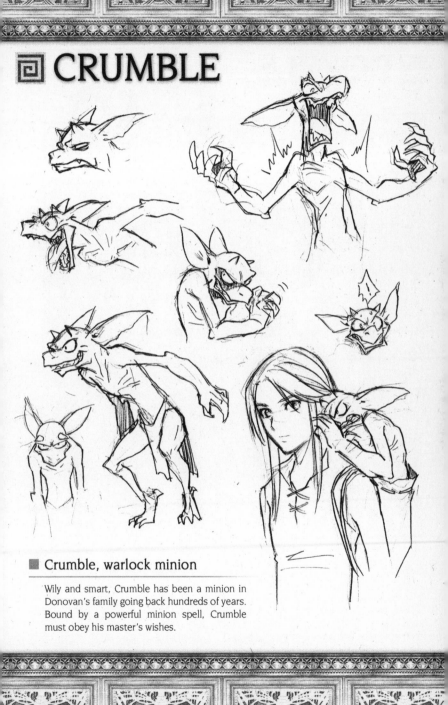

■ Crumble, warlock minion

Wily and smart, Crumble has been a minion in Donovan's family going back hundreds of years. Bound by a powerful minion spell, Crumble must obey his master's wishes.

FRIZZLE

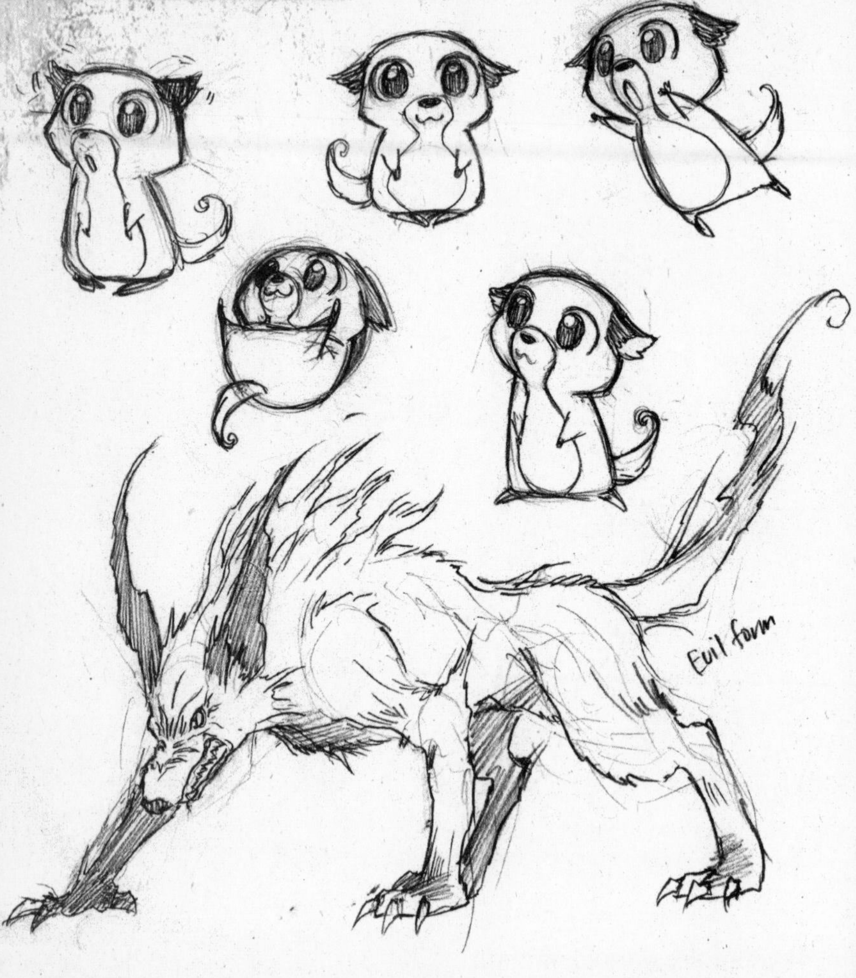
Evil form

Frizzle, warlock minion

Frizzle is a shapeshifting minion recently bound to Donovan. Frizzle enjoys making magic with Donovan and unlike most minions, he is fun-loving and likes to improvise.

DREAMER

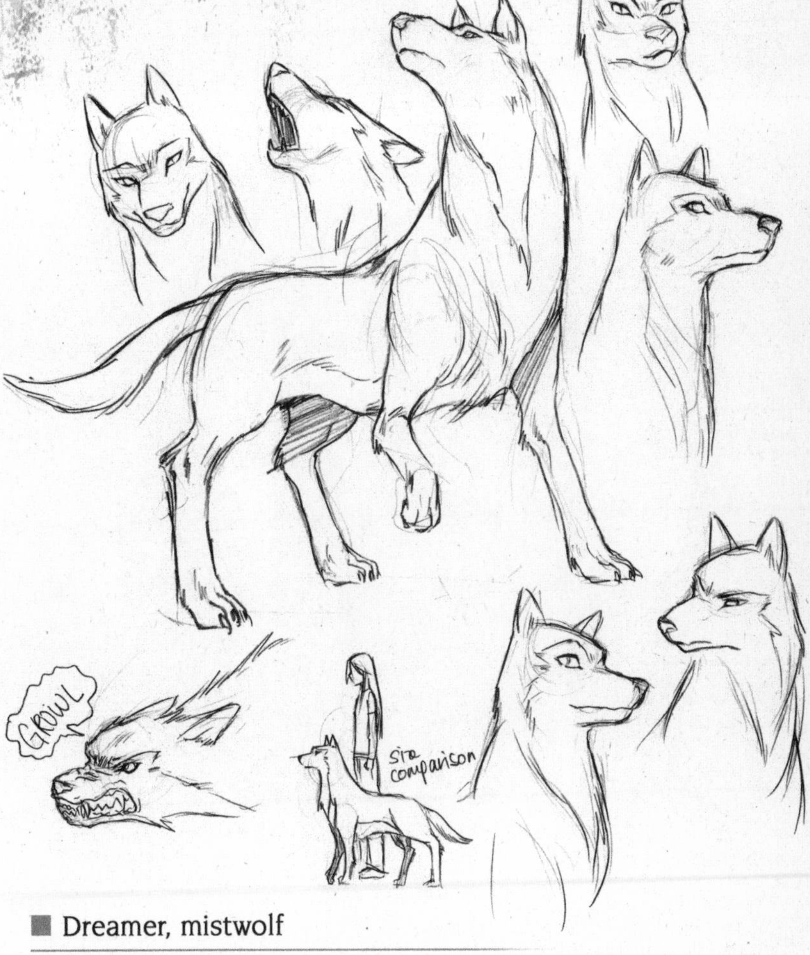
GROWL
size comparison

Dreamer, mistwolf

Orphaned on Aldenmor, Dreamer was given to Adriane by the mistwolf pack mother, Silver Eyes. Raised by Adriane in Ravenswood, Dreamer has a deep bond with the mages and animals. Like all mistwolves, his bloodline goes back thousands of years, enabling him to tap into memories and visions of the past.

LYRA

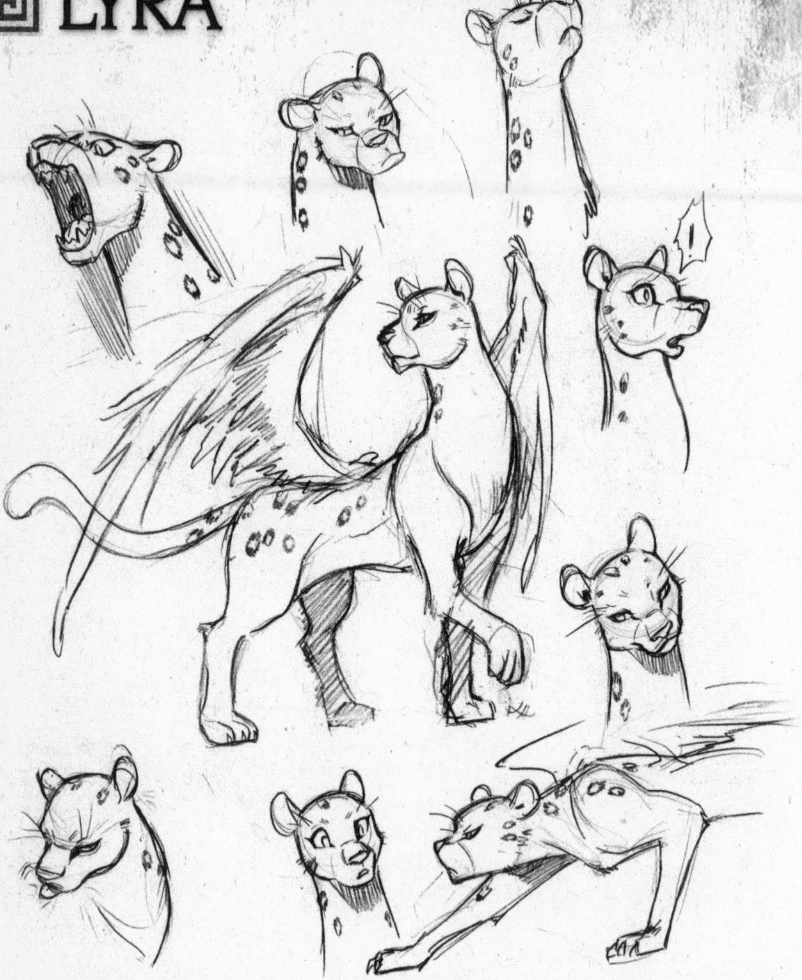

Lyra, magical flying cat

A magical, winged, leopard-like cat from Aldenmor, Lyra is dignified and very smart. She is extremely intuitive and can sense things no one else can. A fierce fighter, she is very protective of her bonded mage, Kara. Only mages can see Lyra's beautiful golden wings.

GOLDIE

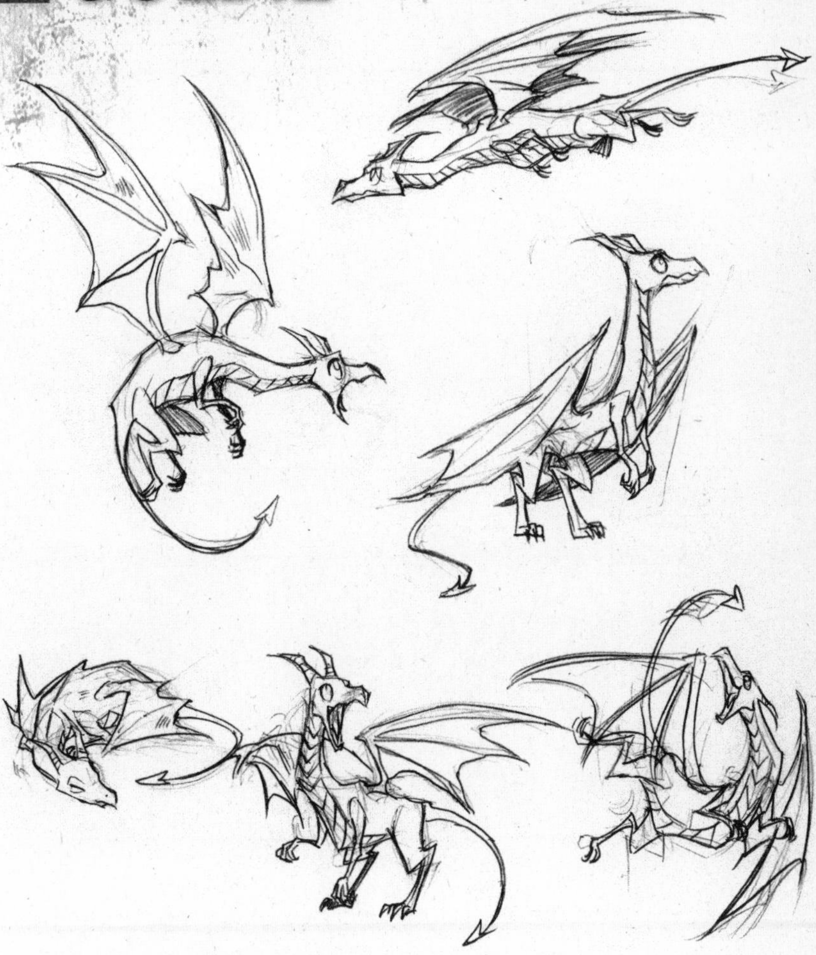

Goldie, dragonfly

Goldie and her buds always come whenever Kara calls them. Dragonflies are fairy creatures that can travel without the use of a portal. They can be used as dragonfly phones to help mages communicate with each other. Goldie has a special bond with Kara, having gone on many adventures with the blazing star.

BULWOGGLE

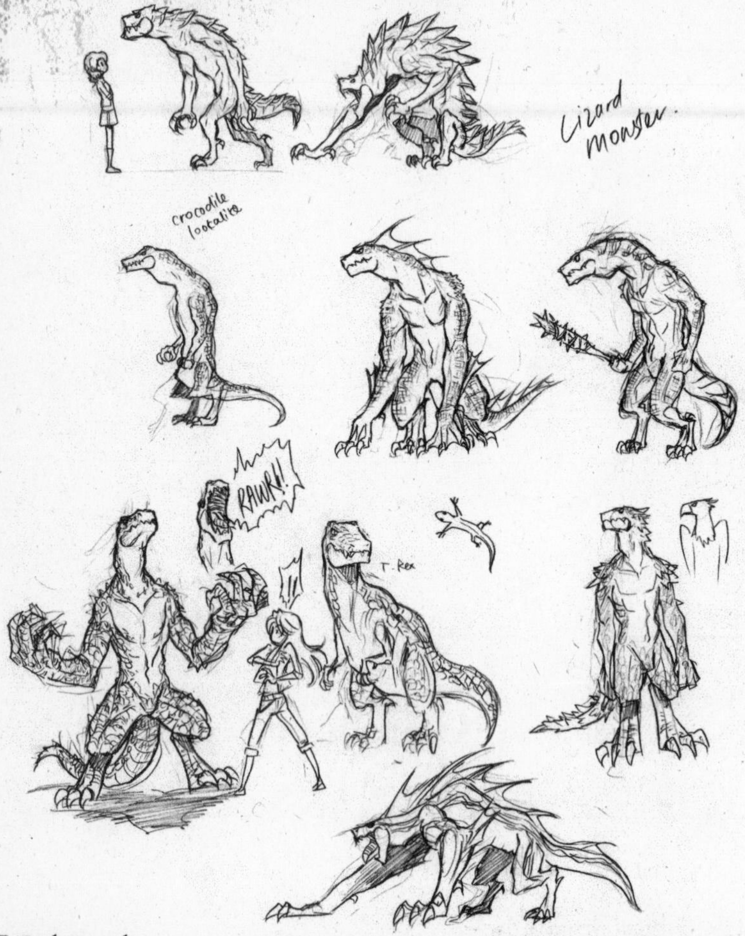
Lizard monster
crocodile lookalike
RAWR!!
T. Rex

Bulwoggle

Large lizard-like creatures, Bulwoggles are strong, ferocious, and quick-tempered. Bulwoggles hunt the web searching for magic. They hire out their skills as magic trackers and mercenaries to anyone willing to pay for their services.

�回 GOLEM

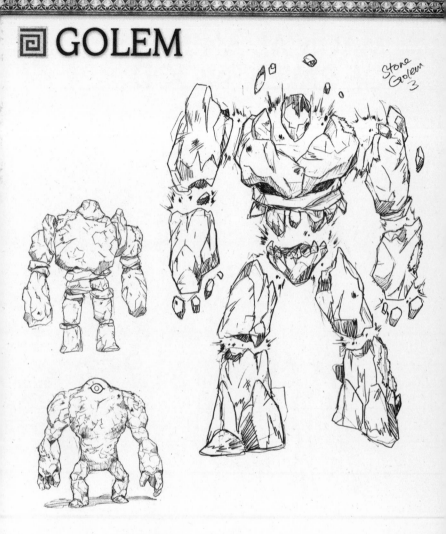

Stone
Golem
3

◼ Golem

A golem is constructed from an inanimate object like stone and brought to life by a powerful warlock spell. They are usually made to accomplish a single goal.

MAGICAL ANIMALS OF RAVENSWOOD

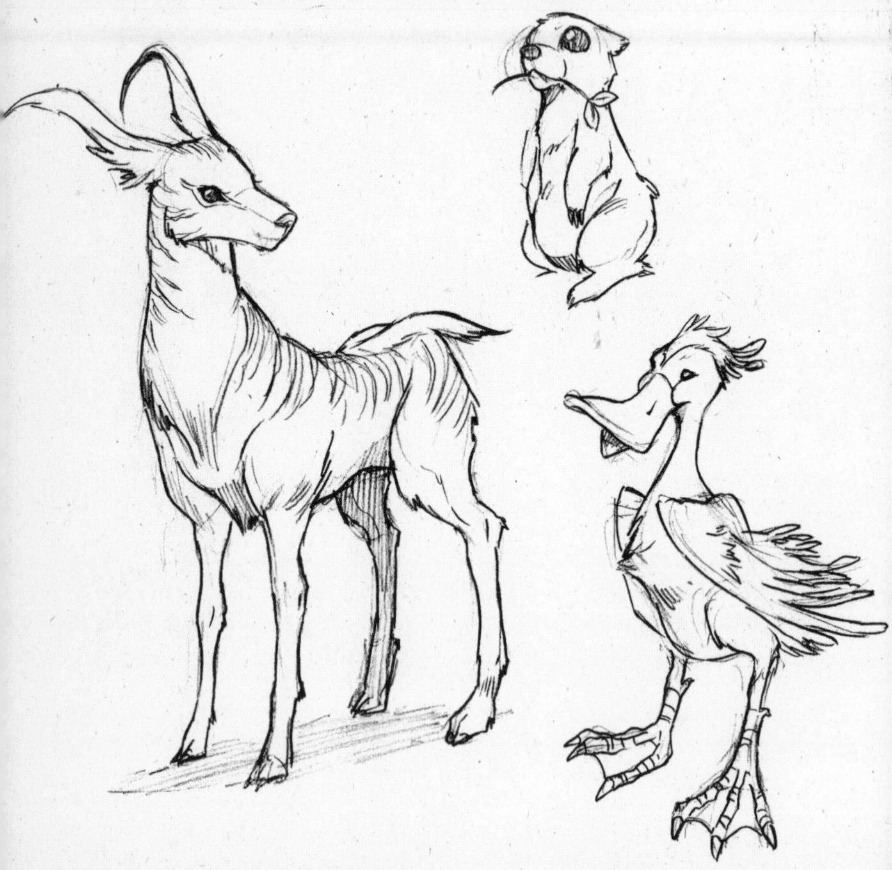

Jeeran / Wommel / Quiffle

Animals from Aldenmor who came through the Ravenswood portal seeking sanctuary at the famous animal preserve for magical animals. They now live there, helping to protect the forests and practice making magic with the mages.

FRIENDS & CLASSMATES

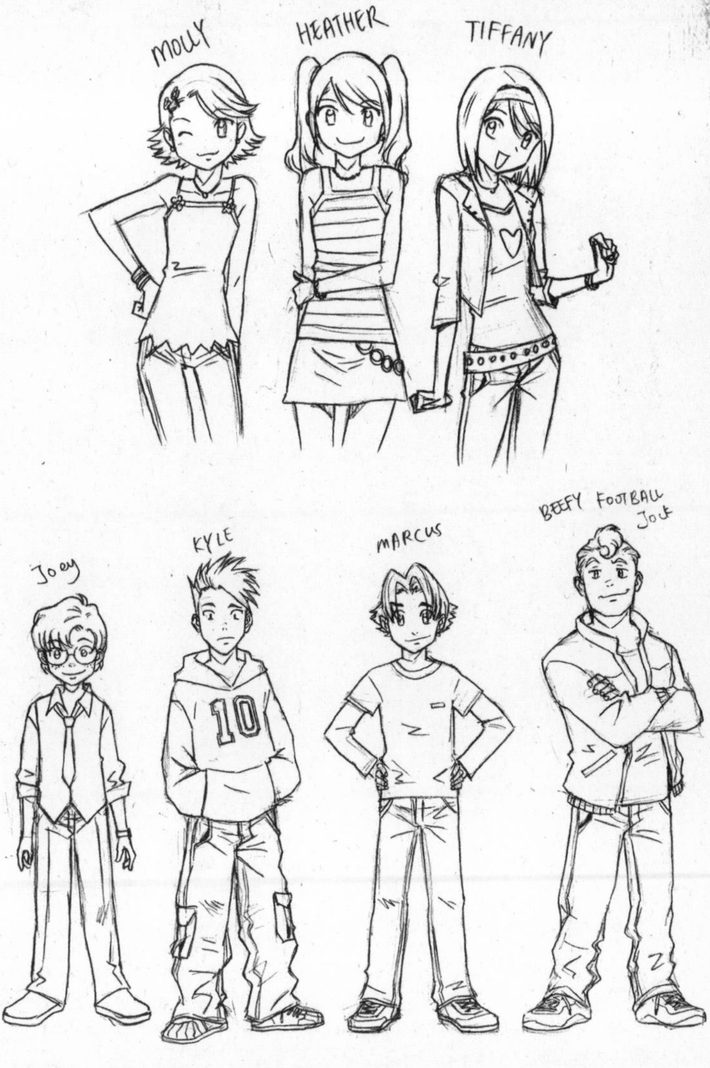
MOLLY
HEATHER
TIFFANY
JOEY
KYLE
MARCUS
BEEFY FOOTBALL JOCK

Magic Jewels

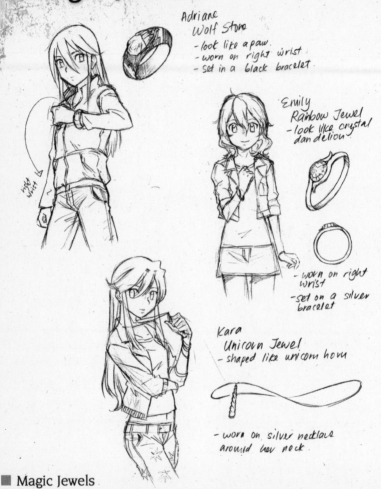

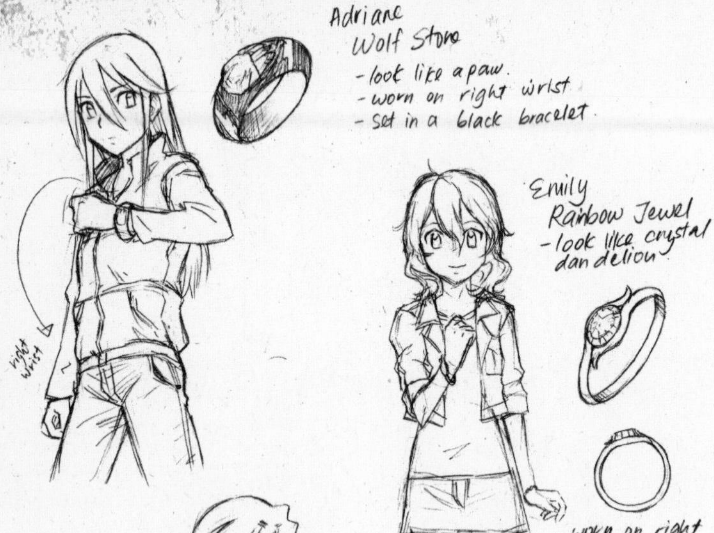
Adriane
Wolf Stone
-look like a paw.
-worn on right wrist
-Set in a black bracelet
right wrist
Emily
Rainbow Jewel
-look like crystal dandelion
-worn on right wrist
-set on a silver bracelet
Kara
Unicorn Jewel
-shaped like unicorn horn
-worn on silver necklace around her neck

Magic Jewels

Magic jewels are formed from concentrations of wild magic. The jewels focus magic and change as the mages' powers evolve. Each jewel is totally unique and its powers can only be fully used by the mage it's tuned to. Adriane and Emily found their jewels in the Ravenswood Preserve. Kara's is a transformed unicorn horn.

回 Comparative Magic Chart

MAGE MAGIC	WARLOCK MAGIC
Bonded animals work with mages, creating renewable magic that becomes more powerful as friendship grows.	Powerful spells bind minions who must obey their warlock masters.
Jewels amplify and focus magic created with animals.	Spells, charms, and potions store magic.
Uses elemental magic based on the five elements of nature: earth, wind, air, water, and time.	Uses spells based on arcane science handed down through generations.
Improvisation, flexibility, and adaptability are key – each mage has a unique approach.	Extremely rigid, every warlock practices the same unchanged, ancient methods.
Emotions power and direct mage magic.	Must be unemotional and scientific.

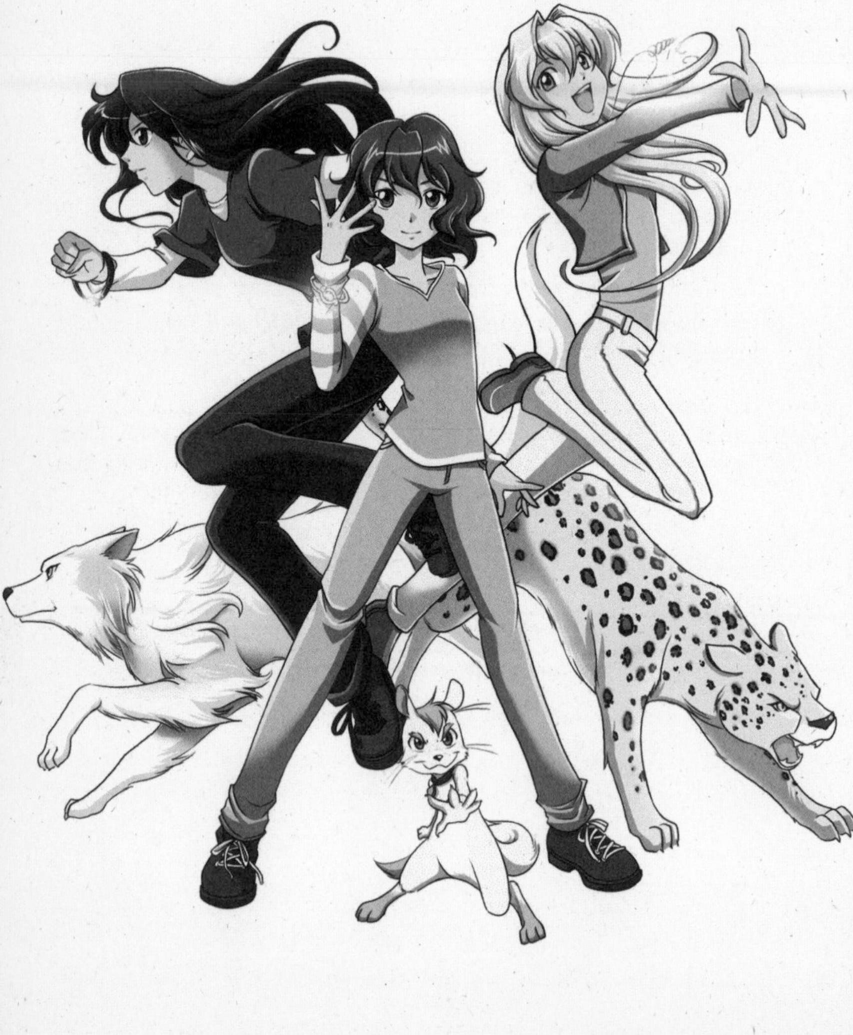

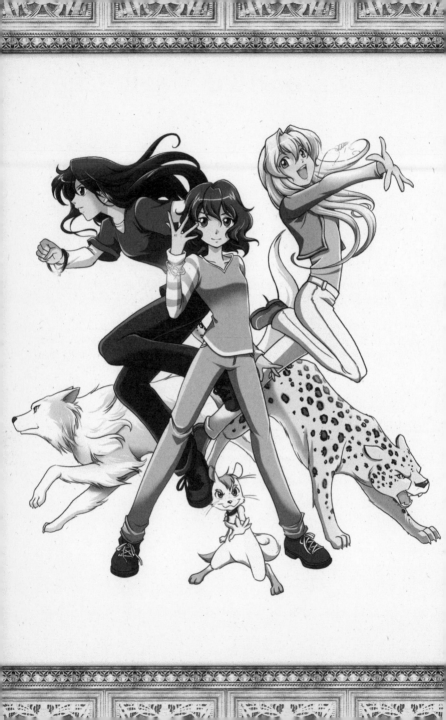

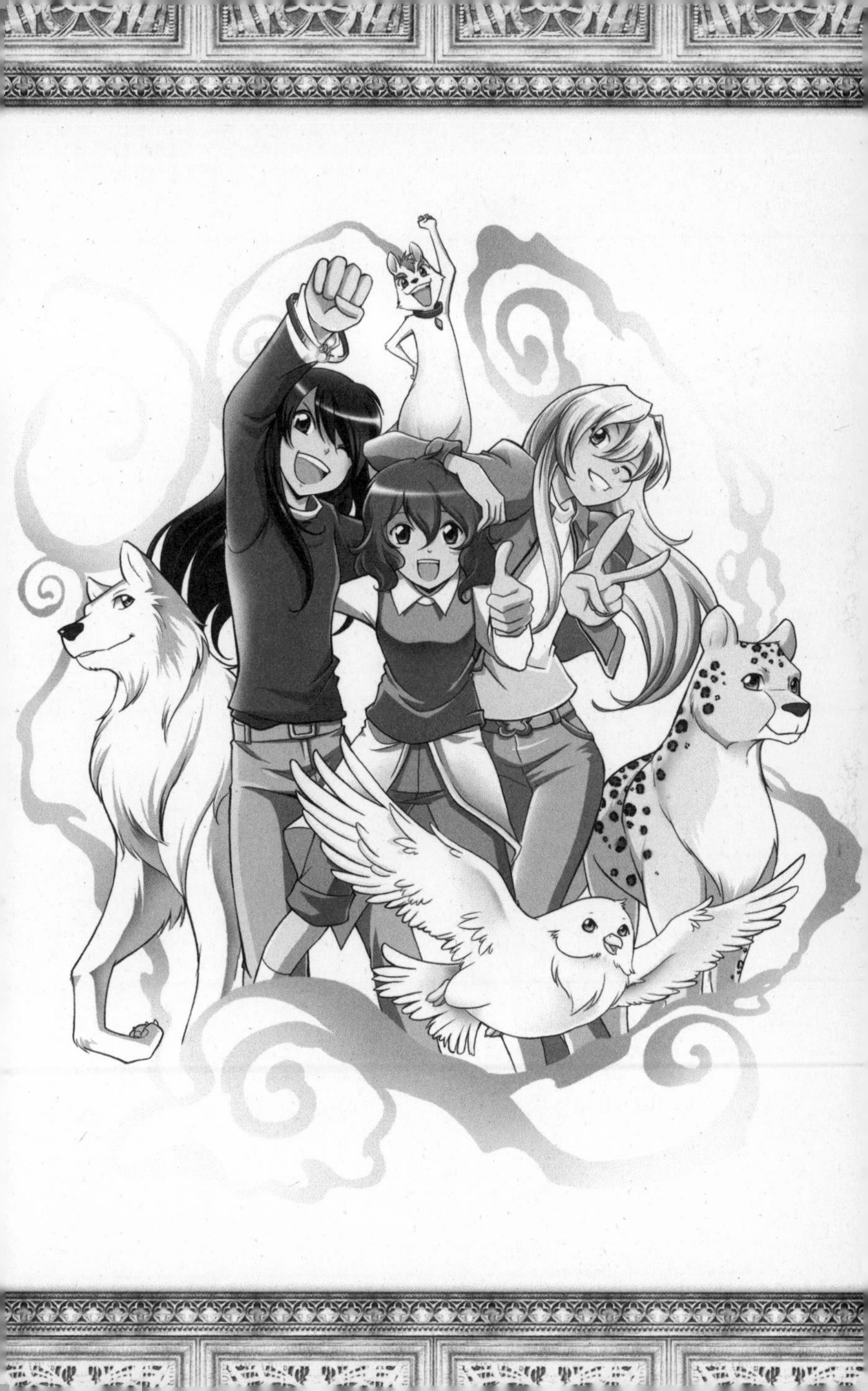

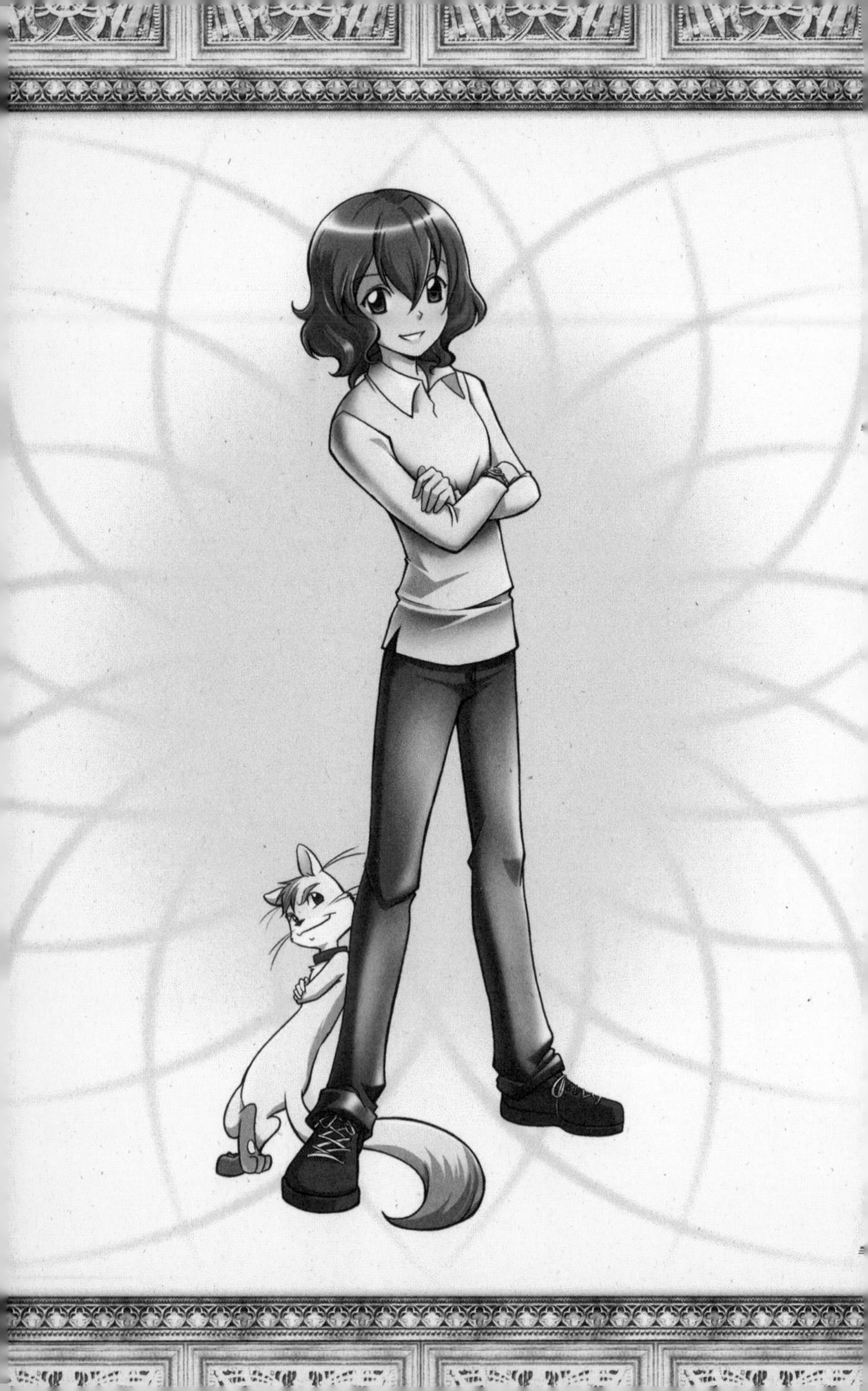

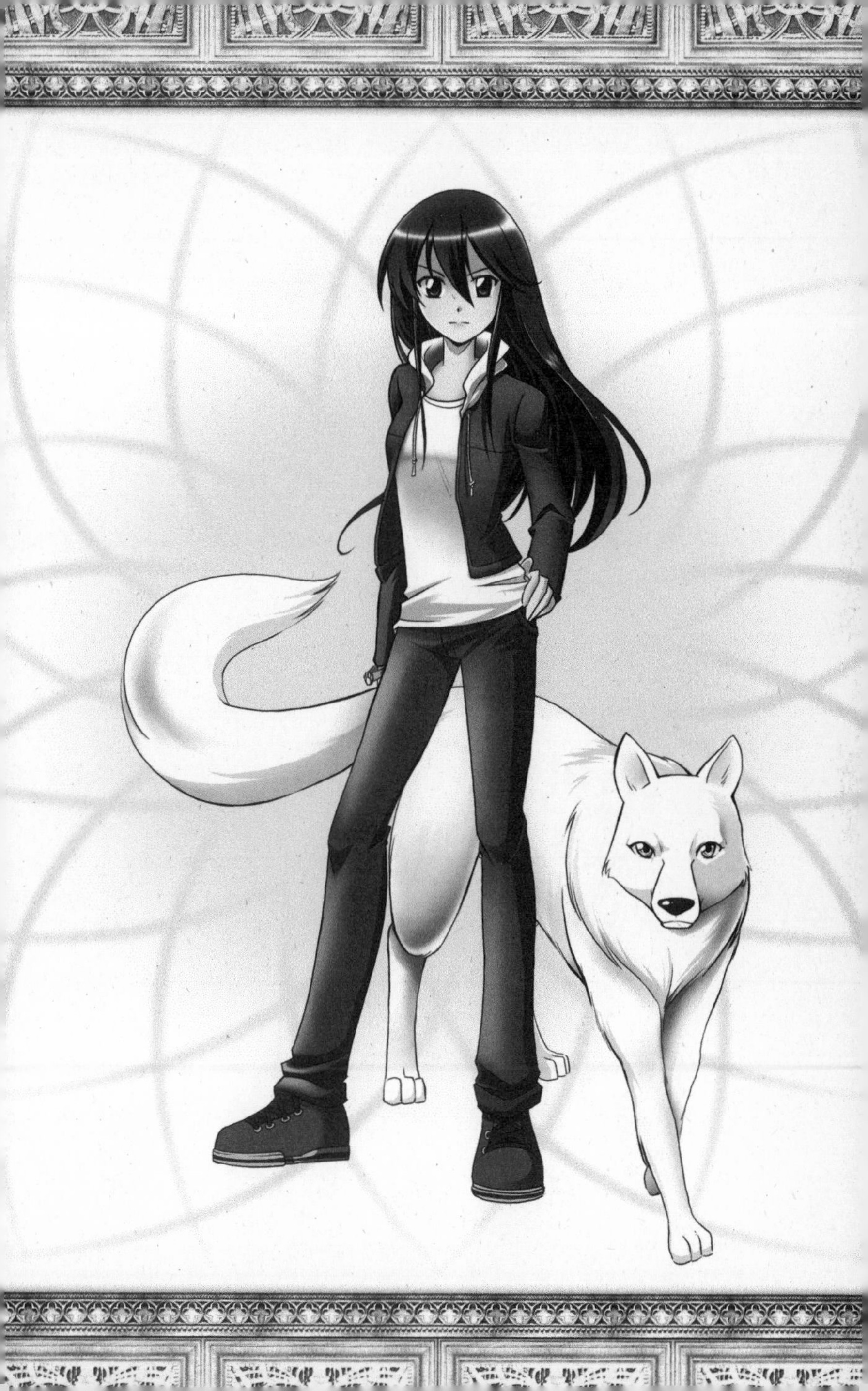

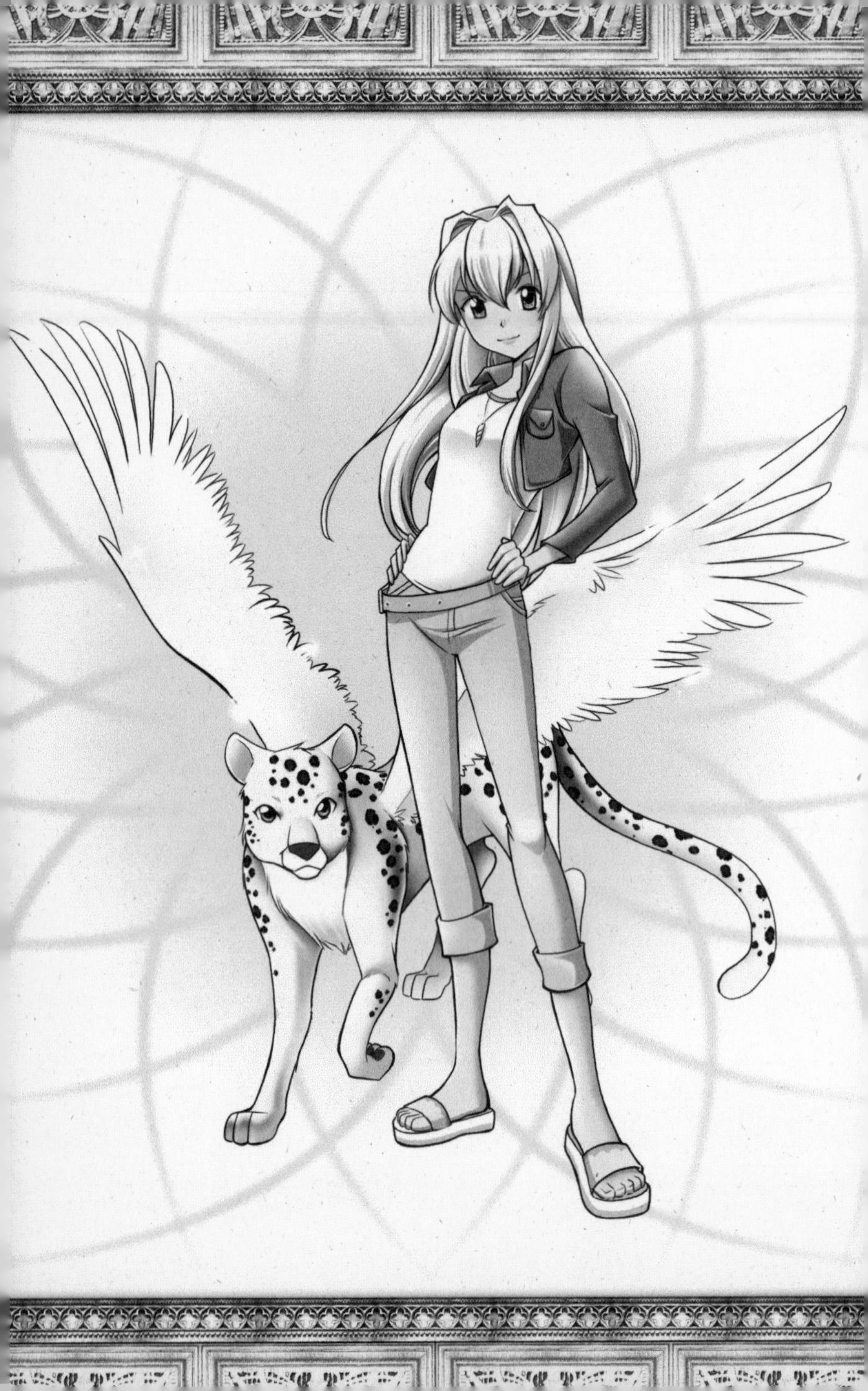

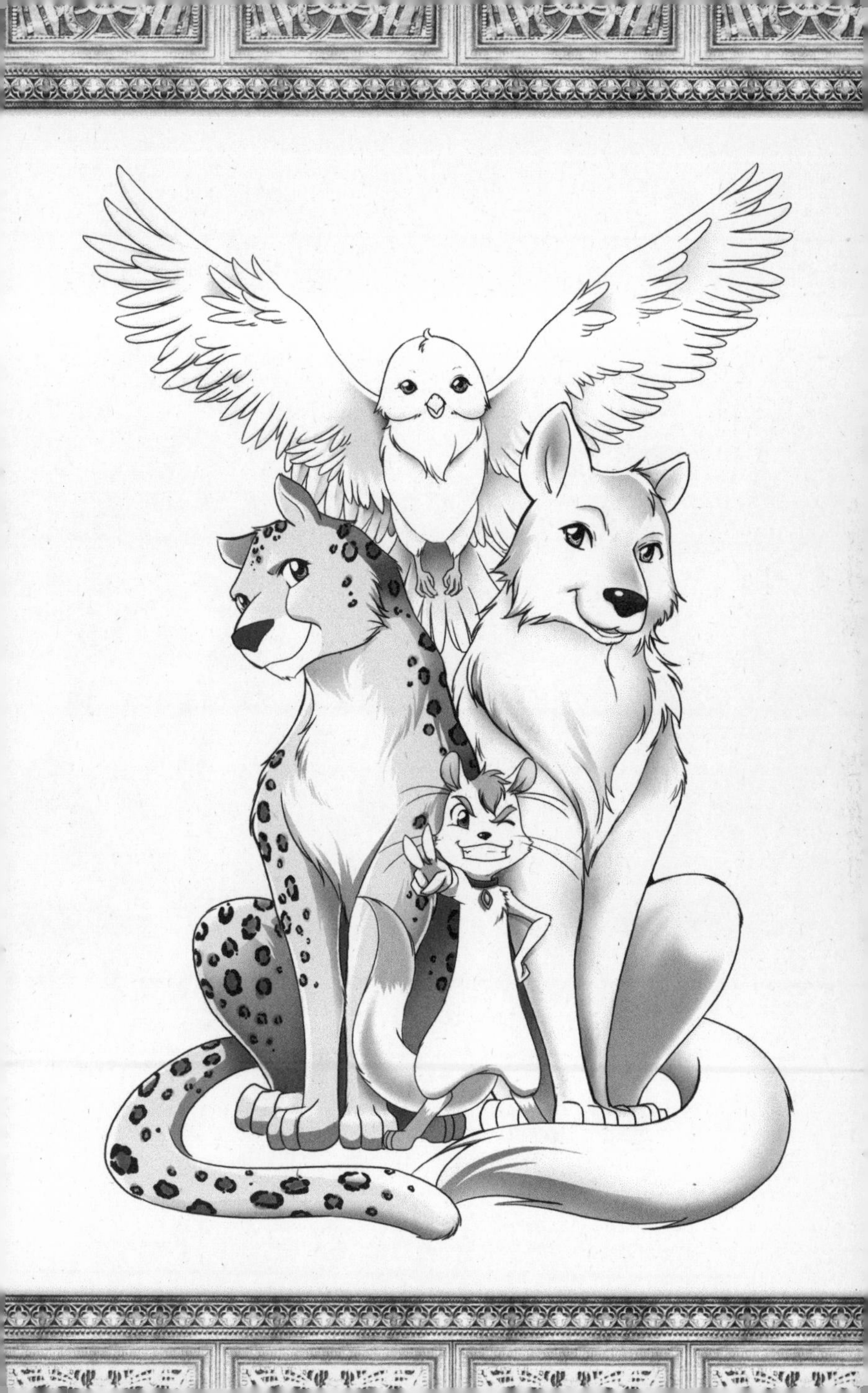

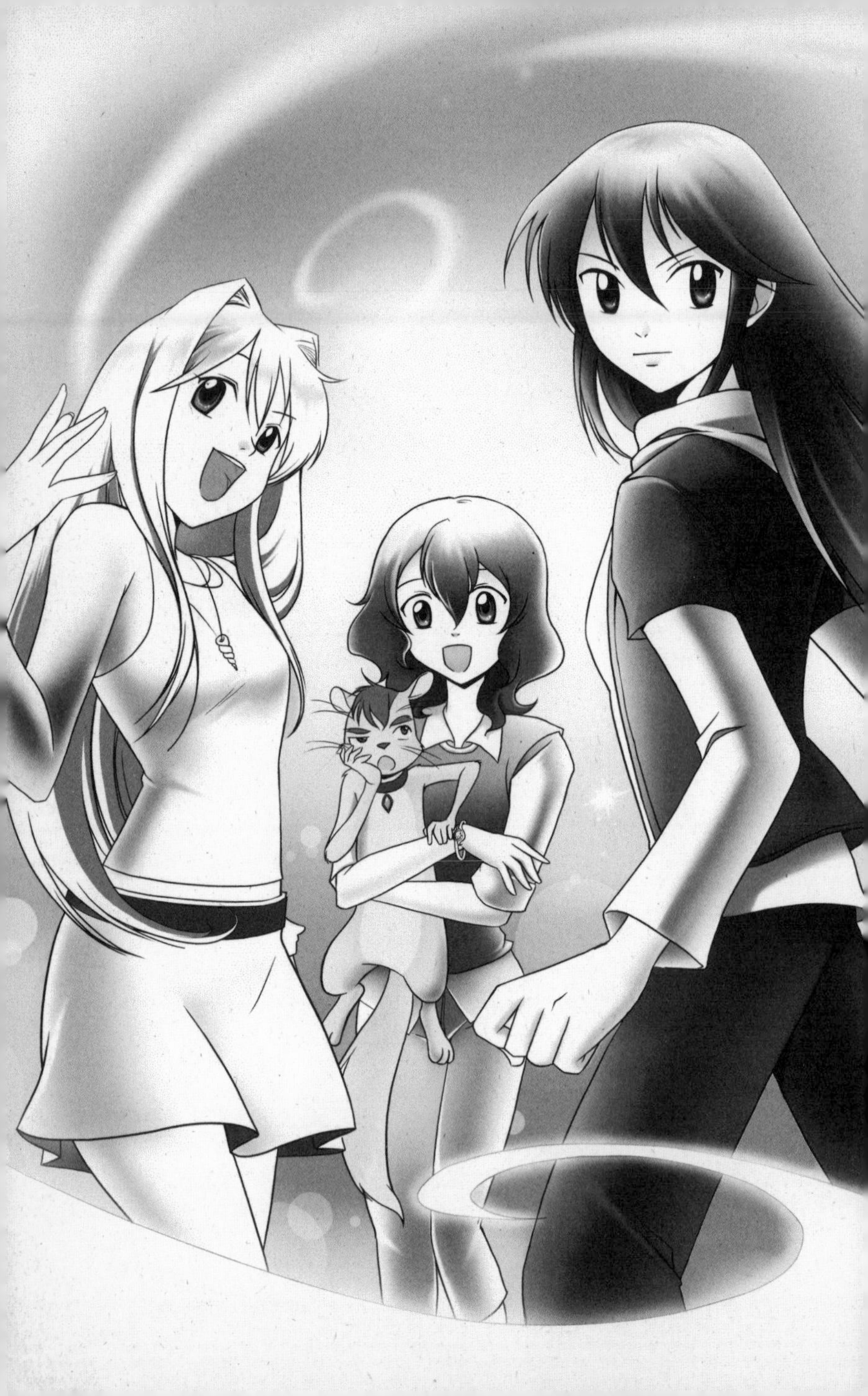

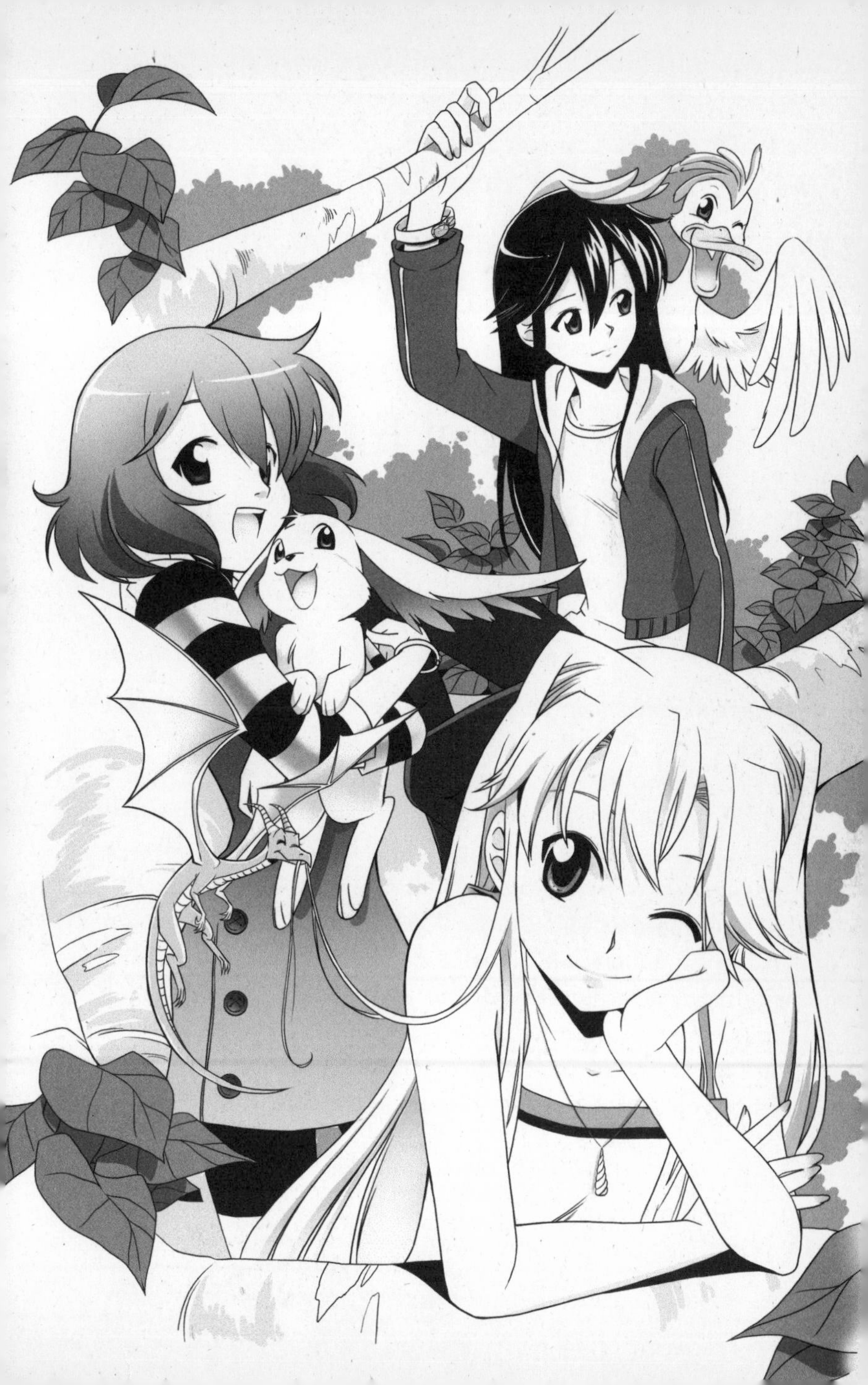

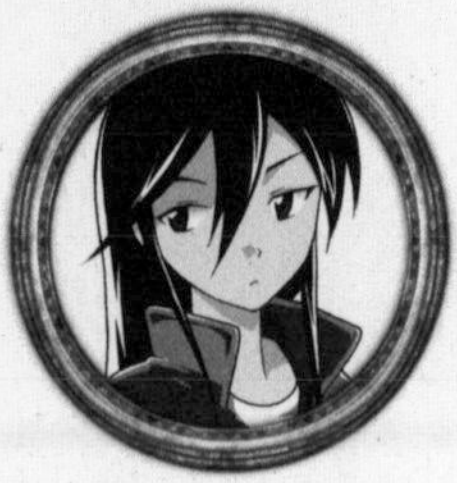
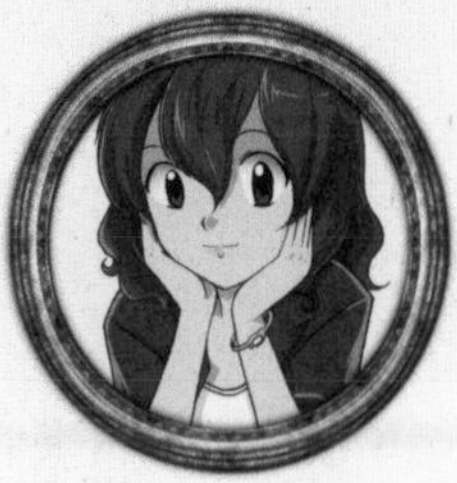
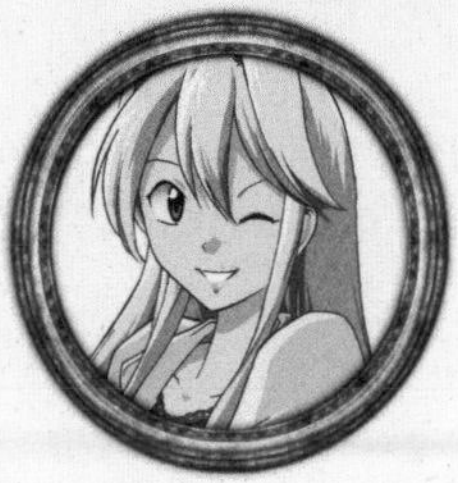

Circle of Friends with Rachel Roberts

Hello, mages!

Special thanks to Team Manga for contributing so much creativity and talent to *The Warlock Diaries*. You might think an author works alone in a room with her kitties, but that's only the first step. It takes a team to complete the vision and bring the adventure to you and your bondeds. Team Manga has proven what Avalon is all about: working together with friends makes good things happen. This story may have come to an end, but that means new ones are on the horizon. And wherever our journey takes us, we hope you'll come along. Until then, it's up to you to keep the spirit of Avalon alive. No matter who you are or where you come from, you've got magic to share.

Your friend,
Rachel Roberts

Legend of the LAOA

PART 1

Zach bent low over Drake's neck as the red dragon soared over rolling green hills and verdant farmlands. The village of Arahoo Wells passed below. It was full of busy elves, their ox-like colgees pulling wagons through the crowded streets. When they saw the mighty dragon soar overhead, a diminutive, pointy-eared group stopped to cheer, tossing their hats into the sky in celebration.

The teenage boy-turned-mage waved back. Zach remembered the first time the elves had seen the enormous dragon in the skies above their home. They had run in terror, hiding from the monstrous flying creature.

But that was during the reign of the Dark Sorceress. Things were different now. Once the elves understood that Zach was a mage and Drake his bonded, they welcomed the pair joyously, even fell all over themselves to see who could find the best food for the ever hungry dragon. Zach and Drake were heroes. They, along with the mistwolves, were the protectors of Aldenmor.

Outside of town, Drake eyed the expanse of farmland where dozens of elves now pointed to their ripe crops. *"Rutabagas!"*

"We'll stop for lunch later." Zach stroked the dragon's soft scaled neck. "Right now we have to check out the report."

Ozzie's cousins, Schmoot and Tonin, had reported seeing a strange object soaring over Dumble Downs. They immediately sent a message to the Fairimentals at the Garden, the sprawling magic research center and animal preserve. What had once been burned out Shadowlands controlled by the Dark Sorceress was now acres of beautiful rolling meadow, home to all species of magical animals.

The guardians of Aldenmor's magic had sent Zach and Drake to check out the sighting. The suspicious object had first appeared south of Wizard's Crossing, then east in the Silver Forests, and now north over elf country. Whatever it was, the strange thing seemed to be erratically popping in and out of portals.

"I got something," Drake told his rider.

The ruby dragon stone set in the leather band on Zach's wrist flared in response to the dragon's strong senses.

With a tap of the boy's foot, Drake banked left and soared over the Moorgroves. The great forest covered a huge section of central Aldenmor. Through the canopy of trees, the waters of Dream Lake shimmered in the afternoon sun.

Light blossomed on the horizon, a quick flare highlighting the trees in bright gold.

"Let's go in for a closer look."

On Zach's command, Drake skimmed over a clearing splashed with yellow, purple, and blue wildflowers. They buzzed over a herd of large furry animals drinking from the gleaming waters of Dream Lake.

"*Wilderbeasts!*" Drake trumpeted happily.

Zach's heart swelled with pride at the sight of the magnificent creatures. The Dark Sorceress had nearly hunted them to extinction, but ever since the mages released magic to heal Aldenmor, the mammoth creatures were flourishing once again. The handsome dragon rider flashed on a pair of dark eyes and a warm smile. Adriane would be so happy to see how well the animals of Aldenmor were doing now.

"*HoNK! I miss Mama, too!*" Drake said, picking up on his bonded's thoughts. Drake had imprinted on the warrior mage when he first hatched. He was being raised by Zach and now both mages shared a bond with the incredible dragon.

"Where is it?" Zach asked, hands tight on the reins.

Blinding light exploded beneath them in a rush of wind.

"*Right below us!*" Drake exclaimed.

A ball of light hurtled over the startled wilderbeasts. Then, it disappeared into the trees.

"Let's fly!" Zach shouted, gripping the saddle as Drake's powerful wings shot them deep into the forest.

The ball of magic reappeared, hurtling through the trees, bouncing like a glowing pinball.

"Try to head it off!" Zach commanded.

The globe of light suddenly doubled back toward the dragon and rider, screaming over their heads. Wild magic crackled like lightning—and in its sparkling bright center, Zach could make out the shape of an animal. It was alive!

"It seems to be making its own portals," Drake observed as the object disappeared and reappeared below.

"Then it must have powerful magic!" Zach responded.

The glowing sphere shot from around a clump of trees and whooshed into the sky.

Magic twisted from the creature—then without warning, it coiled around Drake like a rope.

"It's taking my magic!" Drake struggled to stay airborne as the thing twirled around them, wrapping them in rings of dazzling light.

Zach raised his jewel, firing quick bursts of magic, but he couldn't see anything.

Drake lurched sideways, nearly pitching Zach out of the saddle as the creature pulled them down. Flashing light swirled over them in dizzying waves.

"Drake!"

They were plunging from the sky like a stone, Drake up side down, Zach clinging fast to the saddle. A dense canopy of trees zoomed terrifyingly close.

In a mighty flap of wings, Drake flipped himself over, belly grazing treetops and snapping off branches. The dragon soared into a clearing, his big feet catching saplings and brush as they crunched to a halt.

"That was close!" Heart hammering, Zach leaped from the saddle, checking his friend for injuries.

"Heads up!" warned Drake.

Blazing out of the skies, the bright globe dove straight for them like a meteor.

With a flick of his wrist, Zach hurled a shimmering swath of light. Spikes of magic shot from the dragon stone, blazing into a red shield.

The thing ricocheted off the magic shield, sending shock waves rattling up Zach's arm.

A blackened trail sliced through the forest floor as the creature crash landed in a smoking trench.

Silently, Zach followed the clouds of glittering steam rising from the crater. Bonded and mage crept toward the edge, jewel raised and dragon fire ready.

Bright beams sliced through plumes of smoke as a shadowy shape loomed in the mist. Colored lights sparkled from its body in a shifting halo.

An eerie wailing emanated through the clearing.

"*Sounds like a werebeast,*" Drake speculated, his golden eyes narrowed.

"Or some dark creature from the Otherworlds," Zach added grimly.

In a whoosh, the smoke swirled away.

"Stand back!" Zach warned.

Two small furry ears, pointy and alert, appeared above the crater wall, followed by a snuffling nose. A small silver cat peered up from the smoking ruins. Large prismatic eyes shone with every color of the rainbow, studying the boy and dragon. Magic crackled along its silvery coat as it focused on the dragon stone.

"Rowleep!" The cat-like creature emitted a loud musical note.

Drake and Zach were blown backwards by a powerful gust of wind.

Drake edged closer and stared down at the strange little beast. Scales along the dragon's back shimmered with iridescent magic.

"Brooraaaoal!" the cat yowled in a frenzy of sparks. "prReeeIP!"

Drake turned his large head to Zach. *"I can understand him."*

"What's he saying?"

"PrreeeIp!"

"What?"

Drake shook his head. *"He says he's my brother."*

"Broo preeeip!"

"Big brother," Drake corrected.

"How can you understand him?" Zach asked.

The small cat slinked around Drake's legs, sniffing at the dragon's magic.

Drake's golden eyes followed the little creature. *"His magic is like mine."*

"What are you doing here?" Zach asked the strange cat.

"Zooooom baya!" it crooned in response, rubbing against Drake.

"He's trying to find his way home," the dragon translated.

"ooo, bobay." The cat eyed the smoking trench, his fluffy tail drooping between his legs.

"He didn't mean to hurt anything."

Zach kneeled and eyed the little animal. Smiling, he

asked, "Where is your home?"

"Aarayaaa!" it sang, showering sparkling embers over the forest floor.

Drake snorted a surprised burst of flame. *"Avalon!"*

"Avalon?!" Zach repeated, stunned. The legendary home of all magic was hidden somewhere along the magic web. None of the mages knew what lay inside Avalon's gates. If this creature really came from Avalon, it would be a major breakthrough in their quest to find the home of magic.

"oooweeeEE!" The cat arched his back, shooting spirals of light into the air.

"Easy." Zach brushed sparks from its silver coat. "We have friends who can help you."

Zach held up his dragon stone, about to send a message to the Fairimentals.

The jewel pulsed deep red in warning.

"Drake!"

The sky blackened like an impending storm cloud.

"Incoming!"

A swarm of creatures corkscrewed from the skies, shrieking like banshees. Their bat-like wings sliced though the air, descending on the little cat. Skeletal fingers reached for their prey.

"Shadow creatures!" Zach fired bolts of magic fire from his fists, disintegrating several monsters into smoke.

Drake roared, letting loose a jet of magic fire.

In a burst of light, the cat creature turned to pure crystal. "Hiyoot!" It spun like a tiny tornado, deflecting magic off its prismatic body.

The shadow creatures swarmed, snatching at the cat's magic, their ghostly bodies becoming more solid with each successful grab.

"Rrrriial!" The glittering creature spun and suddenly halted, its crystalline form glowing, ready to unleash a barrage of wild magic.

"No, they're feeding on your magic!" Zach cried.

The cat blinked jeweled eyes at the mage and smiled. "Pweeblee daacoo."

"He said it has been a long time since he's made magic with friends," Drake said.

In a whirl of billowing smoke, the creature let a clear ringing note echo across the clearing. The musical sound warped through the air, engulfing the monsters in sparkling mist.

When the smoke cleared, there was no sign of the monsters—or the cat.

The amazing creature was gone.

"What happened? Where did he go?" Zach spun around.

One last note echoed through the forest.

"What did he say?" Zach asked.

"Thank you," Drake snorted.

Suddenly a thought occurred to Zach. "Drake, I've heard legends about animals like this. They're called LAOAs."

Drake blinked. *"What's that?"*

"Lost Animals of Avalon, powerful magical animals that lived long, long ago."

"Wow."

"So if the LAOA is your, uh, big brother, does that mean you're from Avalon, too?"

Drake's big golden eyes widened. *"I was hatched on Aldenmor, but my egg was very old."*

"A real LAOA," Zach said hopefully. "I wonder where all the others are?"

"Maybe our new friend will tell us," Drake rumbled.

"I just hope he lands somewhere safe," Zach said, jumping into the saddle. "Let's get to the Garden and report to the mages. I can't wait to tell Adriane we met a LAOA!"

With a beat of his mighty wings, the dragon and his rider took to the skies and headed home.

Legend of the LAOA

PART 2

"I feel like there's someone missing," Sierra Sanchez said worriedly.

"Tex counted them all," Tyler Branson replied as he helped the teenage girl close the barn door.

"Yeah, so did I." Sierra's brown eyes scanned the desert that lay beyond the Happy Trails Horse Ranch. Spooked by a pack of wild animals, her horses had broken out of the corral. Her friend, Tyler, from the Twin Forks Ranch had helped her wrangle them all back in.

"You know your horses." He brushed a lock of sandy blond hair from his brow.

Sierra wasn't so sure. Something tickled at the edge of her mind, almost calling to her. She couldn't put her finger on it. But she had the strongest sense there was another horse still out there.

"I'd better head back to Twin Forks." Tyler swung onto his black gelding, Shenandoah. The horse neighed and bobbed his head, ready to jet. It seemed all the horses were skittish tonight.

"Thanks, Tyler, couldn't have done it without you and

Shenie." She patted the black horse's neck, settling him down. "You two going to be okay?"

"Probably just a pack of coyotes or wild dogs. Shen can outrun anything on four legs." He slipped his iPhone into his shirt pocket. "Call if you need anything."

Sierra nodded. "Don't forget, I've got us booked for barrel racing at the County Fair next weekend."

"Got enough room for another trophy?" He grinned.

She returned his smile. "I'm building a new shelf for Apache."

Sierra and Tyler had known each other since they were kids. Now in high school, they still shared a love of horses. She lived with her Uncle Tex, training horses and giving riding lessons to visitors at their ranch. Most of the Happy Trails horses had come from Tyler and his family, including her favorite, Apache. Twin Forks was famous for breeding paint ponies.

Sierra watched Tyler and Shenandoah gallop out the main gate. The sun dropped below the horizon, sending a last burst of pinks and purples across the darkening sky. Night was coming on fast.

She grasped the turquoise pendant on her silver necklace, a gift from her grandfather in Mexico. It always seemed to ease her fears, but tonight it wasn't working. Sighing, she turned back to the barn when she heard a soft whinny. Something was calling her. Was it in her mind or had she heard it?

Quietly, she crept behind the barn. There in the dirt was a fresh set of hoof prints, but all the Happy Trails horses wore shoes. These unshod prints led out to the desert—almost as if the mysterious horse had come to visit and then left in a hurry. A cool breeze ruffled her short dark hair. It would be completely dark soon, and whatever had spooked her horses was still out there. Sierra shivered.

She followed the tracks past the arenas and the guest cabins only to see that they abruptly stopped. There was nothing but open desert all around, no place the horse could be hiding. It was as if the horse had simply disappeared.

She looked skyward. A glow streaked across the heavens, trailing a tail of dazzling light.

Sierra gasped. "A shooting star!"

But instead of vanishing into the night, the star soared over the ranch and plummeted behind a sand dune a few hundred yards away. Sierra watched, transfixed.

Atop the dune, a lone horse stood, silhouetted against the flickering light, hooves pawing the air.

"I knew it!" Sierra blinked against the intense flare. But when her vision cleared, the horse was gone.

"Wait, come back!" She dashed into the desert toward it, her cowboy boots digging deep in the sand.

Her jewel felt warm against her neck as she scrambled up and over the dune, sliding down the other side. She leaped to her feet—and froze. The air was filled with iridescent sparkles as if a thousand fireflies danced before her eyes.

Then she heard a musical sound, strange and lilting, as the cloud of twinkles washed away. The horse wasn't there, but something else was. On the desert floor sat a small silver cat with pointy ears. Fragments of rainbow colors shimmered along his coat. It didn't look like a native desert animal and it seemed completely tame, staring at her calmly with strange, shining eyes.

Sierra slowly knelt to inspect the amazing creature more carefully. "Where did you come from?" she whispered.

"Aldenmor." A tinkling voice sounded in Sierra's mind.

She stared at the cat. "Did you just say something?"

"Meeeeeeyooooo," the mysterious cat yowled.

Sierra rubbed her eyes. "Geez, I must be really tired."

"Me too."

This time there was no mistake. The cat had spoken. "How can you talk?"

"Only those who have magic can hear me," the sparkly cat replied.

"Magic?"

The creature cocked his head, regarding her with eyes that seemed to be every color of the rainbow. *"Yes, aren't you a mage?"*

Sierra flashed on her friends from Ravenswood, Emily, Adriane, and Kara. A few months ago they had introduced her to thirty baby unicorns. She'd been emailing with Emily, and knew they were mages, users of magic. They were on a quest to save an entire world of magical animals.

"Where's your bonded animal?"

"Apache? He's in the barn."

The cat's fluffy tail twitched. *"Mages really shouldn't wander around without their magical animals. It's dangerous out here."*

An eerie howl echoed across the desert.

"What was that?" Sierra asked nervously.

"That's what I'm talking about. They must have fallen through the same portal that I did."

"Portal, as in..."

"A doorway which connects two points along the magic web," the cat informed her.

"What are they doing here?" she gulped. A sense of uneasiness filled her.

"Hunting."

Out of nowhere, six huge wolf-like creatures with black shaggy hair, pointed snouts, and glowing yellow eyes sped toward them in long loping strides.

"What do we do?" Sierra cried.

The cat arched his back, silvery coat gleaming as his fur transformed into shimmering crystal. Rings of blinding light swirled from the cat's compact body.

Sierra shielded her eyes, gasping as her pendant erupted in brilliant sparkles.

The wolf creatures yelped, stumbling away in a spray of sand and rocks.

"That won't hold them off for long," the cat warned. *"Call your bonded animal."*

"I don't understand," Sierra stammered.

Suddenly, the thunder of galloping hooves shook the dune as something barreled through the stunned creatures. In a cloud of swirling dust, it skidded to a stop. Standing before her was a magnificent red roan mare.

The cat shook his furry coat as he regarded the amazing horse. *"Ah, there you are. Here's your mage."*

The mare's deep brown eyes locked onto Sierra. *"We must hurry."*

Sierra stared in astonishment. This was the horse that had been calling to her, she was sure of it.

"What are we waiting for?" The cat leaped onto the mare's back.

In the light of the rising moon, the dark creatures were regrouping, yellow eyes flickering with malice.

There was no time to think. Sierra grabbed the mare's russet mane and swung herself on. The horse took off at a full gallop. But the wolf creatures were fast. They sprang after the horse, snapping at her hooves.

With a fierce growl, one of the monsters launched itself at Sierra, dagger teeth flashing from its open maw. She hugged the horse's neck. Her jewel blazed with light, sending the creature hurtling to the ground.

Turquoise sparkles raced up and down her arms. Sierra should have completely freaked, but somehow she knew the horse would protect her. The mare swerved, galloping up the steep incline to Stony Ridge.

"Wait, we'll be trapped up there!" Sierra shouted. The ridge ended in a sheer cliff.

"Trust me." The horse gathered speed, rocketing toward the edge. She was going right over—with her on top!

Sierra screamed, terrified as the mare leaped. For a second, they hung suspended in the air, then plummeted straight down. Something brushed against her legs. Glimmering copper wings spread from the mare's back—and suddenly they were flying!

The breath rushed from Sierra's lungs as the mare wheeled through the sky, soaring over the gully far below.

The cat casually scratched his ear as howls of frustration faded behind them.

Sierra's elation was short-lived. The pack of creatures had turned away, only to head back down Stony Ridge and make for Happy Trails.

"We have to stop them!" Sierra cried.

The mare snorted agreement. *Let's send them back through the portal.*

Angling her wings, the horse banked left and dove over the creatures. She hit the ground at a full gallop directly in front of the leader. Coppery wings sparkled once and vanished as hooves flashed across the sand.

The monsters howled in fury and gave chase.

The mare suddenly skidded and whirled around to face the oncoming predators. The beasts closed in at full speed, jaws snapping. Finally, they would have their prey.

The cat glanced at Sierra. *Go ahead.*

"What do I do?" Sierra cried.

Focus on your jewel, send me your magic, the horse instructed.

Now! The cat fluffed out and blazed like a beacon in the night.

With all her might, Sierra willed her strength to the

horse. She wasn't sure she was doing it right, but her jewel responded with a powerful burst.

She felt the magic erupt behind her as they shot straight up in the air, the horse's wings open and flapping.

The monsters were coming on too fast. Unable to stop, they barreled headfirst into the magical doorway.

With a fierce yowl, the cat shrunk the portal into a point of light and it vanished.

The horse floated gently downward, gliding to the ground.

Sierra leaped off and stroked the mare's silky neck, admiring her deep copper mane and tail. "Thank you," she said.

The horse whinnied. *"I came here to find you, but the creatures followed me through the portal."*

"But why me?" Sierra asked, amazed.

"I am your bonded."

Her glowing turquoise jewel reflected in the horse's deep brown eyes. Sierra had always sensed that her jewel was special. Now she knew why.

"That was amazing!"

Sierra whirled around.

A teenage girl was walking toward them, a train of long moon and star patterned robes swirling behind her. She held a glowing handheld device—and she was green!

"A most excellent display of mage and bonded animal magic."

"Uh, hi, I'm Sierra."

"I know." The strange dark haired girl smiled. "I'm Tasha, I work with Emily, Adriane, and Kara."

"But you're green!" Sierra exclaimed.

"I recycle," Tasha replied, scanning the cat with her handheld device. The cat had transformed back into his silver furry shape and was purring like a lawnmower. "Zach told me about you. I've been searching all over but I couldn't find you on my magic meter!" The small device blinked and beeped. "But your magic seems to have stabilized."

The cat rubbed his head against Sierra. *"The mage and her bonded helped me."*

"Your healing magic must have stabilized the LAOA's portal popping," Tasha told Sierra.

"How did I do that?"

Tasha pointed the meter at Sierra. "Fascinating! You're a healer mage with elemental fire magic bonded to a flying horse." She showed Sierra several glowing lines on the magic meter. "Look, a bit of warrior, too."

"Wow." Sierra could hardly believe this was really happening.

The cat stretched his lithe body. *"When I felt the time of magic had come back, I left my hiding place, only I found out I couldn't control my magic anymore."*

"Are there other LAOAs?" Tasha asked excitedly.

"There are many of us. We have been away from home for so long. I must find my friends."

The mare lowered her head to snuffle the cat. *"How can we help the Lost Animals of Avalon?"*

"You already have," the cat replied.

"Portals are opening and closing all over the web," Tasha confirmed. "This portal here is now a key access point to the web. I have to tell the mages right away!"

"Whoa, does that mean other things are going to come through here?" Sierra asked.

"Well, be on the lookout. You never know who else might drop in for a visit," Tasha said. "But don't worry. I'll send the dragonflies to weave you a dreamcatcher. It will only let creatures with good magic through."

The cat strode over to Tasha. *"You're friends with my little brother Drake, then?"*

Tasha nodded. "I'm sure you two have a lot to talk about."

"Speaking of talking," Sierra patted the mare's silky neck, "what do we do now?"

"I can stay with you…" The red roan lowered her head shyly.

"I don't know how I'm going to explain the wings, but we'll figure it out."

"Only those with magic can see my wings," the horse assured her.

"Oh great, so everyone else is going to see a floating horse."

"Good luck," Tasha waved as the cat zapped open the portal. "You're our mage on the magical frontier. How exciting is that!"

Sierra waved back as Tasha and the cat vanished, leaving

her alone with the horse. The mare's coat gleamed like burnished copper under the desert moon.

She smiled at her bonded. "What's your name?"

The horse snuffled close. *"I guess we'll have to find out together."*

Legend of the LAOA

PART 3

Music resonated throughout the Crystal Keep, filling the chambers and floating down the hallways in a bright flurry of sounds. On the top floor of the large building, a pretty green teen studied the source of the harmonic melodies.

"Bravo!" Tasha, Goblin Court Sorceress, and her assistants applauded the amazing music of the mysterious cat she had recently brought to The Garden.

"Thank you." The silver cat sat in the middle of a round table, preening his shiny coat as he took in his new surroundings.

Sunlight streamed through the crystal dome, casting rainbow prisms over Tasha's busy laboratory. Along one wall, row upon row of dazzling crystals were neatly placed in specially built shelves. A group of elves and dwarves climbed up and down ladders filing crystals full of magical data. Pixies fluttered about, organizing the top rows. Friends from all over the web had been lending Tasha important volumes of magical lore. Her assistants had recorded all the data in specialized jewels, making a crystallized library of magic.

On the lower floors of the keep, aisles and aisles of shelves stored charms, amulets, enchantments, and elements of magic collected from all over Aldenmor and beyond. With Tasha's help, The Garden was becoming a top-notch magical research center.

Tasha scratched the cat's back, smoothing down his furry hide. "We need to get a reading so I can study your musical signature." Her dark eyes scanned the crowded worktable. "Where did I put my—"

A fuzzy blue paw gave her a small handheld device with a touch screen.

"Thank you, Harvey." She took her magic meter and patted the helpful brimbee who had suddenly appeared on the table beside the cat. "Now if I could just find those—"

The fuzzy trunk of a wilderbeast plunked a container full of data crystals on the table.

"Ah, there it is, Bartleby," the goblin sorceress said gratefully. "All the readings I take with my magic meter will automatically be input and stored in these data crystals."

"*Impressive,*" the cat said, jeweled eyes brightening as he sniffed the crystals.

"Call for Lady Tasha!"

Tasha whirled around at the sound of the voice. Behind her, several large mirrors formed a semi-circle, each set on speed dial to her most important contacts. A green-faced hobgoblin in a tight vest appeared in the center mirror. "Is she available?"

"Of course I am, Twon. You're looking right at me." Tasha powered off her handheld. Instantly, Goblin Queen Raelda, stout and stately, materialized in the mirror. "Lady Tasha, how goes your work at The Garden?"

"Fantastic, Your Highness!" She pointed to a set of documents spread on the table. "We've had excavation teams mapping these tunnels for months. The Dark Sorceress did a lot of magic research here. I've found many interesting things in her old lair."

"Very good. I see you are working with your new guest."

The silver cat greeted Queen Raelda by way of a few tinkling notes.

"I am pleased to meet you, too," the goblin queen chuckled. "We all thought the Lost Animals of Avalon were a legend. Until now."

"And I had never seen a goblin until I met Tasha," the cat replied, paws twinkling.

"I'm going to write a whole new lecture series on 'Legends of the LAOAs!'" Tasha exclaimed.

"An excellent way to open the Mage Academy," Queen Raelda approved.

"The school is ahead of schedule," Tasha said proudly. "I have every animal at The Garden cataloged and filed."

Thanks to the resounding success Emily had matching the baby sea dragons with young dragon riders of Aquatania, the kings and queens of the Fairy Realms were eager to get the Mage Academy started in The Garden. Young people from all over the web would be coming to study magic and get a chance to bond with one of the incredible magical animals being raised here.

"We have several candidates from the Fairy Realms who

can't wait to get started," Raelda said.

"We're working on the mage manual now, Your Highness." Tasha couldn't hide her excitement as she thought of the brightest magical minds on the web all gathering at the new academy.

"Castle Garthwyn is very quiet without you here." Raelda said with a smile. Her perfectly square teeth gleamed in her wide mouth. "Do you need any more pumpkin cookies?"

"No thank you, Your Highness." Tasha returned the smile warmly. "I'm still working through the five boxes you sent."

"How is Dorchester working out?"

"He's a very able apprentice."

"Excellent, keep me informed on your progress with our new friend."

With that, the image of the goblin queen vanished.

Suddenly, the doors to the lab flew open with a loud commotion and dozens of animals piled in, pushing past a tall, red-faced goblin.

"There he is!" The newcomers, tweeting and honking excitedly, surrounded the silvery creature. A pair of pooxims peered into the cat's pointy ears while a baby wilderbeast raised a velvety trunk to snuffle his snout. Curious fluffy kittens and feathery quiffles scrambled onto the table and stared into his prismatic eyes.

"Out, out, out!" Dorchester, oversized robes billowing behind him, scooted behind the animals, trying to shoo them back out.

"It's okay, Dorchester, I asked them here to help," Tasha

reassured her frazzled apprentice.

"I am happy to meet all of you," the cat purred.

Dorchester lifted a handful of jewels from his pocket and projected holographs of three different lists. "Lady Tasha, I have troll artifacts to store and label, the shipment of grooming supplies and hamburger niblets from Ravenswood is expected later today, and I'm still printing drafts of the mage manual for your review." With every word, his nose pointed higher toward the crystal dome. "We really have no time to fool with a LAOA, they don't even exist."

"Interesting theory." The cat stretched, tail twitching with amusement.

"Hey, Dorie! I'm going to need a fresh crystal," an elf called out from high atop a ladder. "The Legend of Ozymandius is now on Volume Eight."

"Can't you see we're working, Schmoot?" Dorchester adjusted his tie.

"So are we. Ozzie is a real hero!" Tonin, another of Ozzie's cousins, rolled a tall ladder past the perplexed goblin. "The first official elf hero since Cromeo and his juggling bear! Oh, and while you're out getting that new crystal, pick me up a grain taco and fries."

"I'll take a bubbleberry shake!" Schmoot added.

"Elves. I've never met a species that ate so much!" Dorchester grumbled.

Tasha scanned the cat from the tip of his bushy tail to his pink nose, making the creature sparkle with light. "Your composition is very unusual," Tasha noted.

Dorchester peered over her shoulder. "Elemental particle distribution changes his molecular structure for optimum magical resonance."

"He's a cat who looks like a jewel," Bartelby observed.

"That's what I said." Dorie rolled his eyes.

"Fascinating, you're part animal and part jewel…" Tasha paused. "I'm sorry, I don't know your name."

In response, the cat released a flurry of notes.

"Look at that!" Tasha's magic meter reacted with its own tuneful chords. Flowing bands of color floated across the mirrors and around the dome. "Your name has the same frequency as a spellsong!"

"My name is in the ancient language of Avalon." The cat purred notes that rose and fell in a lilting melody.

"A musical language, it's amazing!" Tasha's mind spun just imagining a brand new section of her crystal library.

"We already know music can make powerful magic," Dorchester observed dryly. "That doesn't prove this cat is a LAOA."

Inspired, all the animals hummed and hooted, matching the cat's notes with their own and creating a whirlwind of glistening magic.

"Arg! Stop the music!" Dorchester covered his ears.

"Why don't I just call you Lyric," Tasha suggested.

The cat purred his agreement, then shifted his gaze to assess Tasha's bank of mirrors. *"You know, portals would really be more efficient."*

Dorchester arched a bushy eyebrow at the cat. "We can't

just place a portal wherever we want. For a LAOA, you sure don't know much."

The cat's ears twitched. *"I can make a portal."*

"Nice," Tasha said, then blinked. "What?"

"That is what crystal cats do," Lyric informed her.

"Any unicorn can open a portal," Dorchester commented, unimpressed.

"Yes," the cat said, swishing his tail. *"But those portals only last until the unicorn gets where it's going. I can make* real *portals."*

"The actual fabrication and construction of permanent portals?" Dorie sputtered. "Why that could…"

"Revolutionize interweb travel!" Tasha could hardly believe her pointy ears. "Think of it Dorie, we could build direct portals to key points of magic all over the web!"

"I evaluate magical facts, accumulate fantastical data, and assimilate legendary lore," Dorchester scoffed. "And nobody but nobody knows how to make a permanent portal anymore."

"I am descended from cats that once lived in Avalon," Lyric explained. *"Before the crystal city fell to the dark mages long ago, a group of very powerful animals left Avalon. Each magical animal carried with them great secrets of magic so that one day they could be given to good mages."*

Tasha listened to the cat, astonished. "So Avalon was really a library?"

The cat nodded. *"Now the LAOAs live all over the web, hiding in pockets of magic, protecting the ancient knowledge."*

"Wow," she whispered.

A sad note emanated from the cat's gleaming body. *"But after centuries of protecting our secrets, they are still in danger."*

"What happened?" Tasha asked.

"Dark mages have been tracking me ever since I left my home. Now I can't find my way back to warn my brothers and sisters."

"Dark mages," murmured the animals worriedly.

Tasha shared their concern. She had heard rumors of dark mages living along the web, hunting animals for magic. Without any proof, she had thought they were nothing more than stories. But if the crystal cat was right, then no animal on the web was safe.

"The Garden is protected by powerful friends," Tasha reassured the distraught cat. "Mages of good, the healer, warrior, and blazing star. They won't let anything happen to you."

"This really is like Avalon," Lyric sang.

"Using your magical signature, we can help you locate your friends on the web," Tasha offered. "If we can make a direct portal path between The Garden and your home, the dark mages wouldn't be able to follow you."

The animals all nodded in agreement.

"What do you think, Dorchester?" Tasha asked.

The goblin apprentice scowled, clearly not convinced this was possible. "Behind the Fairy Ring there's a meadow with plenty of room. I suppose we could try, for the sake of magical research."

"Perfect!" Tasha enthused. "Let's go!"

The excited group of goblins and magical animals circled down the staircase and barreled out of the Crystal Keep. With Lyric in the lead singing a spritely melody, the group made their way down the rock path that twisted past the lake and over to the Fairy Ring. Soon every animal in The Garden fell into step behind them in a long trail, singing, hooting, squawking, and tootling along.

"Coming through!" A flying creature called out.

Tasha ducked as several pixies whizzed by, water splashing over the edge of the bucket they carried. The purple winged fairies dumped the bucket into a bubbling hot spring. And in that spring sat a familiar red dragon.

"*Hi!*" Soapsuds went flying as the dragon leaped from the pool, dousing the pixies with bath water.

"*Little brother!*" the cat vanished and reappeared an instant later atop Drake's head.

"*Hello, big brother,*" Drake trumpeted happily. "*I'm taking a bath!*"

"We have a match." Tasha studied the read-outs on her magic meter. "Lyric's magical signature is identical to Drake's."

Dorchester, eyebrows fluttering, checked the readings. "Fascinating, different species, same magical frequency. Maybe there is something to this LAOA after all."

"*I'm glad you're okay,*" Drake rumbled.

"*I'm trying to find my home,*" Lyric said, smoothing Drake's ears. "*Your magic would be a big help.*"

"We're going to make a portal!" the animals cried.

"Don't be absurd, man," Dorchester lectured a small brimbee. "If you jump through a portal without tuning it, you can end up anywhere!"

"If we can find Lyric's friends on the web, we will all help tune the portal," Tasha said excitedly as she set her magic meter to the magic tracking app. They were about to do something that hadn't been done in hundreds of years! She took a deep breath. "Okay, Lyric, go ahead."

The silver cat raised his head and sang a series of notes. Concentrating, his paws and tail flashed to crystal. Light glinted off his body.

"Everyone sing together to help Lyric focus," Tasha instructed.

The animals gathered close, crooning and trilling in harmony.

The cat's silver fur began to shimmer. In a flash, he turned to blazing crystal, glittering like a diamond in the sun.

"That's it!" Tasha exclaimed, encouraged.

Magic beamed in a bright halo around the cat. He began to float, rising into the air until his magic formed a perfect portal sized circle.

"Drake, help me stabilize the portal," the cat said.

Drake closed his leathery eyelids tightly and released a small lick of flame. Lyric glowed with warm dragon magic and the circle of light began to shift and swirl.

Satisfied, the red dragon roared confidently. Magical fire poured into the halo, surrounding the cat. Wind whipped through the meadow as the air itself wrapped around the small glowing cat. With a blinding burst of silver, a portal opened. Inside, strands of glowing web lay like intricate highways, star points glittering in the distance.

Tasha's eyes darted from her magic meter to the portal, confirming readings. "We're halfway there!"

"Not bad, but it won't hold," the ever-doubting Dorchester observed.

Lyric's mournful song grew stronger and louder, a call across worlds to all who might hear it.

Kaleidoscopic images began to swirl inside the portal. Different sites appeared and disappeared in a blinding blur—dense forest, barren desert, and wind washed beaches. The edge of the portal rippled and shifted as Lyric tried to find his hidden home.

"Hang on, I'm getting something," Tasha exclaimed.

"Powerful earth magic." Dorchester stepped closer to the portal, eyeballs fixed on his handheld jewel. "I can't quite see what—"

The images lurched to a stop as something that looked like a bouquet of green leaves and branches fell through the portal and landed on Dorchester in a heap.

"By the great tree!" A small figure made up entirely of twigs and leaves scrambled to his feet, adjusting the turquoise jewel hanging around his neck. "I detected immense amounts of portal power, what are you doing?!"

"Good timing, Tweek!" Tasha patted the little guy. "We could use your help."

Dorchester smoothed his robes and examined the small

Experimental Fairimental. "We are attempting to construct a permanent portal to the LAOAs."

"O' me twig!" Tweek's quartz eyes twirled.

"Lyric, look out!" Tasha cried.

A strong force was latching onto the cat's magic, pulling the portal connection away from Ravenswood.

The portal's location shifted and blurred to a dark, misty place.

"Where did it go?" Tweek projected a map of the web from his jewel, trying to triangulate.

Suddenly, dozens of yellow eyes gleamed through the mist as a mass of black shapes advanced. Low growls rumbled through the portal and into The Garden.

"Find somewhere else, Lyric—fast," Tasha urged.

"I am trying, but the creatures are very strong."

"Werebeasts!" Tweek screamed.

The ferocious wolf-like creatures snarled and leaped for the portal. Long teeth snapped as they tried to grab the cat.

Lyric's crystal body shot silver bolts, deflecting the monsters' attack.

Instead, the thwarted beasts grabbed the creature closest to the open portal and heaved him inside.

"Help!" Dorchester's scream was cut off as the portal flickered to a new location before they could help him.

"Where'd he go?" Tasha asked Tweek.

"Portal flux must have bounced him over the web," the Experimental Fairimental fretted. "Wait, something's happening!"

"Here I am!" Dorchester flew topsy-turvy across the open window as the animals all tried to grab for a foot, hand, or nose.

"Careful you don't fall in!" Lyric warned them.

"This is going to get bumpy, Dorie!" Tasha yelled, then faced Lyric. "Hurry, we have to get him back before he winds up somewhere even worse!"

"BlAAAhaalp!" Dorchester flew the other way as a swarm of giant mothmooses flapped after him.

Drake roared, creating flames that spun around the portal's edge. The cat absorbed the magic and glowed as golden as the sun.

"HellPPP—dooof!"

The bright lights in the portal faded away as a steady image wavered into place. The portal had settled on a field of something blue and furry.

A pair of goblin feet stuck out of the mysterious stuff.

"Dorie, are you all right?" Tasha called out.

"Blech!" Dorchester sat up.

The blue fuzz was suddenly replaced with a giant eyeball staring with great curiosity at the group in The Garden.

"Ahhh!" The animals backed away in fear.

"No, wait its Bluebell!" Lyric mewed happily.

An enormous smile appeared in the portal as Bluebell recognized little Lyric. A booming musical note swept through the portal, blowing everyone across the meadow.

Lyric blasted his own greeting, and then beamed at Tasha. *"That's my home. Let's lock this portal in place!"*

Rainbow lights streamed from Lyric's crystal body, spinning around him in flares of magic. The edges of the portal became smooth, until the magical doorway was a perfect circle.

"One more blast, Drake, and the portal will be stable!" Lyric instructed his little brother.

Drake's magical fire hit the portal with a brilliant flash, sending sparks rippling through the air and showering over The Garden.

"Holy webweaver!" Tweek cried.

"We did it!" the animals in The Garden bounced with joy.

"With this new portal, we can always be connected," Lyric said. *"There are lots of new friends to meet."*

Other creatures had appeared behind Bluebell: a huge bird with flaming orange and bright green feathers and a tall horse with deep blue crystal wings.

"I don't believe it!" Tweek cried. "LAOAs! Look, a Ki and a Thundercloud Pegasus."

"Thank you for helping me find my way back home," Lyric said. *"It is time we shared some of our secrets with good magic users."*

"You have to come back when the Mage Academy opens." Tasha reached up and hugged Lyric, surprised to find his crystalline body warm to the touch.

Two giant furry arms wrapped around Dorchester as the goblin apprentice stared at the big, blue, bear-like creature.

Bluebell studied the astonished goblin with huge, wide eyes.

"Dorie, she likes you!" Tasha exclaimed.

"I guess we can always learn something new." Dorie lay over the creature's arms. "At least we know LAOAs enjoy intelligent company."

Lyric floated into the portal as Bluebell gently guided Dorchester through to The Garden.

"Welcome back, Dorie," Tasha said.

Dorchester's eyes gleamed with tears. "I'm going to miss those LAOAs so much!"

Tasha smiled. "I have the feeling we're going to be seeing them again soon."

Bright sparkles danced around the incredible creatures as the portal closed, a promise that the ancient magic of Avalon still lived on.

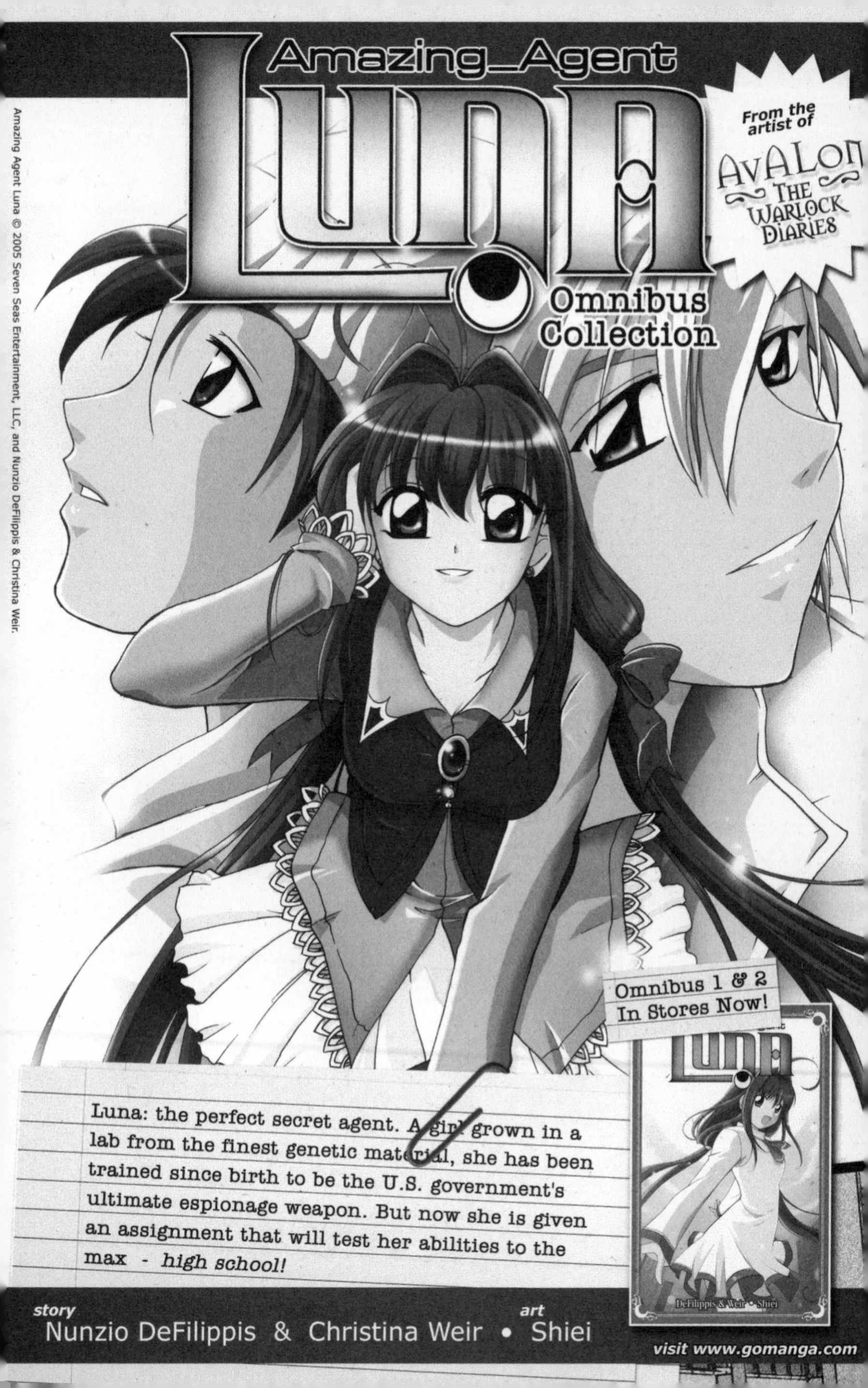
Amazing Agent
LUNA
Omnibus Collection
From the artist of
AVALON THE WARLOCK DIARIES
Amazing Agent Luna © 2005 Seven Seas Entertainment, LLC, and Nunzio DeFilippis & Christina Weir.
Omnibus 1 & 2 In Stores Now!
LUNA
DeFilippis & Weir • Shiei
Luna: the perfect secret agent. A girl grown in a lab from the finest genetic material, she has been trained since birth to be the U.S. government's ultimate espionage weapon. But now she is given an assignment that will test her abilities to the max - *high school!*
story
Nunzio DeFilippis & Christina Weir • art Shiei
visit www.gomanga.com

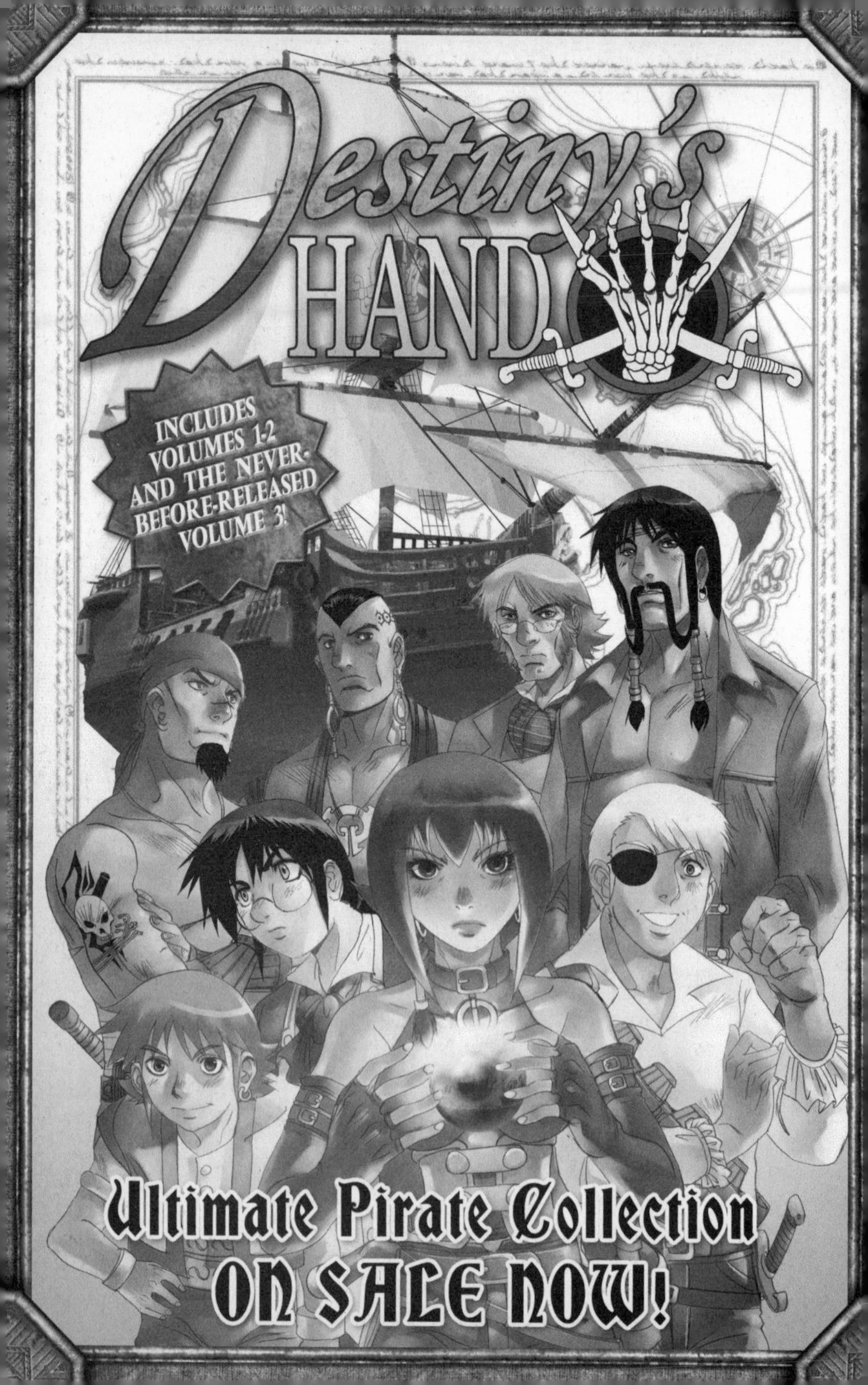
Destiny's
HAND
INCLUDES VOLUMES 1-2 AND THE NEVER-BEFORE-RELEASED VOLUME 3!
Ultimate Pirate Collection
ON SALE NOW!

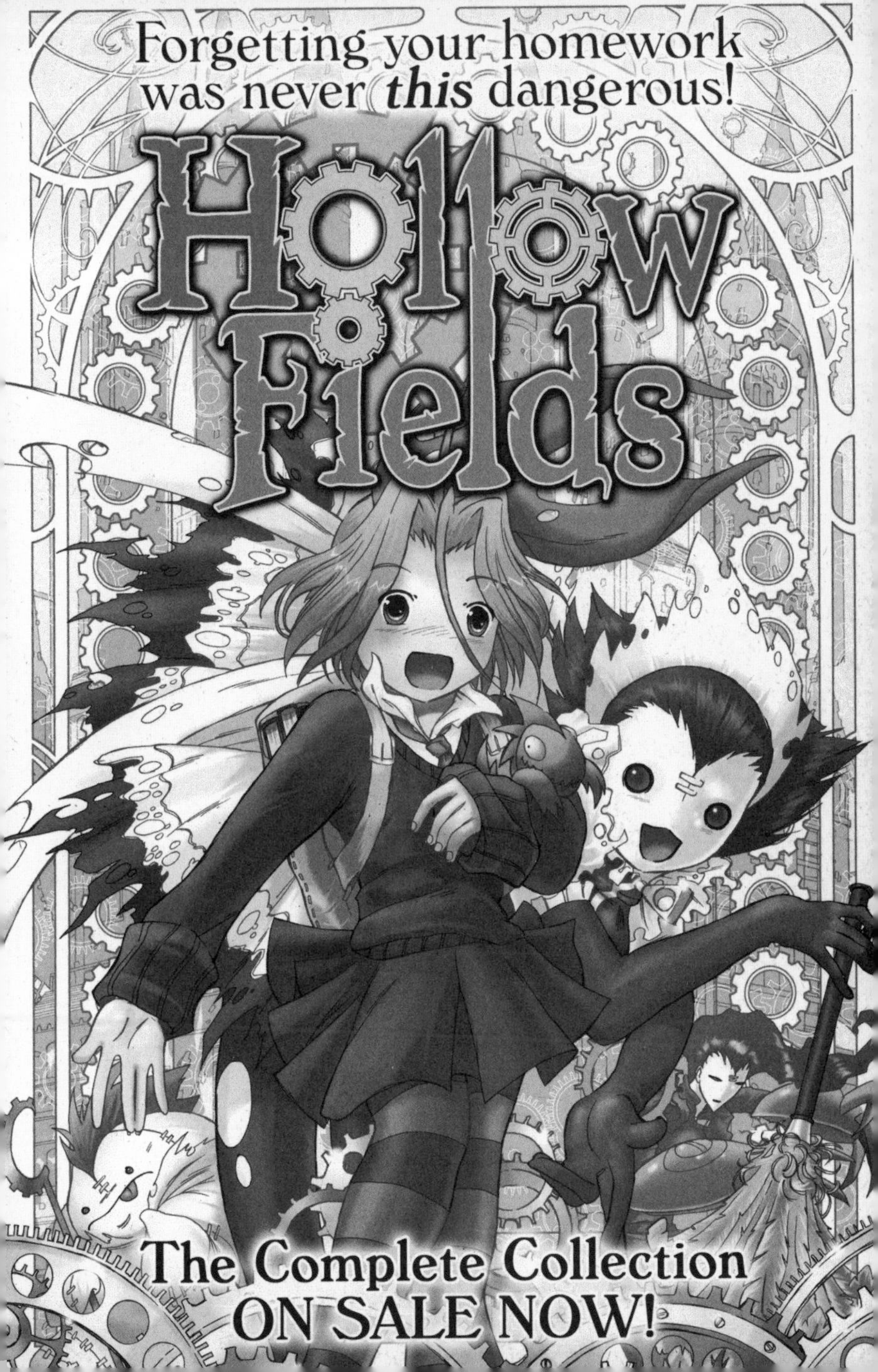

Forgetting your homework was never *this* dangerous!
Hollow Fields
The Complete Collection
ON SALE NOW!

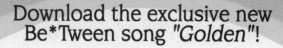

Download the exclusive new Be*Tween song *"Golden"*!

Be*Tween worlds
Be*Tween sounds
Be*Tween the magic
Lies the music

In the song the mages sing with Be*Fuddled,
who is the magic in between?

Enter the answer at
www.avalonmagic.com/secret.php

Rock on, mages! Music is magic!